New Wilderness

New Wilderness

Brian S. Matthews

New Wilderness by Brian S. Matthews

This novel is a work of fiction. Names, characters, places and incidents are the product of the author's imagination or are used fictitiously and any resemblance to actual persons living or dead, events or locales is entirely coincidental.

Manufactured in Canada.

National Library of Canada Cataloguing in Publication

Matthews, Brian S., 1971-
New Wilderness / by Brian S. Matthews.

ISBN 1-897242-01-8

I. Title.

PS8576.A83123N48 2005 C813'.6 C2005-905373-9

Cover art by Bill Richards

Aydy Press
www.aydy.ca

In loving memory of my father
And for my mother
The strongest person I know

Let us make man in our image,
and let them have dominion over the fish of the sea,
and over the fowl of the air, and over the cattle,
and over all the earth, and over every creeping thing.

Genesis I, 24

1. June 10th

Sheets of snow gusted across the landscape, like frozen ghosts seeking refuge. A polar bear's yellowed muzzle stood out against the white in the hunter's cross hairs. The hunter, a large man—also in white—lay flat against the ice, the rifle gripped loosely in his hands. He turned to a similarly camouflaged man who studied the bear through small binoculars. They waited. The bear was slowly wending its way closer with steady, rhythmic steps of black claw and shaggy leg. The hunter's rifle contained tranquilizer darts, a botched bullet being so dangerous to the coveted pelt. He liked to wait until the last possible minute, that way he didn't have run too far to deliver the final, surgically precise blow. No part of the animal would be wasted. The skin was headed to a real estate broker in Hong Kong. The organs were likewise bound for Hong Kong, where they would be packaged and sent all over the world. This bear was going places.

The second man gave a questioning look, which the hunter caught and ignored. He liked scaring his partner, it was half the fun. He pushed it a little further every time, no matter what the prey. The bear, however, would soon be too close for comfort. The hunter eased the rifle's stock into his shoulder and placed his eye to the scope.

With a sudden impact the rifle was gone and the hunter was flipped over. He stared into the face of another bear, this one much closer. Blood-matted fur peeled back from mountains of teeth. The bear roared. There were popping sounds as the second man fired a pistol. The bear turned and bounded towards the gun-wielding poacher.

The hunter reached for his handgun. The gun wasn't there, neither was the holster. He looked down his body to see the weapon right where it should be. It was his hand that was in the wrong place. The hunter's right arm was severed below the elbow. Bone and ragged flesh protruded from a shredded down-filled sleeve. His disembodied hand and forearm lay a few metres away, its path across the ice marked by a long red smear. A combination of shock and hard will clamped down, crushing panic. His own scream stopped, and he heard wet ripping sounds from his right. The hunter turned his head and saw his partner being torn apart like a padded rag-doll. Feathers fluttered gently in the wind as the bear tossed the man back and forth, losing one jaw hold and finding another.

A roar from above him flipped the hunter onto his stomach. The first bear, the pelt and organs, was charging. Gobs of saliva flew from its mouth to spatter and freeze on the hard terrain.

Kate Thurlow dropped the sponge in a bucket. The dirty water resisted at first, then accepted and swallowed the offering.

"Noah, c'mon. I need some clean stuff," she called, slight irritation in her voice.

"Coming, Mom," said a sandy-haired boy of about ten. He held a second bucket by the handle with both hands. The bucket was levered off his stomach and it sloshed sudsy water with every knee that hit it.

Kate rubbed a hand through her short, blond hair She pulled it out quickly, looking at the grime that covered her fingers. The jeep she was washing was filthy. Sticks and leaves clung to racks mounted on its top and back. The winch on the front looked like it was growing a small bush. She plucked futilely at the embedded foliage while Noah dropped the bucket near the front wheel. A third of the water still remaining, splashed out, taking with it the last of the surface suds.

"Remind me never to have you fetch beer," said Kate.

"Huh?"

"You'll get it when you're older." She dumped the water out of the first bucket and groaned when the sponge hit the driveway. Sure enough, the sponge picked up pebbles and bits of gravel like a magnet in a pin box. She handed the empty bucket to her son.

"Get me another bucket of water. Don't fill it all the way, you'll hurt yourself. Get me a new sponge. Your dad's probably hogging them all in the backyard. Tell him to forget about his precious kayak and come help me."

"Okay, Mom."

Kate picked a few pebbles off the sponge, then gave up and dropped it in her clean bucket. "Mom?" Noah said from behind her. "I think there's something wrong with Sharky."

Reflected in the jeep's window, she saw her son standing in front of the dog. She crossed the front lawn and put her hand on Noah's shoulder. A few feet away, Sharky, a seven-year-old Golden Retriever, stood tensed, alternately growling and whining.

"What's wrong, Snucks?" asked Kate, squatting a little.

A look of almost human indecision held the dog's face, then something was settled in Sharky's eyes and the strange expression was replaced by one of vacuous hunger. Kate pulled Noah behind her and backed away, slowly.

"It's okay, Sharky, it's us, it's just us...RANDY!" she called to her husband, praying he wasn't wearing his Walkman. "It's just us, Sharky. RANDY I NEED YOU!"

Sharky cleared the distance between them in the blink of an eye. Noah went sprawling as the dog struck Kate in the chest with all its weight. She fell backwards over her son. Kate pushed at Sharky, then pulled, not wanting to hurt the animal. By the time she realized she would have to harm her beloved pet, she'd sustained too much damage to do so.

Brad and Darcy stood near the end of the line, hands interlocked with the people on either side of them. Both of them were sixteen, and among the youngest that made up the human chain between the loggers and the timber line. For Darcy, this was heaven. This was right where she wanted to be, protecting Mother Earth from greed and destruction. For Brad, this was a chance to show his new girlfriend how sensitive he was to Gaea's plight and, hopefully, earn some major boyfriend points. He scanned the faces of angry lumberjacks to see if any of them were checking out Darcy's legs, so nicely bare below her denim cutoffs.

"We've got the law on our side," said a wide-faced man, heading the wedge of loggers. "The last batch of you tree-huggers was hauled off to jail, and the same will happen to you. I'm trying to be polite here, but you people are really starting to piss me off!"

At the far end of the line from the teenagers, stood an off duty RCMP officer named Sid Halbert. He eyed the Chinese hand gripping his black fingers and thought it looked like a multicultural society's logo. He knew he was risking his job, but the cause he had joined was more important, it was bigger than him. If things got out of hand, he didn't know what he was going to do. He couldn't allow violence to occur, but at the same time, he'd be arrested himself if the authorities were called in. Two weeks ago, he'd been one of the authorities doing the arresting.

"We're not going anywhere," said Dr. Monroe, a woman of about sixty, standing in the centre of the line. Her silver hair hung loosely, just past her shoulders. "Our reports have been bogged down in committee hearings, but you're over-cutting and you know it."

"Oh this is ridiculous," said the logging foreman. He threw down the court order he'd been brandishing like a cross and stomped off to his truck. The other loggers remained and the staring contest continued.

Brad looked at Darcy's curly, reddish-brown hair and squeezed her hand. She smiled at him and squeezed back. Sunlight glinted off a silver dolphin necklace Brad had given her the week before. While waiting for the impending convoy of land rapists, Dr. Monroe had tried to teach them a couple of resistance songs. Except for Darcy, none of the new recruits could sing all that well, so they'd settled on a silent resistance.

At his truck, the foreman loudly explained his situation into a CB mic. He struggled through a miasma of political correctness training. Essentially, he was trying to get permission to bust some heads. This had been the third time in a month his men had been blocked. Though the other faces changed, Dr. Monroe was always in the middle. Injunctions and restraining orders didn't phase the woman. The jail time she was surely facing would only add to her valiant sacrifice. The farther behind schedule his crew became, the more careless they would be in their haste to catch up. Accidents happened. Lives were lost because of these eco-freaks. Why couldn't they understand that?

A scraggly blonde man to Sid's right spat a wad of tobacco at the feet of the nearest logger. Sid could almost hear the clicking of wheels in the logger's head as he weighed consequences versus crime.

A raccoon appeared from the tree line and wandered boldly between the opposing sides. It stopped over the glob of spit.

"What are you going to do?" asked the blonde man. "Kick it?"

The logger, who towered over his antagonist, squinted and looked away, straining to maintain his composure. His head jerked down and he yelped as the raccoon bit through denim into tender flesh.

"Yahoo!" called Brad. "Nature gets her own back!"

The logger brought his leg up and swatted at the animal that held on strong.

Dr. Monroe broke the line and rushed to assist the logger. The bitten man was sitting now, pushing with both hands at clamped jaws, tearing his own tissue in an effort to dislodge the raccoon.

"No, stop, you'll hurt it," said Dr. Monroe as she slapped at the logger's white knuckled grip. "It doesn't know what it's doing!"

The raccoon had reached bone. The logger clung to macho like it was a lifeline. The scream he held back with his teeth was coming out his eyes.

"What the hell is going on here?" said the foreman as he jogged back from the truck, leaving the mic dangling out the window. "Jesus! Get that off his leg!"

Dr. Monroe gripped the raccoon on the top and bottom of its head. "Everybody back away," she ordered. "This animal is rabid."

The foreman pushed Dr. Monroe away and broke the raccoon's skull with a steel-toed boot.

Brad sneered at the gasping logger, but when he looked for approval from Darcy, he saw only sympathy in her eyes.

Dr. Monroe cradled the animal in her arms. She steeled herself and spoke to the foreman. "You'll have to take this man to a hospital as quickly as you can. You might as well give this up for the day."

The foreman, who was applying pressure to his man's wound with a handkerchief, looked at Dr. Monroe with utter contempt. "I don't believe this. I've got a man down, and you use it to...fuck off, Doc."

"Don't you talk to her like–" Whatever else the blonde man was going say was cut off by his scream. A second raccoon was chewing into his leg.

The line of protesters split and scattered as raccoons raced from the tree line, clamping onto anyone not fast enough. Brad, who'd lost Darcy the moment panic ensued, tripped over a fallen protester and landed face to face with a brown squirrel. Brad blinked. The squirrel growled, then bit a chunk out of Brad's nose with teeth designed to crush walnuts.

"JESUS FUCKING CHRIST!" yelled the foreman as his men flew in all directions. People screamed and fell under a wave of fur and bushy tails. There were hundreds of woodland creatures. They dropped from trees and flowed out of the forest. Cougars joined the squirrels and coons, and the mammoth frame of a grizzly bear lumbered from the timber and into the fray.

Sid held a bleeding arm tightly to his chest and smashed at animals with the butt of his back-up piece; a black, snub-nosed revolver. He aimed the gun at the bear when something landed on his back and bit his shoulder. Something else bit his ankle, and Sid fell into the swarm of critters.

Dr. Monroe, a strip of flesh dangling from her cheek, looked into the face of the cougar that stood on top of her. "Why are you doing this?" she asked, her voice choked with panic and confusion. "We were trying to help you!"

The cougar hissed and made Dr. Monroe the martyr she'd always wanted to be.

The waves were gentle, just the way Lena liked them. The *Xingyun Shui Shou* rocked just the right amount. The sun was far past its zenith and whitecaps sparkled in a cone that came from the horizon and stayed with the boat despite its passage. She leaned over the railing and cast her eyes at the water, imagining the wonderful mysteries that transpired beneath its opaque surface. Her father joined her at the rail.

"It's a nice night," he said.

Normally he didn't waste breath on stating the obvious. Lena knew he was working up to something.

"Ni zhida Luis jia xia zhou yao juxing yici wuhui–"

"Father," said Lena, "I've asked you to speak English while Marty's around. Please. It's impolite."

Mr. Wong inhaled, then spoke in English, but in a much lower voice.

"The Luis are having a party next week. I would like it if you would come with us."

"A night avoiding Mia and Sue-Ling? Delightful. The Luis don't even put out a good spread. What's the point?"

"Henry is back from Harvard. He plans to stay for a while before returning to his thesis."

Lena pushed away from the rail. She flicked a strand of long black hair away from her face and grimaced at her father. "Dad, Marty is just below deck. How can you be so rude?"

"Oh, please," he said as he put his hands on her shoulders. "He's fine, Lena. He's a nice boy, but you'll be graduating soon and you have to think about what you'll be doing afterwards."

"Is that what you think? That Marty is just my university boyfriend? No, that's what you hope."

"Nandao shi wo cuole ma?" he asked.

Lena dropped into her father's native Mandarin.

"Yes, you're wrong. He's white, Dad. He's a bright white man and I love him."

"But don't you want to give your mother grandchildren?"

Lena didn't understand the question for a moment. Mr. Wong misinterpreted her lack of response.

"*Lena? Are you…?*"

This she understood perfectly. *"No, but I wish I was. You'd have to accept him then."*

Feet pounded up the stairs that led down to the tiny galley and lower bridge. Marty stepped out onto the deck. He had a nicely shaped face, but it held more freckles than would be considered attractive by most people.

"Mr. Wong," said Marty, "there's something funny on the sonar. I think it's pretty big."

"I told him to watch the sonar to keep him out of the way," said Mr. Wong. *"He can't even do that right."*

Lena shook her head a little, then said to Marty, "My father doesn't think you can read a sonar."

Mr. Wong looked wide-eyed at his daughter, then turned to her boyfriend and stammered, "Come on then, let's see what you've found."

The two men went below, and Lena watched after them. Her father was making this so difficult. He'd promised to behave himself when she'd agreed to this trip. Lena felt the boat slow to a drift. Mr. Wong came up the stairs, he was smiling and waved excitedly.

"Look over the side, look over the side," he said.

Marty emerged, followed by Mrs. Wong, who'd been doing the piloting.

Lena's face lit up as the back of a killer whale broke the surface not twenty feet from the boat. Its massive tail rose in a spray of brine, then it sank beneath the waves. The four people scanned the water in all directions, hoping for another glimpse of orca's majesty. Water covered their backs as the whale leapt from the ocean on the far side of the boat. As they spun, the whale crashed back down and an even greater deluge hit them in their faces.

Marty gasped and rubbed salt water out of his eyes. "Wow! Do you get to see this often?"

Lena and her father were at the other side of the boat, searching for the next appearance. Mrs. Wong wrinkled her nose as she wrung out her sweater. There was a dull thud from below and the boat rocked violently. Marty and Mrs. Wong fell, but Lena and her father kept their footing by clinging to the rail. A few feet from the boat, the whale surfaced. Its huge dorsal fin curled over near the top. It fixed one eye on the boat, then opened its mouth and water roared as it rushed out. The whale let out a high pitched squeak—so incongruous to its massive bulk—then melted into the sea.

Mr. Wong ran from one side of the boat to the other, anxiously searching for the leviathan. Marty went below deck.

"Dad," said Lena, "why did it do that?"

"I don't know. Maybe it's protecting young." He turned to his wife. "Nancy, take us out of here."

Mrs. Wong hustled up the steps that led to the upper bridge. She fired up the engines and turned the boat towards shore. Land was very far away, it would take them at least forty minutes at full speed to reach the docks. From below deck, Marty's voice called urgently.

"Mr. Wong? You've got to see this!"

Lena's father pulled himself from watching the ocean and went below. He was back up in a shot. He yelled at his wife as he jumped the steps to the upper deck. "Turn around! Turn around!"

The boat shuddered and heaved as a killer whale slammed into the prow. There was a crunch of wood and fibreglass. Mr. Wong was hurled to the deck. Lena fell and slid back and to the right. Mrs. Wong somehow kept her balance and hauled at the wheel. Another impact tossed the boat starboard and a third almost rolled it over. Mrs. Wong was thrown into the sea.

"MOTHER!" screamed Lena.

The *Xingyun Shui Shou* lurched and groaned the first of its many death rattles. It was taking on water fast. From all around, orcas rose and watched the boat flounder. Mr. Wong pulled himself to the life-boat—a zodiac with a motor—and tugged at its restraining ropes. Lena stumbled to the stairs. Water lapped at the bottom of them.

"Marty!" she screamed. "Marty!"

The boat was almost lifted into the air by the next impact. It split the *Xingyun Shui Shou* in half. Icy water knocked the air out of Mr. Wong's lungs as he fell in and under. His chill was short lived as mighty jaws cut him in half.

On that first day, millions died. The military was desperately needed, but military bases in most places had their own dogs, and rats—thousands of rats. People barricaded their doors and pulled whatever fire-arms they had from top shelves of closets and basement gun racks. Zoos around the world were chaotic, but none more so than San

Diego Zoo, where a clever gorilla got its fat fingers on a keeper's keys and deftly jangled the other animals to freedom. The main thoroughfares of most cities were clogged by accidents—so many people drove with pets in their cars. It didn't matter anyway, where would anyone run to? The woods certainly weren't an option.

People in the sprawling metropolises discovered the exact meaning of commensal wildlife. Mice and rats, once perfectly content to hide in the walls and occasionally wander into a snap trap, now flowed from holes behind fridges, and up the pipes of baseboard heaters. For some people, locking the doors was the worst thing they could have done. Stray dogs joined feral cats in taking care of the homeless problem once and for all. Animal rights activists everywhere got their fondest wish as research animals turned on their tormentors. Petting zoos were a tragedy of children versus strong-jawed and hard-hoofed ponies. Old goats gained new strength and steers smashed through fences to reach those who had stolen their virility. In Spain, the running of the bulls started early, and didn't stop. What few circuses that still had animal acts gave North American audiences a taste of what was happening in villages all over Africa.

At a marine centre on Grand Bahamas Island, one of their best attractions, swimming with the dolphins, turned into a nightmare. Bystanders' cameras dropped to the ground as their family and friends bobbed in the water, held up by BCDs and blood-soaked neoprene. Aeroplanes and helicopters alike fell from the sky like meteors as flocks of birds hurled themselves into flight paths. Wild animal preserves offered a variety of horrors. In Tenaru Nature Park, a keeper wet himself beside his jeep as he watched gibbons tear through the roof of a rag-top car and dismember its occupants with hideous enthusiasm. By some quirk of fate, that keeper's torso wound up draped over a sign that read, "Please Do Not Leave Your Vehicle."

On the evening of the first day, sparse lines of gun-wielding troops and volunteers prayed to their gods as they faced the relentless waves of slavering animals that wended their way towards the hospitals, back lit by burning cities.

For the first twenty-four hours the single most common emotion felt on the planet was mind-numbing panic. Overnight the world had become a giant ball of widows, widowers and orphans. By day two, the death toll was immeasurable. By day three, some control had been reestablished in certain areas. Fenced refugee camps had been set up and tanks rolled through city streets, pushing and crushing cars as soldiers leaned from the turrets and sprayed machine-gun fire down dark alleys and into rustling bushes. Small towns everywhere were a complete loss. Any hamlet unlucky enough to be exposed to its native predators was on its own. For dingos, jackals and hyenas, jubilee had come, but for humanity, it was Hell on Earth.

China blamed the CIA. Religious zealots glowed with vindication—Sodom and Gomorrah were once more being swept clean. Old survivalists locked in their underground bunkers blamed the Commies. The younger ones knew it was Iraq. Xenophobes screamed that the aliens were using animals as a first wave before colonization. Some people said the Japanese were behind it. None of these people lived in Japan, where animals behaved just like everywhere else, and even the gentle snow monkeys sprang from the trees to gore soldiers and civilians alike. In every part of the world, someone blamed the Jews.

Where there was power, people stared in glossy-eyed droves at their window on life; the television. Somehow, it was still more real for people to watch transmissions of the Change on the tube, than it was for them to just look outside.

On day four, a new force joined the attack on mankind, an army whose soldiers numbered in the billions; the insects. Not all of them, just one lowly order; the hymenoptera—bees, wasps and ants.

The last station to go off the air, supported by satellite access far exceeding that of other networks, was CNN. It was an historic moment, the kind of thing that would be replayed again and again by those with the equipment and the power to do so. Tom Westlaw, a field reporter whose hair was perfect even after three days of chaos, stared straight into the camera as angry swarms rose behind him. There was no where left to run and he and his cameraman had decided to make their last stand amid the tortured streets of Anywhere, Europe. As tiny bodies lit on his skin, Westlaw raised his hands and screamed, "If you're out there Lorne Greene, here's your God-damn New Wilderness!"

Even though most people didn't know Mr. Westlaw was referring to a naturalist long in the grave, the vehemence of the statement could not be denied. Despite being made on June 13th, the declaration was made retroactive by its audience. Many titles the world over were attributed to June 10th, but the name that stuck and held was New Wilderness Day.

2. Ten Years Later

A pack of dogs wandered through the scrub. They ranged in size from medium to large, individual breeds were indiscernible, but it was possible to pick out a bit of wolf in some of them. The brush thinned at a cracked four-lane highway. Without maintenance and the constant weight of traffic, the earth beneath the blacktop had begun to reclaim its surface. Plants sprung from cracks and a small tree had thrust out between a split seam near the crest of an upward incline. Near the tree, a rusted minivan lay on its side. Some of its windows were broken out, but wind and time had removed any fragments of glass from the road. The interior of the van was blackened by a fire, caused when sunlight through a spider crack in the rear window had ignited something within. Two of the dogs sniffed around the van. One of them jumped inside and emerged with a long bone, most likely a femur. There was no meat on the bone, as beetles had long since removed the last of the soft tissue, but a bone was still good to chew on. A large dog with dark, shaggy fur and a wolfish muzzle claimed the middle of the highway and snarled. The bone carrier dropped the femur and backed away. The pack's alpha male nudged the bone with its paw, then cocked a leg at the minivan. An unusual sound, like the roar of the river, but different, came from beyond the crest. As a group, the dogs pricked their ears and turned their heads. A hurtling shape of black rubber and dented metal broke the crest, smashed the small tree, and left the alpha male a bloody smear across faded yellow divider lines.

"Wuhoo!" exclaimed a gray-bearded man as he looked back over his shoulder. "Didja see it fly? That was the best one yet!"

In the passenger seat, a young man with messy, sandy hair and a short brown beard, sat austerely, facing the oncoming road. Strong steel mesh covered the cracked windshield, as well as all the other windows. It made sight-seeing possible, but not altogether pleasant. The grizzled driver swerved to avoid a large pothole and noticed his companion's lack of enthusiasm.

"Would you quit moping already? If you don't start having some fun, kid, I'll turn this car around right now!"

"Do it!" said the young man, a mixture of hope and relief gripping his features.

The driver sighed. "That was a joke, Noah. I guess I shouldn't be too surprised you didn't get it."

Noah, clearly disappointed, hunched his shoulders and slumped further into his seat. He reached into the neck of his shirt and withdrew a small dogskin pouch on the end of a leather thong. "This sucks," he said.

The driver slapped Noah in the shoulder without taking his eyes off the road. "Live with it. Sanderson makes the decisions. She's doing it in everyone's best interests."

"Sanderson can get locked outside for all I care."

"I'll tell her you said that," said the driver. "That'll make her change her mind."

Noah looked out his window. Bushes thrived and wild flowers had sprung up among the scrub. They went by in a semi-blur of blue and violet. Wasps and other insects met their deaths on the windshield and many more would be buzzing around the flowers, but Noah thought he'd gladly risk leaving the car if it meant returning home with a pretty bouquet.

"I still don't understand why Jenny couldn't come. Why is it just us, Bacon?" Noah rubbed the dogskin bag between his finger and thumb.

"I told you this already," said Bacon. "It's dead-man's boots only where we're going."

"Well maybe I'll just kill someone when we get there."

Something large enough to make the car shudder went under the wheel. Bacon looked in the rearview mirror. "Coon squash!" he said. "Look, kid, I'd get over little Jenny quickly if I were you. Nobody at Compton Pit is going to give a cat's carcass about your wounded heart. You won't make any friends if their first impression of you is as a snivelling baby."

"I'm not going to get over her, and she's not going to get over me. You should see how broken up she was when I told her."

Bacon gripped the steering wheel a little tighter. "She just did that for show," he said quietly.

Noah turned angrily in his seat. "Dogshit! She loves me. She gave me this." He dug into the little bag and produced a tiny ball of blue-tinted glass.

Bacon looked at the crystal, then shook his head and snorted. "I'm sorry about this, but it's for your own good." He struggled in his seat to reach a pocket, pulled out an almost identical dogskin pouch, and tossed it into Noah's lap.

Noah picked up the bag and felt the round object inside. He opened it, and his confusion increased. There was a crystal in it just like his. "Where did you get this?"

"Where do you think I got it? From Jenny."

"But why did she give it to you? She gave one to me because I…" Noah's jaw dropped. "Bacon?! You and her? When? She never told me! How long ago was it? She must have been just a kid!"

"When's not important. Jenny's got a whole sack of those things. She keeps it at the bottom of that big trunk of hers. I'm...there's a few of us with those crystals."

Noah held the two crystals together in stunned silence.

"Now don't go gettin' into your head that she's like some bitch in heat. She's a good girl. We all do what we can for the community and this is her contribution. She makes some of us happy and gives us these crystals for luck. I never go outside without mine. Since I'm still here, I guess it works. She's not that mature, Noah. Some of you young 'uns got stuck as kids in the head."

Noah snarled and dropped Bacon's crystal to the floor of the car. He cracked the door, and threw his own crystal, and the pouch, out into the slipstream.

"Maybe you're still stuck there too," said Bacon. "You're going to regret doing that tomorrow. Give me mine back. I plan on keeping it."

The road narrowed to two lanes, and turned gradually. High brush and trees obscured what lay ahead. They passed a place where a score of cars had been pushed to the side of the road. Bacon slammed on the brakes and hauled the vehicle into a fishtail, coming to a stop just before hitting a long bus that lay across the road.

"Goddamn," breathed Bacon. "That wasn't here last time."

Noah blinked at the rusted underbody, scant inches from mesh and glass. The bus's long drive shaft had split from corrosion. Bacon backed the car up into a T-position with the overturned vehicle. He eyed the scrub on both sides of the road.

"Just drive around it," said Noah.

"You see those posts on either side?"

Noah squinted through the mesh-covered glass. Close to the ground, he could see the remains of thick, rectangular posts—now only powdering nesting sights for ants and fungus.

"Those held guardrails," said Bacon. "Now the posts are rotted, sure. But where's the rail? Metal is metal to a scavenger, but we're kind of far out. There should be something left. And look at that." He indicated the underbody of the bus. "There should be a motor there. The wheels are gone, even the ones that would be pinned to the road. That'd be a big operation, and I don't see any signs of a fight. There'd be something, a carcass, a boot...something. I don't think this bus got here under its own power."

"Who put it there?"

Bacon said nothing.

"Is there another road?" asked Noah.

"Nope. Not without a lot more fuel. That armour around the tank reduces capacity. Makes us heavier too. Not good for mileage. This is the only road we've got."

Noah considered. "Well then, I guess we'll just have to turn around."

"About that, we passed the point of no return just before noon. Didn't want to worry you."

Noah punched the dashboard, "OH THIS SUCKS!" The cracked vinyl was unforgiving on his fist, and he nursed his fingers as he turned to the driver. "What else are you lying to me about?"

"I ain't lied to you about nothing!" Bacon said angrily. He calmed down and continued. "Did you ask me how much fuel we had? Did you ask me if Jenny...forget it. We go around."

Bacon picked the right side of the road, and slowly eased the car into the brush. There was furtive movement as animals, drawn by the rumbling engine, scattered out of the way. The car scraped against the side of a boulder as they skirted the front of the bus. Through the bus's empty window frame they could see no seats inside, not even for a driver. A raccoon landed on the hood and clawed at the mesh. Noah's brown eyes widened in shock.

"Get off of there!" barked the driver. He pulled a knob on the dashboard, and spring-loaded, foot-long spikes shot up from in front of the mesh. The raccoon squealed and ran up the windshield. Noah heard it patter across the roof, and then it was on the trunk, clawing at the mesh on the back window. The right side of the car dipped sickeningly as incline took it. For a moment it seemed the car would roll, then the wheels gripped again, and they spat out back onto the road on the other side of the bus. The raccoon was still at the back window. Bacon gunned the engine and the animal gripped the mesh tighter. The gray-haired driver pulled a second knob on the dashboard and spikes popped up from the trunk, one of them neatly impaling the coon. After a few minutes, the car stopped and idled. Bacon tapped the fuel gauge, but it didn't move.

"It's your turn," said Bacon.

"What? Here?"

"Nowhere we can reach that's better or worse."

The younger man frowned, then reached into the back seat for a mosquito-netted helmet and a jacket-wrapped bundle. He undid his seatbelt, forced his arms into the jacket then donned the helmet. He tucked the netting under the collar of the jacket and zipped it all the way up. One at a time, Noah brought his feet up and tucked his pant legs into the tops of his boots. He cinched them tight with a draw-string. He reached into the back seat again and pulled out a shotgun and a red plastic jerry can.

"Ready?" asked Bacon.

Noah nodded and left the car, shutting the door quickly behind him.

"Hold your breath," said Bacon as he pulled yet another knob. Insect repellent puffed out from nozzles all around the vehicle. He killed the engine and locked all the doors. "Hey, kid, while you're out there, change the tire, will you?"

Noah, always looking at the outside world through mesh, saw that the rear tire closest to him was flat. He looked at Bacon, who was laughing himself silly behind the wheel. Noah flipped the door handle a few times and smacked the window with the palm of his hand.

Bacon stopped laughing long enough tell Noah to reset the spikes. Then he was chortling again, but he did get his own gun from the back seat; a short-barrelled rifle.

Noah refilled the tank first, not wanting the gasohol to be a risky backstop if he did have to shoot something. When the gas cap was back on, he gave Bacon a thumbs up. Bacon gestured towards the back window. Noah nudged the coon with the barrel of his gun. It was safely dead. He yanked it off the spike and was about to toss it into the trees, but instead put it on the roof of the car, hoping the scent of the insect repellent would mask the smell of blood. Noah pulled a lever near the base of the rear window and the spikes retracted. As soon as he had done so, the trunk popped open, triggered from within the car. The vehicle was a misshapen hodgepodge of other cars. It was a wide two-door, with long hood and trunk. It may, at one point, have been a Toronado. Despite its awkward appearance, it was exceptionally well welded and sealed. Airflow on the inside was accomplished through vents with multiple screens between exterior and interior. The windows couldn't be opened, and if it was hot outside, you baked inside. Sanderson had kept saying she would get air conditioning in all of Underbel's vehicles, but so far, only hers had been so outfitted. The gray and green paint on the car was scratched in many places; a new coat would be needed soon. The car had been jacked up on its frame, in order to accommodate larger, tougher wheels.

Noah used a steel rod to lever out the heavy spare. He grabbed the jack and looked curiously at the oblong wooden crate and skinbags—hide-wrapped bundles—that occupied the trunk. All of his own possessions were in a rucksack in the backseat. This stuff must be Bacon's. He sure had a funny way of packing. Noah placed the jack under the edge of the frame and raised the car. He removed the bolts from the flat tire, then took up the shotgun and searched the tree line, looking for signs of movement. Satisfied that there wasn't any, he placed the shotgun on the roof of the car, next to the coon. Noah used the metal rod to lever off the bad tire, and then with teeth-gritting effort, lifted the spare into place, and slid it home. He placed the bolts back on and tightened, then released the jack.

"KID!" yelled Bacon. "GET BACK IN THE CAR!"

Noah heard brush being torn aside and heavy feet striking the ground. The passenger door swung open and he dove inside. Bacon gunned the engine and the forward momentum closed the trunk, shut the door, and sent the shotgun and coon skittering to the road. A bull moose burst from the scrub, skidded to a long-legged stop, then charged after the escaping car. In the mirror, Bacon saw that one of the skinbags had flown out of the trunk before it closed.

"Well dogshit," he said. "I wonder what that one was."

The moose gave a good chase, but eventually surrendered, and walked off into the trees.

"We lost the tire," said Noah.

"It was flat. Wouldn't have helped us anyway. It's the jack and shotgun I'll miss. We're lucky whoever set up that bus wasn't hanging around, not that they could really. Not without so much protection it would be obvious they were there. You okay?"

"Yes, no thanks to you. What if that moose had gotten me? Huh? Would you think it was so funny then?"

"Ah, Bullwinkle didn't have chance. You're too fast."

"Bullwinkle?"

"Oh c'mon, you've gotta remember Bullwinkle. He was a cartoon. Hung out with a squirrel that wore pilot's head gear all the time."

Noah stared blankly.

"Hey Rocky, watch me pull a rabbit out of this hat," said Bacon in a fuzzy voice.

Noah's eyes lit with comprehension.

"Yeah, you got it," laughed Bacon. "Only now it would probably be a human head." This notion wasn't as funny as Bacon had thought it would be. The two were silent for a few minutes.

"We lost the jerry can as well," said Noah. "How much farther?"

"Maybe an hour and a half if we're where I think we are. If we pass a gas station with the hulk of a one-ton through the front it, then I'm not far off."

In a short while they passed the landmark. The wreckage had been picked clean by scavengers, but parts of the building and the skeletal truck weathered away on the broken concrete lot.

"Why us?" asked Noah. "Why not Grearson and Max? Or even Loretta? She's learning."

"She doesn't know as much as you, kid. The Pit's solar-panel engineer got animal bit. Freeland, I think his name was, and he needs replacing. Loretta can't fix much without one of us looking over her shoulder. She's smart, but she's got a ways to go."

"Why us?" asked Noah again.

"Underbel's the closest place to draw from. Sanderson worked out a deal with the Pit's boss. He's a good man. Tough, but fair. Don't try to joke around with him, he doesn't have much of a sense of humour left."

"How do you know him?"

"Heh. We've got a little history. Trust me, you're gonna love it there. Just pull your weight."

Noah shrugged off the last of his outside gear and dragged his duffle bag from the back seat. He extracted a piece of jerky—hopefully cow, but probably dog—and chewed on it.

"Will we ever get to go back?"

Bacon hesitated, and shifted his wide girth before answering. "Maybe to visit, but not to stay. If you don't work out, though . . . what the hell am I saying? You'll be fine."

The road drifted by. Sometimes they had to slow to get around shells of cars and trucks, or to traverse truly broken bits of highway, but for the most part it was smooth going. They passed a few more rotting gas stations. At one point they drove beside the remnants of a long fence, its posts and boards splintered and fallen, like a long line of broken teeth. A dairy farmer's field once lay behind it. Now wild cattle roamed the countryside, providing meat for predators and man. Hunting was a necessity, not a sport. It was treacherous and required well armed and well trained people. A successful hunt brought bragging rights not earned for centuries. Despite the elevated status of kill or capture, there were few mounted trophy-heads. Not many people wanted to look at an animal's open mouth unless they had to.

The scrub gave way in places to accommodate a cluster of fallen buildings. There were seven in all, one of them may have been as high as three stories. In front of a crumbled facade of bricks, a large black "T" jutted out of the ground. One of its arms was shorter than the other, and it was rough in the middle at the top. It had once been a magnificent obsidian cross. Someone had told Bacon that the people of this town had remained unharmed in the church for two months at the beginning, and that they were only picked off as they ventured out for food. Bacon didn't know if there was any truth in the animals acknowledging holy sanctuary, but he hoped there was. Past the church was an overgrown cemetery. One patch of it, about four graves worth, was well maintained.

"That's risky," said Noah, indicating the short-cut grass. There were flowers on one grave that might have been put there fairly recently. "Bacon, who else died?"

"What?"

"Dead-man's boots, you said. There's Freeland, that's one, but who else died?"

Tires squealed as the car turned hard. Noah was jerked within the confines of his seatbelt.

"I almost missed it," said Bacon. He'd pulled off the highway onto a much better maintained road. There was patching over some potholes and all vegetation had been cleared. The brush vanished to reveal a large clear area surrounded by a tall, wire-mesh fence. In some places, the fence was supplemented with piles of wrecked cars, and walls of sandbags. As they got closer, Noah could see the shape of an echelon of solar panels. Near a radio tower was something that Noah vaguely identified as a satellite dish. The only two structures were thirty-foot-high towers, one far in the distance, the other closer, just inside the fence line. Some birds flew way up in the sky, but there was not an animal in sight. Bacon stopped the car and got out, no netting, no gloves. He cupped his hand over his eyes and looked up at the tower.

"Delivery from Underbel!" he yelled at the tower.

A section of the fence rolled sideways, pulled by chains that ran over pulleys and disappeared into the ground. Bacon returned to the car and they drove through the newly appeared gate. The road descended into a ramp that led to huge steel doors. After a moment, the doors slid apart, slowly and with some protest. They pulled into a concrete bay three and half times the length of the car. The doors sealed behind them and the sun was replaced by fluorescent lights that ran the length of the high ceiling. Another set of steel doors were closed at the far end of the bay.

Beside the doors was a speaker. A woman's voice issued from it. "Please place the vehicle over the central grate, and do not open your doors."

Bacon pulled forward over the middle of three grates that ran from one set of doors to the next. There was a loud hiss and yellowish pyrethrum gas filled the air around the car. The grate stopped blowing and started sucking, pulling the gas back down, to be partially reclaimed by condensers. The interior set of doors opened, reddish metal sliding into concrete.

"Come on in and park anywhere," said the voice from the speaker.

Bacon drove the car from the airlock to the motor pool. It was much larger than the previous chamber. A tractor-trailer rig, a mishmash of metal plating and primer like the car, was parked against one wall. There were three smaller vehicles and a motorbike with a high curved windshield and fine steel mesh that would completely surround the rider. Bacon parked next to a reconditioned milk truck. They got out of the car and the older man eyed the semi. In an alcove near the bike, a door opened. A thirtyish-looking woman with auburn hair stepped out, accompanied by another woman and two men. The lead woman wore khaki coveralls with a black-and-red stripe over one breast. The skin around her right eye was pulled tight and a patchwork of crescent-shaped scars lead from the eye to just below her full lips. The left side of her face was unmarked. She had a holstered gun at her hip, but she appeared to be the only one armed. One of the men wore a tool belt over faded jeans.

"Glad you made it in one piece," said the armed woman. "I'm Darcy McCullough, chief of security. Welcome to Compton Pit."

3. Compton Pit

Once outside the car, Noah's traveling companion was fairly tall. He strode towards the welcoming committee and extended his hand.

"I'm Hyacinth Backenbridge, but my friends call me Bacon."

Darcy took his hand. "Am I a friend?"

"Your predecessor was. I'm a little shocked that he's not here. What happened?"

She lifted her chin higher. "Travis Jones was lost to us some months ago. I remember him talking about you. It's nice to meet a friend of his."

"Were you two close?" asked Bacon.

"The boss told me to send you up as soon as you got here," she replied. "Miranda will show you the way."

The second woman, older, with dark hair, inclined her head. She wore a sleeveless, low-necked top that showed a bit of cleavage and a jagged scar that ran from sternum to left shoulder. There were additional scars on both her forearms. She went through the door and Bacon followed.

"Hey, what about me?" asked Noah.

"I'll be taking care of you to begin with," said Darcy.

"Don't worry, kid," said Bacon. "I'll see you later."

He left and Darcy spoke to the two men. "Start unloading. Check the car out once Burle has everything." She gave Noah the once over. "So, you're our new panel jockey? You're kind of young, aren't you?"

"I'll be twenty-one in a month," he said defensively.

Darcy looked him over again. He was only five years younger than her, but he looked only sixteen or seventeen, by the day's standards—even with the beard. It must have been the quality of his skin.

"Okay, twenty-one in a month, follow me. I'll get you settled."

The two men left with the wooden crate and the hide-wrapped bundles. Noah indicated his duffle bag in the back seat.

"What about that?" he asked.

"What's in it?" asked Darcy as she eyed the bag speculatively.

"All my stuff."

"Is it heavy?"

"No."

"Well then you carry it. Where do you think you are?" She spun on her heel and left.

Noah grabbed his bag and caught up with her. They walked quickly down a well-lit hallway. The motor pool's lighting had been augmented by three bar-covered skylights. In the hall it was more fluorescents.

"Where do you get so many light tubes?" he asked.

"We make them ourselves."

Noah looked up with new respect for the Pit. Underbel had few fluorescent lights that still worked, and new bulbs were hard to come by. Darcy turned and went through a curtain of thick strips of translucent plastic. Noah parted the curtain and found himself in a room filled ceiling to floor with guns. Mostly there were rifles and shotguns. One section was reserved for more powerful weapons, assault rifles and a few Uzis. A trunk marked "grenades" sat under a rack holding compound bows and wooden arrows.

"This is the armoury," said Darcy. "If necessary, you come here and Burle will issue you a weapon. His office is next to the doorway we came in. Otherwise stay away from them. Only security and certain others are allowed to walk The Pit armed. We don't separate the firing pins, everything here is kind of on the honour system. Don't think that means you can break the rules."

She exited through another plastic curtain before Noah could say anything. He hurried after her again.

Another hallway led to two doors. The scent of animals filled the corridor, and it made Noah nervous. Darcy didn't seem to care. She knocked on the first door, then pushed it open. There was an examination table in the room, as well as a large desk, behind which sat a clean- shaven, middle-aged man of East Indian descent.

"Harpreet, this is Noah Thurlow. He's our new sun boy. Noah, this Dr. Patel."

Dr. Patel rose and extended a hand. "Good to meet you, my boy. Welcome to the Pit." He spoke with a slight British accent. Noah shook his hand.

"I'll leave you now," said Darcy. "I'll be back in about an hour. If you're finished early, Harpreet, give him a tour of the infirmary."

"I thought you were taking me to my digs," said Noah.

"Check-up first, then you get your hotel room. See you." She left.

Dr. Patel handed Noah a can of shaving cream and a straight razor.

"Can you use that?" the Doctor asked, indicating the razor.

"Yes. Uhm, what do you want me to shave?"

"Your beard. The Boss doesn't like men to have beards here. Women can't grow them to cover their facial scars, so he prefers it if we don't either."

"I don't see any scars on you," said Noah.

Dr. Patel pulled up his shirt to reveal jagged lines starting below his right nipple and descending into his pant line. He dropped his shirt and gestured to a sink and mirror beyond the examination table.

Noah stroked his beard. "But it just started filling out. Besides, I've got no facial scars."

Dr. Patel shrugged a can't-be-helped, and nodded at the sink.

Reluctantly, the young man stepped to the sink. There was no bucket of water or pump next to the basin. Curious, he turned a faucet handle. Clean water came from the tap. He looked at Dr. Patel's reflection in the mirror. "These actually work!" He put his hand under the stream of water and quickly pulled it away. "This water is hot!" Noah plugged the sink with a rubber stopper and added cold water. He soaped up his face, then lathered and shaved.

"We also have hot showers," said Dr. Patel.

Noah dried his face. He stained the white facecloth with a few drops of red. He'd given himself some small cuts, but nothing that wouldn't be healed in a day or so. His rounded chin was unblemished, as were his high cheekbones and aquiline nose.

"Now take off your clothes," said Dr. Patel.

Noah complied, then sat on the table once he was nude. Dr. Patel studied his patient, drawing his eyes slowly from feet to head. The intense scrutiny made Noah a bit uncomfortable. He was conscious of his pale skin, but then who could go out and tan?

"Please stand and turn around," said the doctor. Noah did so.

"I don't believe it," said Dr. Patel, walking a circle around Noah. "You have no scars. None at all."

"Of course I do," said Noah. He raised his left arm and pointed to a three inch line of white that came up from the elbow. "I got this from a piece of broken glass while scavenging a few years ago. I got stitches."

"Yes, yes, I saw that. I mean you have no claw scars, no bite marks. Did you grow up in a refrigerator?"

"No. I've just been very lucky."

Dr. Patel had Noah lie down and examined him thoroughly. He checked blood pressure, pulse, eyes and ears. He took a throat swab, and some blood samples. Noah replied negatively to questions concerning history of diseases or allergies. Eventually, Dr. Patel finished and Noah put his clothes back on.

"If your blood checks out, you'll be the healthiest person I've seen in years."

"I'm sorry to hear that."

"How have you kept your nutrition up at Underbel?"

"My section's cook feeds us some of the grossest things. Bacon wouldn't let me get away with not eating them. He even made me eat this root on the drive up."

"Bacon's with you?" asked Dr. Patel with a smile. "That's excellent. I assume he's with the Boss. Here, take these." He held up a small plastic jar of pills. "Take one a day. If you forget one, don't worry about it, but try not to miss too many days in a row."

Noah took the jar and looked at the small, cream-coloured pills. "What are they?"

"Sperm inhibitors," replied the Doctor. "You like women, don't you?"

"Sure," said Noah, not completely understanding the question.

"The Boss doesn't like children here. In fact, pregnant women are sent elsewhere, usually without the fathers. These are easier to make than BCPs for women, given the materials at hand. Ironic, isn't it? They don't really affect us after the first few days."

There was a number of reasons for not wanting babies at a settlement. New life distracted people, they dragged on resources and robbed the community of workers. But those were only little reasons. Animals no longer actively sought humans like they did that first year, well, at least not as much. In every part of the world, however, one or two species took up a special duty. The elite corps were always small, clever creatures, able hunters of the night. In the Pacific Northwest, that banner was carried by raccoons. Raccoons hated babies. They could sense them somehow, they were drawn to squalling infants from who knew how far away. Raccoons in pursuit of a baby took enormous risks, often suicidal ones. When one of the bandit-masked animals did get to its prey, it was savage. No hunger was satiated in the act, all remains were left where they landed.

"If you don't want the pills," Dr. Patel continued, "I could give you a vasectomy. Many of the men here take that option. We could do it right now."

Noah unconsciously pressed his legs together. "No, I'll take the pills, thanks. I don't think I'll be jumping into bed with anyone soon. I just got here. I don't know anybody yet."

Dr. Patel chuckled and wagged his finger at the young man. "Well, you have to wait a couple of weeks for the pills to take effect, and I have to clear you of VD, but I don't think it will be long before one of our ladies works her charms on you. Especially once word gets around about your unblemished skin. They'll want to see it for themselves."

"How is word going to get around? I'm not going to flash people in the hallways."

Dr. Patel smiled an apologetic grin. "I have to have something to talk about."

"Where do you get these pills from? I've never even heard of these. What other medicines do you have?"

"You'll be amazed at what we have here."

There was a short knock and the door opened. Darcy entered the room.

"Are you finished with him?" she asked.

"Quite," replied the doctor. "He's absolutely clean, in every possible way."

Noah shot the doctor a dismayed look. Dr. Patel laughed.

Darcy didn't get what the doctor meant, but also didn't care.

"Alright, Thurlow, come on. I'll show you your new home."

As she turned to leave, Noah caught the left side of her face in profile. Without the scars visible, she appeared much younger. Her small, freckled nose made her look almost girlish. She left, and Noah had to grab his bag and hustle once more. In the corridor outside the infirmary, he caught the scent of animals again, but it vanished as they walked back through the armoury.

"Where'd that smell come from?" asked Noah.

"Animal research is down the hall from the infirmary."

"You keep animals *inside*?"

"Look, I'm just checking you in. I'm not your tour guide."

She took him past a number of doors and plastic-curtained archways, and led him into a large room with different sized tables and chairs of numerous colours and styles.

"This is the mess hall," she said. "Breakfast and dinner are announced by a double ring of the bell. If you miss one, you don't eat until the next, but you can usually get jerky from the kitchen. Supper's passed, but if you're hungry I might be able to scare something up, what with you being new and all."

"No, I'm fine," said Noah.

"Good. That door," she indicated a wide steel door, "is off limits until you're cleared by the Boss. The living quarters are through here." She pushed through another curtain and into a long corridor. Darcy didn't slow as she walked him past multiple doors, all with numbers on them. Some doors had posters or handwritten signs stuck to them. Noah didn't get a chance to look at any of the decorations closely, but one door had a large poster on it of a young boy with his foot caught in a railway trestle. There was a collie sitting on the track, baring its teeth and drooling. The caption underneath read, "Lassie, fuck off."

Darcy stopped suddenly and Noah walked into her. He pressed up against her for the barest moment, and felt firm flesh and hard muscle beneath the coveralls. Embarrassed, he stepped back.

"This is your room, number 26. There's no locks, but once again, it's the honour system. Don't enter someone's room without permission, or knocking first if you know they're in. If you're caught stealing, you'll be locked outside, it's that simple. There are bathrooms at both ends of the corridor. They're co-ed, so be polite. The showers are in the bathroom at the far end. You'll be allowed to shower twice a week, the Boss will let you know when your scheduled time is." She opened the door to Noah's room. It was larger than his digs in Underbel, but not by much. There was a single army cot, a small desk, and a chair. Two folded woolen blankets sat on a footlocker in front of the bed. Amazingly, an electric lamp on the desk provided light. Noah attempted thumbnail guesstimates of the power required by what he'd seen already. The lights alone would take...

"Those coveralls are your uniforms," said Darcy, indicating a dark blue cloth bundle on the cot. "The colour denotes that you're in science and a yellow stripe over the pocket shows that you're in the photovoltaic division. This gives you a certain amount of rank here, but don't expect some people to acknowledge it until they get to know you. There's a section of the workshop that is also yours. Your tools and equipment are all there. You'll get the whole tour tomorrow. In the meantime, this is where I leave you."

Just like that, she was out the door.

Noah dumped his duffle bag and dropped heavily onto the cot. It creaked. He looked at the bare walls of his new home. At the top of the wall above his desk was an air vent, covered by fine mesh. There would probably be many such screens throughout the entire duct system. The place was far cleaner than Underbel, and the showers were only one of many luxuries, but it wasn't home. Noah thought about Bart Grearson, and Max Reagan, who, along with Bacon, had taught him everything he knew about photovoltaics, as well as physics and related sciences. He thought about his friends and Sanderson, then he thought about Jenny. He punched the mattress, but it was more an affectation than actual anger. He already wanted back the dogskin pouch and its lucky crystal. He remembered the letter he'd left with Max to give to her, and felt like an idiot. He'd seen a leather thong around Max's neck on occasion, but never wondered what was on the end of it.

There was a knock at the door.

"Come in," said Noah.

The door opened and behind it stood a man with thin black hair, long at the back and receding in the front. He wore a green T-shirt with the words "Kill Benji" printed on it.

"Wow," said the newcomer. "You *do* look young. I'm Caps. Well, Rick Scagling, but everyone calls me Caps." He stepped into the room and held out his hand. His scars crisscrossed from the back of his hand to just beyond the wrist, where they joined in a reddish mass. The last two fingers of the hand were missing. Noah shook without even a thought. Missing digits were as commonplace as two eyes and a nose. The hand was usually the first thing thrust out for protection, or offered as a sacrifice.

"Why Caps?"

"I do cartoons and stuff, with captions. Captions, Caps. Y'see?"

"Is that your poster?" asked Noah. "The one with Lassie?"

"Yeah. Like that, do you?" Caps looked at the bare walls. "You need a housewarming gift. Come on."

Noah followed him into the corridor, checking his room number as he shut the door. Two doors away they entered Caps's digs. It was crammed with stuff. There were posters and sketches on a variety of materials stuck to the walls. On a white paper plate was a drawing of a big truck driving over a small dog. The caption read, "Rin Ten Ton." The outer edges of the plate were shaded to look like the treads of a tire. An angled easel made of knocked-together wood touched one wall and pushed against the cot on the other side. A big piece of cardboard was held to it by a wooden clothes pin. The cardboard had the preliminary sketches of a pack of dogs surrounding a giant mousetrap. Next to the easel was a battered metal-and-wood contraption that Noah didn't recognize. A metal rack held T-shirts of all colours. Some were hand-stitched, some were decade old manufactured. Circular bins in one corner of the room held rolled up paper and other long items.

"Look around," said Caps. "If you see something you like, I'll tell you if you can have it."

Noah looked through the T-shirts. They were printed with the same style as the posters.

"Where did you get all of these?" asked Noah.

"I make them myself. That's a silk-screen over there." He nodded at the odd contraption.

Noah pulled a light-blue shirt depicting a white dog with an enormous, curved muzzle, chewing on the leg of a little black-haired girl. The word balloon beside her head read, "Is it because I kept pulling the ball away?"

"Anything catch you yet?" asked Caps.

Noah let the shirt swing back. "Uhm, do you have anything besides dogs?"

"Sure, plenty of stuff. Hey, I know, what about this?" He grabbed a large scroll out of the bin, unrolled it, and held it up to Noah. It showed a fleet of cement trucks dumping their payload into the ocean. The caption read, "Pave the Whales."

"I made it for someone else," said Caps, "but they didn't want it."

A memory stirred in Noah. It was one of warmth, and the taste of popcorn. He felt tears coming to his eyes. Noah blinked them away and took the poster. "This will do fine. Thanks."

"Great. I've got no room for it in here, and I prefer it when my work is displayed. Are you crashing or do you want to yak for a bit."

"You're being very nice to me. I appreciate it."

"Don't mention it. It's not often I get to talk to someone who hasn't heard all my jokes." Caps pushed a pile of stuff off the cot.

"Here, have a seat. I do requests by the way. Shirts, and posters I mean. I don't like, sing, or anything."

Noah sat down as Caps kicked a crumpled blanket till it pushed up against the bottom of the door. He reached under the cot and pulled out a strange box. The box had a hooded, circular vent on top. In the middle of the vent was a small ceramic bowl. A rubber tube came from one end of the box and ended in a wooden mouthpiece. From a small drawer in the box's side, Caps removed a clear plastic film canister with a greenish herb inside. He took some of it and put it in the bowl.

"Do you smoke?" asked Caps.

Noah shook his head.

Caps lit the herb with a metal lighter, and drew on the mouthpiece, then immediately closed the hood and flipped a switch on the side of the box. A fan inside spun, drawing away smoke from the herb. Deprived of oxygen, it went out. Caps opened the hood, and exhaled into the vent. The smoke from his mouth was sucked up. He closed the hood and slid the box back under the cot. There was a slight odour left in the air, a hint of something sweet and heavy.

"I'm not supposed to do this," said Caps. "The Boss knows, but as long as nobody smells it, he doesn't have a problem."

"What do you do here?" asked Noah. From what he'd seen so far, Caps was entirely out of place.

"Do? Well, I help out in hydroponics, but mostly I make people laugh. What did you think of our chief of police?"

"Darcy? She's kind of brisk."

"Yeah, but real easy on the eyes, huh? She's pretty cool, actually. She's just stressed right now because of her promotion, and other stuff. You'll warm up to her. You're from Underbel, right?"

"Yes. Been there ever since...well, since I can remember."

"Underbel's only been going for nine years. You look older than that. Not much, though."

"I don't think about my childhood. Clear recollection starts at about twelve."

Caps nodded in understanding. "Why's it called Underbel? Is it named after someone?"

"No. There used to be a town topside called Bellingham. And a huge shopping mall. Underbel started as series of sewer tunnels and the underground parking lot. It was called Under Bellingham at first. It grew once they got gas for the rats. There's a few above-ground buildings now. They're building more of them too, or reclaiming parts of the mall. We have tunnels that go up to it, and poison moats around the outside, kind of like your guard towers. Why's this place called Compton Pit?"

Caps rooted through a pile of papers under the easel. He withdrew a faded picture of a thin man in a jogging suit. "This is Russell Compton. He was a billionaire crackpot that owned this place. It was supposed to be an underground hotel, shopping mall, theatre, the works. He saw a future where people would want to take vacations away from the sun and outside air. Lucky for us, eh? We've done a lot of expanding, since then."

"Where's Compton now?"

Caps curled his hand into a claw and drew it across his throat. "I wonder what he had sometimes, a couple of Dobermans maybe? Rich folk used to like Dobermans. Maybe he was exotic and had a pair of leopards. We have leopards by the way, I've seen them, so have a few others."

Noah shuddered at the thought. He'd read about leopards in old animal books. They were sleek and powerful, impossible to outrun.

"I came here with a friend, Bacon. You wouldn't know what room he's in, would you?"

Caps looked puzzled. "No, as far as I know there's only one empty room. At least it was empty until you got here."

"Where are the other rooms?"

"These are all of them." Caps gestured in the direction of the door. "There's two more hallways, but they're all full up. Unless your friend is being put in one of the guest rooms, but the Boss has always insisted we keep four empty. He could also be in the barracks, there's twenty bunks in there, but I'm pretty sure those are full too."

"How many people are here?"

"A hundred and twenty-six permanent. We have a few people that stay for a while, that's what the guest rooms are for."

"A hundred and twenty-six?" Noah was stupefied. "There's over two thousand at Underbel. How many panel jockeys have you got?"

Caps made an exaggerated display of scanning his room for something that wasn't there, then focussed on Noah. "One."

"Dogshit."

"No, really. Lots of people can do the work, but here we like specialists. You're it. I'll tell you something, you keep our roof going, you've got a cushy job. Hope you like to read."

Noah stood and picked up the poster. "Thanks for this. I'm going to bed. I guess I'll see you tomorrow."

"Hold on a sec," said Caps. He pulled a piece of putty off of a larger chunk stuck to the side of the easel. "Take this, you'll need it to put the poster up. It's hard to put a tack through concrete. Man, you sure do look young."

4. Breakfast and Lies

In Noah's dream, he sat between his mother and father in a darkened theater and watched an educational video on solar panels. His father wore a life jacket over his dark blue suit, and Kate Thurlow sniffled melancholy tears and wiped them off her cheeks with a raccoon pelt. An usher's flashlight bobbed towards the row in which Noah sat.

"There you go, sir," said the usher.

From the light of the screen Noah could make out Sharky. In the dog's mouth was the handle of a large, green plastic bucket filled with popcorn. Kate got up to help Sharky with the bucket. Noah wanted to tell her not to, but he couldn't speak. He tried to grab her arm, but he couldn't move. The popcorn glistened with something that wasn't butter. Noah turned to find his father missing. A pounding noise filled his ears. On the movie screen, Randy Thurlow was rhythmically thumping an oar against a solar panel.

"Kid? You awake?" It was Bacon's voice.

Noah opened his eyes. Fragments of the dream slithered away like silverfish, leaving him with only a feeling of muddled discomfort.

"Yeah, come in."

Bacon stepped in and looked around. He read the poster, which was puttied to the wall above the desk.

"I've seen a few of these around," said Bacon. "Nice room you've got here."

"And to think I just got my own private room at Underbel a few months ago. What's your room like?"

"A lot like the one back home. Let's get going." Bacon threw a pair of coveralls at Noah.

The young man struggled into his one-piece and laced on his boots. The coveralls were a bit large, but not uncomfortably so.

"Is it breakfast?" asked Noah. "I didn't hear any bells or anything."

"Nope, food's not for another half hour. We've got some stuff to take care of in the motor pool."

Noah cleared the fog in his head as he blindly followed Bacon through hallways and doors. When they reached the motor pool, a lone man stood near the rig against the far wall.

"Noah," said Bacon, "this is the man you'll come to know and love as the Boss."

The Boss was almost as tall as Bacon. His dark purple coveralls were meticulously tailored, and a single stripe of gold was affixed to the left breast. A twin line of pale scars stood out against black skin, starting at the left ear and curving over and down the cheek, to join a cicatrix patchwork that covered the side and front of the man's neck.

"I'm Sid Halbert," he said. "I'd tell you to call me Sid, but like your friend just pointed out, you'll wind up calling me Boss. Welcome to The Pit. Bacon's told me good things about you."

Noah held his tongue. Halbert was an imposing presence, and the young man didn't want to say the wrong thing on their first meeting.

Sid grasped Bacon by the shoulders. "It was good to see you again. Empty roads. I'll leave you two alone." He turned to Noah. "There's a meeting of senior staff after breakfast, that means you too. I'll see you there."

Noah watched his new superior leave, then turned angrily at the sound of the semi starting up. Bacon jumped down from the cab and checked a tire.

"What's going on?" demanded Noah. "Why do you still have a beard? I had to shave mine."

Bacon waved an arm at the rig. "Someone's got to drive that thing back to Underbel."

"How are you getting back?"

"I'm not, kid."

Noah crossed his arms and looked away. When he looked back, Bacon's look of apology angered him even more.

"You said you were done lying to me!"

"I didn't have the heart to tell you. You were so miserable about coming here in the first place, I thought it best...look, here's the whole thing. In the back of that rig, is clean water, fluorescent bulbs, medicine, and a whole bunch of other stuff. The cargo and the rig are the pay-off for you. You've been traded Noah, but you have been traded up. To tell you the truth, I envy you."

"So switch places with me."

"Can you drive this rig?"

"I'll learn fast."

Bacon thrust his hands into the pockets of his jacket. One of them encountered the dogskin pouch. "The deal was for you kid, not me."

"But you know more than I do."

"Which is why Sanderson wants me back."

Noah turned around and grabbed his head with both hands. He saw the car. The spikes were still sticking up in front of the windshield. "What about the bus? You can't go around it with that truck."

"With this big fella I'll be able to push it out of the way. The car's staying here."

"And all that stuff in the trunk?"

Bacon pulled his hands out and rubbed them on the front of his pants. "Yup, also part of the deal. I've got to get going, Noah. I hope I'll see you again."

Bacon climbed into the truck and drove through the doors to the airlock without looking back.

The airlock doors slammed shut on the last of Noah's comfort zone. He was completely alone. Again. Anxiety twisted his stomach and the walls of the motor pool seemed to swim away. Noah sat down in the middle of the floor, heedless of anyone who might happen by. Pain from the loss of his crystal was more acute than he would have thought possible. He looked at where the semi had been parked moments before, hoping to see a puddle of some vital fluid, requiring the recall of the truck. Against the wall was a CB rig that had probably been pulled from the semi. Apparently being able to call for help wasn't part of the deal.

A bell rang in two short, loud peals.

Noah wandered out of the motor pool, pausing on the way to reset the spikes on the car. He found the mess hall by following other people. He couldn't see the greasy stain on the rump of his coveralls. In the mess hall, smells of food both familiar and not, awakened hunger. Noah followed example and grabbed a plastic tray from a stack near a long line of steam tables. As he passed, various items were dumped on the tray by nameless faces. At the end of the line, a portly Japanese man in green coveralls placed a large glass of water and a small glass of milk in slots in the tray designed for that purpose. Noah took some mismatched cutlery from a bin near the end, and turned to face the throng of diners. Some people wore coveralls, some didn't. He looked for Caps, or Dr. Patel, or even Darcy, but couldn't find them.

"Noah! Hey, new guy!" The man's voice came from Noah's right. After a few misses he found the source. Caps stood at a round table only big enough for five or six. There was one empty chair at the table. Noah sat down and Caps put names to faces.

"This is Miranda, she works in the farm—"

"We met yesterday," said Miranda.

"This is Lena."

A Chinese woman smiled and nodded. Her face was unblemished, but her dead eyes bespoke scars that ran far deeper than skin.

"And tall boy in the white coveralls is Burle. He'll be your best friend for the first little while."

"Welcome to the Pit, Noah," said Burle, bunching his white eyebrows and smiling through a cracked and wrinkled face. "I'm head of stores. You need something, you get it from me."

Noah nodded greetings at each of the people in turn. He picked up the milk and sipped it. It was different from the milk he was used to. It was thicker, richer, it tasted like..."This is real!"

"That's right," said Caps, savouring his own.

"I haven't had this since...since..." Noah knocked the milk back in one glorious shot, and started to get up. Caps stopped him with a hand.

"No seconds, sun boy. That's all you get. There'll be more before the end of the week."

Noah looked at his empty glass. "That's it?"

"Mmhmm," said Miranda. "Next time, sip it. You'll appreciate it more."

Noah sat back down, a little chagrined. "Where did you get it?"

"Where do you think?" Caps asked. "From a cow."

"How did...how did you milk it?"

"Very carefully."

"Don't let Caps fool you," said Lena. "The cows are lobotomised. We have four of them. They eat, they crap, they make milk."

A hawk-nosed man with hair almost the same colour as Noah's approached the group and placed a prosthetic leg on the table.

"It's done, try it out," he said.

Lena did some shuffling under the table, then placed another prosthetic leg next to the first. She took the new one and affixed it to the stump of her right knee. She got up and walked around the table. The first few steps were awkward, but then became fluid.

"This is good," she said. "Decent action in the ankle. Were you up all night?"

"Most of it," said the man. "You know me, once I get started. If I could only mass produce these things."

Lena sat down. "Pull up a chair."

"No, I'm going to get back to it. I'm working on something for you-know-who. I want to get it finished, stay in his good graces and all."

The man walked out, stopping on the way to grab a glass of milk and some bread. Noah started eating and everyone else returned to their trays, completely unaffected by the artificial leg still on the table.

"What do you do, Lena?" asked Noah as he cut into a strip of meat.

"SatCom," said Lena between bites of steamed vegetables.

"What's that?"

"Oh, man, you've just got nothing back at Underbel," said Caps as he popped a birth-control pill. Noah patted his pockets, then remembered that the bottle was in his old pants. Caps slid a pill over. "Here, take one of mine. You might forget and you'll want to be primed as soon as possible."

Noah felt vaguely uncomfortable by the exchange, but he took the pill anyway. He caught Miranda looking at him speculatively. She used getting her water glass as a pretense to look away.

A single female voice cut through the mess hall's melting pot of conversations.

"So lock him out then! He got his damn room, let him follow the rules!" Darcy got up from the table she shared with Sid Halbert and a few others. She walked quickly across the hall and out the door that led back to the motor pool and a dozen other locations.

Caps and Lena exchanged glances.

"I got her last time," said Lena.

Caps looked at what was left on his plate, pushed away from the table and exited through the same door as the security chief.

Noah studied the ceiling of the room to avoid being nosy. If information wasn't volunteered, he was too new to ask for it. High in the ceiling were a number of skylights like the ones over the motor pool. Only a few of the banks of fluorescents were on. Sunlight was doing most of the work by itself. Sid was talking to the other people at his table, but Noah could neither hear nor make out what was being said. At one point The Boss glanced towards him, and Noah started to lift his hand in a wave, then pulled it down quickly and returned to his food.

"Do you know any Campbells in Underbel?" asked Burle, "Natalie or Jessie?"

Noah thought for a moment, then shook his head. "Sorry, no. When would they have gotten there?"

"I don't know if they did. Just asking."

Lena gave Burle a quick, sympathetic look, then picked up her tray, and placed it on a bus cart. She left.

Burle finished the last of his food and started to rise himself.

"Uhm, Burle," started Noah, "I've got a meeting with Halbert, do you know where that will be?"

Burle sat back down. "I'll be there myself. Finish up. You can follow me."

Noah polished off his breakfast and followed Burle out the door through which Caps had pursued Darcy earlier. They went away from the motor pool, and after a few more confusing twists and turns, arrived in a room with a single large table. There was a sheet covered cart against one wall. Darcy and Caps were already there, sitting at the far end of the table, talking quietly. Lena sat with Dr. Patel and the hawk-nosed man was there as well. Noah sat between him and a dark-skinned bald man who appeared to be in his fifties. The dark-skinned man introduced himself as Dr. Odega, and welcomed Noah in a subdued tone. Burle sat on the other side of Darcy from Caps. He took one of the security chief's hands in his and said something with a smile on his face. She laughed. Everyone turned in their chairs as the Boss entered with another man, white, garbed in the khaki of security. Sid took the seat at the head of the table.

"Okay, people," he said, "If you haven't met him yet, Noah Thurlow there is our new photovoltaic engineer."

The hawk-nosed man, who'd been lost in his own train of thought, snapped his head around like Noah had suddenly appeared out of thin air.

"Sorry I'm late," said a rail thin woman with shoulder length graying brown hair as she quickly took a seat opposite Noah. Her coveralls were the blue of engineering. There was a green stripe over her breast. She looked at Noah. "You the new sun boy? You're pretty. Come by some time, I'll change your diapers." She winked. There was polite laughter as Noah blushed.

Sid's voice ended the chuckling. "Noah, this is Dr. White. She's the head of hydroelectricity and hydroponics. She calls it H&H."

"Call me Momma," said Dr. White. She winked again and there was more laughter.

The Japanese man that had served Noah his food entered and pulled up a chair.

Sid rolled his eyes and did a head count. Satisfied that everyone had finally arrived, he resumed speaking.

"According to Bacon, and our new man here, there's a bus across the south road, in the snaky bit, where the guard rails used to be. From the description of the obstruction, it's probably the one that used to be by the road near Goat's Head Rock. Now it wasn't moved far, but it still took some effort. Any guesses on who might have done it?"

"Shangly?" Darcy offered.

"That's my guess," said Sid. "Can anybody think of a reason besides to just piss us off?"

"He couldn't hold the position for long," said Dr. Odeg. "Too many teeth out there."

"Did they think maybe it would stop us from using the road?" asked Caps.

"No," said Sid. "Shangly would know we could move it without too much trouble. I think it was to stop people from getting to us. Obviously it didn't work, but then our friend was never that bright. Still, I am concerned. We go back to patrolling the outer perimeter in four shifts. All of you find people in your divisions who are interested in getting some sun. If you can't find volunteers, Darcy will pick them. I'll take a turn or two myself so nobody can grumble."

Noah raised his hand.

"He thinks he's in school," said Dr. White. "Do you have an apple for teacher?"

"That's enough, Sara," said Sid. "Go ahead Noah. In future, just speak up."

"Who's Shangly?"

Caps groaned.

"Why don't you answer him, Richard?" said Sid.

"Here's the deal, Noah," said Caps. "Shangly is a mean, smelly scavenger who plants his ass out east a bit. He's got a bunch of doglickers with him and they forage all over the place for anything they can get. Metal, electronic equipment that might still work, you know the drill. Anyway him and his pack used to come around and trade with us for supplies. The Boss cut him off a few months back. For a couple of weeks they made life interesting, then they just took off."

"Why'd you stop trading with him?" Noah asked Sid.

"The last time he showed up here he had things that I knew came from a settlement to the southeast. It was a small place, called New Found Hope, on what used to be the border. A couple shelters, a couple of above-grounds with poison moats...they could have made a go of it there. Shangly sacked the place. He must have been desperate."

"How do you know he didn't just show up after an animal attack?" asked Noah. Small settlements were sometimes overrun by a sudden attack of numerous creatures.

"Shangly had some new recruits with him. I recognized them as young 'uns from New Found Hope. They told me what happened after I convinced them I wouldn't let anything happen to them. One of them is still here. The other was pregnant, and I sent her off to Underbel. You may have met her, blond girl, missing an eye?"

Noah shrugged his shoulders. The description didn't exactly narrow things down for him.

"Well, doesn't matter. Until this bus thing, I thought we'd heard the last of them. Dr. Odega and I took a trip up that way last month, so it's since then that the bus was moved. It may be nothing, but let's not get caught napping. Okay, anything I need to hear from anybody?"

A few people shook their heads. The hawk-nosed man perked up. "Did my hinges come in?" he asked.

Sid smiled and looked at Burle. "Go ahead, give them their presents."

Burle rose and pulled the sheet from the cart. On it was the wooden crate and hide-wrapped bundles Bacon had brought from Underbel. The skinbags had grown tags attached with wire twist-ties. Burle looked at each tag as he distributed the items. The first bag he gave to the hawk-nosed man, who breathed a sigh of satisfaction as he opened it to reveal various hinges and metal brackets. Dr. White got some soil samples in ziplock bags, a hairbrush and an assortment of seeds in faded paper packets.

As the bundles moved across the table, Sid spoke up. "One of the packages was lost on the way. Richard, I'm afraid it was yours."

"What a gyp! Why'd it have to be mine?"

"Quit your bitching," said Dr. White. "You're doing fine with the stuff we make."

"I'm almost out of gold. We can make all the other dyes, but metallics? When's the next shipment going to be?"

"Not for at least a month," said Sid, "but I sent the same request with the convoy to Drum East. Maybe they'll find some for you there."

"Drum East?" Caps was not enthused. "We couldn't get a decent bucket of mud from Drum East, never mind gold ink."

The last presentation was the wooden crate. Burle dropped it smartly in front of Dr. Odega. The dark skinned man rubbed his hands together and pushed the lid off the crate. Inside was a model kit for a remote controlled aeroplane, a miniaturized Sopwith Camel. The picture on the box was faded, and one corner of the lid had been pushed in, but upon opening the box, Dr. Odega discovered all of the pieces were present, and intact.

"Are we finished?" asked Dr. Odega, like a child wanting to leave the dinner table.

"Yes, I guess we are now," replied Sid. "Everybody have a good day. Noah, stay for a few minutes."

Everyone left the table and sauntered out, clutching their acquisitions like kids at the Christmas Tree. Caps bitched to Lena about not getting his paints.

"How did Underbel get all that stuff?" asked Noah, once he was alone with the Boss.

"Bellingham had a hobby store that remained relatively intact. Your former chief, Sanderson, stockpiled the inventory, as well as that of a hair salon and hardware store. She occasionally remembers she has certain things when we have our trading sessions. We never give up our full export inventory either. It's standard practice. Richard was right, we don't have a chance in hell of getting his paint from Drum East. We should get some steel piping though. They've started a little foundry up there, if you can believe that."

Noah had never been to Drum East, or anywhere near it, so he neither believed nor disbelieved what Sid had told him.

"So you might be asking yourself how a lowly panel jockey becomes a ranking member of our group."

Noah nodded. "I was also wondering about the cook. Why is he involved? Or Caps? I like his posters, but are they vital to the Pit?"

"What did Richard tell you he did here?" asked Sid.

"He said he helped out in hydroponics and told jokes."

Sid chuckled. "Unofficially, Richard is the chief of the pool. He'll be overseeing the refit of the vehicle you brought us. He's the best mechanic I've ever seen. He won't wear any colours, so he won't take the position on the record. And he does make us laugh, so I give him leeway. The cook is vital because he's the man that feeds us. We've accomplished what we have because the moral is so high. Part of the reason is that we eat good meals. I can't remember the last time I didn't like something Roshi put on my tray. He only cares about one thing, getting his ingredients. If a decision would effect his ability to provide for us, he'll know it, and the rest of us might overlook that department. You are equally as vital. Anyone with the specs can assemble a solar power array, but we use a lot of juice here. More than you realize. We have two sources of power, the small hydroelectric generator we have, and your panels. I want you to get to know every wire, every photocell, every circuit. If something goes wrong, I want you to know where to look before you even go into the battery bay, or topside. If there's a way to provide more power, I want you to come up with it. I need you to come up with it. There's a lot to our system. You'll understand once you've had a chance to examine it. I'll have to restrict you to the Pit and topside within the fence perimeter. I can't let you go on hunting or exploration trips."

"I have no problem with that," said Noah.

"Well, you'll be too busy to worry about it at first anyway. Why don't we go topside right now?"

They walked down the hall that led to the motor pool. Sid stopped along the way to grab a rifle. They had almost reached the outer doors to the airlock when Noah asked;

"What about gloves, or net-helmets?"

"Don't worry about them," said Sid.

"Uhm, due respect sir, but it is the middle of summer."

"When I say you don't need something, then you don't need it."

The Boss gave a hand signal, and somehow, someone saw it and the outer doors opened. They stepped out into bright sunlight, and for the first time in a decade, Noah looked at the summer sky through nothing but his eyes. Beyond the barren ground, in and around the fence-line, majestic trees spread their foliage. High grass and bushes obscured tree trunks. Just like when he had arrived the day before, there was not an animal in sight.

"There's an access hatch that leads directly to the panels," said Sid, "but I wanted you to approach from the front the first time."

They walked across the field towards the army of panels. Noah looked everywhere for wasps and bees, but found none, and was soon captivated by the sheer number of photovoltaic cells before him. The collection of panels sprawled across the field. There must have been over four acres of them. There were all types; large concentrators—moving imperceptibly, tracking the movement of the sun on pivoting supports—static panels of both jet black monocrystalline and fragmented polycrystalline, and on every pipe and bracket, every rounded surface in fact, Thin Film, flexible panels, were affixed, so not a centimetre of surface was wasted. Cables both thick and thin snaked their way between the supports and brackets, winding their way towards a central, metal hub, which was also covered in Thin Film. It was the type of setup Edmond Bequerel could only have dreamed of in 1839, when he first discovered electrons could be excited by beams of light.

Under normal circumstances any joker with a manual and some duct tape could have performed the routine maintenance, but this monstrosity required so much more. Noah felt it would be years before he discovered every nook and cranny.

"Impressive, huh?" asked Sid rhetorically.

Noah suddenly remembered he was outside with only another man's rifle for protection. He looked about, but still found no sign of animals. He didn't even see any tracks in the dirt.

"Is the fence electrified?" he asked.

"No. It used to be, but the dogs learned that as long as they weren't touching the ground they wouldn't get shocked. They took to throwing themselves at the fence and bouncing off so that they were well away when they landed. We watched a pack of them one day take out a section in less than an hour."

"You just stood there and watched?"

"It was...fascinating."

"So did you drive them all off? How many of them did you kill?"

"Oh, we killed our share of them all right. We'll kill a lot more of them too, but we have other methods of keeping our haven. You'll figure it out once you're here for a while."

Noah ran his hand along a thick cable. "The other guy, Freeland, Bacon said animals got him. Wasn't he restricted to the Pit?"

"Your predecessor was...I locked him outside, Noah. He broke the rules."

There was another half-truth Bacon had told him. Noah's situation took on a heavier gravity.

"What did he do? Did he steal something?"

Sid stared off into the distance. "Nope."

"So what was his crime?"

"Rape."

"Hey, Boss," called a short man in security colours. He was walking towards them, armed with a rifle. He also wasn't wearing any headgear or gloves. "Darcy asked me to take over baby-sitting the new guy. She asked if you could meet her at the tunnel."

"I'll see you later," said Sid to Noah. "Sit with me at dinner tonight. In the meantime, you've got your work cut out for you."

Noah spent the better part of the day lost in cables and panels. At one point his guard was replaced by a lithe girl who introduced herself as Cass. She brought Noah a sparse tool kit and a pad of paper for taking notes. She also brought him some schematics of the panel array. Numbers and letters were marked on the edges of some panels in red ink. There seemed to be no rhyme or reason to the markings at first, but after checking the schematics, Noah learned that each set of figures identified which cable went where, and which of the batteries below the respective panels charged. Noah jotted figures down and did some figuring. According to the schematics, the array produced a lot of juice, almost triple what Underbel's array could. Banks of mobile reflectors ensured that each of the panels received the optimum amount of sunlight for as long as possible. Something picked at the power output Noah had calculated, but he couldn't put a finger on it.

Along one perimeter, two newly appointed guards walked the fence line. They carried M16's and wore gloves and net-helmets. Noah's skin crawled. He spun to look at Cass, who was leaning on one of the larger panel's support posts. She had her head tilted, and a contented smile curved her lips as she basked in the sun. Her dark hair, tied back in a ponytail, was draped over a Thin Film covered pipe. The rifle rested against her leg, its muzzle held loosely between two fingers.

"Why are they wearing nets?" asked Noah with a little urgency, "Shouldn't we get some? Should we go inside?"

Cass casually flipped her ponytail as she looked at the guards. "It's just for show. If someone in the towers spots something, we head inside through the access panel over there." She tilted her chin at a trapdoor near the cable-hub. "The guards stay out. Not a good idea for people to be seen topside without gear on. Might give some folk ideas."

"How do you keep stuff away? Is it a gas or something? I don't smell anything."

"I don't know how much I can tell you. Just ask the Boss, okay? What do you think of our roof?"

Noah looked at the netted guards again, then scratched the back of his head. Nobody was telling him much of anything, and when they did tell him something, it turned out to be less than the truth. "You're not wearing colours. What do you do here?"

"I'm a tanner."

Noah was downwind of her. He sniffed the air. "You don't smell like one."

"I showered last night, and I kind of ditched work today."

The trapdoor opened with a metallic creak and a model aeroplane rose from it. The plane was placed gingerly on the ground by a pair of hands. Dr. Odega clambered out of the trap, quickly followed by Dr. Patel and the Boss. Dr. Odega picked up the plane and walked a short distance from the panels.

"You're in for a treat," said Dr. Patel to Noah. "We might make history here."

The guards on the perimeter caught sight of Odega and stopped their patrol. Sid stood by the plane and Cass picked up her rifle and sauntered off to join them. There was a definite swing in her hips as she walked. Dr. Patel stared after Cass appreciatively for a moment, then said to Noah, "Come on, keep your fingers crossed."

"What's going on?" asked Noah.

They reached Dr. Odega. The guards were coming over as well, but at a look from Sid they returned to the fence line. They resumed their patrol, but netted faces kept turning back to look at the plane.

Dr. Odega knelt by the plane and fiddled with a small gadget affixed just behind the propeller. Satisfied that the gadget was secure, he stood, and looked dramatically at the people around him.

"Alright, Ted, make your speech," said Sid.

Theodore Odega took a deep breath and began his oration. "Ladies and Gentlemen, I bring you a new dawn, a return to the skies." He gestured grandly at the air. In the distance, a few seagulls swooped and arced as they caught different air currents. "Those feathered menaces will no longer be a concern." He favoured Noah and Cass with a look. "Attached to this little warrior is an object of my own, humble design. Using acoustical projections, it will soar unhindered as avians swoop harmlessly off balance." Dr. Odega extended the antennae on a black plastic control unit, then he knelt and started the plane. With a push of a joystick, the plane began taxiing across the field.

Birds rarely attacked people on the ground. There were stories of mass bird attacks on settlements and travellers, but Noah had never seen one, nor had any of the people whose stories he trusted. The birds, however, aggressively defended the air. Anything larger than a small balloon that went up, came down fast. Kites were torn to shreds, model rockets were savaged as they began their parachute assisted descents. The last plane attempt Noah knew about had been a rebuilt Cessna seven years previous. The plane had been covered entirely with reflective material, it was hoped that it would be camouflaged by mirrored sky. It hadn't lasted ten minutes.

The miniature biplane jumped into the air and ascended. The buzz of its motor was strangely familiar to Noah. In the sky past the fence line, the birds still circled and dove, heedless of the Sopwith Camel. All heads were turned skyward. Each person, in their own way, was lifted from the ground by the little plane. If this worked, larger versions of the device could be made. After time, it might be possible to fly again. Large scale exploration could begin once more, and travel between distant settlements could be accomplished. If, of course, enough planes and helicopters could be found and restored.

The gulls grew from black shapes to white feather as they altered course to intercept the remote controlled intruder. Dr. Odega thumbed a switch, crudely drilled into the side of the control unit. The birds had almost reached the plane. It held a steady course as the birds flew past it on either side.

"Yesss," said Dr. Odega.

"That's one," said Sid. "Bring the plane around."

The plane banked to the right as black dots appeared on the horizon. Other birds—gulls and crows—were drawn by the motor. The large shape of an eagle was on an intercept course from the northeast. The first flock of seagulls beat their wings furiously in an attempt to catch up with the Camel. Some crows had entered the plane's flight path. Dr. Odega put his toy into a short dive. The crows flew through a place near where plane had been. Even more birds were coming. Noah recognized robins and sparrows. Mostly it was crows. A turd hit the ground near Dr. Patel's feet. "We should have brought umbrellas," he said.

"Here comes the big show," said Dr. Odega.

"That's Icarus," said Dr. Patel to Noah. "He nests here every summer. We've yet to get a launch past him."

As the eagle ascended an updraft, the little plane began to bank from side to side.

"Don't, Ted," said Halbert. "If this is going to work, it has to do it without evasive maneuvers."

So high up it was barely more than a speck to the people on the ground, Icarus folded its wings and began an attack dive that would reach a speed of over two hundred miles per hour. Odega held his breath as the speck grew in size at an alarming rate. Icarus smashed through the little plane with ease. As the other birds darted about, shrieking and clawing at fluttering bits of balsa wood, the eagle pulled out of its dive and disappeared into the horizon. The main body of the plane struck the ground just outside the fence line, kicking up a cloud of dust. Dr. Odega watched the dust settle, then sadly collapsed the control unit's antennae. Nobody said anything for a few seconds. Even as they had flown with the plane, they'd crashed with its demise.

"Maybe the acoustical projections don't work on a long range attack dive," said Dr. Odega. "Or maybe the generator couldn't overcome the engine."

"You'll have to go back to kites," said Sid. "Those planes are too damn expensive. I'm glad we didn't announce this test over the whole Pit, though I'm sure everyone will know about it by nightfall. Dinner's in a few minutes, let's go inside."

Sid and Patel went through the trapdoor. Cass placed a hand on Dr. Odega's arm. One of the guards trotted over with the Camel's wreckage. He handed it over to the animal researcher. Dr. Odega looked at the splintered wood in one hand, and the control unit in the other, then he howled at the sky. He hurled the plane and controller at the ground and swung impotent fists at birds high overhead.

"I'll kill you all!" he shouted. "I'll build a ladder a hundred feet high and break your necks with my bare hands!"

Ted Odega stomped off towards the trapdoor, his shoulders hunched, rubbing his forehead and temples with both hands.

Cass hooked an arm through Noah's. It was a sudden, intimate contact that startled the young man.

"Come on, sun boy," she said. "Let's go eat."

"Will he be okay?" asked Noah, indicating Dr. Odega.

"He'll be fine. This always happens, but I guess he thought he really had it this time."

Noah used a thin piece of bread to soak up a puddle of gravy. His small steak had vanished like it hadn't been there at all. The Boss sat at the far end of the table. Dr. White and Dr. Patel were arguing over the respective benefits of certain herbs.

"Your shower time is Tuesdays and Fridays at oh-six-hundred. If that doesn't work for you, you can try to swap with someone else. You have ten minutes in the shower."

Noah looked up from his tray to see if Sid was talking to him.

"The next slot is at six-fifteen, but use the five to dry off. Maintenance doesn't like mopping puddles in the hallways. Don't go overtime. You probably will at first, but you'll know what ten minutes feels like to the second after a few showers."

Something clicked in Noah's head. "Hot water! There isn't enough power in the system to heat water, or heat the base for that matter. What does Roshi cook with?"

Dr. White stopped her conversation with Dr. Patel and looked askance at the Boss. Sid nodded. She turned to Noah. "Geothermal. We have hot springs here, underground. What do you know about the Pit's history so far?"

"Caps told me about Russell Compton and his hotel," said Noah.

"Well," said Sara White, "the guy knew what he was doing. The springs provide our heating, freeing up the electricity for everything else. There's some above ground springs about a kilometre from here. Care to go for a bath?"

Noah missed her inference and looked at Dr. Patel. "Do the animals stay away from the springs?"

Sid answered before the doctor could. "No. We can only keep them away within the Pit and about a hundred or so feet around it. I'll have someone show you everything tomorrow. Did you enjoy the steak?"

"It was amazing. Do you keep beef animals here?"

"No, not enough space. We have freezers. Not many, but Roshi stretches the meat out."

Noah looked around the mess hall. At one table he saw Cass. She glanced his way and smiled.

"Where's Dr. Odega?" he asked.

"Probably sulking in his lab," said Sara. "It's not like I go to pieces anytime a crop fails."

"Theodore had a pilot's license," said Dr. Patel. "He had a small plane, too. He's described to me what it was like to fly by himself. You know he misses it terribly. He views the birds as if they're his enemy, and his alone."

"I miss things too," said Sara with genuine remorse in her voice, "but I still don't throw tantrums. Honestly, he acts like such a child sometimes."

"You're closest to him, Sara..." Sid said, letting the rest of the sentence hang.

Sara gave the Boss a long glance. "What are you suggesting?"

Sid held his hands up, palms out. "I'm not suggesting anything. I'm simply saying that maybe Ted seems more broken up than usual. He worked on that displacement device of his for a long time. His preliminary tests were successful. This is more than just another disappointment for him."

Sara ran a finger along the table edge. "Maybe I'll visit him later."

This brought back the loneliness that had gripped Noah with Bacon's departure. The people here were more than sharing a compound. There was a caring and familiarity between them that separated Noah unintentionally. Maybe Caps would be up for talking after dinner.

A hand gripped Noah's shoulder. He looked up.

"Care to pop down to stores?" asked Burle. "I have something for you."

Stores turned out to be a long room filled with bins and lockers. A stack of flattened cardboard boxes stood next to a hopper filled with animal hides. A thick manifest of curled paper rested on a tabletop. A strange device leaned against the table. It was made up of a steel shaft, with a small pull-cord motor at one end and a bell of green plastic at the other.

"What's this?" asked Noah, running his hand over the small motor.

"You've never seen a weed whacker?" asked Burle in response.

Another memory tugged at Noah. Gardening wasn't a big occupation anymore, but the name gave the device a purpose in his mind.

"What do you use it for?"

Burle placed a skinbag on the table. "I do a little trimming once a month. There's a cemetery up the road. I keep some graves clean."

"I saw that coming in. Your family?"

"My wife. My grandchildren. Well, my wife for sure. Never did find my grandchildren."

"Is that who you asked me about this morning? Natalie and...and..."

"Jessie. Yes. I had to bury their clothes. Never did find a hint of them. I keep hoping, but I know they're gone."

"Isn't it dangerous going out there to do that?"

"It doesn't take long. I pack a gun. The Boss understands that I need to do it. My Rachel deserves it." Burle's eyes glazed slightly, as if he was lost in a memory.

Noah gave the store master a moment, then pushed at the skinbag. "What's this?"

"Freeland's stuff. Nobody wanted it, so as his replacement you're the closest thing to next of kin."

Noah pulled back from the hide-wrapped bundle as if it might suddenly grow teeth and bite. "What makes you think I want it?"

"You probably don't, but that's your decision. Mine is to give it to you." Burle flipped to a page in the manifest and handed Noah a pen. "Sign here, please."

Noah looked at the line indicated by Burle's finger.

"Sign?"

"Or just put your initials. I know, it seems silly, but the system makes me feel better. Indulge an old man, would you?"

Noah scratched his first name on the page. It was rough, but legible. "My first name good enough?"

"I guess that will do. We don't have any other Noahs here, but if another one turns up, I'll have to add your last name."

Noah realized the old man was joking, and they both chuckled a little. Burle patted the panel jockey's hand.

"You'll fit in here just fine, son."

"Thanks. I sure hope so."

Noah took the skinbag back to his room, holding it in front of him like it was a ticking bomb. He dropped it on his table, deciding he'd open it tomorrow. He changed out of his coveralls and into his old clothes, then went to see if Caps was in.

"Ted?" Sara pushed her head through the door to animal research and scanned the dim interior. She stepped inside. Even after all this time she had to push down the discomfort animal odours instilled in her. Most of the lights were off, as was normal procedure for downtime. What wasn't needed, wasn't used. Dr. Odega's computer was still on, though. A schematic for some technical device glowed on the screen. The computer's keyboard was on the floor a few feet from the computer desk. The cable that attached the keyboard to the tower dangled from the edge of the desk. Frayed wires protruded from the gray rubber.

Odega was slumped in a chair by a metal shelving unit overflowing with thick books and scraps of paper. His back was to the door Sara had entered. There was a bottle in his hand.

Sara stooped and gently removed the bottle from Dr. Odega's hand. From the smell it was whiskey. She took a swig. It was smoother than the stuff Dr. Patel distilled, and the yellowed label identified it as old world product, Canadian Club. She nudged Odega's shoulder.

"Hmmph, whuzza?"

"Where'd you get this?" she asked, swirling the few fingers of amber liquid left in the bottle.

"Mmmph. Private stock. Kept it special. For celebrating." Odega blinked a couple of times, then slumped further in his chair. "We'll never get off the ground. Nothing I do gets off the ground."

Sara took another swig from the bottle and offered it to the drunken researcher. "I didn't come here for another one of your bouts of self-pity."

"S'true though. I don't know why Sid wastes the electricity on me. Can't make the birds go away...can't make a Mimi. Waste of juice." He took the bottle from Sara, eyed the two or three swallows that remained, and placed it on the floor.

"You done?" Sara asked.

"No...maybe I just don't want to waste what's left. S'my last bottle. There's some home-brew in the box by the computer."

Sara lifted the lid of a scratched, wooden box and withdrew a cylindrical metal flask. She unscrewed the top, and took a slug. She grimaced as the liquor burned her throat.

"You're pathetic, Ted. We all face setbacks. Your gizmo worked on the kites, but the kites don't have buzzing motors on them. Have you thought about rigging up a hot-air balloon?"

"Where are we going to get one of those?"

"Where do we get half the stuff Sid and Burle dig up? Use your head. These slumps of yours are why I broke it off with you, remember? I don't have the strength to be your nurse."

"It's not just the birds." He tilted his chin at a thick metal door that occupied the far end of the room.

Sara looked at the door, then back at Odega. "Ghandi?"

"Go see for yourself."

She opened the door, and flipped a switch, lighting a long room with cages lining the concrete walls. Some of the cages were empty, but most held animals: cougars, a raccoon, some dogs and cats. The furthest cage held a rangy mutt with clear signs of husky in it. The different colored eyes—one brown, one white—had survived generations of crossbreeding. Sara walked past the other cages. The animals looked at her with quiet hatred. She knelt in front of Ghandi's cage.

"Ghandi? Here girl," she said in a quiet, anxious voice.

The dog launched itself at the bars, snarling and biting. Sara was so startled she fell over backwards. The other animals, stirred by the dog's attack and Dr. White's position of vulnerability, threw themselves against their prisons, snapping teeth and growling. Sara's head whipped back and forth in panic and she bolted to her feet, but none of the animals could reach her. Her breathing steadied, and she calmed down. She looked at Ghandi, her face contorting in loss and disappointment. Sara wiped at tearing eyes with the back of her hand, and realized what remained of the good whiskey was not going to last another minute.

5. Things Revealed

It was not as if Noah had never had a shower before. On the contrary, he washed whenever he got the chance. The shower he was under now, though, was like a cannon to a pea shooter when compared with what he was used to. Water ripped into his skin, a hundred steaming hot needles exorcising dirt and sweat. It was cleansing on so many levels. And to think he could do it twice a week. He pictured Bacon standing under a red-flaked metal drum, pulling a chain to receive a sprinkle of sun-warmed water. No wonder the older man had been envious.

Everything he'd seen so far dwarfed Underbel's capabilities. Maybe Sanderson had these luxuries, but in Compton Pit, they were available to everyone. The doctor seemed competent and well supplied and the food was delicious, but this shower, this was the most amazing thing of all. The experience, however, was over almost as soon as it began. Noah backed out of the stall, and took a towel from the rack. As he rubbed his head, he saw a woman drying herself off. She was standing with her left side to him, bent at the waist, squeezing her long hair with a towel. White cicatrix peppered both calves, and one large claw mark, a set of three parallel lines, hugged the curve of her hip. The dark reddish thatch of pubic hair stood out in contrast to the fair hair that grew on her legs. Her breasts were full, but not overly large. The woman stood and rotated towards Noah, her face still wrapped in a towel. A portion of her chin emerged, and Noah saw her flat belly at the same time as he recognized Darcy's mouth and cheek.

Noah threw himself into the stall as her towel came down. He turned his face to the wall and wrapped his towel around his head. Unexpected arousal vied with shame for dominant emotion. The slap of bare feet approached from behind him then stopped.

"I think your time's up." It was a man's voice.

Noah turned to see a naked, stocky, close-eyed man with hair the colour of soil.

"How do you know it's me?" he asked lamely.

"I recognize everyone else. You the new panel jockey?"

Noah peeked his head out and turned to where Darcy had been, hoping she was gone, wanting her to still be there. She must have grabbed her robe and left almost immediately.

"Yes, photovoltaic engineer, that's me. The name's Noah."

The man was running his eyes over Noah's body. The examination wasn't sexual in nature; at least Noah didn't think so.

"You're pretty clean, Noah. I'm Ray. I work the farm. Nice to meet you, but you're eating my time."

Noah apologized with a shrug and stepped out of the stall. He could feel Ray's eyes on him as he took his robe from a hook and left the bathroom. As he padded down the corridor to his room he wondered how he could be so lucky. Of all the people he could share a time-slot with...his predecessor must have enjoyed the same privilege. Freeland. Noah stopped dead in his tracks. The old panel jockey had shared shower time with Darcy. She'd been not unkind, but cold to Noah ever since he'd arrived. Freeland had been locked outside for rape. Protective rage swelled Noah's chest. Whatever animal or animals had gotten Freeland couldn't possibly have been as cruel as justice deserved. Common sense whispered through the anger, telling Noah he didn't know for sure that Darcy had been the victim. The image of her body as she towelled off replaced the enigmatic one of Freeland being ripped to shreds by a dog pack. He would get to see her twice a week. He held his towel in front himself to cover the bulge under his robe as he walked the rest of the way to his room.

Freeland returned to Noah's mind abruptly as his eyes fell on the skinbag that crouched on the corner of the desk. He approached it warily, curious but fearful of what lay within. A tug on a cord opened the parcel. The skin fell away to reveal an assortment of objects. Noah picked up a gold pen with an engraving on the side that read "University of Regina, 1995, We are, we are, we are the Engineers." There was a handful of photos: a chubby man with thin blond hair and blue eyes sitting on the hood of a shiny blue pickup truck; the same man in a drafting room with two other men, one short and Chinese, one tall and caucasian; a small sailboat with the name, "Sun Dancer." The last photo was of a different type. Noah recognized it as a Polaroid. Grearson had a clunky Polaroid camera. On very rare occasions, he would use it to capture a moment. The instant picture from Freeland's skinbag was of the chubby man from the previous photos, sitting on the doorstep of a house. Another man, white with brown hair, sat next to him. Both of them looked tired, their hair was messy and the brown-haired man had a dirty bandage wrapped around one arm. Both of them held rifles. Noah studied the blond man in all three photos. He wasn't the slavering maniac Noah had wanted to see, but then maybe he wasn't Freeland. None of the photos had writing on them. The other objects included a single palm-sized monocrystalline solar panel, a scratched wooden ruler, and a tin-soldier, about the height of Noah's thumb.

The soldier wore a long red coat, and had a tall, funnel-shaped black hat. It held a rifle against its shoulder as it stood at rigid attention. Noah's eye twitched. He dressed and checked his tool case, then returned to the soldier. It felt good to hold it, despite who its previous owner had been. The paint was chipped in places, but maybe Caps could touch those up.

A double bell announced breakfast. Noah pocketed the pen and the Polaroid. He grabbed his tool kit and joined a small herd in their journey to the trough. His mouth was already watering. He was disappointed when no milk came from Roshi. The cook caught Noah's look.

"Don't worry, you still be surprised. There's fresh peppers in the eggs."

Noah scooped some egg into his mouth with his fingers. It was delicious.

"You see. Go, go eat it at a table, you're blocking the line."

Noah found Caps at the same table as the day before. Only he sat at it so far. Noah put his tray down and slid the pen across the table to Caps.

"Do you think you could grind that for gold paint?" asked Noah.

Caps picked up the pen and ran his thumb along it. He read the inscription.

"Where'd you get this? Was it your father's or something?"

"It was Freeland's. It was with some stuff Burle gave me."

Caps regarded the pen with loathing. "Oh I'll grind this down alright."

Noah put the Polaroid on the table. "Is that Freeland? The blond guy?"

Caps slapped his left hand down on the photo with such suddenness, Noah jerked back from the table.

"Put that away," said Caps, pushing the photo at Noah. "Burn it."

Burle and Lena sat down together. They were discussing the barter value of slightly damaged motherboards.

"Do we get window today?" Caps asked Lena

"We should. Around thirteen hundred." She noticed Noah's hair. "You just have a shower?"

Noah nodded as he savoured his spicy, scrambled eggs.

"So what did you think?"

Noah swallowed. "Heaven."

A woman joined them. It was Cass, the tanner who had brought Noah his tools the day before.

"Hi, stranger," said Caps. "Someone take your usual seat?"

"No, I needed a change of conversation. Got any new jokes?"

"I tell you the one about the two dogs and the fisherman?"

"Son, you've told everyone that joke," said Burle.

"The hunters are due back today," said Cass. "Anybody want to bet on empty seats?"

"That's not funny," said Lena.

Noah didn't have to ask what they meant. In Underbel most hunts were day trips, but some groups would head out for a few days. The number that came back wasn't always as high as the number that left.

"Can anyone hunt here? Or do you have specific hunters?"

"Once in a while," said Caps, "non-hunters go on a day trip, but we have people who have that as their sole job. We haven't lost one in almost six months. Not since Toffee took over. You'll meet him."

"Oh yes," said Burle. "You'll meet him. You might not like him, but you will meet him."

Noah had cleaned his tray completely. He fought the urge to pick it up and lick it.

"Sun boy, I'm completing your tour," said Darcy from behind Noah.

"Now?" he hoped he wasn't blushing.

Caps watched Noah and Darcy leave, then turned back to his breakfast companions.

"Did you see the look on the kid's face? I think someone has a crush on someone."

Burle clucked his tongue. "He'll get over that quickly."

Cass's eyes narrowed and a small, predacious smile quirked the corners of her mouth.

Darcy walked quickly, keeping Noah half a step behind her.

"I'm not taking you to the workroom or the battery bay. You can find those yourself. I'm taking you to the Pit's secret. Sid decided quickly on you. Your friend Bacon must pull some heavy weight with the Boss."

"The secret? You mean what keeps the teeth away?"

"That's it. Everyone in the Pit keeps their mouths shut on this one. You'll understand."

They marched through archways and down corridors. Noah didn't say anything. He didn't trust his tongue. He had no clue as to whether she'd seen him in the shower room. She would see him sooner or later, but he hoped she hadn't seen him gawking. Darcy pushed open a door and the smell of animals hit Noah, setting off all sorts of personal alarms.

"This is the farm. Come on, you're totally safe."

Noah gingerly stuck his head through the doorway. Darcy grabbed his arm and pulled him through.

People moved back and forth between various stalls in the huge room. The clucking of chickens could be heard from the far end. Some people looked up and nodded at Darcy, then returned to their work. Noah saw that there were indeed four cows. Each was in a stall constructed of waist-high corrugated metal. The cows were tethered to posts, and their big, beautiful eyes stared blankly as they chewed away at food from troughs mounted on the metal.

Ray, the man from the shower, scooped manure into a metal pushcart. In another enclosure of bent metal, a group of sheep wandered about mindlessly. Noah, keeping up with Darcy, didn't have time to take in every lobotomised animal. He focussed on Darcy's back and forced back the fear of being surrounded by so many four-legged creatures.

"This is the secret?" he asked. "How does this keep the other animals away?"

"This isn't how we do it. We're almost there."

She led him past a wall section made up of four rows of seven crates, stacked on top of each other. Each crate had an open front covered in mesh. The chickens within supplied the Pit with eggs. A short corridor led to a metal door, with a big lock plate by the handle. Darcy stopped at the door.

"Through this is a series of caverns," she said. "We discovered them a few months ago. We were getting ready to expand the farm. Sid figures we can get a few of those ostriches out there. Tough to handle, but we'll just drill their brains out. Anyway, we broke through to these." She unlocked the door with a slim key, and pushed it open. Behind lay uneven walls of rough stone and dirt. There were powerful lights spiked to walls and hanging on stands. They provided good illumination, but many passages twisted off into darkness. Noah could hear rushing water.

"Our water and hydroelectric power is provided by an underground river," said Darcy. "You haven't seen our hydroelectric generator or the water station yet. It's through the steel doors in the mess hall. We always knew we'd hit the rest of it as we expanded, but we didn't expect this. These caverns surround the entire Pit. We can't grow anymore in any direction without opening into these. They go on for miles and we haven't had a chance to explore them fully. We've lost people down here."

Noah searched every crack and crevice the lighting allowed him to.

"Won't there be rats in these caves? And other stuff?"

"Yes, the…Travis Jones, the security chief before me was swarmed by rats in one of these caves."

"That wasn't that long ago, was it?"

Darcy paused before answering. "It happened in March."

"But you act like you've been here forever."

"I've been here for five years, same as Sid. We came here together."

"Oh. I thought it was, uh, dead-man's boots. That you would have been brought here to replace this Jones guy."

"You were brought here because we didn't have anyone to promote, really. I was second in command of security. Sid had no problem giving me the job."

"So who got Jones's room?"

Darcy's eyes grew dark. Her cheeks reddened a little, making the scars on her face stand out more. "The new hunter got his room."

Noah didn't know how, but he'd plainly offended her. He needed to change the subject. "You came with the Boss, how long have you been together?"

"Are you writing a book?"

She set off down one of the well-lit passages. Noah was getting sick of the way she just took off on him. He wanted to yell at her, but he didn't know what to yell. She stopped at a white metal box mounted on a tripod. The box was a thirty-centimetre cube, and covered on one side with extremely fine black mesh. The mesh faced away from the Pit, but a power cable from the box lead back down the passage.

"This is it," said Darcy as she rested a hand on the box. "This is how we keep the teeth away from the Pit. It's also how we keep the bugs away."

Noah looked at the box from all angles. Nothing indicated how it was responsible for such a miracle. "What is it?"

"Ultrasonic acoustical generator. We call it a Screaming Mimi. We have six of them down here. The rest are hidden topside, about fifty feet outside the fence. They keep out everything: dogs, cats, rodents, even ants and bees. Behind the Mimis, we're completely safe."

Noah stared at the Mimi, then Darcy. At Underbel he'd taken his turn at mesh-enshrouded animal patrol. Being a panel jockey had granted him few privileges back home, and freedom from guard duties hadn't been one of them. He remembered times where someone wasn't watchful enough, or fast enough. Sometimes their bodies were recovered, most times they weren't. A shift on guard duty was hours of boredom, broken up by seconds of terror. Even with people out on animal watch, people lived in fear of sudden swarms of teeth.

"How can you be so selfish?" he blurted angrily. "How can you keep this to yourself? Everyone should have this!"

"I said the same thing at first."

She said it so calmly, Noah's anger all but disappeared.

"What changed your mind?"

"Follow me. I'll show you."

Darcy set off back the way they had come. Noah followed the Mimi's power-cables with his eyes. They ran into rock near the door to the finished portion of the Pit. A number of other cables snaked in from the darkness to create a nexus of metal and rubber. Darcy led Noah back through the farm, and into a set of hallways he hadn't been in previously. She didn't walk as briskly as before. They pushed through a curtained archway into yet another large room. Two skylights in the high ceiling supplemented fluorescents. There were various work stations set up, some attended to, others vacant. Noah didn't get a chance to check them out, as he was soon led to another archway.

"That's the workshop," said Darcy. "Your workstation is in there, but you'll want to see this first."

They stopped at another door, this one with two locks on it, and a guard. The khaki garbed woman stepped aside to allow passage. Darcy unlocked the door and led Noah to the heart of Compton Pit. Two chest-high, blue metal boxes were joined together by a series of flexicoil hoses. Presumably they were for protection of vital cables, rather than for airflow. A number of smaller metal boxes, also blue, were linked to the larger ones by cables of standard type. More cables ran in a tight coil straight up through the roof, supported by a skeletal metal framework.

Darcy placed her hand on the closest large box. "This is Gershwin, it runs the Mimis. It was named after some composer by Gerard Fritz, the man who built it two years ago. There's no user interface beyond a diagnostic. The code is encrypted. Noah, this is all we have. Gerard kept all the information in his head, or in records he destroyed, or we just can't find. We've taken apart two Mimis, but couldn't get them to work once we put them back together. One other Mimi just stopped functioning. We don't know why. We can't get replacement parts, and even if we could, we don't know how to make more. We can't risk the ones we've got left on reverse engineering. Moving the six we did down to the caverns, weakened the system topside. We'd share this out if we could, but we can't."

"What happened to Gerard Fritz?"

"He snuck off one day to test a portable Mimi. We found most of him, eventually. Noah, this is the Pit's biggest secret. If others learned of it, they'd come. Explaining that we couldn't move the system, that we couldn't duplicate it...that wouldn't matter. It's a miracle we've kept it quiet so long. As long as Gershwin and the Mimis work, we can research and build here, free of animals, free of insects. Do you understand?"

Noah ran his hand across Gershwin's cold metal surface. "You keep this a secret because you think you'll be able to give it to everyone one day, but you need time."

"Right. If you leak it, you'll be locked outside. More importantly, you might cost us all a chance at reclaiming civilization. These are Sid's words. I guess I've picked them up along the way."

Noah pulled his hand away from the metal. This was, perhaps, the biggest thing he'd ever come in contact with. The future of humanity hinged on cables and delicate microchips. "I won't tell a soul. Do you have any idea at all how this system works?"

"You ask a lot of questions, you know that? Do I have "information" written on my forehead?"

Noah was taken aback by her sudden return to near hostility. He didn't want to run afoul of the security chief, especially with the unexpected attraction he had to her, but he could only take so much.

"What is your problem with me? Just because I'm a panel jockey doesn't make me Freeland!" He regretted the words as soon as they hit the air.

Darcy looked at him quizzically. "What's that supposed to mean?"

Her reaction was not what Noah would have expected under the circumstances. Maybe he'd been wrong. "I...I don't know. I thought maybe you held some sort of grudge."

"Why? Oh, who told you?"

"The Boss."

Darcy rolled her eyes. "And that's my problem. Okay, sun boy, I'm the chief of security here. That's my job. The Boss is rolling out the red carpet for you on the say so of some old friend of his. He also has me taking you everywhere when I have better things to attend to. If I'm curt, I'm sorry, but I have other things I'd rather be doing."

Noah paused, then nodded. "Thank you for your honesty. Could I ask you a favour?"

"What?"

"My name is Noah. Not Thurlow, or sun boy."

Darcy gave him a half smile. "I'll try to remember that. About Gershwin, I personally don't understand it, but then that's not my job. Lena or Eggerson could explain to you better—"

"Eggerson?"

"You met him at the meeting yesterday morning. Tall. Nose like a beak."

"The prosthetics guy?"

"That's not all he does, but yes, that's him. What I can tell you is this; the Mimis work on a TDMA system. That's Time Division Multiple Access. Each one of them has to synchronize with

Gershwin. They each have a lithium battery that keeps them in sync when they're unplugged from main power, so we can move them. When we open one up, its power is cut, and we can't get them to resynchronize when we turn them back on. Gershwin constantly changes their frequencies to adjust for air-pressure, humidity, etc. That's all I know, and more than I think you should be told. Enough?"

"Yes. Thank you."

The Pit's alarm system issued one long bell, followed by two short ones. Darcy's expression of mild annoyance disappeared, to be replaced by a flat, closed look.

"What does that signal mean?" Noah asked.

"I've taken you just about everywhere else, you might as well see this, too. Come on."

Darcy led Noah back to the main corridor. From the direction they were going, he knew they were headed to the motor pool. A number of people were there already. Caps was standing by the car Noah had arrived in. The car's hood was up and bits and pieces of the motor were on a tarp next to the front wheels. Burle and Roshi leaned against the wall next to the airlock doors. With a groan the heavy metal slid open, and two vehicles drove in. One was a wide jeep, which Noah recognized as a Hummer, the second was a long van. Both vehicles rode high on fat tires, and were covered in mud. The Hummer was standard primer, with patches of an old camouflage pattern showing in certain places. Steel mesh covered all windows, and bits of foliage stuck out from a wide, angled piece of metal on the front, called a brush cutter. The vehicles came to a stop in the middle of the pool. The Hummer's doors opened and two men stepped out. The driver was a stocky man of Polynesian descent. His gentle face lit up in a smile as he surveyed the people who waited to greet him. The second man, who emerged from the passenger side, was another story all together. He was tall, maybe six foot four, or more. He was wide at the shoulders and his eyes were cold and hard. His chin was square, and covered with a week's worth of growth. Steel-gray hair covered his ears, and reached down past his collar line. There was a depression in the bridge of the hunter's nose where something had bitten a chunk out of it. A fist sized skinbag hung from a leather thong around his neck, and he cradled a long black hunting rifle in his arms. Had Noah known anything more about firearms, he would have recognized the rifle as a .300 centre-fire. Brown leather gloves covered the man's hands. He had an aura about him, almost animal in nature. Noah wouldn't have been surprised if the man started growling instead of talking. As the doors to the van opened, the tall man approached Darcy. He stopped in front of her and let the rifle slip until its stock rested on the floor.

Darcy did a head count as two men and a woman exited the van. All of them wore camouflage patterned coveralls.

"I see you brought everyone home again," Darcy said to the chief of the hunters. "You must be proud."

"I don't waste pride on easy accomplishments." The man's voice was quiet and rough, like sandpaper rubbed on stone.

Darcy folded her arms across her chest. "This is our new panel jockey, Noah Thurlow. Noah, Ethan Toffee."

"I've heard people talking about you," said Noah. "It's nice to meet you." He extended his hand.

The hunter turned his head to Noah slowly, then looked at the proffered hand. He turned back to Darcy, Noah completely dismissed. "Were you worried I wasn't coming back?"

"Worried isn't the right word." The security chief's voice was flat as a board.

Noah fought to keep from wrinkling his nose. Toffee stank. All the hunters did. It wasn't just that they'd been out for days without washing, they'd rubbed manure on their skin and clothes to cover their scent. After a while, regular hunters didn't even notice the smell.

The hunters had opened the side door of the large van and a cart had been positioned by the doors. Roshi gasped in delight as the body of a buck wapiti—the largest of the caribou—was pulled from the van by a multi person effort. The wapiti was joined by a smaller deer, and then a new cart was loaded with some dogs and various fowl. Overall, it was a good haul. The Polynesian man took a heavy looking hide wrapped box from the back of the Hummer. The box jerked in his hands. He set the bundle down, and Burle pulled the hides away to reveal a small black bear cub in a cage. The cub sniffled and emitted a mournful cry.

"Good lord, Seth? Where's Momma?" asked Burle, peering into the van to see if bear would also be on the menu in the coming days.

"Don't know," said Seth. "Don't care."

Burle re-wrapped the cage, and directed one of the people in the pool to take the cub to Dr. Odega. For maybe a few days, people would come to animal research to touch the cub, to play with it. The very young of certain animals were unaggressive. Newborns behaved in a manner that bordered on affectionate. It didn't last long, however, and all too soon the party was over.

"Where'd you find that?" Darcy asked.

"We saw it along the side of the road as we were coming back," Toffee replied. "It was Seth that went out to get it. Fool. We were on our way again before its mother showed up. It was a good hunt. Mike had a few interesting moments with a bobcat. You should come out, Red, do you good to get some air."

Darcy grabbed Noah's arm and dragged him back into the Pit's main corridor. "Come on, I'll take you to the last few stops."

She let go of his arm once they were well away from the pool.

"So that was Toffee, huh? Bit of an asshole if you ask me."

"Did I ask you?"

"No. Uhm, how long until the hunters shower? Are they going to stink like that until their turn comes around? At Underbel I never would have noticed, but here..."

"They get to shower as soon as they've unloaded. One of the privileges of being a hunter. As long as they're at the Pit for a while, they stick to a schedule like everyone else."

Once through the steel doors at the end of the mess hall, the sound of rushing water was loud. It echoed through the short concrete passageway. Another set of steel doors opened to the river itself. The viaduct was about a hundred feet long, and twenty to thirty feet wide. Water rushed from a grate-covered opening in the rock at the end farthest from the doors. A Screaming Mimi was set up to cover the vulnerable opening. At the exit point, the water passed through steel grates. Churning rotors could barely be heard over the sound of the water's passage. Another set of steel doors stood at the river's exit point, on the far side of the water. The doors could be reached via one of the two foot bridges that crossed the expanse.

"Those doors lead to hydroelectric maintenance and the water filtration system." Darcy had to raise her voice to be heard over the water. "You don't really need to see that, but now you know where it is."

"Are there any fish in this?" Noah asked, also raising his voice.

"Not any small enough to make it through the grate. We've discussed fishing in the river through the caverns I showed you, but we can only extend the Mimis so far. Were you thinking of playing Huckleberry Finn?"

"What?"

"You know, kicking off your shoes, fishing with a pole?"

"I'm sorry, I have no idea what you're talking about."

"We're done, Noah. That's it," she said abruptly, and took him back into the mess hall.

"Thank you. What is that—"

"I said we're done. I have work to do." She strode off at her usual fast pace.

Noah sat at the table he'd shared with the Boss and company the night before. The comment Darcy had made about Huckleburton Fin, or whatever, had seemed like the first good-natured thing she'd said to him since they'd met, and Noah had blown it through straight ignorance. Noah was also confused by her reaction to his calling Toffee an asshole. There was obviously no love lost between the chief hunter and the chief of security, but his insult had failed to garner a positive response. Noah pushed himself away from the table and stood up. He had his own work to do here, and he hadn't been bought and paid for by the Boss to spend his time brooding.

With only a little back tracking, Noah was able to find the work room. The people he'd seen earlier were absent. Only Eggerson was in the large room, adjusting some gadget made of metal strips and ring-clamps. The engineer looked up briefly, his small close-set eyes blinking in vague recognition, then returned to his creation without speaking. Noah found his own work station almost by accident. He was trying to identify the numerous half-made machines that were scattered across the tables and desks, when his eyes fell upon a photovoltaic schematic. He sat down in a creaky chair that had once been a very comfortable example of ergonomic design. One of the pivots had seized and the padding was compressed to the point of being hard. Noah didn't notice. The desk that was now part of his domain was covered in papers. He attempted to organize some of them, but gave up and simply swept the papers on to the floor next to the desk, planning to assemble them in some sort of order later in the day. Underneath the papers was a plastic box. He lifted the lid to find that it was a laptop computer, fixed to the desk, with two cables running down through a hole in the desktop. The cables disappeared into a wall off to the right. Noah found the power switch, and to his surprise and delight, the words "logging on" appeared on the screen.

Noah called out to Eggerson, "Is this mine?" When there was no response, he called again, louder. "Excuse me? Is this computer mine?"

Eggerson looked up. "Who else would it belong to?" The bird-faced man returned to his tinkering.

Noah used a small roller ball nestled between some keys to move a pointer around on the screen. His access included panel-array schematics, power conversion spreadsheets, and information on the various components in the battery bay. There was also a screen that monitored efficiency in power input and output. Noah was delighted. He'd occasionally had a chance to play with some of the computers at Underbel, but he'd never had one of his own before. He'd never even dreamed of having one of his own.

"Eggerson," he called out.

"Oh what do you want? I'm busy here."

"I'm Noah."

"I know who you are."

"Is Eggerson your first name?"

"Of course not. Who on Earth would name their child Eggerson?"

"What is your first name?"

Eggerson looked surprised, possibly it was a question he hadn't been asked in a long time.

"Neil."

"Can I call you Neil?"

"Why...yes."

"Thank you. Neil, are there really ostriches topside? Or was someone just pulling my leg?"

"Ostriches. Big birds. Interesting mating rituals."

"I know what they are. Are there actually some around?"

"Yes. There used to be an ostrich farm not far from here. I can remember a time when ostrich farms were popping up all over the place. Driving along the highway, seeing the cows, seeing the sheep, then a field of ostriches. Just when I was getting used to the llamas. Very disconcerting. That was in the old days of course. Not a lot of farming going on topside now. But then you know that. Anything else?"

"Yes, where's the battery bay?"

Eggerson gestured at a door in the far wall to the left of the photovoltaic station. Noah thanked him and went through the door. Eggerson watched after the young man for a few moments, a bemused expression on his face, then shook his head and returned to his work.

The battery bay was twice again as large as Noah had expected. Batteries of all sizes, from knee-high to chest-high were crammed into every space available. They were in a multitude of colours, and cables snaked in from holes in the walls, and down through the ceiling. The batteries were connected to capacitors and resistors. Converters were hooked up to allow the power to be piped into outlets throughout the Pit, and other devices were in place to keep the batteries from overcharging. A few old fashioned meters were interfaced in the system. Numbers were etched on the batteries in the same red ink that marked the solar panels above. Some of the thicker cables were also marked. Against one wall were racks of rechargeable batteries. Noah recognized size designations from AA up. There were empty slots in the charging racks, dark holes among dingy silver. Noah lost himself in the battery bay. He probably would still have been there when the dinner bell rang if Caps hadn't appeared at the door, and called Noah away from his work.

"Come on, new guy, I want to show you something."

"Well, that makes you different from Darcy," said Noah, rolling up his paper battery chart. "Why didn't the Boss have you give me the tour?"

"I don't have all the keys. What did you think of Gershwin?"

"I think it's really crappy that...Fritz, right?...that Fritz didn't keep any written records. What do you want me to see?"

"One of the finer points of Compton Pit."

"You mean there's more?"

In a well lit room not far from the engineering workroom, Lena sat in front of large monitor. HF radio equipment was set up on one table, but all other surfaces were covered with computer equipment, sound filters, equalizers and other contraptions that Noah simply didn't recognize.

"Hello, Noah," said Lena. "Welcome to SatCom."

"She means Satellite Communications," Caps explained.

"I saw the dish up top," said Noah. "That thing actually works?"

"No," said Caps. "Lena just pretends it does so the Boss doesn't make her muck out stalls in the farm."

"How often do you use the HF?" Noah asked Lena.

"Only when it's necessary. I'd gab all day long if the Boss would let me."

Communication, once as commonplace as leaves on a tree, now was as rare and as valuable as flawless diamonds used to be. Functioning transmitters were coveted, and all radio operators were wary of those who listened to the airwaves, hoping to find radios to steal. The HF at Compton Pit was safe, but few people could say the same. All other systems of global communication had fallen to entropy. The sky, like a giant aardvark, reached down with tongues of lightning and picked off transformers and communication towers. In the new world, nobody would be going out and replacing them. Only the satellites, way up in the sky were safe, but they had their own problems. Very few of them were autonomous. They all required telemetry from Earth, and without it, orbits decayed. Low and medium orbit satellites burned up in the atmosphere from lack of course correction. Even if the satellites could guide themselves, eventually they would have run out of fuel. The self-reliant geosynchronous satellites, however, twenty-two thousand miles up, used much less fuel keeping their fixed positions in relation to the Earth.

"What satellites do you communicate with?" asked Noah. "How many are still functional?"

"There are twenty that I know of," Lena replied. "The Telstars, some LANLs. GEOS-9 is still going strong. The problem is that most of them are spinning up there. Whether it's from lack of fuel or malfunctions doesn't matter. I can hit them, but it doesn't help if I can't bounce the signal. I have windows to play with, where some line up with others and I can get the weekly world news. I'm going for London today. We usually get about four hours out of this connection."

Taking up a quarter of the large screen in front of Lena, was a black window with a red countdown in the centre. The numbers were ticking down from one minute, twenty seconds.

"London," Noah breathed. "We're going to talk to London? As in London, England?"

"Mmhmm. There's a fellow named Lancaster I usually talk to."

"Do they live in the city? Above ground?"

"Not really. There are a few sealed buildings, but for the most part it's like everywhere else. People get to venture topside more in the fall and winter when the hymenoptera have gone to bed for the year. London has a well established below, connected undergrounds left over from World War II. They still have to deal with rats and all. Topside has some exotic stuff, what with the massive zoo they had there, and all the wild animal parks. There's a similar setup under Glasgow, but there's no SatCom there."

"They still hold to the monarchy," said Caps. "Chucky was on the polo field on New Wilderness Day, but Harry is alive and kicking.

Y'know if there were two Englishmen left on the planet, and one of them was the king, the other would still bow and scrape."

"Harry is the king, I take it?"

"Noah, Noah, Noah..." Caps clucked his tongue. "For a guy high up in our science division, there sure is a lot you don't know. You were what? Ten? Eleven? Can't you remember anything from back then?"

Noah ignored the question. "What do you talk about with London?"

"Oh the usual stuff," said Caps. "We exchange tales of misery…The woif got eaten by bleedin' rats, so she did! Still, must keep one's chin up."

"Here we go," said Lena. The timer on her screen reached zero, and the black window turned white. A small animation on the bottom of the screen showed curved lines emanating from a satellite dish. Numbers scrolled down a column beside the window at a good rate. Telemetry data from the first of the geostationary satellites in the chain, Telstar 5, was being piped back, even as signals were being sent up from the Pit. Something on the screen made Lena unhappy.

"It's not hooking, is it?" asked Caps. He was leaning over the back of Lena's chair, and had a hand on her shoulder.

Lena waited a few more seconds before answering. "No. Dammit. I'll keep trying but when I don't get it right away, I usually can't get it at all."

"Is the satellite still there?" Noah asked.

"Yeah, it's there, it's just that its spin cycle has changed again. I've been missing with this one about every five rotations. I wasn't expecting to miss again until next time. I'll have to chart new window schedules," she looked up at Caps, raising her thin eyebrows. "Do you think the Boss will let me have the juice?"

Caps patted Noah on the back. "I'm sure sun boy here can put in a good word for you."

Lena looked hopefully at Noah.

"How much will you need?" he asked, uncomfortable about being put on the spot.

"Not that much more."

Noah ran some figures through his head. Lena's computers didn't take that much power, but the transmitter sure would. He hadn't looked at all the individual power readings on his laptop yet, but he did know that there was already a fragile balance between collection and use.

"Do you just have conversations? Do you just yak to each other?"

"No, we exchange data as well. Animal research, weather patterns, you know."

Noah scratched his head. "Can you give me figures?"

"Would tonight be soon enough?"

"Sure. How much will you need to rotate the dish?"

"I'll need to triangulate, but one, maybe two moves."

"I can't promise anything, but—"

"Modesty doesn't become you," Caps said, patting Noah's back again. "You'll find the power."

Dr. White entered the SatCom room. "Sorry folks, got to cut your parlay short. The Boss has called a meeting." She looked at the computer screen. "Missed again, huh?"

Lena got up. "Yep, on four this time, not five. I hope Lancaster can find the new windows as well."

"Hey Sara," said Caps. "What did the blacksmith say to the raccoon?"

"Aaaaahhhh," the doctor replied, "Get off me! Let go of my arm! Come up with something new, will you?"

Sid sat at the table with Dr. Odega on one side and Toffee on the other. The hunter had showered and shaved. His hair was tied back in a ponytail and he'd changed from his camos into a black coverall. He still wore his gloves, though. Sara took a seat beside Odega. Noah sat down next to Caps.

"We've got problems," Sid said, "and something that's disappointing. As a few of you know, Ted's been keeping a dog that acted like an old dog."

Dr. Patel raised his eyebrows. "Ghandi?"

"Yesterday afternoon Ghandi started behaving normally."

"If she'd kept quiet for a few moments longer, I would have opened her cage," said Dr. Odega.

"Was she a puppy?" Noah asked.

"No, Noah," said Sid. "She's mature. Old, actually, for a dog. We found her walking the fence perimeter one day. We don't know how she got past the Mimis, the topside field was still at full strength. Ted, your turn."

Dr. Odega's eyes were a little bloodshot. He spoke quietly, but his deep, resonant voice easily reached the furthest end of the table. "I apologize to those of you who were kept in the dark, but Sid didn't want to get your hopes up. We guess Ghandi was about a ten years old when we found her. The West tower reported her first, and Travis went up to shoot her. When she didn't try to bite at him through the fence, he brought her inside. I don't know why she was nonaggressive, I don't know why she stopped being that way. There is no difference I can discern between her today and last week. The only difference is...now she acts like a dog."

"No surprises there," said Caps. "The only good dog is a burnt dog."

There were nods of agreement from around the table. Burle didn't join in the chorus of approval, in fact he looked quite dismayed. He'd kept six dogs in his old life, and he had loved each and every one of them. Until the Change, of course.

"I have a new bear cub," Dr. Odega continued. "I'll let people see it for the next two days, but then it's off limits. I'm sure you all know by now my latest attempt at unmolested flight was a complete failure. Does anyone care to go bird shooting later?"

Dr. Patel and Lena raised their hands.

"No target practice," said Sid. "We can't afford it."

Shotgun shells could be easily made, as could a few other types of bullets, but the birds that flew over Compton Pit had learned to stay high up. Ammunition for high-powered rifles and automatic weapons required a finesse that couldn't be easily reproduced. Weapons were easy to find, but bullets were hard to come by.

"Toffee's filled me in on some other things. The bus across the south road is only the start. There are other roadblocks on both the east roads. It didn't stop the hunters because they can just go off road, but someone, probably Shangly, is making it difficult for other vehicles to reach the Pit. Now he won't attack here. We hold the high ground and we've got way too many people and guns for him to try anything. Rules are different on the road. The convoy from Drum East is due back in two days. We can't reach them with radio yet, so we can't let them know what's going on. Opinions?"

"I think we should take it to Shangly," said Toffee.

"We don't even know that it is Shangly," said Darcy, her eyes flashing challenge at the hunter. "We should all just go charging out to Fenwick, lose a lot of people on a hunch?"

"Have you started thinking it might be someone else?" Sid asked.

"No. But we don't have any proof."

"What's the strategic position of our favourite scavenger?" asked Dr. Patel.

Sid let Darcy answer the question.

"The last report said most of Fenwick Prison's stone wall was still up. There was mesh and plastic over some ground floor windows. Last convoy to go there was almost a year ago. The place could be better or worse by now. Shangly had about forty or fifty back then. According to Gil..."

"That's the kid we got off Shangly," Caps whispered to Noah.

"...he has roughly the same amount. They only use the basement and the ground floor. Gil says they don't keep guards in their towers, but he's not what I'd call a trained observer. We don't know how well armed they are, but we can assume they've got at least a few automatic weapons."

"Shangly only traded arms when he had to," said Burle. "He's probably kept the good stuff for himself."

"So is this some kind of a siege?" Caps asked.

"Looks like it," said Sid. "It could be a good one, too. Until we get the rig back from Drum East, we can't easily clear the road."

"At least let me do some reconnaissance," said Toffee. "I'll take the new fella there."

Noah blanched. The thought of sneaking through the woods at night was not a pleasant one.

"The guards topside have seen nothing out of the ordinary," said Darcy. "We should wait until the convoy is back, and then decide what to do."

"My feelings exactly," said Sid. "Sorry, Toffee, you're on standby for now. A few more points, people. It's really dry out there. We haven't had a good rain in a few weeks now. A forest fire could send a lot of teeth our way, Mimis or no Mimis. They might not hit the Pit, but they'll surround us, maybe cut us off. If you're going topside to have a smoke, be careful with it."

"Only you can prevent forest fires," said Caps, saluting with one hand and pointing at the Boss with the other.

"How are the wasps?" Lena asked Toffee.

"The wasps are everywhere," the hunter said, pushing up his left sleeve to reveal red welts. "There are bald-faced hornets filling the trees for about six klicks. From what I've been told it used to be just yellow jackets. The hornets can get through thicker clothing than most. We all got stung a bit till we made it back to the vehicles. Made for a bad morning."

6. Animal Behavior

Noah deleted another line of calculations from the screen and closed the laptop. He'd been up half the night before, trying to squeeze more juice out of the system. What he'd found today was that privilege urged for more privilege, until abuse set in. Everyone kept the lights on in their rooms a little longer then they should have. Lena used a touch more juice with her HAM than she was actually allotted. There was a few minutes more on one thing, just a little extra from another. Those touches added up. Hydroponics, oddly, was exactly within its parameters. The abuse of the power had increased since Freeland's last entry in the logs. Even Sid was over his share. With the long summer days the power loss wasn't really noticeable, but the panels couldn't supply what was being used and keep the battery bay charged to its fullest. In case of an emergency, those batteries had to be one hundred percent. Noah was going to have to crack the whip.

Sid hugged the bear cub to his chest. The warm body squirmed and its tiny heart beat against Sid's. The cub licked his ear.

"You're getting tired aren't you?" He held the cub out at arms length. Its little paws flopped in the air, and it yawned, showing a pink tongue.

Dr. Odega took the cub gently from the Boss, and laid it in a cage lined with soft hides. "There you go, you've had a busy morning haven't you?" He shut the cage.

"It's always a shame when we have to kill them," said Sid.

Dr. Odega gave the cub a thoughtful glance. "Yes, but it'll make a good stew, won't it?"

The door opened and Noah was led in by Daniel, a tall, dark haired man that was Darcy's second in command.

"If you've come to see the cub," said Odega, "I'll have to disappoint you. I've put it to bed. Come back later."

"Actually I came to see the Boss," said Noah. "I don't want to see the cub."

"What can I do for you?" Sid asked.

"Uhm, who set the power limits for the various departments?"

"I did."

"Well, they're being broken. By everyone. Including...uh...you, sir. We can't keep the batteries at full the way things are going."

Sid let his voice take on a harder edge. "Are you telling me to cut back my usage?" .

"No, sir. Yes, sir. You set the limits. You know they have to be followed."

"You're right. I've been indulging myself. Everyone will have to reign in."

The boy's eyes widened, and he was a doing a poor job of holding back a smile. "Well…uhm, that's all. I'll get back to work now." He turned to Daniel. "Get me to the main corridor and I can find my way from there."

Noah and the security officer left.

"Was that your first test?" asked Dr. Odega.

"My second. Having Darcy show him around was the first. He may well be worth our second rig after all."

Noah walked down the corridor with a little extra spring in his step. He'd made a command level decision, and it had been followed. Without him, the power drain would have continued. Compton Pit needed him.

Toffee appeared at his side as if from thin air. The hunter walked at exactly the same speed as Noah, face front, saying nothing. Noah's eyes flicked from the corridor ahead to the man beside him, intermittently at first, then with rapidly increasing frequency.

"Uh, where are you going?" Noah asked.

"Where are you going?" the hunter returned.

"I'm going to the workroom. The photovoltaic station."

"I'll go with you."

Noah slowed his pace a little, then sped up. The hunter stayed right beside him without missing a step. Noah was quite unnerved by the time they reached the workroom, and relieved when Toffee left his side to talk to Eggerson. Noah sat down at his station and, with a last furtive look at the hunter's broad back, opened his laptop and focussed his attention on the screen. After clicking through a few screens, Toffee's shadow engulfed the desk.

"That the power schematics? Show me something."

"What do you want to see?" Noah slouched deeper into his chair.

"Show me panel output."

Noah clicked through some screens, not knowing why the hunter would be interested in power displays. "How much do you understand about this stuff?"

"When I don't know something, I'll ask you."

Noah didn't know if that was a statement or a threat.

"Okay. Show me something else."

Noah clicked through a few more displays.

"What does that mean?" asked the hunter, pointing to a flashing red icon on the lower left corner of the screen.

"It means...what the?...It means there's an interruption in the flow. Excuse me." Noah pushed Toffee a little, unthinkingly, on his way past to the battery bay doors. He found the problem right away. One of the cables that ran through the ceiling had become detached. He could see the large female adapter dangling on a thick cable from the top of the support frame. He'd have to go topside and fish it up from the hub. Noah was on his way up the ladder in the workroom that led to the access panel when Toffee called up to him.

"If you're going outside, you'll need a guard."

Noah climbed back down. "You're right, thanks. I'll go find Daniel."

"I'll watch you. I could use some sun. Wait here."

Noah sat on the steps and his stomach roiled in confusion. What was up with this hunter? Was the guy trying to be nice? He needed to work on his communication skills, that's for sure.

Toffee returned carrying a shotgun.

Once out among the panels, Noah had a tougher time than he'd expected finding where the cable had been unplugged. The connections at the hub were all twisted together, and it was hard to move some of the cables to look at others. He'd finally found the proper plug when he heard the growl.

A large, gray dog stood between the panels, about twenty feet away. Its tongue lolled from a wide mouth, set in a shovel shaped head. There were black stripes across its fur. It growled again.

Noah's blood ran cold, and his scalp tried to crawl down the back of his head.

"Oh man...Toffee?"

"What?" The man's voice was far too calm.

"Shoot it!"

"With what?"

The dog was bunched, preparing to attack.

"With the rifle!"

"You mean that rifle?"

Noah looked quickly at where Toffee was pointing. The shotgun leaned against a panel column, on the far side of the canine.

The dog charged, closing the distance in an eye blink. Noah threw his arm up and lurched backwards. The dog was in the air. Suddenly Toffee was in front of him. There was a click of metal and a yelp from the animal. Toffee staggered from impact, and an arm hit the ground. Dull reddish wood led to a brown leather glove. The hunter had the dog by the scruff of its neck with one hand, holding the animal impaled on a long blade that protruded from a brace just below Toffee's right elbow. The dog gurgled, then coughed blood on the hunter's chest. Its head drooped as it died. Toffee let his right arm drop. The dog slid from the blade and landed on the ground with a thump and a puff of dust.

Noah fought down his panic and choked for air, searching between the panels for other dogs.

"That was exciting," said Toffee as he knelt and wiped the blade off on the dog's side. Then he picked up the prosthetic forearm and slid it over the blade, locking it in place with a twist.

Noah searched the air around him. Were the Mimis off-line? How soon until hornets swarmed in? Feet pounded the ground behind him.

"Dogshit," said a net-masked guard. "How'd that get in here?"

The second guard stepped away from the panels and waved a signal at the east guard tower. Two quick bells followed by a pause repeated a few times. In less than a minute, armed people were climbing out of the access panel. Some had net-helmets, others didn't. They spread out in a circular pattern, combing the panels, scanning the perimeters. Noah stood in the centre of it all, quivering. Toffee picked up the shotgun and cracked the breach.

"Look at that," said the hunter. "I didn't even load it."
Noah's legs went out from under him.

7. Ice

June 10th, New Wilderness Day

Toffee grabbed his rifle and fired. The shot was unaimed and guided by an untrained hand, but regardless, yellow feathers appeared from one massive, shaggy shoulder. The dart was large and contained a powerful anesthetic, but it had almost a thousand pounds of animal to work through. Toffee rolled and the charging polar bear went sliding past him, but recovered with lightning speed. The bear rose to its full ten feet. It filled the world with its bellow, then pounded down on the ice. Toffee rolled again, staying inside the bear's reach, making it turn. A heavy paw swipe narrowly missed the hunter's face. Cold had slowed the flow of blood from Toffee's severed forearm, but he wouldn't last much longer if he couldn't tie it off. He struggled for his handgun as he twisted. The holster was in the wrong place for his left hand, and he couldn't look at what he was doing. The bear smashed him in the side, sending him sliding. The hunter couldn't feel it, but he knew there were ribs broken. A chunk of Toffee's partner, Ken, landed in front of the bear, momentarily distracting it. The monstrous animal scooped it up, and shook it back and forth, then, eyes unfocused, slumped to the ice.

Toffee got the gun out of its holster and aimed it with a trembling hand. His first shot went wild, but his second took the bear in the forehead. The other bear turned from dismembering Ken. Toffee tried to draw a bead, but his hand was shaking harder by the second. He tried to bring his right hand up to steady the gun.

He almost lost it at that point.

Somehow he focused. The second bear had begun a casual advance. It seemed to have no fear. Toffee pulled the trigger and the .357 magnum nearly jumped out his hand. Snow kicked up behind the bear. Toffee pulled his arm down and steadied the gun's pommel on the ice. He tilted the barrel and fired again. A piece of the bear's jaw exploded in a spray of blood and teeth. The animal jerked back, shaking its head. The next bullet opened a hole in the bear's neck. It took another step, then fell.

Silence rushed in like a tidal wave, swallowing the remnants of violent sound, disputing they had ever existed in the first place. Snow claimed the newly dead, a few crystals at a time. Toffee pushed himself across the ground, spiking the ice with the handle of the gun to help his legs do their job.

He found his partner's shredded backpack a little past what remained of head and torso. The first aid kit was still inside. Yanking the kit open, Toffee reached for a rubber tourniquet, then grabbed a bottle of antiseptic instead. He hadn't survived a double bear attack just to die of gangrene. He had to twist the cap off with his teeth. A bit of the alcohol-based disinfectant spat into his mouth, burning his tongue. Toffee tried to splash the liquid into his sleeve, but kept hitting the down. He put the bottle down and with teeth gritted, yanked the sleeve back from the stump, but it wouldn't pull far enough. He looked down at his chest. A tightly buttoned flap covered the jacket's zipper, Toffee needed two hands to undo it. There was a sharp knife on Toffee's left hip. After fighting with the covering strap, he withdrew the seven inch blade, and held it trembling against his right shoulder. With a little prayer to nobody in particular, the hunter pushed the blade through his jacket and cut along the arm. Padded cloth parted to reveal a ragged stump surrounded by flayed skin.

His vision faded for a moment. Splashes of antiseptic bit little holes through the numbness of the limb. Toffee tied the arm off near the top of his bicep, using his hand and teeth to pull the tourniquet tight. He took a few deep breaths once that was done, then wrapped the stump with a sterilized pad and compression bandage. The pad stuck to the stump, but wrapping the nylon proved to be a difficult task. Toffee had to pin the bandage between his side and shortened arm. It took a few tries. Adrenaline seeped away, and cold burned its way into Toffee's exposed arm.

A trio of foxes approached the bloody snow. They'd shed half their winter coats, and dark patches of fur intermixed with white. By this point there should have been a lot uncovered scrub, but a late blizzard had plunged the landscape into winter again. Normally the foxes would be subsisting on the eggs of snowy geese, but they weren't adverse to a little carrion. One of the foxes nosed at a severed limb. Toffee realized it was his arm.

"Get away from that...you...can't have that." His voice held bewilderment and hurt.

He was a bit woozy, but he could still lift the gun. It might even have bullets left. The foxes sniffed the bears, then moved to a large piece of Toffee's partner. They turned their noses up at that as well, and stalked towards the hunter.

"Fuck off, I'm not dead."

The animals continued their approach, eyes intent.

"I said FUCK OFF!" The gun bucked and the lead fox's head blew apart.

The other two animals stopped in their tracks, but didn't run. The way they were behaving scared Toffee far more than the bears had. Foxes were scavengers and thieves, not pack hunters. One of the animals darted forward. It leapt on Toffee's chest and bit a chunk out of his nose. Toffee got his hand up and under the fox's jaw as it snapped at his throat. The other fox had bitten into material, not leg, but was pulling and shredding the down.

With a massive effort Toffee twisted and pushed the fox away. He grabbed his knife as the fox sprung forward, impaling itself on the outstretched blade. Toffee picked up the gun and levelled it at the last animal. The way the barrel was jerking around he was just as likely to shoot his own foot off. There was a useless click as the hammer fell on a spent round. The fox was completely occupied with tearing the pant leg apart. Toffee pulled his knife out of the animal by his head, and sat up. The earth wobbled. The single fox became three fuzzy ones, then returned to being just one. With what felt like the last of his strength, Toffee drove the blade into furry back, just between the shoulder blades. The animal turned and snapped at Toffee's wrist, then its eyes went glassy, and it spasmed in the snow.

Desire to sleep was very strong in the hunter. The snow would be so comfortable. Even better, he could pull himself a short distance and lie against one of the bears. Will to live overcame stupor—if he closed his eyes now, he would never open them again. He realized the antiseptic would do little for him. He needed warmth, and serious medical attention.

The human mind is an amazing thing. Toffee's world depended on having two arms, and in order to continue, his reality had to be as solid as possible. A part of his mind supplied the missing limb. The arm was still there, he just didn't need to use it right now.

Down an embankment sat a pair of snowmobiles, attached to one of them was a tiny shack on runners. It wasn't high enough for Toffee to stand up in, although his partner could. It took the injured hunter what seemed like an eternity to get to his feet. He opened the door and fell into the insulated shack. After wiping blood from around his mouth, he reached into a duffle bag and withdrew a flask of brandy. The cap was on too tight to be twisted off with teeth, besides, movement of the mouth brought new agony to his nose, so Toffee clamped the flask between his knees and twisted off the cap by hand. The brandy warmed him, the second slug even more than the first. He splashed some brandy on his nose and rocked as pain rasped and burned. Through a small window in the side of the shack, Toffee saw a polar bear, striding purposefully towards the snowmobiles. There was no doubt as to its intent.

"Oh…no…what is going on?"

A high powered rifle stood in one corner. Toffee smashed the barrel through the glass, and flipped off the safety. He sighted down the scope, but it twitched in his unsteady grasp. The bear broke into a run. The first shot missed, as did the second. The tiny shack skewed sideways with impact, then fell over on its side. The stock of the rifle jammed into Toffee's chest, but the barrel, now pointed at open sky, still protruded from the window. A massive silhouette blocked the sun as the bear climbed onto the fallen shack and roared.

"I…hunt you," Toffee said. "I HUNT YOU!" He pushed the rifle's muzzle into gaping jaws and fired. The bear, missing the top of its head, crumpled to the shed.

Toffee let go of the rifle. His arm flopped down and his head lolled to the side. The flask was upended against what was, only moments before, the floor. Precious brandy puddled out, and was quickly absorbed by insulation.

The way the shack had fallen had pinned the door to the ground. The window wasn't big enough for exit, and the bear's weight made it impossible for Toffee to move the shack, even if he was at full health. It didn't matter anyway. The snowmobiles had their throttles on the right side. Toffee wouldn't have been able to drive them.

Toffee didn't know how long he drifted in a state of semi-consciousness; his watch was high up on his wrist, and the hunter couldn't pull the sleeve back far enough with his teeth. Time had no frame of reference under a midnight sun. He was going to die here, in an insulated coffin with skis mounted on the bottom. There was no thought of heaven or hell for him. Those places had no meaning. No reincarnation either, no "I'll get it right next time." Toffee had spent most of his life intimately associated with death. A creature lived until it stopped, end of story.

A scratching and pattering across the wall that was now the ceiling drew his attention. A fox appeared at the window. Though Toffee couldn't get out, the fox could get in. A drop of saliva fell from the animals mouth and spattered on the hunter's cheek. Toffee fumbled for his rifle. The fox flew from the window, a firearm's report followed a fraction of a second later. Time passed, there were a few more gunshots, then a head looked down at Toffee through the window. The face was surrounded by furry parka, and goggles covered the eyes, but the colour of skin and shape of face exposed was that of an Inuit.

"Ruski? English?" asked Toffee's rescuer.

"Yes...English."

"Going to cut you out. With ax. Stay still."

The face disappeared. There was another gunshot, followed by silence before wood splintered from above. Toffee closed his eyes as wood chips and bits of insulation covered his face. The Inuit was small, but surprisingly strong. He had to almost dead lift Toffee out of the shack. The little man was injured himself. There was a gash in the Inuit's pant leg, and a reasonable amount of blood stained the padding.

"Bear?" Asked Toffee, indicating the wound. "Nanuk?"

"Tuktu."

"Tuktu. Deer. Deer?"

Toffee was draped over the back of a snowmobile. He felt himself being strapped down somehow, and then he finally let sleep take him.

8. In Security

"I don't know if it was deaf or not. Both its eardrums are intact," said Dr. Odega as he placed an aurascope on a steel tray and pulled off tight gloves made from dog intestines. "I'm not even sure what all went into this one. There's a lot of mastiff, but this striped fur?"

"It's an English Mastiff," Burle said. "Purebred, and a good example of the breed, if I'm not mistaken."

Darcy looked from the dog, stretched out on an examination table, to the chief of stores. "Did you ever have one?"

"No, not me. West aways, though, and a little north, there was a breeder back when. Guess they held together."

"This one could be a driven off male then," said Dr. Odega, "or maybe the pack has drifted here. If they all can get through to us, not just this one…"

Toffee leaned against one wall, arms folded across his chest. His narrow eyes twinkled. "If others come through, I'll gut them, too. Save me a tooth, Doc, a big one."

Darcy looked off at a corner of the room. Her features tightened for a moment. The scars on her cheek crept a bit closer to her eye. She turned to Toffee. "Wait outside."

"Just like that?"

"Just like that. Shut the door."

Toffee took his time pushing off from the wall, then he stepped into the hall, and with a last expressionless look at Darcy, closed the door behind him.

"Burle, how far away was this kennel?"

Burle's eyes went to the ceiling and he pursed his lips. "Let's see. It was before the river, so...no it was after. It was after, but before the turnoff for the rest stop, so fifteen miles, give or take. Took their time getting here, didn't they?"

Darcy did some conversions. "Fifteen miles, about twenty-four klicks. Burle, could you leave us please?"

Burle raised his eyebrows in surprise, then smiled and inclined his head. "Yes ma'am."

Burle opened the door, and gave Toffee a shrug as he walked past the hunter. Darcy closed the door.

"Could you or Harpreet tell me if the dog has been tranqued recently."

Dr. Odega looked at the carcass, as if somehow his eyes alone could find the answer. "Sure, expensive tests, though. Are you thinking it was delivered?"

"You have my authorization for any tests you need to do. This is between you and me. Don't even involve Harpreet if you don't have to."

"Do I tell Sid?"

"I'll tell Sid."

Darcy came out of Odega's lab with her body in tight control. She shut the door behind her quietly. Toffee pushed off the far wall of the corridor and took a step towards her. The security chief uncoiled like a spring and shoved the much larger man back up against the wall.

"Wha—" he started.

"How did that dog get here?" Her words were hard, sharp.

"How should I know? The sound net is weak, there are gaps in the fence."

"Dogshit. Did you know where to look for that monster or did it just show up conveniently?"

She dropped her hands from Toffee's chest. Toffee adjusted his coveralls, then held his hand up, palm forward. "Kind of ungrateful, aren't you? What with me saving the sun boy's life and all."

"Lucky for him you just happened to be there. Nice touch, not loading the shotgun."

"I guess Burle can't remember everything."

"If I ask Burle, will he remember giving it to you?"

"Oh, that's right, I just grabbed it. Didn't see a need to sign it out."

"I could have the dog analysed for tranquillizers."

Toffee cupped her chin, drawing his thumb down her cheek. "But you won't, will you?"

Darcy smashed his arm away with an audible thump of bone on bone. Her voice was quiet and intense. "Never touch me again."

Toffee rubbed his arm against his side, then smiled. "Taken a shine to little Noah, haven't we? Must be that pretty face of his."

Darcy's self-control was fragile at best. She could have easily pulled her gun and put a bullet through the hunter right there. "Noah Thurlow is too valuable to be a toy in your games."

"He was never in any danger."

"He was never in any…? You're restricted to your quarters. Get out of my sight."

Toffee nodded a little, then smiled again as he turned to leave. He called back over his shoulder before exiting through a plastic curtain. "Even if the dog was tranqued, that still won't prove I was the one who done it."

Darcy squeezed her eyes shut. She pushed open the door to animal research. Dr. Odega looked up from calibrating a spectrometer.

"Forget about the tests, Ted."

"Really? Are you sure?"

"Yes. I'm sure. When you're done with that thing, send what's left to the tanners."

The corridor blurred past as Darcy marched to...where? She wasn't going to brief Sid yet and she wasn't going to her room. The main corridor was the longest in the Pit, the place where she could walk the farthest without stopping. It eventually led to more secure areas, and to the caverns. Darcy walked the length of the corridor, taking turns that led her to the uneven passages that surrounded the Pit.

"Hello, Chief," said Patricia, a large solid-jawed woman in khaki coveralls. She was armed with a shotgun.

The security door slipped from Darcy's fingers, swinging shut with authority.

"You scared me, Pat. Didn't expect to find anyone here."

"Boss's orders. This dog thing has got everyone a little edgy. It's not like it's the first time, but still...what are you doing here?"

"I think I'm going for a walk."

"Need an escort? You could okay me to leave my post. It's kind of dull."

"No. I'll be fine."

Darcy took a flashlight from a small recharging rack near where the power lines and hook-ups flowed through a hole drilled into the rock. Her choice of passage was inevitable. Past outcroppings and jagged stone, she followed the cables for a Mimi all the way to the box on its stand, then she went a little further. The flashlight's spot passed over a large dark stain. Smaller stains of the same colour covered the ground and were spattered a little way up the tunnel wall. Darcy knelt and touched one of the spatters. She couldn't help but be drawn to this spot again and again. To stare and revisit a death she hadn't been a witness to. Her eyes clenched shut. The tightened skin around her right eye allowed only a poor seal, and a tear escaped, bulging, then trickling down her cheek. It stopped on a pucker of scar tissue, and dried there.

"Toffee's everything I said he was," Darcy said to the stains. "I need you. Why aren't you here when I need you?"

It was chilly in the cave, and her nose was stuffing up. She had to go back. It wouldn't do for her subordinate to see her with red eyes. Dr. Odega's cub sprang to her mind, but that wasn't an option. Darcy never let herself touch one of the rare, young animals that were brought to the Pit. It was too painful. She'd had a kitten, a creamy ball of fluff that chased house flies and stalked things that weren't there. Its name was Bono, and it always loved her.

For Darcy and the rest of humanity, it was a blow from which they would never recover. Everybody lived in a petless society. Animals could never replace human companionship, but in some ways, theirs was a superior comfort. It didn't matter that you hadn't done your hair up, or what stupid thing you'd done that day, pets didn't care. They provided simple, unconditional love.

Travis Jones had given Darcy the next best thing. He was a beautiful man, son of a black border guard and a Lakota Indian dental assistant. He'd inherited the best features of both races. In Travis's arms Darcy was clean again. Her scars vanished under the caress of his fingertips, and his deep voice, quiet in her ear, returned the world to the way it once was. He had taught Darcy how to control her temper in a way that Sid had never managed. Many would have referred to Travis as a puma, were it still complimentary to compare a person to an animal. His confidence and strength had led him to this cavern to scout the best places for Mimi setup. On one hunting trip, he'd beaten two coyotes to death with the butt of an empty rifle, but no amount of physical prowess or skill could save a man from a rat swarm. Like a beady-eyed flash flood, the rodents would appear out of nowhere by the hundreds. They'd climb over each other on their way up a body, moving so quickly, two or three would reach stomach and chest, before their victim fell into the teaming mass of teeth and ropy tail. Travis should have waited for the flamethrower that incinerated the rats. So many people believed the former security chief was indestructible, he'd started to believe it himself.

"Find anything new?" asked Pat, as Darcy stooped to return the flashlight to its charger.

"No. Nothing that could help me. How long have you been on?"

"Four hours or so."

"I'll have someone relieve you in a while. Good night."

Darcy found Sid in his room, one of the six that were extra large. At first Sid had planned to have them split into two rooms each, but then decided rank should have its privileges. The other double rooms were held by Odega, Darcy, Patel, Burle, and now, Toffee. This was another burr under the security chief's saddle. Sara should have gotten Travis's old room, while Toffee could have moved into the smaller one. Sara hadn't made a big deal about it, but Darcy was sure it bothered the doctor.

Sid's room held very little that marked it as personal quarters. Instead of decorations, the walls held blueprints of the Pit, a topographical map of the surrounding area, satellite pictures of the same ground covered by the map, and various other informative displays. The only purely aesthetic wall hanging was a glass case, that held a police officer's badge, and a signed declaration of appointment to the position of chief of Compton Pit."

The Boss had allowed himself the conceits of a double bed and a larger table. He had his own gun rack, containing a shotgun and an assault rifle, as well as a suit of RCMP riot gear, hung out on display.

Sid barely looked up from a map he was studying when Darcy entered.

"I want Toffee out of here," she said.

"Yes. I'm sure you do. I was informed you've restricted him to his quarters."

"Who told you?"

"He did."

Darcy closed her eyes and flexed her fingers, willing stress to drain from her body. "I didn't give him permission to stop by for a chitchat. Where is he now?"

"In his room, and he didn't come by. We passed in the hall. I want you to rescind the order first thing tomorrow."

"He brought a dog inside! Deliberately!"

"Do you have proof of that?"

"I don't need proof. I didn't even want him here in the first place, but oh no, you just had to let him in."

"We need him." The statement was one of finality. There would be no arguing this with the Boss, but Darcy did anyway.

"The hell we do. He's arrogant, belligerent—"

"Sounds like you."

"HE BROUGHT A DOG INSIDE!"

Sid raised a hand to stop Darcy's outburst. As he did, the map on the table rolled up to his other hand. He rolled the map back out and placed a handgun on it to hold it in place. The gun was the same one he'd had on that first day, so long ago.

"I had one of the Mimis repositioned. It's possible there was a gap," he said as if that would take care of everything. She wasn't buying it. "Darcy, do you realize what's going on around us?"

"How do you mean?"

"Here, in the Pit, everywhere else. We're gaining ground in many ways, but we're falling back in others. Toffee is capable of things. Trust me, we need him."

"Seth is an excellent hunter, and he's a good man. Everyone loves him—"

"That's just it, he's a good man. Toffee isn't. That's why we need him."

Darcy pulled out a chair and dropped into it. She noted that the map on the table was of the area around the Pit, but large enough to include Fenwick Prison.

"Why do we need a raccoon like Toffee?"

"Be nice, now."

Darcy wouldn't withdraw the insult. She crossed her arms under her breasts and raised her chin.

After a moment, Sid inclined his head. "It's getting ugly again. We're running out of things we never thought we would. There was just so much of it to stock pile. Canned soup, batteries, car parts…"

"That's not our problem. We make our trade goods, or recycle them. Our medicine alone could—"

"And when people run out of things to trade to us? What then? Do we give it away for free?"

Darcy knitted her eyebrows. She had come here to talk about Toffee, not bartering. "No we don't give it away, we work out another arrangement. That's our whole point."

"If we get the chance. There's plenty out there that would split the golden goose."

"That's an old one."

Sid chuckled. "Yes it is. Can't forget them all I suppose. We're guilty too, Darcy. We keep clean and we have lots of toys. It makes us think we're better than everybody else. Do you realize I bought a man?"

After all this time, Sid could still completely lose her.

"What?"

"Noah Thurlow. I paid water, medicine, light and chocolate for him, and he's mine!" Sid punctuated the sentence by closing his fingers tightly. He rotated his hand as he did it. It was flashy, like a conjurer's gesture.

"Are you out of your mind? Thurlow's not a prisoner."

"Isn't he? I'll never let him go outside. Not to hunt, not to explore. For the rest of his days, all he'll see is the inside of the Pit, and the ground within the Mimis."

"Oh, come on. It's not like he's a slave. He gets a room, he gets fed for his work. There are people who haven't been outside for years. Miranda hasn't even been topside since before we got here."

"But they can leave if they want to. It's different."

The undeniable shriek of a steam kettle cut the air. Sid rose and walked towards his hotplate. "Coffee?"

"Definitely. What kind?"

"Freeze dried. One of those things we're running out of."

"Sugar?"

"Sorry."

Sid placed a steaming mug of straight black in front of the security chief. The mug had been painted with one of Caps's offerings. A grizzly bear sat beside a picnic table and a garbage can. There was a basket on the table and a foot protruded from the bear's mouth. A wooden sign beside the bear read, "Feeding the Bears Can be Dangerous to Them and You."

Darcy picked the mug up by its handle and blew across the surface of the coffee. "I don't believe you're not going to let Noah go outside. I get to hunt, if I want. Harpreet and Odega go the strangest places on their expeditions—under heavy guard of course, but you let Burle go out by himself! For gardening of all things. I still object to that, by the way."

"But I made you coffee," the Boss said, with hurt in his voice.

Darcy took a sip and grimaced. "I don't come this cheap. I'm having Burle escorted from now on." She went on quickly, cutting off Sid's attempt to protest. "It's a security decision and you know I'm right, especially with what's been going on lately."

Sid conceded the point with his eyes. "Okay, but be diplomatic about it. Burle can handle himself. He shoots better than people half his age. Noah on the other hand...did you hear how he reacted earlier?"

"I was told he fainted."

"Doesn't exactly inspire confidence. Good thing Toffee was—"

Darcy slammed the mug down on the table. Coffee splashed on her wrist, burning flesh, but she ignored the pain.

"Toffee brought the dog in. What is it with him that—"

"Why would Toffee do that?"

Darcy's temper was threatening to burst, but the pain from her scalded wrist helped give her focus. "How should I know? Alpha male dogshit. Scare the crap out of the new guy, kill the big bad wolf. I'm surprised Toffee didn't just piss on him."

"That's only done in the military."

"Huh? What's that supposed to mean? No. You're not going to distract me again. I want Toffee locked outside. He broke the rules. It's a done deal."

"Why would he do what you're suggesting? When would he do it? The hunters were out when Noah arrived. Toffee didn't know anything about him. If this was a setup, he would have had to sneak out last night and bag an animal..."

Darcy nodded quickly. "Seth wouldn't do it, but maybe Mike, or Senna! He must have had help."

"Drop it."

Darcy's eyes widened in shock, then narrowed in suspicion. "What does he have on you?"

Sid licked his lips, then smiled as he leaned back in his chair. "So, I'm not a god, then?"

Darcy was lost again. In the face of her anger, and apparently in the face of justice, Sid was playing.

"That's the first time you've ever thought I might be a guilty party. I'm proud of you."

At first Darcy thought it was another deflection, but he'd said it so sincerely...

"You've come a long way. You're the chief of security in every sense of the word. You still can't dispose of our hunter. There may be tasks ahead that I can't give to Seth, or to you. Toffee is loyal in his own way, and as far as you're concerned, the most you have to worry about with him is damage control. You'll just have to trust me on this. Darcy, I'm tired, and I have things to finish." He gave her one more brief smile, then looked down at his map.

Darcy struggled with her emotions. One moment she'd been furious, the next filled with an unexpected warm glow. Ironically, it angered her more that Sid had made her forget her temper. Now she'd been dismissed. She looked at her mug, it was still half full.

Sid glanced at her. "Take the mug. Bring it back though, I like that one."

Darcy stood in the hall and looked at the Boss's door. Sid had said he was proud of her, but she may just have been completely fleeced. As she walked to her room, she realized her belief couldn't let the Boss be anything but on the level. He'd saved her life that first day, and on many occasions after that. He'd been her father, her older brother...he was one thing that she could completely count on. Without that, there was nothing.

Lying in bed, Darcy replayed the events of the day in an endless loop of disbelief and frustration. Travis's face danced in her mind, hovering over everything, then suddenly looking straight at her with accusation in his eyes. Darcy had a physical reaction to the waking dream; she jerked on the bed and sat up, swinging her feet to the floor.

Numbered doors bobbed past as she padded down the hall. Lena might still be up, and if she wasn't, she soon would be. Darcy stopped at door thirty-one and prepared to knock. A half heard sound stayed her hand. She pressed her ear to the door, breathy whispers and soft moans could be heard within. Darcy closed her eyes and listened to the sounds of sex. Travis returned unbidden to her mind, to be overshadowed by Toffee, with his steel eyes and cratered nose. Her eyes snapped open and the hunter's face was replaced by empty corridor. She looked down at what little she wore. It wouldn't look right for someone to see the chief of security listening at a door in nothing but a shift.

In bed again, Darcy tossed and turned, then drew her knees up and hugged them to her chest. She lay that way for a long time.

9. Logging Road

June 10th, New Wilderness Day

Darcy stood in the clearing, her hands squeezed her bottom lip so hard, it bled. Men and women thrashed on the ground and stumbled to reach the trucks. Bushy tails bobbed and weaved as animals scampered from victim to victim. Darcy had the insane image of a collection of subterraneous bumper cars, with only their tail-adorned antennae peeking through the ground. In front of her, Brad jerked to his feet. Blood flowed from between fingers clamped to his face. Darcy, who had somehow been holding back a scream, let loose a howl of such primal terror, it could be heard above all the other cries around her. This was not happening. She'd waited weeks for Brad to ask her out in the first place. She'd hung around him, dropping subtle hints, touching him with increasing frequency. Now her sought after boyfriend was staggering blind in front of her, and the very animals she so dearly loved were the cause. Darcy's mind blocked everything else, Brad being the only thing it could handle at the moment. She lunged for her boyfriend but he'd moved away, and something was on her leg. Darcy looked down and saw a martin, a dark furred, ferret like creature. It dug in with claws and bit into soft thigh. Darcy screamed for Brad, and swatted at the animal as she turned her head. Her boyfriend lay on his side, his hands were away from his face, but she could only identify him by the color of his shirt. Her gaze opened to include absolutely everything that was happening. Darcy's sanity frazzled at the edges and her thoughts became like the snow on a broken television set.

"Get to the trucks!" came a voice from far away.

There were two martins on her leg now. Before her, a brawny logger crushed the windpipe of a raccoon with this forearm, while another raccoon tore shreds of skin out of his back.

A thick smell assaulted her nostrils, and an impossibly hard blow struck her hip. The martins were thrown free as Darcy hurtled through the air. She landed on wet dirt. The sensation awoke something in her, a different Darcy, one who could handle this, one who could make choices. Her shorts were shredded across one hip, flesh pushed out through the denim and blood was oozing between the slashes and running down her leg. The grizzly was so much bigger than she would have imagined. Its lower jaw dropped open and it gave her a look that was almost questioning, then it raised its paw and lunged forward. A metal jerry can struck it in the nose.

"C'mon, try me, you piece of shit," said the foreman. He was bleeding from a dozen wounds, but from the look on his face, he couldn't feel any of them.

Two gunshots rang out, but Darcy couldn't tell where they came from. The trees on either side of the road stood in mute witness as cries both defiant and pathetic issued from the clearing.

The bear looked from Darcy to the foreman. She could see the change in its eyes as it made its decision. The bear took two steps towards the foreman, who looked for all the world like he was going to take the animal on with nothing but his fists. Another shot rang out and the bear shuddered. With a fourth shot, the grizzly turned and stumbled, then crashed to the ground. Darcy had no idea where the bear had been hit, but she saw who held the gun. It was the black man Darcy had noticed earlier. He'd been quite attractive a few minutes ago. Now he looked like an extra in a zombie movie. The man had open wounds on his face and neck and blood was splattered on him everywhere.

Darcy pushed off from the ground, preparing to stand, when one of the martins reached her leg and bit in again. A raccoon darted in front of her and snapped at her throat. She jerked back and the raccoon caught the necklace Brad had given her and pulled with surprising strength. The chain was of good quality and held as the animal yanked her into its embrace. The raccoon pushed claws into the right side of her face and bit in just above the cheekbone. Darcy felt the skin beside her eye stretch and then tear. The wet, ripping sound was that much louder due to its close proximity to her ear. Panic threatened to paralyse her again, but she rose to her feet, with the weight of the raccoon pulling on her cheek. She was sure there were two animals on her leg again.

The foreman was tossing animals off himself like a television superhero. One of them would latch on, and he would break its neck with his strong hands. The cougar had set its sights on what it perceived to be the most dangerous of the humans. There was a glimmer of fear in the foreman's eyes as the cougar swiped with a meaty paw. A bullet took the cougar behind the head, and it went down.

Darcy held the raccoon in her hands, supporting its weight, begging it not to take her face off. One of the animals on her leg was climbing higher, but she could only tell by pressure, because her nerves were numb from the hip down. She dragged the leg a few steps, then a logger was beside her, helping her with the raccoon. The logger fell away, pulled by she knew not what. A bloody hand grabbed the raccoon, and something heavy smashed the animal in the head, it went limp, and fell from Darcy's face. Nausea rose, and she vomited as a strong hand pushed her towards the trucks.

The foreman lit a zippo and threw it into a puddle of gasoline. Flames danced and leaped across ground and animals, even a few people. Burning fur and skin joined the stench of fear and released bodily fluids. Animals skittered away, but did not retreat completely. Those on fire raced in circles, shrieking in fear and agony. Darcy found she actually felt sorry for them. She reached the truck and her leg gave out. She struck her head on a giant tire as she fell. The foreman, who somehow was already inside, grabbed Darcy by her hair, and dragged her into the cab. The man with the gun was in right after her.

Darcy slumped into the space behind the seats, something chittered, and she realized there was still a martin on her leg. She was hysterical in her thrashing, she couldn't take anymore. Her hands flailed at the creature, but she hardly hit it at all. The foreman grabbed the animal off her leg and broke its spine against the dashboard, then threw it into the back again. Darcy jerked away from the carcass, her shredded hip dragging along rough floor matting.

The foreman had started the truck and thrown it in reverse. The truck's warning beeps sounded ludicrous as animals landed on the hood and clicked across the roof. Two men and one woman ran for the truck. The foreman shifted into forward gear, and the men jumped for the back bumper. One of the men couldn't quite reach the truck, and the woman jumped off again. Both of them were taken down. A new bear had arrived, as well as two more cougars.

"Get off! Get Off! Get Off!" yelled the foreman at a raccoon clinging to the windshield wipers. A spray of cleanser shot up from the hood and splashed in the raccoon's eyes. It flinched, then flew off the hood as the truck swerved.

"What the fuck?...the fuck!...what the fuck?" The foreman's vocabulary was reduced to meaningless obscenities.

The man with the gun turned in his seat to look at Darcy. "Are you okay?"

It was such a logical, commonplace question, but coming from a man who was holding his neck together with his hands, it struck Darcy as funny. She realized she was also holding skin in place with her hands. She giggled.

The foreman looked back at her with disbelief, then reached for his CB. The handset fell from his grasp. The foreman looked at his hand. One of the fingers dangled by a strip of flesh. The gunman grabbed the mic and held it up for the foreman to speak.

"Reynolds to base, over!" There was no response, "REYNOLDS TO BASE, OVER!"

The foreman glanced at the gunman, who released his grip on the mic's button.

"Base here, go ahead, over." It was a man's voice that came from the speaker.

"You're not gonna fucking believe this..."

"Base here. Reynolds, do you read? Over."

Reynolds took the mic from the gunman. His hand was slick with blood, but he finally got a decent grasp and depressed the button.

"Send ambulances, and guns, I've got men down!"

"Reynolds, please repeat. Over."

From where she lay, Darcy couldn't see the road ahead, all she could see were the tops of trees going by. Her whole body numb, she couldn't remember who she was.

"Kid," the gunman was talking to her. "Could you see if there's a first aid kit back there?" His voice was thick, and slurred.

"YOU HEARD ME THE FIRST TIME," yelled Reynolds. "GET THE GODDAMN COPS UP ROAD SIX!"

"You have men down? Over."

"YES, GODDAMN IT!"

"Nate, calm down. How many men? Over."

"How many...ALL OF THEM YOU FUCKING IDIOT! OVER!"

Darcy tugged at coveralls and papers that occupied the back area with her. She found a white plastic case with a red cross on the front. She offered it to the gunman. The kit seemed to weigh a hundred kilograms.

"Stop swearing on the air, Nate. You've been warned about that before. Are you telling me a bunch of eco-freaks took out your whole crew? Over."

The foreman looked at the mic with something beyond exasperation in his face. "The eco-freaks are down, too! I think one of them is on the back of the truck, but it could be one of ours. Over."

"Nate, are you drunk? Over."

"NO I AM NOT...we were attacked by animals, base. Hundreds of them. I have two of them in the truck with me, we all need urgent medical attention. Over."

"You have two animals in the truck with you? You're not making any sense. Over."

"No, I have two of the...MY FUCKING FINGER IS HANGING OFF!" He ripped the mic out of the CB, then cursed at the exposed wires dangling from his hand. The gunman half slid, half fell from his seat. He'd taped gauze pads to his face and neck. He pushed himself halfway into the back of the cab and took one of Darcy's hands.

"I'm Sid. I'm going to take care of your leg first."

Reynolds muttered to himself as he drove. It had become dim in the back of the cab, and passing trees seemed like pointed shadows. Darcy looked down at her waist as Sid cut through her shorts and panties with a sharp pair of scissors. For a moment it looked like he would collapse across her, but he recovered. He had to peel the denim from her hip. Darcy had soiled herself and her cheeks reddened with shame.

Reynolds glanced back at his passengers. "What's that smell? Jesus Christ...fuck..." He turned back to the road.

"I think it looks worse than it is," Sid said. He reached for one thing in the kit, then another, unsure of what to do first. He settled on a large gauze pad which came from a rather small cardboard box. He place the pad over her hip. "Can you hold that in place?"

Darcy didn't want to take her hands away from her face.

"Please?"

She shifted one hand and used the other to apply pressure on the bandage. Sid secured the bandage with tape. She had to raise her pelvis a couple of times in order to help him do it. When he'd wrapped the tape a few times, he cut it with the scissors, and moved to her face.

"Why do you have a gun?" asked Reynolds. "Were you going to shoot us?"

Sid glanced at the back of Reynolds's head. "No. I'm a cop. RCMP."

"So you were undercover?"

"More like under a delusion."

Sid's hands trembled as they applied gauze and tape to Darcy's cheek. When he was finished, he pulled coveralls over her. "You're in shock, you have to keep warm."

"S-so do you," she said. Her tongue was thick in her mouth.

"Don't worry about me." He pulled himself back into his seat, dragging the kit with him. "Let me see your hand," he said to Reynolds.

"Not while I'm driving."

"I have to take care of your hand."

"NOT WHILE I'M FUCKIN' DRIVING!"

Sid backed off, and disappeared from Darcy's view. She heard the sound of fabric being cut.

Reynolds looked over at Sid, then back at Darcy. "You did a shit job, you know that?"

The truck came to a stop, its large motor rumbling quietly under the hood. Reynolds leaned into the back of the cab and took Darcy's head in his hands. He looked at the padding on her face. "That's not good enough, don't they teach you cops anything?"

"...was the best I could do." Sid's voice was losing strength. "Get...the truck moving again."

"I'll patch you two properly then—"

"Here they come..."

The cab rocked as something smashed into the driver's side. The impact came again, and the door buckled inwards. Wide antlers appeared in the window, followed by the head of a moose. The head disappeared.

"There's another one," said Sid, half to himself.

Reynolds darted into his seat and slammed the truck into gear. Heavy antlers smashed into the truck along its body as the foreman gunned the engine.

"They've all gone fucking crazy," he said, as he stared at the side mirror. "I hope that guy got into the back."

Darcy pulled herself into a sitting position. Her gorge rose and she dry heaved. Snot ran from her nose, its salty taste mingled with the copper already in her mouth.

"Y...You have to keep warm...too." She pushed a pair of coveralls off of herself, and onto Sid's leg.

"Jesus, girl, there are blankets back there," said Reynolds. "You're lying on them."

Bunched under her legs were folded blankets. Nausea took her again, and she had to lie back for a moment before she could move. She pulled at one of the blankets until she could give some of it to Sid's waiting hand, then she pulled at another one until it covered her. She lay back, and looked at the ceiling of the cab with one blurry eye. Something sharp dug into her neck, but it wasn't another animal, at least, not a real one. Darcy repositioned the dolphin pendant on her necklace, and thought about Brad. This was her fault. It was her idea to skip school and come all the way out to protest. Once she had her hooks into the boy, he could deny her nothing. What was she going to tell Brad's mom and dad? Would she be expelled for this? The irrelevance of this last concern didn't enter into her mind.

"We all need shots," Reynolds was saying. "Tetanus, rabies…those animals didn't look rabid. Did those animals look rabid to you?"

Sid had wrapped himself up well, only his head emerged from what Darcy could see.

"Turn on the radio," said Sid.

"You want music?"

"I want news."

Reynolds turned the radio on, scratchy static came from speakers by Darcy's head. Reynolds fiddled with the tuner. "We won't get much out here."

Static was replaced by a blurb of something as Reynolds passed a station. He tuned back and a strained woman's voice filled the cab.

"...all over. This is no joke folks, our lines are flooded here. Willy? My producer is shaking his head, he can't get through to any of the authorities. We'll keep trying. Please don't call the station, we know what's going on. For those of you just tuning in, we're getting reports of animal attacks from all over..."

The announcer went on to list examples. It wasn't just creatures of the woods, people were being attacked by their own pets. One man on a cell phone claimed he couldn't leave his car because of the twenty odd cats waiting on the outside.

Darcy heard, but didn't grasp, the reality of the litany of horrors spewed by the shocked DJ. As vibrations from the road and her own exhaustion lulled her to sleep, Sid turned off the radio.

The first thing Darcy noticed when she awoke was how high the ceiling was. Its green, corrugated metal must have been thirty or forty feet up, and curved like the roof of an igloo.

"Oh, you're awake," said a soft, feminine voice.

Darcy rolled her head to the side. A woman sat on a stool with one of Darcy's hands in hers. She was a pretty woman, with thin blond hair. Hard lines came from around her mouth, but there was nothing but compassion in her eyes.

"I'm Anne. What's your name?"

"Darcy. Where..." She saw someone lying on a cot behind Anne. The person's face was completely swathed in gauze. Darcy pulled her hand away and touched her own face, it too, was bandaged. Disjointed images of horrifying clarity beat against the inside of her skull.

"Noooooooo...noooooooo..." Darcy rocked back and forth as she uttered her plaintive denials. Strong hands reached out to steady her.

"Stop honey, you'll pop your stitches. Russ, get Sid."

Anne cradled Darcy's head in her arms. The girl sobbed, and Anne had to fight to keep from crying herself.

"Hush, child. I'm here, I'm right here."

"Where am I?" Darcy asked between sobs.

"You're at Chisselha Emergency Airport. We're in the hanger."

"I have to call my parents."

"Oh, honey..." Anne leaned over the girl and hugged her through thick blankets.

Sid shuffled to the side of the bed. He favoured his right leg, and leaned on a wooden pole. His face was bandaged, the left side completely covered. "Hey kid, remember me?"

"Her name's Darcy."

"Hello, Darcy. I'm Sid."

An image of the man stumbling towards her, his cheek hanging open, rose up in Darcy's mind. She looked at his bandage wrapped head and neck, and thought he'd gone from being a zombie to a mummy.

"I remember you. Did you...did you lose your eye?"

Sid patted the left side of his face. "No, it's fine, but the skin around it's a bit worse for wear."

Darcy suddenly realized she had an eye covered herself. Her hands flew to her right socket. "Did I lose mine?" She couldn't feel anything beneath the padding.

"No, the doctor says your eye is fine as well."

"I have to call my parents."

Sid sat down on the side of the cot. He looked quite relieved to do so. "You can't. Seems that everyone in the world is trying to call somebody. The lines are all tied up. Nobody can get through to anyone."

The implications of this were not immediately apparent to her. "Is there a radio? I could talk to someone at home, get a message through."

"Where's home?"

"Vanderhoof."

Anne and Sid exchanged glances. A staccato of gunfire came from outside the hangar's walls.

"What's going on?"

Sid put his hand on Darcy's. "There are some people outside...shooting animals."

"You mean we...the animals...it's not over?"

"We're safe in here," said Anne. "There's a high fence with barbed wire on top. The mesh is too fine for small stuff to get through..."

"Except mice," Sid said.

"...except mice. The birds let up on us after they downed the second plane."

"Birds? I want to go outside."

Sid shook his head, "Kid, Darcy, you don't. You really don't."

"The hell I don't!" She went to swing her legs out from under the sheets. Pain tore through her hip, stealing breath away.

"Lie still. It's okay, honey, just lie still." Anne held Darcy down by the shoulders, and cast about for something, or someone.

A woman appeared at her bedside. She looked like she was in her late thirties, but without the bags under eyes, and with her dark hair combed, she would probably look younger.

"You're awake, good. How are you feeling?"

"Darcy," said Sid, "this is Dr. Nash. She stitched you up. She stitched us both up."

"I want to go outside."

The doctor stooped by Darcy's side, "I'm afraid you won't be walking for a few days."

"Then bring me a wheelchair. You seem to have everything else here."

"They're on order, I'll let you know as soon as one arrives. I'll be back to check with you later."

Dr. Nash walked away. Darcy followed the retreating back with her eyes. There were a few other people on cots, some of them in much worse shape than her or Sid.

Darcy pushed Anne's hands away, and looked at Sid. "I'm going outside if I have to crawl. I want to see."

Sid looked at Anne and shrugged his shoulders.

"Russ," called Anne to someone out of Darcy's field of view, "Can you be a wheelchair for a few minutes?"

Russ turned out to a burly man with a shaggy, brown beard. His arms were bigger than Darcy's legs, and his stomach certainly hadn't suffered too many nights away from the beer keg.

Anne gave a hopeless look at the big man, and said, "This is Darcy, she wants to go outside."

Russ looked at Sid, who nodded.

"Okay," said Russ, clearly not thinking it was a good idea.

Anne pulled the sheets aside, and Darcy saw she was wearing nothing but a long, black T-shirt. Her right leg was wrapped all the way to the ankle. Russ slipped an arm under her back, and the other under her legs at the knees. With a gentleness that belied his girth, he lifted her from the bed, and carried her to a door set in the wall furthest from her cot. Darcy's T-shirt rode up, and modesty forced at her to tug it down again, for all the good it did. Russ didn't seem to notice her state of undress. He had a far away look in his eyes, like nothing before him was actually real.

Sid opened the door, and Darcy was borne into sunlight.

The fence surrounding the hangar was high indeed. The wire mesh was marked by countless dents, surrounding quarter sized holes. A few carcasses littered the ground inside, and blackened earth showed where gasoline fires had been lit. Beyond the fence lay scores of dead animals, of all shapes and sizes. Darcy focussed on a caribou, looking serene and harmless, the tip of one antler keeping its head from completely touching the ground. A man walked past, splashing gasoline from a metal jerry can, preparing another firewall. She recognized the foreman coming towards them. His right hand was bandaged and he carried a rifle.

"Hello, girl," said the foreman. "You got a name yet?"

"Darcy McCullough. I'm sorry, I don't remember yours."

"Nate Reynolds. I didn't think you were going to make it. We couldn't wake you up earlier."

"Did the doctor save your finger?"

Reynolds looked at his bandaged hand. "No. Not exactly a major hospital here."

A shot rang out. All heads turned to see a raccoon jerk on the barbed wire, then get hung up on the metal spikes. There were a number of other creatures stuck to the wire in various places along the fence line.

"Sid," said Nate, "We're almost out of ammo. I've got eight rounds left, Kyle's got a little more. We have no more shotgun shells. I don't know if the next wave of mice'll fall for the firewall. The last one fell back pretty quickly. If the birds start diving again..."

Darcy noticed a shape on the ground, obscured by the edge of a long shed. "What's that? Move closer." She directed Russ by pushing on the back of his head with her hand.

"You don't need to—" Sid's warning came too late. Russ had already moved enough to allow the girl to see behind the shed. Ten or eleven tarp-covered shapes lay in a line. From beneath one tarp, a pair of boots protruded, from another, a hand peeked out.

Darcy's mind reeled. This wasn't happening, this wasn't how it was supposed to be. Her sweet-sixteen summer was upon her. Darcyland included long days tanning by the lake, trips to the big city for rock concerts, horseback riding and drunken bush parties. She buried her face in Russ's chest. "Take me back. I can't look at this...I can't look at this!"

The tone of her voice, so lost, so hopeless caused nearly physical pain in Sid.

With Darcy back in bed, Sid sat on the stool, his hand resting on the girl's arm through woolen blankets.

"Sid, is it a disease? Is it a virus or something?"

"Dr. Nash says it could be a strain of mutated scapies, but that usually only goes for sheep. Besides, it doesn't add up."

"How far? Is it all over the province?"

"It's everywhere, kid. Everywhere in the world."

Darcy took a moment to absorb this. "My parents?"

"Maybe, but the radio says small towns got hit the worst. They had no warning, and lots of animals already inside people's homes. Did you have any pets?"

"A kitten, and...and two dogs. Malamutes...they're my...they're my dad's. He...l-l-loves them..." Darcy was wracked by uncontrolled sobbing. From the dampness under her bandage, she could tell her right eye was exactly where it was supposed to be.

Sid held her as tightly as he felt he could. "It's okay, Darcy, I'll take care of you. I'll take care of you now."

10. Pulling Strings

Noah was out of bed a few minutes before the bells sounded for breakfast. As he fastened the top button of his coveralls, all thoughts of food were banished by recollection of what had transpired the day before. His eyes squinted as he tried to will the memory from his brain. Noah paused before opening his door, imagining contemptuous looks from people as he walked to the mess hall. In the face of danger, he'd passed out. Even a little kid could have done better. He walked the length of the corridor with his head down, not making eye contact. The glass of fresh milk he received lifted his spirits only a little. He started towards his "usual" table, and stopped. Maybe he couldn't sit there anymore, maybe he wasn't worthy. It would have almost been better, he thought darkly, if Toffee hadn't saved the day. At least Noah wouldn't be alive to face this embarrassment. Far from being grateful to the hunter, Noah resented him for his skill.

"How are you feeling?" asked Caps as Noah sat down.

"Kinda stupid."

"Don't sweat it," said Lena. "We can't all be big and strong. That's why Toffee's a hunter and you're a panel jockey." Her comment wasn't the least bit helpful.

Burle held his glass of milk up as if to make a toast. "I wouldn't worry about it kid. Here's to dead critters." He knocked the milk back in a shot, then gave Noah a big smile.

Noah was surprised at first, then returned the smile and chugged his milk as well. Caps, Lena and Cass joined in the gulping. They all laughed at their cavalier waste of the precious fluid, then looked regretfully at their empty glasses.

A tapping of metal against glass quieted conversation and drew everyone's attention to what was considered to be the head table. The Boss stood with a roll of papers in his hand.

"Listen up people, I have an announcement to make. As of right now, all unauthorized use of power is to cease. Violating personal limits will result in immediate suspension of privileges. Violation of departmental limits...well there won't be any will there?"

There were a few depreciative sounds and comments.

"This order comes straight from our chief of photovoltaics, Noah Thurlow."

Noah's jaw dropped. Heads turned to look at him.

"Wow," said Caps, under his breath. "The Boss can be a real prick sometimes."

"Furthermore," continued Sid, holding up his roll of papers, "this is the list of all batteries that have been properly signed out. There's a discrepancy between what's on this list, and what's been taken from the recharge racks. If the manifest doesn't balance by eighteen hundred, we start tossing rooms."

Noah turned to Caps. "I didn't order that! I haven't even checked the battery manifests!"

A comment came from one of the tables nearby; "If he tries to take my batteries, I'll sic a dog on him."

Sid silenced further complaints with a wave of his hand, then sat and returned to eating as if nothing had happened.

Noah faced his companions, but he could feel eyes picking at his back.

"Looks like The Boss is on a character building crusade," said Caps. "You should feel privileged Noah, he's given you special attention."

"Everybody's going to hate me. This sucks."

"Here's some good news," said Cass. "You're clear of STDs."

Noah was getting pummelled from all sides. "How do you know that?"

"Dr. Patel posted it on the notice board outside."

Caps and Cass shared an amused look.

Lena laughed and clapped her hands together. "You've never been hazed before?"

Burle patted Noah on the back. "If you can't grow a thick skin, drop by stores, I'll see if I can hook you up."

At ten o'clock people started arriving at Noah's desk in the work room. Some of them said nothing as they dropped off batteries. A few apologized and asked if they could legitimately sign them out, others made barely veiled references to Noah's incident topside. One of them, a bald man in hunter's camouflage, barked at the panel jockey, reproducing the sound so accurately, Noah flinched. The hunter went off laughing.

"That wasn't very nice of him," said Eggerson.

"No, it wasn't. At least you're not making fun of me."

Eggerson held up a series of hinged pieces of metal, connected by a cable. "Haven't had the time. I've been too busy making you a backbone."

Noah leaned over the desk and buried his face in his arms.

At twelve o'clock Cass appeared and dumped six D batteries on his desk.

"What did you need all those for?" asked Noah.

"None of your business." She winked at him, then left.

Noah didn't get the thrust of her insult, but shook his head, and wished that everyone would just leave him alone. He noticed Eggerson was still working on the "spine." It had grown ring-clamps and some extra metal plates.

"What is that thing? Neil! What are you really making there?"

"What? Oh, flexible leg brace." He held it up and demonstrated by bending it in his hands. "For stabilizing multiple leg fractures in the field. Just something new I thought up."

By sixteen hundred all but two AA batteries were accounted for. The recharge rack was properly stocked, and Noah awaited the dinner bells and his eminent encounter with the rest of the Pit's occupants. He wondered if he could just eat in the workroom. From the crumbs and other organic detritus around Eggerson's desk, the engineer did it all the time. Something shiny and red poked out from under a hide on one of the tables. Noah pushed the pelt away and discovered to his amazement a child's puppet, a marionette of excellent quality. The puppet had a bright smile, a red coat and dark pants. It had a rifle in one hand, and Noah found, that with just a little practice, he was able to make the little soldier walk across the floor quite realistically.

"Where did this come from?" Noah asked as he marched the puppet to Eggerson.

"Oh dear, that should have gone out on the last convoy. Just like me to forget."

"Did you make it?" Noah made the puppet crouch, then leap to the top of Eggerson's desk.

Neil stopped working on his leg brace and took the puppet from Noah. "Yes, I made it. That's what I did before. I was a toy maker. Last of dying breed I'm afraid. It's the same thing you know, making prosthetics, just bigger puppets, that's all."

"So you weren't an engineer or anything?"

"Oh no, not at all. Ah, you've heard some refer to me as Dr. Eggerson?"

Noah nodded, though he'd heard nothing of the sort.

"The title is purely honorary. An attempt at flattery I suppose. I still make the marionettes when I get the chance. I wish I could see the looks on children's faces when they get them. I just make people now of course, not much call for animals."

Noah studied the puppet's face. "This looks kind of like one of the hunters. Seth?"

"You see the resemblance? Seth thinks it looks nothing like him. I use his face on most male puppets. It's easy to carve, and he looks so friendly, doesn't he?"

"Who do you use for the females?"

"Lena for the young ones. Asians have such a timeless quality, don't they? I use Dr. White for the older ones, but don't tell her that." Eggerson's eyes gleamed as he touched a finger to his lips. He placed the puppet in one of his desk's drawers, careful not to tangle the strings, then returned to his leg brace.

Noah flipped through screens. He'd remapped schematics to suit his own way of looking at power flows, and found that if he skimmed a few seconds off of a number of departments, he could quietly give Lena the juice she wanted for her dish. The computer couldn't cut off power flow to any one place by itself, but with just a look at certain diagrams, Noah knew just what plugs to pull, and when. It occurred to him to check the screen that monitored power usage, to see if personal power reduction was being met with the same zeal as battery returns. He noticed a small red icon on the bottom of the screen. It was one he should have seen hours ago, but his eyes kept skipping past it. Noah looked up at the ceiling access panel like all the teeth in the world were waiting on the other side of it. He squared his shoulders and climbed before resolve failed him. He was halfway up the ladder when Eggerson called to him.

"Why are you going up there?"

"I didn't reconnect the cable yesterday. Neither did anybody else."

"You should take an escort."

"I...I can't. I have to do this alone."

"At least take a weapon. Toffee's shotgun is still here. He left it by that table over there."

Noah had to twist his neck in order to see the gun. "But it's not loaded."

"It is now."

Noah descended and took up the shotgun. He broke the breach, and sure enough, two shells lay nestled, side by side. Noah walked over to Eggerson.

"Thanks."

"What for?"

"Didn't you load the gun?"

"Why would I do that?"

"How did you know it was loaded?"

"I checked when I came in this morning. Don't you check to see if a weapon in your presence is loaded? Guns you know, never can be too careful."

The access panel flipped open and Noah emerged gun first, ready to blast anything that even looked like it might have fur. He studied the shadows between panels, his heart pounding against his ribs. In a crouch, he moved from column to column, always keeping something at his back. Soon there was nothing between him and the cable hub. Marshalling his courage he darted between two risers and threw himself to the ground by the hub. He swept the air in all directions with the shotgun and saw a pair of perimeter guards, leaning on the fence and watching him. Noah felt like an idiot. His grip on the shotgun went limp and his shoulders slumped. Not being able to see faces under the guards' net helmets made things worse. The guards resumed their patrol.

Noah found the proper cable fairly quickly, hooked the loose plug from within the hub, and reconnected the line. The barrel of the shotgun dragged in the dirt as he walked back to the access panel.

"See anything interesting while you were up there?" Eggerson asked.

"I didn't, but someone else did."

Dinner wasn't as bad as Noah had feared, although he heard a few snippets concerning his death defying attack on nothing. Caps was on a rant about the world changing being the best thing that could have happened to popular music, considering the direction it had been going. From the noncommittal responses of the others at the table, Noah could tell it was a tirade they had all heard before. Burle was at the table, as were Lena and Cass. Noah wondered absently why Miranda had been supplanted so easily. He scanned the tables for the older woman, but before he saw her, he realized how many people were talking and laughing. Obviously, they were all talking about him. Despondently, he turned back to his tray and resumed pushing steamed vegetables around with his fork.

"You're a quick learner," said Burle. "Most people are here months before they figure what bad cook Roshi really is."

"Yeah, sun boy," said Caps. "What's up with your appetite?"

Noah opened his mouth, but nothing came out of it. He didn't know what to say.

"Buddy, ease up on yourself. Okay, pay attention. You see that guy, brown hair, funky mouth that hooks up on the left?"

Noah followed Caps's finger and nodded.

"That's Eric, been here two years. On his second night he got himself locked outside by accident. He didn't know where the access panel was. The Boss found him at midnight, pounding on a skylight and crying like a baby."

"Didn't the tower guards see him?" asked Noah, shocked.

"Sure, but they didn't feel like helping him. They don't keep lights on at night, so Eric thought the towers were empty. See her? That's Veronica..."

"Who?"

"...sorry, green coveralls, talking with her hands...got her? Good. She wasn't here a week before someone got her drunk and let her loose in the farm. They told her that it was a solar-induced lobotomy, and at night, the animals went back to normal."

Noah looked disbelievingly at Caps.

"Oh, yes. She bought it, hook, line and sinker. It took Dr. Patel two days to calm her down. The Boss was pissed. She held up though, never said who did it. Now she works in the farm, works hard, too. Now look at that guy..."

"I get it. Everyone here has done something stupid."

"Well, I haven't."

"Sure you haven't," said Lena. "Noah, if someone doesn't screw up by themselves, someone does it for them, at least lately. I bet Caps had something nasty planned for you."

Caps put on a hideous sneer. "Be grateful you never have to find out what it was."

"So what was done to Toffee?" asked Noah.

"Nothing was done to Toffee," said Lena.

"I'll do something to him," Caps said, tapping his fingertips together.

Burle raised his eyebrows. "You go right ahead, son. I'm sure Harpreet could use a patient."

Caps lifted his empty tray. "I'm finished. Noah, could you scout ahead, make sure there's no teeth between me and the exit?"

"Very funny. Ha ha."

"C'mon, sun boy, if your friends can't hack on you, who can?"

Noah took in the whole mess hall with a sweep of his arm.

"Yeah, alright. Point made. We should take him to the head room."

The conversation had made Noah suspicious of everything. "Head room?"

"Yeah, it's on the second level."

"Second level? There's another level?"

"Where did you think hydroponics was? Haven't you been looking at the power charts?"

"I guess I never noticed level designations."

Caps dragged Noah up by an arm. "Anyone else?"

"No thanks," said Lena. "You boys go have fun."

"Me neither," Cass said, holding a hand up. "That room still gives me the creeps."

Burle finished the last of his food, then swapped his tray with Noah's. "You don't mind, do you?"

"No, go ahead."

The second level wasn't as well lit as the first. There were no skylights, and only a single string of lights ran the length of the corridor.

There were almost as many doors as above, and Noah felt if he became separated from Caps, he could get lost for hours.

"What else is down here?" Noah asked.

"Pipes, mostly. Access to water filtration, geothermics, the park—"

"Park? As in trees and stuff? How do you..."

"No, it's a section of corridors that people use for jogging. We just call it the park. Can't remember who came up with the nickname. Oh yes, it was me."

"The Boss called me the chief of photovoltaics. Why am I a chief? It's not like I have a staff, or anything."

"You can conscript people."

"Huh?"

"Let's say you need one of those big panels moved, or something. You can round up some folk and make them do it."

Caps walked a few metres before he realized Noah had stopped dead in the corridor.

"You mean I can order people around?"

"Just about everybody 'cept another chief. You've got to have a reason though, you can't just Shanghai someone into giving you a pedicure. You know what Shanghai means, right?"

"I've never heard it, but I get the context. That's...that's good. I can order people around. That's really good."

"Don't start ego tripping on me now. This way, chop chop."

After a few more turns, Noah stopped again. "Can I order *you* around?"

"Nope, I'm the chief of the pool."

"The Boss said you hated titles."

"Not as much as I hate being told what to do. C'mon, we're almost there."

Caps wore a capricious expression on his face as they turned corners and pushed through plastic curtains.

"Caps, I don't want to sound ungrateful, but why are you being so nice to me? You don't even know me."

"You've got some confidence issues, you know that? Okay, from a purely selfish point of view, you're the juice man."

"Excuse me?"

"Did you figure out how to get Lena her dish time?"

"Yes."

"There you go. Piss you off, and oops, no power to my room. So sorry, yes, I know you'll get to it as soon as you can. If I need a favour though, better to be on your good side. But then I shouldn't be telling you this, makes it too easy for you. We're here."

From the hallway they turned into, Noah could see stairs up to the first level.

"This is where we came in. You just took me in a big circle."

"Mmmmm, caught that did you? Well, it gave us time to chat." Caps gave Noah a thoughtful look, as if deciding whether or not to say something. "Ah, what the hell. Let's see what happens."

Caps pushed the door open and three dogs stared Noah in the face. A moment before falling over backwards, he realized they were just stuffed heads mounted on posts.

"You brought me all the way down here just to scare me again?"

"Get over it, you'll like this."

There were other types of animal heads on posts—a caribou, a cougar, some raccoons. Some of them had glass eyes, others just empty sockets. All of the heads were in bad shape, seams were ripped and stuffing protruded in places. They had their mouths open, and there wasn't a full set of teeth among them.

"Choose your weapon," said Caps, offering Noah a choice of two wooden clubs. "This was Harpreet's idea. It works for some people, doesn't for others. Go ahead."

Noah took a half hearted swing at the head of a raccoon. It bobbed, the motion made it look as if it was laughing. Noah hit it again, harder.

"Wouldn't you rather beat a dog?"

Noah looked at the three canine heads. He chose the one closest to him and gave it a whack. It felt good. He hit the head again and felt energy surge through his arms. His arms swung back and forth as he hit his target over and over. It was well stuffed, and mounted with punishment in mind. Noah raised his club over his head and poured all his frustration and hatred into the blow. The head split across the forehead, a chunk of it fell to the ground.

Caps raised his hand to his mouth and called out, "Wench, bring me a fresh head!"

"Would some booze do instead?" Lena's voice scared Noah half out of his wits.

"Couldn't resist us could you?" asked Caps, as he took a metal flask from Lena.

"I can here. Let's go to the Enchanted Forest."

Noah followed the two of them out, but not before giving the torn head one more hit, and turning off the head room's lights. After taking a more direct route than what he'd been led on before, the three arrived at large bay filled with old pipes. Condensation beaded along the metal. Spurts of steam hissed from valves and weak seals. Caps pulled some power cables from behind a wooden box and began hooking up strings of coloured lights wrapped around pipe supports.

Noah looked at the sheer number of bulbs and groaned. "Most of the lights down here shouldn't be on anyway. This...I don't even remember seeing anything like this. What battery do these lines come from? What's the designation?"

"Take a load off, juice master. This is one of those favours. 'Kay Lena, kill the mains."

Lena flipped a switch and the bay was plunged into darkness, then lit with reds and greens as Caps gave power to the coloured lights. In a few seconds, the lights began to blink on and off in sequence. The steam took on a mystical quality, and droplets of water glistened. It was beautiful.

The flask was pushed into Noah's hand. He drank, then gasped as his throat erupted in flame.

"Not the smoothest stuff," said Caps. "That's why I prefer this." He brought a stone pipe from his pocket, then filled the bowl with aromatic herb from a small skinbag. The herb glowed a cheery red as he inhaled, then offered the pipe around.

"No thanks," Noah said, rubbing his throat. "I've had my fill for the night."

Caps angled the pipe at Lena.

"I don't know," she jiggled the flask. "I don't like to mix chemicals."

"Fine, more for me."

They sat on wooden crates and watched the lights for while. Caps moved down to the floor and Noah had another slug of whatever was in the flask.

"The Human Torch!" Caps blurted, spreading his arms wide, "Then I could burn all the wasps as I flew around and terrorized the birds! Fry you little bastards! Zzzzzt! What about you, Noah?"

"Huh?"

"It's one of his games," said Lena. "Choose some fictitious character you could be. Just go along with him, it's easier."

"So who would you be?" Caps's eyes were glossy, and he had a stupid grin on his face.

"I don't know. God?"

"Fictitious character," said Lena.

"He is a—"

"Whoa, whoa, whoa!" Caps shook his hands in the air. "That's a discussion for another time! Lena, don't even get started. Noah, God's off limits. Someone else."

Noah pondered. "I can't think of anyone."

"Who were your heroes?" asked Caps.

"Uhm, Bacon's kind of my hero, but I wouldn't want to be him."

"That's the guy you came here with, right? I mean heroes from when you were a kid."

"I can't remember."

"You watched TV right? Saw some movies?"

"Sure, I guess."

Lena lit Caps's pipe and took a small hit. "Noah, where did you live?"

"Underbel. It's about—"

Caps put a hand on each of Noah's legs and leaned into him. "Sun boy, for the rest of the evening, assume that every question we ask you is about pre-Change events. Comprende?"

"I lived in Seattle."

"We have a breakthrough! Lena, do continue."

"What was your Mom's name?"

"Kate."

"What did she look like?"

"I can't remember. I dream about her sometimes, but when I wake up," Noah shrugged. "It's the same thing with my dad."

"What did your house look like?"

"I dunno."

Caps stood up. "Let's go straight for the big one. Noah, where were you on New Wilderness Day?"

"I don't remember."

Caps gave Lena a long look. "We've seen this before, haven't we?"

"Rick, don't."

Caps hitched up his voice to sound like Burle. "You've got no future if you don't know your past." He took the pipe and offered it to Noah. "You'll need this. Go ahead."

There was something Noah had always felt fundamentally wrong about smoking marijuana, but then Bacon did it once in a while, and Caps looked so sincere. The smoke was acrid, but full of flavour. He held it his mouth, then blew it out.

"No man, you have to inhale it. Like this." Caps demonstrated, then returned the pipe to Noah. Lena intervened.

"No, don't smoke that. Rick, he's already had a couple of swigs of Harpreet Surprise, don't make him do this stoned."

Noah got up. Whatever Caps was planning, he wanted no part of it.

"Hey, sit down, trust me. This'll be good for you. Did I steer you wrong about the heads?"

Caps's face washed green and red, giving him the surreal cast of a beckoning sorcerer.

Noah sat down against his will.

"I'm going to ask you a series of questions. Answer as quickly as you can. What is your room number?"

"Twenty-six."

"What's your favourite colour?"

"Don't have one."

Caps gritted his teeth at hitting a hurdle so soon into his interrogation. "I guess we'll just stick with facts. Here we go. Who is the chief of stores?"

"Burle."

"How many hours in a day?"

"Twenty-four. I don't get where this is—"

"Just answer the questions. How many fingers do I have on my right hand?"

"Two and a thumb."

"Where were you on NW Day?"

"I don't know."

"What is the square root of sixty-four?"

"Eight."

"Who is the chief of security?"

"Darcy McCullough."

"What does C represent in an equation?"

"Speed of light."

"Where were you on New Wilderness Day?"

It was like a jolt of electricity to the back of his head. Noah's lips tightened against his teeth.

"Stop..."

"I know it's hard, we're almost there. How many guard towers do we have?"

"Two," he answered automatically

"What days do you shower?"

"Tuesday and Friday."

Angry hornets buzzed and stung at Noah's brain.

"What is pi to the fifth decimal place?"

"9.23256."

A bubble was forming from the primordial soup of Noah's mindscape, what lay within seethed and twisted.

"Where were you on—"

"STOP!"

A short alarm sounded, one bell, pause, two bells, pause, repeat.

"Oh shit," said Lena.

"What does that mean?" Noah felt like he'd run a hundred klicks.

"Meeting," Caps said. "We're busted."

They huddled outside the door to the meeting room. Caps straightened his hair with his fingers while Noah pressed his lips together and tried not to giggle. The vile miasma of suppressed memory had faded almost immediately, leaving behind only the barest tendrils.

"How are my eyes?" Caps asked Lena

Lena squinted and brought an arm in front of her, shielding her view from an imaginary glare.

"That bad, huh? That doctor of ours...makes birth control pills but can't make me any freakin' Visine."

"The Boss'd know anyway. You're terrible at hiding it. Noah, you ready?"

Noah said nothing but nodded. Nervous laughter almost got the better of him as Lena opened the door. All conversation stopped.

The Boss looked casually at the three of them. "Glad you could join us."

Caps walked to his customary seat at the far end of the table. He nodded with great seriousness at each person he passed. Burle looked at Caps's face, then gave a smile that only the elderly are capable of, the one that said, "Ah, the glory of youth," at the same time as it said, "You stupid kid."

Noah went for the first empty chair he came to, but Lena beat him to it. He had a clumsy moment of reversing direction when her body suddenly appeared in the seat. As Noah steadied himself on the table, he locked eyes with Darcy. She looked at him quizzically, then indicated an empty chair with a tilt of her head.

"We finally contacted Drum East," said Sid. "Something I had expected you to be doing, Lena."

Lena touched her fingers to her chest, "Me?" Her voice took on a patronizing tone, like she was explaining something to a child. "I know it was my shift, but I'm allowed to delegate to a subordinate. That's why I'm a chief."

Sid spoke as if he hadn't noticed the insolence. "It turns out the components they needed to fix their radio had to be cannibalized from the CB's in both the rig and the escort vehicle. So now Drum East can't get a message through to them either. Dammit, where is Toffee?"

"Oh, shit," said Darcy, bunching her hands into fists. "I forgot to let him out. Daniel?" Darcy's second in command rose and left.

"Let him out? From where? There's no lock on his door."

"I found him wandering the halls around four a.m. Since he obviously couldn't be trusted to stay in his room, I put him in lockup. I meant to let him out at breakfast, but it slipped my mind."

"Wow," said Caps. "Toffee all alone in a little room. Do you think he passed the time intimidating himself?"

Noah knew his perception had changed. He didn't know how, exactly, not being familiar with the stages of intoxication, but he did know Sid was bigger, Caps was sillier, and Darcy was gorgeous. He'd thought she was attractive before, but now she glowed. She was the most beautiful woman in the whole world. Noah wondered why Caps had wasted so much time on animal cartoons, when he could have been drawing pictures of Darcy.

Sid's voice stabbed through Noah's reverie like an icepick.

"What is wrong with you people? Darcy, you disobeyed my instruction…"

She slapped her hand on the table. "He disobeyed mine!"

"...I'm talking. You listen now! You didn't present me with the new situation. And you three," Sid somehow managed to look Noah, Caps, and Lena in the eye at the same time, despite their scattered positions around the table. "I'll deal with you three later." The Boss took a second to compose himself. "We have another, more urgent situation. Explorers have found an entrance to the caverns from outside. The opening is past the northeast crest, out of line of sight of the towers. Makes a nice little shortcut right to our most secure areas.

We need to block off that entrance, but the bushes outside are swarming. You'll notice Dr. Patel is not with us at the moment. He assures me that Connie will make a full recovery. Darcy, assign a burn crew. Everybody else, we need to hide the Mimis. Bury the cables, camouflage the boxes, just like we did topside. If there's one entrance, there'll be more."

"You really think this is a problem?" asked Sara.

"I don't think there's anyone skulking in the woods, but I still don't like the idea of back doors, especially ones that are outside the sound net."

"Sounds like there's gonna be a storm in my office," said Burle. "I'll go get the necessities ready."

Burle ruffled Noah's hair as he passed. It was a comforting touch that the boy very much needed. While Noah felt somewhat reduced in size, Sid had grown even larger, the twin scars down his cheek seemed to thicken and throb. No sooner had the door closed after Burle, then it swung open again. Toffee strode in with Daniel a step behind him.

The hunter looked at Darcy, his face no less intent for its lack of emotion. "Feel better?"

Sid didn't give Darcy a chance to reply. "Toffee, assemble a group. Take what you need and go meet the convoy. In lieu of communication I want October escorted. They're taking the river road through the mountains. "

"You want me to leave right now? I just got out of lockup."

"You should be well rested, then. Go."

"Fine, I want Darcy on my crew."

"She has duties to attend to here."

Something passed between Sid and the hunter. The two were engaged in a contest, like wolves measuring each other for leadership of the pack. Without saying a word, Toffee turned and left.

Sid stared at the closing door as he spoke. "Everybody else, grab some bodies and get to work. Try not to use anyone who doesn't already know about the caverns. Take your orders from Darcy until I get there."

Chairs slid back from the table, people started leaving.

"Not you, Richard," Sid looked at Noah and Lena. "You two stay as well."

When it was just the four of them, Caps tried to apologize.

"I'm sorry, we set a bad example, but how were we supposed to…"

"Shut up, Richard. How have you become so complacent? What year do you think this is? Chiefs don't get more freedom than everyone else, they get less. Which one of you has the booze?"

Without thinking, Lena touched the flask in her hip pocket. The Boss raised an eyebrow at her, and she slid the liquor across the table.

Sid opened the flask and sniffed. "This is Dr. Patel's brew, this isn't for sipping. Caps, Noah, on your off time...but Lena, ditching a shift to get hammered! If you think liquid courage allows you to insult me in front of the senior staff..." Sid's cheek had started to twitch. "And you," he burned into Noah with his eyes, "four days and you appear before me with grease and bits of dog fur on your clothes! Bacon spoke very highly of you. I'm sure he'd be disappointed. Where were the three of you? Down by the steam pipes?"

Caps and Lena shared a guilty look.

"I thought so. When you've finished with the Mimis, you will take all those coloured lights down. Now get to work!"

Noah shoved cables against the cavern wall and wiped his forehead with the back of his hand. Although it was chilly in the caves, sweat glued Noah's clothes to his skin. He'd already taken down the top of his coveralls and knotted the sleeves at his waist. His undershirt was covered in dust, as were his arms and face. The work would have gone much quicker had it just been straight cables that needed covering, but the caverns were serpentine in nature, and there was more to hiding the Mimis then just kicking rocks over things. Noah would position cables, two men with hacksaws would cut sections of plastic pipe to fit flush to the wall, then someone else would secure the pipe with spikes and a hammer. They couldn't just let the cables run along the ground, so Noah had to hold the lines up for prolonged periods of time. Once the last bit of pipe was installed over the cables, all joints were checked and when final touch ups had been done, the entire thing would be painted with gray primer. Each Mimi was surrounded by a metal frame, after which strips of scrap paper were applied to the outside with paste. Noah's little crew had reached the end of the line for tunnel number six. It was after three in the morning, and everyone was punchy. Noah returned to the first tunnel to see how Caps was doing. If he hadn't known the pipe was there, he never would have seen it. Black and dark gray paint had been added to the primer in patches that followed the contour of surrounding stone. Small rocks had been placed along the pipe to hide its regular shape. The artistry to which the piping had been disguised was nothing in comparison to what Caps had accomplished with the paper covered frame. It looked like part of the rock. Caps had matched color and tone to the degree that even under the spotlight, his creation appeared natural.

"How long have you been working on this?" Noah asked.

Caps dropped a paintbrush in a pail of water and took a step back. "Got started as soon as the paste dried, so about two hours. I've got about another twenty minutes left. How many of these do I have to do again?"

"Five more. My end of this is done, I guess I could take care of the Enchanted Forest."

"No you don't. You're not finished until the job is done, neither is anyone else. And my Christmas lights aren't going anywhere. Y'know where the Boss was on NW Day? He was at a logging protest. Now he wants to clear-cut the Enchanted Forest. No way. You did say five more of these didn't you?"

"That's lookin' good, Caps," said Darcy as she dangled a small bucket with dark splatters along its top. "I need more paint."

"Already? Take it from the second bucket from my foot. I hope you're not just splashing that stuff on."

"You're not the only one with talent around here. Noah, what are you doing?"

"I guess my hands are free." *Great* he thought, *now I get to sweep.*

Darcy compared her paint to the colour on the wire and paper outcropping. "What gray is this?"

Caps nudged a can with his toe. "This one, I mixed it."

"It's much better. Mix some for me."

"Awe c'mon, I've got five more of these to...yeah, you're right. Grab some dirt, this'll take a few minutes."

Darcy hunkered down into a relaxed squat, her rear not touching the ground. Noah flopped against the wall, earning a sharp stone to the lower back. Paint cans made pleasant popping noises as their lids were pried off.

The security chief pushed two fingers into the fake rock, testing its resilience. "How do we get into this for maintenance?"

Caps examined the shade he was creating, then stirred in a few drops of white. "I don't know. I guess we just rip it open and make a new one later."

"That's inefficient."

Noah had thought the same thing while twisting and shaping the wire. "I know what to do. We cut a square out somewhere near the cable ports, then hog-tie one side of it back to the frame. Caps can blend the pattern, and we've got a little door."

"Thanks for the extra work, Noah. How do we keep it shut?"

"We can use that putty you've got for putting up posters."

"Hey, that's just for my works of art."

Darcy finished her inspection of the camouflage, "Caps, this is a work of art. How's that paint coming?"

"Just about...okay, here." Caps held a paint can out to her.

"That's the colour you used for the rock?"

"Yes."

"Good, you don't need this anymore. " Darcy took the can of paint Caps had mixed for himself. "C'mon Noah, break's over."

Caps sighed and decided the paint he'd mixed for Darcy could use some improvement.

Noah followed the security chief to the hub where the passages met. "You might as well start cleaning up," she said. "Pick up all the wire cuttings, pipe shavings, etc. You know the drill."

"What are you going to be doing?"

She waved her paintbrush at him. "What do you think I'm going to be doing?"

"Can I paint, too?"

"I don't know, are you any good at it?"

"I might be, I haven't done it before."

"Have fun taking out the trash." She disappeared into the second tunnel. There was a spring in her step that managed to invigorate Noah as well.

A repetitive sound came from just around a corner, taps and then clinks. Noah rounded the curve and saw the bald man that had barked at him the day before. The hunter sat on a crate, chipping away with a small hammer at a fist sized chunk of rock. Stone chips were bunched on the cavern floor, next to a pile of rocks waiting to be reduced. The hunter looked like he was peeling the world's hardest potatoes.

"What's your name?" Noah asked.

The hunter gave a look of contempt before answering. "Chris."

"Chris, that's all the chips we'll need right now. I want you to go through the caverns and pick up all the junk we've left behind, wire, pipes and stuff."

"Why should I do that?"

"How well can you read in the dark?"

Chris chucked his hammer aside and grabbed a wheelbarrow. "I'm doing this by myself?"

"I'll find someone to help you. Start in the third passageway and work to six."

Noah watched Chris trundle off into number three, then headed down the passage Darcy had taken. "I like being a chief," he said to himself.

Darcy had taken down her coverall top and knotted it as well. Streaks of paint stood out on her arms, and a couple specks had found her nose.

"What are you doing here?" she asked.

"I delegated. Teach me to paint."

At first he thought she was going to refuse, then she reached into a pocket and handed him a paintbrush.

"Watch what I'm doing. You see the grain of the rock? The way it curves? Try to match the lines. Put down a line, then blend it with side of your hand." She demonstrated. It looked easy. "Try to join in with the rock beneath the pipe. Caps and Sara will be doing final blending later."

"Who's Sara?"

"Dr. White, remember? Your Momma?"

"Oh, her. She's an artist as well?"

"Not an artist...this is kind of like make up. It's all in the blending. I'm good, but Sara's amazing. You should see the stuff she did topside. I was good with it myself, as a kid, so this isn't too hard."

Noah found the task to be more challenging than it first appeared. While Darcy's lines followed the stone, his were ugly smudges. She handed him a rag to wipe his mistakes before they dried.

His rag was soaked through by the time he got the hang of it. Sections of pipe faded into the rock, Noah working at quarter the speed of Darcy. The security chief hummed quietly to herself. The tune was ancient and familiar to Noah, a tendril of memory tightened its grip. When she noticed her audience, she hummed louder, and let a few words slip through her lips.

"What was that?" he asked, once he'd decided she'd finished.

"*Dreams.* You remember it?"

"I think maybe...I think my mom liked it. You get off on this no sleep stuff, huh?"

"How do you mean?"

"You said in the meeting that you caught Toffee at oh four hundred, and it's past that now again, so you've been up for like, two days."

"I caught a nap earlier. I feel like I'm setting up a high school dance. All this painting. We should paint a big banner that says 'Welcome, survivors of the Change!' Sorry Noah, but if you can't pick up the pace, I'll put you on something else."

Noah smudged his next three lines in haste and had to redo them. "When's the Boss coming down?"

Darcy struck pipe with the end of her paintbrush. It made a wet slapping sound and produced an ungainly splatter. "Sid will show after he wakes up. He'll come in here when it's time to give the order to knock off, and everyone will love him for it." She took her own rag, which barely had any paint on it, and wiped up her mess.

Noah blew his next line; he was going slower instead of faster. "Do you know any other songs?"

"Sure. My dad taught me this one."

Darcy half hummed, half mumbled the first verse, but when she wasn't interrupted, she opened her throat and sang. Not loudly, but clearly, filling the passage with her voice. The cavern's lighting had been augmented quickly, bare bulbs hung from wire supported by outcroppings of rock. This song was even slower than the first. It was sad, about the ocean, and being alone. Shadows curved along the walls, and Darcy's voice rolled across cold waves of stone. A clanking noise approached them. Darcy quieted, then stopped singing as Caps trudged past, laden with paint cans and brushes. When the sound of his awkward percussion receded, Darcy finished her song.

Painting was time consuming but not physically intensive. Cool air raised goose bumps along the backs of Darcy's shoulders. She shrugged on her coverall top, and as her bare flesh disappeared, Noah restrained himself from darting forward and kissing it.

"Did you like that one?" she asked.

Caps applied zigzags of black to a white plaster peak. He heard Darcy begin her third song, something he didn't recognize. Through a haze of drug burn out and sleep deprivation, he was proud of Noah; the kid had discovered a secret. As long as he kept the security chief singing, he would hardly have to work at all.

11. Convoy

October Neriah had the longest legs in the world, at least that's what *Style Nation* magazine purported in the last April edition they ever ran. She had the enjoyment of world fame at the same time as complete anonymity, because though millions had seen her, very few had seen her face. October's legs graced the covers of pantyhose packets, appeared in shoe commercials and demonstrated how flattering split seam skirts could be. In two major motion pictures, the camera had panned up her legs to reach a different woman's face. Despite the money and perks of international travel (why it had to be her gams on a street in Paris she never understood) what October liked to do most with her legs was push the pedals of a big-ass truck. Her father and brother had both been truckers, and until a man with a business card approached her on the beach, she'd fully intended to join the family trade. The money she earned went to establish a trucking company her brother ran, and when she tired of the lights of the runway, she looked forward to the lights of the highway. October's legs were insured with Lloyds of London for five million dollars, not that it helped on June 10th, when the horse she was riding along a California beach threw her to the ground and stomped on her knee in front of two cameras and six people. It was her photographer, Blair, that dragged her to safety. He took a kick to the side for his efforts. From inside her contract specified motorhome, they watched the horse go to work. It was a palomino, specially trained to kneel on command, or stand on its hind legs and flail at the air. The skill of its trainer showed as the animal galloped behind fleeing people and caved in their skulls with lightning strikes of iron shod hoof. Blair drove away from the photo shoot only to find he had to keep on going. Along the way they picked up fellow refugees. Blair taped the windows and air vents up on day four when the wasps set in, and made everyone believe it would be okay. When October had healed enough to drive, Blair let her take over everything, went to sleep and never woke up. The photographer had sustained lethal injuries. He'd kept himself alive by sheer force of will. She'd never expected the man to have that much strength.

October turned away from Los Angeles miles before reaching it. Her passengers looked blankly at endless traffic jams and human corpses born of bullets, not teeth. They siphoned gas at night, and went north.

She was amazed – everyone was amazed – at the devastation that swept the next few years. As if the animals and bees weren't enough, bizarre weather—summer hail storms, fatal heat waves—continued for the next half decade. Diseases so easily curable in the past now wiped out entire settlements. Even the finest mesh was no defense against viruses and bacteria.

October's twisted left leg would only make the pages of a latter day medical journal, but it could still push a clutch. Drifting from settlement to settlement, always upgrading her quality of life, October arrived at Compton Pit and knew she was staying on. It took her twelve miles of bad road to convince Sid Halbert of her value. She spoke continuously as the truck shuddered over cracked pavement and fallen trees, regaling the Boss with tales of shaving time off tough runs. She'd been the chief of transport for going on two years, ever since the former chief had taken a permanent stress leave.

Cool slipstream, barely hampered by fine steel mesh, rushed past October's ear, pushing dark brown hair against her cheek. Her skin, once tanned all year long, now held the pasty white of all Caucasian underground dwellers. The steel mesh and bars over her window prevented her from even the consolation of a trucker's arm. Not that she could get a tan late at night anyway. She'd been impatient; satisfying Drum East's needs had taken longer than expected and she was behind. There were no bonuses for beating a clock, but what kept order in October's life was making a run in less time than she quoted.

"Can I put on some tunes?" asked her cab mate, Ian. He had scruffy blond hair and a crescent scar that swept under his mouth, giving him a permanent smile.

"As long as it's not more show tunes. Put on that one." She pointed at the CD rack, indicating a blank disk in an unmarked jewel case.

"What is it?" said Ian, turning the disk over in his hand.

"I can't remember, that's why I want to hear it."

Ian spotted a tiny etching on the jewel case, the letters CT. "No way, not again. This is Conway Twitty." He fished out another case. October traded for them whenever she got the chance. Her collection was almost as diverse as the one she'd had in the old days. Ian slid a CD into the player and Tragically Hip jangled out of the speakers.

"I can live with this," said October. "How are our boys doing up there?"

"I can't see them either."

She hated not having any radio contact. The escort vehicle, an augmented Range Rover, was supposed to keep its tail lights within view of the rig at all times. She could signal the Rover with her headlights, while her escort could flash her with a headlight mounted on back. It was common enough procedure, radio contact was avoided whenever possible, but with it gone as an option completely, the Rover's break from formation was that much more irritating.

"Why can't Sam just slow down? We can't go any faster than the rig."

"I still say we should have waited till the morning. Or at least taken Wide Road."

There were two available routes for the convoy to take back to Compton Pit. What their original names had been was irrelevant. When the world had changed, people had a need to rename things, as if to say, "We still own this place, we'll call it whatever we want." Wide Road, in places, was an eight lane highway. It never narrowed to less than four. It was certainly easier ground to cover, but it was also easier ground to watch. The River Road was less travelled, more secure.

"I see them," Ian said. "Nope, gone again. They're not that far ahead of us, it's just the road hiding them." He jerked back from the windshield as a wall of rock loomed in the headlights, impact was certain. The rock fell away as October effortlessly curved around it.

"Wake you up?"

"Damn. I fall for that every time. How many trips is it now?"

"This'll be seven. That little settlement is doing well for itself. The foundry is a go. I like their wind generators. We should try and push those on Sid again."

The road straightened, far ahead the taillights of the Rover disappeared over a crest.

October reached for her CB, then pulled her hand away in frustration. "Where does he think he's going?"

"He wants to get laid. He's always like this on the way back, but usually I ride with him and keep him tethered. Stuart doesn't care one way or the other."

"At least Stuart likes Conway Twitty."

"No, he just doesn't care."

A screech of tires ended in the crunch of metal and glass. October's hands tightened on the wheel and she accelerated. Past the crest she found the Rover skewed sideways across the road. One headlight was smashed, but the other shone on a similar vehicle flipped on its side. There was no sign of movement from Sam or Stuart.

October's stomach tightened. "Shit! Why were these people on the road? How long until cougars get here?"

Ian cocked a shotgun. "We'll be gone before then."

The driver side door of the overturned vehicle swung open. A woman with long straggly hair, heaved her pregnant bulk through the portal and dropped to the blacktop.

"Oh no..." October drew her pistol and jumped to the ground. "Ian, get her scent out of the air. I don't care how badly she's hurt, put her in the truck." She approached her escort vehicle while Ian moved to assist the woman. The men in the Rover sat motionless as October wrenched open the passenger door. Stuart hadn't been wearing a seatbelt and the dashboard had not agreed with his head. Sam had been belted in, and although broken glass glinted on his legs and chest, there was nothing to account for the gash in his throat. The chief of transport heard something metal clatter to the concrete. She turned to find Ian, his hands up, held at gun point by the woman. Icy metal pushed into the back of October's neck. She raised her hands and someone took her gun.

The pregnant lady took a handful of her own hair and yanked it off. Under the wig was a crewcut.

Rough hands pushed October against the Rover. A man stepped into her view.

"Shangly! What the hell do you think you're doing?"

Whereas most people tried to ignore their scars, Victor Shangly augmented his. On his cheeks, vivid tattoo scars joined real ones. Emerging claws had been inked in a way that made it appear his face was being shredded from the inside. A similar effect had been accomplished on his arms, though there were no real scars there. Hair so black, it was almost blue, was tied in a ponytail that hung to the middle of his back. He held up a roll of duct tape. "Want to trade for some of this?" He tore a strip off and covered October's mouth. Ian tried to come to her side, but another of Shangly's henchmen knocked the man out with the stock of a rifle. More scavengers appeared from the shadows. They stripped Ian naked and rifled the truck. One of them brought Shangly a fluorescent bulb.

"Yes, we can always use more of these."

October muffled something under the tape. Her arms were pinned to her sides, and somebody was wrapping her hands. Shangly reached forward and ripped the tape from her mouth.

"Those won't do you any good," she spat. "They're burnt out."

"Why would you trade for burnt out bulbs?"

"We can't make the tubes, we're not a glass factory. We refill them. The whole cargo is worthless to you."

The bulb shattered as it hit the road. "You won't be refilling that one. I know you didn't come all this way for a truck full of empty glass."

"Let us go! Do you know what Sid Halbert will do?"

"He'll suffer." Shangly taped her mouth shut again.

The man who had taped October's hands was tattooed as well. A puckered scar on the back of one hand had been made to look like the upper lip of a mouth filled with sharp teeth. He drove a fist into her stomach, knocking the wind out of her and driving her to her knees. The front of her coveralls were ripped open.

"You leave her dressed!" said Shangly. "Don't want you boys getting distracted. Give me another burn circle!"

Off in the darkness, a flamethrower ignited bits of scrub. The leader of the scavengers hauled himself into the cab of the truck, then jumped back down again, satisfied. "A CD player even. This rig will make our lives a whole lot better. Take it away boys." Two men jumped in the cab, other scavengers cleared the way. The rig rumbled forward, pushed the fallen vehicle out of the way, and disappeared around a curve.

October struggled to her feet, only to be knocked down again. She fell back against the open door, and felt Stuart's cooling flesh push into her back. Sam's body was pulled from the vehicle and a scavenger tried in vain to turn the motor over. In the back of the Rover was a shotgun, and Stuart had a pistol on his hip. Concrete rubbed skin off her knuckles as she twisted against her restraints. The engine could barely muster a few revs.

"Forget it," Shangly said. "Get stripping. Lot, go ahead and pull the tape off. Let's have a conversation with the lady."

Fang hand pulled the tape off slowly, letting it peel her lips.

"My rig better be clean when I get it back! You're a dead man for this."

Shangly cupped his hands to his chest. "Alas, fair lady, my heart is already dead," he said whimsically, then his voice turned serious. "Halbert killed my wife. A little bit of his doctor's penicillin, and Kristy would have been fine. I'd have traded anything for it."

"There are other places you could have gotten penicillin."

"I had time for one trip, you were my best bet."

"You should have thought about that before you sacked New Found Hope."

Shangly sneered, the claws on his face slid up to the cheekbone. "That place got swarmed."

"That's not the story we heard."

"Those two kids? We found them huddled in a storm cellar, gave them a chance. I guess they didn't like our way of life. The boy told Halbert just what he wanted to hear."

"You're lying."

"I'm going to kill you. Why should I lie?" He kicked her in the jaw.

She heard a voice in her head. It was the southern twang of the chief of transport she'd replaced at the Pit. "Whatever happens, never leave your truck." Sound advice; often given, rarely followed. October pulled herself back into a kneeling position, refusing to let despair take her. She was going to die in her sleep at the age of eighty, not now, not on this stretch of road, and certainly not at the hands of some tattooed scavenger. Before she could speak, Shangly kicked her again, knocking her flat. Lot covered her mouth, wrapping the tape all the way around her head. Pavement pushed against her face as the man knelt on her back and taped her legs. The Rover was stripped in a remarkable short period of time, so were Stuart and Sam. October heard a few gunshots and the flamethrower light up again. A wide jeep pulled onto the road. From the glare of its headlights she saw that Ian had been shot through the back.

Shangly pulled her head up by a handful of hair. "I lost my woman," he said, rubbing something wet on October's face. "Now Halbert loses one of his. And oh yes, did you manage to get everything on this list?"

He held a piece of paper out to her, shining a flashlight on it so she could see it better. October's eyes grew wide. She pulled at her bonds with renewed vigour.

Soon after the last set of taillights vanished into the night, soft paws padded up the longest legs in the world and sharp teeth punctured an anonymous neck.

12. Respite

Three down, three tunnels to go, Noah could barely lift his arm. Darcy had sung herself raw, so had a few others. For the latter part of the work, other voices had joined Darcy's, a disembodied choir that danced and echoed throughout the caves. Noah didn't know any words, and hadn't even tried to join in. Caps on the other hand, knew many words, but though the guy could paint, he sure couldn't carry a tune. Fortunately, he knew that, and had only interrupted with involuntary discordant bursts that ended as soon as he realized he was singing. Noah's hunter-turned-lackey even bounced out a few words during something called *Take It Easy*, as he guided his wheelbarrow past the chief of security.

Lena, her hands blackened with paste, wobbled on her feet as she glued her thousandth stone chip to plastic pipe. She'd slowed her pace to stay in close proximity to Noah and Darcy. Despite the protection of the Mimis, and the camaraderie of the songs, the caverns were not a place people liked to be alone.

Burle sauntered down the tunnel. He'd only been there an hour. "Darcy, couldja let me back in?"

Darcy tossed a key ring to Burle. "I'm not walking back and forth. Block the door open and bring me back the keys." The stores master stood in place, looking at the key ring. "It's the yellow one, Burle, you know that."

"Whu…? Oh. No, I was thinking about key chains. I had a lucky rabbit's foot. Hmmm."

Lena watched Burle's retreating back. "He could have been helping us you know. That 'weak old body' of his comes and goes conveniently."

Darcy finished off Noah's can of paint. Hers lay empty on its side. She cupped a hand to her mouth and bellowed, "CAPS!"

"What?" came a hollow reply.

"I NEED YOU!"

Caps appeared, heralded by the sound of scuffing feet. "What?"

"I'm out of paint. Bring me more."

"Aw, why didn't you just come for it?"

"I'm..." she quirked a smile at Noah, "...delegating."

Caps swore under his breath and scuffed even louder as he returned to his gear.

They rested until the chief of the pool returned. Lena dozed off. The can Caps brought was only half full. "You'll have to make do with this. I'm running low."

Darcy eyed the paint. "You just mixed this? It's all gummy on top. You brought what you've been using. Fine. You'll have to make this trip again twice as soon."

"Good work people!" Sid thundered down the tunnel. "Take a break, get some food, start again at fifteen hundred."

Faded gratuities and praises to deities followed the Boss's declaration.

"What did I tell you?" Darcy said to Noah. She checked a watch on the inside of her wrist. "Great, I get to shower now and be filthy again by tonight."

Lena left her paste jar and bag of chips behind in a heap.

I get to shower, too, thought Noah.

Caps sealed the cans and paste jar, then grabbed the brushes. He caught up with Noah, who had left on Darcy's heels.

People shuffled wearily from the tunnels, bottlenecking at the locked security door. Sid hadn't left it open after shouting his clemency. People looked at Darcy and waited for her to open the door.

She patted her empty pockets. "Sorry folks, push the buzzer."

"I did push the buzzer," said one of the men that had worked with Noah earlier.

Noah cursed himself. The door buzzer was on a circuit he'd considered non-primary. He'd cut its power for Lena's sake, planning to give it juice before he went to bed.

"So what do we do?" Caps asked. "Draw straws? Chris, you look pretty juicy."

The door opened. Burle was pushed against the corridor wall as escaping workers squeezed past him. He handed the key ring to Darcy with an apologetic smile. Noah had become separated from the security chief among the bustle, and he tried nonchalantly to force his way closer.

Caps caught his arm. "Hold up, sun boy."

"But I'm going to–"

"I know where you're going, to the showers."

Noah tugged at Caps's grip. "I don't want to miss my slot."

"Sure you don't. Hang on."

Noah relented, and soon everyone had passed them. Once the crowd's movement created a moat of empty hall, Caps started walking.

"I've gotta tell you a few things, Noah, about your new love."

Noah's cheeks burned. "I don't know what you're talking about."

"Whatever. You and her? Not gonna happen. Nothing personal, but, no way."

"I'm crushed." Noah changed the subject. "How does the power structure work here? The, uh, chain of command. I like it, but it's new to me. Darcy ordered everyone around. Is that just this time, or is that a permanent thing?"

"It's sort of casual military. The Boss is the boss, period. Darcy comes under him, she's also second in command, sort of. Then it's the great doctor, Sara, and believe it or not, Toffee. You, me, Lena, the rest of us share the same line after that."

They reached the main corridor. Smells of food already emanated from the mess hall. "Where does the cook fit in?"

"I guess he's below us, but sometimes I think he outranks the Boss."

There was still an hour to breakfast, but some people had planted themselves at tables, determined not to move until they'd eaten.

"Who made Sid the Boss?"

"It was sort of democratic. Our old boss, his name was Jason Worthy, he'd been losing it for a while before Sid showed up. The Boss…there's just something about him. There was no question of giving him the job. Burle, Patel, the chief of the hunters then…what was his name? Felix. and someone else, maybe the chief of security before Travis…they signed him in. I made up the document, it's pretty official looking."

"Is Worthy still here?"

"Nope, he was losing it remember?"

In the corridor that led to the showers, Noah picked up his pace. Caps grabbed his arm again. "Hang on, Noah. Trust me." He took Noah to door thirty and knocked.

"Hello?" came a sleepy woman's voice through the door.

"Susan, want to swap shower slots with my friend here?"

"What, permanently?"

Noah shook his head vigorously.

"No, just today. It's in about five minutes."

"You bet!"

There was frantic shuffling beyond the door.

"There you go," said Caps. "All taken care of. Now you get to shower tonight after we're finished. Come hang with me until breakfast."

Caps sat on his stool, Noah flopped on the bed. There was a new drawing on the easel, it depicted a good caricature of Noah, levelling a rocket launcher at a mouse.

"Nice," said Noah. "That for the notice board?"

"Relax, It's for you and you alone. I forgot to cover it, didn't want you to see it until it was finished."

Noah bunched sheets in his hands and looked longingly at Caps's pillow. "Who did Freeland rape?"

"Yuck! Stay up all night and you come up with the weirdest questions. Why do you want to know?"

"Well I thought it was…I thought it was Darcy, but I guess I was wrong."

"It sure wasn't Darcy. Man, I wish he'd tried with her. She'd have messed him up so bad. You haven't really met who it was, and it's not my business to tell you."

"Why'd he do it?"

"How should I know? He was," Caps tapped his head with a finger, "a nutcase. He kept his mouth shut around the Boss, but when other people would listen…Freeland thought the animals were the cleansing hand of God."

"I know lots of people who think that."

"How many think that the cleansing's being done for them? Freeland believed that when redemption came, he'd be the one leading the way. Went on and on with Bible quotes that supported his claim. I checked up on a couple of them, but they weren't in any Bible

I looked through. I even shoved a Bible in his face once. He said I'd had a false one printed to confuse him. This is my favourite; he said the Pope had put a price on his head, and the animals were God's protection. He probably thought his victim was a gift from above. Doglicker! I hope he died slow."

"That's not the craziest thing I've heard." Noah propped the pillow against the wall and leaned back. "So why don't you think Darcy would go for me?" he asked in a tone he hoped was casual.

"I knew it! For one thing, she's sort of taken."

"Oh. Is it the Boss?"

"That's a laugh. They're close, but he's kind of like her dad. No, you're competing with a dead guy. Travis Jones, the last security chief. She adored him. Even if she wasn't still in mourning, you're not her type."

"What, not big and strong? We were really hitting it off in the caverns."

Caps snorted a tired laugh. "She'd hit it off with a cougar if it wanted her to sing. Wait a minute, you weren't just distracting her…you…heh. She won't admit it, but she's really vain about her voice. Can't really blame her. It's not often she gets such a durable audience. You're too young, Noah. Look at you, not a line on that face. Darcy likes her men older, or at least looking older. Anyways, you couldn't handle her, man. She's got some moods."

"Sounds like you tried for her yourself."

"No way. She's my friend and I'm just fine with that. Trust me, look elsewhere. If I could make a suggestion…"

The breakfast bells rang, Caps didn't finish his sentence.

At the steam tables, Noah cast a regretful look at Darcy's wet hair. Though they stood next to each other, she hadn't even acknowledged him. His brain was too addled to start a conversation.

Lena was absent, probably asleep, but Burle and Cass were at the table, rested and awake.

"You look like a dead raccoon," said Cass, as Noah sat down.

"I feel worse. You still don't smell like a tanner."

"I'm not anymore, didn't you notice the colours?" She was wearing khaki. "I swapped with Patricia. She already had some experience and I think Devon likes her. Devon's the head tanner, not quite a chief."

"Pisses him off too," said Caps. "Why'd Pat want to be a tanner?"

"She hates guard duty. Says long periods of time standing around doing nothing isn't her bag. Go figure."

Breakfast passed in a blur, Noah and Caps chewing mechanically until their trays were empty. Noah barely got to the bus carts, and had no idea how he made it to his room before passing out, fully dressed.

Noah shovelled another load of dirt on his mother's head. She was buried up to her chin in the vegetable garden behind their house.

"Hurry up," said Randy Thurlow. "It's almost dinner time."

Kate whistled a Janice Joplin tune until her mouth was covered. She winked at her son one last time before her eyes were lost from view. When she was completely buried, Noah's dad took the shovel away.

"Good job, son. Lets head in."

They sat in chairs in the kitchen looking through the window at the backyard. There were so many things Noah wanted to ask his father, but he couldn't put them into words.

Sharky wandered into the backyard and sniffed the ground.

"This'll be fun," said Randy, taking a pull from his beer bottle.

Sharky rooted around for a while, then pawed at the screen door and whimpered.

"What? It's not my problem if you can't find her."

The dog barked once, then returned to its search. Dread stirred in Noah's stomach, though he couldn't put a finger on why. Sharky moved closer to the mound that covered Kate.

"So how was work today?" Randy asked.

"Long day, probably a long day tomorrow as well." Work? Noah didn't have a job, he was in the fifth grade.

Sharky dug his nose into Kate's hiding place, barked enthusiastically at the house, then started digging.

"Damn, he got her again. We'll have better luck tomorrow, kid. Maybe we should put her in a tree." Randy Thurlow vanished.

The kitchen became the inside of a semi's box trailer. Noah sat huddled against the vibrating side, wrapped in a blanket. Other people sat in the trailer, and although Noah knew none of them, he had a feeling they all knew him.

"This is for you," said a man. It was Burle. Noah didn't know why he hadn't recognized him before.

He accepted a skinbag from the old man. "What is it?"

"It's the hand of God."

The hide fell away and a large foam hand with a pointing finger popped out to its full length. It was the kind of hand Noah's father had bought for him at a basketball game. Words on the hand read; "We are, we are, we are the engineers."

"Sign here, please." Burle held out a clipboard and pen. Noah initialled where indicated.

The truck stopped vibrating.

"We're here," said Burle.

Sunlight blinded Noah as the door slid up to the ceiling. Beyond the open door, as far as the eye could see, was a roiling, inky black sea. Swirls of brackish yellow chased blobs of crimson across the water's surface to a central point a stone's throw away. They coalesced into a mass that swelled as it rushed towards the trailer.

"We'd better close the door," said Bacon. How long had he been there?

Burle pulled the door closed with a loud clank just before the oily bubble could cross the threshold. The trailer rocked as it was struck again and again.

"NOAH!"

The mouth was so close to his ear it actually hurt. The legs of Noah's cot scraped as they moved back and forth across the floor. Caps stopped shaking the bed when he saw Noah's eyes open.

"Up and at 'em!"

"What time is it?"

In reply, Caps held out a paintbrush.

13. Three Days on a Porch

June 13th, three days after the Change.

The chair was the last solid thing. Burle's grandfather made the rocking chair, back in '34, or there abouts. He died in it in '56, and Burle's father took up the vigil, rocking on the porch, drinking in the woods. Pneumonia came in '83 and the duty passed to Burle.

A Lee Enfield rifle slid forward and back on the rail, guided by the movement of Burle's knee, where the rifle's stock rested. There were only six rounds left in the clip, and no bullets waiting to replace those. There had been seven bullets before Burle shot the radio. Despite his lack of ammunition, the old man felt it was a round well spent. Absence of human voice did not leave him feeling lonely. He was kept company by regret.

Flies buzzed merrily over animals that remained where they'd fallen. Burle had tried to keep clean. For the first two days he'd piled carcasses in a heap behind the house, but he'd grown tired of that pointless activity. The heap included Tennessee, Pinecone, Rufus, Clark and Emma. Digger, a great Dane and largest of Burle's dogs, was absent. Best not to think about it.

Birds sang in the trees. Their tempo and tone was the same as it had been the week, or the year before. The imagined meaning of their music had changed irrevocably. None of them had swooped down, like the radio had reported in other places. Burle waited patiently for them to start, confident he'd be able to get inside when they did. It was the only thing, however, that would make him leave the porch. Outside was now, inside was then.

"C'mon Grandpa, it's just activity day at school. There's no classes or nuthin. Please?"

Jessie gave Burle that look, the one that made him melt, and worse, she'd taught her younger sister how to do it.

"You're not going up there to meet boys are you?"

Jessie flashed a smile at Natalie. "No! Of course not. Thank you Grandpa."

"Mmhmm, well you take Digger with you. He'll keep any friends you might come across on their best behaviour."

Natalie's expression soured. "Digger always goes in the river and gets all smelly."

"Well, you'll just have to give him a bath then. Go on. I'll call the school and tell them you've got summer flu. You be back by three–"

"Grandpa!"

"–thirty, and you clean the living room tonight."

Burle had cleaned the living room that night. He hadn't looked at it since.

"What happened to Jessie and Natalie?" asked Rachel. "Is their visit over so soon?"

Burle squeezed his wife's leg. She had her good days and her bad days. This was one of the latter. "They're out by the river. They'll be home soon. Honey, they're not visiting, they live here."

"Oh yes, so they do. Is Robert with them?"

Burle took her hands in his as he kissed her forehead. "I'm sure he is. You stay right here."

Something thumped violently as Burle passed the cellar door. He picked up his rifle from where it leaned against yellowed corn row wallpaper. In back of the house was a large dog run, defined by a metal fence too high to jump. The old man yearned for any reason to change his mind, but the radio had been quite clear, and his dogs' behaviour did not aid in their defence. Other evidence had been provided by a raccoon, who had always been thought of as a member of the family. Burle raised his rifle. Four bullets, four dead friends.

From the house came the sound of a door being rattled.

"Who's in there? Who got locked in the cellar?" His wife's sweet voice.

"RACHEL, NO!"

"Tennessee, is that you?"

Some bushes rustled, Burle tensed, but it was only wind. He'd been lucky, sort of. Animals only trickled from the forest, one or two at a time. Going by the news, they were drawn more by large groups of people, rather than individuals. Burle was small change in comparison to the school or the town. He still held hope for Jessie and Natalie, if they kept their heads together, if somehow Digger hadn't…

Burle had buried his son and daughter-in-law three years ago, and got on with the job of raising his granddaughters. The rocking chair was Robert's by tradition, but Burle had resigned himself to keeping it warm for a great grandson. Some of these modern women kept their maiden names when married, so it was possible another Campbell would take Burle's place, or at least a hyphenated Campbell.

Digger, when on his hind legs, was taller than Natalie. Best not to think about it.

He knew he could never make the river by himself, not on the first day, and not now. Without a wall behind him, he wouldn't stand a chance. All he could do was sit on the porch and wait for the Angels.

They'd arrived the day before.

"You got any gas?" asked the first man to dismount.

Burle kept his gun at the ready, despite wanting to rush down the stairs and embrace each of the bikers in turn. Their motors in the distance was the first non-animal sound he'd heard since he shot the radio.

"Got some out back. I'll need it for my generator if the power cuts out, but I'll trade some for .303."

There were six of them, all bearded. Their leathers were caked with dirt, but they seemed exhilarated, not weary. One of the bikers, a man with black hair and his hand wrapped in cloth, leaned on his handlebars. "We could just take it from you."

Burle hoped it wouldn't come to this. "You could, but I'd rather save my ammo for the critters."

"That's right!" said the lead biker. "Barry, how much you got?"

Barry, wide and heavy, patted a saddlebag. "Not a lot, I can give…five shells?"

"Not good enough," Burle said. "But you do me a solid, and I'll kick in some food. My truck's at the garage in town, I can't go by myself."

The lead biker (his name was Ray, Burle found out later) patted the seat of his Harley. "You want a lift out of here? Can you hang on and shoot at the same time?"

"I'm not leaving. I have to stay here in case someone arrives. I've seen you boys around a few times. Do you know Clippers Bend, where the river…"

"Yeah, we know it," said the black haired man.

"My granddaughters went there. I need you to find them."

Ray shook his head. "We were there three days ago, didn't see nobody."

It was Burle's turn to shake his head. "Take the road just east of here, that's how they went. Bring back…bring back…"

"I got you," Ray said.

He let them into the house and fed them in shifts, two always staying on the porch. They traded information until Burle couldn't listen anymore. The Angels had been through town. Barricaded survivors had haled them with cries of relief instead of the usual looks of caution and scorn. Minister Asher had offered them space in the church, but refuge meant missing out on a whole lot of fun. The church held four men and three women, no teenage girls. There was nothing the Angels could do at the school. The building was old and had so many windows, but that was a moot point at best. Everyone had been outside, running races, playing games. Birds, apparently, had played a part in that one.

Burle was making coffee when his benefactors returned. He met them on the porch. The host of Angels had been reduced by one. He eyed their saddlebags, picturing within torn scraps of cloth, a tooth-marked shoe.

"Sorry, old man," said Ray. "We found nothing. Not a soul on that road, or at Clippers Bend."

The black haired biker shouldered his way past Burle into the house. Ray gave a look of near apology as the rest of the bikers followed.

"What've you got to drink?" one of them called.

"Down in the…it's in the cellar."

A door opened, heavy feet thumped down steps. Burle watched strange men wander his home and paw at things. It didn't matter. Nothing mattered now.

Barry returned, his arms laden with bottles. "So who's the stiff in the–"

Ray silenced his man with a squeeze to the back of the neck. "It's his wife, you asshole."

Black Hair rooted through kitchen cupboards, knocking things to the floor as he dug deeper and deeper. "Hey, old man, you got any smokes?" He swore when Burle shook his head.

"Did you see a dog at the bend?" Burle asked. "A Great Dane?"

Ray pursed his lips, "No. Did any of you guys blast a Dane? That's a big fucking dog to you, Walsh."

Walsh had flaming red hair and beard to match. "I've killed a lot of big fucking dogs."

"Didn't see a Dane, Ray." said Barry.

Ray knocked a bottle from Walsh's hand. "Nobody gets drunk yet. Burle, ride behind me."

"I can't leave, you found no sign of my granddaughters. What if–"

"I'll crack your skull and tie you to the back, old man. You can't stay here. We're taking everything we can use, too. I saw that pile out back. Nice set of kills."

The church provided excellent protection against animal attacks. Heavy front doors could withstand multiple blows, while the high stained glass windows were out of reach of all but the birds. Next to the church was the town graveyard. While bikers grudgingly unloaded some of their supplies, Burle stared at headstones, vowing that Rachel would get a proper burial.

Walsh was the first to be stung. He cursed and slapped at his neck, then his cheek. Within seconds the biker's red hair disappeared under a mass of tiny bodies. Barry slapped at his friend's head repeatedly, killing ten or twenty wasps with each hit. The swarm leapt from Walsh's head to that of their attacker. Burle caught only a glimpse of swollen skin as Ray grabbed his arm and dragged him into the church. Barry's screams were muffled as wasps filled his mouth.

They stuffed cloth between and under the doors. It was an effective, if hasty, bug proofing.

"He stepped on a ground nest, right?" asked Shannon Crew, only two days a widow. "That's what happened right? He just stepped on a ground nest..." Her voice was reaching hysteria.

Ray looked deep into Burle's eyes, "Is that what you think? Those things just defending themselves?"

He'd been about as collected as anyone could be up until that point, but Burle could tell a part of the biker wanted to hear a lie, and would be willing to believe it.

"I've stood my ground and pumped Ficam right into a nest. Got stung once, maybe twice. I've never been chased by a swarm." He put his ear to the door. "And I've never had them try to get at me through a wall."

Later on, his head wrapped in cheesecloth, Burle stood on Ray's back (the pews were bolted down) and plugged small holes under windowsills. In total, about thirty wasps met their deaths in the church, swatted out of the air or crushed against skin. They'd sting where they landed, but most them went for heads.

Shadows crept across pews and carpeting, thrown by clusters of wasps on the windows. Minds already strained to the breaking point snapped under the incessant buzzing of thousands of tiny wings. As sunlight weakened, so did the swarm. Its numbers gradually reduced as wasps returned to their nests. By nightfall, the air was clear again.

Ray, who had been drowning his terror with Burle's alcohol, shoved open the church's doors and staggered outside.

"We ride!" he called out to the night.

Without thinking the other Angels shrugged on their leathers and stumbled to the bikes.

"You can't be serious," said Minister Asher. "At least stay the night."

"Not a chance, preacher. Burle, come with us." He gestured at Walsh's Harley.

"You can't give him Walsh's ride," said Black Hair.

Ray gestured at the bike again. "I can do whatever I want. The rules have changed. Come on old man, you'll die in that church and you know it."

"Can't go," Burle said. "I've got things to take care of."

Ray glanced at the cemetery and laughed. "Your funeral." He kick started his bike, and that was the last Burle ever saw of the man.

Asher's prayer for the Angels was cut short by a blast from Burle's rifle. A raccoon flew backwards, head over tail. It had only been a few feet from the clergyman.

"Let's go inside, Minister," Burle said.

As the double doors shut behind him, Burle realized his fellow survivors were looking to him for leadership. He had none to give.

Nocturnal hunters made escape by night an impossibility. Would the wasps return with the dawning of a new day?

Best not to think about it.

14. Anger Management

Toffee guided the wheel with his artificial hand. It was one of many things he could do well with Eggerson's creation of wire and wood. The hunter's previous prosthetics had been simple, enough to give the illusion of completeness. The hand he had now had moveable fingers and wrist. It wasn't something Toffee could control with the muscles of his arm; he had to use his left hand to rotate dials, but it was a far cry from motionless, useless plastic. The only drawback was that under the glove his hand was clearly a construction. Fitted joints and steel pins made up an extremity that Toffee found far more freakish than the long blade underneath.

Compton Pit was an hour behind when Seth grew tired of Toffee's silence. "I was told you were restricted to quarters. I'm impressed you stayed in your room so long."

Toffee's eye twitched. "I was in lockup, since about four in the morning. I left my room to take a piss."

"Who stuck you in lockup for going to the bathroom."

"Darcy. She must have been camped outside my door."

"You…you let her…for going to the bathroom?"

"She is the chief of security." Toffee's voice was heavy with sarcasm.

"Aren't you mad?"

The look Toffee gave Seth could strip the primer off a car. "What do you think?"

Silence reigned in the car once more. Seth and Toffee were in the Hummer, with the hunters' van behind. One hunter and three security officers made up the rest of Toffee's crew. He'd selected people he knew wouldn't hesitate to shoot a human if the need arose.

As the Hummer shuddered over cracked road, Seth watched moths flash in the headlights, and decided to get some sleep. He was woken abruptly when the car screeched to a halt. It was still dark out. Toffee killed the motor and stepped out into the road.

"What's happening?" asked Seth, grabbing his rifle from the back seat.

"Stay in the car," Toffee said quietly. It was an order, not a suggestion.

The second vehicle came to a stop. Daniel called to Toffee through his window. "Why are we stopping?"

"I need to kill something."

"What? What's out there?" The doors to the van opened.

"STAY INSIDE!" roared Toffee. When he was sure his order was being followed, he unbuttoned his shirt, then doffed his prosthetic, exposing the blade to moonlight. He drew the blade across his chest, and let the scent of blood hit the air. "Come on," he said to the woods, "come and get me."

Inside the van, Senna, blond hair made pale by the moon, turned to Daniel. "What the hell is he doing out there?"

"Why don't you get out and ask him?"

Toffee moved closer to the tree line. "COME ON! WHAT ARE YOU WAITING FOR?"

Seth scanned the foliage beyond the chief of the hunters. He flipped the safety off his rifle.

A low growl issued from the trees, leaves parted and a sleek, lupine form stepped out to answer the hunter's challenge.

"Get back in the car," Seth's calm voice belied his unease, "before the rest of the pack shows up."

"No." Toffee locked eyes with the wolf. "This one's a loner. Aren't you, boy?" He raised the blade, pointing it away from the animal. "Go ahead, I'll give you the first shot for free."

The wolf bunched, its hackles raised, then it lowered its head and vanished back into the trees. Toffee blinked after it, then put his arm back on and returned to the car. "Well I guess that's good enough. Let's go."

Daniel let go of the breath he was holding. He turned to the others in the van. "Have you ever seen anything like that?"

"Shit, give me my shades," said the hunter as morning sun broke the mountains and lit up cracks in the windshield like streams of electricity.

Seth reached into a container between the seats. He put on a pair of what could have been Raybans at one point, and handed Toffee a pair with silver frames and tiny circular lenses. Broken concrete disappeared behind the two vehicles, and the sun cleared the mountains completely, leaping into the sky. Summer was truly the cruelest season. It brought wasps and bees, making the very air a threat. Ants swarmed from the ground, their numbers increasing exponentially year by year. They didn't chase humans the way their yellow and black cousins did. Ants just tunnelled and reproduced, moving inexorably closer to human settlements. Few ants were capable of stinging bites, but woe betide anyone who was asleep when the insects came, or too injured to move. Carpenter ants could chew through wood in a remarkably short period of time. Human flesh was much less of an obstacle.

The request for shades were the first words Toffee had spoken since he'd resumed driving. Seth used the break in silence to start talking. "You ever do that before? Stare down an animal?"

"First time." A grin stretched Toffee's face, the tiny black lenses made him look like an aging pre-Change rock star who'd stuck his nose in a blender.

"When do you think we'll hook up with October?"

"If they make good time, nightfall. Provided there's no roadblocks too big to push out of the way."

"What did the Boss say about going after Shangly?"

"He's soft on that one."

"What do you think of October?"

The change of subject was not lost on Toffee. His second in command respected him, but was ultimately loyal to the Boss. It wasn't surprising. Toffee had tested Seth a few times, subtly, even using the fact that he'd been passed over for promotion. Each of the people exposed to Toffee's careful scrutiny was completely under the Boss's beguilement. "I think she drives like a man," he said

"Sure doesn't look like one, though. I miss dating. Working your way closer to someone in the mess hall…it feels childish."

"Think of it like stalking. Take your time. Get a good look before you bring down the game."

Seth bit a chunk off some jerky. "Listen to you," he said as he chewed. "I feel sorry for whoever you've got your eye on. Do you have your eye on someone?"

"I did." Too bad Travis Jones had died before Toffee could finish. The pursuit had not been sexual; the hunter preferred the company of women in that regard. Animals were anything but a protected species, but there were other things to poach, like a man's life. Not his breath or heartbeat, it was easy to take that. The challenge lay in finding the game's sources of pride, and making trophies of them, one by one.

The jerky was thrust under Toffee's nose. He half bit, half tore a piece off. Jerky was such a common flavour, it tasted the same no matter what or where it came from. He could have been eating human for all he knew.

"We need a bar at the Pit. Y'know, a social place, use one of the storage rooms on two. Should be easy. I'll bet we could even make little paper umbrellas. You gotta admit, we've got a right to be proud of ourselves."

"Proud? I'm ashamed of us."

Seth was caught completely off guard. "Ashamed? Why?"

"You had your eyes closed these last ten years? It's just animals, and look at us. The whole damn planet fell apart. India and Pakistan nuked each other by the second day. China...great time to have a revolution boys and girls. If the birds over here were as active as they were over there...We used to build space stations and now an underground YMCA is the best we have to offer."

"Well, I'm still proud of us, but you're right, some things don't change. Shangly or whoever, putting up these roadblocks...it should just be people versus animals. I'll be glad when this is over."

"This is just beginning." Toffee's alarm bells went off as they entered a blind curve. He didn't know what exactly he'd noticed, a pattern of broken branches maybe, something out of place with nature. He slowed till trees and rock face eased by the window. The van slowed as well, not asking questions, keeping radio silence until Toffee broke it. Had they been going faster, they would have run right into the pile of cars. There were five of them, two on top of three.

Seth whistled. "These are in the right place. Exactly where I'd put them on this stretch of road. What tipped you?"

"Don't know anymore. Brain just sees things."

"That's why you're the chief," said Seth, a little regretfully.

They pulled on their suits and net helmets, tied off wrists and ankles, then grabbed their guns. Toffee toggled a spray of repellent from the car's gas spouts. A few moments later, similar gas puffed from the van.

"I don't see any tractor treads," said Senna as she scuffed the road with a steel-toed boot. Evidence of track covering was immediately apparent under closer inspection. Weaves of branches had been placed to conceal crushed saplings and broken branches.

Toffee ran his finger along a straight line scored in the ground near the end of one wreck. "They didn't have a tractor. They used a ramp. Drove the top cars up there, then stripped them. Efficient. He did it at night, there's flare scorches over there. Okay, we blow it."

"Won't that be a little loud?" Daniel asked.

"Your point being?"

"If there are people waiting for–"

"Saves time when they come right to you, doesn't it?"

Seth unloaded dynamite from the Hummer without being told. It was, after all, his specialty. The US Army had invested years and money in making Seth a demolitions expert. His last name, Boomatay, was of particular amusement to his commanding officer. That training had gradually faded as it went unused. Given a chance, Seth would gladly have brought down acres of forest, but people had learned the hard way not to do that. Mass destruction hurt far more than it helped. A group with enough ammunition and sufficient will could decimate the animal population in a given area. Large amounts of poison would have the same affect, and the same consequences. Without the animals, insects took over and the land died. Attrition had forced humanity into balance, but that was life at the bottom of the food chain.

"What's our fire risk here?" asked Daniel.

"Minimal," replied Seth as he measured fuses. "This stretch is getting a reasonable amount of rain. That's it, let's back off." He waited until the van was out of sight, then lit a central fuse and bolted for the Hummer. Toffee backed the vehicle off slowly, waiting for Seth to look uncomfortable.

Shrapnel tore through the trees. The top two cars now lay on their sides on the road. Two of the bottom three had been pushed apart. It was easy for the Hummer to nudge them out of the way. Toffee accelerated.

"Do you think there'll be more?" asked Seth.

"How much time is someone going to spend dragging wrecks? It'll be clear for a while. I'll bet you Danny boy still keeps radio silence."

Seth glanced back at the van. "I think there's a cop gene. Doesn't matter where you are, you give a guy a badge, he pulls his pants two inches higher up his butt crack."

The chief of the hunters was correct in his assessment; hours passed with no communication from Daniel. Seth napped, smiling in his sleep. On some level, Toffee envied that. At a peak in the road, where green branches receded to reveal a rock formation that looked like a crooked finger, he brought the Hummer to a stop and checked his watch. Even with the light weakening behind him, Toffee could still see a good stretch down the road. There were no more obstructions, but there was also no convoy.

Seth awoke and, recognizing where they were, cast his eyes at klicks of road that snaked away beneath them. "Are we early?"

"No."

"This isn't good."

Toffee floored it.

15. New Flavors

The unmistakable odor of sweat and fire was carried to Noah by a slight air current that ran through the caverns. The smell was followed by the distinct jingling of metal, then the burn crew appeared, making their way home. They were well within the sound net, but Noah could tell by the dust on their faces that they'd removed their net helmets long before that. Not that there were wasps deep in caves, but there were ants. Noah watched the burn crew pass without speaking. Their job was done, he still had hours ahead of him. Not that he would have wanted their job, it was much tougher. The Boss had not only ordered the cave blocked off, but hidden as well. Not an easy task considering the amount of fire damage that had to be done in order clear the area of stingers. The burning itself had to be controlled, as the dry weather would make mistakes disastrous.

Once the crew had passed, Noah was alone again. Caps was a tunnel over, Lena a tunnel back, and Darcy off somewhere, periodically using security duties as an excuse to ditch the caves for a while. The panel jockey had become quite good at blending paint to stone, another reason Darcy had left it to him. She always seemed to be there when Sid showed up. Nice trick, that.

Noah's mind returned to thinking about ants. They terrified him. There could be millions of them just out of range of the Mimi's, waiting for a power failure, or a new generation that would be immune to Gershwin's intricate weave of frequencies. One of the great legends Noah had heard was about the giant anthills in

Alabama. They were supposedly forty feet high or more, filled with billions of fire ants. Supposedly, ants were the reason for everything. The batch that sprung up in the summer of the Change had human extermination hardwired to the system. They knew they couldn't do it alone, so they pulled in everything else. The giant anthills were brain centres. All the colonies within did was spend the whole day psychically transmitting, "Death to the humans!" Noah didn't believe a word of that, but there was definite strategy to the insects' method of kill.

Wasps and bees driving an animal away from their nest still behaved the way they always had, swarming angrily but rarely giving chase. Stinger attacks on humans, however, were far more calculated. Everyone was taught to keep their mouths shut tight if swarmed, because the insects' goal was to sting the inside of the throat. A signal was sent once that had been accomplished a few times, and the stingers would move on to a new victim or simply dissipate if none were available. Swelling in the throat cut off air supply. In this manner, small swarms could kill a number of people in a very short period of time. To Noah, the ants were worse.

Except for the fire ants (which now infested over a billion acres in what used to be America's south) and a few other species, most ants didn't have much power individually. What they did have was numbers. Ants took sleepers mostly, only attacking once enough were assembled on and around their unfortunate victim. Bacon had told him the worst part about ants was that you went insane before you died. Noah had never been in an ant attack personally, but seemingly at will he could summon the feeling of tiny carapaces moving up his nose and down his ears. Even in the new wilderness, some people took pleasure in scaring themselves.

"We'll be quitting in a few minutes," said Darcy, appearing at his shoulder. He almost dropped his paintbrush—she moved as quietly as Toffee.

"How do you know?" asked Noah, recovering.

"Dinner."

"Oh. I thought that had already come and gone."

"We'll get you a watch, sun boy."

Instead of taking the lid off her paint can, she picked it up and left. A few minutes later, Sid's voice called knock off down the cavern.

Noah was relieved to find they were done for the day. It made no sense to him that he'd been kept away from his real duties for so long. Surely there were other methods of punishment besides labour. Why couldn't Sid have just docked his power allotment? Noah realized how stupid that was as soon as he thought it up.

He was one of the last people to be served that night. Roshi hd taken his tray from him instead of just ladling onto it. He'd handed it back, pointing at some leafy vegetables.

"Where's Burle?" Noah asked, nodding at the empty chair.

"At his cemetery," said Caps, licking his fingers. "Did you get some, too?"

Noah paused, confused, then he moved his greens a little. Beneath was a strip of dark meat. Looking around, he realized not everyone had gotten this treat. He was overly casual as he cut a piece off and snuck it into his mouth. The meat was rich and tender, like beef, only fuller in flavour. "Mmmmm," he hummed loudly, then again quietly. "Is this veal?"

"It's bear cub. Guess I won't be cuddling it tonight."

Lena rolled the meat between her tongue and the roof of her mouth. "You know, this is a new speed record for Roshi. Odega must not have put up a fight at all."

Burle's wasn't the only empty chair at the table. "Is Cass with Burle? What with her being security now?"

Caps looked around the mess hall. "I don't know where she is. Burle always goes out alone, though. Darcy's plenty mad about him sneaking off while she was in caves. She told him he had to be escorted now."

"Is that one of the 'duties' she had to attend to? Fuming after Burle? She sent someone after him right?"

"She couldn't," said Lena. "No vehicles. The hunters are out hooking up with the convoy, and they're late calling in, I might add. The two cars and the bike are out scouting the north and south roads, and Burle took the Pig."

"The Pig?" Noah got an image of Burle on a muzzled pig, beating it with a stick to keep it in line.

"That's the big van," said Caps. "You've seen it. It used to be a milk wagon. We call it the Pig 'cause it handles like one. Won't try to bite you, though. We shower right after dinner. Are you grateful now?"

"Like you wouldn't believe."

If not for the cub, it would have been the first lackluster meal served to Noah since arriving at the Pit. The entree was stew, well seasoned, but stew nonetheless. The meat was tough and chewy.

Back at Underbel, Grearson would have called it meatgum. He said if he chewed it long enough, he could blow bubbles.

Noah was working on his last piece of meat, slowly persuading his mouth to swallow, when he saw Darcy moving towards the bus carts. If he was going to do something, he was going to do it now. He forced the meat down his throat, tensing as it stuck over his epiglottis, then relented. He had to do a quick walk to intercept the chief of security.

"Darcy, I was–"

"What?" she asked abruptly.

"Nothing, it's just that–"

"I don't have time for more questions."

Noah didn't know what he'd planned, but it certainly wasn't watching her retreating back again. Caps was right; the concert had been for her own benefit, not his. Noah returned to the table. If either of his dining companions had noticed his winning style, they didn't say anything.

The shower had a rejuvenating effect on him. The steaming torrent of water washed away his weariness and disappointment. Wearing only towels, he and Caps walked back to their rooms.

"I'll check my station tomorrow," said Noah. "Want to do something?"

"Sorry, got plans."

"Oh? Working on a poster?"

"Something like that."

Ten minutes after returning to his room, Noah realized he had nothing to do. He didn't feel like going to sleep yet, but there also wasn't anywhere he wanted to go. He was sitting on his bed playing with Freeland's model soldier when a knock came at his door.

"Changed your mind, huh? Come in."

"Hi, am I disturbing you?" It was Cass.

"No...uh, sorry, I thought you were someone else." He closed his legs and pushed a flap of towel between them. Nudity in the shower was necessary, but beyond the bathroom walls, it once again became taboo.

"Oh, do you have a date?"

"A date? No, just..." his towel fell apart on the leg facing the door. He hastily tugged it up again. "What can I do for you?"

"There's a lot of things you can do for me."

Noah was sure he misread the tone in her voice. Her dark hair, which was usually in a ponytail, was now out and curled. She was wearing tight pants and a shirt with the top four buttons undone. Cass sat on the bunk next to him and a put a hand on his knee. "So, how do you like it here so far?"

It came to Noah in a flash what was going on. "I get it. Okay, what do you want the juice for?"

She furrowed her brow. "That's a crude way of…oh, you mean power. You think I'm here to hit you up for electricity."

"Well, what are you here for?"

She leaned closer. "How do I smell now?"

Noah sniffed, she was wearing perfume. Her hand darted under his towel and squeezed the top of his leg.

"Have you met someone here yet?"

"N-no," he stammered, "I guess not."

She captured his earlobe with her teeth. His erection pushed the towel aside.

"Well, that answers the rest of my questions," she said.

She helped Noah strip off her pants. He was awash with conflicting emotion. He was flattered at this sudden attention, guilty at casting Darcy aside so easily, and tremendously horny.

"Will my pills have kicked in so soon?" he asked, running a hand up her leg.

"Not a problem, I can't have kids." Her shirt hit the floor. A patch of ruined skin above her navel septum showed where something had torn open her insides. She was lucky to have survived the trauma.

"I'm sorry," he said, touching the scar.

"I'm not," she pushed him back on the bed. "Who wants to bring a kid into this world?"

Noah reached for the light, but Cass stopped him.

"Don't, I want to see you."

This was something new. Jenny hated making love in anything other than complete darkness. Noah didn't have any problems with the light though. Cass had a pretty, rounded face. Her breasts were small but firm. Noah took her by the shoulders and rolled her over, covering her with himself and pushing between her legs.

"Stop! Noah, what are you doing?"

Noah raised himself up on his arms and she squiggled out from underneath him.

"What do you think I'm doing?"

"You've had sex before right? You're not a virgin, are you?"

"No way. I've had plenty of sex." What was going on now? Was she playing games?

"With how many different women?"

"Why does that matter?"

She drew her nails lightly across his scrotum. "How many women?"

"Oooooh...uh...one."

"And you just got on top and went at it? Is that it?" She stopped her caress.

"Well...yeah."

She kissed him, probing behind his teeth with her tongue. "You've got a lot to learn, mister. Lie back."

Noah complied and she straddled him, half way down his legs. The position gave him an excellent view of her body. Yes, lights on was definitely better.

"No foreplay, huh? You play with her tits at least?"

"Sure." Noah brought his hands up. She slapped them back down again.

"Not yet. Just behave." She used her fingers to trace delicate circles around his areolas. The sensation banished any qualms he had about letting her be dominant.

"Patel was right, your skin is so smooth. You're beautiful." She leaned forward and licked a nipple. Her belly rubbed his groin as she did so. Her breasts brushed against him as she kissed her way down his body. He was so glad he'd swapped shower slots. When she took him in her mouth Noah's head lolled and his back arched. Jenny had done this only once, and then only for a few seconds. Cass moved slowly at first, then faster. She continued rubbing a nipple as she did so. She took him to climax in no time at all. It was mind shattering. She stroked his chest and stomach gently as he recovered.

"Wow...that was...just give me a five minutes and..."

"Five minutes? God, I love young men!"

"Young? How old are you?"

"Flatterer. It's never nice to ask a woman her age, especially after she's given you a blowjob. Now it's my turn." She moved up his chest and straddled his face.

"Hey!"

"Don't complain. Trust me, you'll like it."

The smell was unpleasant at first, as was the taste, but both grew less so as he persevered under Cass's encouragement and guidance.

When her hips started bucking, it was difficult for him to stick with the spot she'd guided him to, but he managed. At the end she said "yes" about fifty times and banged the wall with her fist. Then she flopped down beside him and snuggled into his side. He was ready for more and tried to roll on top of her again.

"Not yet, not yet. Let me enjoy my afterglow."

"I was good? I did okay?"

"Couldn't you tell?"

Jenny had never put on a display like what he'd just seen. "I guess so."

"Okay, I'm ready." She was up again, this time she perched over his groin and guided him in, slowly. When he was fully engulfed, she placed her hands on his chest and moved slightly, back and forth. Noah pulled her closer, capturing a nipple with his mouth.

"Not so hard," she breathed. "Just like before, gently."

It took longer this time, but soon Cass was bucking and writhing again, alternatively pushing her face into his neck and arching her back as she ground against him.

Noah allowed her to instruct him throughout the night. For her part, she travelled every inch of his skin. A stroke of the wrist sent trembles through his whole body, a delicate touch between the buttocks took his breath away. He did eventually turn out his light, knowing that he'd gone overtime, but it was special circumstances after all.

Cass called it quits after what she called her third "big O". Noah was more than willing to continue.

"You just relax now," she said. "Save some of that energy for next time."

The cot wasn't large enough for two people to fit comfortably. As his leg teetered on the edge, Noah realized Cass had established herself across a lion's share of the mattress. He didn't mind. "So, there'll be a next time?"

"Mmhmm," she sighed contentedly.

"Uhm, do you have a boyfriend here?"

"Had. He was out root collecting."

"I'm sorry."

"It happens."

"Why me?"

She trailed her fingernails across his chest, barely touching him. "Because you're so fresh. Like a new day."

16. Fallout

Darcy had to compose herself before hitting the transmit button again. "Anything else? Over."

"Nothing important. Dee out." Daniel's voice vanished into hissing static.

She took her headphones off and dumped them beside the mic. Lena took her hand and squeezed. The two women looked at each other. What was there to say?

"Do you want me to come with you?" asked Lena.

"No. I'll be fine."

Most of the Pit's residents were already in bed—asleep or otherwise. Lowlight settings had gone into effect a couple of hours before. Previously a single line of flourescents lit the residential corridors. Noah had reduced this even further. Now only every other bulb was lit. A wedge of light protruded from beneath the Boss's door. Darcy knocked.

"Come in."

Sid rolled up a map as she entered. Before the topography completely vanished into a crumpled scroll, she saw small marks in red and black ink had been made in one area. He was expecting bad news. She could tell by his body language. He could probably tell from hers that he wouldn't be disappointed.

"Go ahead."

"Daniel reported in. They found them. Stuart and October..."

"Go on."

"Stuart and October were easily identified. Sam was, too. Ian…there were a few more parts than bodies to put them on. Those were, uh, Toffee's words. The Rover was stripped. There was another vehicle, placed, not driven. No sign of the rig. Sam and Stuart were naked, but it seems October was dressed…and taped."

"Taped?"

"Daniel said duct tape. A lot of it. He said it was what was holding her together."

"Anything else?"

"Senna has a minor injury. The crows don't like being chased off. Shall I call a meeting?"

"No. Go on, I'll call it when I'm ready."

"Sid?"

"Not now. Please."

Darcy had people to wake. Might as well do the hardest ones first. She knocked on 57.

"Who is it?" It was a woman's voice, catching on the last word.

"It's Darcy. Can I come in?" Silence. "Lorraine?"

Sid had married them less than ten weeks ago. Sam and Lorraine Williams. Roshi made a cake with real flour. It had been a small cake.

"Lorraine?"

"No!"

Darcy squeezed her lip until the pain made her stop. She turned the doorknob. Lorraine sat on a bed made of two cots jammed together. The sheets bunched around where her hands clenched tightly to the fabric. Medium length brown hair splayed out bedhead style around a face that was rigid with denial.

"No! You're not coming in!"

"Lorraine…"

"If you're coming in it's to tell me something's happened to Sam, so you're not coming in!"

"I'm sorry…"

Lorraine's face changed so dramatically, under different circumstances, it would have been comical. What colour could be seen from the light in the hallway, drained away. Her mouth dropped open and she seemed to stare through Darcy at something a million miles distant.

"He's dead?"

Darcy nodded.

"I felt him…" Her eyes gained focus. "I felt him but I thought I was just being…" her voiced choked off as she wailed without making a sound.

Darcy didn't know what else to do. She sat on the bed and wrapped her arms around Lorraine. So forceful was the woman's grief, the chief of security felt tears flowing freely down her own cheeks, despite her best efforts to hold them back. Her strength was draining rapidly, and she still had one more like this.

"I'm sorry, I have to go. There are other people I need to tell."

Lorraine looked up, her face a decade older. "Ian, too?"

"All of them."

Sam's widow took a few deep breaths. "I'll tell Susan." Transport wives, like the spouses of police officers in times past.

Relief overrode guilt. "Thank you. It'll be better coming from you."

"How could it be?"

October wasn't connected romantically to anyone, she'd been holding out for the Boss. Stuart was also single. It was generally believed he too, was holding out for Sid Halbert.

Darcy should have ordered support to Drum East the moment she'd heard about the first roadblock. Travis never should have let security slack off in the first place. It was definitely Shangly, they had their confirmation. They'd assumed the scavenger had given up harassing them when things died down. It had been months. Sid had let his guard down too, but that didn't matter. It was her job to see that he didn't have to worry about security matters. They'd lost four good people and two vehicles, and it happened on her watch. She informed certain department heads right away. Sid called a meeting at five a.m. He'd had no sleep but held himself at the table as if he'd just come out of three days in a feather bed.

"So that's it. The duct tape was his message to us."

Noah raised his hand, then remembering previous instructions, pulled it down. "Why duct tape?"

Darcy gave her head a mental shake. Why couldn't he ask his questions afterwards?

Sid stifled his own annoyance. "The last time he came to trade, he had two boxes of duct tape, the shrink wrap still on them. A lot of barter value in that. Wrapping someone up in it is a waste, unless you're doing it to send a message."

"We should have hit Shangly as soon as this started," said Dr. White.

"Sara, please. I'm going to have this discussion with Toffee, I don't need to have it with you, too."

She conceded the point with a nod of her head. Toffee would definitely not pass up an opportunity to say "I told you so."

Sid waited for anyone else to say their piece, but all heads were turned towards him. On the day to day problems, two people came up with three opinions, but in this instance, it was all on the Boss.

"We'll need a new chief of transport. In fact, we need almost an entire transport division, but that's secondary considering we don't even have a transport vehicle. We can't afford to run trade in the Pig, and the hunters' van can't be put on other duties. We traded our other rig to Underbel because they needed one and couldn't afford to get one from Gascan. We, on the other hand, can."

Peter "Gascan" D'Abo held a compound five days by road from Compton Pit. He'd killed every animal for miles around his base, burned the scrub and poisoned the land. He had almost no food production whatsoever, but it didn't matter, he had gas. In the early years of chaos, D'Abo led a group of people to take and hold one of the largest reservoirs of refined petroleum ever to be built in North America. Solar, wind and hydro power were used for installations, but vehicles still needed oil and gas. D'Abo stepped on his gas with alcohol and other fillers, like any other pusher. Anything he needed, he traded for. His home was filled with toys that would have been the envy of any pre-Change playboy. He was also the only person who could almost always be counted on to have vehicles available. For trucks, like his gas, he traded dear.

"Lena, get a hold of D'Abo and tell him we need that rig sooner than expected. Dig into the possibilities of getting two from him, in case we can't recover ours. Burle…"

Burle, lost in his own thoughts, didn't hear the Boss.

"Burle! You with us?"

"Oh…sorry. My mind was wandering."

"Understandable under the circumstances. Did you hear anything I just said?"

"Well, no."

"In a nutshell, sit with Lena when she contacts Gascan. Negotiate a two truck deal, but don't make anything solid until you've talked to me, got it?"

Burle nodded.

"Now the next order of business is this; we're going to get our rig back, and whatever is left of the cargo."

"What are we going to do about Shangly?" Caps asked.

"That's what we're here to discuss."

There was silence around the table. Darcy felt the answer was pretty obvious. "We lock him outside."

"Yeah, right!" Caps said. "We just march on over to Fenwick Prison and kick him out."

"Works for me," said Toffee as he pushed through the door. Seth was right behind him. Toffee sat down smoothly, whereas his second in command flopped into his chair.

"Welcome back," said Darcy, directing the comment to Seth, not Toffee. "How close were you when Daniel wired in?"

"A lot closer than he was," replied the chief hunter.

"You separated?" Sid was flabbergasted, a state that Darcy rarely saw him in. "Have you lost your mind?"

"Relax. He's second security, he can take care of himself. He should be here soon."

The Boss's muscles tensed. He almost stood, but resisted the impulse. "You were leading a team."

Toffee leaned back in his chair, legs apart, real hand lightly gripping artificial. "I split the team. Daniel's in charge of his. I brought mine in safely."

Seth shrugged. Who was he to argue with his direct superior?

Sid's eyes narrowed, then his face relaxed. He spoke in a measured voice; "Lena, get Daniel on the horn, find out where he is. Toffee, we'll talk about this later."

"I'm looking forward to it," the hunter produced a torn sheet of paper. "This was taped to October." He gave the sheet to Burle. Lena took a peek at it as she left.

Burle looked it over then got up and walked the page to Sid.

"This is the cargo manifest," said the Boss after he'd examined the offering. "Shangly's little reminder about what he stole from us." He gave the manifest to Darcy without looking at her.

The page was difficult to read. Besides being torn, it was also stained with blood.

"This isn't the manifest," she said. "This is what we wanted, not necessarily what we got. October writes...wrote her manifests in blue ink, always. This is black."

It took a moment for her statement to sink in. Caps spoke up first.

"So Shangly's got someone in Drum East. Burle, did you recognize the handwriting?"

"You mean hand printing? No. October might have."

"So what now?" asked Toffee, oblivious to the mood of those around him.

"Darcy, there are two maps on the table in my room, bring them please. Take Seth with you. Everyone else, dismissed. Toffee, you stay."

The chief of security would have given her eyeteeth to witness the chewing out Sid was no doubt delivering. Instead, she walked towards the residential corridors with Seth and Odega. Behind her, Noah pelted questions at Caps.

"You should have seen Toffee stare down that wolf. It was amazing."

Darcy had no idea what Seth was talking about. "What wolf?"

"Toffee hopped out of the car to…uhm, he was pretty pissed at…Anyway, this wolf shows up, he gives it the evil eye, and the thing just took off."

Dr. Odega stopped and grabbed Seth's arm. "It didn't attack?"

"No. I just said that. Ouch, you're squeezing pretty hard there, Ted."

The scientist released his grip. "Sorry. How far out were you?"

"I don't know. I guess we'd been on the road about an hour or so."

Odega gave Darcy a queer look, half bewildered, half hopeful.

"Excuse me, I have to check something in my lab." He turned his wide back on them and walked quickly in the direction from which they'd come.

"I guess that had more meaning to Ted than it did to me." Seth looked back over his shoulder, then trotted to catch up with Darcy, who was already a few strides ahead of him.

Toffee stabbed a finger into a ridge southwest of the prison. "There. We come down from there."

"We can't come down from there," said Darcy. "Have you ever been out to Fenwick? He's burned that ridge clear. No cover. He'll spot us coming in a mile away."

"It gets us close enough to use the rocket launcher." The hunter looked at Seth for support. He didn't get it.

"No can do. We've only got three rockets. We'd need more to guarantee a sufficient hole through the wall. We'd be picked off as we were doing it anyway. Doesn't matter. We've got too much brush to come through if we're not using the road. Could we get someone in under the guise of negotiation?"

Sid considered. "No. It would be suicide. Shangly wouldn't negotiate. Not at this point. He'll have cleared a back road, though. Rats like to have an escape route. Odds are it won't be as heavily guarded as the main road. It might not be guarded at all. He'd never attack us directly. He won't be expecting us to try it on him."

Toffee was looking at the second map. Whereas one was topographical, the other showed roadways, or at least what had been roadways in 1983. According to the map, Fenwick Prison lay almost two hundred klicks from the nearest town, a tiny burg called 170 Mile House. There hadn't been much to the town to begin with: a gas station, some houses and a restaurant. Darcy's family had made a point of stopping there whenever they could. The restaurant served buffalo burgers and sold buffalo steaks out of its freezers to anyone who knew well enough to ask.

"What's this?" asked the hunter, running his finger along a thin line north of the prison.

Sid looked over Toffee's shoulder. "It's a logging road. Surprised it's on this map. Wouldn't be paved. I doubt the road's still there."

Toffee grinned. "It's much easier to clear a road, than make a new one. This spills out a few klicks away, but this map's old. I bet that road wound up going all the way to the prison. Convicts made for cheap labour."

Darcy pulled the road map towards her and turned it around. "Canada didn't believe in prison labour. Sid, you've been looking at these maps for days. Why don't you just tell us what we're going to do?"

"I like unprejudiced options."

The door swung open. Dr. Odega came in like a pack of dogs was at his heels.

"I need a Mimi. A functioning one."

"What?" Sid was shocked by the outrageous demand. "Why?"

"I can't say right now. I need a Mimi in my lab. Which one can I have?"

"None of them. The topside net is weak enough as it is. I can't just pull one out. What are you thinking, Ted?"

Odega's jaw dropped. He'd been so wrapped up in his needs, it hadn't occurred to him they wouldn't be met.

"Well?"

"I...fine!" The doctor slammed the door behind him.

"That was interesting," said Toffee.

Sid just shook his head, then placed his hand flat on the road map. "We can't hit the prison with a full out assault. We'll be slaughtered. These maps don't tell me what I need to know. We can question Gil again, but I need proper recon. One team, five people. We come in along the river, here." The river curved just before intersecting with the road. "We have a pretty tough inflatable boat in storage. Burle's never been able to trade it for anything. It means shooting some rapids, but it can be accomplished."

"Who makes up this team?" asked Darcy.

"Toffee, Seth, Daniel, Senna and Norman."

"Why not me?"

Toffee placed his shoulder against hers. "The Boss likes to keep you safe at home."

She shuddered in revulsion and pulled away.

"That'll be enough." Sid's voice was weary, not angry. "You two work out your differences another time. Seth, Toffee, go get some sleep. You head out tonight."

Seth gave the map one more apprehensive look, then left. Toffee nodded, flashed a smile at the chief of security and followed his second. Once they were gone, Darcy rounded on her mentor.

"It undermines my position when you leave me out of these things."

"I'm not leaving you out of these things. When have you ever done a covert operation? You're not qualified. I've got too much on my plate right now to worry about your ego."

"I've hunted plenty of times."

"Animals don't have guns. Some or all of the team might not come back. If it comes to that, we can make do without them, but I need you. Maybe I am keeping you safe at home, but that doesn't change my decision."

The door opened again. This time it was Lena.

"Daniel will be here in hour. He's not very happy."

"Thank you, Lena. How soon can you contact Gascan?"

"I should be able to in about two hours. I doubt he'll be out of bed till later though."

"Fine. Get some rest, I'm going to do the same. Darcy, when Toffee's 'second team' gets in, send them to bed."

"You know, one problem is solved; there's something the other settlements can trade to us."

"What's that?"

"People."

Sid forgot his maps when he left. Darcy rolled them together and tucked them under her arm. She was at a loss as to where to go. It was the weak spot in her position. When everything was falling apart around her, she had to be the strong one. Before her promotion there was no question of going to Lena or Caps, and there had always been Travis. Now there was a distance, not one created by the others, but by her. Darcy knew this, but only on rare occasions could she forget it.

She dumped the maps on her desk once she arrived at her office. A man with the unfortunate name Purtricil (Purty) held watch. He'd been with the Pit for three years now. A small man—thin with only a remnant of hair the colour of straw—he was nonetheless capable of diffusing a situation with words, and equally adept at force when words failed.

"Morning, Chief. You're here early. There a problem?"

"I'll brief everyone in a few hours. Purty, could you get me some coffee?"

He scanned the blank surface of the watch desk. "Yeah, I think I can step away for a moment. Milk today, innit?"

"Oh yes, please. Tell Roshi it's for me. Get yourself a cup as well." She checked her watch, deciding to wander down to the airlock in about twenty minutes. She'd have to get the sun boy a watch as well. It was one of the little things that kept being forgotten. Purty returned shortly with steaming, brown coffee. Darcy took it gratefully. The nice thing about delivered coffee was that usually it arrived at just drinkable temperature. She wasn't disappointed as she knocked back a huge swallow, completely free of burns to her mouth and throat.

"So do I get a hint?" asked Purty, licking his lips after sipping his java.

"Victor Shangly hit our Convoy. Took the rig. No survivors. Daniel found them."

"Shit!"

"You got that right."

Noah entered the office, peering through the far door to get a look at the lockups.

"Shouldn't you be in bed?" Darcy asked, raising an eyebrow.

"I'm up. Breakfast is pretty soon, I figured I'd just do some work." He gave Darcy a once over, quick, but she caught it anyway. There was an unreadable expression on his face.

"So, what do you want?"

"Uhm, a key. You know, to the caverns. If I need to get to the Mimis fast, I don't want to have to come looking for you."

Darcy leaned back in her chair. "There is a guard posted on the other side of the door. Just knock, identify yourself, you'll be let in."

"Oh. Okay." His voice held disappointment.

"Wait a minute, you want a key 'cause it'll make you feel important, right?"

The sun boys cheeks flushed red. He looked uncomfortably at Purty. For his part, the security officer tried not to smile.

"Forget it. I'll get you a key. You're the chief of photovoltaics, but you've probably figured out you're pretty much the head electrician as well. You should have access to everywhere."

"Thank you. I'll uh…I'll be going now."

Purtricil allowed himself a laugh once Noah was gone, but the void left by the chief of photovoltaics was quickly filled by the weight of Darcy's announcement. Purty's laughter died on his lips, and he turned to his boss to find her staring at a structure marked on a map.

17. Snake in the Gas

Lena sipped her tea (with milk!) and watched the time anxiously. She'd been told by one of Gascan's underlings to reconnect at precisely nine o'clock. Though she had only a couple of sips left, Burle had barely touched his. If he didn't drink it soon, it would get cold. She finished her tea.

"Are you going to drink that?"

He looked at his mug. "Not really thirsty."

"Well, you're the one always saying we shouldn't waste anything. Can I have it?" He passed her the mug. "Burle, we're all shaken up, but I need you at a hundred percent. Should I put off this negotiation? I'm sure the Boss will understand."

Burle glanced at the computer screen. "It's time, Lena. I'll be fine."

Lena punched some keys, thinking it was the second time she'd heard someone say that in less than twenty-four hours. The display on the screen changed, indicating contact.

"This is Compton Pit. Are you receiving?"

"Hello, Miss Wong. I've been looking forward to your call." The voice had an unmistakable sliminess to it. Lena and Burle exchanged a look, Gascan never answered satellite communications himself; he always had a subordinate notify him.

"Hello, Peter, how are you?"

"My, my, pleasantries. I'm very well, thank you. How's everything in the pits?"

"Same old, same old. We'd like to talk some business."

There was a pause. Lena imagined she felt smugness conveyed by the silence. "And here I thought you called me up just to say hi. Young lady, you know how to intrigue even as you disappoint."

The screen changed. The icon of a projecting satellite dish was replaced by a man's face. It was fat, and unshaven. Small eyes perched above a bulbous nose and a mop of gray hair crowned an almost spherical head. "Why don't you turn on your camera, Lena? I like to conduct business face to face."

She took a deep breath and tapped a key. On the screen Gascan smiled.

"Burle, too? I sense an ambush. Should I be nervous?"

"We need to jump ahead the schedule for our rig, Peter. We also need it delivered."

"COD, huh? That means sending an escort vehicle. My price goes up. Why the change?"

"We'll pay the extra," said Lena. "Some circumstances have arisen that make it difficult for us to send a pickup. We'd actually like two trucks, in case we ever run into scheduling problems again."

Gascan nodded. "Scheduling problems. I see. You wouldn't be short a large quantity of copper wiring, would you?"

"What?" Lena felt Burle's hand on her shoulder. "Uhm, excuse me for moment, Peter." She cut audio and visual. "Copper wire? I don't get it."

Burle tipped his head at the screen. "Part of the shipment from Drum East included copper wire. He knows, Lena. He knows we don't have any rigs. I'll take over from here."

Lena keyed on sound and picture, then slid her chair sideways to make room for the chief of stores.

"Were you in on this, Gascan? You a thief and a murderer, too?"

Gascan wasn't taken aback by the accusation. If anything, his smile grew wider. "Burle? Whatever happened to your exceptional bartering skills? I've no idea what you're talking about. All I know is Victor Shangly contacted me with some serious buying power. I just put two and two together."

"I suppose he had some tool bits to offer as well? Maybe some ammunition?"

"He didn't mention any ammunition. I suppose that's something else you have to worry about. That information comes free. It's none of my business where he came by his fortune. All I do is provide hard to find items for trade."

"How did he contact you?" burst in Lena. "Does he have satellite capability now?"

"Now that information will not be free. I'll tell you what. Two trucks, extra fuel, the answer to your question and rush delivery, all for the low, low price of…"

"Ridiculous!" said Sid, slamming his fist on Burle's desk. "Dr. Patel and all his pharmaceutical equipment? Is he out of his mind?"

"He knows we're over a barrel here," said Burle. "He's pretty much cornered the local market on fuel, now he wants to own the drugs as well."

"And he thinks we'll trade our doctor for a pair of trucks."

"Why not? We traded one of ours for an electrician. There's more, Sid. Lena talked to a few other people. D'Abo beat us to them. Apparently everyone within earshot has been informed that if they trade us a rig for anything, they don't get anymore gas."

Sid's eyes narrowed. "An embargo? He put an embargo on us? And the others have agreed? After all we've–"

"They need gas, Sid. Everyone needs gas."

The Boss paced for a few moments. "Old friend, once we take care of Shangly, we should pay Gascan a visit."

"With what? You got a tank hiding somewhere I don't know about? Even if you did, Gascan's got a couple of howitzers sitting topside. I'm sure he still has shells for them."

"And he won't trade for anything else?"

"Nope. Harpreet and the lab, or nothing."

"No deal."

"I know. So what do we do now?"

"Wait, Beverly, don't disconnect." Lena had failed to find anyone she could contact that hadn't already placed themselves under Peter D'Abo's thumb.

"I'm sorry, Lena, I can't help you."

"When you needed a rig, we helped you out."

"Don't try to guilt me. Noah Thurlow was a valuable member of our community. It was a fair trade. By the way, tell him Bacon and everyone say hello. I forgot to tell you that earlier. Goodbye, Lena."

The chief of communications threw her headphones down and stood, almost falling over. Her mind and body did an amazing job of redistributing weight to accommodate for one leg when two were expected. Lena sat down again and grabbed her prosthetic from the desktop. She'd removed it earlier to rub her stump, which always itched when she was upset. There was no point in trying Gascan again. He'd made his position very clear. D'Abo had always been mercenary in his trading, but it surprised her that he'd be so willing to profit by the Pit's misfortune. The fact that October and her transport team had been murdered didn't bother him one bit. Sid had traded hard when he had to, but he'd never considered an embargo, never mind enforcing one. It occurred to her that even if they did recover their truck from Shangly, Gascan might hold onto his twisted trade scheme, demanding the doctor for gas instead of vehicles.

It won't last, she thought. *Sooner or later someone will need something from us more urgently than they need fuel. No, it won't last, but right now, we're in trouble.*

"Any luck?" asked Caps, bringing her another mug of tea, also with milk.

"None. Thanks, but I've already had two cups."

"But this is the last of my milk in here."

"You drink it."

"I don't like milk in my tea."

Lena dropped her leg and hopped forward, wrapping her arms around Caps, pushing her head into his shoulder. He put the tea down and returned her embrace.

"It's okay," he said, stroking her hair, "we'll be fine. We've faced worse."

She pulled her head back, he kissed her forehead.

"Have you cried yet?" she asked.

"For October? Yes. I might again. Care to join me?"

"Okay."

Darcy watched the Hummer disappear into the distance. The boat, already inflated, looked completely out of place strapped to the top of the vehicle. Dusk wasn't for another hour, and the eastward sun blasted into the watchtower, making her shield her eyes with one hand.

"We'll have to get you some tinting," said Darcy.

"I've been saying that for years," said Chiu-Keung. His lean form was silhouetted in Darcy's peripheral. "Are we going to be attacked?" He'd had his orders to set up the 50 cal., clean it, load it and man it. It was in perfect working order, but he had less than seventy rounds for it. The northwest tower only had forty. On the field below, a pair of shielded tripods had been positioned by the gate, additional heavy machine guns. He had no idea how well supplied they were.

"I doubt it," said Darcy, hoping she wasn't telling a lie. "In any case, we'll be bringing a rocket launcher up here before nightfall. You'll get a watch partner. Any preferences?"

"Did Cass Owens transfer to security?"

"Yes. You want me to set you up in the middle of a crisis?"

"You said we weren't going to be attacked. I like her conversation. She sat with us at meals until recently. It gets boring up here."

"Cass is on cavern rotation. She switched with Patricia, got her job, got her post. Cass doesn't have any heavy weapons training. We don't have the rounds to give it to her."

"Fine, is Redge going to be topside?"

"Yes, but on a different shift."

"So what are my choices?"

"Collin, or me."

"Chief? I didn't know you felt this way."

"Don't flatter yourself, Chiu. Think you can handle having your boss looking over your shoulder?"

"No offense, but I'll take Collin. At least we can tell dirty jokes."

"You'll have to tell me what this is about, Ted. I can't believe you're keeping something from me."

Dr. Odega's mouth tightened. He shut a drawer a little too forcefully, then turned to the Boss. "You know I don't like revealing things until I know."

"What do you want to do with it? I can't let you take it apart."

"I won't take it apart. I just want to turn it on."

"In the lab? To what end?" Sid turned his eyes on the door that lead to the cages. "You want to torture the animals."

"I don't want to–"

"Is it for kicks? Do you want to see blood coming out of their ears?"

"Sid! If you won't let me bring one here, let me work with one outside. It'll be worth it."

"That's not good enough. We went to a lot of trouble to hide the topside Mimis. I can't just have you setting up a workstation right next to one. We can't afford the exposure."

"HOW OFTEN–" Odega clamped his teeth together. When he spoke again, it was in a quieter voice. "How often do I ask you for things?"

"All the time."

"I mean big things. This is important, Sid. You just have to trust me."

"Are you going loopy on me? I've watched my senior staff crack up one by one over the years. Are you next?"

Odega's voice remained calm, though his eyes showed his outrage. "If Darcy asked you for a favour you'd give it to her immediately."

"How long have your hands been trembling like that?"

Odega shoved his hands in his pockets. "I haven't been getting much sleep lately."

"How much are you drinking, Ted? There's too much going on right now. I don't mind you and Harpreet having your little piss-ups once in a while, but if you're hitting the bottle every night..."

"Lock me outside then. At least I'll get to work near a Mimi."

Fatigue was getting the better of the Boss. He had no desire to keep talking in circles. "You can't have a Mimi, Ted. End of discussion."

Burle and Dr. Patel waited for Sara. She looked up from her cards, spooned some sugar from a small cup beside her into a pitcher in the middle of the table, and said, "I'm in. I'll take two."

Burle separated two cards from the top of the deck and passed them to her. "Bet's to you, Harp," he said.

"Raise three," Dr. Patel spooned his bet into the pitcher.

"Call," said Burle.

"Call." Sara put the last of her sugar in the pot.

"Three queens." Patel spread his cards out on the table. Sara groaned and threw her hand face down. Burle dropped his face-up.

"Burle, you've got nothing here," said Patel, pushing through Burle's hand. "You can't bluff by calling."

Burle got up. "We shouldn't be doing this, it's not right."

Dr. Patel sighed. "If she were here right now, she'd tell us to keep playing. She'd like it that we were saying goodbye this way. Sit down, Burle."

"I'm out of sugar," Sara said. "Why don't we all just get drunk?"

Eggerson blew lightly on his carving and examined its curves. It was almost October, but not quite. He'd never tried to carve her face before, and was finding difficulty in remembering it clearly. Though he'd seen her so many times, he'd never really paid attention to the little details. A small pile of wood shavings had accrued on the table before him. He used to do his whittling in his room or at his station, but he'd discovered that Devon from tanning came to the mess hall at nights to strum his guitar for a small, but appreciative audience. The tanner, like many of the people at Compton Pit, was multi talented, capable of making guitar strings from catgut. Neil set the head down and picked up a lock of Miranda's hair. It was the same colour as October's, at least he thought it was. When this puppet was finished, both its legs would be straight and slender and it would sit on a shelf in his room, part of a permanent collection that included Eggerson's late wife, Princess Diana of Wales, and Travis Jones.

"That's good work you're doing there," said Darcy. He hadn't heard her approach. Before he could say anything, Devon called out to her.

"Darcy, come sing with me."

"I'm not in the mood."

There were a few murmurs of disappointment from the musician's audience.

"There's no better time for it, Chief. C'mon."

Darcy moved around the table and took a place next to Devon. He strummed the first few chords, and she started, recognizing the piece.

Worlds change and time moves on, everything we knew is gone,
takes a lot to keep a body moving.
Watch the trees as they pass by, no point in wondering why, it's a
matter of picking life when choosing.

Money, it can't buy a thing, I don't want no diamond ring,
give me peace to close my weary eyes.
Someone wake me when it's done, when there is no need to run,
when Summer brings only empty skies.

Devon's voice joined in on the chorus, adding his baritone to her alto.

Far away from tooth and claw, out of reach of cougar's paw,
underneath the stony ground, we'll find our home again.

Darcy and Devon sang two more versus, then the security chief excused herself. The song was of the tanner's own composition. It was better than most of the songs he wrote, and the lonesome tune made up for what Eggerson considered to be only fair lyrics at best. Nevertheless, their harmony had released something in the former toy maker, some last rope that held back grief. Not for October, specifically, but for the overall loss, for Lorraine Wilson, for Susan Thomlin, for children that would never come.

The mattress rocked gently as Cass slowed to an easy, swaying motion. Noah sat upright, clinging to her torso, losing himself in her arms, her breasts, her hair.

"Noah…Noah…" she gasped into his ear, "this is how everyone should mourn."

18. A Change in Plans

They unloaded the boat at midday. It was about an hour to the prison by water. Norman would stay with the vehicle while the other four took their trip. The worst part was the boat would only take them one way. They'd have to stash it or trash it, and make their way back on foot.

"This plan sucks!" said Senna, trying to scratch her nose through her net. The gloves made it even clumsier.

"I think it'll be fun," Seth said, pushing the boat with his boot. "It's been a long time since I've gone whitewater rafting."

Toffee looked up and down the river. "Okay. Get our little surprise."

Seth removed a case from the back of the Hummer.

"What's that?" asked Daniel.

Toffee grinned through his mesh. "Bypasses if Shangly's wired his bridge. A couple of our own explosives if he hasn't."

"This wasn't part of the plan. The Boss said recon only."

"So he can fire me when we get back. Let's go."

Daniel grabbed Toffee's arm. "Wait! No contact. Those were the orders. We go, we look. That's it."

"Take your hand off me." Quiet, so quiet.

Daniel pulled his hand back. "I won't let you do this. You overestimate yourself."

"Do I now?"

Seth stepped in between them. "Cool it! Daniel, we'll set the charges if there's an opportunity. Otherwise, we keep our heads down."

Daniel was appeased, for the moment at least. He stepped back.

"Good choice," Seth could hear the grin in Toffee's voice. "You should wait until Darcy's around for our little showdown, that way she can see just what a loyal dog you are."

Daniel was fast, he swung his fist from the hip as he lunged forward. Toffee was faster. The second of security could feel blood trickling down his face as he picked himself up off the ground.

"Attempted assault on a superior officer. Be a good boy and I'll leave that out of my report." Toffee got in the boat.

Seth moved close to Daniel. "Forget it. We've got a job to do. If you have to, wait until we get home. Even then, forget it."

"Thanks for the advice." Shame burned his cheeks.

"Act like a boy, get spanked like a boy," Senna said under her breath.

Norman had shrunk to a few inches high when a bend in the river made him disappear from view. The current was strong, but not dangerous. The journey would become much more interesting in all too short a time.

"OH I HATE THIS!" Senna's scream was barely audible above the roar of water. The prow of the boat rose a full six feet before crashing down again. All of the boat's occupants were drenched. Water glued mesh to skin, making everyone look like dishevelled bank robbers with nylons for masks. While gripping tightly to the rope, Seth attempted to check the plastic covering of their equipment. The boat heaved starboard and fishtailed. In front, Toffee held his position firm, kneeling forward, his artificial hand clamped to one rope, his real hand clinging to another. He took the deluge full on, like some hero out of Greek mythology.

"YOU'RE GETTING A REAL BUZZ OUT OF THIS, AREN'T YOU?" Seth yelled. A blast of water hit him in face, filling his mouth. The boat heaved port, lifted, then slammed down again. *He's doing this on purpose,* Seth realized. *He's deliberately making the ride rougher.* Another lift and drop. Daniel felt like a giant had kicked his backside. A huge rock loomed ahead. At the last possible moment, Toffee heaved on his ropes and the boat turned. The back end caught the rock, setting the boat to spin. For a gut-wrenching moment, the boat was airborne. The landing nearly tossed Senna into the water, then the gyrations slowed and the four calmly floated, aft first, down the river.

Toffee rolled onto his back and rested his head against the prow. His posture was that of a man on vacation, without a care in the world.

"Glad that's over," said Seth. "Who needs to vomit?"

Senna pulled herself into a more upright position. "Not me. I'm too skinny already."

Daniel needed to, but he wouldn't. He refused to give Toffee the satisfaction.

"This is the easy part," said the chief of the hunters. "The walk back won't be as much fun."

They had no choice in the matter. The river would get them in close to the prison, but they had no idea how much cover there would be. The current only went one way and they didn't have an outboard for the boat. It didn't matter anyway. The waterfall they jumped was only three or four feet high, but utterly impassable for a return journey. It could be they could just crouch for a while, but odds were they'd have to bellycrawl for a klick or more.

Seth pointed at a formation of rock. "There's our landmark. Get ready."

As the boat hit the next curve, Toffee and Seth guided the boat to shore with small, plastic paddles. They jumped out, and pulled the raft up and out of the water.

"So do we hide it?" asked Senna.

"Are we really going to come back for it?" Toffee pulled his knife and cut a long gash along the side of the boat. "Takes too long to deflate it the other way."

Daniel kept watch as the other three stamped and jumped on the boat. Senna was taking particular pleasure in putting boots to her vehicle of torment. When the erstwhile raft was flat, they buried it.

After checking his charges, Seth loaded them into a backpack and swung it over his shoulder. The ammunition looked dry enough. They all carried sidearms, only Toffee had a rifle.

Seth gestured down the river. "The bridge should be half a klick that way."

They climbed the embankment, both relieved and perturbed to find quite a bit of scrub at the top. It would make hiding from people easier. It would make dodging teeth a lot harder.

Toffee took the point, Seth next with Daniel bringing up the rear. They all had their guns out. The problem with being out in the open was that even if you were downwind of some things, you were always upwind of others.

A small bird—a thrush—landed on a branch in front of Toffee.

"What the hell do you want?"

It dove into his face. The hunter managed to jerk his head aside but the bird's beak tore through his mesh and into his cheek. He grunted and grabbed the bird, crushing it one-handed.

"I hate birds." He drew them up short.

Seth pulled a first aid kit from his bag.

"Make it quick," said Toffee.

The hunter second dabbed alcohol on a pad and wiped Toffee's cheek through the hole in his mesh. "We need to patch your mask."

"No time. Damn, that stuff burns."

They moved ahead. The brush ended abruptly. From where they were, they could see the bridge, and the top of the prison. The ground around for at least two hundred meters had been burned away.

Seth handed Toffee a pair of binoculars. The hunter surveyed the area. There was no safer vantage point.

"There goes our surprise attack. I can see the back road. I count three...four guard boxes. I don't know if there's anyone in them."

"Can we make the bridge?"

"No chance. We can make the ridge, though."

They doubled back, swinging up and around. The scrub had been burnt back from the top of the ridge as well.

"See anybody?" asked Daniel, wishing for his own pair of binoculars.

"No. You two stay here. Seth, let's eat some dirt."

Toffee and Seth bellycrawled to the edge. Dry earth sucked greedily at the moisture in their clothes. By the time they reached their destination, a film of dust covered them head to toe. From the precipice, Fenwick Prison spread out below them.

The prison had been built in 1936, designed by an architect hand-picked by Judge Arthur Fenwick. There was no doubt as to what the structure's purpose was. Large blocks of gray stone massed together to form a building that screamed despair long before its first tenant ever arrived. The outer wall was overshadowed only by three high towers from within. Barbed wire stretched across the top, as if anyone could ever climb those walls in the first place. At its peak,

Fenwick Prison housed over six hundred inmates. It was decommissioned and scheduled for demolition in the year of the Change. Those walls long outlived the man who'd signed the order. There wasn't a single break that Toffee could see. The only way in was across the bridge, and through the main gate.

"Do you see the rig?" asked Seth.

Toffee handed the binoculars to his second. "Far corner. I think that's it."

Within the ring of magnification, Seth could make out the top of a large vehicle, just past the prison wall. Toffee slapped the binoculars down.

"Hey!"

"I saw a light spot on the wall. We're reflecting all over the place. Let's go."

As they turned a person stepped out of the brush. He or she carried a shotgun, and while similarly apparelled as Toffee, there was a raggedy, mismatched quality to the gear.

"Who the fuck…?" It was a man's voice.

Senna appeared from behind and drove her knife through the back of his neck. The point made a tent under the mesh as it pushed out through where the man's Adam's apple would be. He gurgled, then fell.

"Come on!" Toffee did a crouching run to the foliage. They dragged the man into the bushes and did a quick search. Seth pocketed the man's shells, but left the gun. Daniel cut a leafy branch and crawled to the edge, then slinked backwards, sweeping his makeshift broom to eradicate any evidence of passage.

Senna sat with her back against a tree, not saying anything.

"Been a while since you've had to kill someone, hasn't it," Toffee said, not unsympathetically. She nodded.

"Wouldja look at what this guy did to his own face?" Seth had pulled the net-helmet off. Large fangs were tattooed, descending from a bald head. A second set of fangs came up from either side of his chin. It looked as a if something was swallowing his head from behind.

"Let's make his wish come true." Toffee took up Senna's knife from where it lay on the ground and split the man open from throat to groin. The wet, tearing noise and smell that followed made Daniel's gorge rise again.

"We're gone. Looks like we don't get to hit the bridge after all. Happy, Daniel?"

"Do you think he was up here alone?" asked Senna.

"We'd know by now by if he wasn't."

They waited until they heard the sound of snarling animals from where they left the body.

"Just leave a body anywhere in the woods," said Seth, " and let the teeth dispose of the evidence. The Mafia could have used this."

"How do you know they don't?" Toffee pushed branches aside and led them back to the river.

"Any ideas?" asked Seth.

"Short of waiting for Odega to figure out how to get a bomber in the air, no."

19. Housekeeping

Sid waited until everyone was seated. "Lena, you start."

"The good news is Gascan's embargo only applies to rigs. Apparently people can still trade other stuff to us. The bad news is…Burle?"

"Hmmph, make me tell them, huh? With everyone delivering, our costs go up. Plus the word's out that we're in a bind. I'm sure people will take advantage of that. We took a big hit losing the cargo from Drum East. There were a lot of raw materials in there we needed. We can take care of ourselves for now, but as far as export is concerned…it's like starting all over again."

Sid let his head fall back against his chair. "All from losing one convoy. I'd forgotten how precarious our position really was. Let's get the little things first. Sara?"

Dr. White gave the Boss a sarcastic smile. "Little things? I like that. I'm fine on my end as long as nothing breaks down. My share of the export will still arrive on time, I just hope it doesn't rot before everyone else gets their ass in gear."

"Roshi?"

"Need new cookware. Some things burnt! Black! You get my pots from bastard Shangly or you taste the difference. You see! People won't be happy."

"Eggerson?"

"I'll get by. Don't worry about me."

"Harpreet?"

"Same as Sara, for now. What we were going to buy after processing some of that cargo…one month, maybe six weeks at the most, well, the drug store will have some empty shelves."

"Noah?"

"I'm fine as long as there's no major disasters."

"What would that constitute?" asked Caps. "A light burning out? Boss, there were a lot of things on that convoy I needed. The car from Underbel needs a serious brake job. I'm a hair from taking it out of service. The underbody is pretty banged up, too. The hunters' vehicles need refits just about every time they come back, especially since Chief Drive-It-Into-The-Ground took over. I guess I can handle things for about as long as the two doctors can."

"Burle?"

The stores master waved a sheaf of papers at Sid. "Where do you want me to start? We're low on ammo, especially if you're going to start a war. We've got no bulbs to fill, part of our main stock and trade, I don't need to remind you. The convoy from the coast is due sometime next month and if we don't figure something out, we won't have our end of the trade. We've diversified too much, setting up complex deals like we have…you ever line up dominoes when you were a kid? A month and half, then we're in trouble. If we get our rig back from Shangly, that's a different story."

"We'll need to hit him soon," said Darcy, "before he can pawn off everything he took from us. I say we strip the place, make up our losses from their stuff."

"Wait a minute," Dr. White said. "What about the scavengers, what do we do about them?"

"We're just going to take care of Shangly," said Lena. "Right?"

Caps snickered. "Yeah, and if you just shoot the lead wolf, the rest of them run away."

Lena gave the mechanic a reproachful look. "So what's your suggestion? Kill all of them?"

Caps shrugged.

The senior staff waited for an answer from Sid. The Boss held his tongue.

"No," said Sara. "We can't just wipe them all out. That's razing a settlement you're talking about. Not one we've always gotten along with, but they are a legitimate settlement. We can't punish them all for the crime of a few."

"Could we recruit them?" asked Noah. He flinched from the glares he received. "Sorry, that sounded stupid, even to me."

"So?" Sara's eyes burned into Sid.

"So we wait until Toffee gets back, then we decide."

"But whatever we decide," said Caps, "it's a shopping spree at Fenwick Prison, right?"

"Yes, Richard, it's a shopping spree."

"What is it from there you want so badly?" Dr. Patel asked.

"All their tattoo gear. I can see the sign now," Caps spread his arms wide. " 'Scagling Ink: finest tattoos in the Pacific Northwest.' They'll come from miles around."

"Do you know how to do that?" asked Noah.

"How hard can it be? I'll practice on the cows."

"No you don't!" Roshi said indignantly. "You infect them. Make milk poison!"

The Boss cleared his throat. "Anything else major? Might as well hit me with it while I'm in the mood."

"Are we having a burial for the transport team?" asked Lena.

"No. The only remains we have…had, were October's. It would be a disservice to the rest of them. There will be a service tomorrow night for those that wish to attend. Could someone please put that on the board."

"Consider it done, Boss," said Caps.

"That's it then. Meeting adjourned."

Caps stuck the notice to the board outside the mess hall. The note read; "Memorial Service: Thursday, 20:00, Holy Ground."

"What does Holy Ground mean?" asked Noah.

"It's what we call the…uh…I'll have to show you. Follow me."

They took a corridor that turned off just before reaching Burle's office from the mess hall. At the end was the fanciest door Noah could remember seeing. It was of a dark, burnished wood. Scroll work trimmed the edges of the door, and a feather-like pattern spread out from a central point.

"Neat, huh? This was originally going to be Russ Compton's office while at the hotel. He had it furnished before most of the place was even built. We've redecorated, of course." Caps pushed the door open and ushered Noah in.

Six long wooden benches stood on faded blue carpet, at the front and either side were curtains the same colour as the floor. Carved woodwork and brass fittings marked gaps between the curtains.

"This room is huge!" Noah gasped. "I could fit my room in here five, six times."

"Tell me about it. There was a lot of fighting in the beginning about this place. Some people figured the space could be put to much better use, me included. So what are you?"

Noah examined the edge of one bench. Scratched into the wood were the words; "why why why".

"Huh? What do you mean, 'what am I?' "

"Are you Catholic?" Caps pulled a golden rope that hung from the ceiling. The curtains opposite the door slid open. Behind them hung a large wooden crucifix. The carving of Jesus captured exquisite agony. "For those of you who like your prayer guilt free…" he spun the crucifix. Reversed, it was a simple cross, bereft of weeping saviour.

"No, I'm not a Catholic."

"Are you a child of Moses, then?" Another curtain parted, behind lay a wooden podium and a polished oak cabinet. A six-pointed star adorned the front of the cabinet. "And before you ask, yes, there really is a Torah in here. Don't ask me how we got it."

"A Torah? I don't know what that is."

"Not a Jew. Okay, here's a long shot…" The last curtain parted. A carved statue about three feet high sat on a platform with candles and incense burners. The statue was of a serene fat man, sitting cross-legged.

"Hey, I know him. That's Buddha."

"Right in one. So, worship him much?"

"No. I don't worship anyone."

"Except Cass, right? So this is it. It's a temple, a mosque, a church or a synagogue, depending on when you're here. That's why we just call it Holy Ground. The last time I was here, it was for a wedding. Sam's wedding. I don't worship anyone either." He crossed to the crucifix and turned it so Jesus once again cast his pain across the room. "You hear me? I don't worship anyone." He gave one of the crosspieces a shove. The crucifix rotated slowly in place.

"Who leads the services?" asked Noah, sniffing an incense plate by Buddha's bare feet.

"No one really. The Boss performs the marriages. There've been five since I've been here. Everything else…We had a Rabbi, but he was also a hunter. He gave up on Kosher killing, never mind, it's a Jewish thing…compassion to the animal…so instead he tried to bring game down on the first shot. The bear that got him wasn't so compassionate. We had an ordained minister, he died of natural causes. We had a Catholic priest, he killed himself. I guess he forgot his own rules. Heh."

"I don't get it."

"Catholics believe suicide is the express route to hell. It's probably a pretty short road from here, though."

"Did you used to be something?"

"I used to believe in a higher power, but I was never into organized religion. Lena can't make up her mind. She's half Christian, half Buddhist. I keep saying she should get Buddha on the cross, but Happy Jack over there is so fat he'd probably fall off. Don't tell her I told you that joke, she'd kill me."

"Caps, are we at war?"

The crucifix had stopped spinning, Caps gave it another shove. "I guess that's one way to put it."

Noah sat on the bench closest to him. "What happens now? Nothing like this ever happened at Underbel."

"I should have brought my pipe. I love smoking up in here. I don't know, buddy. We've had problems with a few people over the years, but never before...Shangly and his crew have it coming, but be glad you won't have to know most of the details."

"So I won't have to go out and fight?"

"You? No way. Not me, either. It'll be the hunters and security, except Darcy. She'll want to go, but the Boss won't let her. And some people who are, uh, more expendable."

"Well, I'm glad Darcy won't be going."

"You still stuck on her? What with all the lovin' you're getting from slim, trim and horny? Wassa matta with you, boy?" Caps flicked Noah in the head with a finger.

"I love the sex. Wow, do I ever love the sex, but Cass...I don't think she's that caring a person."

"What gave you that impression?"

"She's mentioned past boyfriends that died. She made it seem like, stubbing a toe or something."

Caps flopped down onto the bench beside Noah. "Has she told you how many boyfriends she's lost?"

"No. I know there's two."

"Nine. In the last six years. She came here and prayed the first few times, but eventually reality and bad luck knocked the faith right out of her. She's been celibate 'till you showed up. You're just what she needs."

Noah puffed up his chest. "You mean young and good-looking?"

"Nope, breathing...and restricted to base. But you're still carrying a torch for the sheriff, huh?"

"I...could you close those curtains please?" The crucifix had stopped again, Jesus side out. Caps closed the drapes. "Thank-you. Who do you tell about these talks of ours? This is private right? Just between you and me?"

"Yeah. You bet."

"I can't stop thinking about her. Bacon would have said I had a crush, but here I am sleeping with Cass, and still thinking about Darcy. It gives me a headache."

Caps slapped Noah's knee. "That, my friend, is the definition of women."

"You weren't serious about that tattoo stuff were you? I sure as hell don't want one."

"Relax. I don't want the gear, I want all that ink. They must have buckets of it."

"Are we going to kill all of the scavengers? Is that really what's going to happen?"

"If you want my guess...no, forget it. I'll go with what I said earlier, be glad we won't know most of the details."

Darcy watched Dr. Patel rewrap the arm. She was relieved when the last of Connie's welts disappeared under white bandage. One of the senior security officers, Conrad never had the brains to be considered a leader. The last of his dark hair had been conquered by gray two years previous, but he still had most of the muscle that had come from hauling cable for the movie companies. Darcy had never seen him so weak. A dull redness showed in his cheeks, and his right arm would be useless for a while yet.

"How many stings do you think you took?"

"I lost count at eleven. I don't know, twenty-five? Thirty? Too many."

"And you won't go out with a rip in your suit again, will you?" Dr. Patel chided.

"I guess I won't be invited to the party at Fenwick Prison, huh?"

Darcy laughed. "No, and consider yourself lucky. I guess you probably want to take a flamethrower and burn every nest for miles."

"Nope. Actually, I like wasps."

"What?"

Dr. Patel gathered his supplies and moved towards the plastic curtain that separated his office from the infirmary. "I've heard this story too many times."

"I need to talk to you, so don't go anywhere," said Darcy.

"Yes, ma'am." The curtains whispered as he passed through.

"So go on, why do you like wasps?"

"Well, let me start by telling you this isn't the worst I've been stung. The worst was on New Wilderness Day."

"Excuse me for calling you a liar at the start of your story, but the stingers didn't start in till a few days later. I was there, you know."

Connie pulled his bandaged arm to his chest and plucked at the gauze. "Hush, girl. Let a man tell his story."

"Girl?"

"Out there, you're my boss, but in here, I'm thirty years older than you are."

Darcy leaned forward and kissed his forehead. "Tell me your story."

"I was working the cable truck on this crappy film called Legend of the Jade Idol."

"Yuck."

"Tell me about it. It was pretty high budget, but a Raiders rip-off all the way. The producer was nuts for animal stuff. He had critters I'd never seen before. Some of these things had no business being in the same place, but willing suspension of disbelief, right? Like cobras pop out from behind fir trees every day of the week. He even threw in a wasp swarm. Here's the scene; our hero, Dirk Manly..." Darcy groaned as if on cue, "and the heroine, Stacy Curvington, are trapped in a Mayan temple. Dirk steps on a loose stone, and all these wasps come pouring out of the walls. 'Cause you know, them Mayans knew how to keep wasps alive in bare rock for thousands of years without food and drink." Conrad took a cup from beside the bed and sipped some water.

"And you were the stunt double for this?"

"Hell, no! I was lugging these boxes of wasps around. They were made out of wood frames and steel mesh."

"We've got a couple in animal research. I know what you mean."

"We must have had about a dozen of the things. So here I am standing there with who knows how many wasps in my arms, and I hear someone start screaming."

"Was it Dirk?"

"No, but he got it too. It was one of the animal handlers. Buncha monkeys…well, you know. I'm just standing there watchin' it happen, I don't know what the hell to do. Then other folk start screaming and I see a lion, its name was Timmy, rip the innards out of one of the caterers. I'm lookin' around for a good place to run when one of the monkeys gets a look at me. We locked eyes, me and that little demon. I've knocked the tar out of guys bigger 'n me and never thought twice about it, but that little monkey scared the shit out of me."

"What did you do?"

"I remembered I had a box of wasps in my hands and I threw it at him. I missed, but the box broke and he jumped away, then he chittered at his buddies. They looked at him, then they looked at me. I ran right into the stack of boxes, broke every one of them. The wasps went nuts. I got stung everywhere. They buzzed all over the place."

"How did you survive?"

"Well, they weren't after me, they was just scared that's all. Now I didn't know that at the time, and maybe the monkeys didn't either, but they sure knew they weren't coming anywhere near the swarm while there were other people to pick off."

"So you ran?"

"Don't know. I woke up the next day in the back of a truck, feeling kinda like I do right now. Me and twenty other people made it off that set alive, out of a crew of over sixty. If it wasn't for the wasps, those monkeys would have torn me limb from limb. Even after this, me and the wasps got ourselves a deal; they don't come near me when I'm sleeping, and I don't burn them out unless I have to."

Darcy pushed herself off the side of the bed. "How come you never told me this story before?"

"I thought I had."

She patted his unstung hand. "Rest up, Connie. I want you back in uniform ASAP."

"Place just falls apart without me, right?"

"No, I never want to hear you call me 'girl' again."

She took Connie's cup with her, promising a refill before she left. Her subordinate had taken stings to the chest and legs as well. He was lucky the wasps weren't able to make it past the tight collar of his net-helmet. Dr. Patel was doing an inventory of his sutures when she exited the infirmary.

"How prepared are we?" she asked. "For real."

Patel shook his head. "Not good. Under normal circumstances, fine. If a van load of bullet-ridden people shows up here, not good at all. You're in this pile." He patted a stack of cards. There were four stacks in all.

"What are those?"

"Blood types. I'll expect a lineup of donors if I need it. You'll help with that, right?"

Darcy picked up her stack and flipped through it idly. "I don't think we'll need to force anybody." She stopped at a card that was newer than the rest. "So me and the sun boy are the same blood type. Don't tell him that, he'll think it means we have something in common." Noah's card moved to the bottom of the stack. "Maybe the Boss will have you along. Seth is about the closest thing we have to a combat medic, and it was never his specialty."

"What, you mean do a house call on the slaughter? I charge extra for that." Dr. Patel suddenly beamed and snapped his fingers. "That's it! Maybe D'Abo didn't have such a bad idea after all!"

Darcy's eyes narrowed. "What are you talking about?"

"I never go anywhere! Once in a while a special patient is transported here, but I never go to them. I could do rounds, people would trade for that. Most places have a doctor of sorts, but there aren't that many surgeons available. Or even better yet, instead of lobotomising an animal and shipping it off, I could go places and drill what they've already captured for themselves. I don't need a big truck for that."

Darcy dropped the stack and picked up another. "That's the best idea I've heard all week. Sid will need convincing, but he'll go for it. Hey, look at this. Caps and Toffee are blood brothers. If crater-nose comes back needing some plasma, plug the two of them right into each other. I'm sure it'll be a bonding experience worth remembering."

"Oh yes, giving CPR to Caps after removing an IV stand from his rectum is exactly what I need to brighten my day."

20. open Door Policy

Noah awoke at the first heavy knock, but the door opened before he had a chance to grant entry. Darcy and Daniel stood at the door.

"Up," said Darcy. It was an order, no question about it.

"Sure, what time is it?" He fumbled for his watch on the table beside him. Burle had signed it out to him the day before. It was a wind-up, as were all the watches. Its face was scratched and the wrist strap was worn, but it was his.

"Never mind the time," said Daniel, stepping into the room and pocketing the watch.

Noah stopped pulling the sheet aside just short of exposing his nudity. "Uh, could you give me a minute?"

"No." Darcy held herself rigid. There was thinly veiled accusation in her eyes.

Noah braced himself and got out of bed. Daniel took a single step back, giving Noah room, but not that much. He was glad Cass had pulled night watch and wasn't with him—that would have been embarrassing. He stole a glance at Darcy to see if she was checking him out. She had her eyes fixed on him alright, but not in a nice way.

"What's going on?" He pulled on his coveralls.

"You'll find out soon enough," replied Daniel. "You won't need those."

Noah hesitated, then dropped his right boot.

"This way." Daniel took his arm, firmly, but not painfully.

"Where are we going?"

"I don't want to hear anymore of your questions," said Darcy, taking the lead.

Noah padded barefoot down the corridor, guided by Daniel's grip. The corridor was vacant except for them. His mind raced over anything he could have done wrong. He'd falsified an entry in the battery log for Cass, "vibrator" not being something he wanted to record permanently. Certainly that didn't merit this kind of treatment.

He was led through the mess hall, where Toffee sat drinking coffee with Seth. The chief of the hunters looked speculatively at the photovoltaic engineer as they passed.

It was the second time Noah had been to the security office. This time he got a much better look at the cells. There were two of them, barely wide enough for a person to lie down in. Daniel pushed him into the first.

"Sit down," said Darcy.

Noah sat on the cot. Daniel left and was replaced by the balding security officer Noah had seen that last time he was here.

"We haven't been formally introduced," he said. "I'm Purtricil. Call me Purty."

"Uh, thanks…what…"

Darcy leaned in close. The veil was gone, her face held pure contempt. "How long have you been working for Victor Shangly?"

"What?" The question was so outrageous, it was almost surreal.

"So you're deaf as well as stupid?"

Purty placed a hand on Darcy's shoulder and pulled her back gently. "Noah," he said, "it'll make it easier on all of us if you just come clean."

A light gleamed in Noah's mind. "I know what this is! You're hazing me! It's a little late isn't it?"

Darcy slapped him so fast he didn't realize it had happened until he saw her hand pull back. A red warmth spread through his cheek.

"Hey! What was that for?" Noah started to stand but the chief of security shoved him back down.

"I think," said Purty, "we'd all be more comfortable if you just stayed sitting."

"How long have you worked for Victor Shangly?" Darcy asked again.

Noah brought his hand up to his cheek. "I don't know what you're talking about! I'd never even heard of the guy before I came here."

Purty sat on the bed a few inches from Noah. "So, he didn't contact you until after your transfer?"

Noah looked back and forth between the two security officers. "You're not joking! You think I've done something. What do you think I've done?"

"How does he contact you?" asked Darcy. "How do you send messages to him?"

"I told you, I…"

Darcy bent over at the waist, putting her nose almost in contact with Noah's. "Very convenient that everything started just when you got here, isn't it? Asking all your little questions. It's nice that you told us about the first roadblock. I'll bet you and that porkchop fellow put it there."

"How could we have…wait a minute. You think Bacon did something, too? He would never…"

Purty eased Darcy back again. "Noah, we're not interested in your friend right now. We're interested in you."

Darcy stepped back and folded her arms across her chest as she leaned against the bars. "Your friend's in really big trouble if we have to go all the way to Underbel to get him. If that's where he really is."

"That's right, Noah," Purty's voice was gentle. "You can help him if you help us."

Daniel returned and handed a small solar panel to Darcy. "That's about it," he said. "No radio equipment."

Darcy tilted the panel in her hand so it caught the light from the ceiling and reflected it directly into Noah's eyes. "What were you doing with this? Going to give it to your boss so he can see what kind of cells we have? Or are you partners? Do you think he's going to try to rescue you?" She lowered her voice. "You're on your own, sun boy. You're screwed."

"I HAVEN'T DONE ANYTHING!" His mouth was dry, but he could feel tears starting to well up in the corners of his eyes. He turned to Purty. "Please. I don't know what this is about. You have to believe me."

Purty looked deeply into Noah's imploring face, then nodded. "I believe him," he said to Darcy.

The security chief sighed, then squeezed her lower lip between a thumb and finger. "I do, too. Sorry, Noah. You were the second most obvious suspect. Well, third. Purty, take him back to his room."

"Thanks." Relieved gratitude was replaced by anger. "Hey, hold on! You slapped me. What's going on?"

"Tell him, Darcy," said Sid's voice, from the front office.

"Come on, Noah." She waved him up with a hand. Sid sat on one of the desks. Daniel was there, as well as two other people in khaki that Noah didn't recognize. Darcy sat at her desk and motioned to an empty chair.

"Shangly, or some of his crew, was in the Pit last night," she said. "They came in through the caverns. The door to Gershwin's room was open. Someone let them in. They must have been scared off by Odega's dog."

"Odega's dog?"

"Dr. Odega was down there with Ghandi, that's the dog. It looks like the mutt took a chunk out of someone, there's blood leading to the caverns. It took a few tries to get her back into the cage that was there."

Noah was bowled over by this statement. "You mean the dog attacked someone, but not Dr. Odega? How?"

"We don't know. Odega's in a coma, he took a bad blow to the head. Ghandi turned normal soon after we got her into the cage, but for a while there, it looks like she actually protected him."

"How do you know it was Shangly?"

"We know."

Ice rippled down Noah's spine. "How did the intruders get past security?"

"Cassandra Owens was on duty. She's dead."

The way she said it, so matter-of-fact, she couldn't have known about Cass and Noah.

"Noah," the Boss said, "why don't you wait for me in the mess hall. Roshi's up, there'll be some early breakfast."

Noah rose and walked glumly out the door. His head ached. Cass is dead, I just saw her. Cass is dead, we made love before her shift. Cass is dead, Darcy thought I had something to do with it. Cass is…

"Come sit with us," said Toffee as Noah entered the mess hall.

He forced back tears, determined not to cry in front of the chief of the hunters.

"You get interrogated?"

"Yes. I can't believe–"

"Don't think you're so special, she grilled me first. She slap you?"

Noah touched his cheek. "Yes."

"It's a good move." The hunter turned his head to show a fresh bandage. "I took a bird hit, she opened it up again. Did that on purpose. So, you a traitor?"

"No. I can't believe she thought I was."

Toffee slapped him on the back, hard. "Neither can I, little man, neither can I. Shame about Cass Owens, she was a sweet little thing, wasn't she?"

Noah's eyes went wide. His teeth clamped together and his hands bunched into fists. He pushed back from the table and tried to keep his voice from quivering. "Excuse me, I have to go."

Seth also stood, giving Toffee a look of disbelief. "Yeah, me too."

"We toss rooms during breakfast," said Darcy. "Look for radio equipment, maps of the Pit. Daniel and I will handle the rooms for senior staff. Dismissed."

The security officers moved into the hallway, each of them eager to be the one who caught the spy.

"It could still just be luck on their part," said Sid, once he was alone with Darcy. "They took the key from Cass, and it's not that far to Gershwin."

"I don't believe that anymore than you do. They knew right where they were going. Someone told them everything. All Odega did was save them the trouble of breaking in. Cass's key was still on her."

"They might have put it back to keep us off guard. Information could have been tortured out of the transport team. We'd never know if it was."

"Only October knew about Gershwin. The cave opening was found after she left. We're limited to about twenty suspects, plus anyone they might have let a few things slip to. I can't believe we have a dog to thank for keeping them from doing…whatever it was they were going to do."

Sid moved from the relief desk to Darcy's. "You were a little hard on Noah, don't you think?"

"I…in hindsight, yes."

"Did you know he was sleeping with Cassandra?"

"Oh. No, I didn't. I owe the boy a bigger apology, don't I?"

"Yes, you do owe the *man* a bigger apology. I also question your choice as to who was the tough for this one."

Darcy put her head in her hands. "You're picking now to give me a lesson?"

"Best time is when the mistake is made. You've noticed his feelings towards you?"

"I've picked up on them. Okay, Lena told me. You're saying I should have been the sweet one with him."

"Yes. Never let an advantage slip by. The slap was too much."

"You didn't object to it with Toffee."

"I didn't see anything wrong with it in that case, though you could have used the other cheek. Did Noah's crush on you influence your decision after all?"

Darcy pursed her lips, then shook her head. "I guess it did. Why would he have a crush on me if he was...oh, Sid, why didn't somebody tell me? If Cass was his girlfriend and I...I'll worry about it later." At least she hadn't told him about the cuts on Cass's torso, or the duct tape across her mouth.

"Change the locks on the cavern door, and Gershwin's room, just to be safe."

"Yes, sir."

She'd wanted Toffee to be guilty. Denied that, she wanted Noah to be the one. She needed someone to blame, someone to punish. The convoy had been so far away, but this was a violation, a penetration of the Pit itself.

She searched Sid's room as a matter of procedure. Daniel would search hers for the same reason. Dr. Patel had a good supply of sugar stashed under his bed, and Caps was hiding some pot, but no surprises there. At the same time as she felt like she'd hunt until she found her prey, she was completely devoid of energy. She took a rest in a wooden rocking chair in Burle's room. Procedure, she was just following procedure. There was only one place in each room to really hide something. All the long term residents had discovered it, probably thinking they were the only ones. She pulled a screwdriver out of her pocket and went to the air vent in the wall beside Burle's bed. Toffee had a few things in his; a thick gold ring, a button made from a tooth, an American twenty dollar bill and some vials of a sticky yellow substance. She knew what those were without opening them. She'd been so sure she had the hunter this time. She'd grilled him for almost half an hour. She'd still be grilling him if Sid hadn't stopped her.

She left one screw in at the bottom of the grate to act as a hinge. Burle's stash was like the others—a few personal items, but nothing incriminating. She picked up a tarnished silver bracelet. Engraved on it was a caduceus—twin serpents wrapped around a sceptre. It was a medical alert bracelet. She hadn't seen one in over a decade. On the back was inscribed; "Jessica Campbell," and "Penicillin Allergy." She dropped the bracelet back in the shaft and picked up Rachel's wedding ring. It made her think of Lorraine. Too many widows. Someone was going to pay dearly.

The door opened and Daniel stepped in. "Nothing in Lena's room, not that she'd need it. Are we going to question her? She is the chief of communications, if anyone could be transmitting, it would be her."

"It's not Lena, it's not any of the senior staff. Find anything interesting in my room?"

"Apart from the spare chip for your shoulder, no."

Darcy swung the grate up and held it in place. "Don't you start, too. Here, screw this in."

She'd posted guards at the doors from the mess hall to the residential corridors. The other rooms would be searched, one by one, in teams of two. There'd be some contraband—booze, a little pot maybe—but nobody was going to be busted for that. Somewhere there would be a transmitter, though. There had to be.

"How is he?" Darcy asked, running her fingers down the tube that lead from an IV bag to Dr. Odega's limp arm.

Dr. Patel smoothed a hand across his friend's forehead. "Alive. That's all I can tell you. Vital signs are good. He could wake up any second. I'd kill for an X-ray machine."

"You've said that before. We do keep trying, you know. Does he know we're here?"

"I hope so." Dr. Patel leaned in close to Ted's ear. "How did you tame the dog, Ted? Who hit you?" There was no response. "When you wake up, I'll be here."

By a little after noon, each of the rooms and the barracks had been searched. Nothing germane to the case at hand was found. Darcy dispatched teams to search the lower level, as well as hiding places in the different work areas. It would take days, during which time the culprit, (Darcy couldn't allow herself to believe there was more than one person involved) could move or dispose of any radio equipment. The Pit was on lock down. No one was allowed in or out, save the security patrols. The cavern entrance had been resealed and the surrounded area searched. Nothing was discovered. Every person with direct knowledge of Gershwin or the cave entrance was questioned thoroughly. After the senior staff interrogations were complete, Darcy allowed Purty and Daniel to take over.

"More?" asked Lena.

Darcy nodded. Lena punched a button and the columns on the computer screen were replaced with almost identical columns.

"Every single transmission we've made is recorded in this log? Every signal we've received?"

"Yes. You asked that already."

"How many more screens are there?"

"How far back do you want to go?"

Darcy rubbed her eyes. She didn't know how Lena could stare at that screen for so long. "I don't know. I guess seven months should cover it."

"Then there's," some clicking followed, "thirty more screens."

"Could a transmission be left out of the log?"

"Not out of this one. It's my own log, supplemental to the standard one. I don't think anyone else even knows about it."

Darcy squeezed Lena's shoulder. "You're legitimizing yourself as a suspect."

"That's not very funny, Darcy."

"No, it isn't. I'm sorry. Give me the next screen."

Noah didn't even look up at her as she entered the workroom. He focussed intently on his computer screen, as if he could fathom the secrets of the universe from it. She briefly pondered talking to him, but decided it would wait until later.

"We've got to change some locks," said Darcy.

Eggerson got up and moved to a dull, gray tarp. He pulled the cloth aside to reveal a key cutting machine. Nestled beneath the table upon which the machine sat was a large cardboard box. The engineer leaned over and flipped up worn corrugated flaps.

"We have three locks left." One the main reasons for the honour system on most doors was simply for a lack of locking mechanisms. "How many do we need?"

"Two. The caverns and Gershwin."

Eggerson blew metal filings off the machine, placed a key in one slot and a blank in the other. "Well I suppose we would have needed to change Gershwin's lock anyway, if you wanted to make more keys. We're out of blanks for the lock on there now."

"I should have been informed of that. Wait a minute, how many blanks did we have for that key type?"

Neil checked a notation on the side of an empty box. "Four."

Darcy did a count in her head. She had a key, Sid had one, security possessed two that were kept careful track of, and Odega had cut one for himself after conning a master out of Purty.

"How many keys came with the lock originally?"

"Two. There's always two."

"Then we're missing a blank for Gershwin. Someone else cut a key. Eggerson, how many blanks do we have left for the cavern lock?"

"The one you had me cut for Noah was the last one. Hey, we should have one more of those, too."

It was like being punched in the gut. Darcy's realization knocked the wind out of her. Her legs weakened and she had to put her hand on the table to steady herself.

Eggerson reached out to her. "Are you okay, Darcy? What's wrong?"

"Chief of security to communications, chief of security to communications," Daniel's voice boomed from an intercom system used so seldom, most people forgot it was there.

At his desk, Noah jerked his head up. Eggerson started as well, then returned his attention to Darcy.

The chief of security pushed Neil's hand away. "I'll be alright, th-thanks."

"Uhm, if you say so. How many keys for each?"

"However many you think. Eggerson, I'll talk to you later."

Darcy turned and left the room. Once outside, she pushed her back against the wall and doubled over. A pain ten times more acute than her worst menstrual cramp twisted at her insides.

"Chief of security to communications, chief of security to communications." This time the voice was Lena's.

With a hand against the wall for balance, Darcy straightened, and forced herself to walk.

"Burle, come in please," Lena said into her mic, as Darcy entered. Daniel had on the second set of earphones. He leaned on the desk and his face was deadly serious.

"What's happening?" asked Darcy.

Lena skewed her earphones, keeping one ear covered while exposing the other. "Burle slipped out in the Pig before the lockdown orders were issued. He's out doing his stupid grave tending."

"What?"

Daniel held his hands up. "I just found out about it myself. Norman was on duty in the airlock. He knew Burle wasn't supposed to be allowed out by himself, but we've always ignored that order. He was afraid to tell me."

"Where are the patrols?"

Lena tapped her mic with a pencil. "One and two are nowhere near the cemetery. Three just came back in the new car."

Rage exploded in Darcy's chest, burning away the pain. She punched the button that activated the intercom. "Pool, this is Darcy. Load the new car, I'm taking it. Daniel, with me."

They ran to the motor pool. Caps had guns and net-helmets waiting for them. Darcy jumped in the driver's seat, Daniel got to his door as she started the engine. The chief of the pool had to jump out of the way as Darcy squealed backward. She gunned the engine as soon as the doors to the airlock were open wide enough.

"Chief, we could have sent someone else after him."

"Suit up."

"What do you know that I don't?"

Darcy wore the face of a demon as she glared at her second. They burned down the road. Darcy barely slowed at the T-junction, setting the car into a hard skid. She regained control and put pedal to the metal. The church hove into sight. The Pig was parked just outside the cemetery. Another vehicle, a wide jeep, was parked about forty feet from it. There was a flash of movement from behind a tombstone.

"Is that one of Shangly's?" asked Daniel incredulously. "How did they get past the patrols?"

Darcy slammed on the brakes, bringing the car to a screeching halt a few metres short of the Pig. As she opened her door, a bullet hole appeared in the metal by her head.

"Dogshit!" She slammed her door. Daniel opened his door and both of them crawled out through the passenger side. Another bullet struck the car as Darcy's feet cleared the running board.

Daniel pushed a net-helmet at her and popped his head up above the car. He pulled it down again just before a shot pinged off the roof.

"There's someone down, by the jeep," he said.

"Do you see Burle?"

"No."

"There's one behind the shed," called Burle's voice from the direction of the cemetery.

Darcy crept towards the front of the car. She cursed the shotgun and pushed it away from her. Daniel put his own down. The shed was out of the weapon's useful range. The chief of security drew her side arm, a 38 cal. Saturday Night Special. Not the greatest handgun, but easy to supply with ammunition.

"Come on out, boy," yelled Burle. "I'll shoot through the shed to get you! Might take three, four hits that way! Come out and die clean!"

Darcy saw Burle crouched behind a granite upright. His Lee Enfield held stiffly in his hands. Burle glanced at the car, then rose and put a bullet through the shed. There was no response.

"You wasted a lot of shots, boy!" called Burle. "You out?"

A hooded figure burst from the shed, arms swinging, legs pounding the ground. The person appeared unarmed.

"He's going for his jeep!" Daniel took up his shotgun and moved toward the back of the car.

The running man threw himself flat behind a row of headstones just as Burle let off another round.

Darcy stood and yelled at the chief of stores. "Hold your fire, we're taking him alive!"

"Darcy?" Burle waved his hand at her. "That you? He's got a gun, don't be fooled."

Darcy fired twice to keep their quarry's head down. Daniel moved from the car to the jeep. Darcy motioned to Burle to move to a flanking position. Daniel came up over the hood of the jeep and fired his shotgun at the ground near the stones.

"I surrender!" came a panicked voice.

The man stood, his hands held at his sides. Burle levelled his rifle.

"I SAID HOLD YOUR FIRE!" screamed Darcy.

Burle held the rifle up for a few more moments then let the barrel drop.

"On the ground," ordered Daniel, approaching the man warily. The man dropped to his knees. Daniel moved behind and struck him down with a blow to the head.

Darcy pulled the mic from her car. "CS to base."

"Base here." It was Sid. "What's going on out there?"

"We have a guest. Dee will bring him in, I'll follow with Burle in the Pig. CS out."

Daniel searched the man and found a roll of duct tape in one his pockets. He held the tape up for Darcy to see.

"Nice of him to bring that," she said.

The security second taped the man's hands behind his back, then yanked him to his feet. He pulled the net-helmet off. There were no wasps in the air, but Daniel might have pulled the man's head gear off even if there had been. The man looked to be in his late thirties, with narrow, cruel lips and completely bald except for a topknot of black hair.

"I know you," called Darcy. "You're Lot."

Lot smiled back. "You could get to know me better."

Daniel hit him in the back with the stock of the shotgun, then wrapped tape around his mouth.

"Take him away, Daniel. We'll be right behind you."

Lot was shoved into the car, after having his head dummied off the door frame. Daniel got in and started the engine.

Darcy approached Burle and took the rifle from his hands. "You tried to shoot again, didn't you? Lucky your gun was empty."

"No!"

"I heard the click, Burle." She raised her gun to the old man's head and wiped a tear through the mesh. "I should kill you right here."

21. Of Betrayal

Burle sat in the passenger seat of the Pig. His hands were bound together with a leather thong, but it was unnecessary. The old man had no fight in him, he slumped in the chair like an empty skinbag.

"How did you know?" he asked.

"Shut up, Burle."

"They said nobody would get hurt. They said..."

Darcy bit her lip. "Shut up, or you won't make it back to the Pit." She took up the mic. "CS to base."

"Base here," Sid was still on the mic.

"Have the motor pool clear. Only Purty and yourself. Over."

"Roger that."

Darcy waited until Purty had left with the prisoner before opening the door and motioning for Burle to step down from the Pig.

"What the hell?" exclaimed Daniel, spotting the stores master's bound wrists.

"He's the traitor," Darcy said to the Boss. "He's been in communication with Shangly. Sid, he cut a set of keys for them."

Sid looked from Darcy to her captive. "Burle, is this true?"

He'd never looked more ancient as he raised his eyes from the floor. "Yes, Sid. It was me. You won't understand, but I had no choice."

"Daniel," said Darcy, "clear the way to security. Let's not let anyone see this."

The security second was still off balance. "Yes, Chief."

"Thank you," said Burle.

"I'm not doing this for you," Darcy's voice was cold as the grave. "I'm doing this for everybody else."

Burle was kept in the motor pool for a few minutes. He wasn't questioned, nor did he try to speak. Darcy returned and led him to the main security office. She shut the door that led to the cells. Sid and Daniel sat by the second desk. Purty stood with his back to the main door, which had also been closed.

Darcy shoved Burle down into a chair. She reached into a pocket and withdrew a silver medical alert bracelet. "You always said you never found anything of Jessie's."

Burle looked at the bracelet. His eyes watered.

"She would have always worn this, you would have made sure of that. You sat with Lena during most negotiations, even conducted a few by yourself, so you knew just about everything about the communications system, even her backup log. Didn't you?"

Burle nodded.

"You cut keys when I gave you my key ring that time in the caverns, that's why you took so long getting back."

Burle nodded again.

Darcy's breathing became heavy. Only Sid or Lena could have delivered a deeper betrayal.

Sid held himself rigid in his chair. "Burle...why?"

"They came to me while I was out at the cemetery. Lot had Jessie's bracelet. They've got her, Sid. Natalie's dead, but Jessie's alive and well. They've got her out at Fenwick Prison. They told me if I talked to anyone...they'd kill her. They said if I gave them the convoy schedules, and some other information...they said they'd bring her to me."

Darcy's anger kept her standing, though her legs had started to tremble. "What about Gershwin?"

"They already knew about Gershwin. I don't know how. They said they just wanted to get a look at it."

"And you believed them?!"

Sid gave Darcy the floor. He didn't trust himself not to lose control if he spoke again.

"I didn't have a choice. Sid, Darcy…I'm not long for this world. Ask Harpreet, he knows. I had a chance to bring my granddaughter home, I made a promise."

"You made a promise to us, too."

"I'd already given them the keys when we heard about the convoy. I went out to kill them today, not help them anymore."

"Why should we believe you?" asked Daniel.

"I'd already killed one of them when you showed up. I'd have killed Lot in another minute."

Darcy squeezed her legs together to steady them. "And completely covered your ass. Daniel, lock him up."

Burle looked pleadingly at the Boss. "Sid, please, you have to let me talk to Lot. I was furious out there, but now he could tell me what they've done to Jessie."

The Boss couldn't even look at his former chief of stores.

"Sid, please!"

Daniel locked Burle in the first cell and took Lot from the other.

"You still don't remember me, do you?" Lot asked Burle as the cell door opened.

"Of course I remember you."

"But you don't *remember* me." The scavenger licked his lips and chuckled.

"Shut up," said Daniel, propelling the prisoner towards the door.

Sid and Lot measured each other as Darcy once again closed off the lockup.

"How's it goin', Halbert? Going to question me now? Why don't you ask me about your trucker lady?" Lot waggled his tongue.

"You're lucky I need you conscious," said Sid.

There was a knock at the front door.

"Who is it?" asked Purty.

"Toffee."

Purtricil opened the door allowing the chief of the hunters to enter.

Toffee sneered at Lot, then spoke to Darcy. "So, I'm really off the hook now. Disappointed?"

"Always. You have somebody pick up that jeep from the cemetary?"

"Chris brought it in."

"And that other thing is ready?"

"Just like I told you."

The chair was set up in the head room. Lot's ankles were tied, his hands bound behind him. He looked at the dog heads mounted on either side.

"Those supposed to scare me?" he asked.

"What are your orders?" asked Darcy.

"To come here and fuck you."

Toffee hit him across the mouth. The scavenger's head rocked to the side. Lot spat blood on the floor.

"You guys won't kill me. You're just a bunch of bleeding heart wimps."

Toffee reached behind the chair and picked up a box made of wood and mesh. There was a hole in the bottom of the box. He placed it over Lot's head, then fitted plastic around the neck and sealed it off with duct tape. "Thanks for the tape, we can always use more of this."

"What the hell are you doing? Trying to make me look stupid?" Lot moved his head around, looking at the box they'd mounted on his shoulders. There was a circular opening in the top.

Toffee handed Darcy gloves and a net-helmet. "The seal's good, but there's no point in taking chances." He left.

"What...what the fuck is this?" Lot was starting to get worried.

Darcy leaned forward. "We don't expect you to answer our questions, we just want to watch you die. Slowly."

"What? You won't torture me, this is just a bluff."

"Here's a question; how long can you keep your mouth closed?"

Toffee returned with some flexicoil tubing and another mesh box. This one had wasps in it. They buzzed angrily and tried to find holes through which to escape. The chief of the hunters fixed one end of the flexicoil to the box over Lot's head. He attached another end to a funnel and held it up to a hatch on one side of the wasp box.

"What are you doing? Stop this!"

Toffee slid the hatch open and jammed the funnel up against it. The opening to the funnel was larger than the hatch.

Darcy put a hand on Lot's shoulder. "The man you injured was our animal researcher. He's been doing some good work with how wasps communicate, but he's never had a chance to study a kill close up. I'll write a report for when he wakes up."

One of the wasps found its way into the funnel. Toffee closed the hatch. Lot tried to keep his eyes from bulging as he heard the wasp vibrating along the hose.

"Stop this! You can't do this to me!"

The wasp entered the head cage. Lot clamped his mouth and eyes shut. The insect landed on the scavenger's face, just below his lips. Lot jerked as he was stung, then stung again.

"Let a few more in," said Darcy, "but take your time."

"Yeah," said the hunter. "I want to enjoy this, too."

As the wasp stung Lot's face, it released a pheromone that drove its kin into a fury. Their volume increased as they bit at the mesh with tiny mandibles, trying desperately to follow their instinct to kill.

Lot suddenly opened his mouth. The wasp darted inside, and the scavenger clamped his jaw shut, crushing the insect between his teeth. He spat the bug out against the inside of his head cage. "I'll talk! Whatever you want to know, I'll tell you!"

Toffee let the funnel drop to his side in disappointment. "Damn, boy. You made that way too easy."

"What were your orders?"

"To take anything we could from your sound computer. We didn't expect it to be so big. We also weren't expecting the dog. Could you take this thing off me?"

"No. Did Odega have anything to do with you?"

"Who's he?"

"Mmmph. Do you have other contacts here besides Burle?" It pained her even to say the stores master's name.

"No. Just the geezer."

She nodded at Toffee. The hunter moved the funnel closer to the wasp box.

"I swear! Just the geezer, nobody else!"

"Where's Jessie Campbell?"

"Take this box off my head, and I'll tell you."

"What's the use? Toffee, let him have it."

"OKAY! Okay! She's dead. She's been dead for ten years."

"Come again?" Toffee put the funnel down.

"Me and a guy named Walsh found these two little girls out by the river on NW Day. I remember them real clear, 'cause it was a few hours later everything got weird. We had some fun with them." Lot glanced at the wasp box, preparing to be swarmed. "I took the bracelet as a souvenir. I always take a souvenir. I didn't connect her to Burle until Shangly mentioned pickin' him off while he was at the graves."

"How did that make the connection?"

"Ten years ago, your old man asked me and my pack to find them little girls. They was already dead, but our leader didn't know anything about it. They had this big dog with them. It would have killed them if we hadn't, and they would've enjoyed it a lot less." Lot forgot where he was. "Me an' Walsh laughed at that stupid old coot the whole time we was searching. Memory's like that, isn't it? Rememberin' those little girls, but forgetting the old man."

A great emptiness opened beneath Darcy. Burle had betrayed them for nothing. She knew he'd never given up on his granddaughters, even with his graves. It was small comfort that Burle had forsaken one duty for another, but at least it was there. Now that was gone, too. She rushed out the door.

Lot smiled in his cage, the swollen lip adding lunacy to his visage. "Whadaya think, man? Untie me and we'll do her together."

Toffee put the wasp box in the scavenger's lap.

"GET THAT OFF OF ME!" He jerked in his chair as best he could, bashing the back of his head against the cage in an effort to distance himself from the wasps.

Toffee held the box steady while he reached up and yanked the flexicoil from the top of Lot's bizarre helmet, exposing the opening. "I'm going to take my hand away. You keep struggling like that, the box'll fall and break." Toffee stepped away and opened the door.

"You can't leave me here like this!"

"Just keep still, you'll be fine."

Darcy stood in the corridor with her back to the door. Her hands were pressed up against the far wall. Her breath came in short, quick gasps.

Toffee moved close and squeezed her buttock as he spoke into her ear. "We work well together."

Darcy pushed off the wall and stomped her foot. Toffee barely avoided having his instep crushed.

"I told you what would happen if you ever–"

"Good. Now you're angry instead of pathetic. Let's go in there and finish this."

Darcy still perched on the balls of her feet, but her hands lowered from a striking position. Toffee opened the door to the head room. The rancid odour of urine invaded the hallway.

"Smells like he's ready to me," said the hunter.

Sid opened his eyes after what seemed a long time. He reached out to the declaration that hung on his wall, the largest of its signatures was Burle's.

"So do we tell him?" asked Darcy. She'd left the truth about Jessie until the last.

"I don't see what purpose that would serve. It's bad enough that tomorrow I have to lock him outside."

"I'll lock him outside."

Sid looked to Toffee for support, it only made Darcy more determined. There was more to the act than just shoving a person out the door. The execution meant driving the condemned a sufficient distance away that it would take at least a day to walk to the nearest settlement. Unarmed, practically naked, none had ever survived the ordeal, at least not to Sid's knowledge.

"I'm chief of security, Sid. I'm not a figurehead. I caught him, and it's my job."

"Darcy…"

"I'm not your little girl anymore! I was never your little girl in the first place. It's my responsibility. Or isn't it?"

"Fine. You want it, you do it. Now I want you to get some sleep."

"How am I supposed to do that?"

"I don't care. Toffee and I have some talking to do." Sid raised a hand to halt Darcy's response. "You're no good to me like this. I'm not your father, but I'm still your boss. Good night."

Toffee, for a change, kept silent as the security chief left.

Her lamp wouldn't go on despite furiously jiggling the switch. She moved it to a different outlet. Nothing. Light from the corridor cut a wedge across the floor. Thurlow must have cut her juice. It was a mean, childish thing to do, but then the sun boy had been kept out of the loop. All he knew was they'd captured a scavenger. In addition, Darcy felt that maybe she deserved it. The timing of Noah's arrival was suspicious, and she had cut him a key…but it was Noah Thurlow. The boy – man – had no more guile in him than a footstool. But then she'd thought the same thing about Burle…and Travis.

It was too much. Physically she was drained, but mentally she couldn't stop running. Her head filled with images and sensations; Burle holding her at Travis's funeral ceremony, October trying to teach her to walk the runway, Toffee's hand on her buttock…

She was at Lena's door before she realized she was going there. From habit, she placed her ear to the wood. Lena had company. Why did it have to be now? Darcy almost left then, to find her own solace, but she remembered what happened the last time she was this messed up. She knocked. The sounds of frenzied movement eased, then stopped.

"Who is it?"

"It's me. I'm sorry, I really need you right now."

There was a pause. "Alright, come in."

Caps sat in the bed, his back against the wall. The sheets covered him to the waist. Lena had her head in the crook of his shoulder.

"Aren't you a little old to be crawling into bed with mommy and daddy?" Caps asked.

Lena looked at him.

"I get the message. I'm gone. Darcy could you...oh, never mind."

He stepped out of the bed without regard to his nudity. Darcy tried not to glance at his erection, but failed. Simple, human nature. He dragged on a pair of pants, grabbed the rest of his clothes, and left.

Lena patted the bed. "Come on, honey, what's going on?"

Darcy took a chair instead. She needed companionship, but couldn't stand the thought of contact. She opened her mouth to speak, but words wouldn't come yet.

"This is going to be heavy, isn't it?" Lena leaned from the bed and pulled open a drawer. She took a flask from it. "Do you need some of this?"

Darcy had to look away from the flask. "That's how I got into this mess."

"What mess? Darcy?"

"Burle's the traitor."

Lena dropped the flask. "What?"

Darcy told her everything. Lena left the bed and hopped to her friend's side. She lowered herself for an embrace but was pushed away.

"Please. I'm sorry, I don't want to be touched right now."

"Well, screw you! I need a hug."

Darcy held on until her stomach roiled. She moved from the chair and sat on the bed. After retrieving the flask, Lena sat in the chair. She'd pulled a sheet from the bed to cover herself.

"I was handling it fine," said Darcy, "well, handling it better. Until Toffee touched me."

"Touched you? Where?"

"He squeezed my ass."

"I can't believe that son of a bitch! You're frazzled and he uses it as a chance to cop a feel?"

"It's not the first time he's touched me. The first time...I was crazy in the head. I came to see you, but you and Caps were...you guys screw a lot, you know that?"

"He's good at it. I'm good at it. Seems to me you and...sorry." She took a pull from her flask, then offered it to Darcy. This time, the chief of security took it.

"Yeach!" Darcy forced saliva down her throat to soothe the burn. "That's the stuff all right. I tried going back to my room, but I wound up in the mess hall. I guess I knew I needed to talk to someone. It couldn't be Sid...there was nobody there, so I just started drinking..."

"I should just knock on her door!" Darcy said to the empty hall. "Who cares if she's getting it on? They can do it again tomorrow..." The flask, only a quarter full, slipped from her fingers. "Oh, don't you spill on me, too." She picked up the flask and stood it up in the puddle of rotgut.

"Why'd you do it, Trav?" Her voice was raised, thoughtless of who might overhear. "Why'd you have to do..." The tears started again. "Why'd she have to tell me?"

Senna had come to her earlier that day, with her catlike walk and pale blond hair.

"Darcy," she'd said, "I have to get something off my chest."

And so she'd unloaded. Travis and her had slept together, after a hunt. It was the day they'd lost Felix, the day before Toffee took over. The group had been out to get a cow. Cow hunting was more dangerous than cougar hunting. With the cougar you shot it and you were done. With cows, it wasn't so simple. If the bovines caught wind of where you were, the entire herd would turn and stampede, right at the hunters. Slaughtering the herd wasn't an option. You did that too many times, soon there were no more cows to hunt. This particular hunt had been even more dangerous, because they wanted the cow live. That meant tranquillizing the chosen animal, and hoping to hell they could pick it up before the sedative wore off. It wasn't like cows could be driven away with a few shots in the air, that just gave them a target. Felix had gone down under a thousand tons of stamping, cloven hooves. That night, while Darcy was on duty, Senna and

Travis had comforted each other. Felix had been a good friend to both.

"I can't believe she told you," said Travis, when she'd confronted him in her room.

"That's what you're mad at?"

"You didn't need to know. It meant nothing. It never happened before and it hasn't happened since. We were in pain."

"You're supposed to come to me with your pain!"

He'd taken her by the shoulders. "It was three months ago. Nothing had changed before you knew."

She pushed his hands away. "How can I trust you?" Senna had no scars on her face.

Anger crept into Travis's eyes. "I've got a job to do. We'll talk later."

He'd left and Darcy hadn't raised a hand to stop him.

Now she sat bitter and alone, getting smashed on Dr. Patel's finest.

"Mind if I join you?"

Darcy looked up at the hunter. At any other time she would have told him where to go. She didn't like the way he looked at her.

"Go ahead. I don't care."

"I guess you're not on duty." Toffee picked up the flask, sniffed the contents, then took a swig.

It wasn't that Toffee looked at her with lecherous intent; he did, but with no more or less desire than he looked at Travis's mark of office, or his room. She could tell right away that the hunter was after the chief of security's position in the Pit, in all ways.

"I didn't say you could share my drink." She snatched the flask from him. "I don't like you."

"I know." He grinned. "Travis told me. You just don't know me yet."

She poked him in the chest. "I know you. You were a poacher. Sid tells me everything."

Toffee's smile dimmed a little, but didn't vanish completely. "I doubt that. Honestly, do you really hate me for poaching back when it was still a crime? Hmm? Do you have any sympathy for the trophies I took?"

"S'not the point. You were a criminal. The ends don't...um...the ends..."

"I get your point. I disagree with it. How much of that stuff have you had?"

Darcy shook the flask, it still held fluid. "Not enough." She drained it.

"So what are you doing, getting drunk by yourself?" His voice seemed to hold a note of genuine concern.

"I'm the security second. I can do whatever I want."

"That crap you're drinking has a bad taste to it. Would you like to try something else?"

Suspicion crawled its way through Darcy's drunken haze. Her chair felt a little unsteady, like it was going to abandon her. "Like what?"

Toffee reached into his pocket and produced a small, glass vial. There was something golden inside.

"Is that...hash oil? I could lock you up for that." Maybe she would, too. Even if he was a chief. She had the authority, or at least she thought she did.

"I don't use drugs. Besides, hash's darker in colour, and much less valuable."

He unscrewed the vial one-handed, pinching the bottle against his palm with his fingers, while using his thumb to rotate the cap. He then tilted the vial until a slow drop accrued on a fingertip. He held it out to Darcy. "Try it."

Darcy looked at the sticky glob on Toffee's finger. "Is that...no way." Her tongue darted out of its own accord and lapped up the honey.

"Mmmhhh! That's wonderful!" The hunter kept his hand extended. Darcy had to stop herself from licking the residue.

"Here," he said, placing the vial before her. "It's all yours. See, I'm not such a bad guy."

She closed her hand around the vial. There must have been at least a tablespoon worth in it. She was about to take another taste when her suspicion kicked in again.

"Who did you steal this from?"

"Nobody. I brought it with me."

Honey was one of the rarest and most valuable commodities around. Honey Bees had been dying off for years before the Change, victims to a tiny mite that nested in their bodies. Without constant effort to restock populations, the Honey Bee population of the Pacific Northwest was as-near-as-makes-no-odds zero. Even if it wasn't, who would be a bee keeper? Now she had a whole vial of honey, all to herself.

"How much do you have? Does Sid know? He'll make you give it to Burle. Roshi will want some, too."

"Ssshhh. Nobody knows. Just you and me. It's our secret." He winked.

This was a side of the man she hadn't seen before. His usual aura of aggression was gone, like he'd taken off a mask, just for her.

She felt herself slipping in the chair. A warm sensation was moving up her belly, spreading through her chest.

The next thing she knew, Toffee's arm was hooked under her shoulder. He was helping her stagger down the hall.

"What happened?"

"You sort of passed out. Either you don't drink too often, or you had way too much."

Her feet dragged as they stepped. She giggled. "I hope no one sees me like this."

"Ssshhh, you keep talking that loud and someone will."

They were getting closer to her door. "Where's my honey? I don't have my honey."

"I've got it. It's right here in my pocket."

Once through the door, Toffee let her drop to the bed. He handed her the vial.

"Put it on the desk, I don't want to lose it. Thank you for helping me. I guess I can sleep now."

Toffee sat on the edge of her bed. "I thought I might stay a while."

She wondered why he would want to do that. Then she heard his boot hit the floor.

"Hey, wait a minute…" The second boot dropped. "What do you think you're…"

His fingers stroked her cheek. "You're beautiful. The colour of your hair, the way your eyes burn…"

She turned away from his touch. "My face is ugly. I used to be beautiful."

His hand was on her belly, moving slowly.

"I think you should leave."

Toffee covered her with his weight. His lips touched hers, tentatively, then forcefully. Darcy heard another thud and realized it was his prosthetic. She pushed at him, but not with much strength. At the same time as she resisted his attentions, there was no denying her arousal. She realized she was kissing back. Her clothes seemed to melt off her, as did the hunter's. She neither helped nor resisted. Toffee maintained contact the entire time, stroking her with his fingers when he didn't need his hand, licking or kissing when he did. He seduced her with a gentleness she never would have expected from him. His caresses remained soft only as long as they had to. Soon she needed more aggressive participation and Toffee supplied it—in spades.

Darcy was lying in the circle of Toffee's arm when the knock came at the door. Warm afterglow vanished in naked realization of what had happened. What would Travis do when he came in and found her like this? The knock came again.

"Darcy?" It was Daniel, the security third. "Can I come in? I'm afraid something's happened."

Lena moved to the bed and hesitantly put her arm around the chief of security's shoulder. "So when Travis was swarmed in the caves, you were…Oh, Darcy." This time Darcy accepted the hug. "Did he drug the honey?"

"I wanted to think he did, but no. I wanted to get back at Travis and…it was all me."

"I'm here to see Burle." said Toffee, daring Chiu-Keung to deny him access.

"I'm under orders that nobody sees him. Take it up with Darcy."

"Do you think her orders really included me?"

Chiu stood up. He didn't want to wake his chief, and Toffee was the third in command. "I'll have to frisk you."

"You think I'm going to slip him a file?" The hunter spread his arms as the security officer patted him down.

"No, I think you might be going in there to kill him. I've contemplated it myself. You're clean."

Toffee moved to the lockup door.

"Uhm, sir? Your arm."

Toffee slipped his prosthetic off. His sleeve hung limply from the elbow. "I left the blade at home." He threaded the arm up his dangling sleeve and locked it place with a twist.

"Sorry, just doing my job."

Burle sat up as Toffee closed the door behind him. The old man's eyes were red. He'd been reclined, but not asleep.

"Oh, it's you. What do you want?"

Toffee tapped the bars with a knuckle. "You really tore a chunk out of Darcy."

"It had nothing to do with her."

"You couldn't have hurt her more if you'd raped her."

Burle held the hunter's eyes for a moment, then lowered his head. "I could no more rape her than you could beat me at patty cake."

The hunter's mouth twisted into a sneer. He detached his arm and held it out, hand pointed down. "She's going to lock you outside tomorrow." He upended the prosthetic. A coil of rope fell from the open end and landed just inside Burle's cell. "Why don't you save her the trouble."

22. Fenwick Prison

Victor Shangly sat with his feet up and his head back. The woman who stood before his desk had put him in a contemplative mood. The rich mane of hair Diane Fuentes had worn in her youth with pride had been shaved off. She'd done this to allow her tattoo artist a larger canvas. A trail of ants that started from just behind her ear, curved over her head, down one cheek and ended at the corner of her mouth. The ant near her lips had been the most painful.

"So?" she asked.

Shangly pushed his legs against the desk and leaned back even farther. "I was married to Kristy seven years, and you think you can fill her shoes."

"Why not? I already fill her bed."

He let out a bellylaugh and spun in the chair. It was a fat, cracked leather armchair that Shangly claimed once belonged to Fenwick's last warden. In truth, the prison had been devoid of furnishings when the scavengers moved in. The chair had been found by the side of the road. The desk had come from somewhere or other, as did the empty file cabinets and throw rug. Despite the changes he made to his body, for decor, Shangly clung to fixtures of a pre-Change executive.

Diane moved around the desk and dropped into Shangly's lap. "You're not answering me."

He grabbed her cheeks and pulled the olive coloured skin tight around her mouth. "Yes!" he said.

He pushed her off and flung open his office doors, revealing bare earth and the stone wall beyond. "LEON! GET YOUR ASS IN HERE!"

"You mean now?" Diane gasped.

"Why wait?" Whereas most people would choose to put their office far from a structure's entrance, Shangly had chosen the prison's main foyer for his. General movement into, and out of the prison, was conducted through a set of side doors in the south wing.

Leon came to his master's call. He was a short man, but stocky. Tight curls of dark brown hair surrounded a square face. He was bare chested, and knife scars criss-crossed below the breast. At the end of each scar hung a noose. From each noose dangled a different animal. Leon had done the work on himself, both the tattoos and the scars.

"HEY EVERYBODY, COME WITNESS!"

From throughout the yard, people were drawn to the gaping maw of Fenwick Prison's main doors. They were a motley crew of all shapes and sizes, all of them tattooed. One woman had a squirrel on her neck that pawed at her ear. A man had hands that looked like spiders. Double rows of eyes were inked on the second knuckles, and all the fingers looked like legs. They hauled themselves from couches made of torn-out car seats. Some carried their weapons, others left them on the ground. Each of them was an outcast in their own way. Many had been kicked out of other settlements, a few had voluntarily joined the ranks of Shangly's scavengers. Had the world been the same as it once was, and Fenwick had not been decommissioned, most of the scavengers would still be residents. If not of Fenwick, then of other prisons.

"What's happening?" asked Leon.

"Me and Diane are getting married."

Leon was their sculptor of both body and soul. Being the tattoo artist made him the closest thing they had to a priest. He gave the bride a thumb's-up. "Okay, do your vows."

Shangly turned to Diane and looked straight into her eyes. "You're mine. I own you. You stray, I'll kill you." He drew back his hand and struck her across the face.

She put her hand on his chest to steady herself, then raised her chin. "You're mine. All of you is mine. You stray, I'll kill you." She delivered a blow to the side of his mouth.

Shangly staggered back a step, then looked at Leon.

"Go ahead," said the tattoo artist. "You may kiss the bride."

They kissed passionately, the blood from their lips intermingling. Leon whooped.

The crowd parted at the sound of running feet. Kramond arrived, his beer gut kept jiggling after he stopped. "Hey, Victor, the jeep's back."

"About freakin' time."

Diane followed her new husband as he strode out the door. Leon and Kramond fell in step.

"Gus is holding him at the bridge," said Kramond.

"Why?"

"He won't answer radio calls. He's just sitting in there."

Shangly stopped. "He? He who? Is it Lot or Terry?"

"We don't know, he's got a net on. Won't get out of the car. Maybe he's hurt or something."

"Or maybe it's not either of them." Shangly took off at run. Diane and Leon kept pace but Kramond was left halfway across the yard. He'd managed to run the distance once, he couldn't do it twice.

At the gate, Leon turned a crank that winched back a heavy wrought iron fence. Beyond the gate, Shangly could see the bridge's guardhouse, with Gus outside, training his rifle on the jeep. The vehicle sat, perched on the far side of the bridge.

"Has he said anything?" asked Shangly, once he reached his guard.

"Nope. He's just sittin' there. Oops, he's moving now."

The jeep's driver stepped out, holding hands open and apart.

"Lot, is that you?" called Shangly. "What the hell are you playing at? Where's Terry?"

The figure reached up and pulled off the net. Beneath was a face much older than either of Shangly's scavengers.

"Burle..." he breathed.

"I'm here for my granddaughter, Victor. You send her out, and I'll show you what I've got in the jeep."

Shangly recovered quickly from his surprise. "Where are my boys?"

"Lot's been captured. Probably dead by now. I know the other fella's dead."

Diane took Shangly's arm. "He's lying."

Shangly put his hand on hers. "How do you know Terry's dead?"

"Was that his name? I killed him."

"You...get down on the ground!"

Burle stuck his thumb out at the jeep. "I've got something for you. You send me Jessie, and I'll give it to you."

"GET DOWN ON THE GROUND!"

Burle bit his lip, then dropped to his knees.

"ALL THE WAY DOWN!" Burle complied. Shangly turned to Leon. "Get some people out, sweep the perimeter. Go in twos. Shout at each other, keep constant contact. Go!"

Leon jogged back across the yard, shouting orders, transforming wedding guests into soldiers.

"Is there someone hiding in the jeep?" Shangly called out.

"It's just me, you peckerhead! You broke the deal. You said you weren't going to hurt anybody."

"No, I said I wanted to send a message. If there's someone in the jeep, I'll kill you." He nodded to Gus.

The guard moved quickly across the bridge, bringing his rifle to bear on the car's windshield. After changing angles a couple of times, Gus indicated that it was clear.

"What's in there?"

"Just some skinbags," Gus called back.

"We shouldn't be exposed like this," said Diane.

Shangly's eyes flicked anxiously to the foliage beyond where he'd burned out the land.

"Gus, get him in here, then drive in the jeep." The newlyweds moved back within the safety of Fenwick's wall.

Gus motioned Burle up with the rifle, then pushed him across the bridge and into the yard.

"Did you really kill Terry?" Diane asked.

Burle didn't acknowledge her. He spoke only to Shangly. "I had to. I'd of killed Lot too, if security hadn't showed up. They were on to me. I had to cover my ass."

"But you didn't kill Lot."

Burle spat on the ground. "Nope. What the hell did you have to tape up the cavern guard for? I go to all that trouble so you can sneak in and you just announce your presence?"

"Was the guard a woman?" asked Diane.

"Yes."

Diane punched her husband in the arm. "Lot just can't control his dick! I told you he'd do something like this."

Shangly reached behind his back and tugged on his ponytail; something he only did when stress was getting the better of him. The claw tattoos on his cheeks curled up as he clenched his teeth. "You've got a lot of balls coming here."

"Where else was I supposed to go? They were going to lock me outside. Now where's Jessie?"

Shangly put his hand on Burle's throat and squeezed, gently. "How did you get away?"

Shouts of "All clear!" and "Nothing out here!" travelled over the walls.

Burle tried to pry off the choking hand, but he wasn't strong enough. "Someone slipped me a rope…"

"What for?" The grip increased in pressure.

"To hang myself. What do you think it was for? They were all ashamed of me. Thing is…please, let go." The hand eased off a little. "The thing is, a rope can be used as a garrote. I choked out the kid they had guarding me." Behind him, the jeep rumbled into the yard. "The motor pool's right near security. I got in your jeep and came here."

Shangly yanked Burle closer. "So every car in Compton Pit is headed my way?"

"Not a chance. I kicked over three barrels of gas, fired the whole pool. They'd have caught me by now if I hadn't."

Victor opened his hand. Burle stepped back gratefully and rubbed his throat.

The scavenger's face shone with glee. "So you're telling me…"

"The Pit is crippled. If the pump tank blew, they might not even be able to get the airlock open." A look of remorse crossed Burle's face, but it didn't last long.

Fenwick's inmates came through the gate in pairs. They formed a rough circle around their king and queen. "No one's out there, he's alone," said one of them.

Shangly opened the door to the jeep. "You're sure all the vehicles were in the pool? There weren't one or two on patrol, maybe?"

"Halbert called them in for the night. No transportation, anywhere. You can go and take them at your leisure. What have you got, about forty people?"

"About that." Shangly turned to his subjects. "Folks, this here is Jessie Campbell's grandpa. You all make sure you treat her with respect while he's here."

Burle scanned the faces around him. "If anyone of you has touched her…"

Shangly put his hand on Burle's chest. "I can promise you, not one of them has laid a finger on her."

There were mumbled agreements from the scavengers. Leon stifled a laugh.

"So what did you bring me?" Shangly patted the jeep's hood.

"Send out Jessie first."

"This isn't a negotiation. Somebody give me a gun." He held his hand out, a pistol was placed in it instantly. "Why don't you take those bags out slowly and place them on the ground."

There were four of them. People stepped back involuntarily as Burle undid the first one. Inside was a white metal box. There was a grid on one side, a power jack on the other.

Shangly picked it up and examined it on all sides. "Is this what I think it is?"

"Mmhmm. That's a Screaming Mimi. There's two more here, and a control box."

Diane took the Mimi and held it out critically. "I thought these things couldn't be detached from the Pit."

Shangly levelled the gun at Burle. "Yeah, that's what you said."

"No. I said the Mimis plugged into Gershwin couldn't be detached. This is a portable set. Runs off lithium batteries. It's for the hunters, so they can have a safe base camp."

Shangly took the box back from his wife. "You didn't tell me about this."

Burle unwrapped another Mimi. He sighed. "Most people don't know about it, not even some of the chiefs. It wouldn't do to have folk knowing there's a sound net that can be carried away."

"And you'd sell out your friends without even a second thought?"

Burle started to say something, then stopped. A thousand lines crinkled around his mouth and eyes. "They were going to lock me outside. Halbert didn't care about Jessie. I know what's important."

Diane didn't like the newcomer. This was her wedding day, she was supposed to be the star, but Burle had stolen all her thunder. She stepped forward and put her foot on a Mimi. "If you had to take off so quick, how'd you manage to grab these?"

Burle shook his head at her ignorance. "I told you, this is for the hunters. It was stowed in the off-road van, and the van was in the motor pool."

Kramond and Leon leaned against the walls. Diane sat on the desk while Shangly studied the control unit. It was made out of black metal. There was a numeric keypad on it, a switch and two lights.

"So do I just turn this thing on?"

Burle tugged at the control unit. Shangly didn't want to give it up at first.

"You'll have to place them first. Once you turn it on, they can't be moved again."

"You said they were portable."

"Only to a degree." Burle placed the control unit on the desk, just out of Shangly's reach. "That's Little Gershwin, or LG for short. When you turn it on, the three Mimis gauge their position in relation to each other. Once the net is going, moving a unit breaks the pattern. When you turn them off, LG needs to be plugged back into Gershwin before it can be used again. The control unit can't move either. A couple feet either way won't matter, but I wouldn't risk even that."

Shangly leaned forward and put his elbows on the desk. Burle nudged LG a little farther away.

"So once they're on, that's it. That's what you're telling me?"

"That's it."

Shangly ran a hand down Diane's leg. "So what do you think hon, trade it or have an ant free home?"

"Ant free home. Definitely."

Kramond stepped up to the desk and picked up a Mimi.

"Lemme see that," said Leon.

The portly scavenger made as if to toss the unit. Burle snatched it from him quickly, but carefully.

"Don't do that. These are delicate pieces of equipment."

Shangly got up and opened the doors. Most of the scavengers still milled about outside. "Hey everybody, ant free home!" There were some cheers, and a couple of catcalls. "I want to see these things work. Somebody go get an animal." There were no volunteers.

"You don't have to do that," said Burle. "Just watch the tree line. The birds will scatter."

"How much range are we talking about here?"

Burle stepped to the doors and scanned the yard. "If you set them up right, about a quarter mile past where you've burned."

"Very nice."

With Burle's guidance, the scavengers placed Mimis in locations that would optimize the net. Shangly wanted to keep them all inside, but the thick stone of the outer wall would hinder their function. The first was placed in the guardhouse for the bridge, the second against the north wall, on the opposite end of the yard from where the vehicles were kept. As the third was secured to the west wall, Burle scanned the ridge.

"We paid you a visit, you know."

"Come again," said Shangly.

"A squad from the Pit came in by the river, checked you out from that ridge. They killed one of your men."

Shangly's jaw dropped. "How long were you going to wait before giving me that little tidbit."

"I just remembered it now. Didn't help them anyway. The squad came back saying there was no place to attack you from."

Once the final sound unit was secured, they returned to the foyer office. Little Gershwin was duct taped to one corner of the desk.

"Okay, old man, how do I do this?"

"There's a code. Punch in the wrong code twice, the whole thing shuts down."

Shangly drummed his fingers on Little Gershwin. "You're not going to give me the code, are you?"

Burle leaned over the desk. "I haven't seen your end of the deal."

Diane flicked an imaginary piece of dirt off her tanktop. "We could torture it out of you."

"Lady, I'm almost eighty years old. How much torture do you think I can handle?"

"We could torture Jessie," said Shangly.

Burle kept his mouth closed and waited.

"So now we deal. What do you want?"

"The first thing I want is to sit down. My back's awful sore. That chair of yours looks right comfortable."

Shangly rose and gestured to his chair, overdoing his attempt to appear magnanimous.

Burle sat down and rocked the chair a little. His shoulders drooped and his lip trembled.

"Comfy now?"

The former stores master hardened his resolve. "I won't tell you the code, but I will punch it in."

"In exchange for?"

"Me an Jessie leave here in that jeep I brought in. I earned it, what with what I did at the Pit. We'll need a few days basic supplies, and gas."

"Where will you go?"

"It doesn't matter."

"You could stay here. Help us mop up Halbert's crew."

"We leave. Jeep, gas, supplies."

"You've got a deal." Shangly stuck his hand out.

Burle folded his arms across his chest. "Spit on it. I seem to remember that means something to you."

Shangly smiled and brought his hand up to his mouth. "You punch in that code, you and your granddaughter will be together." He spat on his palm. Burle did the same and they shook.

Burle flicked the switch. One of the lights glowed red. Leon and Kramond moved closer to the desk.

"Wait!" Shangly opened the doors. He did it with gusto, flinging the large portals so they banged the wall on either side. "IT'S SHOWTIME!" He turned to his wife. "I'm going to watch this from the guardhouse. No more worry when a baby's coming! We can open the upper floors. Wait until my signal. This is great!"

"I'll be able to go out at night and sit in the trees," said Leon. "That'll be nice."

Burle stood and walked out to the yard. A couple of scavengers, age indeterminate, stood by the doors. The rest, like their leader, were off by the sound boxes, like kids waiting for fireworks.

Someone waved a hand by the gate. Burle returned to Shangly's chair. He rocked a little, squeezing the armrests, trying to recapture a feeling he'd once had.

"I'd like Noah to have my chair," he said, then he hit the zero key three times.

Up on the ridge, Sid pulled headphones off as the three Mimis and Little Gershwin detonated simultaneously.

"I'll make sure he gets it."

23. Even Small Wars are Hell

"Everybody go," Sid said into his radio.

As soon as the scavengers had declared the perimeter clear, the Boss's soldiers had moved stealthily into position. It was a nerve wracking experience for everyone. The hunters moved quickly, using compound bows to take down animals. They couldn't afford the sound of a gunshot. The birds had left them alone, as was their want in recent years. Shangly's treatment of the land had left the surrounding forest mostly clear of fauna, but there was always something wandering around.

"Aren't you glad he didn't kill himself?" Seth asked Toffee. The chief of the hunters didn't reply. They hunched their shoulders and sprinted for the prison.

Sid had gone to the lockup an hour after Toffee had. He needed closure, he needed Burle to make him understand. He told Burle what had really happened to Jessie. It didn't change the fact that an execution had to be carried out, but it did open the door for a different method. Toffee and Seth smoothed out some edges, but mostly it was Burle's plan. They needed a Trojan Horse, and they got one.

Seth had used remote control equipment cannibalized from Odega's broken planes, and the very last of the Pit's high-yield explosives.

The combined force of hunters and security—minus Darcy, Connie and Chiu-Keung—moved through the newly opened holes in Fenwick's walls. From within the walls came two gunshots, that was all. Sid had turned away a second before the scavengers clustered around the west Mimi had met their end. Toffee, however, watched the whole thing.

"We got it," came Toffee's voice through the headphones. "We've taken the prison."

It took Sid and his escort a few minutes to work their way down the drop-off. It was dangerous, but quicker than going around and back to the river. True, the recon expedition had failed to determine a successful attack route, but Toffee had picked out places to watch from.

Sid forced himself to look at a leg that protruded from a pile of charred stone. He moved through the hole and into Fenwick Prison.

The surviving scavengers were herded into the centre of the yard. There were only seven of them, two of them wounded. Seth went to check out the rig.

Senna took in the fleet with a sweep of her arm. "Are we taking them all?"

"I don't know. Caps will want the parts, but maybe we should leave these people with something."

"We're taking the tow truck, right?"

It was a dingy, gray, three quarter ton with a rusty hook hanging from the crane.

"Yes. We'll take the tow truck. Now we know how Shangly was making his roadblocks."

The smell of death was in the air. Prisoners of war looked accusingly at Sid as he made his way to the prison's foyer. None of them had met him, but they all knew the Boss of Compton Pit was black, and they could tell from body language who the real leader was. The double doors were undamaged, though one of them hung crookedly, having lost half its hinges. Smoke and dust wafted out through the portal, accompanied by the odour of cordite. What remained of Burle Campbell would never be separated from what was left of the chair.

Toffee stooped and jiggled a burnt head. It was impossible to tell if it had been a man's or a woman's. "I wonder if this was the guy that wanted to sit under the trees." Toffee worked at a tooth until it came free. He pulled on the thong around his neck and withdrew a small skinbag. Opening it, he dropped the tooth in. "I've never kept a man's tooth before, but this is an occasion worth remembering."

"That might have been the woman." Sid toed through the rubble, looking for anything that could be identified as Burle's. There was nothing.

"Boss?" Daniel's voice said through the headphones. "I'm down by the bridgehouse."

"Can you identify Shangly?"

"There's a lot of, uh, gore here. If he was right next to it when it blew…sir, he could be anything."

"We've got more people," came a different voice. Sid thought it might have been Purty.

From a side door in the prison, two of Sid's men led a cluster of terrified scavengers into the yard. There were children in the group. One woman carried an infant. Sid's crew shot looks at him, wondering what they should do.

"Daniel, you and Mike get back here." Sid pulled his headphones off and let them drop to the ground.

"We didn't really think about the civilian population, did we?" asked Seth. Dr. White had not been included in any of the planning sessions, neither had Lena.

"We're not going to hurt any of you," said Sid to the survivors.

The woman with the infant hugged her child closer, and glared at the smoking ruin that had once been her leader's office. "How can you say that?"

"It's your mess, Boss," Toffee whispered. "I'm going to start inventory. Seth, how's the rig?"

Seth pulled his gaze away from a girl of seven or eight, with a cat's eye tattooed above her nose. "It smells like someone had sex in the cab. A lot of our stuff is still in the trailer. Maybe Shangly was getting ready to deliver it to D'Abo. There's a twenty footer we can tow as well. Maybe we can relocate these people."

"Relocate us where?" A man, burns on his arm, moved towards Sid. He was stopped by Senna's rifle. "Where you gonna take us? We were kicked out of everywhere else."

"You win," said a woman. She came to stand next to the man. "Big Bad Halbert. Congratulations. You've wiped us out."

"You'd have done the same to us," said Senna. She spoke to the woman, but kept her gun on the man. That was her mistake.

The woman produced a small knife and lunged forward. Sid jerked back, but not fast enough. The tip of the knife dug into his chest, just below the sternum. Toffee shot the woman through the side of her head.

"Noooo!" screamed the man. He slammed into Senna. They fell to the ground, grappling for her rifle. The rifle went off before Toffee could incapacitate the man.

"Everyone on the ground!" the hunter roared without raising his voice.

Sid pressed his hand against his chest, amazed at the red that seeped through his fingers.

Someone screamed. Senna, not yet having gained her bearings, looked for the source of the anguish. The little girl with the cat's eye lay sprawled on her back. She now had another circular mark on her forehead. There was only a small trickle of blood. Senna doubled over and vomited.

Sid stared numbly as Seth cut open the front of his camouflage coveralls. The hunter second examined the wound, then was flung away, as if swatted by a giant hand.

Toffee spun towards the source of the gunshot. He, like everyone else, had been distracted by the little girl. A man stood by the semi, he'd dropped his rifle and was preparing to throw a grenade. Toffee's bullet took him high in the chest, knocking him off his feet. The grenade rolled under the cab.

"No–" Sid had time to say before an explosion blew the tires out from under the cab. The fuel tank ignited, not in a fireball, but with a dull whump that sent flames licking up the sides of the vehicle.

Seth staggered to his feet. He pressed his hand hard against his shoulder. He knew from experience that his collarbone was shattered.

In a few more seconds, the entire cab was engulfed in flame. Heat waves made the wall behind shimmer, as blood ran down Sid's naked stomach. The victorious army fell silent, the only sounds being crackling flames, and the muted sobs of a heartbroken mother.

"Oh shit," said Toffee. "Crows."

Unnoticed, hundreds of the black birds had found their way to the top of the outer wall. More were on their way.

"Everyone inside," said Sid. "Move!"

Victors and vanquished alike forgot their differences and bolted to the doors, escaping from a less discriminating enemy. The crows began to launch themselves from the walls as their prey sought refuge. It took Toffee and two other people, one of them a scavenger, to haul the broken door into place. Feathered bodies thumped against the wood. The glass from Fenwick's windows had been removed and traded long ago. Only bars and steel mesh held the birds at bay.

"We have to go below," said a young boy, pulling at Sid's sleeve. He was right. The covering on the windows was made to keep out wasps, not crows.

From an intellectual point of view, it was fascinating to watch a crow attack. No matter how many of them there were—and crows could gather in numbers that were unimaginable—only one or two crows cawed. The rest skirmished with only the sound of flapping wings as their cry.

Steel gates were pulled open, the Comptonites followed the scavengers through a barren corridor and down stone steps.

The lower level of Fenwick Prison reeked of unwashed humanity. Rooms were cells. There was no electric lighting. The boy that had talked to Sid ran ahead, lighting kerosene lamps. Toffee waited by the top of the stairs until he heard crows winging down the corridor. He slammed the door, but it bounced open again. There was no handle or lock, both had been stripped out for trade.

"Bring me something to block the door!" shouted Toffee. There were two places the birds could get through; the hole where the handle used to be and a tiny window. The steel mesh that once had been there, was also gone.

"Come on!" The foyer's windows must have been completely stripped away, or else the broken door had fallen open. It sounded like a whirlwind. From down the corridor, one of the generals cawed its orders.

Toffee blocked the hole with his artificial hand, pushing on it with the real one. Steeling himself, he turned and put his back against the window. He was tall enough to do that.

"Come on! Halbert!" The first beak hit him in the back. He sucked breath in through his teeth. The window was small enough that only one crow could attack him at a time. It dug in with its claws. Toffee shoved his body sideways, scraping the bird off against the side of the window. The same crow or a different one dug in right away. It used Toffee as leverage and tore away strips of cloth and flesh.

Senna came up the steps with a large book. Toffee jerked away from the door and slammed his back against the wall, crushing the bird that clung to him. Senna covered the window with the book, putting her full weight into holding both it and the door in place.

"Watch the handle!" warned Toffee.

A black head appeared through the hole. Toffee lurched forward, intending to break its neck, but in his haste he forgot himself, and reached with his wooden hand. His jointed fingers succeeded only in swatting at the bird as it shot out the hole and down the stairs.

Senna pressed her hip against the opening and prepared to endure the same torment Toffee had. The pounding against the book was continuous, she had to use both hands to keep it in place.

"There's one coming down!" the hunter shouted.

There was a cry and a flapping of wings, then Daniel, bleeding from his scalp, was there with a roll of duct tape and a wad of cloth.

"Nnnggh!" Senna winced as pain stabbed up her hip.

"Move!" Daniel covered the hole with his cloth and taped over it quickly, then he and Senna did a small ballet as he hurried strips of tape over the book, while she jerked her hands to give him room, but still keep the book in place. When it was done, Daniel took over and Senna slumped against a wall.

One of the scavengers came up the steps with a metal bar. He fitted it through clamps on the door and frame.

"Why isn't that kept up here?" asked Toffee.

"We was usin' it for something else."

Under Seth's instruction, Purty administered first aid. The Boss only had a flesh wound. It was disinfected and taped shut easily. Seth's shoulder was bound. The bleeding wasn't the problem. Understanding the process didn't keep the body from going into shock.

"I'm glad we don't go to war too often," said Seth. "We suck at it."

Toffee's back would need stitches. He'd have to sleep on his stomach for a while. Senna's hip was tricky, because any movement of the leg would open the wound. There was little Purtricil could do for the scavengers' burns, but he did set a broken arm. The hunters and security officers not wounded kept the scavengers under guard. They huddled in a wide area that might have been a guard station. It was a bad situation. Even children could run circles round them in the unfamiliar, dimly lit corridors.

"You, big fella," said a scant woman with genuine scars on her cheeks. "You kill Jerry, or just knock him out?"

"Who's Jerry?" asked Toffee.

"The guy who grabbed your girl's rifle."

"I just knocked him out."

She looked up at the ceiling. "Well, he's dead now."

Seth let out a groan as he shifted his position. He couldn't allow himself to pass out, not yet, not while their situation was so precarious. "Those crows…there's so many of them. How'd they get here so fast?"

"They've probably been sneaking in for days," said Toffee. "Somehow they just know when a feast is coming. There'll be coyotes, too, and dogs. They follow the crows. By nightfall every animal for miles will be up there, fighting over barbecued meat. You're right, we do suck at this. Hey, kid!"

The lamplighter's eyes were apprehensive. He had a mop of sandy hair, though it was hard to tell in the dim light.

"Yeah, you. Come over here."

The boy looked up the guard closest to him, then rose and shuffled over to the hunter.

"What's your name?"

"Bill."

"How many ways are there into the basement?"

Bill's lips moved as he counted in his head. "Five."

"Why don't you take me to them, and we'll make sure nothing can get in here."

The boy glanced down the corridor. "Uhm, that's already being done."

Toffee did a headcount. He guessed there were six people missing.

"They'll be back," said the woman with the infant. "We've got worse things to worry about right now than fighting you."

"How are you for rats?" asked Sid.

"We get a few. We have a flamethrower down here."

"We'll have to secure that," said the Boss. He gestured to one of the hunters. "Let her take you to the flamethrower, bring it back here. Bill, I know there's a radio here, could you take me to it?" The boy shook his head. "Please? I have three more people out there, just a short drive away. They're waiting for my signal. My handset won't reach them from underground."

"It's upstairs," said Bill.

"They might be on their way here now," said Toffee. "Not much they can do though."

Senna unleashed a scary, almost insane laugh.

"What's so funny?" asked the Boss.

"You…heheh…you know what a flock of crows is called?"

"Yes."

"Well...we're stuck in prison...on account of a murder!"

Topside, there was indeed a feast. Though the charge in Little Gershwin was the smallest of the four, walls had reflected the blast inward, reducing most everything to cinder. Outside, bodies had room to fly. Even separated limbs landed cooked, but intact. The crows did comical sidesteps as they tore meat from bone, glutting themselves on conflict's spoor. Dogs and coyotes, other animals willing to eat the newly dead, filtered out of the woods. Though the murder of crows far outnumbered walkers, birds were easily chased away by a snap of teeth, or a low growl. That much of nature's hierarchy remained unchanged.

Not all the crows were at dinner, however. Within the main building, feathered jailers perched on refuse and window sills, fulfilling a duty that had not been performed in almost twenty years. Air, propelled by flapping wings, drifted through the corridors like a contented sigh. Fenwick Prison once again had inmates, not residents.

Wheels creaked as one of the security officers pushed a lawnmower down the hall. It was a gas-powered model. Part plastic, part rusted metal. It would have been quite funny to watch the man mowing the hall, had Sid not known where the machine came from. It was part of the cargo from Drum East. A tasty bit offered over a brief communication. If Drum East had told true, the mower was fully functional. Eggerson and Odega wanted it badly. They felt they could make a tough, mobile ground unit out of it. In short, an ROV. Though they'd outlined the benefits of such a tool, Sid suspected Eggerson just wanted to make a big toy, and Odega needed to justify the accumulation of remote control leftovers that was crowding a box in storage. The scavengers had decided to keep the item. Leon wanted it as a parts vehicle for the gas-powered generator that supplied electricity to his tattoo parlour. Apparently, what Leon had wanted, Leon got.

Seth drew back his blanket to look at the ugly discolouration slowly engulfing his swollen arm. It was no better than it had been five minutes ago, but the hunter second couldn't resist torturing himself. He poked at it to see if it hurt any less. It didn't. Their first aid supplies were woefully inadequate. They had plenty of stuff to bandage people up, but they hadn't planned on long term care. The good stuff was in the van, back down the road. Fenwick had an infirmary, of sorts, but it was upstairs. The woman with the infant, her name was Menka, had grudgingly taken over for Purty at tending to the wounded. She was moderately knowledgeable about what she was doing. Some things everyone knew, like letting an animal wound bleed a little before bandaging it, allowing the body to do its own cleansing. Tetanus killed almost as many people as the animals did. They'd all had tetanus shots, but that wouldn't prevent gangrene, or septicaemia, or…Menka rolled back a sleeve, revealing serpent scales that covered her entire arm.

"Where's the tattoo gear?" Seth asked her.

"It's down here. Won't do you much good without our artist."

He pushed himself up until he was half sitting against the wall. "What do you have there to fight infection?"

Menka rubbed her hand along the serpent arm, then she yanked the sleeve back down. "Nothing. We were getting it from you, remember? What little we can afford from elsewhere is in the infirmary. We haven't had a new 'too in months. Leon's been…was painting murals to keep from going nuts." She stooped over Sid. "How's the cut?" She reached out as if to poke it.

Sid pushed her questing finger away. "Thank Shangly for that. We don't trade with pillagers."

"What's pill-a-chers?" asked a little girl of Asian descent. Her black hair was knotted and tangled. Mottled scars, possibly from a raccoon, ravaged the landscape of her legs. They hadn't been tattooed yet.

Menka knelt and tried to comb the girl's hair with her fingers. "Pillagers are people that kill and take what doesn't belong to them."

The girl pointed at Purtricil. "That man said they were taking our tow truck, and…and…other stuff! Is he a pill-a-cher?"

Sid tried hard to meet Menka's stare. In the end, he found a particular bit of ceiling much less hostile. She was right. Shangly had killed five of Sid's people. Six if he included Burle. In retaliation, forty plus scavengers—and there must have been some children, too—were scattered around like so much detritus. But Shangly had violated the Pit, violated Burle! Still, it wasn't everyone's fault, no more than Senna or Purty could be blamed for the explosives. Even Seth was just following orders as he cultivated death with wire cutters and diodes. Sid had come here with the intention of stripping everything out, right down to the last bottle of ink. The survivors, who couldn't just be shot in cold blood, had been an abstract thing, to be dealt with later. Relocate them, indeed! It wasn't just that they had nowhere to go; Fenwick Prison was their home. Shangly had opened locks, Sid had knocked down walls. The Boss had come personally, deluding himself that it was purely out of duty. A part of him had yearned to lord over a humbled prison, to stride through smoky rubble. Despite the greater reward of creation, Sid had thrilled at the instant validation of power destruction wrought. Still, he wasn't completely inhuman. He knew what would have happened had Toffee helmed the attack. The hunter confirmed Sid's suspicion with the utterance of his next plan.

"It's simple; we toss a couple of these scavengers out the door, then we make like hell for that second corridor. We can get to the vehicles." He spoke quietly, so the natives couldn't hear.

"What's the vehicle capacity?" asked Sid. He knew the answer, but was in the habit of guiding people to things. Toffee was a step ahead of him.

"Yeah, so we've got more bodies than seats right now, but how many of us do you think'll make it all the way?"

"Not good enough."

"Fine. We throw all the scavengers outside. That'll give the birds something to work on while we hustle."

Sid was dismayed to find Toffee wasn't the only one who'd thought this.

"It's too much work, Chief," said Mike, one of the hunters. "They'd struggle, we'd have to shoot them. The kids wouldn't last long enough anyway."

Sid tried to gain focus. This was what he did; come up with solutions. It was why people followed him. It was a reputation as much as a fact. Only limited information would be given out back at the Pit. It would simply be another grand triumph by the Boss. That was, of course, if they made it back to the Pit. Darcy might just wind up running the whole show. The problem, he had to simplify the problem. Crows. They were fast and clever; rats of the sky. They coordinated their dives so as not to collide when dive bombing a victim. They loved to pluck things out of bodies; organs, tissue, and eyes. Individually, crows were annoying because they couldn't resist…

"Menka! Can we get to a tower?"

She was caught off guard by Sid's urgency. "Sure, to it. Not up it. Putting guards up there just pissed the birds off. Anything over thirty feet… We couldn't afford to keep replacing the mesh. Or the guards.

Since we stopped using the towers, we haven't had any sky problems." She didn't need to add *till now*.

"Where's your air compressor?"

"Upstairs."

"Upstairs. Damn, everything's upstairs. The generator, is the gas for it down here?"

Menka looked askance at Toffee. The hunter almost shrugged.

"Yes. At least one full can."

Sid picked up a blanket, tested its resiliency, then discarded it. "Do you have tools?"

"Some. Most are topside. What are you thinking?"

"I'm thinking we need a lot of files."

Toffee pushed the hatch up. The effort reopened his wounds, but then he'd never really let them close. It was dark outside. Even the crows had to sleep. Nocturnal critters would be nosing about, but probably not many. The animals would all be bloated from the feast. Their full bellies would slow them down, but an all out run across the yard was not an option. Through the smallest of gaps, he scanned the ground. The closest thing seemed to be a pair of coyotes curled up, about thirty feet away.

"Toffee to Radu," he said into his handset. No reply.

The hunter pushed the hatch a little higher. Below him, Daniel gripped an M16 uselessly. If he sprayed bullets up the hatchway, he'd hit Toffee more than anything else. With a larger slice of the yard available, the hunter could see a cougar had deigned to join the banquet. It slept near a piece of torso that must have been dragged a long way from a detonation site. It rolled over, swinging its tail and stretching its claws before once again becoming inert. In the distance, Toffee could hear some scuffling. There were very few crows. Maybe they'd retired to the building, or were high up on the outer wall, hidden by the darkness.

Toffee dropped the handset and reached down, waving for the rifle. He brought the gun up and rested the barrel on the ground. He chose the coyotes. He had a feeling they'd wake before the cougar. Pinching the rifle's stock between his side and shoulder, he retrieved the handset.

"Toffee to Radu."

"Radu here! Where are you?"

"What's going on topside?"

"Mae drove back far enough to radio Compton Pit. She's staying there to relay. Reinforcements are on their way here. Dr. Patel's coming."

"We can't wait that long."

"How are you going to get out?"

"Bring Mae in. A little after dawn, come in through gate, turn left, park by the vehicles. You'll know when." One of the coyotes moved. It was a jerk reflex.

"Yes, sir. How is everybody?"

"Some better than others. Maybe the doctor should meet us halfway."

Everyone was bone weary. Even the children looked shell shocked. They'd been at it for hours. Kerosene light reflected off bars shinier than they'd been the day Fenwick opened.

"This has got to be enough," said Daniel, handing the Boss a skinbag.

"This'll do it." Sid examined the contents, closed the bag and set off down the corridor. Menka went with him.

"This is insane," she said. "I thought it was nuts living here, but your Pit must be a loony bin if this is what their leader's like."

Sid didn't reply. He continued down a corridor. Absently noting rough piles of possessions in certain cells. Up a twisting flight of steps, three scavengers stood by the door. The lawnmower had its handle off and leaned on its front wheels, the blades exposed.

A number of skinbags were piled by a door, like cannon balls beside a powder keg. They were in the ground level of the northeast tower. The stairway above had been sealed with bars, wood and anything else that could be found lying around.

"We do this for you," said Menka, "and you go."

"What will you do?" asked the Boss.

"The meat up there won't last that long. The crows will leave soon. We can make it until then. We still have *our* cargo. You won't have time to steal that."

"Are you the new boss here?"

She thought about it. "Yes, I suppose I am. I'm queen of the prison."

"When I get back home, I'll trade with you."

"I won't trade with you."

Sid pulled her a few feet away from her subordinates and lowered his voice so only she could hear. "This is over now. If we have to come back here, my hunter, Toffee, will be in charge. You understand what that means, don't you?"

"I understand perfectly," she spat in reply.

Just after dawn, the morning sun broached the tree line. It shone straight through the front gates, bathing the front of the prison in yellow light. The crows shook themselves from rest, and lazily returned to another fine day of picking. Birds that had patrolled prison corridors the day before, took their turn at the trough. They seemed to have forgotten that there were still people hiding somewhere, or maybe they just didn't care.

The door in the northeast tower swung open and the buzz of the lawnmower drowned out a cacophony of caws. From the side of the mower, a billow of silver erupted into the air. The sunlight reflected off of countless facets, creating a constantly rippling haze of sparkles. Tiny bits of flashing metal drifted up and around the front of the tower. The crows forgot everything. En masse they hurtled towards the wondrous thing, the shiny curtain, the infinite twinkles. As they approached their destination, gouts of flame spewed from the doorway, roasting feathers and denying the crows their prize.

The hunters' van, the Pig, and a car zoomed through the front gates. The crows didn't care. The vehicles stopped by the burnt-out rig. The door from the southeast tower opened, and Compton Pit's warriors bolted for the van. Daniel carried Seth across his shoulders.

By the mower, Menka dumped another bag of metal filings into the blades.

"They'd better hurry up, we've got two bags left." Sweat covered her face and arms, either from her anxiety or from the proximity of the flamethrower.

The door to the Pig slammed closed, then slid open again. Toffee jumped out and hit the ground running.

"What are you doing?" yelled Daniel from the driver's seat.

"Go without me!" called Toffee.

The teeth had only been momentarily distracted by the glittering cloud. They closed on the vans, then altered course for the hunter. Toffee made it to the cab of the tow truck just before jaws snapped at his leg. He slammed the door shut on the coyote's head, then again. The animal whimpered and dropped. The keys were inside. He started the engine and roared off after the rest of Compton Pit's vehicles.

Menka glared at the departing truck as one of her new subjects pulled her back inside. The tower door slammed shut, abandoning the lawnmower to crows, who learned quickly not to go near its spinning blades. In the air above, the birds darted this way and that, trying to catch shiny objects that flashed, then disappeared. Any semblance of order had vanished. Birds cawed in excitement or frustration. Their vision told them there were flashing things all around, but the metal filings were too small to be easily captured. Some of the crows broke off their attempt to capture prizes, perhaps realizing they'd been had. Near the tower door, a coyote bit down on roast crow. After all, meat was meat.

24. It Works Both Ways

Toffee couldn't reach the other vehicles with the radio in the tow truck. He'd lost his handset at sometime or another, but this wasn't a problem. After the conflict, the hunter preferred to keep company with his own thoughts. If it hadn't been for the old man's bombs, this would have been impossible. The expectation had been to get no more than half of the scavengers with the initial explosion, but create enough confusion to make for an easy attack. When they'd breached the walls, all that had awaited them was non-combatants.

Had Toffee been in charge, those survivors would have joined their dead in minutes. Leftovers bred revenge. The rig would have been out the gates and on its way back to Compton Pit before the children had been discovered. Certainly Menka should have been killed. It was probably her that moved the children inside when Burle showed up. Toffee had never met Shangly face to face, but the new boss of Fenwick Prison seemed far more canny than the former. Sid came across as hard, but underneath that, he still had values that weren't much use in the new world. Still, Toffee blamed himself for the crows. He knew they came after a pitched battle; he'd faced them before under similar circumstances.

There was no surprise that the truck smelled bad; everything at Fenwick Prison did. It handled well, though it pulled a tad to the right. The seat had become uncomfortable, its padding long since compacted to the hardness of rock. The wounds on Toffee's back scratched against the fabric of his undershirt and coveralls. He craned his head back. Behind the seats, a tattered blanket covered unidentifiable objects. Toffee, keeping his left hand on the wheel, reached back for the blanket with his right. It had been a decade since he'd had fingers that responded to neural impulses, but that didn't stop him from trying, still thinking that one day wood and screws would curl of their own accord. His hand hooked the fabric and turned, bunching the fabric around and around. He pulled, but the blanket caught on something. One side flipped up, revealing an open box of dynamite.

"Well, look at that," he said out loud. "What were you going to use those for, Shangly?"

Ahead, the Pig slowed and stopped. Only one of its brake lights still worked. Unknown to the hunter, Sid had once insisted on all lights of a vehicle being in complete working order. His reasoning was that convoy vehicles could run into each other in the darkness without the glowing red indication of change of direction, or cessation of movement. In actual fact, it was a holdover from the Boss's days as an officer of the law. Ensuring proper vehicle safety was one of the things still under his control.

Toffee brought his tow truck to a halt and allowed the motor to idle.

Radu, a tall Croatian with graying hair and mirthful cheeks, stepped out of the Pig and walked to the tow truck's door.

"Switch off," he said. "Dr. Patel will be here soon and the Boss wants you up ahead with Seth and Senna."

"Watch out for the candles in the back," said the hunter as he stepped from the truck. Radu glanced at the box, raised an eyebrow to Toffee, then got in and closed the door.

From the southeast tower, Darcy watched, and waited. Three wounded. Four, actually, if she counted the stab wound the Boss passed off as nothing. One dead, but that death was inevitable. There was no rig coming back, though the chief of the hunters, seemingly of his own initiative, had seized a tow truck. After what seemed an eternity, the four vehicles appeared at the top of Compton Pit's driveway. Through binoculars, she scrutinized the new acquisition. It was rusty and dented. It leaned moderately to the right, probably a suspension problem. Caps would have a field day with it. It could easily be refitted to pull a trailer. They might not be able to get a complete rig, but there were still a few twenty footers lying around that could be brought in and fixed up.

The hunters' van was the first to arrive at the gates. They slid open and Darcy dropped her binoculars, preparing to make the trip down to the motor pool in order to welcome the returning conquerors and place the mantle of leadership back where it belonged. Her brief stint as boss had been quite unpleasant; dealing with the initial loss of contact, and then the horrid report of birds. She'd sent out a reinforcement group made up of farmers and labourers. She knew that the second group could do no more than hide within the confines of their vehicles and shoot a few birds at most, but she had to do something. Darcy had taken the eventual contact in stride, keeping calm on the outside, but inside, buckling with relief. She was already halfway down the stairs when the airlock doors opened, and didn't see the tow truck break off from the group.

Radu's head throbbed. He failed at his first two attempts to rise. His vision wavered and the road, where he lay, pitched and yawed beneath him. On the third try he made it to his knees. After a brief rest, he got his feet under him and examined his surroundings. He remembered taking the truck from Toffee. They'd waited until Dr. Patel arrived, then the convoy had resumed its homeward journey. Now he was here, wherever here was. Running his fingers through his hair, the security officer found a tender lump on the back of his head.

Victor Shangly's face was pulled back in a rictus of death. The one eye he could see through fixed on his target and held.

When the Screaming Mimi had gone off, Shangly was standing on the bridge. The force of the blast hurled him off the bridge and onto the soft edge beside the river. He must have blacked out, but not for long. He was up from the river and shambling towards the gate, still not sure of what had transpired. The guardhouse was a pile of cinders. Those in it and leaning up against it, must have been killed instantly. How had this happened? Did Kramond cause a short when he mishandled the sound unit? The smoke issuing from Fenwick's foyer answered the question. He dove under the rig when camouflaged soldiers appeared. Two scavengers were shot in an instant. As his people were herded to the middle of the yard, Shangly ran through his mind the options available to him. He had no weapon, but there was dynamite in the tow truck, a whole box of it, plus a lighter to ignite the fuses. His physical weakness bespoke injuries above what he could see on his body. It wasn't until he tripped over his own feet that he realized his depth perception was gone. His left eye was sightless. Examining his face, he found one side crushed and broken. That was when the pain started.

Huddled against one of the rig's large tires, Shangly eyed the open ground between him and the tow truck. The grenade going off was the distraction he needed to cover the distance. Once inside, he was unable start the engine. The keys were there, but he had no strength. He pulled himself into the space behind the seats, covered himself with the a blanket stored there, and passed out. The next time he'd opened his eye, black birds perched on the hood of the vehicle, and, it seemed, everywhere else. The king of Fenwick Prison pulled the blanket over his head, and allowed sleep to take him once more.

Motion of the vehicle awoke him. He peeked out from beneath the blanket. The man driving could only have been Sid's hunter, Toffee. The vehicle was being taken back to Compton Pit, and that was just fine with the king of Fenwick Prison. He'd wait until the tow truck was safely inside, then make his move. The change in drivers had made for a different plan of action. Shangly had no delusions about being able to take out the big hunter, even with surprise on his side, but the other man looked much less capable. Shangly waited until he felt the vehicle slow for a turn, then revealed himself and struck with a tire iron. It had only taken one blow. With the rest of the vehicles out of sight, the scavenger shoved his enemy out an open door, taking control without missing a beat.

Now, he held the wheel steady with one hand while he fished dynamite from the behind the seat with his other. His shame of being so easily hoodwinked by the old man, his rage at the destruction that had been visited upon his home, all this coalesced into a single, burning desire for revenge. Halbert had cost him two wives. Shangly would take from him the Pit itself.

Daniel looked as if he would fall to his knees and kiss the concrete floor of the motor pool. Seth was taken to the infirmary on a stretcher, Patel beside him, holding an IV bag the whole time. The procedure of gassing the vehicles while sealed in the airlock was forgone, in order to expedite the hunter second's delivery to surgery.

"Where's the truck?" asked Caps, peering from the pool into the airlock, at the same time as a triple-bell alarm rang from above.

"Who's driving the truck?" asked Darcy.

"Radu," said Toffee, staring above.

Darcy ran through the airlock and up the ramp in an instant. Behind her, hunters and watchers, felt like they'd awoken from nightmare, to find they were still in one.

The first explosion threw dirt and photovoltaic crystal way up in the air. The second hurled even more. Darcy had her gun out and aimed before she knew what to shoot at. From above, the southeast tower's 50 cal. poured bullets into the tow truck. From a forest of panels, another explosion reduced vital solar collectors to burnt metal and jagged, twisted frames. From behind came Toffee's voice, yelling at her to wait.

The 50 cal. ceased its deadly staccato, either for lack of ammunition, or because the chief of security had entered its field of fire. Black crystal crunched underfoot as Darcy wove between the support columns. She saw him then, standing next to the hub, a stick of dynamite, as yet unlit, in his hand. She had no clue why she didn't just shoot.

"Stop!" she ordered.

Shangly vanished behind a column like a puff of smoke. Assistance was right behind, but Darcy didn't wait. She moved forward, gun held in both hands. She heard the sparking fuse arcing over her head.

"Down!" she yelled behind her.

The blast threw Darcy to the ground. Debris showered her back, and a terrible ringing filled her ears.

Shangly's kick took her in the shoulder, then her own gun pressed into the back of her head.

A mosquito buzz gradually became a voice. "…Halbert's little princess. Don't you move a muscle, girl." Then, "Drop it! Get down on the ground! I mean it!"

There was a thump, then a scuffle.

"You were in the truck. My sense of smell must be going."

The pressure from the gun barrel increased, squishing Darcy's nose against the ground.

"You're Toffee. I know you. Back off."

"Not gonna happen, doglicker."

Darcy's hand scrabbled over the ground, searching for a shard of crystal, a length of pipe. She pictured the field from above, trying to gauge lines-of-site, places where her people could get the drop on Shangly. A stick of dynamite was shoved into the ground beside her head, its bottom twisted into the dirt.

"You light that candle, I'll come for you."

Why was the hunter waiting? Her life shouldn't have meant spit to him. Once she was gone, Toffee could take her place. It was what he'd been after, wasn't it? From the sound, she guessed there were about ten people moving about beyond the panels. The dust hadn't quite settled, but visibility shouldn't have been completely obscured. She didn't want to die, but she knew it might come to this. It had been made very clear to her before she took the job.

"SOMEBODY SHOOT HIM!" she bellowed into the dirt, "THAT'S AN ORD–"

The gun came away from her head. She rolled over, narrowly avoiding Shangly's swipe.

The stick was lit. A bullet pinged off a column near her head, at least someone had obeyed her command. She heard Toffee scrambling to his feet. Shangly scooped the dynamite and casually tossed it to the hunter, who caught it by reflex. Darcy didn't see what happened next, she was too busy striking out. Her legs swung forward, attempting to hit Shangly behind the knees. Her foe skipped away, then another explosion smashed through the array. The chief of security shielded her face as the shockwave peppered her body with tiny missiles. From the direction of the blast, Toffee must have thrown it away from approaching friendlies, but farther into the panels.

Shangly was beside her. For the first time, she got a clear look at him. The left side of his face was ruined, the skin dimpled and flaked around scorch marks. Dead skin surrounded an empty socket. There were burns to his shoulder as well. The hair on the end of his ponytail was frazzled.

"I'm gonna kill you slow, princess." The scavenger was crawling towards her. Between the tattoos and the fresh wounds, Shangly was a beast. His humanity was covered by ink and burned away by fire. Killing him was no worse than killing a raccoon.

Shangly's hands closed on empty air. Darcy twirled behind him. She grabbed his ponytail and wrapped it around his throat, pushing down on his back with her knee as she pulled up with all her strength. It was like fishing, she thought. Her father had taken her fishing, some of her fondest memories. Shangly lay beneath her and struggled like a salmon on a hook. Froth bubbled from the side of his mouth and he clawed at a garrote that couldn't be removed.

By the time Toffee reached the contest, dirty and bleeding from a myriad of pin pricks, his assistance was no longer required.

His feet amid a litter of char and crystal, the useless tool kit on the ground beside him, Noah stood in the ruin of his garden. In the dying light, empty frames and malformed columns washed black, like the distant skyline of a broken city. Noah had stopped counting what didn't work, finding it quicker to inventory what did. Cables on the outside of the blast areas were fused. Panels not destroyed were out of alignment. The entire bar of concentrators, those monochromatic giants of the team, were splayed in opposition to each other. The axles were so bent, there was no way for the panels to track the sun. They were stuck in place, capable of only getting what direct light the day offered. Thin film was blown from the columns. Shrapnel had scratched and chipped the surfaces of cells still intact.

Despite the damage, it could have been worse. Much worse. If Shangly hadn't focussed on tormenting Darcy, if he'd gotten a stick down the hub, into the battery bay…there'd still be heat and water, but no lights, and no Mimis. The hydroelectric generator couldn't support the network.

Later, Noah would feel guilty that his sorrow over panels overwhelmed his grief for Cass. Though Gershwin was the voice, the panels were the lungs. They were Noah's domain; the reason for his position, the halo around his head. It meant no difference to him over forty lay as bird food in Fenwick Prison, or that Radu still hadn't been found. Seth might as well have been in Gascan D'Abo's pleasure palace (which was something of a legend in Underbel) as in the infirmary. That Noah hadn't been the one to light the fuses, didn't change the fact that during his short tenure, the panel array had gone from a masterpiece of engineering, to a feeble ruin of crumbling cells.

Someone, part of the clean-up crew, took Noah's arm. "Sir, I've been told to tell you, meeting."

It was sombre at the table. The faces that met Sid's were as tired as his, even those who had stayed out of the action.

"Small things first," said the Boss. "Dr. Patel tells me that Seth might not ever recover full use of his arm. It doesn't matter. He won't need it in his new position as chief of stores. Daniel, I'm promoting you to chief of transport. Congratulations."

Daniel nodded a thank-you, but his face didn't echo the sentiment. There was no joy in how the position had been vacated, and currently, there was no transport team.

"Lena, you're now chief negotiator. Officially you're just chief of communications, but you understand what I mean."

She licked her lips. "Boss, I...thank-you. Maybe under normal circumstances, but now, shouldn't you–"

He cut her off with an upheld hand. "You've handled your share of tough barter sessions already."

"Yes, but that was because I always had Burle to fall back on."

"So you'll work without a net. It's what being a chief's about. Patricia is back in security. She wasn't happy, but we need her. Her position in tanning will be filled by–"

"What about seconds?" asked Toffee. "Darcy and I just lost ours. Do we get to decide, or do you?"

"That's your decision to make."

"Fine. Senna's my new second."

"That's not an option, Toffee. Senna is a tanner now."

"What?" blurted the hunter and Darcy at the same time.

"We discussed it on the ride back. She never wants to hold another gun again, or a knife if it's for killing. She can skin an animal like the best of them, she's done tanning before. Devon will appreciate her help. So who's your second now? Choose carefully. Darcy?"

"Chiu-Keung's the better fighter, but Purty's the better diplomat. I'll have to think about it."

"Fine. You'll have plenty of time to do that." He didn't explain what he meant. "Sara, Burle's room is yours. You can move in as soon as you want." Dr. White, far from being grateful, looked at the table with remorse. "We have four rooms to fill from the barracks, which means four bunks to fill from somewhere else. Five, I suppose." There wasn't much chance for Radu, now. "Lena, put the word out we have space."

"Maybe that's not such a good idea," said Noah.

"Go on," the Boss urged.

"I was overly optimistic in my first report to you. We've shut down a lot of the Pit, but we need to shut down more. I don't think we need to keep this room. I'm turning off Holy Ground. It's going to be daylight, with slight augmentation only. I'd say we're at less than twenty-five percent draw. With work, we can get back up to thirty. Maybe even that's optimistic. We need panels, Boss. Lots of them, and soon."

The Boss's expression was unreadable. "Tomorrow at breakfast," he said, "I'll announce that Burle Campbell was lost during the attack. He died while protecting Compton Pit and its interests."

Darcy let her eyes wander the room. Beyond the senior security, Toffee, Seth and the Boss, nobody knew the real story. Nobody, except Lena, which meant that Caps probably knew, too. He'd keep his mouth shut. For all his talking, Caps was good at keeping secrets.

"Tell me about the truck, Richard."

"It's not as good as a rig, Boss. The truck's not a factory model, that's for sure. Its suspension has been reinforced, badly I might add. The motor was put together by a maniac. It'll take me a while to figure out all the ins and outs. It's well armoured, but that reduces its towing capacity. That's all moot, though, considering the damage. The fuel tank wasn't ruptured, but the roof's a mess. The dashboard's gone, so we have to start it from under the hood. If we could start it. The tranny's damaged and the stick shift got blown off. We actually had to tow it into the pool."

"Can you fix it?"

"Not without a transmission. Guess who we can get that from."

"I'm sure I can find a tranny…" started Lena.

Sid shook his head. "Harpreet, how's Odega?"

"Same as last time. He's stable, vital signs are good, but he won't wake up. He could be opening his eyes right now, or dying for that matter. Without a CAT, or MRI, or even an X-ray, I couldn't tell you for sure. I'm not about to open up his head just to take a look around."

Sid stood and walked around the table. It was a rare thing for him to do. He looked at each of his chiefs in turn. Finally, he returned to his chair, but stood before it.

"We need at least one rig. We need solar panels. We need raw materials. I know a place where we can get all three."

Darcy was the first to cotton on. "You can't mean…"

"We have to go to the city."

All except Noah were stunned by this announcement.

"Which city? How are we supposed to–"

"You mean Vancouver, don't you?" asked Lena. It was the most logical choice considering geography.

"That's right," said the Boss, "Vancouver."

"Whoa," Caps spread his arms wide. "Dogcouver? Ratcouver? Antcouver? Who the hell are you going to send there?" There'd been an expedition four years ago. Like the one before it, nobody had returned.

"You, for one."

"Me?!" Caps shook his head like a cat snapping a mouse's neck. "Not a chance. Colour me terrified."

"Has to be you, Richard. There's fleets of trucks there, just waiting. They'll be broken down, partially stripped...if we can't find one that runs by itself, you'll have to make one. I'm hoping for two."

"But why me?" his voice had taken on a pleading quality.

"Because your people are good mechanics, but you're an artist. We need to get in and get out as quickly as we can." Lena's expression was sour. Sending Caps to the city was about the same for her as locking him outside. "Don't worry, Lena, you're going, too. You know our second objective better than anyone. You went there."

"Went, uh, where?" She looked at Caps. She couldn't tell which one of them was more horrified.

"Noah, you too."

The chief of photovoltaics felt like he'd been kicked in the chest. "I..."

"Say, ' yes, sir,' " said the Boss.

"Yes, sir."

"Freeland told me about a cache of solar panels, better than anything we've got here. It was never worth the risk before. Noah, you and I will go over all the details. You'll understand."

Darcy could stay seated no longer. "Who's leading this expedition?"

"I am."

The room exploded. Patel called it foolish. Sara called it suicidal. Darcy refused to let the Boss go anywhere after being stabbed. Caps argued the logic of stripping the Pit of four of its senior staff.

"Five," said Toffee. "I assume I'm coming, too."

"Yes," said Sid. "That's why you need to choose your second carefully. Until we return, he or she will be chief of the hunters."

"Then it's six," said Darcy. "If you're going, I'm guarding you." She shot a look at Toffee.

"You have to stay behind," said Sid, gently. "You're the boss while I'm gone."

She reached forward and gripped Sid's wrist. "I'm. Going. With. You."

Noah sat in his new chair and rocked anxiously. The tiny panel he'd found in Freeland's skinbag lay on the bed, an evil, spiteful thing. He'd test it against sunlight the next day, but he had no doubt it would prove as efficient as the Boss had told him. An experimental set of panels, in a basement under the University of British Columbia. How much was actually there didn't matter. Sid only had a vague idea of where it was; faded reports, scribbled notes, all from Noah's predecessor. It was a straw, but it was the only one Sid had. Nobody would be foolish enough to trade solar panels away.

Noah's light was on, against his own orders, but it didn't matter, not now.

"Is that comfy?" asked Caps, taking a deep draw on his pipe.

"Yes. Why'd Burle leave it to me? I thought he would have given it to Darcy."

Caps looked at Lena as he handed her the pipe. She shook her head slightly.

"I guess he really liked you, Noah. Maybe he hopes you'll put some children in it one day."

I will not drive them out from before thee in one year,
lest the land become desolate,
and the beasts of the field multiply against thee.

Exodus XXIII, 29

25. Preparations

"You've lost your mind," said Toffee.

Senna looked up from a patch of leather. She had a small mallet and a metal punching tool in her hands. She grimaced, then hammered another hole through the material.

Bang.

"Was this Halbert's idea? Did he convince you you couldn't take it?"

She placed her tools on the desk. Her room was decorated with animal hides. Empty pegs, where rifles used to be, occupied the wall behind her bed. She'd been ordered to take a few days off, so she'd taken some scrap material to fill her time. Senna wasn't up early, she just hadn't gone to bed.

"The Boss tried to talk me out of it. This is my decision."

Toffee eyed the empty pegs with disdain. Never give up your weapon; it didn't matter who you were. "You've made a bad choice. I know what it feels like to kill someone–"

"Dogshit! You've never regretted killing anyone in your life."

She was right. *Well, there had been one man.* Toffee banished the thought. "You had to kill that man on the ridge. He would have gotten off a warning."

She fingered the mallet's handle. "I know that."

"And you didn't kill that kid. That could have happened to any of us."

She whipped her head around angrily. "It couldn't have happened to you!"

Oh, couldn't it? I drove halfway here with Shangly right behind me. "You're a good hunter, the best I've got–"

"You haven't got me."

"I want you to be my second."

Her anger turned to fear. "Did Seth…I thought it was just a shoulder wound…"

"He's promoted, not dead. Chief of Stores. Be my second, not a tanner. Trust me."

"I did that before. Remember? 'Clear the air with Darcy,' you said." She picked up her tools and set metal to leather. "I don't know why I told you about Travis. I never should have told her."

Bang.

"It's not like we were sisters, but at least we were friends."

Bang!

"You know what Travis called me? His last words to me? He called me a selfish bitch."

BANG!

"I didn't like that word, even before it meant what it does now."

People gave Toffee a wide berth as he moved through the mess hall. No one wanted to offer him a target. The word had gone out; Toffee had hand-delivered an enemy into their ranks. He must have been furious, looking for any target. Surprisingly, they couldn't have been more wrong. Toffee was furious, but it was an anger so deep, he could only channel it at himself. Missing a shot, stubbing his toe, these were things that could be assuaged by someone else's discomfort. This bungle was monumental. It had tangible effects. Only sunlight lit the mess hall. The kitchen, having no skylights, worked under limited flourescent. Food was burnt.

Like anything he chose to possess, Toffee owned all of the blame. Radu was his fault. The security officer had been out there for almost forty-eight hours. Even if he hadn't been killed outright by Shangly, he was dead now. Toffee's status in the Pit had been unalterably changed. Physically, people would still view him as formidable. Mentally, however, he would be seen as somewhat less than that—the idiot who drove Victor Shangly right through the gates. He'd dropped from being a demon to a mere bully. He'd even been denied the small redemption of killing Shangly. He sure liked the way Darcy had done the job, though.

The way other people felt about him was secondary to how he felt about himself. Toffee had only felt this low, this worthless, one time before. There'd been no witnesses to that, though. Well, there had been one, but she must be long dead by now. Toffee would still destroy the first person that cracked wise to him, but only because it was expected. There'd be no satisfaction in it. Unless it was the painter. That would feel nice.

In contrast, opinion for Noah Thurlow had grown tenfold. Instead of the dog-scared geek with the tool box, he was a brave adventurer, daring the untold dangers of the big city. At the same time he'd gained the respect due only to the soon-to-be dead.

"Man," said Noah, "it's like I'm equal to the Boss, or something."

"Yeah," remarked Caps. "You seen how they're treating the Boss?"

In a closed meeting, Sid had explained his reason for choosing his team. The Pit was wounded. They had one shot at getting what they needed before the wound became fatal. Gascan could starve them out, strip the place of everything he wanted. Economic warfare was every bit as devastating as that fought with guns. If the mission failed, it wouldn't matter who was running the Pit. The Boss wanted his specialists. He admitted that he should have picked Darcy in the first place.

"This sucks." Caps scraped black bits off his eggs. "You know, sun boy, when we get back from this, you're gonna be beating the ladies back with a stick."

"Won't you be, too?"

Caps almost dropped his knife. "Wow." He turned to Lena. "Wow! Noah, you are just blind to some things."

Noah searched Caps's face for whatever he'd missed. "What?"

"Me and Lena," he took her hand, "we're a couple." After a second, Lena pulled her hand away.

Noah was aghast. "Why didn't you tell me?"

"I didn't think I had to."

"But, but, I've never seen you kiss, or hold hands or anything."

Caps shrugged. "That's Lena's idea. She thinks it's bad luck to have PDAs."

Lena answered Noah's look of confusion. "Public displays of affection. Also, it's mean. Everyone here has lost someone. I think it hurts people to see others holding hands."

Noah thought about Cass. She'd never touched him around others, either. He looked around the mess hall. Even between people he knew to be couples, there was no indication of anything other than platonic friendship.

"I've never noticed that before. You know, in Underbel, I once saw two people screwing in a hallway. How long?"

"A while now," said Caps. Lena looked uncomfortable even talking about the subject.

"Are you two getting married?"

Lena almost choked on her breakfast.

Caps watched another person pass by, ignoring the empty chairs to find room at more crowded tables. The artist stood up. "Hey! There's two empty seats here! We gonna leave them that way forever?"

The other diners, both those standing and sitting, stopped in their motions and looked at the chairs. One was Burle's, the other had become Cass's. There was a general feeling of discomfort. People watched for someone else to turn away, nobody wanting to be the first. Patricia, once again in khaki, walked over and sat down. That was enough for some to resume eating, but Burle's chair held the others. Who was worthy?

At the head table, a seat pushed back. Darcy walked with the bearing of a queen, as she carried her tray of burnt food and took Burle's chair without a word.

There, thought Sid, *rest in peace, old friend. All is forgiven, if not forgotten.*

"Why not me?" Sara smacked her hand with a fist. "I already run H&H, plus the farm, practically. You can't leave it to him!"

"And why not?" asked Dr. Patel, with equal ire. "If I can run an OR, I can certainly make snap decisions."

The Boss was the only one seated. The meeting room was still lit. It was the closest thing Sid allowed himself to an office. He looked from Dr. White to Dr. Patel, and waited.

"Snap decisions?" The skin around Sara's mouth tightened. It was something that happened before she said something evil. "You'll make drunk decisions."

"I like that! And you aren't enjoying your share of my product?"

Sara stood on her toes and mimed waving a bottle. "Trade what away?" she said in Patel's accent. "HIC! Okay. Turn what back on?"

Sid had seen enough. "You've made your point."

"Sorry, Harpreet," she crossed her arms. "I won't let this place fall apart with him holding the reigns."

"And I won't take orders from this harpy!"

Sid had hoped for better from Patel. "You'll do it together."

Sara and Dr. Patel exchanged a glance. Patel was defiant, she was regretful.

"Fine," said Sara, giving up. "Let him do it. We'll butt heads too much. Nothing will get done."

Sid leaned back, satisfied. "Good. Sara, you're the boss."

Dr. Patel's expression went from vindication, to shock, then to defeat. "I don't believe it," he said, "you went Solomon on us."

Lena sat in her chair and stared at dead equipment. Noah had shut her down. The computer still operated, and the radio was on, but no satellite. Standing orders were for passive radio use only. Monitor transmissions, but give no replies. Not a word of Compton Pit's condition could be risked. It wasn't just D'Abo that had to be kept in the dark. Drum East, Piper's Cove, even Underbel needed to be guarded against. Who really knew what they'd do if they saw the mighty Pit laid low. Even radio silence might be useless. By now, one of Shangly's survivors might have traded information to Gascan. According to Lot, Fenwick Prison had no satellite capability, but there was some sort of radio relay; prison to settlement, settlement to communications truck. D'Abo had a few of them out there, lurking on the airwaves, reading market trends whenever a frequency was discovered.

Today, Lena could have linked to either London or China. She could only pick one, the geosynchronous dance giving her both windows for the same brief period. Now, she didn't even have that. She longed for a chance to say good-bye to at least one of her distant friends. Seeing their faces proved that there was still a whole world out there, not just the teeth infested corner she shared with equally endangered settlements.

"Screw it!" she said. She put on her headphones and punched up her communications screen. Checking the satellite dish orientation, she selected China and fired off her signal. The dish didn't have to move. As long as nobody was watching the usage screen on Noah's computer, she could do this undetected. She deserved it; she was going to the city.

Noah leaned over Bob "Duff" Dufferin's shoulder and watched the man flick through screens.

"Now tell me what capacity the battery bay is at."

Duff, a man shaped like his nickname, swallowed a retort and did as he was told. Who did this kid think had held things together before he showed up? Still, the chief was the chief.

"Yes, sir." As soon as the screen came up, a blue and red graph on a yellow background, Noah shouldered him out of the way.

"That's not right," said Noah.

"What?" Duff didn't see the problem. The batteries were still over three quarters. With the additional cuts Noah had outlined, they'd be brought up to full.

Noah ignored his subordinate. The capacity was lower than he had set it. Power was going out somewhere. He clicked through a couple of screens and caught the leak. SatCom. Noah clicked back to the battery screen.

"My mistake," he stepped away from the laptop. "Everything's the way it should be."

Daniel sat on the edge of Darcy's desk. He didn't want to take the chair. "So, I'm still not a chief?"

"Sure," said Darcy, "You're chief of security."

He pointed to the patch over his breast. "This still says second."

"Daniel, there's no point being chief of transport without a truck. Right now I need you here. As soon as I come back–"

"And if you don't come back? I have to know what I'm getting into. Traditionally, chief of security is second to the Boss. How long do you think Sara's appointment will last?"

Darcy finished cleaning her gun, and began to reassemble it. "I've thought about that. So has Sid. What happens, happens."

"So," Daniel rapped the desk with a knuckle, "not that I want it to happen, but do you think I could be the Boss?"

"You want honest?"

"That bad, huh?"

Darcy had to smile. Her second had eight years on her, but sometimes she was very much the big sister. "You need moderation. You've got it mostly, but you still let your anger get to you. That's sometimes good in a chief, but not in a boss."

"The same could be said about you, Chief."

"I know. I don't want to be the Boss."

Daniel snatched a vital piece of the gun's inner workings, forcing Darcy to stop and look up at him. "Is that why you insisted on going? You'd rather die than lead the Pit?"

"We're all coming back, Daniel." But she didn't know that to be true. What she did know, was that she'd rather die than live without Sid.

Toffee flipped his desk over and checked the legs. They weren't hollow either. He worked with a flashlight, not because Thurlow had cut his power, but because both lamps had been disassembled. The hunter shoved the upside-down desk a few inches across the floor and moved to the bed. It was a double, unlike most of the cots in Compton Pit. He'd inherited the bed from Travis Jones, as well as all the other furnishings. Darcy had taken some things, but the rest were still where they had been. Toffee pulled the mattress and box spring off the frame. He tapped the wood in various places, hoping to find a void between the flats.

At the foot of the bed, an empty thunk signalled the end to his search. The frame was ingeniously constructed of interlocking boards. No screws or nails had been used. This was the first piece of good luck to find the hunter all day. He slid two boards out to reveal a space just a bit bigger than what he required. Removing a screwdriver from his pocket, Toffee held the flashlight in his mouth while he removed the grate from over the air vent. Honour system was all well and good, but the hunter didn't trust people not to come nosing around once he was gone. If they wanted his honey, they'd have to earn in it. He took the collection of vials, wrapped them in a shirt, and wadded it into the space. The gold ring and American deuce he didn't care about, but the button held his attention for a moment. He picked it up and turned it each way under the flashlight's beam. Placing the button in the skinbag hung from his neck, Toffee removed the wad from the frame, withdrew three vials, then placed the bundle back, and reassembled the bed.

The bovine moved a little at the touch of cold hands on its udder, but it was reflex, nothing more. No annoyance showed in its thoughtless eyes. Once, Miranda would have warmed her hands before milking, but she didn't bother anymore. It wasn't that she wished discomfort on the animal, it was just that it didn't seem to care, so why should she? She'd given up long ago wondering what went through the lobotomised heads of these creatures; the cows, the pigs, the sheep. The pigs were an addition only six months old. There weren't that many left running around in the woods. When the squealing creatures were found, they were usually shot on the spot. It was Roshi's idea to bring a couple in, to fatten them up. The cook had a dream of a pig roast, the whole show. Pig on a spit, apple in its mouth. The apple was actually more difficult to obtain than the pig. There was a valley only a day's drive away filled with apple trees, but it was also filled with bees.

Miranda looked the stereotypical farmer's wife as she worked the udders; walnut coloured hair tied back in a bun, wide hips spreading out on the stool. She was built that way, as had been her mother and grandmother. She'd grown up on the Malkovich family farm, a little north of Spokane, Washington.

Among the other animals, they had a tame ocelot. Three times the size of an average house cat, its tufted ears had earned it the name "Sagebrush." Sagebrush was fed on table scraps and occasionally, a raw steak. On June 10th, New Wilderness Day, the beloved animal had decided it wanted a different lunch, namely Mr. Malkovich. His daughter should have known better than to wrestle with the animal, but it had never hurt her before. It was Miranda's mother that pulled the trigger, euthanising the pet with a 38 cal. bullet from twenty feet away. Miranda had gained permanent marks on her chest and arms. Her father wasn't so lucky. Neither was her fiancé. He'd been safely away from the farm on New Wilderness Day, comfortable on his second week in the new, air-conditioned office. She never did find out what happened to him, but she knew by day three that he wasn't coming home.

For the next ten years, Miranda had shunned the touch of men. She rarely covered her scars. She wore them openly. Not because they didn't disgust her, but to hide the fact that they did. Her only physical comfort had come since moving to Compton Pit. Though some might find it perverse, the soft resistance of cow's teat had mitigated her need for human contact, at least a little. She felt she had a great deal in common with the animal; both of them big-eyed, both with large hips, and both mutilated, body and mind.

The chief of the kitchen wore a look of childlike innocence as he handed Noah the tray. The dinner served was different from what others were receiving. No attempt had been made to hide the fact. While others were getting yet another dose of stew, Noah's tray held a slim cut of meat, accompanied by vegetables on a rice pilaf. It had been a long time since Noah had eaten rice.

"Saffron!" said Roshi, pointing at the rice, like it was supposed to mean something.

"What's saffron?" asked Noah as he sat down. Caps and Lena were there already.

"Only the most expensive spice in the world," said Caps. "It was even before the Change. I think this is the last of Roshi's rice, too."

Patricia sat down. She had stew, but made no comment about the fancy dinner her table mates had received.

"Won't everyone else be jealous?" Noah asked, spooning rice into his mouth.

"If they were leaving tomorrow," Lena waved at the mess hall with her fork, "they'd get this, too. Ever hear of a last meal?"

The rice, melting deliciously in Noah's mouth, turned to ash.

"Did Roshi tell you this was saffron?" asked Darcy, taking a chair. "I wonder how long he's been sitting on it."

"Please," said Caps, "this meal is hard enough to eat without thinking about the cook's big butt on it."

They ate in silence for a few minutes. Patricia had nothing to offer, she was just filling a seat.

"So," started Caps, feeling the quiet had lasted long enough. "Are you going to sit with us once we get back?"

Noah stared at his tray intently, dreading the answer. A week ago, he'd have been overjoyed at a yes, now he desperately wanted a no. His feelings towards Darcy had changed. Unlike the hunter, Noah was, as yet, incapable of truly pinpointing the source of his negative emotions. Guilt at thinking about Darcy while with Cass had become a betrayal of his late lover by the chief of security. He didn't rationalize it. Transference didn't work that way.

Darcy flicked her eyes at Noah, then shared a look with Lena. "No. By then other people will sit here. My place is still by the Boss." She was prepared for Noah's shift in posture. His shoulders slumped with relief, and the piece of meat that had stopped halfway to his mouth, completed its journey. Despite being aware of the panel jockey's change of tune where she was concerned, it still hurt a little to find him happy that she was not a permanent addition. She'd left apologizing to him for too long. It was too late now. Darcy was surprised that she actually missed having the young man dote on her, even though she didn't feel a mutual attraction.

At the head table, the hunter, chewing automatically on his gourmet meal, sat alone. Two chairs—Seth's and Darcy's—separated him from the Boss. Nobody sat opposite him. His face was a study of what had befallen the Pit; a scabbed and harried metaphor of cratered nose and punctured cheek.

"Check out big boy," said Caps. "Looks like he stuck his face on a grill. How'd you avoid that, Darcy?"

"I shielded my face with my arm." She demonstrated. The fork, still in her hand, stabbed into her neck. "OW!"

Serves you right, thought Noah. He remembered the sting of her slap.

Darcy shot her eyes right and left, trying to see who had caught her little faux-pas. Noah was looking everywhere but at her.

Well I hope that made you happy, she thought. It didn't occur to her that this was the first time she'd cared about what went through the sun boy's head. Except when she'd been interrogating him.

For his part, Noah had forgotten the chief of security was even at the table. He was examining his cut of deer. It was cooked exactly right. Examining the other trays, he saw that nothing was burned this time around. Either the cook had gotten proficient at low-light cooking in a remarkable hurry, or he'd used more lights than he'd been allotted. Noah was going to have to make physical cuts to the system, rather than just virtual ones. If everyone sneaked just a little more, the batteries would be empty in a matter of days. He'd be up all night.

It was Caps that started tapping his glass first. Soon other utensils took up the percussion, along with cries of "Speech! Speech!"

The Boss resisted for the expected period of time, then stood and silenced the din with a sweep of his hand.

"Ladies and Gentlemen…I appreciate the sentiment. Anything I have to say to you, I've already said. Either personally, or through your department heads. If you need something more, you'll have to get it elsewhere." The Boss turned his head towards Caps.

The artist actually managed a blush as he stood.

"Unaccustomed as I am to public speaking…" a smatter of laughter, "…I'll make this as a quick as possible. I know how much all of you want to get back to your rooms, so you can sit in the dark." Rueful chuckles, a groan. "We've had it real tough here the last week or so, what with the boredom and all. But I figure things will pick up if we just keep our fingers crossed." More laughter, some of it genuine. "Don't think of it as less time to read, think of it as more time to have sex." Cheers went up, along with some applause. Lena would bust his chops for that crack later, but right now, it was worth it. "The worst thing is you'll have to live without my daily cartoon."

"Try weekly!" called someone.

"Try monthly!" came another voice.

"Yes, alright, I've been slacking off, I admit it. But I'm out of fresh material until I see someone do something stupid."

"Get a mirror!" called Dr. White. There was resounding laughter for that, it never being too early to butter up the new boss.

A dozen clever retorts vied for position on Caps's tongue. He used none of them. He couldn't hack on Dr. White, it might undermine her position. Caps winked at her; *Okay, Sara, you got me.* Once the mirth had died down, the artist resumed. "If I could be serious for a minute–"

"I'd rather you were funny for a minute!" called Mike, the hunter.

This was a safe target. "Mike, you're living proof that some dogs can still sit at the table."

They roared. Caps had them in the palm of his hand. He silenced the crowd by raising his glass. It was water, not liquor, which tradition called for, but there'd be a lot of real drinking going on later. Not for the Deep Six—as Caps had taken to referring to himself and his teammates—they couldn't afford hangovers the next day. Around the mess hall, glasses of water floated to the air.

"To October, Ian, Sam and Stuart, and to Burle. We've lost some friends, but we've lost a lot more enemies."

Lena smiled as she drank, but she wasn't happy with the toast. Caps had justified the loss of five people, with the slaughter of forty more. The denizens of Compton Pit didn't care, though. They whooped and hollered until Caps took them once more with a casual shift in the position of his arm.

"As for us, we'll be back in no time." He gestured at the ceiling. "And the lights will all be on again right after that. But if we're not...since I opened with a cliché, I'll close with a cliché. Those of us about to..." Lena grabbed his leg behind the knee and dug her thumb in. "...not get much sleep, salute you."

Everyone cheered, and shot back water with all the gusto of schnapps.

"Unaccustomed as I am to public speaking?" taunted Darcy as Caps sat down.

"Hey, even old jokes are good jokes if nobody's heard 'em for a while."

Roshi waited as long as he could, but the mess hall was not going to empty completely. Without light in most of the rooms, night owls sat at tables and read, or talked. The next day's voyagers sat at the head table, held there by the Boss, at Roshi's demand. There was one more course to serve. Roshi carried the tray to them like it contained the secrets of the universe. He placed the dish on the table, then pulled away the cloth. On it was a single cake, eight inches by four, shaped like a brown brick.

"Chocolate cake," said Caps. "Thanks, Roshi."

"It's not chocolate," said the cook. An assistant placed a stack of plates on the table as Roshi cut slices. Heads around the room came up, but no one rose in attempt gain a piece.

The cake had taken the last of many things: baking soda, cinnamon, real brandy, and one other ingredient.

"Mmmm," mouthed Darcy, trying not let a single crumb escape from her mouth.

Caps took a bite. "Oh man, oh man! Roshi, what is this?"

The chief of the kitchen beamed. "Honey cake."

Noah gauged how much of the cake was left, before setting his mouth to top speed.

Sid shook his head and gave Roshi a wistful smile. "I was amazed at the saffron, but honey…how long have you been keeping that a secret?"

The cook shrugged, then cut himself a slice. Lena looked at Darcy, who shook her head, then glanced at the hunter. Toffee stared off into the distance, his mouth chewing, no expression on his face.

"Who is it?" called the Boss. No answer. The knock came again. "Who is it?" he asked again, a little perturbed. He'd almost been asleep.

"Sir?" a voice whispered. "Sorry to disturb you…"

"Hang on." He dropped out of bed and pulled on a natted, terry-cloth robe. Clicking on the lamp, he said, "Come in."

The door opened. "Were you…were you asleep?"

"Miranda? Is there a problem?" She'd never come to his door before. She'd never even spoken to him in the mess hall.

"No. No problem. I'm sorry, I should just go." She turned to leave.

Sid moved to close the door.

"No, wait," she said. She seemed to be struggling with something. "Sir, I'm not looking for a promotion or anything, and I wouldn't expect nothing once you came back…"

Sid stood frozen, with his hand on the door. What was going on here?

"I know Caps's speech and all, but you might not be coming back...and...uh..."

"Miranda, what is it?"

She pushed past him into the room. "Sir, I'm not built like Darcy, or pretty like Senna, but...I know it's been a long time for you, too. If you want company tonight, then..." Miranda looked at the bed, then at the floor.

The Boss's mouth went dry. He'd been propositioned before, and dealt with it well, but there was something different this time. Miranda was a farmer. He had no relationship with her other than that they both lived and worked in Compton Pit. If he refused her it would not be for the reason she'd suspect. He'd never thought of Darcy in a sexual capacity, except, perhaps, in the most abstract way. Nor did he desire Senna or her type, leaning towards woman with more meat on their bones. His abstinence was by choice, for the sake of propriety, all part of being the chief of chiefs. Despite not really knowing the woman, he somehow understood how much courage she'd had in coming to his room; to offer herself like this to any man, never mind the Boss.

"Miranda," he said as he took her hand, "I'd like that very much."

26. The Chaucer Effect

The Deep Six showered together as most of the Pit was just waking up. For each of them, it was a different experience. Noah couldn't stop thinking about Darcy, just two stalls away. He tried to envision Cass, but his lover's dark hair kept changing to red. Desire picked at his animosity. It made him feel weak. The object of his confusion was also uncomfortable. Toffee stood back from the stalls, using a cloth so as not to get his stitches wet. Darcy could feel the hunter's eyes crawling over her, and she despised giving him any access to her body.

"Oh, am I gonna miss this!" Caps danced in the spray, making sure to get every nook and cranny.

Lena couldn't move like her boyfriend. She stood one-footed on wet tile, washing with one hand, while leaning on the other. She'd fallen before. They went hand in hand for her; water and imbalance.

Sid couldn't believe how quickly he learned to take things for granted. In some ways, it felt like any other shower; hot, cleansing and short.

Darcy wrapped a towel around herself and left, while the others stayed where they were to dry off. Noah thought it was because of him.

"One at a time, people." Sid's hands were already full with "shopping lists." Roshi wanted cookware, of course, and an assortment of foodstuffs that might have been packaged right. Sara wanted seeds for a number of things, as well as hydroponics equipment and some hair care products. Apparently, some conditioners did have a decade-long shelf life. Patel's list was the longest.

"You've got to be kidding me," said Sid, scanning down the list. He didn't even know what some of the things on it were.

"There are a number of hospitals where my requests could be found. I've listed them at the bottom. I know you'll at least be passing close to Vancouver General."

The department heads had fought like children over city maps and a 1994 telephone book. Devon was hopeful that the group would somehow find themselves on a Granville Street, where a rather large leather shop might be visited. The tanner hoped for some fancy stamping tools.

"Okay," Sid held up the lists, "thank you for all going completely overboard. Harpreet, we'll try for the x-ray machine. Roshi...if we pass a mall we can get into...Sara, I don't know about–"

"Sid, you're going right past a nursery."

"What do you think it'll be like now? Devon, I'm sorry, but this address is way off our course. Plus, it adds an extra bridge, and puts us right by Stanley Park."

Devon took the map from Patel and pointed at one side. "Like the university isn't sitting in the middle of," he checked the map, "the Endowment Lands. Looks like a lot of green stuff to me."

Sid tugged the map from Devon's possession. "We *have* to go the university."

"If you do happen to get to this leather shop," Dr. Patel hadn't heard a word the Boss had said, "you'll be right near St. Paul's Hospital. I think that was a big one."

"I still disagree with this," Sara said, pointing to the Pig. "You should be taking the hunters' vehicles. They're the best we've got."

"And that's exactly why we're not taking them. We've already been through this."

Dr. White's fists pushed into her pelvis like she was trying to break it. "So you take the most expendable vehicles and the least expendable people? Where's your logic?"

Sid shook his head and thrust the shopping lists into Darcy's hands. There was something more important for him to worry about. "Toffee, who's your second? You still haven't told me."

The hunter tossed a rifle into the backseat of the car. He acted like he hadn't heard Sid's question.

People from other departments trickled into the motor pool. Miranda entered. She and Sid shared a long look, but neither of them spoke. At the arrival of another person, Toffee's head perked up.

"Leaving without saying goodbye?" asked Senna. She wore the camouflage coveralls of the hunters. The patch of a second was pinned above her breast.

Toffee looked her over, then resumed loading the car. "What changed your mind?"

"Travis Jones. He was right. I am a selfish bitch. I'm the best hunter here, next to you. Seth, or no Seth. You better make it back, though. No way am I going to be chief."

Devon groaned and gave Sid an imploring look. "Boss, how am I supposed to keep my department up when my personnel switch in and out every other day?"

Sid squeezed Senna's shoulder, then turned to Devon. "Not my problem. As of now, I'm not the Boss."

Devon wheeled on Sara, who pursed her lips, then stared daggers at Sid.

Senna stood near Darcy, forcing the chief of security to look at her. "Darcy, I want to…"

"When I get back, we'll talk."

The new hunter second nodded. With a quick glance at Toffee, she left.

Caps wedged a final skinbag into the trunk of the car. "All aboard!" he chirped as he climbed into the van. Lena was already inside. Sid got into the driver's seat. Darcy and Noah bumped shoulders as both of them tried to enter the van at the same time.

"Hey," called Toffee, standing beside the car, "am I riding alone?"

Darcy and Noah looked at each other. She shrugged, then darted into the van. Toffee watched her door close, then his eyes settled on Noah. The hunter's grin was only slightly evil.

With feet that weighed a hundred pounds, Noah shuffled towards the car. He took a last look around the motor pool. Its concrete walls, so foreboding less than two weeks before, now were as hard to leave as a mother's womb. He briefly considered the back, but that would mean moving things. With a sigh, he dropped into the seat that had carried him to Compton Pit in the first place. Both motors started simultaneously. The van pulled around and faced the airlock doors. Toffee turned the car to follow. With a groan that sounded to Noah like the snarl of some great beast, the doors opened. People formed twin lines on either side of the airlock. They must have gone out through the central access panel and snuck around to the front.

"Touching, ain't it?" asked Toffee.

There were no cries or cheers as the vehicles drove slowly past the honour guard, just quiet respect, and silent prayers. As the car topped the ramp, Noah glanced back at his solar panels. They'd be cleaning up the rubble for days.

"Hah!" barked Caps, shoving a shopping list in front of Lena's face. "Look at this, he wants us to get him a tricorder. Who says the Doc doesn't have a sense of humour."

Darcy sat with one leg crossed over the other, and a foot on the dashboard. The van rocked and jounced as it passed over blacktop laid by the lowest bidder. Darcy finished her set of lists and passed them back to Caps in trade. Sid hadn't said too much. They'd only been on the road for four hours. They had a long way to go before the reality of their situation was too heavy to deny. The city's skyline would appear soon enough. For now they could still pretend they were on a road trip. It was hardest for Lena. She hadn't been outside Compton Pit in over six years.

"There's nothing on but Top Forty," said Darcy, playing with a tuning knob that did nothing. It was an old joke, but still worth a chuckle.

"See if you can get some Motown," Sid suggested.

Darcy popped open the glove box and pawed through it. Some things were just natural, no matter what state the world was in. Under a first aid kit and a spare net, she found a vehicle registration in a plastic bag. Caps tried to have one in every vehicle because it amused him to do so. She looked at the name on the slip.

"This was once owned by a Vera Krudentup. Uhm, it's expired. Try not to get pulled over."

"Want to sing something?" asked Lena.

"Let's save that for later," Sid said, before Darcy could choose a song. He liked her voice, but he wasn't ready to hear it yet.

"So do we play a road game?" asked Caps. "How 'bout scars?" It was another of his stoned creations. The object was to come up with best non-animal related story about how one's markings were obtained.

"No!" said Lena and Darcy at the same time. The artist could joke off his missing digits, but the two women couldn't discuss their own disfigurements without thinking about their true history.

Lena reached between the front seats and plucked a Vancouver street map from where it lay, folded incorrectly. She opened the map and flattened it against the back of Darcy's seat.

"I thought you didn't want to look at that until you had to," said Caps.

"I've run out of scabs to pick." Her finger traced the streets she'd taken every day. Forty-Ninth Avenue to West Boulevard, West Boulevard to Tenth, then all the way to school. There was a bakery she'd stop at least twice a week.

"Red bean buns. I haven't thought of them for years."

"Excuse me?" said Caps.

"Here," she indicated with a finger, "at Forty-Third and West Boulevard. Red bean buns. You could get them everywhere, but the ones from this bakery," she paused to swallow the saliva that had suddenly appeared in her mouth, "were the best. Hands down. Forget chocolate. These buns were the way to go."

"Bean buns?" Darcy didn't find the name too appealing. "You'd take beans over chocolate?"

"Chinese delicacy. You'd have to try one, Darcy."

"So what was the name of this bakery?" Caps was gently tugging at the map.

"Can't remember," she flicked at his hand.

"What was a Chinese bakery doing down there? I thought Chinatown was here, up around Hastings."

Lena slapped her forehead. "What was I thinking? You're right. They'd never let us past the ghetto walls, never mind set up a bakery."

Caps drew back, suitably chagrined. "Sorry, don't know what I was thinking."

"Hongcouver. That was one of 'em," her mouth turned up in a sad smile. "UBC: University of Billion Chinks. That was the other. Something else I'd forgotten about. "

"I know what you mean," said Sid. "S'funny, what brings us together. A common enemy, the most powerful unifying force in human history. When a man says coon he means raccoon and that's all he means. But you know, I'd gladly let someone call me a nigger if it meant sitting on my front porch, with a cold beer and my dog."

"I didn't know you had a dog," said Caps. "What kind…no wait, let me guess." He brought his hand up and stroked an imaginary beard. "You strike me as a Rottweiler type."

"Not bad, Richard. Rottweiler-Shepherd cross."

"What was its name?"

"Quota. For what I would have to fill to get a better posting. You had two dogs right? Let me see if I can guess you."

"That's not fair, you know what I had."

Sid locked eyes with Caps in the mirror. "You're getting egotistical again, Richard. Just because you told me, doesn't mean I remember. I know they were different. You had a Daschund and a Irish Setter."

"Wrong and wrong! An Irish Setter? I'm insulted. Sooooo, do you remember what happened to my dogs?"

"Please, Boss, think hard." Lena had heard this story more times than she'd eaten breakfast.

Sid did think hard. Vague details flitted about, but nothing to tie them together. It bothered him a little that he couldn't quite recall. "Might as well tell me again. We've got time to kill."

"OWW! Fuck!" The wrench slipped again, and Rick skinned his knuckles for the third time. The bolts were rusted in place. He was going to have to cut them off. He pulled himself out of the pit, and rolled from beneath the car. The torch sat amongst a jumble of tools. Rags littered the floor of the garage. The entire place was a fire hazard. Lighting the torch made Rick think about sparking a joint, and since he'd been working on the car for almost twenty minutes, he did deserve a break.

The door from the garage led to his house, or at least the house he lived in. He walked past a living room/studio as messy as anywhere else in his abode. He hoped one day to make his living solely as an artist, but for now the closest he had come was doing the CD cover for a psuedo-grunge band that would never make it past small pubs and high-school gymnasiums. The basement of the house was Rick Scagling's third place of work, his little farm. Twenty-six plants, grown from British Columbian seeds, were only days away from harvest. Soon, a select group of Seattle's citizens would pay for the opportunity to be carried away in a euphoric haze. The illegal power-tap Rick used to supply his operation would get him in almost as much trouble as the plants themselves. He'd be more worried if one of his most loyal patrons wasn't a cop.

His stash was kept in a container disguised to look like a can of shaving cream. The fact that the container was usually on Rick's living room table, next to a pack of zigzags and a roach clip, somewhat defeated its camouflage. He flopped down onto a cracked naugahide sofa and started rolling. On the wall behind him was a representation of the last supper. Everyone at the table was a dead rock icon. Jim Morrison was in the middle. It was yet another of his creations that he couldn't bear to part with once completed. With a practiced lick, and twisting of the ends, the joint was ready. His lighter was a disposable with the setting as high as it could go. A three-inch tongue of flame licked the end of the zigzag. Rick leaned back, took in three deep hits and put the joint out.

He considered himself a functional pot-head. Rick smoked every day, but still kept the bills paid and his head above water. He was proud of the fact that he never smoked before one in the afternoon. This restriction was made easier to follow by the fact that he usually didn't roll out of bed until noon. In the distance, an ambulance wailed.

The munchies set in almost immediately. Caps went to the kitchen and set the oven to 350 degrees, then yanked open the freezer. He'd long since outgrown potato chips and chocolate bars.

"Now what's it going to be?" he asked his stockpile of food. "Battered mushrooms or smoked-salmon squares?" he turned to an imaginary overhead light board. "Survey says? Ding! Salmon squares."

Rick took the box and dumped a small pile of the flaky pastries onto a sheet of tinfoil. While waiting for the oven to heat up, he looked at his backyard through the kitchen window. He hadn't cleaned for a while, the excrement was starting to pile up. The task had gone from scooping poop to shovelling shit. Hoffman and Dreyfuss were nowhere in sight. Another ambulance siren drifted through the walls. It was soon joined by the call of a fire engine.

Thinking of his dogs, Rick dropped a few more salmon squares onto the tinfoil. He could now identify the distinctive sound of at least two police cars joining the other emergency vehicles.

Must be a big accident, he thought as he opened the kitchen window. "Hoffman! Dreyfuss! C'mon, boys, salmon squares!" When the dogs didn't enter his field of view, dope-induced worry set in. *Crap, they got out again.*

Rick went into the garage and opened the door that led to the back yard. The next door neighbour's kid, little Bruce, must have pushed open the loose board on the fence. Bruce was a frail thing, and his mom wouldn't let him have any animals. She was convinced they'd give him a disease or something. So Hoffman and Dreyfuss had become his surrogate pets. Rubbing and grabbing through the fence had ceased to become enough for the boy a few months back, and the stupid kid had taken to working open a bigger hole.

No less than ten sirens wailed from all directions as Rick stepped out to the shit strewn yard. At the far end, near a haphazard doghouse—knocked together in a single afternoon—the two dogs lay curled up together, enjoying a siesta. Dreyfuss, a Standard Bulldog, was tucked neatly into Hoffman's larger frame. The bigger dog was a hodgepodge of German Shepherd, Black Lab, and Sheepdog. The fence was whole.

"Hey, you lazy pigs, I got munchies coming."

Hoffman cracked one eye, then let it shut again.

"Fine, but if there's none left, don't come begging to me." He left both garage doors open as he returned to the house. They'd be up as soon as the smell hit them.

Rick placed the sheet of foil in the oven, then returned to his stash. He wasn't quite buzzed enough yet to resume work on the car. Judging by the sound outside, every emergency vehicle in the city was off to somewhere in a hurry.

"What the fuck? Did someone burn down a mall?" Rick looked out his front window. He didn't see any smoke in the air, but something nasty was going on.

"Wurf!"

Rick turned to find Dreyfuss standing by the easel. A line of saliva oozed from the bulldog's perpetually drooling mouth, and spattered on the floor. Rick had often thought of filling the animal's mouth with paint to see if he could get some abstract art out of the deal.

"Woke up, didja? What's going on out there? Smell any smoke?" He stooped down and extended his right hand.

Dreyfuss, usually slower than a turtle, darted forward and tore off Rick's pinkie finger.

"Glaahhh!" He fell back, and everything slowed down, like the climax of a John Woo film.

The dog swallowed the morsel, and advanced. Rick looked in utter disbelief at the blood spurting from his hand. Instinct took over. He leaped over the couch. The dog attempted to do the same, but its stumpy legs kept it from getting higher than the cushions. Rick stumbled to the kitchen, where Hoffman took another finger.

"Enough already!" said Lena. "Skip the screaming and the chase around the house, okay? Just get to the garage."

"Yes, dear. So I'm in the garage now. There's blood all over the place, and I've made a mess in my pants."

"I can sympathize," Darcy said. "You left that part out when you told me this before."

"Hoffman and Dreyfuss are right behind me and the only thing I can think of is the car. I yank the door open and jump inside..."

The dogs followed right after him. One of them got a jaw-hold on his pant cuff as he fell through the door on the other side. Rick pulled with panic-driven might, leaving behind a scrap of material. He slammed the door on Hoffman's head, rolled over the hood, and shut the other door. Now the dogs were trapped inside. Dreyfuss's flat muzzle slammed against a window. Hoffman howled. Rick backed away from the car, his ruined hand held tightly against his chest. His head pounded as sirens outside sounded the call of Armageddon.

I'm gonna get rabies, was all he could think, over and over again.

In the kitchen, Rick pushed a wad of paper towel against the stumps of his fingers and dialled 911. It was busy. Next he called his best friend.

"Hello?"

"Jamie, I'm hurt man, you gotta come get me."

"Hello?"

"Jamie, it's Rick. My dogs attacked me..."

"What?"

"My dogs, I'm hurt pretty bad, man..."

"What?"

"I SAID I'M–"

"Hah! Fooled you, this is my machine, sucker! Leave a message at the tone."

The phone dropped from Rick's trembling hand. "Fuck." Jamie had gotten that one from him. He'd had the message on his machine a couple weeks ago, and fooled every person that had called.

At first he thought the buzzing was coming from his own head, then he realized it was the alarm on the stove. The salmon squares were ready. Shock was setting in, bringing with it nausea and loss of peripheral vision. Rick shook his head, then shut off the buzzer. He realized he'd have to kill his dogs. That's what always happened at the end of Old Yeller, no matter how many times he watched it. Rick didn't own a gun. A few friends had suggested that he get one, but he figured he'd just wind up shooting himself. He pulled the pastries from the oven and got a box of rat poison from under the sink. He sprinkled the deadly powder over the squares, looked at them critically, then sprinkled some more. After burning himself twice while moving the squares from the foil to a plate, he carried the toxic hors d'oeuvres out to the garage.

"Hey boys," a tear ran down his left cheek, "dinner's here."

One of the back windows was cracked a couple of inches. The dogs, who had been destroying the upholstery in frustration, growled at Rick as he tilted the plate, and dumped most of the salmon squares into the back seat of the car. Dreyfuss and Hoffman paid no attention.

"Eat them, and get it over with, okay? Please?" Sharp claws scraped against the glass. "Fine, I'll just have to make you eat them."

The walls of his house were bowed and elongated as he staggered to the living room, like something from an M.C. Escher print. Rick took the joint and lighter and returned to the garage. He lit the joint, took a deep drag, and blew the scented smoke through the cracked window. He continued to do so until the roach burnt his fingers, and fell to the floor of the garage. The dogs' snarls became confused whines. Rick fell back against the car and slumped to the ground. From within he heard his pets begin to scarf down the pastries. Two of the squares still sat on the plate, which now occupied the floor next to him. Without thinking, he picked one up, and popped it in his mouth.

"As soon I realized what I'd done, I ran to the bathroom and threw up. You know, I didn't even have to stick my finger down my throat. Which is good, 'cause two of my fingers had already gone down throats."

"Richard, that's an awful story," said Sid.

"C'mon, you missed the point. In the middle of all that, I still had the munchies. You just can't beat that BC pot."

"Actually, I think the point was dope kills." Sid reached an arm back to Caps. "Give it to me, Richard."

"Give you what?" Sid's hand didn't move. "Okay, you win." Caps reached into a pocket and withdrew his pipe and a small skinbag. He placed them in the waiting palm.

"Chief of Security, dispose of the contraband." Sid dumped the confiscated items in Darcy's lap. She cracked the door and tossed the pouch and…

"NO! Not the pipe. Please?"

Darcy faked turfing the pipe, then dropped it in her breast pocket and closed the door. "You can have it back when we get home."

Lena knew her lover had left out the real end to the story. The poison hadn't killed the dogs. He'd done it later with a heavy wrench. It was the first time Caps had killed anything bigger than a cockroach. The crunching of bone had somehow changed the artist more than the loss of his fingers. He loathed dogs for what two of them had made him do, not for what they'd done to him. It was sickening how love could turn to hate.

Caps turned back, as if to see his tiny stash through the Pig's small, mesh-covered back windows. He caught sight of the car. "I wonder how Noah's doing back there. I hope Toffee hasn't talked his ear off...or bitten his ear off."

Noah sat hunched in his seat, and resented everything; Darcy for sticking him with the hunter, the Boss for dragging him out, the car for taking him places he didn't want to go, and Toffee for just being Toffee. Silence reined supreme. The hunter didn't say anything, and Noah certainly didn't have anything to say to him.

Something small and brown flew from the Pig and disappeared off the side of the road.

Noah looked at the hunter. Toffee raised an eyebrow, nothing more. The panel jockey had been keeping as still as he could, fearing any movement would draw disapproval from his travelling companion. His back was getting stiff, and one of his legs had gone to sleep.

"So say something already."

Noah's face stretched wide in shock. "What?"

"You did good. Kept your mouth shut, but you're a talker. We've got a long drive. Go ahead, talk."

"What do you want me to say?"

"What do you want me to say?" Toffee mimicked. "You weren't such a wimp when you wired my lamp."

He knows, thought Noah, his gut twisting up in a knot. It had been a stupid thing to do, but he was so angry at the hunter's crack about Cass. He'd almost booby trapped Darcy's lamp as well, but settled for just cutting her power.

"Gave me a good shock. Lucky for you it didn't burn me."

For a moment, Noah thought he could see right through Toffee's arm, to the blade beneath. "You deserved it." His voice caught at the end, robbing the statement of the brave defiance he'd intended.

"Maybe I did. Gutsy little whelp, thinking you could be the one to give it to me."

"So what now? You going to push me out the car?"

"Thought about it. Halbert needs you on this. Tell me why."

Noah wasn't to tell anyone the reason. The Boss had been explicit on that point. This mission was scary enough as it was.

"C'mon, out with it. Don't make me beat it out of you."

He hesitated, then figured, why not scare the hunter? Noah told him.

Instead of being worried, Toffee smiled. "You don't say. And you can do that?"

"Yes. I'm a physicist. At least that's what Bacon told the Boss. I guess I am. I don't just know the hows. I know the whys."

"Bacon, huh? I've heard about him. Big fat guy, right? He teach you that stuff?"

"Yeah. Him and a couple other guys. Didn't know why I needed it, but they crammed it into my head anyway. Who taught you how to hunt?"

"We're not going to talk about me. Do all animals make you faint? Or just dogs?"

Noah's lips drew tight together. The road blurred past. He wondered how much it would hurt to just jump out. They'd have to stop. Noah could ride up ahead. His fingers actually toyed with the door handle.

"Okay, I'll ask you something else. How 'bout the traditional icebreaker; where were you on NW day?"

"I don't know."

"Dogshit. Everyone knows. What are you doing over…heh. You'll have to unlock the door before you can open it."

Noah looked at the sunken lock pin. "I wasn't–"

"Yeah, whatever. You'll have to undo your seatbelt, too. C'mon, where were you on NW day?"

"I told you, I don't–"

"I ain't asking you when you lost your virginity, you stupid idiot. Answer me or I'm gonna start hitting you. One more time, where were you on NW Day?"

Like an avalanche, like a hurricane, images rushed at him from the darkest corners of his mind. The hunter's bullying smashed through walls no gentle prodding had ever breached. The noxious bubble swelled and burst. Noah Thurlow remembered everything.

27. Beasts of Myth

June 10th, New Wilderness Day

Noah sat in the middle of his bedroom floor and unpacked his bag. The necessities of life were taken care of by his parents, leaving his backpack free for a more important cargo; toys. Batman had dirt in all the little holes where fantastic gadgets could be placed. The doll had also picked up a new crack in one leg, the result of a nasty fall from a branch. That these were the worst of its injuries was amazing considering the dangerous journey it had taken to rescue Duke Nukem.

The Duke, which had spent all its time safely tied to a sapling with shoelaces, was none the worse for wear. A plastic Hummer with a machine gun mounted on top was the next item removed from the backpack. This was the personal vehicle of Batman's worst enemy. The rigid plastic figure was still wedged behind the steering wheel. Wearing only a red Speedo, the Horrible Hasslehoff gazed over the hood of the car, painted eyes just a touch malevolent. Noah upended the backpack and dumped the rest of the scantily clad figures on the floor. Why his grandmother had given him the entire Baywatch collection, he'd never know. He certainly didn't ask for them. They did however, make excellent fodder. Usually one doll apiece went up in flames, got crushed flat in a vice, or met a similar fate during Noah's grand adventures. His favourite had been the Giant Cuisinart of Death. Slivers of plastic—like shredded, pink carrot—had coated the inside of the cylinder as justice was served. His allowance had been docked for three weeks to pay for a new blade.

The hollow drumming of a bucket being filled drifted through his bedroom window. Noah frowned. Mom and Dad were washing the car now. Lately they'd taken to doing that as soon as the family returned from camping. There was one chance that Noah would still be safe. He put down his favourite dolls and moved to the window. Mom was by herself near the jeep. That didn't mean anything yet, but it wasn't encouraging. Down the stairs and through to the kitchen, Noah saw through the window that the kayak was in the back yard. Right now it was on its bottom, but if Dad…

"Shit!" said Noah quietly. His father had flipped the boat over and poured some soap on it. That meant Mom would want help.

As Randy Thurlow turned his hose on the kayak, Noah decided he'd have to start injuring himself on the last day of camping trips. He'd get away with it two, maybe three times. He cast a regretful glance up at the ceiling, knowing Batman and the Duke would be delayed in their vengeance against the evil Baywatch lifeguards.

"NOOAAHH!"

Noah pushed a chair up to the hall closet, then pulled it away again so he could open the door.

"NOOAAHH!"

"I'M GETTING IT, MOM!"

He climbed up on the chair and pulled down a green bucket. He had to work it off the shelf with his fingers. His father had no consideration for the vertically challenged when installing new shelves.

Noah took the bucket to the kitchen sink and squeezed in a healthy dose of dish soap. He wasn't allowed to fill up in the bathtub. Mom said he made too much mess. He could have used the utility spout in the basement, but that would mean carrying a full bucket up an extra flight of steps. The kitchen faucet took forever to fill the bucket. While he was waiting, Noah caught his father looking at him through the window. Randy tapped an ear and mouthed, "Walk-man," then winked. The boy smiled and ran from the kitchen into the living room. Leaning up against the sofa was his Dad's khaki backpack. He found the Walkman in a front pocket. It had cool headphones. They were silver and really sleek. Noah fitted them onto his head and thumbed the volume switch. As the newscaster's voice sounded through the minute speakers, the boy imagined he was receiving secret intel from an orbiting satellite spy station.

"…emergency rooms clogged with people claiming to have been attacked by their own pets."

Noah walked out the back door, waiting for instructions on how to save these victims of obviously alien-controlled animals.

"...an epidemic of rabies, possibly spreading as a result of the increasing rat population in many parts of the city. If you think your pet may have been bitten by..."

"Thanks, slugger." Randy scooped the headphones, and placed them in his own ears. He pushed the play button and muted music replaced the announcer's voice.

"Dad, what's rabies again?"

"What?" He pulled one earphone out, the plastic tensing to snap back in again the moment he let go.

"What's rabies?" Noah knew; he'd snuck downstairs one night and silently watched most of *Cujo* before being hauled back up to bed. He just liked being scared by his father.

"Oh, it makes dogs grow twice as big, and all they want to do is eat little boys!"

"Dad, could Sharky ever get rabies?"

"He did look a little larger this morning. Who knows what might have got to him out in the woods." He snapped his teeth a few times. Noah giggled.

"NOOAAAHHH!"

Randy tussled his son's hair. "That's you, slugger." He let the earphone return to its post, and winked again.

Noah ran back into the house. The bucket was full, as was the sink. Most of the runoff was on the floor in front of the counter. Some had splashed into Sharky's bowl, and the crunchy brown food had produced a murky sort of gravy. The boy hastily shut off the taps, then spilled a quarter of the bucket's contents as he hauled it from the sink. Water puddled onto the floor, enveloping the bottom of a table leg, disappearing under the fridge. Maybe there was some way to blame it on the dog. There were still suds on top, so that was okay. He was out the kitchen door when his mother bellowed again.

"NOAH, C'MON! I NEED SOME CLEAN STUFF!"

"Coming, Mom."

She turned with a look of vexation. She had mud and a little stick protruding from her strawberry-blonde hair. Noah spilled water with every step he took. He couldn't hold the bucket away from his body, and he kept hitting it with his legs. His arms had just about given up when he reached the jeep. With a silent groan he let his burden drop to the cement. There went the suds.

"Remind me never to have you fetch beer."

"Huh?"

"You'll get it when you're older."

That was something he'd been hearing for as long as he could remember. How many years would have to go by before he was older? His mother emptied the bucket she'd been using and handed it to him.

"Get me another bucket of water. Don't fill it all the way, you'll hurt yourself. Get me a new sponge. Your Dad's probably hogging them all in the backyard. Tell him to forget about his precious kayak and come help me." She was frowning as she said this, but a smile sparkled in her eyes.

"Okay, Mom." He wondered how much time he had before someone came into the kitchen. Dad would probably laugh. Mom definitely wouldn't. He had to remember not to use the good towels this time.

Sharky stood between Noah and the door. The boy stopped in his tracks. There was something funny about their pet. The Golden Retriever seemed to be whining and growling at the same time. Did he also seem a little bigger?

"Mom? I think there's something wrong with Sharky."

Noah felt his skin growing cold as his mother approached. She squatted down beside him.

"What's wrong, Snucks?" she asked.

The dog's gentle face turned evil. Kate yanked Noah behind her and started backing up.

"It's okay, Sharky, it's us, it's just us...RANDY!"

Sharky was bigger, no doubt about it.

"It's just us, Sharky. RANDY I NEED YOU!"

The dog was huge, it was ten feet high. It was bigger than the house. Noah wrapped his arms around his mother's legs and clung to her with all his might. Then she was falling, and so was he. The boy was trapped as horrible ripping sounds came from above him.

"MOM! GET HIM OFF! GET HIM OFF US! MOM!"

An elbow struck him in the face as his mother flailed at the animal. Something warm and wet covered his cheek.

Bits of flesh landed on the grass. Kate Thurlow's thrashing eased as her muscles went limp, and only the dog shook her body. Noah screamed so loud he didn't hear the impact as a wooden oar smashed Sharky's skull. Nor did he hear his father screaming. As Noah turned his head, all he saw was the monster. It was the hydra, it was Cerebus, it was every vile thing Hercules had fought, all wrapped up into one.

Ropy tentacles interlinked the creature. It already dragged one victim behind it. Noah recognized the poor teenager. It was Mark, the skinny fellow who walked the neighbourhood dogs, adroitly managing ten or more leashes at a time, always with a plastic bag at hand to help keep the sidewalks clean.

Noah watched helpless, pinned under the wreck of his mother as the monster charged. Noah's voice gave out, but he kept howling as his father went down without killing a single head.

A long-muzzled head rose up, its mouth clamped on Randy's lip and cheek. The facial skin pulled taught, then stretched and separated from the skull. Noah's mind did the only thing it could do. It shut down. The edges of his vision went black, until the cruel beast was framed like an image on a television. Meaningless loud noises accompanied bursts of red from the creature. There were more noises, and the creature was split, trying to go in two different directions. It pulled at its own body as it shuddered. Heads went limp. Legs tangled. Then the television screen went fuzzy and narrowed to a single white dot.

"Well at least this one's not hurt," said the adult. Noah was inside somewhere. Maybe it was the school.

"What's your name, kid?" asked another adult. "Kid? Can you hear me?" A hand waved in front of Noah's eyes. It was dirty. "Oh, yeah. He's not hurt. He's healthy as a horse."

"I can take one more." The speaker was a large man with a salt-and-pepper beard. It was dark out. A big truck rumbled in the street.

"What about that one?" The short man pointed at Noah.

"The blond kid? Silent Sam?"

"He's no good to us here. Shit, Hy. How many more trips can you make before the sun comes up?"

Hyacinth Backenbridge rubbed his hands on the front of his pants. "This is the last one. How are your windows?"

"Not good. About a hundred of them got in this morning. Janice was allergic. Not that it mattered. And we're still getting rats in the basement. Is there another truck coming?"

"Nope. Other places, Bill. I'll see you tomorrow night."

"I sure as hell hope so."

Hy took Noah by the shoulder and gently guided him towards the truck. "We're going somewhere safe, kid. Try to snap out of it. You're too young to go nuts."

"Noah? Do you know who I am?" A Spanish woman. Army cots. Someone crying. "Noah? It's Renata. I'm a friend of your parents. Do you know where your parents are?"

Time passes. Weeks turn to months. The nights get colder. Renata doesn't come by anymore.

The bearded man tugged at Noah's lapels. They were green. So was the little hat he was wearing. "There you go, boy. You're a perfect little elf."

"Bacon, this is just stupid. Going out for these suits…"

Hy stood and patted his ample belly through the huge red and white jacket he wore. "The kids need this. And don't call me Bacon."

"Yeah, and what are we going to give them as gifts?"

"I got the costumes, didn't I? I'll find gifts."

He dropped into a chair and hoisted Noah up to his knee. "So tell old Saint Nick, what's your heart's desire, kid?"

The elf's lips curled back over his teeth. "I want my mom."

Hy was ecstatic as he crushed the boy to his chest. "You talked! Kid, you talked!"

Then Noah did more than talk; he howled, he thrashed, he kicked Santa in the nuts.

"Jesus!" exclaimed Max, helping Hy pin Noah to the ground. "I NEED A DOCTOR!" He bellowed down the hall. "What is he, an epileptic?"

"Get his leg! He sure is strong for a little guy. It ain't epilepsy. It's shell shock."

28. Bumps in the Road

Toffee stared in dumb amazement at the thrashing demon in the seat beside him. Worse than the flailing hands was the impossibly loud keening that ignored ear drums as it drilled into his brain. One of Noah's hands bashed the hunter across the sunken bridge of his nose.

Toffee slammed on the brakes and blinked stars out of his eyes. He curled the fingers of his right hand into a fist against the dashboard, then swung from the shoulder, smashing Noah across the forehead.

"What the…?" Darcy snapped her head back as the Pig decelerated.

"They've stopped," said Caps. "I don't see any animals on the road."

All four of them craned their necks back, waiting for Toffee to break radio silence. Instead, they saw the door open and Toffee, sans net, stepped onto the road.

"He's bleeding," said Caps.

Sid threw the van in reverse and backed up to the car. The hunter was looking a little shaky.

"What happened?" asked Sid as he stepped from the van.

Caps donned a net-helmet as he handed one to Lena. Darcy was already out the door, so the artist grabbed one for her and the Boss.

Toffee gritted his teeth and gestured at the car.

"Noah!" said Lena, hopping down to the road. "What did you do to him?" She pulled open the passenger door. Noah was limp in the seat, and bleeding from above one eyebrow.

"I didn't do nothing. He went tooth crazy." A moment of vertigo took the hunter and he rocked on his heals.

"What's wrong with you?" asked Darcy.

"Little whelp punched me in the nose."

"You hit him!" Lena was on her knees, examining Noah's face.

"You got into a fight?" Sid demanded.

"I told you, he went tooth crazy. I knocked him out before he could kill himself."

Darcy scooped a rifle from the back of the car as Lena and Caps lay Noah out on the road.

"How could he have killed himself?" she asked.

"He might have hit me again."

"So he just snapped?" Caps's accusing glare was lost behind mesh. "One minute he's normal, the next he's throwing punches at you?"

The hunter had regained his balance. He drew up to his full height and fixed his eyes on Caps. "That's it. We were just talking, then he goes nuts."

"Noah?" Sid slapped the young man lightly on the cheeks.

Noah's eyes flew open. He screamed into Sid's face, then nearly took Sid's head off with a swing of his arm. Lena and Caps jumped back as Noah thrashed and beat himself against the blacktop.

Darcy dropped onto Noah's chest and pulled his arms over his head. One of the arms got loose. Caps grabbed it and held it to the ground. Lena and Sid each had a leg.

"Noah! It's Darcy. Noah! Get a hold of yourself!"

The sun boy's head swung from side to side.

"Toffee, get his head," ordered Sid.

The hunter stooped beside Noah and punched him once across the jaw.

"That wasn't what I meant!" said the Boss as his subordinate went limp. "C'mon, everybody into the van."

They bound Noah's wrists and ankles together, and laid him down in the back of the Pig. Lena drew a blanket over him.

"What were you talking about?" asked Darcy.

"Just stuff. Small talk. I don't do it too often."

Lena sat in the back with the patient. Sid and Caps were in the front seat, while Darcy interrogated Toffee behind.

"What did you say that set him off?"

"Everything's my fault, isn't it? I was asking him questions."

"About what?"

"I asked him where he was on NW day. I had to smack him five seconds later."

Lena's mouth fell open. She looked at her boyfriend. He shook his head almost imperceptibly. *Not now, Lena. Not now.*

"We have to abort," said Caps. "We need to get him to Harpreet."

"Not an option. The doctor will want to hold on to him for weeks. We don't have the time."

"We don't have the time?" Lena held her hands out, palms up. "We'll lose one day. We can bring someone else."

The hunter leaned forward and spoke quietly in Sid's ear. "No we can't, can we?"

"Toffee, get back to the car. You're riding alone. Lena, is he secure back there?"

"Yes, but..."

"But nothing. He'll just have to snap out of it."

Caps broke his pencil tip against the sketchpad for the third time. He sighed, and whittled at the pencil with a small knife, adding more wood shavings to a pile beside the door. It was difficult to sketch with the van bumping, and it showed in irregular lines and smudged spots of shading. Still, it was possible to make out what was being depicted. A caricature of Toffee, the divot in his nose increased to the size of a lunar crater, getting the drop on a raccoon. The hunter looked really proud of himself. Two massive bears were creeping up behind him. The pencil was just about sharp when the tip broke again. In the back, Noah dozed soundlessly with Lena hunkered down beside him.

"This is my fault," said Caps after a few hours had passed.

Sid knotted his brow. "Go on."

"No, Richard, this couldn't possibly be your fault," Caps said, bobbing his head from side to side. "Thanks."

"So what did you do?" asked Darcy.

"He found out Noah had a memory block," said Lena, pushing a blond curl off Noah's forehead. "He tried to break it."

The Boss kept his eyes fixed on the road. Darcy fastened hers on Caps.

"How did you go about doing that?"

"It's this old trick I learned way back. You distract the mind with a bunch of random questions, then go for the gold. It was good for remembering the name of a movie, or where someone last saw their keys. I had some friends with bad short-term memory."

"But this is a little bigger, right?"

"I found out I could use this trick to make people remember a bunch of stuff. You know 'power corrupts' and all that jazz? Well it seems Noah had buried, oh, the first decade or so of his life. I guess there was a good reason for it, but I was tripping and..."

"So, he flipped like this before?"

"No," Caps held his thumb and forefinger about a centimetre apart, "but he came this close."

Sid closed his eyes, then remembered he was driving. "In the future, Richard, stick with lost keys."

"Hey, I helped Lena get to details about NW Day that she'd suppressed. She didn't freak or anything."

"I guess you weren't paying much attention," said Lena, a little sadly.

"Okay, I'm a dog. I feel as low as a dog." He sounded like he meant it. "Everybody happy?"

Darcy opened her eyes and stretched. It was dark enough outside that she could pick out the range of the headlights. Lena drove while Sid lolled in the back seat and flipped though reports from previous expeditions to Vancouver. They were brief, and he'd memorized most of them, but he kept hoping for some little missed detail.

"Sid, we should relieve Toffee soon. Caps, I'll take over with Noah."

Caps clambered up from the back and stretched himself as best he could. Darcy and him squeezed past each other.

"How you doing there, sun boy?" she asked as she hunkered down and patted his arm. Noah made no reply, other than to intensify his breathing for a moment. His eyes twitched back and forth under closed lids. She felt Noah's shoulders and arms. The muscles were tense. He was going to be exhausted when he woke up.

"I'd sure hate to be having your dreams." Almost without realizing it, she began to stroke his hair. He'd been a jerk to her the last few days, but the way he looked now, so helpless, like a...like a kitten. The cut had been cleaned and butterflied. It might scar, but the eyebrow would hide it.

In a surge of empathy, Darcy picked at her own NW day experience. She hovered just beyond it, close enough to sample the emotions, but not be overwhelmed by them. It was something she'd learnt to do with Travis, and now Burle. It seemed like the last ten years of her life had been spent accruing memories that needed to be handled with kid gloves. Acclimatization: the human ability to get used to anything. Those that didn't have it, or didn't have enough, went tooth crazy. Some just acquired the distant stare of a lobotomized animal. The "walking wounded" was a term used for them, supplied by veterans of both Vietnam and the world around them. Others gradually became a different person, always a change for the worst, and some just went ballistic.

Noah's eyes flicked open, they captured Darcy's with a look of pure love, of unfettered need.

"Mom?" his arms came up and wrapped around her waist.

Too shocked to move, Darcy stared, as Noah's eyes closed, and he slumped back to the floor of the van. She cupped his cheek, envious of, at the same time as mournful for, the loss of the woman who'd deserved that look.

"Did he say something?" asked Sid, looking back over his seat.

"He said 'Mom.' His eyes are going again. What do you think, Sid?"

"I think he's tougher than we give him credit for."

"Really?"

Sid returned to his reports.

"Surprised you're riding with me," said Toffee.

"I drew the short straw." Darcy shifted her shoulders in the seat and gripped the wheel a little tighter. "Aren't you going to ask how Noah's doing?"

"Why should I care? I beat him up."

"You're off the hook. Noah had blocked NW day completely. Caps had been working at him for a while."

"So funny man played his bucket out and I dropped the lucky quarter. Nice pay-off."

"Why'd you give honey to Roshi? It's not like you."

"Who says I gave him anything? I cut a deal."

"What kind of deal?"

"None of your business. A little extra consideration at meal time."

"Should have known better than to think you'd do something selfless."

Toffee leaned a little closer. "Do we have to fight? This is a good time to get to know each other better."

"Does a punch to the nose always have that effect? Take your balance away like that?"

"Yeah, ever since..." he suddenly realized what he'd admitted to, what he'd given away.

"There. I know you better already." She fought hard not to grin.

Toffee grunted, then turned his face in to one shoulder, and closed his eyes. If he didn't actually drop off to sleep, he did a damn good job of pretending.

Visions of nature's victory paraded through the arc of light that preceded the car. An old tire now home to a colony of puffy fungus. Signposts perforated by ant galleries. A desiccated VW convertible in which a tree had taken residence. Roots curled over the hood and sides of the car, reaching down to precious soil. It appeared as if the tree had captured the vehicle, rather than growing around it.

Darcy took note of the tree as a landmark. This trip was more than just a smash and grab. If they could safely enter and exit Vancouver, they'd have a place to strip for months before other settlements started in. The city was a trove of pirates treasure. Its dark borders had become a thing of legend.

It was impossible to tell exactly how many people had vanished into the city. Settlement-produced teams were recorded, but surely other fortune seekers had met their fates while operating under their own auspices. Cut off from the rest of the land by the mighty Fraser River to the south and east, and imposing mountains to the north, Vancouver could be reached by one road, the former Number One Highway. It was already a death zone by the time Sid and Darcy had worked their way down the province towards it. A city in a forest, or a forest in a city, depending on one's point of view, it was home to raccoons, skunks, coyotes, and of course the usual domestics: dogs, cats, ferrets, rabbits, etc. Ants had kept a whole plethora of pest control companies in business. The income from eradicating colonies during the summer had kept them afloat for the entire year. There were also a lot of rats. It was those rats that killed the city. Or more accurately, the fleas on the rats. As an international port, it was impossible to keep immigrant rodents from sneaking in; hiding in shipping crates, nesting in amongst the cargo. Incidents of Bubonic Plague were rare, and kept very quiet, but they did occur from time to time. One had occurred on June 8th, two days before the Change, amid the squalor of an East Vancouver flophouse. As if the city didn't have enough to worry about.

The Pit's last expidition was four years earlier. Two vehicles, carrying irreplaceable satellite communications equipment, left Compton Pit and went out of contact shortly after passing the city's limits. A year before that, a string of Gascan D'Abo's radio vans set up a network. He'd lost three vehicles that way. Underbel had made two attempts. One brave group had come all the way from New Portland. Scavengers had safely stripped out everything within a kilometre of the city, but past that…

What was known as Vancouver (or as Caps had mentioned earlier, Ratcouver or Antcouver) was actually comprised of many cities: Surrey, Burnaby, Coquitlam, Port Coquitlam, Richmond, Delta, North Vancouver, West Vancouver, and Vancouver itself. They'd all blended together with time. Darcy only remembered the names because Sid kept referring to them as he plotted their course, even if they weren't going anywhere near some of the sections.

The most recent information they had from within the city was nine years old, supplied by Dr. Sara White. She'd stayed with a group in the buildings of Simon Fraser University, Vancouver's other noted post-high-school think tank. In the end, she'd had no choice but to leave. Lena was just outside of the city on the day the world changed. Her rescuers had given Vancouver a wide berth on their way to relative safety.

Whatever lay within the city was allowed to stay there. Settlements had deemed further expeditions as a waste of resources. It had become a modern Bermuda Triangle, a spot on the map where "here be dragons" was written.

Beside her, Toffee made an amusing snuffling noise. He had to be asleep, there was no way he'd make that sound voluntarily. Darcy wondered if she could sleep were their positions reversed. Could she allow herself to be unconscious while alone with the hunter?

She'd tried to tell herself that her transgression had been solely for revenge. In her inebriated state, any man could have found his way to her bed that night. That it was an obvious rival of Travis's made it so much the better. That was all a lie, though. Part of her had been strongly attracted to Toffee. Even at his age—he couldn't be much younger than fifty—he seemed more powerful than anybody at the Pit. Not that he was everybody's superior strength-wise, but he was so…capable. Darcy took quick glances at the sleeping hunter. Was she still attracted to him? She gradually allowed the memories of that night to fill her; the pressure of flesh on flesh, the soft wetness of his tongue. She stopped just short of actual nausea. The twisting of her stomach faded, but what didn't was the need for a shower.

"There isn't enough water at Compton Pit," she said quietly.

She had to acknowledge that Toffee had her beat in one department. He'd bought himself some luxury for after the trip. He had every intention of collecting. For her part, Darcy felt she was going to die. The thought came matter-of-factly, no remorse attached to it. People died everyday. Faces disappeared. It was just one of those things. Now it was her turn. Wonderful thing, acclimatization.

29. Camper World

The building was small in comparison to the six acres of concrete that surrounded it. It was built of red brick and had few windows. Two stories high, with no style to its architecture, it looked like a child's building block amongst a field of canopies and campers. The glass was still in place; there was a taboo against scavenging from it. Camper World was the last haven before Vancouver. The final, completely intact building to spend the night. For that reason, it was left that way.

The two vehicles pulled into the lot, passing beneath a sign that read; "Camper World: For all your camper and canopy needs."

The lot wasn't home to a single independent unit. Everything there had to be mounted on the back of a pickup. The canopies ranged in size from quarter-ton fitted boxes, to large multi-person sleepers that only a one-ton could accommodate. A huge placard by the building read; "If we don't have it, we'll get it."

"Ah, Camper World," said Caps, looking out the window. "Funny, the roller coaster is smaller than I remember. When is the guy with the little donuts getting here?"

Sid checked his watch, "I think we missed him by about ten years."

"Darn, so close."

"What the hell are you guys talking about?" asked Lena, once again sharing the back area with Noah. "Caps, have you been here before?"

"I passed by years back, on a trip to 'Couver. I was coming up for a comic book convention. The sign back then said; 'Camper World: Bring the whole family' so me and Jamie, that was the guy I was riding with–"

"You've told me about him."

"We joked about the place being an amusement park. It's funny, the things you remember."

"So were you coming up to corner the market on collectibles?" asked the Boss.

"Nah, I read my comics too much to keep them in collector's condition. I was going to be an artist. I had a portfolio drawn up, and there was a guy from DC supposed to be looking at submissions."

Lena clambered up to the front seat. "Did he like your work?"

"I didn't even get the chance to see him. There were about six thousand people in the line ahead of me, and some of their work made mine look like kindergarten stuff. I picked up some old issues of *The Shadow*, and then me and Jamie spent the rest of the visit in strip clubs. Jamie's idea, not mine."

"But you went along with it?"

"Jamie's car, Jamie's rules. I seem to remember I was bored shitless."

Sid parked the van next to the building. Darcy brought the car up next to it. One by one, the travellers exited their vehicles, and stretched.

Sid tried the door. It was locked. He put his hands on his hips and turned slowly, surveying the lot.

"Do we kick the door down?" asked Caps.

Lena put herself up against the door. "No way, bad karma."

"There's a key around here somewhere." Sid walked up to the closest pile of canopies. A mottled pattern of gray and green covered the stack, weathered plastic providing a home to a thin moss.

Caps jiggled the locked handle. "If this place is for anyone, why lock it?"

"Tradition, Richard. There should be a clue somewhere."

"Could it be this?" Lena pointed at a black "3x3" written in black marker at the bottom of the door.

Sid walked three stacks over to the right, tried the third canopy from the top, then the third from the bottom. He repeated the process to the left. From one canopy, a tarnished key hung by a thick, leather cord.

They carried Noah inside and laid him down on musty orange carpet. While Caps and Lena checked the ground floor, Darcy scouted the second. The upper floor, as expected, was empty.

"Karma or no karma, I'm surprised this place hasn't been stripped," Caps had emerged from a back room, the pitcher from a coffee maker in his left hand. "There's some instant back there. Can we make a fire?"

"We might be able to do better than that," Sid said. "Toffee, you're with me."

Behind the building was a wasteland of rusted propane tanks.

"This one's empty, too," Toffee tossed the canister back in the pile and selected another one. "You actually expect to find a full one?"

The hunter's answer came way of a brief hiss from behind him. With a satisfied smile, Sid shut off the valve and hoisted the canister to his shoulder.

Lena brought jugs of water from the van. Toffee loaded his rifle, while Caps hooked the propane up to a Coleman stove inside the building. The empty canister that had been in place was tossed through a window, to join the pressurized graveyard out back.

"How long are we staying?" asked Darcy, forcing some water between Noah's lips.

Sid put a hand on Noah's forehead, then pulled himself upright and looked out a window. "I guess we'll leave tomorrow. I don't like losing a whole day, but I know I could use some sleep in a horizontal position, and I hate the idea of hitting the city at night. How are we for beds?"

Darcy dabbed with the edge of her sleeve at a bead of water that ran down Noah's chin. "Plenty for everyone. There are large cushions upstairs, pulled from the campers, I guess. I agree with Caps; even for tradition's sake, this place is well stocked."

"Oh, I think you'll find most of the campers have been stripped of piping and other components; light bulbs, valves…we might find some bar fridges though. I've been thinking of putting one in my room."

"Java time!" called Caps. He entered the building's foyer with a tray of steaming mugs.

"How much gas've you got left in there?" asked Toffee.

"Quite a bit," Caps handed the hunter a mug. "I'll unhook it and leave it beside the Coleman. Keep the next person from having to search for one. And I'm not doing it for karma," he shot at Lena as he caught her smile. "This place is...nice. That's all."

Toffee threw on a net-helmet, shouldered his gun, and strolled out the door. In a short while they heard a gunshot, then two more. Toffee returned with the brutish carcass of a St. Bernard over one shoulder. He dumped it just outside the door, not wanting to add blood to the smelly, but relatively clean carpet.

"How many of us are you planning to feed?" asked Darcy, surprised at his choice of game.

"Big dogs make easy targets. I'll butcher it in one of the campers."

"Was it by itself?" she asked, picking up her own rifle and checking the safety.

"No, there's a pack. What's the closest settlement to here?"

"As far as I know, we are." Sid took up a gun and moved to a window. He didn't see a dog pack, but the piles of canopies could have obscured it.

"You won't see them," said Toffee. "They were creeping in, but backed off when I shot the big fella. Didn't give me any trouble when I collected. Not that they didn't want to."

"What are you saying? That they knew gun range?"

"I still could have got any of them, but yeah, they knew gun range."

Sid tapped the barrel of his M16 lightly against the glass. "So they were driven off from somewhere, or else they get shot at a lot. We watch in twos tonight. I don't like the idea of a settlement that hasn't tried to make contact. Did you, uh, see any crows?"

"None more than usual, if that's what you're asking."

After moving the propane out to a surprisingly intact camper, Caps and Lena roasted the meat in a tiny oven. A shallow tray, which came with the camper, caught sizzling bits of fat that would be used for gravy. Darcy and Sid passed the time staring between the canopies, while Toffee sat on a vinyl couch and paged through a dog-eared paperback he'd found. Suddenly, Caps and Lena burst through the door.

"There's a car coming," said Caps hastily, grabbing a shotgun from by the couch. "It's not one of ours."

Lena squatted by Noah protectively, as her companions moved to the front windows.

"Underbel?" asked Darcy.

No one replied as a battered jeep pulled into the lot. It stopped halfway down a row of canopies, the driver presumably spotting the Deep Six's vehicles. After a while, the door opened, and a man stepped out. He carried a long-barrelled rifle hung from a strap over his shoulder. He had thin brown hair, and an uneven beard.

"Why is a raccoon better than a stranger?" asked Caps.

Toffee supplied the punch line; "You know right away you have to shoot the coon."

"Toffee, upstairs. Do not shoot unless you have to." Sid motioned to Darcy. "Go out the back and flank him. Be careful. He might have friends in the jeep." It was impossible to tell through the bars and mesh that covered the windshield.

Darcy grabbed a net-helmet and slipped away, only the briefest squeak of the back door marked her passage. Outside, the stranger held his ground, waiting for first contact.

"Hello? I'm not looking for any trouble." Evidently, he'd become impatient.

With a nod to Caps and Lena, Sid raised his gun and opened the door.

"I'd appreciate it if you'd put down your rifle," Sid called.

Oh you would, would you? was what the stranger's face seemed to say.

"It would be in your best interest."

"Thanks for the advice. Why don't you drop yours first. You must have someone else on me. I would."

Sid ignored Caps's hiss of "Don't do it, Boss." The stranger had a point. Sid leaned his rifle against the inside of the doorpost.

"Now you."

The man turned his head to the left. "Do you want me to just put it down, or give to the guy you've got coming in on me?"

Sid hated the tension of meetings like this. Words were useless, assurances became lies when backed up by gunpowder. How much leeway would Toffee give the stranger?

"At ease, Darcy."

She stepped out from a stack behind the jeep. Her gun was in her hand, at ready, but not aimed. "He's the only one," she called.

The stranger, surprised to hear a woman's voice come from under the mesh, inclined his head. "M'lady." He held the rifle sideways and raised it slowly, until the strap cleared the top of his receding hair. He considered the hood of the jeep, then offered the rifle to Darcy.

"Unload it," she said.

Up close, the man's beard was full of colours; grays, white, browns and reds. It looked like an ancient calico cat had crawled up and died on his chin. He ejected the clip, then cleared the breach. A shell skipped a few feet across the ground. Darcy stepped in close, and took the clip.

"Please turn and place your hands on the vehicle."

The stranger grimaced, as if disappointed, but complied. Sid walked from the building to the jeep. He frisked the man quickly and efficiently, with a motion that was as familiar and as forgotten as riding a bicycle.

"Can we go inside?" asked the stranger.

Darcy parked the jeep next to the building as Sid led the man inside. Toffee came down the stairs as they stepped through the door. He introduced himself as Donald Graff. No, he wasn't from any local settlement. Yes, he was travelling alone. Then he told them what he did.

"A cartographer?" asked Caps. It was a job he'd considered doing for the Pit himself, but it required a rigidity of line that was beyond his level of discipline.

"That's right. A vital function, if not a particularly popular one."

"Who do you work for?" asked Lena, handing the man a cup of coffee.

"Me. Everyone needs the lay of the land."

The wording he used sparked a memory in Lena. "Wait a minute, you're *that* Donald Graff?"

He smiled, showing uneven, yellowed teeth. "It's so nice to be recognized."

In the years before the Change, Donald Ripley Graff, a child of extremely old South Carolina money, had travelled to the most unforgiving places the world had to offer. He supplied maps and information to those few who needed it. It was discovering the new that drove him. In the last decade, everything was new. The land hadn't changed in shape, except in a few places where earthquakes had hit. But population-wise, whole cities had vanished and new settlements sprung up like volcanoes in the ocean. Equally important was the viability of the land. How defensible was it? What were the predominant animals in a given area. What trade could be obtained?

An independently-wealthy nobody in the old world, Graff was now one of the few published authors in North America. About every year or so, a new issue of *Graff's Graphs* would be printed in

Oregon, then spread out across the continent, following the trade routes. The Pit had two editions, VI and VII—the mail was slow these days. The legend at the bottom of each edition was "Everyone needs the lay of the land."

"What are you doing up here?" asked Caps.

"This year I'm doing my Haunted Cities edition. It'll still have the trade conditions and emotional tone of the settlements I hit on my way. Vancouver was the last on my list. It's one of two that I didn't go into. Well, not that far. Hey, what's wrong with him?" Graff had finally noticed Noah. He covered his mouth and backed towards the door.

"Don't worry," Sid said, moving to stop the cartographer, "he's not sick. He got hit in the head."

Graff looked about with uncertainty, then decided to trust what he'd been told. Certainly the discolouration on the forehead and around the eyes supported the claim.

"Were you planning on mapping the city?"

"Good lord, no. I'd need an army for that. Sooner or later, someone will send one in there. I hope to be there for that. No, I caught wind that a satellite truck had disappeared in there a few years back. I was hoping to find it close to the city limits, maybe scavenge some gear. I drove in about a quarter mile, then pulled out. I admit it, I got spooked."

"What did you see in there?" asked Darcy.

"What's the information worth to you?"

"We've got roast dog coming," said Caps.

"What breed?"

"St. Bernard."

"Ah, a gourmet treat."

Graff sat on the couch, his long legs stretched before him. He was a bit taller than the boss, but shorter than Toffee. The hunter looked up occasionally from his paperback as he cut slices of meat with his knife and stabbed them with the tip. Sid and Darcy stayed by windows while they ate. The cartographer dined with silverware that came from a wooden box. He had extra for Caps and Lena.

Darcy noted that the man had yet to ask them where they were from, or why they were there. She wondered how long that would last.

"So what did you say?" asked Lena, eager for conclusion of Graff's story.

"What else could I say? I told the woman she didn't need to curse my soul for eternity, and I'd be happy to impregnate her daughter."

"Have the rituals changed, now that chickens don't just wait to be slaughtered?" Caps was jealous of the attention Graff was getting, but he was just as interested in the man himself.

"They hood the chickens and wrap the claws in balls of cloth, but Voodoo is still Voodoo, although Loas are always angry now. Loas are spirits or gods, for those of you who might not know. I was lucky enough to observe a possession by Baron Samedi himself. Not many outsiders are allowed to attend the All Soul's Day rites. Apparently my union with the houngen's granddaughter was blessed by the Guede. The Guede is the collective of all the Voodoo gods."

"And you believe that stuff?"

"I neither believe, nor disbelieve.

"Did they dance…the…uhm. That sex and violence dance."

"The Banda? You know your stuff, Caps. Or at least you used to. Yes, they danced. Yes, I was attacked, but not hurt too badly. It was an interesting experience, but not one I'm likely to repeat. They claim the Guede keep the alligators away, but I'm more inclined to believe the settlement just killed every one of them for miles."

"Dogs coming in," said the Boss.

Their plates left on a coffee table and the floor, the people took up weapons, and moved to the windows. Graff had reloaded his rifle.

"Which one do you think is the alpha?" asked Toffee.

The canines weren't coming straight in. They flitted between the stacks, working their way closer. One particularly fluffy creature popped a long-muzzled face out from behind a camper, then disappeared.

"That was a standard poodle," said Caps. "It's mine. I love shooting poodles, especially the big ones. Freaks of nature."

The off-white dog seemed to be the pack's forerunner. Its nature-permed coat preceded all the other animals.

"I think you've got your answer," Sid cracked the window an inch and slid his gun barrel out.

"A dog pack led by a poodle. That's something a man should never have to see." Caps already had his gun exposed to open air. He aimed, tensed on the trigger as the big pompom darted to another canopy, but didn't fire. "If these dogs are gun shy, they'll scatter as soon as one of us shoots. Then we'll go through this all over again." He moved back from the glass, and let Toffee take his position.

The hunter waited until the poodle moved again, then aimed and fired at a canopy that had once been fire engine red. There was a yelp. The poodle's head was exposed as it fell from its hiding place. Furry creatures retreated between the stacks. Toffee's second shot took the poodle's head off.

Sid closed his window and stood down. "If that was the alpha, we might not have to deal with them again today. They'll be too busy picking a new leader."

Toffee went outside to check the animal. He returned with the disappointing news that the poodle was a bitch.

"Probably the alpha's main squeeze," said Graff, taking another bite of his dog chop. "We might be eating their leader right now."

"Doubtful," said Caps. "Bernards are big, but not aggressive enough within the workings of the pack.'"

"Spend a lot of time with them?" asked Toffee around a mouthful of meat.

Sid turned the attention back to Graff before the artist could retort. "So you've been fed and entertained. Tell us about Vancouver."

Donald tapped tobacco from a small container into a pipe. He lit it with a wooden match, acrid smoke filled the room. "Nobody minds, I hope?"

"Maybe you shouldn't do that near our patient," said Darcy. The smoke drifted in a lazy cloud over the unconscious man.

"I do beg your pardon." Graff moved from the couch to a chair on the far side of the room. "What I saw in Vancouver was what I expected to see. Smashed cars, broken pavement and empty buildings. No mysterious creatures rose from manholes to drag me to my doom. In fact, I didn't see anything padding about at all. I believe that's what scared me off. There's always something hanging around the periphery. Especially so with a city like Vancouver, all those trees and such. People say not to enter the city, that's good enough for me."

"So why did you come all the way out here, then?" asked Darcy.

"I like to see things with my own eyes. As I said, it was the last city on my list."

"That's it?" Caps was clearly disappointed. So was Sid, but he hid it better. "That was hardly worth the meal."

"That's why I've been supplementing with other tales."

"I have a feeling you'd tell us those for free, Mr. Graff." Darcy arched her back and stretched. The cartographer pulled his eyes away the moment she caught him staring.

"Guilty as charged, m'lady."

"Where are you going next?" the chief of security asked as she finished her stretch.

"There's a settlement southeast of here that's supposed to be fairly interesting. Compton Pit. I was going to stop on the way up, but decided to get the city over with. People at a place called Underbel told me about this safe house. Are you from Underbel?"

"No," said Sid quickly, "and I'll save you the trouble of trying to reach Compton Pit. Rockslide. Road's completely closed off. We were hoping to get some supplies there ourselves."

"Oh," Graff chewed thoughtfully on the end of his pipe. "How disappointing. I understood they had some rather interesting laboratories there."

"Were they expecting you?" Sid probed.

"No. I never call ahead. I like to show up anonymously, get the feel of how a settlement responds to a newcomer. That's one of the things I put in my books, but I know at least one of you has read my work." He waggled his pipe at Lena. "None of you has mentioned where you're from, or what you're doing here. I doubt you came for a canopy."

"We're from east of here," Sid evaded, "looking to skirt the city, see what's left on the edges. You might want to come with us. Strength in numbers. Maybe you'll see more than you planned."

"There's not much there for you. I didn't see anything that would be easy to remove, but knock yourselves out. You seem like a capable bunch. Come with you, eh? I somehow doubt you'll be satisfied with stopping at the outskirts. Hmm. No, as appealing as the chance to chronicle my own painful death is, I have a schedule to keep. Pity I didn't run into you on my way in."

"Here they come again," said Toffee, already cracking a window.

Graff told a few more tales, then went upstairs to get some sleep. He'd volunteered for the early morning shift, planning on leaving just after sunrise. Sid had finally brought down what they felt was the alpha, a scruffy black thing that was the result of a big mutt mounting another big mutt. By now the gunshots and the scent of blood would be bringing in other creatures. It would be a long night. While Lena rested her forehead against the glass, cradling a shotgun in her lap,

Darcy worked Noah's legs. It was something she'd watched Dr. Patel do with Odega, lifting and bending them to keep the tendons stretched. Noah hadn't been out that long, comparatively, but she felt she had to do something. To her knowledge, his eyes hadn't opened again. Caps had brought some pads down from the upstairs, and he and Sid had moved the photovoltaic engineer onto them. While Darcy was rotating Noah's left foot, she heard Caps chortling in a back room, the one they'd taken to calling the kitchen. He came out into the foyer with Toffee's paperback in his hand.

"Look at this; *Desire and Ice.* It's a bodice ripper." The cover had a man and woman in parkas, embracing passionately under a pastel aurora borealis.

Darcy wasn't the least bit surprised. Those books, laughed at by most men, were instruction manuals for seduction. In the heyday of world media, Penthouse and Hustler sold dangling genitalia and grunting trysts, while romance novels offered the soft touch of silk, and foreplay that lasted for pages, chapters even.

Caps skimmed text, then stopped at something that caught his interest. He whistled, then held the book open to Lena. "Honey, we've got to find an igloo."

Heavy feet thumped down the stairs. Caps tossed the book on the couch as Toffee entered the foyer.

"You usually move a lot quieter," said Darcy. "You still unsteady?"

Toffee replied with a glance, not words. He turned to Lena. "My turn. Get some sleep."

She handed him the rifle, then went into a back room, indicating to Caps with a look that he should come with her.

"Think they're going to hump?" asked Toffee as the door closed.

"Maybe. They liked your taste in books. You find that here, or bring it with you."

Toffee looked out the window a long time before replying. "I found it here. I suppose painter had something clever to say."

"He got caught up in a juicy bit before he had the chance. Read a lot of those?"

"Yes and no. You read one, you've read them all."

"I'll bet you find them extremely informative."

The hunter turned to her. His eyes moved from her feet to her face slowly, lingering briefly at her ankles, stomach and her neck. A shiver ran down Darcy's spine and she dropped Noah's leg. It thumped to the floor. It took a moment for her to realize what the hunter had done. Had he focussed on her crotch and breasts, the look would have been crass, but by choosing other places instead, he conveyed lust for her whole being.

"You will never have me," she said, voice quiet and firm.

"I already did. You came twice, didn't you?"

Only once, you smug son of a bitch. "Sometimes I go slumming when I'm drunk."

"Whatever you say, Red. You don't seem to be leaving."

"This is my shift. I just haven't gone to bed yet."

"So are you going to take a window, or keep playing with the sun boy?"

"I'm thirsty," said Noah.

Darcy was so shocked, she flinched from the voice. Toffee licked his lips and grinned wolfishly as Noah tried to drag himself to a sitting position. The engineer's eyebrows knitted together in a look of pain. He lowered himself back to the floor.

"Sid!" Darcy called up the stairs. "Get down here!"

There was the sound of movement from above, then feet on the stairs.

Noah tried to sit up again. Darcy stooped to help him.

"How long have you been awake?" she asked, worried about how much he'd heard.

"I just sort of...where are we?"

"We're at Camper World. It's a safe house. You're not going to take a swing at me, are you?"

"Could I have some water, please?"

Sid was by the panel jockey in two quick strides. "Noah, how are you feeling?"

"Thirsty."

"What's going on?" demanded Caps, bursting into the room.

Toffee returned to the window. At least he hadn't forgotten what he was supposed to be doing.

"Hey, Caps," said Noah, turning his head quickly, then immediately regretting it.

"Oh, buddy. I'm so sorry, man."

"Sorry about what? How long have we been here?"

"Ah, the sleeper has awakened," said Graff, leaning on a banister. He was wearing a lavender robe, and looked like an aristocrat that had let himself go.

Noah's expression became even more confused.

"Noah, this is Donald Graff," Sid said. " He's a cartographer. You had an attack of some sort. Like a seizure."

The young man rubbed his forehead, then jerked his hand away upon encountering the wound. "Did I…did I hurt anyone?"

"Nobody that matters," said Darcy.

Noah was moved to the room Lena and Caps had taken. Sid shut the door and warned Noah not to let anything about Compton Pit slip to the cartographer. Darcy and the hunter kept their watch in the foyer, while Lena held Noah's hand, happy that her friend was his old self again.

"And this is the first time you've come out with your memory intact?" asked Caps.

"Yes. The last time this happened was years ago. I was seventeen. I fell into the back of a truck filled with hides. I think it was all the fur that set me off."

"What was it about Santa Claus that flipped you?"

"The fur collar, the pressure of Bacon's hug. He wanted me to be an elf the next Christmas, but I wouldn't. Not because of what happened the first time, but because I thought the real Santa was dead."

"Why?"

"Someone told me the reindeer ate him."

The light of a new day was no kinder to Camper World than that of the day before. The canopies were still worn and weathered, forgotten relics of a different time.

Toffee and Sid dumped animal carcasses on a pile of bones just off the concrete. There was no tradition behind the pile, it was simply where others had left remains before. Judging by the condition of the skeletons, it had been a long time since the last funeral, deepening the mystery of how the dog pack had become gun shy. Caps and Lena, somehow taking on the domestic responsibilities, tidied the building. They left the camper a mess, though. Noah sat on the couch, watching others work. His dizziness may or may not have been genuine.

"Where are you going from here?" asked Darcy, as she tossed the last of Graff's skinbags in the back of the jeep.

"Underbel, then southeast. There's a dairy farm I'd like to look at. Heard they have forty head, hobbled and beaten into submission. Seems to me the only way they'd submit is if they were dead. I wonder what types of cheese they'll have. It's been a long time since

I've had cheese. After that I'll work my way back to New Portland, then on to Terpris."

Darcy jerked back from the car, hand streaking to the pommel of her gun.

"There's no animal under the car," said Graff, yanking a strip of fur from the wheel well. "Coyote. Don't worry, I scared myself a couple of times."

"Aren't you scared, travelling alone?"

He wiped his hands with an embroidered handkerchief that appeared out of nowhere. "I find people become quite tiresome after prolonged exposure." He bent from the waist and kissed the back of Darcy's hand. "I might make an exception, in your case."

The chief of security withdrew her hand politely. "I think I might find you tiresome after a while," she allowed just a hint of laughter to enter her voice.

"You might at that, my dear." He flashed his best yellow-toothed smile, which was charming, in a hideous sort of way. Then he belted himself in and turned on the motor.

"Empty roads," said Darcy.

"And to you." Donald Graff pulled out of Camper World, and headed south.

Caps found Lena in the kitchen, looking out a window and shivering. He put his arms around her from behind. She turned her head to one side and rubbed her cheek on his bicep. Outside, the final carcass was being dragged off.

"I don't like this," she said.

"I know, honey. I don't either."

"This is why I don't leave the Pit. It never stops. Why won't it ever stop?"

Caps was battling with the same feelings she was, but he wouldn't give into them. Not this early. He was saving up his energy for the mind-ripping panic that was sure to come. At least in the Pit the animals were always *out there*. After a while, they became something a person just heard about.

"Well, at least Noah got to sleep through most of it."

"That was a horrible thing to tell a boy," said Lena. "About Santa Claus getting eaten by reindeer."

"What's the alternative? I remember the Christmas I spent with the Jameson family, at that settlement I stayed in the second year. They had a tree and everything. The father hands his kid a shotgun with a bow on it and says 'There you go boy, just like the one old St. Nick used to blast Rudolph.'"

"You told me this...his tree ornaments were painted raccoon skulls."

"That's the one. Merry Christmas."

Toffee pawed through his bag again, then shoved it roughly into the car's backseat. He went into the building, scanned the foyer, stomped upstairs, then checked the two other ground-floor rooms. The others ignored him as he searched the premises. He went out to the van and pulled the side door open. After eyeing the interior, he turned his face to the direction that Graff had gone.

"Asshole stole my book. What the hell am I going to read now?"

Sid drew his finger across the map, going over their route one more time. Caps tried to pay attention, but they were going to just follow the road, and he wasn't doing the driving anyway.

"We should have killed him," said Toffee, glancing out the window.

Sid licked his lips. "I understand why you think that. But we can't, even if he wasn't who he is. Damn. I wish we could have taken him with us."

"Do you think he'll bypass the Pit?" asked Lena.

"He's got a long drive ahead of him, he might just take us on faith. All it does is re-affirm how tight our schedule is."

They did one last check around the building, locked it up, and returned the key to its hiding place. Toffee showed no reluctance to drive alone as he got in the car, and everyone else boarded the Pig. The vehicles left behind a field of fibreglass for another stretch of rock and trees. It was raw, beautiful land. The highway was slowly being broken up like a scab pushed off by new skin.

"Hey," said Caps, indignantly, "you passed another point of interest. Aren't we going to stop at any of them?"

"Enough, Richard."

Graff drove with his journal open on the seat beside him. People often asked him how his publisher paid him. His wage was the same currency it had always been—paper. No ugly faces stamped on it this time. The paper was nicely bound in blank books, three hundred pages in length. What the publisher got in exchange for his information was none of his concern. Mundane things, most likely: gas, food, other sundries. Graff could write as much as he wanted, and he did. Nothing of interest escaped being noted. His eyes moved from the road to the journal, one hand flipping pages.

"Halbert! I just couldn't remember that."

Graff was ruthless in acquiring information on the important people of a settlement before he arrived. Everyone needs the lay of the land. Sid Halbert; "The Boss," scars on left cheek and neck, commanding presence, black. Darcy McMillan (?)—Chief of security, red hair, scars on right cheek. He skipped over Dr. Patel and Burle Campbell.

"I've got you here somewhere, sleeping beauty."

He jerked the wheel suddenly to avoid a rather large rock, then almost as if it hadn't happened, went back to the journal.

"Ah, yes. Thurlow. Panel jockey. Swapped for a truck." Underbel had been a wealth of information. It helped being known as a fact gatherer. Some people were so eager to impress with their own vault of knowledge. Not Halbert and his bunch, though. Friendly, but scarce on facts. The cartographer could read while he drove, but not write. He pulled over to the side and fished a fountain pen from a small skinbag. It was his most valuable possession. In the old days, he'd used it as a mark of finesse. Now it was a necessity. Ballpoint pens were a thing of the past, or almost. Gone was the disposable world.

"Now why would the Boss, and a young scientist abandon their home to go to the city?" He always posed his questions aloud. "And why would they not want me of all people to visit the settlement?"

A raccoon dropped on the hood. It growled, then clawed on the window.

Graff tapped the windshield with the barrel of his rifle. "Go on, off!"

The raccoon scampered up to the roof, made a lot of noise, then jumped off to the side.

"Oh, what are you up to?"

The coon stood on its hind legs, presenting itself as an easy target.

"Just step on out and shoot you, shall I?" He pressed the tip of his rifle against the ceiling and pulled the trigger. The boom was deafening. The body of a second raccoon rolled down the windshield and dropped off the hood.

The first raccoon bent down, one claw raised. People who didn't think animals' faces were expressive had to be blind. This coon looked downright sulky.

"Go on then, find another friend and try again, you nasty little beast." He looked at the new hole in his ceiling. "I hope it doesn't rain."

Graff drove further down the road, looking for a place to park that wasn't under any trees. He wondered how far-spread that trick was. Other animals had learned to draw humans out into the open.

A rocky promontory, its point-of-interest sign long since gone to powder, provided an uncovered vista overlooking a river. He wadded cloth in the hole as a temporary measure, then set pen to paper.

"Man, your mom and dad. Right in front of you too. Brutal." Caps shook is head.

"It's no worse than other stories I've heard," said Noah, "but I wish I could block that and keep everything else. My parents...they always put me first, I think."

Darcy twisted in the front seat in order to make eye contact. "What was your mom like?"

"Really cool, but stern. She wore the pants in the family, so to speak. Dad adored her. Would have died for her...I guess he did..." Noah took a pause to collect himself. "Sorry guys, it's just that...well, it's like being reunited, sort of. Mom was tough. If I hadn't grabbed her legs the way I did..."

"You were a terrified little kid, Noah. You can't blame yourself. Uhm, what colour was her hair?"

"My mom's? blond."

"Oh." Darcy sounded a bit disappointed. "Was she pretty?"

"She was beautiful."

"What boy doesn't think his mom is beautiful?" asked Caps. "Not that I'm saying your mom wasn't or anything. At least you know what happened to your parents. It's not nice what happened, but at least you know. Mine moved out to Boston a few years before the Change. My sister had started pumping out babies, so they went to be with their grandchildren. In my mind, I buried them years ago. If they are still alive, they probably did the same with me."

"What about your parents?" Noah asked Darcy.

"Same as Caps. Didn't see bodies or anything, but it's a pretty safe assumption."

"Lena?"

"I'd rather not talk about it. No offense."

Caps shot a look at Noah over Lena's head, *I'll tell you later.*

"My father died young," said Sid. "Cancer got him. He wasn't even sixty yet. Mom remarried a few years later. It was weird, having a new dad in my late twenties. I never really knew what to call the guy. I liked him I suppose. Would have liked him better if he hadn't been sleeping with my mother."

"Noah, could you move your feet, please?" Caps was on the floor of the van, looking under the seats. He swept an arm through the darkness, grunted and rose to his knees. He scanned the back area, then looked up front.

"What are you looking for?" asked Lena.

"My sketchbook. I put it under the seat here."

"Are you sure? You lose stuff all the time."

"My short term's fine today." He jerked a thumb at Sid. "I'm sure I stowed it under the seat."

"Did you take it into the building?"

"No. Maybe I packed it away." He crawled up onto the seat, forcing Lena and Noah to move aside, and hooked a rucksack up from the back. "Hey," he said, pulling a .357 Magnum from the bag, "this isn't my stuff." He rummaged through the rucksack and produced a single, left-handed work glove. "Dogshit! This is Toffee's."

"Oh, that's funny. That's real funny," said Toffee, holding the artist's sketchbook against the middle of the steering wheel. The drawing showed six pairs of disembodied eyes hovering in the darkness. The caption underneath read; "How many Toffees does it take to blow out a light bulb?"

The next page had a caricature of the hunter eating salad with a giant spoon that protruded from the stump of his right arm. "Been thinkin' about me a lot, haven't you, painter?" He flipped to the next drawing, a sketch of Noah standing on a hilltop with his hands over his head. The perspective made it look as if the panel jockey was grasping a burning sun in his hands. The next one showed Halbert with a full head of Rasta dreadlocks, smoking a fat joint.

"You really shouldn't leave this lying around, boy. Never know who might see it." He glanced from the pad to the road, then back again. A few more caricatures passed by. Toffee laughed out loud at one of Eggerson handing chocolates and flowers to an ostrich. He flipped through it backwards, moving from newest to oldest. Some of the middle pages were crammed with drawings, collages of faces and body parts, mostly hands. Toffee stopped at a page that held three nudes of Lena. In each, she was posed in such a way that her half leg was hidden by the full one. Artful use of shadows gave the sketches a touch of class. "Nice body," he said, as he stroked the contour of one charcoal-rendered breast. The next drawing was a single, full-page nude of none other than the chief of security. Once again shading had been used for effect. The entire right side of Darcy's face was in darkness, as was one hip and the side of the exposed leg. All scars were hidden. Her hair flowed out like a lion's mane. Toffee thought she might have posed for it, but then realized the breasts were wrong. Close, but wrong. There were head and torso studies of Odega, Dr. White, and more of Halbert. There was a nice profile of Felix, Toffee's predecessor, and then a cartoon depicting a group of scarecrows running away from a flock of birds. The next drawing was an absolute work of art; Lena in a wedding dress. Every ruffle, every nat of lace was detailed. The dress Caps had conjured up would have cost thousands of dollars in the old world, were it real. Multi-layered, with a high collar and puffed sleeves, the bridal train went right off the paper. On an impulse, Toffee flipped the sketch and looked at the back. Sure enough, the train continued on back, and ended with a little girl, Asian, holding the lace off the ground. He flipped back to the front. Hearts and doves were suggested in the folds of the dress.

A cruel smile pulled at the corners of Toffee's mouth. Was this just daydreaming or plans? He'd toyed with the idea of seducing Lena. There was no doubt in his mind that he could do it. Her half leg discouraged him. Despite being an amputee himself, Toffee liked his women whole. Now, though...the skill at which the drawing had been produced, the time it must have taken...this was more than just wishful thinking.

"You go ahead and marry her, painter, then I'll do my thing." Toffee closed the pad, then opened it again to the nudes of Lena, and tossed it on the passenger seat.

"Please?"

"We're not stopping," said Sid.

"Well, let me use the radio."

"Relax, will you?" Lena squeezed her boyfriend's leg. "It was just a mix up when we loaded the vehicles."

Caps kept craning his neck, looking at the car. "That was my last pad, I just hope I didn't lose it."

"Sure," said Darcy, open amusement in her voice. "You don't want him to see that drawing of him with the spoon."

"You've gone through my pad?" He was aghast. "That's private! When did you look at it?"

"I didn't go through it, I just saw you working on that sketch. Why? Is there something about me in there?"

Caps dropped down to the floor and searched the void beneath seats again. "I don't care about the spoon sketch. There's other stuff in there…personal stuff."

"He doesn't even let me see his sketchpads," said Lena, then her eyes went wide. "Rick, is that the one you used to…" she let the rest of the question hang.

"Yeah, that's the one. It's in here somewhere. Why didn't I notice Toffee had a bag like mine? Noah, could you move your feet again?"

Him too, thought Lena, proud of her lover at the same time as she was furiously jealous. *We're going to Vancouver and all he cares about is his stupid sketchpad. Am I the only one who thinks we're all going to die?*

"Alicia's breath stopped as sure as if it was frozen," intoned Darcy. "David's torso was completely exposed as he pulled his shirt off."

"What?" exclaimed Caps, his head popping up like a Jack-in-the-box.

Darcy waggled the romance novel in her hand.

"What's that?" asked Noah, taking in the cover with a look of disgust.

"Toffee's book, now shush…" she prepared to read again.

"Toffee's book?"

"Yes, shush. 'It sure gets warm in these igloos, doesn't it?' he said, as he turned and flexed his broad shoulders.

"The lamplight caressed his solid abdomen, his tanned skin a dark star against the walls of snow. David's vitality increased the heat inside the little shelter and lit a fire in Alicia that started at her belly and engulfed her heart. She toyed with the tassels at her throat, she had nothing but a camisole on underneath. Could she remove her top? Would it be proper? Maybe he would…" Darcy read well, changing her voice slightly for dialogue, and adding just an edge of sarcasm. " 'The snowfall should end by morning,' he said. 'We can tunnel out then. You're shivering. Are you still cold?'

" 'No! I'm just…I'm fatigued, that's all. You dragged me miles across the ice.'

" 'Licia,' she thrilled at his voice saying the diminutive of her name, 'we've got a lot of ground to cover. I'm sure your fiancé must be very worried.'

" 'Yes, I'm sure he must.'

"Edgar would be worried, but not because of her, because of her father's gold mine." Darcy lowered the book, and gave her audience a knowing look. "David moved suddenly, his brawny arm brushing Alicia's shoulder as he bent over to check the candle. The contact sent delicious icy tingles that radiated up and down her whole side. He looked at her, their eyes locked. David rose, uncoiling from the waist like a magnificent wolf. His warm hands took her firmly by the shoulders.

" 'You are cold. Don't just stand there trembling, tell me.' He turned his back on her while he lit another candle…"

Sid snatched the book from Darcy's hand. "You're giving me a headache."

Darcy retrieved the book, but left it closed. "I'm just reading where Toffee folded the page over. Here," she handed it to Caps, "stick it in his bag."

"Uh…could I have a look at it?" Noah asked, his hand half-extended.

"Abbotsford," said Sid.

None of them spoke as the empty township surrounded the road. It had been stripped to its foundations. No glass, no fixtures. Street lamps weathered away with gaping wounds at their bases, where the maintenance plates had been removed to get at wiring. The rusted, weed-filled chassis of cars and trucks were all that remained of countless scavenging expeditions. There was a truck yard, but it too was devoid. Gas stations long drained, a couple of bars a decade past last call, these were the heralds of Vancouver. The city outskirts were barely an hour away. Noah stared out the window at the remains of cars and trucks that littered the roadside. The closer they got to the city, the more concentrated became the automobile graveyard. Nothing of value could be seen on any of them, save preponderant hulks of scrap metal.

All the gaiety, the forced bravado that had buoyed their spirits, disappeared. The reality of their situation was too close to be denied. Noah, mind still unsteady, deflated like a tire with a leak. Darcy's hand found her lip and squeezed. Only Sid seemed unaffected, but inside he longed for the once-convenient placebo of Rolaids or Tums.

Lena gripped the upholstery like she could stop the van that way. Her breaths became rapid and shallow. Then she was flailing, fighting for the door.

"No!" Caps imposed himself between her and the handle. He made a grab for her but she was already on her way to clawing through the ceiling.

"Get a hold of her!" yelled Sid at the same time as Darcy launched herself into the backseat. Noah pushed himself against one side as Caps helped pinion Lena to the seat.

"Honey, deep breaths, deep breaths," Caps's voice was urgent, but not panicked. He'd been through this before. On more than one night he'd been yanked from sleep by Lena in the throes of a waking nightmare.

Sid jerked his head from the road to the back seat, but he wouldn't stop.

Lena's breath slowed. Control returned to her eyes.

"I'm okay, I'm okay," she pushed at the arms that entrapped her.

As Darcy returned to the front seat, she caught sight of Sid's expression—frustration mixed with disappointment.

"Well, what did you expect?" she asked quietly.

30. Black Water

June 10th, New Wilderness Day.

This is a dream, she said over and over to herself, but it wasn't. Pain could make people wake up, everyone knew that, but the pain in her hip and side was the least palpable component of this nightmare. The deck sloped away from splintered wood and she slid toward the water behind her. She was already soaked, but the rational part of her mind informed her how much worse it would be once she hit the frigid ocean. Lena flipped to her stomach and reached out for a rail. Her fingers brushed the metal, but couldn't get a grasp. Odds and ends slid before her: a snorkel, a tackle box, a bottle of her father's imported beer. The lifeboat bobbed near the end of the boat, all but one of its restraining ropes untied. As water rushed up to meet her she reached for the Zodiac, one hand getting the restraining rope, the other scrabbling at the rubber. Then there was nothing around her but ice. She couldn't see anything, she didn't know which way was up, and she was so terribly, terribly cold.

Something white caught light from the surface and moved towards her face, the black lettering, *Xingyun Shui Shou,* still recognizable through the stinging blur of salt water. The boat's aft was coming right at her, to pin her beneath it and push her to the bottom. At least she'd know which way was down. At the last possible instant, something yanked at her wrist, pulling her away and towards the surface. Her head broke water and she fought to draw in air. Her wrist was pulled again, pain burned its way through the numbness of her skin. Her body was spun away from the sinking boat, and towards the Zodiac. The last restraining rope had somehow knotted around her wrist. Her fingers had been robbed of dexterity, and she couldn't free her tortured flesh from its binding. Another wave caught the Zodiac and Lena was yanked again, a slave to the current's whim.

A killer whale rose from waves about ten feet from her. She could see grooves in the rubbery hide where something had injured the mammal long ago. It shot forward with remarkable grace and smashed into the back half of the boat, encouraging it to give up and drown. The front half, where Marty was, where her mother had been, listed to one side, and was sinking straight down. The sound of the impact, and the force of the whale drew a burst from already overactive adrenal glands. Endorphins and stimulants coursed through Lena's body and mind. Fight or flight? Not much choice here. She kicked her legs and pulled at the rope, working her way towards the lifeboat. She'd almost reached it when another wave pulled it away. Lena screamed, then gagged on a mouthful of brine. She redoubled her efforts, desperate, hysterical. The boat was close, then she was at it, then she was in it. Getting into an inflatable from the water is difficult at best, but the young woman was so charged with adrenaline she could have scaled a waterfall if she'd had to.

She allowed herself only a moment to lie collapsed on the bottom of the lifeboat, then she clawed at the guide ropes on one side, and pulled herself to a sitting position. Only the front half of her family's boat remained above water. The whales had disappeared.

"Father!" she called. "Marty! Mother! Motherrrrrr!" this last ended in a shriek that drew nails down the back of her throat.

"Lena…" it was so faint, her mother's voice.

"Mother!" Lena grabbed the motor's pull cord and yanked with all her might. Nothing happened. Her mother was at the prow, clutching at the side of the hull, near a twisted rail. "Mother, I'm coming!" She tugged again, but the motor wouldn't start.

The prow had given up on gradual descent and was now rapidly disappearing beneath the waves. Mrs. Wong was going with it.

"Mother, let go! Let go of the boat!" She yanked again, her arm was losing strength. "Why won't you start, you fucking thing!"

"Hai Yun…Hai Yun…" Nancy Wong called her husband's name.

Lena's head whipped back and forth, looking for her father. Only a few feet of the *Xingyun Shui Shou* was still exposed to air. "MOTHER! LET GO!" She realized with horror that her mother wasn't holding onto the boat, she was attached to it, caught by a sharp piece of broken rail that had pierced her cardigan. The woman didn't have the strength to free herself. "MOTHER!" Then the boat was gone, and so was Mrs. Wong.

Lena almost gave in to her desire to leap from the Zodiac, but the killer whale that rose twenty feet astern changed her mind.

"Why are you doing this?" she screamed at the orca.

It looked at her with malevolent eyes, then dove into the sea at the exact spot Mrs. Wong had gone under.

Another whale appeared, head first, right beside the Zodiac. It shifted its bulk slightly to one side, knocking the boat a few feet. Lena fell to her hands and knees. It brought her eye level with the motor, specifically with an orange toggle switch with two positions; off and on. Currently, it was set to off. The whale let out a short burst of squeaks, then vanished. With a wracking sob, Lena flipped the switch to on and started the motor with one pull. She turned the boat towards shore and opened the throttle all the way.

A whale that had been rising under her, made brief contact with the spinning motor, and jerked away. The disturbance of its movement lifted one side of the Zodiac and tossed it counter to the waves. A rush of water struck Lena and almost threw her from the turbulent lifeboat. Then the tiny vessel was steady and moving in the desired direction. Two whales rose on either side, well away from the boat. They swam forward, keeping pace, but not approaching.

"Go away!" screamed Lena. "Go away, go away, go away!" the last came out in a ragged cry, her throat, burned by salt water and anguish, could produce no more.

One of the whales submerged, then reappeared moments later. Lena zigzagged the boat, thinking the motor scared them, but the whales paid it no heed, simply drifting with her, still keeping up. They both squeaked something, then submerged again.

Lena stared at the water before her, her mind compartmentalizing, then erasing the fact that her own ineptitude had cost Nancy Wong her life. She couldn't handle the guilt for the time being. Cold pierced her through and through.

Beside Lena was a large, waterproof bag lashed to the inside of the boat. It contained water, a first aid kit, flares and...blankets! She reached for the bag and tugged at the zipper, but it wouldn't move. She let go of the throttle, the lifeboat kicking starboard before the motor went idle. Lena studied the water on either side of her. Whatever the whales were protecting, she must have moved a safe distance from it. There was nothing save the waves, though the dying light made for some awful shadows. With both hands she dragged open the bag, pulled on an inflatable life jacket, yanked out a blanket and dragged it across herself. The wind blew at the wool, tugging one flap over the side. Lena lunged for it, not wanting the blanket to touch water. She jerked back as the head of an orca shot up from beneath. The blanket flapped in the wind like a flag, pinned at one end by Lena's death grip. The whale took the free end of the blanket in its mouth with calculated delicacy, then submerged, taking its prize with it.

Lena flew to the motor, then stopped in place, frozen by the gaze of the whale that hovered behind the Zodiac. Then another whale rose to port, then another, then two came up starboard. The entire pod had followed her, staying beneath the waves. They floated there, not moving, just as they had moments before they'd destroyed the life that Lena knew. The last sliver of sun disappeared behind the horizon, and like a light switching off, it was dark.

Lena's hands forgot the motor and plunged into the bag, searching for the waterproof high-powered light she knew was there. Her fingers closed around the handle—it looked like a fat yellow pistol—and switched it on as it cleared the duffel. She shone the beam in a circle around the boat. The whales were all there, not moving.

"What did we do?" she whimpered. "What did we do that made you hate us?" Had the boat struck an infant? Had they somehow injured one the pod's young? Why hadn't they felt anything?

There was another gun-like object in the bag; a flare gun. Her father kept it loaded in there, contrary to safety regs and common sense, but Lena was grateful for it now. She took the gun and aimed at one of the orcas. But what would shooting it accomplish? The most she could do was aggravate the creature, unless she could somehow get a shot right down its blowhole.

One of the whales near the front of the boat squeaked. It was a long series of bleats that ended with a clicking sound. She brought the searchlight forward, to see two of the whales, the ones blocking her path, drift aside, then sink away.

What is this? she thought. *Are they letting me go?* She took the motor in hand and eased the boat towards the offered gap. None of the whales attempted to stop her. When she reached the edge of the circle of orcas, she turned the throttle and leapt ahead at full speed. She dropped the searchlight, picked up the flare gun, and fired it into the air. In the darkness, lights from the distant shore looked tantalizingly close, as if she could reach out and touch them. Above her, the flare initiated its downward arc, and winked out.

Steering with one hand, Lena dragged a radio transponder from the bag. She wondered why she hadn't gone for it first. That was her specialty, communications, even if simply flipping an on switch didn't require a university degree. A red light blinked on and off, indicating that the device, built to take a few hard knocks and keep working, was doing just that. Lena loaded another flare and fired again. The purple light that bathed the water around her boat, showed two…no, three whales keeping pace with her again. One of them must have realized she'd seen it, because it swam closer, and nudged the side of the boat before drifting away again.

They're not letting me go…they're…playing with me. From a larynx already worn beyond belief, Lena managed one more scream. Her mind tottered, one of the lights from shore detached and moved closer. Her eyes were playing on tricks on her.

"Gab war Kay ooware?" a garbled voice called from ahead. "Gab war Kay ooware?" it called again.

It wasn't a trick of the light, there was something close, a boat with a searchlight.

"Are you okay out there?" came the amplified voice, now clear. Someone had seen her flare, someone with a megaphone.

The light struck Lena full in the face, completely blinding her. From the sides of the boat, Lena heard a multitude of squeaks and clicks. That's when she realized her second guess about the whales' motives had also been incorrect. They weren't playing with her, they were using her for bait.

"Go away!" she tried to call, but all that came out was an empty rasp. "Go away, there's whales."

The searchlight jerked away at the same time as impact thundered across the water. Running lights and a lit cabin outlined a boat not much bigger than the one Lena had set forth on earlier that day. The running lights rose on one side of the boat, and disappeared on the other. The cries from the vessel were garbled again, this time by panic, not distance. She didn't know how many people were on it, but self-preservation told her she couldn't save them. She sped away from the shuddering boat as quickly as the Zodiac would take her. Shamed burned in her as she hoped the would-be rescuers would distract the whales long enough for her to escape.

The engine's droning became white noise and she kept her eyes forward, like Orpheus, not wanting to look back into the depths of

Hades, but a flash of light from behind her turned her head as if with invisible hands, and what she saw lost Eurydice forever.

The vessel had ignited somehow. Flames leapt into the sky as the darkened outline of the boat pitched and yawed. Basked in the orange light, orcas leapt from the sea and milled about in gay abandon, their massive shapes now but a thumb-length. There were many of them, far more than the number that had attacked her father's boat.

Lena hastily loaded her flare gun, it being her only weapon. She pulled the cord on her life jacket that released compressed air from a canister. It ballooned and tightened around her. She felt that every drop of water around her held a killer whale, and she was at least partially right.

The Zodiac lifted from the water and flew a few feet before crashing down again, tossed by a blow from beneath. Lena was knocked off balance, and almost over the side. She grabbed a guide rope with one hand, clinging to it as the motor, unguided, shifted into neutral. Her legs slipped off the side and into the water. Ice gripped her lower extremities once more, and her searchlight had been claimed by the sea, its bright spot dimming as it sank. She hauled at the rope, wringing more strength out of limbs already depleted. Something yanked her back by one leg, there was a ferocious struggle, then whatever had caught her let go and she crumbled to the floor of the lifeboat. She rolled on her back. The killer whale was black against the stars as it loomed beside the lifeboat, appearing to savour her terror before lurching forward for the kill.

Without even realizing she was doing it, Lena pointed the flare gun at the mammal's open mouth, and fired. The purple light was impossibly bright as it flashed down massive gullet. The whale pitched backwards, violet haze still emanating as the orca dove to quench the burning in its throat. The light blinked out and Lena waited, eyes watering at the odour of scorched meat that hung in the air. Seconds stretched out to hours, but the creature did not reappear to wreak vengeance. The numbness in her legs was complete, especially in the right leg. She could feel nothing from it whatsoever. Her mother, her father, Marty…all gone…those poor people that had tried to help her…once again self preservation took control. Lena's arms pushed her into a sitting position, then she pulled herself towards the motor. Once again, something caught her leg. From the light of a sliver moon, Lena saw a ragged bit of bone catching the rubber below her right knee, where the lower leg used to be. She hadn't won the tug-of-war with the orca; she'd lost it. If flesh, muscle and sinew hadn't parted, she'd have been dragged to her death as surely as she was bleeding to it now. The roar in her ears drowned the sound of the wounded killer whale rising from behind her. Its brain was fogged by pain and damage, animals too, went into shock. Unseen, it sank into the depths, possibly never to rise again.

Lena would have lain in the boat until she died of blood loss or exposure, whichever came first, had she not seen the distant flare—this one red—that arced out from source unknown. The pinpoint of light disappeared, then was replaced by a second flare. Was someone else floating in a lifeboat, a survivor from another homicidal pod?

"You must live, child," said Nancy Wong's voice.

"Mother? Where are you?" Lena breathed.

"Save yourself. You must live," then the voice was gone.

With hands powered by will alone, Lena turned the throttle, and headed toward the source of the flare.

"We've got you miss. Awe Jesus, Tim!" Strong hands pulled Lena from the Zodiac into a larger vessel. "Watch her leg, Tim! She's a bleeder!" The deep baritone belonged to a stocky man with a black goatee and a red, woolen cap. As she was eased to the deck, a young Chinese man, wire-rim spectacles perched on a pug nose, placed a hand on her forehead and raised one eyelid with his thumb.

"Can you hear me, lady?"

The man who'd first spoken turned to someone out of sight, "We've got her! Let's get the hell out of here!"

"Where to?" came a woman's tired voice. "Back to Vancouver?"

"Fuck no! What are you, nuts?"

"Then where are we going to go? You said the water would be safe, Bernie! You said we'd be okay out here."

The man shook his head, then turned his attention to Lena. He held her head in his hands while Tim sliced open what was left of her pant leg with a pair of scissors. "Miss, are you from *Jasmine's Dream?*"

She shook her head, not understanding.

"We picked up a distress call from *Jasmine's Dream.* Whale attack. Were you attacked by whales?"

"Looks like it," said Dr. Timothy Chung. "This is as much crush damage as anything else. I'm going to have to take more off." He yelled for someone, "Arthur, crush amputation, I'll need something to cut with!"

Lena's eyes bulged and she began to buck and heave under Dr. Chung's ministrations.

"Christ, somebody give us a hand," Bernie said, covering Lena's body with his own.

Lena's seizure gave out abruptly. Her body truly had nothing left, not one iota of energy. Her perception tilted, expanded as she rose from her body and took up a vantage point a few metres above the boat. From this position she watched, detached, as two men held her down and a third gave her an injection of some sort.

A woman, North American Indian, wrapped in a thick jacket, stepped out of the wheelhouse. "Bernie, where are we going to go then?"

"I'm fucking busy," he growled at her. "Do something useful, get some damn blankets." But the woman just stood there, staring at the mutilated girl on the deck. "Is she going to be okay?"

"I don't know, Amanda," said Bernie. "Please get some blankets."

"I know where we go," said the man beside Bernie, his voice a thick French accent. "We go to the pulp mill, yes? So much pollution, no animals for miles."

Another man, also wearing a red woolen cap, emerged from a hatch and handed Dr. Chung a large fish knife.

"You're kidding me," said Timothy, eyeing the implement.

"Best we've got, Doc. Sorry."

"Zingyun Shee Shoo," said the Frenchman, "there, on her life jacket. Is it the name of her boat?"

"Most likely," replied Tim, placing the edge of the knife against Lena's leg. "It means Lucky Sailor."

The dual engines rumbled, the vessel took a lazy turn to starboard, then increased in speed once it reached its new heading. From that same strange place above her body, Lena remembered the motor of the Zodiac, and how she'd utterly failed to rescue her own mother. Her view from above faded to black, and she knew nothing again until she awoke on a cot in a pulp mill storehouse, with a different body, in a different world.

For the first six months she dreamed of the whales every night. She'd wake up screaming, disturbing all those quartered with her, and would have been chastised had she not been one of many doing the same thing. By day she was confronted with the realities of horrors that walked on all fours, and being disabled when healthy people were urgently needed. The guilt and despair that consumed her would have pushed her past the brink had not her mother's voice echoed in her head at times of greatest need; "You must live."

Gradually, any sympathy she had gotten from others diminished, then vanished. There was nothing special about her experience—everyone had lost someone. Many of them had witnessed their loved ones dying before their eyes. In fact, when she chose to recognize it, Lena was in better shape than a lot of survivors. Some had lost more than one limb, or suffered injuries resulting in paralyses from partial to full. Still others had kept their limbs, but lost huge portions of their minds.

In time she became proficient on crutches, and then even more proficient on a prosthetic limb, supplied by none other than Neil Eggerson. Later, under a mock-hypnosis garnered from magazine-ordered textbooks and two trips to Reveen, Caps guided her back to that night in all its detail. It wasn't her fault that her mother had died. Even if she had remembered the switch on the motor, it wouldn't have mattered. The broken rail wasn't just through Mrs. Wong's cardigan, it had been right through her shoulder. And there had been something else, something she'd seen just as her mother disappeared from view, like maybe not all of Mrs. Wong had been in the same place. As much as the revelation was a relief, it was also a tremendous horror. She'd blocked that vision for a reason, it was something she'd never wanted to see again.

The dreams changed after that, but only to the degree that it was no longer her fault that her loved ones died. They still floundered around her, sometimes simply vanishing into the darkness, other times bobbing back to the surface, intestines drifting from severed torsos. In the throes of her nightmare, no rescue boat came. Her leg didn't separate, and she was dragged ever downward through inky-black water.

31. The Boy Inside the Man

They stopped before a crumbling overpass. High weeds effectively masked the ditches on either side of the road.

"Let's suit up. Richard, break out the guns. Somebody go and–" Sid was cut off as Toffee's car went sailing past the Pig and slammed into the overpass's middle support pillar. The back end of the car rose a full three feet off the ground, then flopped down, bouncing slightly off the tires.

Sid threw his door open and raced to the car. The front of the vehicle was empty. Fifty feet back, Toffee struggled to his feet. His prosthetic had come off, and his blade's tip slipped on the concrete each time he put weight on it. It made him look as if he was part crab.

"What...what happened?" Sid called as he jogged to the hunter.

Toffee took a step, almost fell, then took another. He hobbled over to his arm and picked it up.

"Toffee! What the hell happened?"

The hunter bared his teeth at Sid, then worked the prosthetic up his sleeve and twisted. The arm slid down sharp steel, Toffee caught it just before it fell off. He moved it back up and tried twice more to lock it into place, then with a burst of inarticulate rage hurled it to the blacktop. The man's gray hair was splayed in all directions, and his left cheek was a mess of blood. His lips pulled up and trembled in a silent growl.

"No brakes...no doglicking brakes!" His tongue flicked out to his cheek, tasted the blood. The thrush, the slap, the shrapnel, now road rash. "I'm gettin' the shit kicked outta myself!"

Caps stood by the car, his hands firmly clamped on either side of his head. "I told you," he twisted from the waist to look at Lena and Noah. "I told him! The brakes were shot. Why didn't I take it out of service? That's my freakin' job!"

The front end was crumpled in like an accordion. Jagged metal dug into one tire like a fork into a piece of sponge cake. The hood bowed in the middle and flexed up, and steam belched from one side of the metal tent. The engine was in a new and entirely original configuration.

"Well, it's out of service now," said Darcy.

"Everybody, get back in the van!" Sid yelled. He offered an arm to the hunter, only to have it slapped away by the flat of Toffee's blade. Sid grabbed Toffee under one arm and forcibly helped him to the Pig.

Caps risked an arm into the car to recover his rucksack.

"Get in the van, Richard!"

Caps looked around. He didn't see any animals. Sid reached the van and shoved Toffee inside, with the help of Lena pulling from within. The Boss jumped in the driver's seat and without even checking doors, sped off as quick as the van could accelerate, which wasn't very fast. The overpass vanished behind them, and the Deep Six penetrated Vancouver's outer limits.

The gun in Noah's hand was a Colt .45 It was also a green water pistol that shot on a bias and leaked. The rifle across his lap was black metal. It was also white plastic, its ammunition a tiny car that could streak up a ramp and jump through a blazing ring of cardboard fire. He'd fought with the overlapping images for the first few hours of awakening in the Camper World safe house, and gotten on top of them. The smashed car, Sid's urgency, Lena's anxiety attack, they all combined to push Noah's perceptions out of whack again.

"Where are we going?" asked Darcy.

"What are you doing?" asked Kate Thurlow.

"As far as we can get from the sound of that crash," replied Sid.

The Pig turned off the freeway, and into tree-choked residential streets, just as the Thurlow family jeep passed the last fast food restaurant before open highway. Noah clenched his eyes shut and pushed at the memories, trying to force them back into the box from whence they came, or at least limit them to one at a time.

Caps checked the breach on his shotgun, then snapped it shut with an authoritative click. "You gonna tell us what we're running from?"

Mr. Dalton, Noah's fourth grade teacher, tapped his pointer on the desk. "Class, who do you think got the best score on the math exam?"

He hadn't told any of them what was happening inside his head. The last thing he needed was to be labelled tooth crazy. The street lost its trees and gained a strip mall with a great donut place. Noah brought the pommel of his gun down on the back of his hand, searching the pain for focus.

"People, right?" Toffee occupied the back area of the van. "You think there's people here."

"I'm sure of it." Sid looked off to one side of the road. "This'll do." The van pulled into an open, empty garage attached to a lifeless two-story house with ceramic shingles. The house sat behind grass so high it hid the front door. For a tilting moment, it was also a two-story brownstone with a neatly trimmed lawn, and loving grandparents inside.

Noah hit his hand again.

"Kid, what are you doing?" Toffee whispered roughly in his ear. "You trying to hurt yourself?"

"Yes."

"Lemme help." Toffee cupped Noah's cheek, then dug his thumb into a nerve bundle at the top of the jaw line.

The young man's breath caught in his throat as intense pain caused the peripheral vision in his left eye to wink out. The thumb withdrew. Now that was focus.

"Need more?"

Noah grabbed his cheek protectively and shook his head.

"What people?" asked Darcy. "Who's here?"

Sid tightened his collar around his netting. "It's the only thing that makes sense. What did all the expeditions that have come here have in common?"

Everyone except Toffee said their own version of, "They all died."

"We don't know that. What they all had in common was that they were transmitting. It's standard procedure, some vehicles in, always one outside listening."

Darcy wrapped duct tape around the tops of her boots, there was nothing better for the job. "We've heard that one…some group of people waiting on the outskirts, killing everyone that came inside. You're saying they know people are coming by listening to a scanner."

"Again, we don't know they're dead. What we know is that we lost communication with them. That's why I insisted on radio silence coming in. I didn't want to be noticed."

"So what if we came in silent? If someone was here, they'd be watching the road."

Sid took the tape from Darcy and strapped his gloves to his sleeves. "It's been four years that we know of. Long time to watch an empty road."

"We could have no visitors at the Pit for a decade, I'd still never stop watching the driveway." Darcy checked her own rifle, then opened her door.

"That's at the Pit. This is a city. There's never been any sightings of activity along the road. Sooner or later, a long-term watch post would be spotted. I think they're farther in, but forewarned."

Lena buckled her gun belt, and distastefully drew the pistol. She checked the cylinders one more time, then holstered the weapon. "So you're saying a scanner. What about our last expedition? Those were SatCom vans. You saying there's an uplink here? And a locator? Radio's omnidirectional, but satellite is tightly focussed."

"Those two vans," Sid said as he opened his door, "were in radio communication with each other. C'mon, Darce, let's see if we can get this garage door closed."

Caps rifled through his bag, extracted a gun in a left-handed holster, then rifled some more. "Toffee, did you take anything out of this bag?"

"Is it your bag?"

"Yeah, we swapped accidentally when we reloaded."

"Why would I waste time looking at your crap?" The hunter reached into his own bag, fingering the paperback before removing his gun.

"Shit! The camper! We didn't clean up the camper. I took the pad in there when we were cooking. I was sure I brought it back. Damn."

A nerve-wracking shriek of protesting metal echoed through the garage as the door was yanked down on its guides. It wouldn't go the whole way, and a foot worth of sunlight shone beneath the door.

As Sid rolled under the door to check outside, Darcy clambered into the van. "Toffee, take your shirt off." She shut the doors.

The hunter undid his buttons with practiced flicks of finger and thumb, then turned and exposed his back to the chief of security. She carefully peeled back a gauze pad, and checked the hunter's stitches.

They held strong. She'd should have had Patel fixing her coveralls all these years.

Darcy left and went under the door after Sid. Caps and Lena jumped out to stretch their legs.

"Think you can handle that gun?" Toffee asked.

Noah balanced the .45 in his hand. It was heavy, and probably had one hell of a recoil. "I've fired plenty of these."

"Sure you have."

The hunter tied his sleeve off just above the blade, using his hand and teeth. Then he tucked his net into his collar, and left the van. Noah aimed the gun at the windshield, faked a couple shots, then holstered it. Even sitting, it was an uncomfortable load on his hip. The rifle was more familiar territory; Heckler & Koch 12-gauge shotgun, 26 inch barrel with wood stock. Not a long-range weapon by any means, but easy to supply with ammunition, and certainly capable of shredding a dog or raccoon. Shotguns were the most common weapons carried by non-sharpshooters. It needed only to be pointed in the general direction of the animal. Noah stared at the rifle for a few seconds, waiting for it to shift into something else, but the duality that had afflicted him seemed to be in abeyance, at least for the moment.

Noah exited the van and looked around the garage. Various gardening tools lined one wall, rust permanently affixing metal implements to the nails on which they hung. On a shelf under one filthy window were coffee cans overflowing with nails, screws, and other small items used for securing one thing to another. Spider webs, both occupied and vacant, held the corners of the ceiling and most other places where convenient substrate was available. It reminded Noah of an abandoned farmhouse he used to play in when he was a boy. The memory was not accompanied by a shifting of vision.

With a loud creak, Caps opened the door that led from the garage to the house proper. When nothing jumped out, he went inside.

"I don't think you should do that," said Lena

"Relax, it's perfectly safe," came the artist's voice from inside. "There's nothing in here but mouldy rugs."

With a last look of hesitation at the crack under the garage door, Lena followed her boyfriend. Noah stayed in the garage, and waited until Sid returned with Darcy. They rolled smoothly under the door. Toffee followed shortly afterwards, moving carefully so as not to exacerbate injuries sustained when he leapt from his car.

"Dammit," said Sid as he saw the open door. "Richard, get the hell out of there." When there was no response, he entered the house, Darcy on his heels.

"What's out there?" Noah asked the hunter.

"Nothing. More houses. Lots of trees." Toffee shouldered his rifle and went through the door.

After a last look around the garage, Noah followed his companions. He found himself in a large kitchen. A chest freezer sat next to a refrigerator. Noah knew better than to open either of them. The counter held two sinks and a long cutting board. The paring knife and mummified remains of some vegetable sat beside the board. Dishes were piled in one of the sinks, and more dishes were on a circular table. The house's occupants were at some stage of dining when the decision to flee had been made.

"Upstairs is clear," Caps voiced from somewhere above.

Noah moved from the kitchen into the living room. The carpet was mouldy, as was the sofa, loveseat and armchair. The mantle of a gas fireplace held pictures. Curious, he brushed aside cobwebs to reveal a smiling family: Mom, Dad, and two children—a boy and a girl. They were wearing matching turtleneck sweaters and posed before a tree-filled backdrop. Noah waited for the picture to change to one of his own family, but it remained the same. He examined the other photos. There was a wedding photo, and pictures of two older couples, possibly grandparents. Altogether, it was a typical middle-class home, except it probably hadn't seen a human occupant in almost a decade.

Dust filled the air as Toffee pushed curtains aside with his blade. Nothing stirred in the long grass outside. Noah coughed a bit on the thickened air, then retreated to a second hallway. This led to two doors, one closed, the other open to a small bathroom. A green, porcelain dish held sludge that had once been soap. The toilet bowl was stained a dull brown, and empty of water. The bathtub was likewise stained brown. Noah heard muted voices from the living room.

"Satisfied?" asked the hunter.

"I don't hear any other cars. Maybe we lucked out and we haven't been detected."

"You should turn over leadership to me."

"What?!"

"You're an administrator, Halbert. You brought me in to be the Pit's field operative."

"This is different." Did the Boss sound defensive?

"Why? Because you're with us? Maybe that's a liability. I don't think you have what it takes."

There was a pause. Noah had to strain his ears to hear what came next.

"I'll forget you said that, Ethan."

"Is that a threat? I'm trembling."

"You slapped me with your blade back on the road."

"What of it?"

"Touch me with that thing again, you'll be wearing it through your neck."

Noah stood in the abandoned bathroom, unsure of what to do. Had he paid more attention, he would have seen this confrontation coming long ago. Where was Darcy?

"I believe you'd try," said the hunter.

"Sid," called Darcy from the upper level. Noah breathed a sigh of relief.

"Remember your place," said Sid. "I'm still the boss of you." Footsteps moved up the stairs.

Noah jerked back against the tub as the hunter appeared at the door.

"Get an earful?"

"Everybody back in the van!" called Sid. Feet pounded down the stairs. Noah headed out the bathroom, down the hall, and back to the garage. He was the first one to reach the vehicle, Toffee was right behind him. Lena and Caps filled out the back as Darcy came through the door and dropped to one knee, her rifle held at the ready. Sid fell into position beside her.

"What's happening?" asked Noah.

Caps, his hands tightening on his rifle, looked out the back window. "Dogs. About a dozen of them. First teeth we've seen since we got here. Might be just wandering, but maybe they're here for us. Nice. We can't leave without opening the door, and we can't do that without alerting the dog pack. We can't shoot the dogs without attracting attention."

"Attention from who?"

"Ask the Boss. I'm still expecting some sort of sewer monster."

The seconds stretched out like minutes. When no ominous shadows appeared under the door, Sid eased off and climbed into the van. Darcy stepped up to the front seat and shut the door.

"So what now?" she asked.

"We'll give them a few minutes to pass, then we get out of here."

"And go where?" asked Caps.

"Our first objective. Trucks. I think we would have heard cars by now if they were on to us."

"Can you give us more than 'they?' "

"No. Don't know. I'm just sure there're people here. I'm positive of it."

"Why haven't they reached out?" asked Lena.

"They haven't needed to. Anything they need, they've got right here. There is precedent. Right in your home town in fact, Richard."

"Seattle's not a dead zone," said the artist.

"You're from Seattle?" asked Noah, surprised.

"Yeah, didn't I mention? So what's the precedent, Boss?"

"You never heard of the Stadium Ghouls?"

"Oh, them. There was never a mystery about them. They just killed anyone that came near. There's plenty of settlements like that, approach at your own risk."

"That's the only difference, Richard. No mystery. Fear is a wonderful defence. Look how well it's worked here."

"What about the black death?" asked Lena. "It was rife here the year after the Change. If I remember correctly it even upgraded to septicaemic plague."

"Septicaemic plague?" Noah thought he knew all the city killers. This was a new one on him.

"Think bubonic on steroids," supplied Caps.

"Even in the dark ages there were survivors," Sid explained. "As long as they always lanced the boils, avoided contaminated water…that would protect them from cholera as well."

"What if they don't use cars, Sid?" asked the chief of security. "What if they're on foot?"

"Then we'd have heard guns. They'd have to shoot their way to us."

"Fifty-seven minutes," said Darcy, checking her watch. "Congratulations everybody, we've lasted twelve minutes longer than anyone else to come here."

"As I said before," the Boss admonished, "we don't know they died. All we know is they lost contact. Toffee, get someone to look at your cheek."

Toffee leaned forward and stuffed a small first aid kit into Lena's hand. It must have been one he carried with him. He turned his head and presented the wounded side of his face. Lena gently peeled off the bandage he'd hastily applied when he'd first been pulled into the van.

"You didn't clean this very well," she said. "There's still bits of stuff in there."

She dabbed water onto a sterile pad and began to wipe the cheek. Small foreign bodies pulled from the cheek, leaving behind tiny holes that oozed blood. Toffee winced and gritted his teeth.

"Sorry," said Lena as she pulled her hand away.

"No, that's okay," Toffee took her hand and pulled it back to his face. "You've got a gentle touch."

They waited in the van for another twenty minutes, after which they made their way north and west, using side streets, not the main thoroughfares. Many times they had to backtrack when faced with roads too overgrown, or too collapsed to bypass. What would have been a twenty-five minute drive in good traffic before the Change, took the Deep Six hours. Evidence of the initial chaos was everywhere from big things—cars protruding from storefronts, skeletons on sidewalks—to little things, June 10th's edition of "The Province" in a newspaper dispenser.

One spectacular, if morbid, display of destruction drifted overhead about two hours into the trip. A tractor-trailer had crashed through the guardrails of an overpass. The trailer remained on the upper level while the cabover dangled from its fifth wheel and back tires. The windshield was almost parallel to the road. In the cab's interior, lying against the glass were both the fragmented remains of a human being, and a more intact skeleton of a dog. It suggested the final moments of a pet owner, and the long starvation of an animal, unable to escape the vehicle. Possibly it died of heat exhaustion before it had a chance to pass from hunger.

"I can't believe that thing's been hanging for so long," said Noah.

"Good workmanship." Caps looked back as the shadows from the overpass swallowed the hanging cab. "I'll bet the motor would still work. There was damage to the grill, and I'm sure the chassis is shot, but that motor would still work. I think the dog was a retriever."

"You're just making that up. How do you know so much about dogs, anyway?"

"Parents were breeders. Used to do a lot of dog shows. Had a lot of dog books in the house growing up."

"Oh." Noah hesitated before asking, "What dogs did your parents have on NW day?"

"They'd moved to an apartment, no dogs allowed."

"Well, that's good."

"There must have been a gazillion cats in the building. Anytime I paid them a visit there were at least two in the lobby. They wandered in and out of open doors. You could smell the cat food and unchanged litter from some of the suites. They really stank. Wonder what that building smells like now."

They passed a bevy of fast food restaurants along one strip. A giant white and red bucket on a pole, that at one time had rotated from 10 a.m. to midnight, showed the face of a gentle, bearded man. The golden arches still stood, though the building next to it had become the window box of a giant, demented gardener. Rotting foodstuffs had called to insects and birds alike. The droppings from these creatures, as well as whatever organic material was left over from the initial feeding frenzy provided fertilizer for seeds carried in by the wind and more animal droppings. A bush sprouted between the yellow, plastic legs of the restaurant's redheaded mascot, the branches reaching the statue's crotch, making it look like a clown on a leafy bidet.

"Come in and try our special," said Caps. "Mummified fry-guy."

"Ask me something," Noah told Caps.

"Like what?"

"Movies, toys, stuff from before the Change. I can remember everything."

"What was your favourite film?"

"Ace Ventura, it was old. We had it on tape and DVD. Wow, was that ever funny."

"Yeah? Do you know what would happen to the pet detective today?"

Lena shook her head. "Do you have to spoil everything?"

"What was your favourite TV show?" asked Caps.

Noah thought for a moment. "MASH!"

"MASH? No way."

"It was on twenty-four hours a day. You just had to flip channels."

"But you were a little kid. Did you understand the show?"

"Kinda. My dad loved it. I'd watch it with my dad."

"MASH was my favorite show, too. Next to Star Trek. Did you watch Star Trek?"

"Which one? There was like thirty of 'em on the air."

"Did you like Animal Kingdom?" asked Toffee, gesturing out the window with his blade. Rats skittering along the sidewalks on either side of the vehicle, more followed behind. "Halbert, I don't like this."

Noah looked through all the windows. There were a lot of rodents outside. They couldn't keep up with the van, but they followed behind anyway. New rats appeared as others vanished in the distance. Rats were nocturnal by nature, they wouldn't be following the van unless they knew something. He wanted the Boss to speed up, but instead the van decelerated, then stopped.

"There," said Sid as rats began to climb up the tires and the front grill. Ahead of the vehicle, the street was crumbling. A few car lengths farther, it had completely collapsed. "The road's falling into the sewers. We're headed into a pit trap. These rats…" they were beginning to pile up on the hood. Some of them had made it to the roof, "…are here for a quick meal."

Sid put the van in reverse, squashing rodents as he did so. He turned the Pig around, and sped back the way they'd come. Rats flew from the roof and slid off the hood in spread-eagled panic.

"Are you saying they expected us to fall through the road?" asked Darcy. "Sid, that's a pretty advanced grasp of cause and effect."

"It wouldn't surprise me if the animals started throwing nets at us one day."

It was the middle of the afternoon when the Pig jounced over a forgotten railroad and entered into a different world. Gone were the trees and sprouting blacktop, in their stead were straw coloured weeds that rose before a seemingly endless twin fence line. The ground was too damaged to heal itself anytime soon. Beyond the usual concrete and tar that had been heaped upon it, it was also soaked through with motor oil, gasoline and traces of just about every industrial fluid ever pumped, drained, poured or sprayed. Douglas Road was once home to numerous shipping companies from overland freight to Paramount Studio's Vancouver transport branch, interspersed with automotive component supply depots. At least fifty tractor-trailer rigs sat behind those fences, accompanied by anything that was needed to make them run. Noah's jaw dropped at the sheer value of it all. There was a Walken's Brakes & Exhaust,

Allroad Tires, Wonder Shocks and Suspension and trucks, trucks, trucks.

"Holy shit!" Caps gasped. "Look at 'em."

"Can you get one of them to run?" asked Noah.

"Sun boy, I bet I can get all of them to run."

Sid picked a yard seemingly at random. "Why don't you start with one, then get ambitious."

The Pig crushed a number of weeds beneath its wheels as it pulled into the lot. A long dung coloured warehouse was the backdrop for seven trucks, four with trailers, three without. Two of the trucks were cabovers, their taller appearance only an illusion created by the overall boxiness of their shape. The rest were conventional, sometimes known as long-noses. The explorers suited up again, and one by one filed out of the van. Caps examined the trucks as Darcy and Toffee scanned the surrounding area.

"What do you think?" asked the Boss.

"I think we'll start with this one." Caps ran his gloved hand over the driver-side running board of a Ford LTL 9000 sitting closest to the lot's exit, sans trailer. The reddish paint was faded and rust had eaten through the wheel hubs at the front. Weight and time had rotted out the sidewalls of all ten tires. On the passenger side, a small door allowed access to the sleeping area. On the door was the driver's name—Kenneth Bradley—and maximum weight designations; TARE 9000 kg, GVW 43 000 kg. Moss had taken up residence in both the mesh bug stopper over the grill, and in the two engine-cooling vents on either side of the "nose". Directly behind the cab was a strong metal frame, the headache rack, used to protect the driver in case of impact from a loose load.

"Might have hauled logs," said the artist-now-mechanic.

"So how does it look?" Sid prodded.

"Please, allow me to finish examining the patient before I render a diagnosis." He reached out to a red hose that coiled from beneath the headache rack. Caps squeezed the rubber, it crumbled under the pressure and a metal fitting attached to the end fell, bounced off the chassis and landed on the ground in a puff of dirt.

He stooped and picked the fitting up. It was a glad-hand, one of two that together supplied control to a trailer's air brakes. Caps moved down the vehicle, prodding metal, squeezing hoses. More rubber crumbled under his scrutiny and he made grunts of dissatisfaction as he pulled a release handle near the fifth wheel. He struggled with the gas cap on one of the two fuel tanks, eventually getting it open with Sid's help. Caps pulled a long, reedy weed from the ground, inserted it into the tank, withdrew it, then moved to the back wheels. After that he lay down, pulled himself under the vehicle, then pushed himself back out and flipped a hood latch on either side. There were a pair of foot-holes beneath the grill. He stood in these, grabbed the hood and pulled. With some protest the heavy metal covering tilted up, exposing the engine. After manipulating a few more hoses to dust, he climbed up to the driver's door and smashed a window.

"Hey, maybe there are keys in the main building," said Sid.

"Doubt it. See the name on the side? This one's independently owned. Mr. Bradley has the keys to this truck, he probably just parked it here." Caps unlocked the door and pulled himself into the cab. The seats were mouldy, the upholstery was cracked. The air-controlled seat was in its lowest position and the mechanic's head barely cleared the dashboard as he sat down. He checked the dashboard, jiggled the stick shift, then jumped back down. He walked around the truck one more time, glanced at the other vehicles, then finally gave Sid his report.

"The air hoses are rotted out, so are the air bags at the back. The glad-hand seals need to be replaced. The fuel in the tanks has gone to jelly. The air filter needs cleaning. The braided metal for the fuel lines is sound, but the rubber outside is gone. There'll be moisture trapped in the air tanks. The brakes are probably seized...scratch that...the brakes are seized. The tires are useless, all of them. The Playboy Bunny mud flaps are gauche and the pine-tree air freshener has lost its scent. All in all, its in excellent condition."

"I don't need sarcasm right now. How about the other trucks?"

"They'll all be in the same or worse condition. I'm not being sarcastic, Boss. This rig is in excellent condition all things considered. There's a Kenworth over there I'll look at later, but this here's my baby for now."

"You can fix it?"

"Providing I can find replacement parts in these warehouses...I can make it dance."

Sid smiled beneath his netting. "How long?"

"Two days."

"Two days?"

"Hey, a complete refit of this vehicle, without a trained crew backing me up? Two days is amazing."

Sid mulled this over. "And if we can't find the replacement parts?"

"It's not like you to ask stupid questions, Boss."

"Point taken. Get to work."

"Okay people," Caps raised a hand above his head as he spoke, "this is where I take over." He tugged at his net-helmet. "I'm sweating like crazy here."

"Keep your net on, Richard."

"Relax, there's no wasps anywhere around here," the netting was just about out of his collar.

"What about ants?"

"I'll see them coming."

"Oh? Then I guess you're not worried about the ones on your boot."

"Very funny, I…" he glanced down, "Glaaahhh!" A trail of little black ants streamed from a crevice near the truck, over the toe of Caps's boot, and up the pant leg. A few of the insects had stopped where the cuff was sealed. They prodded at the material, looking for a way to reach the flesh they sensed beneath.

"I'm not asleep, you little bastards," Caps blurted as he danced and slapped at his leg.

Toffee sauntered over from the van, a pressurized spray tank in his hand. He depressed the trigger and a mixture of pyrethrin and piperonyl butoxide spewed from the nozzle in a fan pattern. The hunter sprayed a ribbon of pesticide between the crevice and Caps, then turned his attention to the source itself. Tiny bodies scurried from the crack as liquid death rained down upon them. Those affected staggered as if drunk, then curled up into a ball and appeared to chew their own butts off. More ants came from the crevice, some of them making it almost a metre away before their central nervous systems went completely haywire. Noah and Darcy scanned the blacktop for more of the ants or the telltale piles of fine dirt—frass—that usually accompanied a colony's entrance.

"More over here," called Darcy from beside a dirty brown tractor-trailer rig. Toffee moved in as Darcy fell back. The ants were already on their way towards her.

Caps continued flicking insects of his leg, ignorant of the trail approaching from behind.

Lena, who'd jumped up to the front bumper of the LTL the moment Sid had mentioned ants, called out to her boyfriend. "Honey, behind you!"

Caps turned, yelped again, then joined the chief of communications on her higher ground.

Through it all, Toffee moved slowly and calmly, laying down chemical barriers, filling up cracks. Soon the nozzle hissed and spluttered, announcing an empty tank.

"How much of that do we have left?" asked the Boss.

"Another tank load in the van," Toffee jiggled the tank by his ear, "the rest is in the car. Should we go back for it?" The question was rhetorical.

"Are you expecting an apology? Yes, I knew the brakes were going, but I planned to ditch the car here anyway. You're going to miss that arm of yours."

"Fingers were broken, so was the clasp. Eggerson's working on a new one for me anyway."

The hunter had created a poison ring large enough to include the truck. The Deep-Six stood within the protection of that ring. Caps had jumped down to the ground, but Lena was still up on her perch.

"Could we use some fuel and burn out the cracks?" asked Noah.

"Not a good idea." Caps pointed at a pair of dull, metal discs secured to the concrete a stone's throw away. "Those are caps for a reservoir. That's why you picked this lot, isn't it Boss? You saw the caps."

"No, I saw the pump." Past the discs was a fuel pump with a metal cage around it.

"Won't someone have drained the fuel already?" Noah squinted through his mesh.

"The card lock is still on it," said Caps. "This is unbelievable. All these rigs, and all we have to worry about is a few hymenoptera. Damn, it's still stinking hot out here. Toffee, we've got plenty of bug juice. I loaded pesticide into the van's sprayers instead of repellent. Call me paranoid."

Lena's look of relief was palpable.

"Do you think we got all of them?" asked Noah

"Not by a long shot, sun boy." Darcy scanned the outer rim of the circle. "Anybody plan on sleeping tonight?"

While his subordinates watched the ground, Sid surveyed the horizon. He'd heard nothing to indicate approach, but still he was nervous. Getting in had been almost too easy. "Noah, do you know how to drain the spray tanks?"

"Yes."

"Fill the sprayer and expand our safety zone. Toffee, guard him. Lena, get down off that bumper. Richard, where to from here?"

"Let's start with equipment." He looked at the lots on either side of the one they were in. "A truck yard...could we be so lucky? That building over there should have everything we need. Shall we?"

Noah watched his friend and the Boss set off for the adjacent lot. At least Caps had tucked his net back in. Toffee stood by quietly as Noah opened the drain valve on the pig's repellent tank. Yellowish fluid gushed out and into Noah's upheld pressure sprayer. The hunter's blade caught the sunlight.

"Do you ever cut yourself on that thing?"

"You ever punch yourself in the head?"

"No...I getcha. How'd you get that thing? Did you make it yourself?"

"The sprayer full?"

"Yes."

"Then let's get to work."

For the briefest moment, the sprayer in Noah's hands was also a green bucket filled with soapy water. Thankfully, it didn't change again. The panel jockey didn't want Toffee digging at nerve points.

Caps cupped a hand to his mouth and turned to yell at the truck yard's building, then let the hand drop. He grunted in frustration and trotted towards the building, following a long line of rubber hose that led from one cracked door to a socket gun by the LTL. Sid had scolded him for yelling before. He wanted everything done as quietly as possible.

Noah felt the Boss was being ridiculous. The muffled drone of a diesel-powered air compressor that came from the building's interior was louder and more constant than anything Caps might shout. The air compressor was the first thing the mechanic had gotten working. He'd replaced a few gaskets and seals, then cleaned out the small fuel tank and refilled it with diesel brought up from the reservoir with a creaky hand-pump.

Darcy and Lena, off at a distance of thirty-or-so feet, guarded their flanks while Noah pulled crumbling rubber off of fittings on the truck. It was clumsy work what with his gloves and having to see some things through the net. He'd done a pretty thorough job of spraying, but even after going to the Pig and checking himself twice, he still felt like he had ants inside his clothes.

From within the building, the droning stopped. Caps jogged from fitting to fitting, checking the chain of hoses. After undoing, then refastening one of them, he ran back inside and the motor started up again. Noah picked up the socket gun and pulled the trigger. It jerked in his hand as a cylinder at the end of the gun spun with a high-pitched whine.

"We have a winner!" exclaimed Caps as he arrived a little breathless and took the gun from Noah's hand. He pulled the trigger himself a couple of times, then put the tool down and ran back to the building. The droning stopped again.

"How's it going?" asked Darcy, approaching the truck.

"Good, I think," Noah pushed at the socket gun with his foot. "This is working fine, but they shut the compressor off again. I'm hungry."

"Me too. Jerky for dinner unless Sid lets us go hunting."

"See any more ants?"

"No, not that that means anything."

"Where are we bedding down tonight? We're not all sleeping in the Pig are we?"

"I don't know. These trucks are all sleepers, maybe we'll use those."

"Form up, people," said Sid once he reached the truck. "We're going to pay a visit to Kingco's Automotive over there. The truck yard has all the tools and our mechanic here figures Kingco's will have the parts."

They went as a group, crossing the weed-choked tarmac and entering yet another lot. A number of vehicles rotted away beside a large, two-story building with lichen-encrusted aluminum siding. Instead of semis, these vehicles ranged from subcompacts to pickup trucks. Each had "Kingco's Automotive: Where you need it, when you need it," painted on the sides in blue lettering. Caps led them up a short flight of steps to a locked glass door. He rubbed grime off the door with his sleeve and peered inside.

"Uh oh, there's an alarm. Anyone know how to disarm it?" He chuckled at his meagre joke and smashed the glass with the butt of his rifle, then reached inside and opened the door.

Toffee kept watch outside as the other five entered Kingco's office. Caps moved to a bookshelf filled with thick parts catalogues. He ran his fingers along spines until he came to the one he wanted. While he flipped pages, Noah brushed aside cobwebs, and sat down behind a dust-covered IBM on an equally dusty desk. He pulled open a drawer, pawed through an assortment of pens and pencils, then shut the drawer and opened another. Sid jiggled the handle on a door that led from the office to the warehouse. It was locked. Two strong kicks and the door swung open.

"Find what you need?" asked Lena.

"That and more, my dear. Shall we?" Caps offered her his arm.

She stuck her head through the doorway into the darkened warehouse, then pulled a flashlight from her pocket and thumbed it on. "Wow. This place is huge. How are we going to find anything?"

Noah got up from the desk, clicked on his own flashlight and stepped through the door. A ribbon of light came from under the wide slide-up door at the front end of the warehouse, where a loading dock was located. The rest of the area was filled with shelving units that rose to the ceiling, and disappeared into the darkness.

"Can we open the big door?" he asked.

"Not without electricity," said Caps as he brushed past. He'd left his rifle on the desk in the front office, and aimed a flashlight at the shipper's desk by the loading dock. "If there's a hard copy manifest here, we're sailing. Otherwise, we're going to be hunting a long, long time."

The Boss moved to just inside the door and trained his flashlight on the rafters above the shelves. "Watch out for bats, people."

"Yeah, yeah," said Caps, "and mice, rats, coons, skunks and three thousand other things."

"Watch out for ants," said Noah, under his breath.

Circles of light moved from floor to walls as they searched the warehouse's interior. Caps found what he was looking for—a manifest in a green binder, and brought it back to the better light of the front office. He pulled a pad of paper from the desk and began jotting on it with a pencil. He looked up part numbers in the catalogue, then searched the manifest for storage locations. It took him a little while to complete the list. It was a long list. The artist dug through the desk until he found a pair of scissors. He cut the list into five pieces and gave one to each of his companions.

"Here's the deal: on the left are a series of five-digit numbers, those're the parts you're looking for. On the right are letter-number combinations. Theoretically, that's where we'll find these things. Happy hunting." He shouldered his rifle, aimed his flashlight and set off between rows B and C.

Noah looked at his piece of paper, the first part he needed, 65447, was in row F, shelf 16. He hoped that the shelf numbers got bigger closer to the ground, but knew he'd be disappointed.

32. Brief Discussions

Noah finished the retreatment of the safety zone. He'd only been up for a couple of hours and already sweat glued his inner garments to his skin. Caps stopped bitching about the heat after being chastised by Darcy, who, like Toffee and the Boss, seemed unaffected. It had only been a couple of days since they'd dined semi-well at Camper World, but in that short period, Noah had grown to desperately miss the mess hall and Roshi's cooking. All jerky and no milk made Noah a dull boy. A few birds had gathered on the fence a short distance from the semi Caps was working on, crows mostly. They watched with detached interest, occasionally flitting off to be replaced by other avians. Lena was of a mind to shoot them all, but once again the Boss cautioned against unnecessary noise and wasting ammunition.

While Noah stowed his spray tank in the Pig, Toffee stood off to one side, shadow boxing. The hunter would feint to one side, then swing from the other, alternating punches with swipes of his blade. As Noah looked on, knee strikes were added to the violent choreography. There was one sequence of moves that appeared to involve driving a knee into an opponent's midsection at the same time as drawing blade across neck. The hunter moved with a fluid grace, shifting balance from leg to leg, easing from one attack posture to the next.

Suddenly, Toffee turned to face Noah, then flicked his hand in a come-here gesture. Noah looked behind him, then towards the hunter, as if to say, "Who? Me?" Toffee flicked his hand again impatiently.

"What?" asked Noah, stopping just out of arm's reach.

Toffee lunged forward and swung with his left, clipping Noah on the jaw and knocking him on his ass.

"Ow! What the hell was that for?" Noah grabbed his jaw through his mesh and turned to see if Caps or the Boss had witnessed the attack, but the van blocked them from view.

"You were supposed to block that. Get up."

"Block that? You didn't even warn me."

"That was the slowest punch I've got. I said get up."

"I don't like this game." Noah turned his back to Toffee as he pushed himself up on hands and knees. Toffee stepped forward and kicked him in the butt, knocking him flat.

"Hey!"

"Never turn your back on an opponent. Don't you know anything?"

Embarrassment and anger twisted in Noah's stomach as he looked again for help. Unless someone lay down and looked under the van, they wouldn't see his distress. Pride kept him from calling out.

"I said get up!" Toffee grabbed the back of Noah's coveralls and hauled him to his feet.

"Get your hands…uh, hand off me."

"Or what? You'll fall on me? These friends of yours at Underbel taught you book stuff, but you're shit in a clinch."

Noah brushed himself off and straightened to his full height, he was at least a head shorter than his antagonist. "Well nobody appointed you Mr. Miagi!"

"Miagi?"

"Caps would get it."

"Do I look like the painter? Get your hands up."

"You're serious." He flinched as Toffee cocked a fist. "Okay, okay." His hands came up in a posture of defence he thought was correct.

"What's that?" the hunter knocked Noah's arms aside with easy swipes of his arm. So far, the blade remained at his side.

Noah brought his arms up again and held them rigid, but again they were knocked aside. Once more his arms came up. This time, Toffee grabbed a fist and squeezed hard.

"Ow!" It felt like his fingers were being broken. He pulled at the hunter's grasp.

"You've got no strength in your arms and you don't know how to make a fist."

"Well soorrryyy."

Toffee cuffed him upside the head. "Don't be cheeky."

Rage coiled Noah's right hand into a very tight fist indeed. He sent it streaking at the hunter's throat, but Toffee sidestepped, and changed the trajectory of the blow by grabbing the panel jockey's elbow. Noah's fist thudded painfully into the side of the Pig.

"What the hell is going on over there?" asked Darcy, peering around the front of the van.

"I'm trying to teach the boy here something about fighting," Toffee answered before Noah could.

"Oh, taking him under your…uh…blade, are you? Noah, you okay?"

Do I look like I'm okay? he thought, then said, "Yeah, I'm fine. Do you guys need any help?"

"No thanks. Don't injure him, Toffee," then she was gone.

"Nice try, kid. Get your hands up."

He nursed his throbbing hand. "Shouldn't we be watching for animals or something?"

For an instant, it looked as if the hunter was going to let loose with a real punch, then his features softened slightly and he leaned close to Noah's ear. "If I let you in on a little secret, will you stop whining and do what you're told?"

The young man didn't know which worried him more, sparring with the man, or being taken into his confidence. "What kind of secret?"

"It's been a while since I've had nothing on this stump but my steel. My balance is a little off, so you're helping me out, too. Satisfied? Now get your doglickin' arms up."

Darcy shoved the pneumatic jack under the selected trailer, a forty footer with "Reliable Transport" painted on the side. She pumped on the handle until the four rotted tires nearest her cleared the ground. Next she picked up a tire iron—so heavy, just lifting it was good exercise—and set to work forcing nuts corroded to the point where it took all her strength to get them moving. Some of them crumbled under her ministrations and would have to be hack-sawed off. Once Caps was finished with the LTL, he'd be taking care of the air hoses and brakes on the trailer. His intention was to be done by the next morning. Toffee had finished with Noah about an hour ago, and sat on the hood of a blue Kenworth conventional, his rifle across his lap. Noah, a little bruised, and plenty chagrined, held a similar guard position on the truck furthest from the hunter.

"I don't get it," said Lena. "We've been here two days, and nothing. It's like the whole death zone thing is a lie."

"I'm a little mystified myself." Darcy fitted the tire iron to another nut and shoved. "I think we should head back to the Pit now. Come back here in a few days with twenty or thirty people and just start taking. How are you, by the way?"

"What do you mean?"

"I heard you freaking out again last night, while I was on watch."

Lena leaned her tire up against the cart and sighed. She and Caps had taken the sleeping compartment in the back of the LTL, while the other four had taken turns crashing in the Pig. "I'm okay, I had a bad dream."

"The same one?"

"It's always the same one."

"You survived, Lena."

"No, really? Don't you ever dream, Darcy?"

"Like that? I think my subconscious realizes I deal with enough waking crap to torture me while I sleep. Most of the time, anyway. What do you think of Toffee turning teacher?"

Lena glanced over at where Noah sat, rubbing a shoulder. "Maybe he's trying to get sun boy into bed."

Darcy's whole body went rigid.

"Oh, honey, I'm sorry...I didn't mean...I'm sorry. Bad joke."

The chief of security relaxed a bit, then stiffened once more. "Did you tell Caps?"

"No. Honest. I'm afraid of the cartoon he'd come up with. But I've been meaning to ask you, how did Daniel not know? Did you just keep him in the hall when he showed up?"

"Y'know, that's the strangest thing. Daniel got a good look in the room, but Toffee hid."

"Where?"

"In the bed. He didn't cover his head or anything, he just stayed perfectly still and...I don't know...blended. Daniel didn't see a thing."

"Creepy. Do you think he's told anyone?"

A rusted nut fell to the ground. "Toffee? No, I don't think he has."

"Listen, I'm sorry, but for some twisted reason, I have to ask. Was he…good?"

"I was really drunk, Lena. I don't remember."

"Mmhmm. You ever wonder what Noah might be like?"

"You mean if he could stop asking questions long enough?"

Lena laughed. "Yes, if he could keep his mouth shut."

"No. The thought never crossed my mind. Not that it's something I have to worry about now. I'm pretty sure he hates me."

"You think so, huh? Darcy, he'd sit up and beg if you asked him to. There's a lot of guys back home that would. I'm jealous of you sometimes."

Darcy wrapped her arms around the tire she was working on and began to ease it off. "Getting tired of Caps? Give me a hand with this."

Lena got her arms under the tire and added her strength to the endeavour. "No way. I think I'll love him until the day I die. Uhnnn. It's nice to be admired though."

"Yeah? Uhf! Just a little more. You ever see the way Eggerson looks at you? I'm the one who should be jealous."

The tire hit the tarmac with a pathetic *splud*. A shower of crumbling rubber covered the women's arms. Lena patted flakes off her sleeves and looked over to where Noah and the hunter were sparring.

"Darcy, you should patch things up with him."

"Which one?" she asked guardedly.

"Noah. He's good people, as Caps would say. I haven't known him that long, but I really like him. I understand why you treated him the way you did, but he didn't deserve it."

"I know, I know. Anyway, he cut the power to my room, and…" she caught Lena's expression, "I will. When I get the chance. Now help me with the new tire."

Between the three of them, Noah, Caps and Sid removed the two cell-warped batteries from the LTL, and installed new twelve-volts brought from Compton Pit. Caps made some connections, pulled himself into the cab, and fiddled with controls. The truck's headlights and hazard lights came on.

"We've got juice," he said as he jumped down and smiled at the beacons.

"Can you turn the motor over yet?" asked Sid.

"Nope, a few more things to do yet."

"I can't see any spark plugs," said Noah, peering under the semi's raised hood.

Caps patted him on the shoulder. "There's no spark plugs in a diesel, my friend. It's fuel injection. You want to learn this stuff? Or is your curriculum filled with Bruises 101?"

Sid took Noah by the shoulders and turned him away from the semi. "We'll take it from here, return to your post."

"Yes, sir." He walked back to the truck he'd been sitting on—another Ford—and hoisted himself up onto the hood.

In many ways he felt like he had that first day at Compton Pit; a little disoriented, and a little useless. He had a purpose to fulfill later on this mission, but for now he was just an extra pair of eyes, and an extra back when he was needed. Darcy and Lena were swapping tires on the trailer, talking and laughing. Even the hunter seemed to have purpose as he did the same thing that Noah did—sit and watch.

The hunter had showed him a couple of tricks, how to make a proper fist, and a nice leg sweep manoeuver that, if executed properly, was bound to take an opponent off his or her feet.

The double-image affliction came and went in short bursts. At one point the Reliable Transport trailer became a school bus. What he was struggling with now were the voices of his parents and school friends. Old jokes and schoolyard chants drifted through his mind…I'm the king of the castle, you're a dirty rascal…but these, too, were fading somewhat. Toffee's hand-to-hand training brought to mind Ronny Pratt, an ugly kid who had bullied Noah and his friends from kindergarten to grade two, until Mr. and Mrs. Pratt had divorced, and Ronny had been dragged off by his mother to go live in New Mexico, and most likely torment other weaker children.

The photovoltaic engineer didn't believe for a second that the hunter was really off balance. He'd waited the entire time for the hunter to come up with some totally demeaning comment, but none was forthcoming once Noah had acceded to the exercise, simply terse orders to widen stance, brace arms and other similar commands. Apart from some bruises and a sore arm, Noah didn't feel he'd gotten much out of the experience. What worried him most was that the others seemed perfectly fine with letting the hunter bash him around, as long as it was done quietly.

I want a shower, Noah thought suddenly. He could almost feel the hot water coursing down his skin. He wondered how Duff was doing back at the Pit, clearing away broken panels and charred power cables. Something buzzed by his face, snapping him out of his reverie, but it was only a fly, a harmless, little fly.

Noah washed down a long-chewed mouthful of jerky with tepid water, then handed the flask to Lena. They sat in the Pig, reclining in the seats and growing used to each other's body odour. The forty footer had its new tires, as did the LTL.

"How much longer?" asked Noah.

"If Lena is right, we should be hearing that truck start any minute now. We have keys for it by the way. I found them. Rolled over on them, actually. They were hidden in the sleeping area. How's your head?"

"I'm still a little out of it. How's *your* head?"

"I'm okay. It's just weird for me, that's all. I haven't been outside Compton Pit since I took up residence there. I hate the outside world."

"Me too. When the Boss told me I was restricted to base, I could have kissed him. Then this. Though this hasn't seemed too bad. The ants spooked me a little bit, though. Can I have the flask back?"

"Sure. I'm going to head back out." Lena donned her net-helmet and tucked the mesh in. They hadn't seen a wasp the entire time at the truck yard, but Sid was adamant. He hadn't come all this way to lose a team member to carelessness.

Noah took another swig, then put on his own helmet on and followed the chief of communications. At the truck, Caps was using the air compressor to blow yellow-brownish jellied fuel out of one of the tanks. Ochre puddled beneath the truck. Darcy and Sid were pumping diesel up from the reservoir and into jerry cans. There were a number of empty drums that Sid planned to fill as well. One trailer would be solar panels and other items, the second was for nothing but fuel. There was another reservoir nearby, and Sid claimed there was a huge one on some place called Burnaby Mountain. If they were able to get it all, they might even be able to compete with Gascan D'Abo. Lena was under the impression that the Burnaby Mountain reservoir would be drained already by people who had fled the city during the first year.

Darcy brought a jerry can over and poured fuel into the tank already cleaned out. Lena stooped and bestowed a rare, non-private kiss on the back of Caps's head. It was a kiss through two layers of net, but the mechanic reached back a hand and squeezed Lena's leg.

"So?" she prodded.

"I think we're in business here. The air hoses are hooked up, I replaced the air bags, changed the fluids...maybe the brakes won't be so bad after all. Darcy, you done there?"

"No, it'll take more than one can to fill this tank." She tapped the empty jerry can with a knuckle.

"Close the tank, I'm going to try and start this baby." He climbed up into the cab, gave everybody a fingers-crossed gesture, and keyed the ignition. Nothing happened. He tried a few more times.

"What's wrong?" asked Sid. "Didn't we hook the batteries up right?"

"Hell no, they're hooked in fine...oh..." He jumped down from the cab and moved to the back of the vehicle. He pushed a pair of coiled wires aside and examined the area under the headache rack. "Here we go." There was a toggle switch neatly concealed by hoses. Caps flicked it, then climbed back into the cab. "Electrical power kill switch. Some trucks have 'em, some don't. It's so the batteries don't drain out if the trucks going to be sitting for a while. Doesn't help if the truck is sitting for a decade though. I forgot to turn it back on after I checked the lights."

This time when he turned the key, a stubborn growl issued from the motor, like the sound of a large, wounded cat. It growled a couple more times, then turned over and chugged to life.

Caps leaned out the window and flourished his left hand. "I thank you, I thank you."

"You did it," said the Boss.

"In record time, I might add. Can we go home now? No? Didn't think so. Anyway, that's just ignition. We'll find out about a whole bunch of other problems now."

They had to make a foray into yet another warehouse. Their second shopping spree went as smoothly as the first, a simple matter of breaking in, finding manifests and number listings, then hunting the well organized shelves that time had left dusty, but otherwise untouched. It was late afternoon when the hunter asked Lena to redress his cheek.

"It's weeping," she said, "but it looks good. Well, as good as a puss-oozing abrasion can look."

"Thanks." He sat in the backseat of the Pig while Lena knelt on the floor beside him. Toffee shifted a little bit so more of his leg came in contact with Lena's. As expected, she pulled back immediately, probably not even realizing she'd done it. "How are you holding up?"

"No offense, but I don't think you really care."

Toffee grinned. "You're not scared of me, are you?" It was more of a statement than a question.

"I was a chief at Compton Pit long before you showed up."

"Yes, since the last expedition here, right? Your predecessor was on that one, wasn't he?" That did get a reaction, she stiffened and moved as if to leave the van. "Anyway, we're not at the Pit anymore. How do you feel about Halbert's choices now that he's away from the big table?"

"He doesn't need the table."

"Why do you think he brought you? Are you to communicate with anyone?"

"He brought me because I know the university campus."

"Oh really? I thought that's what maps were for. Did it occur to you that you're here to keep your boyfriend happy?"

"What?"

"Halbert dragged you from safety to keep his mechanic…relaxed. Don't shoot the messenger."

She closed the first aid kit and jumped down from the van. "We should be watching for animals."

"Put your neck in a noose, didn't he? I admire him. He gets what he needs, and that's that."

"You don't know what you're talking about."

"You know that scavenger we captured? Lot? Do you know what happened to him?" He rubbed his bandaged cheek, "Don't worry about it, nobody else does." He fell silent and waited. She'd bite, he knew how to bait a hook.

"So tell me already."

"You know those animals in research? Odega's critters? We fed him to them. Kind of barbaric, ain't it?"

"I don't believe you."

"Quite the spectacle, Halbert tossin' bits of the guy through the food chutes…"

"Shut up."

"You know a raccoon actually ate a hand out of my hand. It was so cute."

"Break out some jerky," said Caps, Approaching from behind. Lena's face was turned away from him, but he didn't need to see her expression to know that something wasn't right. "Sweetheart," he broke into a trot, "what's wrong?" He stopped beside her and turned to the hunter. "What did you say to her?"

"Caps," Lena started, "what happened to the scavenger, Lot?"

"C'mon," he said, putting an arm around her, "let's go for a walk." He led her a short distance away.

Sid, Darcy and Noah arrived seconds later. All three of them were tired and dirty, but Darcy still had bounce in her step.

"How are things going over here?" asked the Boss, watching Caps lead Lena off.

"Just fine," replied Toffee. He gave Darcy the once over. "You're filthy."

"Being near you always makes me feel that way."

"You should leave the jokes to the painter."

Sid grabbed a rifle from just inside the door of the van. "C'mon Darcy, let's do a perimeter sweep, make sure nothing's crept up while we've been working. Noah, stay with the van. We'll be back soon."

Once he was alone with the photovoltaic engineer, Toffee stood and flexed his shoulders. "How are you holding out?"

It was Noah's turn to be suspicious. "Fine. How's your cheek?"

"Turned the other way."

"Maybe *you* should leave the jokes to Caps."

"We'll spar later. To bad we can't make noise, I could show you how to use that gun," he indicated the .45 at Noah's hip.

"Are you trying to be my friend?"

"No. Halbert, Darcy, I got no problems with them, but if you wind up watching my back, you sure as hell better know what you're doing."

Noah folded his arms across his chest and looked at the hunter with a firmness he would have been incapable of a week earlier. "What about Lena and Caps? I don't see you training them."

"No point. The painter wouldn't listen to me if his life depended on it, and the girl handles a gun like it might bite her, but you...you're a clean slate, kid. With potential."

"Potential for what?"

Caps and Lena chose that moment to return. She didn't give the hunter even a glance as she pushed past him into the van and pulled out the skinbag that held their food supplies.

"You're an asshole," mumbled Caps.

"Did I lie to her?" asked the hunter.

"If she wanted to know, she could have asked."

"Asked what?" Noah was instantly curious.

Caps and the hunter had entered into a rather unnerving staring match.

"Asked about what? Caps, asked about what?"

Lena kept her head down, busy doling out jerky and a small ration of berries. Caps used his friend's pestering as an excuse to break away from a competition he'd known he'd lose the moment it had begun. "What we did to that scavenger Darcy brought in."

"Didn't you lock him outside? Just let the animals get him?"

"Yeah, I guess that's what happened," Caps prevaricated.

"Uh-huh. So what's the real story."

Lena exited and shoved a flask into Noah's hand. "The bodies of our dead, Noah. Like October."

Caps took Noah by the shoulders. "Buddy, if someone did something really bad, you'd want to punish that person, right?"

"Sure. That's why we lock people outside."

"What if someone did something so rotten it wasn't good enough to assume he got ate, you had to see it for yourself."

Lena was holding a piece of jerky in her hand, but made no move to eat it. Noah's eyes grew wide as he stared at the piece of preserved meat.

"You mean? You don't mean…"

Lena's hand dropped to her side, the jerky going with it. "Thank you, Noah. Thank you for showing me there's something worse. We're not cannibals. We fed him to Odega's research animals." She sat down on the van's running board and tapped the jerky on her thigh.

"That's…that's disgusting."

"It's efficient," said Toffee. "Why waste the meat?"

Sid and Darcy returned from their patrol. "Lena, hand me some jerky," Sid stowed his rifle under the van's back seat. "We're in luck, there doesn't seem to be a thing out here." He caught Lena's expression, then Noah's. "What's going on?"

Toffee rubbed the stubble on his chin. "We're talking about creative sources for dog food."

"Come again?"

"Dog food…milk bones, scavengers."

Sid put his hands on his hips and took in each face before him. "Now isn't the time to disagree with body disposal. It makes no difference whether the remains went to teeth inside or outside.

Except for Burle, Compton Pit has never used graveyards. People die. We move on." He raised his hand to stop Lena's protest. "Actually, I'm glad this came up. I believe we'll get through this unmolested, but if someone doesn't make it, we're going to leave them where they drop and keep going. That's the bottom line. I've decided we'll stick with just one truck this time. We should be able to head to the university tomorrow. We'll load all the panels we find, and get going. With luck we'll be sitting in the mess hall in four days."

Darcy sat on a concrete buttress and watched the road. Moonlight caressed the blacktop, a length of wire mesh fence casting web-like shadows across the weeds and tarmac. She listened to the wind and stroked the barrel of her rifle like she was caressing a baby. The soft melody of a half-forgotten love song seeped from her lips.

From a few feet away, Noah watched her. The moonlight illuminated one half of her face, the unscarred half. He could make out the gentle curve of her cheek, and he longed to touch it. He couldn't make out the words of her song, but her voice was so enticing.

"What's that?" he asked.

Darcy's gun came to bear as she spun on reflex. "Noah, don't sneak up on me. You're supposed to be watching east."

"There's nothing out there. I didn't think I could sneak up on you."

"I was lost in thought. Bad habit. Especially now. I saw you working out with Toffee again. How's that going?"

Noah glanced at that road, then sat down on the concrete a few inches from her. "He says I'm a quick learner."

"Are you?"

He rubbed a shoulder. "I'm learning how to get bruises. He's really fast. When I don't get my guard up quick enough he stops that blade of his right at my throat, every time. The Boss made him wrap some cloth around it, but still…who would win do you think? Between him and the Boss?"

"Toffee and Sid? My barter's on Sid."

"Really? Toffee's so much bigger, and it's like he's just a walking weapon."

"It's that blade of his," she tapped her head, "all psychological. You get a hit on him?"

"Nope. Not even close. He does this thing where he makes me punch the van. I'm scared to swing too hard. You ever spar with him?"

"I guess I did once."

"Who won?"

Darcy squeezed her lip. It was a quick, unconscious movement. "Do you like learning to fight?"

Noah puffed out his chest. "Yes. I bet I'll be really good at it."

"Maybe…maybe when we get back to the Pit, I could give you a few lessons. I don't know what Toffee's teaching you, but Sid taught me Jiu Jitsu, and Travis was teaching me this bizarre street-fighting style. Caps calls it 'Oh look, your neck's broken.' "

"Was that who you were thinking about when I came up? Travis?"

"Yes."

"What was done with his body? Oh dogshit! I'm sorry. That was a stupid question."

"It's…it's okay. The burn crew that took care of the rats…what wasn't eaten was charred. Not much left of him. I gave him a Viking funeral, put him on a raft, set in on fire and sent it down the underground river. It was a really crappy raft."

The pain etched into Darcy's face was palpable. Noah could picture her, hugging herself as a makeshift assembly of wood drifted away. At the same time, he could imagine the despair that must have gripped Travis, facing death in the caverns, like Cass.

"Darcy, what happened to Cass's body?"

"What's got you so fixated on the dead?"

"Caps told me that your scavenger was fed to Odega's animals. Did you do that?"

"No. The thought of it abhorred me."

"Who did it then? Did they kill him first or just…"

"Noah! Why don't you ask Caps this stuff?"

"He's asleep."

"You can't wait until…Okay, some people needed satisfaction. They chose a method they felt would give it to them. I doubt it did."

"What did this guy do?"

She couldn't tell him about Burle, or Burle's granddaughter, for that matter. She wouldn't tell him some of the atrocities Toffee had forced out of the man's mouth in the head room. Even if the sadistic rapist hadn't confessed his sins, they had already accrued some disturbing data from Dr. Patel's autopsy on Cass.

There was no indication from Noah that he knew anything about what Cass had been subjected to in her last moments, but Darcy couldn't help but imprint her own sympathetic hurt upon him. Normally, she wasn't a touchy-feely type of person, but spending hours in the van with the comatose panel jockey's head in her lap, she felt she had the right to touch him, like she owned a part of him in some way. She put her hand on his.

"Noah, I've been meaning to apologize to you for the way you were treated that day."

Her fingers on his hand sent bolts of electricity up Noah's arm. His mouth went dry and blood pounded in his ears. Within his coveralls it felt as if every hair on his body was standing up straight. He placed his other hand on top of hers. "It's okay. I know you were just doing your job. Caps told me you didn't know about us...me and Cass, I mean."

"You must miss her terribly."

"No, not really." It was the wrong thing to say. Darcy's hand withdrew like a recoiling snake, leaving Noah gripping his own fingers.

"So all she was to you was an easy lay? I didn't know Cassandra all that well but she deserves better than that."

"That's not it at all!" Noah spoke quickly, trying to clarify before the sudden warmth left Darcy's eyes completely. "Actually, I was the easy lay for Cass. I didn't love her." He gauged her reaction to that, it was neutral. "I never got the chance to," he said with genuine remorse.

Abruptly, Darcy's expression softened. "Okay, I'm sorry for saying what I did. It's just that..." she looked away, not finishing her sentence.

"What?" Noah urged, risking a brief touch to Darcy's hand.

"Noah, I'm chief of security. You have to understand the position requires a certain amount of rigidity. I'm a hardass because I have to be, otherwise people won't respect me. Sometimes...sometimes its difficult for me to drop out of the role."

"I understand. You don't have to apologize for that."

"Noah, there's something else," she took a deep breath. "It has to do with you. You look so young, and there's a vulnerability about you that...it makes me want to be harder on you for some reason. I can't explain it, but there it is."

"Vulnerability? Are you saying you think I'm weak?"

"Now, don't get all defensive, I'm just telling you how I–"

"I'm not getting defensive! So I don't come across as a tough guy. That doesn't mean you can pick on me for it. Just because you've got scars on your cheek doesn't mean I'm going to call you…" his heart gained control of his mouth a few words too late.

"What? Call me what?"

Noah felt his tenuous connection to her severed. He didn't have time to berate himself before Darcy did it for him.

"I've heard them all, sun boy. Hamburger Face, Squint Eye, Tooth Tracks…was it one of those?"

"No…nothing. I wasn't going to say–"

"I try to talk to you and you hack on me for it. Fine. Whatever. Get back to your post."

She stood and walked a few paces from the riser. From her stance the conversation was clearly over. Not really understanding how things had gone from good to bad so quickly, Noah returned to his position on the far side of the van. "That went well," he said, chastising himself. "Yup, smooth as puppy's fur."

33. Early Arrival

Daniel, alerted by a brief radio transmission from a patrol, stood in the southeast tower and watched the semi grow larger in his binoculars as it made the long trip up Compton Pit's driveway. It was battered and the paint on both the cab and trailer was a uniform gunmetal gray, not the type of rig he'd expected to come from the city, but despite the lack of both escort vehicles and radio contact, the acting chief of security still harbored a faint hope that it might be the Boss and company, making everything right in record time. That wishful thinking was banished when he saw the grills on the windows. They were too finely crafted for a quick job. This was a model of the new world, not the old one. Daniel raised his binoculars to the end of the driveway, where the patrol vehicle—the hunters' van—was turning in off the south road.

The rig came to a stop before the perimeter fence and a man stepped out. He scanned the ruined panel array before turning to the tower and calling up through hands cupped around his mouth.

"Delivery from Piper's Cove!"

Daniel allowed himself an over-dramatic sigh, then pressed a button that signalled below to open the gate. Purty was in the airlock control room, speaking into the intercom as Daniel descended from the tower. Dr. White would be on her way, if she wasn't already there.

"Please place the vehicle over the central grate, and do not open your doors." Purtricil's hand reached for the lever that would spew gas upwards from the grates. Daniel stopped him.

"Don't bother, Purty. We've cut juice to the system."

"Oh…yeah, I forgot."

"Who are they?" asked Sara, sticking her head through the door.

"Fishers. It's one of their trucks."

"What are they doing here so early?"

Daniel shrugged. "Beats me. Do you want to greet them?"

"Yes. No. Do you know them?" she wrung her hands, a hundred minor headaches clamouring for attention at the edge of her mind, not subsiding in the face of this new one.

"I recognize the driver. Name's Bruno, I think. He's the same guy that came the last few times."

"Do we trust him?" She bit her lower lip as Daniel shrugged once again. "Why don't you know? Weren't you security second?"

"Under normal circumstances, yes, sure, let him in. Right now…If you're asking me if Darcy would let him in, I don't know."

"I'm asking if *you* think we should let him in."

"How long are we going leave him stuck in the airlock?" Purty interrupted.

Daniel bent close to the mic and keyed it on. "Gentlemen, we're having a technical difficulty. Please stand by." He released the button and said to Sara, "We need the supplies. Travis used to say fishers were the most stand-up people he knew. Crazy folk, but stand-up.

"That'll have to be good enough. Daniel, you greet him. I have to talk to Seth." With an incoherent grunt, the temporary boss of the Pit spun from the door in search of her chief of stores.

Daniel moved through the plastic curtain, down a short corridor, and into the motor pool. It looked painfully vacant, only the Hummer and the motorcycle were there. The airlock doors opened and the semi pulled inside, like so many had done before.

"Welcome back," said Daniel as the driver jumped down to the floor. "I'm Daniel Silverman, acting chief of security. Bruno, isn't it?"

"That's right, Bruno Kyriakakis," he extended a thick-fingered hand, the skin on which matched the man's heavy brow which jutted from beneath tight grayish-black curls. He had a crooked nose and a scruffy beard that matched his hair. "This is Dominic," he said as his partner, a long haired Indian joined them on the floor. "Acting chief of security? Where's Travis?"

"Rat swarmed."

"Sorry to hear that. He was a good fella. So where's that girlfriend of his? Shouldn't she be chief then, the way you guys work?"

"She's off base right now. We were expecting you next month."

"The Captain sent us off early. What the hell happened topside? Those panels of yours are positively smashed."

"The Boss will answer your questions shortly. If you'll follow me, we'll get you something to eat."

"Don't worry, I know the way." Bruno pushed past Daniel. The acting chief of security had no choice but to fall in behind him.

"Are you L'heit Lit'en?" Daniel asked Dominic.

"Yes, how'd you know?"

"Uh, Travis used the name in Scrabble one time. He said he knew a fishermen named Dom who was L'heit Lit'en."

"Are you allowed to use tribal names as words?"

"No, but he argued that since the name had a meaning as well, it was legit. He also argued that he was my boss."

"What about the apostrophes?"

"Our Scrabble set is kind of a mishmash. Lost tiles are replaced by new ones, the letters etched by hand. Somewhere along the line apostrophes were added. There's two of them, they're not worth any points."

"So do you make a habit of memorizing Scrabble games?

"That was the last one we played. Sticks, y'know. I take it you're a player."

"Not as good as Bruno, but yeah."

Daniel led them to a table close to the serving line. Breakfast had come and gone a couple of hours ago and Roshi was haranguing an unfortunate member of the clean-up crew who hadn't managed to escape. The portly chief of the kitchen turned, his eyes narrowing as they fell on the new arrivals.

"You early. I suppose you want food now."

Bruno folded his large arms across his chest. "It's been a long drive, ain't had nothing but jerky."

"And that's all you going to get. No more cooking till dinner."

"Fine," he shouldered Dominic. "Go back to the rig and kill those lobsters."

Roshi's facial expression brightened like a fluorescent bulb coming on. "Live lobsters?"

"We got our refrigeration tank working again."

"How many?"

"What's it worth to you to find out?"

"Sit, sit!" Roshi pulled out a chair, then he promoted his clean-up man to prep cook and hauled him into the kitchen.

In a surprisingly short period of time, Roshi was back with two plates of steamed vegetables and gravy-laden meat.

"Don't I get any?" asked Daniel, a little surprised.

"You bring me lobsters? Then you wait till dinner."

Bruno and Dominic practically inhaled their food, smacking their lips and smiling like it was the finest fare east of the ocean.

"Mmmhh, good!" said Dominic, wiping his mouth off with the back of his hand.

"Do you have any idea," Bruno said with his mouth full, "how sick a man can get of eating fish jerky?"

"You didn't answer my question earlier;" said Daniel. "Why are you here now? Why didn't you notify us?"

Bruno shared a glance with Dominic before answering. "Why don't we wait until Burle and Halbert get here, that way I don't have to tell it twice."

"About that…" before Daniel could continue, Sara joined them, Seth in tow, walking slowly, his arm in a sling.

"Good morning." She sat down next to Dominic. "Thank-you for your patience. I'm Dr. White, acting boss. This is Seth Boomatay, chief of stores."

Bruno did an amusing double take, then focussed on Daniel. "What's all this 'acting' stuff? *He's* the chief of stores? Where's Sid Halbert? What happened to Burle Campbell?"

Daniel looked down at his hands, not wanting to give strength to Bruno's dismissal of Sara by answering.

"Sid is off base right now," said Sara. "Burle was lost to us last week. Now, why are you early?"

"Burle's dead?" He slumped a little in his chair. "How'd it happen?"

Daniel tapped his chest. "Heart stopped working." It was as much the truth as it was a lie.

"Why are you here early?" Sara repeated.

"The Captain said to talk to the Boss only."

Dr. White spoke in as restrained a voice as she could manage; "As far as you're concerned, I am the Boss. Your…Captain, is it? Should have contacted us."

Bruno's brow knitted as he pondered this unexpected situation. "So you're telling me, your chief of stores is dead, as is your chief of security, and both the Boss and the new chief of security are off base."

Sara kept her mouth shut and waited.

"So I have to deal with a bunch of 'actings' that's what's going on?"

"No, that's not what's going on." Seth had had enough. "I am the chief of stores, not acting anything. Dr. White is chief of hydroelectricity and hydroponics, and Daniel is chief of transport."

"Whoa!" Dominic slapped his hand on the table. "Chief of transport? You said you were chief of security."

"I was security second before being promoted."

"But if you're chief of transport, then..." he looked at Bruno. "So October's gone as well? If you're chief of transport...what happened to the rest of the crew? Ian, Stuart...that other guy? They're all dead, aren't they? What the hell is going on here?"

"For the last time," said Sara, "why are you early?"

Bruno and Dom engaged in one more exchange of unspoken decision making, then the long haired man turned to Dr. White.

"One of our own went tooth crazy. Took the anti-techno route...y'know, no more science, no more animal attacks. He made his point with a shotgun in our communications hub. Killed two people, destroyed a lot of equipment. We didn't contact you because we couldn't. We have a new sheriff as well. That's like your chief of security."

"The guy killed your old sheriff, huh?" Daniel was quite sympathetic at this.

"The guy *was* our old sheriff."

Roshi, who'd been listening from a table away, came over and put his hand on Bruno's shoulder.

"Your old sheriff...Timothy, right? Son of your Captain? You tell him I'm sorry."

Sara's annoyance at the fishers vanished, to be replaced by understanding and a little shock. How similar their situation was. She'd never been to the coast settlement, but she did know their version of locking them outside; suspending them from a scaffold into the water, weights on the ankles, so that only the perpetrator's head was above water. If they survived a night, they were set free. The number of "soakers" as they were called, to see the sunrise was probably the same as the number of evicted Comptonites that showed up at someone's door—zero.

"Was the captain's son shot down, or did you have to put him in the water?" she asked.

"He surrendered when he ran out of ammo. The Captain lowered him in, said it was his duty. Blamed himself for not seeing this coming."

"Let me see your list."

The fisher reached inside his jacket and withdrew two folded bits of paper. After unfolding, and looking at each, he handed one to Dr. White. The other he went to place back in his pocket, then shrugged and offered it to Sara as well.

"This here is a private letter to Boss Halbert," he leaned on Sid's name a little heavily. "It's from our doctor. They're old friends."

"I know of Sid's acquaintance with Dr. Nash. I'll make sure he gets this." Sara placed the letter on the table and unfolded the list. Keeping her face neutral, she handed the paper to Seth. "Look, I'm not unsympathetic to your situation." She took a deep breath. "We've had something like that happen here. Don't ask for the details. The end result is we had a conflict with another settlement. That's why our panel array is smashed. But I don't think we can help you with components for your SatCom. It would mean cannibalizing our own equipment. Why come to us? Why not go to D'Abo?"

"The Captain's relationship with D'Abo is not one of mutual respect if you catch my drift. He knows you trade with him regularly, so he figured if you couldn't give us what we want, you could set it up for us."

"How long's your SatCom been down?" asked Seth.

"Over a month," said Dominic.

"So you've had no communication from Gascan. Hmmm."

"What's that supposed to mean? And what settlement did you fight with? Oh no, you didn't get into it with D'Abo did you?"

"No, not with D'Abo," said Sara. "You've been straightforward with us, basically putting yourself over a barrel, so...we fought with Fenwick Prison. We...won, I suppose you could say. They're wiped out. During the conflict they snuck someone in to do what you saw topside. It's left us in a bit of a bind ourselves. In addition, D'Abo put a trade embargo on us, so we can't just ring him up and get what you need from him. We can't..." She was stopped by Seth's hand, gently squeezing her leg below the table. "I'll need to discuss this with my people. Daniel?" She stood up and backed away from the table.

"If you gentlemen will wait here, I'll have someone show you to your rooms. How long can the perishables stay in your truck?"

Dom glanced at Roshi, "We could unload the live cargo now if you like." He took Roshi's smile as a yes. "Me and Bruno can do that while you guys talk."

Sara nodded an okay and Roshi called his assistant from the kitchen and demoted him from prep cook to mule, then the four of them went back to the motor pool.

"Let's go to stores," said Seth. "I've got something to show you."

Seth directed Daniel to shove a stack of boxes aside in the back of stores. Behind them was a small door.

"I didn't realized that was there," said Sara.

"Probably only Burle, Sid and Darcy did," said Seth, digging awkwardly in a pocket.

"So how did you find it?" Daniel tried the handle. It was locked.

"It's kind of boring lying around in the infirmary, so I came here and started familiarizing myself. Come on, you stupid thing." At last he produced a key ring. "Anyway, I couldn't find a lock to fit this key." He held up a standard key cut from reddish metal. "I figure the Boss forgot to tell me about it before he left, or he was just leaving it as a surprise. Those boxes had numbers on them that didn't match up with anything in the manifest, so I had someone move them for me, and voila!" He unlocked the door and pulled it open. Beyond it was complete darkness.

"Got a flashlight handy?" asked Daniel, looking around.

"Don't need it," said Seth, patting the wall inside the darkened room. "There we go." Bulbs flickered to life, revealing a room—small by the Pit's standards—containing boxes identical to those in main stores, as well as some wooden crates. "This room isn't on the power allocation charts, so Thurlow didn't know to cut power to it before he left. This is Burle's private stock, his primo barter, among other things."

Daniel knelt by a wooden crate and shoved the lid off. He withdrew a bottle and whistled at the label. "Southern Comfort, a whole freakin' bottle. What else is in here?"

"Put it back, Dan. There's also scotch, a couple of bottles of Bacardi rum, Canadian Club, and a big bottle of Kaluha. We'll open one when the Boss gets back. Until then, it stays the way it was, a secret."

"Impressive, Seth, but I don't think you brought us here to show us liquor…oh my!" She'd peeked into a box herself. It contained two laptop computers, presumably fully functional for them to be in the secret room. "Why are these locked up in here? I could always use an additional screen for my work stations."

Seth closed the box before Sara could reach into it. "I don't know. Maybe the Boss figured we had enough computers out and wanted to save these. Doesn't matter. Look in the crate over there, the big one."

Beneath a sheet of charcoal coloured foam, Daniel found a selection of cream coloured metal boxes, some with plastic screens on the front, others with nothing but a few switches and some plug receptors.

"What are these?" he asked.

Seth's trademark smile was just as bright as ever, despite the weariness of his face. "As near as I can tell, it's every bit of SatCom equipment we've replaced with better stuff. I checked some back records, Burle never traded away a single functioning Sat component. He kept upgrades pretty quiet, too. Those fishers need most of this stuff. Means we've got no spares if something of ours goes down, but we can trade with 'em and not have to touch our system."

"I'm glad you didn't let them know that," said Sara. "It's nice to be in a superior trading position again."

"Superior? Their whole cargo isn't worth a fraction of this. We hold the high ground and beachfront. I was going to tell you I'd need some rest before I could go here, but forget that, let's get them to the table. I'd be willing to bet they've got authority to agree to almost anything."

"Chief of security to the panel array!" the muffled voice came from a speaker in the main stores area.

Daniel looked a silent curse at the ceiling. "I've got to go."

"I'm coming with you," said Sara. "Do you think it's another attack?"

"No, I think it's another fight."

Purty held one of the combatants in an arm lock, not exerting enough pressure to cause pain, but enough to let the man know that could change instantly. The other participant in the fight was similarly held by Chiu-Keung. Both men had dirt on their faces. One of them, Purty's, had a bleeding lip that was going to become much fatter than it already was. Chiu was breathing heavy, and may have had a broken finger.

Daniel approached from the hatchway, Dr. White a few steps behind him. He addressed the man with the fat lip. "I thought I put you two on different work rotations."

"You did, I came up for something I forgot and this doglicker started in again."

"Purty, lock him up. We'll bring his friend down in a minute."

"What's the meaning of this?" demanded Sara of the second fighter. The man stared at Sara close-mouthed.

"Boss," Daniel emphasized, "this is George Lethy, in case you can't remember his name. Lethy here has some interesting theories about one of our dead. Isn't that right, Lethy?"

"Theories nuthin'. Everybody knows Ian sold us out. Everybody knows October and them are dead because of him."

"The other gentleman," Daniel nodded in the direction of the hatch, "was one of Ian's best friends. Doesn't take too lightly to having his friend's name tarnished. Lethy, I warned you. Go ahead Chiu, lock him up. Lethy, you and Brennon go at it through the bars, I'll lock you both in the same cell and let you kill each other. Am I understood?"

"Why don't you do that right now? Some of the things that guy said to me...he's got it coming."

Daniel took a small step back, leaving Sara closer to the recalcitrant worker.

"Let me put it to you another way," she said. "If you and your friend continue this, you'll both be locked outside."

Lethy tried to look back at Chiu-Keung, then finding that impossible, implored Daniel with his eyes. The acting chief of security found an interesting spot on the horizon.

"Thanks, Daniel," Dr. White said, after Lethy was taken below. "I want Sid back. H&H is falling apart and I have to deal with this. I'm going to find Seth. Are you joining us?"

"No. I'm going to have to take care of these two. I'm worried it's only the start."

"How could anyone think Ian was the traitor?"

"He's the only one whose body we couldn't positively identify. Stand's to reason someone else could have been left there. We didn't execute anyone for the crime, and enough went on that everybody knows we were hunting for someone. This is the type of fallout Sid should have planned for, but he deals with these things on the fly. If he doesn't get back in time, you'll have to come up with a convincing lie. The rumours...well you can see, they're getting out of hand. I even caught a couple that Sid and Darcy were behind the whole thing, that's why they split."

"I suppose the name Toffee is coming up a lot."

"With Thurlow as a close second."

"Thurlow?"

"He did show up just when the trouble started. It was why Darcy went after him. Plus he cut a lot of power. We got spoiled fast, Boss."

Dr. White brushed some dirt off her coveralls. "I'm going inside. Sid'll be back in a few more days, then he can take his stinking job back. Maybe I should have let Harpreet have it in the first place."

Seth was in Darcy's traditional chair at the meeting table, right next to Dr. White, who had taken the Boss's seat. He pushed the cargo manifest across the table to Bruno, who took it, then looked quizzically at the chief of stores.

"What do you have that's not on the list?" Seth asked.

"The lobsters aren't on there."

"Yes, yes, I know the lobsters. You didn't come here looking to trade food for SatCom equipment, did you?"

Bruno flicked a quick glance at Dom, who hadn't spoken since they'd sat down. "No, not just lobsters, but look, we have a whole trailer-full of cargo. Now your end of it was bulbs, some processed metals, pipe fittings, medicine…"

"I know our end of it," Seth held up his hand. "What's your point?"

"What's my point? Forget your end. Our cargo for whatever you can supply us with. Within reason, of course. If you can't give us everything, we'll need to go elsewhere to pick up the rest. Maybe even to D'Abo, but I'd prefer not to. I don't like that pig much myself."

"Bruno, you and I both know your whole cargo isn't worth what you want from us."

"Your cook and your doctor might not agree with you."

That's why you're talking to me, not them, thought Seth. "I'm sure you brought something else. Something you're not supposed to offer unless you have to, hmmm? Why don't you save us time and tell us what it is."

"Wait a minute," Dom interrupted. "You haven't said what you can give us."

Seth looked at Sara, who nodded slightly. "We can hook you up with all of it. We're your one-stop SatCom shopping centre. Provided, of course, it's worth it to us. Look, we'll help you out, but we're not a charity."

"Could I have a moment alone with my partner," Bruno asked guardedly.

"By all means," said Dr. White, her smile a picture of benevolence.

Bruno waited a few seconds before realizing it was he and Dom who would have to go outside for privacy, not their hosts.

"What do you think?" asked Sara, once the fishers had left.

"I think we've got 'em."

The door opened and the two men returned to their seats.

"Our instructions," said Bruno, "were to trade our cargo for the components we need. It's not just food in there, and you know that. You need our salt just as much as everybody else does, among other things. But that's not good enough for you, is it?" Seth shook his head. "We did bring a few other items...some pre-Change items..."

"Now we're getting somewhere," said Sara.

"We've got some stuff your doctor might find useful. Dr. Nash was hesitant to give it up, but she recognized our need. We've got two kilograms of cocaine, and almost as much in heroin."

"What?" exclaimed both Seth and Dr. White at the same time. They both started talking at once, but Sara cut Seth off with a gesture. "Bruno, we're not running a palliative care unit, neither are we running a junkie's haven. What the hell would we want with that stuff?"

Seth managed to get his answer in before Bruno or Dom could offer theirs. "Boss, Dr. Patel could use them. Cocaine as a painkiller, heroin for...I'm not sure, but if he doesn't use them straight, he can make stuff from them...but," he turned to the fishers, "that's still not good enough, and you know it. What else did you bring?"

"A metal detector, fully functional, and a box of grenades."

Sara kept quiet. Seth tapped his fingers expectantly.

"That's it," said Dom. "That's all our extras."

Here we go, Seth kept his face poker-smooth. "No, it isn't."

"We drove it here, we know what we have."

"Exactly, you drove it here. Your truck."

"You're crazy," said Bruno.

"That's the deal. The SatCom components and a smaller vehicle for your cargo and your rig. Including the coke and the smack. We'll take the metal detector and the box of grenades for the medicine you want."

Bruno's mouth moved silently, trying in vain to formulate a reply. Dom saved him the trouble.

"We can't make a deal like that."

"Dogshit. Without a way to communicate with your Captain, you have all the authority. I know you have at least four rigs, you can spare one. Do we have a deal?"

"We'll have to talk outside again. Bruno, let's..."

"No, it's okay, Dom. He's right, we do have the authority. What vehicle are you offering us? The Hummer?"

"Not a chance. You can take our other spare car."

"That rust bucket?"

"Unless you'd prefer to walk home."

"Okay, deal. Our cargo and truck for that car and the SatCom gear." Bruno extended his hand, Seth took it and they shook.

"Good. If you'll excuse us, I'll have someone load the car as soon as I'm done talking with my boss."

The fishers exited without even a backwards glance at the table.

"Good job, Seth." Sara grinned. "Burle would be proud. You got us a truck."

"Yeah, so I did. Call Sid on his cell phone and tell him to come home. Anyway, that was way too easy."

"Excuse me?"

"They didn't even try to offer us a counter-deal. Bruno's been their chief of transport for a while now I figure, even given our situation he should have been a better negotiator than that. He didn't even try to table an installment plan. Who's chief of the pool right now?"

"Micky Fornten."

"Boss, I think Dr. Patel and Roshi should get those fishers good and drunk, while Micky goes over that rig with a fine tooth comb. I don't think they brought us a lemon, but that was still way too easy."

Dr. Patel gave the cart a cursory glance, opened one skinbag, then closed it and returned to his desk. It was the usual stuff from the coast; shark-liver oil (God only knew how they got that), some seaweed derivatives, other oils and naturally occurring chemicals that could only be found in coastal flora. The cocaine and the heroin were interesting. He knew a few people in the Pit who wouldn't hesitate to chop themselves a line if the opportunity arose. It would certainly be a change of pace from "Harpreet Surprise" as some of the Pit's denizens referred to his homemade rotgut. He'd have to lock it up safely, with the methamphetamines, downers and other mind-altering drugs he'd accrued over the years. He was a junkie's dream, really. It surprised him once in a while that he hadn't succumbed to the temptation to delve into his stash on occasion, and that he could still keep his demons at rest by drowning them with booze.

Pushing the desk aside, he stooped and dialled open a floor safe. He'd need to reorganize if he had any hope of fitting the new batch of narcotics inside. Taking out a few bottles of pills, he shoved aside a plastic bag of small glass vials, and wedged the heroin beside it. The canister of cocaine went in next.

"We need you in lock-up, Doc," said Purty, standing in the door a little breathless.

Patel popped up from behind the desk, almost bumping his head on it in surprise. "What's happening?"

"Brennon McKay strangled George Lethy through the bars separating their cells. We think he damaged Lethy's larynx."

"Oh for...what were they doing in lock-up? Never mind." He slammed the safe shut. "Let me get my bag." He grabbed it from where it always sat by the door, a black leather job that had been old before the Change. The doctor followed Purtricil from the infirmary, a few pill bottles forgotten on his desktop.

34. Cruising

"Look at his face," said Lena, poking Darcy in the shoulder. "He's just like a little kid."

The windows of the rig were covered with fine mesh torn from the grills of other trucks. It was held in place with duct tape for now, all except for the mesh over the broken window. That had a few screws in it as well, punched through the metal for better security. Not that the screws would hold long if something larger than a bug was left at it unhindered. Inside the cab, Caps had doffed his net-helmet and with his bright eyes fixed on his side mirror, allowed Sid to guide him back towards the trailer. The engine didn't exactly sound healthy, it rattled intermittently, and seemed on the verge of stalling a few times, but the mechanic's tinkering was sound, as were all the new gaskets and hoses.

"A little to the right," called Sid, waving his arm in the desired direction. "Okay, good. Now, straight back, bring it in."

It didn't matter if Caps could hear the Boss or not. The man's come-here gestures were clear enough. The tractor eased back, and with a solid metallic clank, became one with the trailer. The engine idled as Darcy and Sid hooked up the glad-hands to the trailer's brake lines. Electrical connections were made as well, and after a brief check of the lights, Sid came to stand in front of the rig.

"Good job, Richard. Everything's a go from out here."

With a huge smile, Caps leaned forward and patted himself on the back. Then he reached up and fumbled for a cord that hung by his head.

"Richard, no..." but the Boss's warning came too late. Caps had already pulled the cord.

The airhorns burped, and brownish guck oozed from around silver muffling plates. The horns sounded a subdued tone, then one of the plates shot off and smashed into the windshield of another truck. The LTL trumpeted like a great beast rudely awoken from slumber.

All the birds on the distant fence launched into the sky.

"What the hell are you thinking? That'll carry for miles!" Sid yelled, pressing both hands to the top of his head.

"Oops, sorry," Caps put his hand to his mouth and tried to look chagrined.

Sid took up his gun and jerked his head to the side, as if expecting the summons to be answered instantly. The others did the same in response to the Boss's sudden tension. All except Toffee. The hunter simply retrieved his rifle from where it leaned against a tire, then watched the birds, waiting to see if flight was the definite choice over fight.

"What do we do now?" asked Darcy. "If you're right, what do we do now?"

"I don't suppose peaceful contact is an option," supplied Lena.

"That's going to cost us, Richard. Shut it off." The Boss moved away from the truck and surveyed the road.

Caps killed the motor and jumped down. His defensive humour had been torn away by the Boss's certainty. He armed himself, and put on his net-helmet.

The birds settled on a section of fence more distant than the one they'd fled. From a pragmatic point of view, Toffee was relieved. Shooting birds ate a lot of ammo. His eyes followed the last of the birds as it dropped to its new perch.

"I say we set up an ambush," said Darcy. "If they come looking for us, we get 'em that way."

As Toffee turned his head, there was a distant blur in his peripheral vision. The birds, all at once, had taken to the air again. The hunter aimed his rifle by supporting the barrel with the side of his blade, then fired. All heads turned as a coyote pack, about twenty strong, stopped in their approach, and darted back. One of the coyotes lay on its side.

"Were they just out there waiting all this time?" asked Noah.

Toffee fired again, and another coyote dropped. "Seems likely. Coyotes are loners." The rest of the pack turned to their fallen companion, confused. "They only bunch up like this when they're bringing down large game, like a caribou." The hunter picked off a third animal before they wised up and fell back even farther, but they didn't retreat. "Or like us."

"What the hell?" Sid took a few steps forward. "What are they? Half gun shy?" He fired and another coyote hit the dirt, its back end flying out from underneath it. It pulled itself to its feet, then fell for the second and final time. This time the pack fell completely apart. Animals scattered in all directions. Two of them ran straight at the Deep Six. Darcy brought down one, Sid felled the other. Off by the far corner of the warehouse, another pair of coyotes stopped running, and turned to face their prey.

Toffee fired a shot in the air, the two animals didn't move. He stepped forward and shot one of them. The other took off like its tail was on fire.

"They're not gun shy," said the hunter with an air of finality. "It's not the sound of the shot that scares them, it's watching one of their own go down while we're over here."

"So what does that mean?" asked Noah.

"They understand we can kill at a distance. They keep falling back, but not out of our reach. Maybe…maybe bow range."

"So what are you saying," Noah's mind filled with cowboy movies, "Indians?"

"Didn't say nothin' about who's holding the bow. Halbert, that pack out by Camper World was the same, remember? They didn't run when one of us missed a shot, only when we hit."

Noah's stomach flip-flopped, he opened his mouth but whatever was going to come out was overridden by Lena's outburst.

"Let's go home! Let's go home right now! I want to go home! I want to go home!" Caps took her in his arms but she pushed him away. "Boss, I don't want to be here. None of us do! Please? Please can we go home?"

"Toffee, would an ambush work?" the Boss ignored his chief of communications.

"Depends on how many we're ambushing. A handful of people, sure. I don't think we're facing that here. Oh, for the love of…" he turned and shot another coyote. The ones that remained fell back again, but just out of gun range this time. "Those critters aren't going to let us hide quietly."

Sid looked at the rig. It was going to make a lot more noise than the Pig, plus it would be harder to maneuver through clogged streets, but leaving it in the truck yard wasn't an option.

"Let's cover our tracks, people. We're shipping out now. Dogshit!" he exclaimed, taking in all the evidence of their presence. "Darcy, coil those hoses. Noah, shove those tools somewhere."

"Boss, we can't just take off now," said Caps, moving to help Noah with the tools. "I need to test drive it a bit, there's a whole bunch of other things that could still need work."

"Then you shouldn't have sounded the victory bugle."

"Sorry, I…"

"Richard, just clean up your mess. Let's get these coyotes stashed somewhere. Hurry up people, we've got to move here."

"I could have stayed behind," said Toffee. "Could have watched the yard from the building, or from inside one of the trucks."

"And what if they found you?" asked Caps.

"They wouldn't have."

Ahead of the rig, the van took a corner narrowed by a pair of rusted cars, partially on the sidewalk, mostly on the road. Caps had to move to the far side of the road and take the corner as widely as he could. The city maps were all up front. If the two vehicles became separated, Caps would be hopelessly lost. He'd wanted the maps for himself, just in case that happened. He'd argued that with Lena in the van, Sid didn't need them. Unfortunately, Lena herself admitted that she didn't know the whole city, and even what she did know hardly looked familiar anymore.

Whereas before, Sid had tried to keep to side streets, now he chose wider routes, keeping in mind the space required by the rig. They were on the freeway, large signs giving instructions that were comical given their present context: "Slower Traffic Keep Right," and "Two Passengers Minimum In HOV Lanes."

The side streets had boasted a few vehicles here and there, but the freeway displayed the bulk of that first week's ensuing panic. Cars and trucks of all shapes and sizes littered the roadsides and the ditch between the eastbound and westbound lanes. Skeletons, stripped by nature and bleached by the sun, lay between the cars like markers for parking spaces. The nearly-intact remains of a horse was just off the road, near a bluish-green astrovan. Farther ahead, the u-haul trailer it might have escaped from, lay on its side, the pickup it was attached to rested on the hood of a black trans-am. As in other places, plant life had taken up residence in the moisture-holding upholstery of the vehicles. That same slime-green fungus that eked out an existence around the windows of canopies at Camper World thrived in the humidity of the coastal city. It spread out from the window frames and door edges like a disease, giving the illusion of eating the metal as well as the rubber.

At some point, presumably during the first year, someone had cleared a path between the strewn vehicles. The shapes of some cars suggested a bulldozer was used for the job. It was unlikely tanks had been employed; the nearest military base, located a few kilometres south of the city, had been shut down years before the Change.

"Man, this place is death's parking lot," said Caps. "We should get out and put up 'for sale cheap' signs on some of these wrecks."

Toffee didn't spare the artist a glance, he was too busy watching the road. He viewed Caps's clumsy shifting of gears with contempt, knowing he could do a much better if he still had his prosthetic. It would have been nearly impossible for him to work the stick with nothing but his blade. In his side mirror, he caught the shape of a bear loping from the ditch and onto the road.

"There's a grizzly back there," he said.

"Where?" Caps looked in his own mirror, then the hunter's. "Are you sure?"

"You missed it. It's gone behind that ambulance."

"How many bears do you figure are in the city?"

"Don't know. Watch the road."

Caps hauled on the wheel in time to avoid a foot-high lip of blacktop that had been pushed up by shifting earth from below. Though the road was in good condition considering its lack of maintenance, there were stretches of it broken and twisted like stale licorice.

Under another crumbling overpass, and past a police cruiser, undented, its doors open, the van turned off the freeway, taking an exit marked by an arrow sign stating "Grandview Highway." Toffee caught a glimpse of a skeleton near the cruiser that looked as if it still held its gun. The semi eased onto the Grandview Highway exit, then accelerated to catch up with the van. They passed beneath yet another overpass, and barely had enough room to pass through a particularly weed-choked bit of road. Then it was more of the same, wrecked cars, weathered skeletons, broken tarmac.

"How much further?" asked Darcy, eyeing a gas station that could have renamed itself Esso Orchard.

The buildings surrounding the roads had changed from houses to long stretches of identical duplexes. The various ways in which nature was reclaiming the structures gave them an individuality that architecture never had. Here a tree limb thrust out of a broken living room window, there a set of porch steps had been tossed aside by long-term growth from beneath. On one side of the road, an entire block of homes had been supplanted by a three-story structure of vine-covered stone. A clock tower rose from the structure, its face now only capable of being accurate twice a day.

"I know where we are," said Lena. "This is Twelfth and Cambie."

"When did we leave Grandview Highway?" Noah asked. "We didn't turn off anywhere."

"Grandview Highway becomes Twelfth Avenue. Soon it'll become Tenth avenue. We go straight to the University this way."

Sid and Darcy may have had memories of Vancouver, brief pictures, the most familiar landmarks seen a handful of times at the most. For Lena, the city was like watching a lifelong friend rot away from wet gangrene. She'd been in her own stomping ground, so to speak, ever since they'd passed the massive intersection of Twelfth and Kingsway. The streets, so familiar as to have been last seen only days ago, and yet so alien. Favourite stores with clothing mannequins scattered behind broken glass, like the skeletons mouldering away on sidewalks out front. Intersections she'd crossed a thousand times, cracked and going green.

Her mind raced ahead of the van, taking one final look at the city as it had been, before having that forever replaced by the ruin it was now. Cars rumbled along the traffic-congested street: busses, dump trucks, luxury SUVs and station wagons trying to be sports cars. She passed attractive but leaking condominiums, quaint houses crouching behind trees, and onto the final stretch, the best part, where the trees…

"I think we should take Marine Drive," said Lena.

"That's south of here," said Sid, keeping his eyes on the road. "Why do you think that would be better?"

"Once we pass Blanca, the streets are canopied…were canopied by trees. You couldn't even see the sun through them on some days. It was like a big, beautiful green tunnel. You see where I'm leading?"

"You're saying we're headed into a giant bush?"

"That's about the size of it."

"Lena, this is the quickest route to UBC. If it proves impassable, we'll turn around. What about Fourth Avenue, that'll be quicker than going down to Marine."

Lena squinted her eyes and looked up at the ceiling of the van, as intently as if a picture of the road was actually there.

"Worse, I think. The Fourth Ave. route takes us through Pacific Spirit Park. Great way to take if we were going to the beach, but too many trees for us now."

"There's the hospital," Darcy said, tapping the window with the muzzle of her rifle.

The vehicles passed Twelfth and Heather, and there it was, Vancouver General Hospital, marked by a tall smokestack, and a dozen signs pointing to various departments: Emergency, Family Practice, Psychiatric, etc. English ivy entirely covered the east sides of the five structures that made up the hospital complex, just as it did the high-rise apartment buildings across the road.

"We could stop here," said Lena hopefully. "Get some of Harpreet's stuff…maybe spend the night. The ICU wards would be well sealed."

"You'd hate it, honey," said Darcy. "Do you know how many corpses will be in there?"

"And ants," said Sid. "Sara said the ants practically owned VGH before she left the city. There was another hospital they'd gotten to as well…Louis Brant? Louis Barnet?"

"Louis Briar," Lena corrected. "It's about thirty blocks south of here. I heard stories. Ants and rats. It was more than a hospital, it was also a nursing home. They didn't stand a chance." The van wasn't even slowing. Still, she tried again anyway. "What do you think, Boss, take a break here?"

Something thumped under a wheel. It was a soft impact, not like going over broken road.

"Hey, look at 'em all," said Noah, more wonder in his voice than fear.

Squirrels, black and gray, their flexible tails undulating, fell from trees and darted into and out of the road. By some forgotten animal-lover's reflex, Sid actually swerved to avoid hitting one of them, then swerved to avoid another.

"Hey look, the Boss is doing the same thing. Cool!" Caps steered left, aiming his tires like steel-belted steamrollers at the furry creatures populating the streets. Unlike the van, no shudders reached the semi's occupants, only red smears in the mirror announced a successful hit.

"Damn, that one was fast!" The squirrel that had dodged Caps's last pass stopped at the side of the road and stood on its back legs. The artist could imagine the critter giving him the finger.

"I'd have gotten it," said Toffee, thinking out loud.

"Oh man, there's gotta be hundreds of them."

And there were. For every one Caps managed to squash, ten more remained unscathed, charging at the vehicles, as if they could somehow halt the thousands of pounds of metal with only their tiny claws. One of them must have jumped a running board. Caps could hear scraping near the bottom of his door.

"He'll chew right through that, given time," said the hunter, listening to the scratching near the bottom of his own door.

Another squirrel had timed its leap right and clasped tightly to the mesh outside the window.

"You better speed up," Toffee said, rolling down the glass. The squirrel's teeth punctured the mesh. It pulled its head back, peeling back a curl, making an entrance. Toffee opened its throat with the tip of his blade. It fell, and the hunter closed his window. "Better speed up."

Ahead of them, the van had stopped swerving, and was now holding a steady course.

"Aww, the Boss quit," said Caps choosing a target. "That's his problem, never lets himself have enough fun." He got two squirrels at once this time.

"They're not car shy," said Darcy.

The closer they got to the university, the more animals appeared from the rotting houses and surrounding foliage. Mostly it was squirrels, but dogs and cats were showing up, as well as raccoons, spurred into diurnal activity by the unfamiliar sounds. Though most of these creatures had never seen a functioning motor vehicle in their lifetime, their reaction to it was instinctual.

Darcy turned to the back of the van, wondering at the emotional state of her two most fragile teammates. Lena was pushing the heels of her palms into her eyes, then looking out the window again, as if hoping the animals wouldn't be there. Noah's attitude, however, surprised her. He moved his head between the two side windows and the back, like a soldier waiting to see the whites of some eyes. He had both his rifle, and his gun out. She thought the .45 looked ridiculous in his hand. She pictured him firing off the shotgun and the handgun at the same time. He'd probably be thrown right off his feet like a rag doll. The expression on his face was disturbingly familiar, but she couldn't quite place it.

"How are you guys doing back there?" asked Sid.

"Loving every minute of it," said Lena, her sarcasm not so much dripping as flowing.

"We knew this was coming, just keep calm."

"Lena, look, look quick!" Noah grabbed her shoulder, turning her towards the back windows. Behind them, a large dog that had been chasing the van, barking its head off, went down under one of the semi's front tires.

"Yeah! Felt that one!" Caps was jubilant, but given the circumstances he was a bit too happy.

"Don't go crazy on me," said Toffee.

"What are you talking about? Hang on!" The cab jerked violently to the left. "Yeah! That was a Siamese. I always hated Siamese. Crack yer window and start shooting, big guy! What are you waiting for?"

"I'll crack you one if you don't reign in, painter."

"Aw, you're just pissed 'cause you can't drive. Shit! These squirrels move like lightening. Hey, there's a coon on the Pig. Shoot it, Toffee! Never mind, it's off. C'mere furball, you're next."

"Look at yourself," Toffee grabbed Caps by the back of his head, and heedless of danger, shoved the man's head into the window, so he could see himself in the side mirror. "Like what you see?" He released his grip.

Caps snapped his eyes back to the road and hauled the wheel to avoid smashing into a black van with the logo for some radio station painted on the side. What he'd seen in the mirror was the face of a lunatic, features pulled back in a rictus of glee.

"That's better," said Toffee. "Don't overcompensate. Be scared, but be in control."

"Yes, Polonius."

"How'd Leartes wind up?"

Caps's eyes widened in shock, he hadn't expected the hunter to get the reference; Polonius, Hamlet's doddering old fool. Nor had he expected such a retort—Leartes, a character of the same play, who wound up dead on account of a stab wound.

"That's right, painter. Keep this rig on the road."

"Okay, I'll tone down on the Mad Max, but..." he wouldn't acknowledge his defeat, "...let me know if you see any poodles."

Noah's soldier persona was fraying at the edges by the time they reached the stretch of Tenth Avenue Lena had described. The motion of animals was constant. New ones appeared ahead as others fell away from behind, waves of fur as relentless as the ocean. The rocking of the van as it shuddered over creatures was inducing something akin to seasickness in Darcy. There were cougars now, here and there. The birds hadn't joined in, and hopefully wouldn't. Suicidal dives into the windshield would ultimately make driving impossible. Darcy thought she saw a couple of small bears, but she wasn't sure, they could have been big dogs. The only thing that kept them safe was the forward motion of the vehicles, and as Lena had predicted, that was about to end.

"Damn," the Boss swore, slowing more than he felt comfortable with, in order to turn away from a thoroughfare that had become a dead end.

Trees weren't just reclaiming the last stretch to the university, they owned it. Thick branches intertwined, stretching from trunks so wide it was astounding. What little road could be seen beneath greenage, was strewn with dead boughs. There was no way they were going through. From the darkness between the branches, squirrels launched themselves into the air, like a barrage of watermelon seeds spat from a giant leaf-encrusted mouth. Many of them made it to the hood and roof of the Pig, its reduced velocity making it an easier target. The Pig didn't have much in the way of animal protection, short of the bug sprayers, and those were empty. Noah had used every last drop of pesticide they had, determined to render the truck yard ant-free for generations to come.

"Hang on." Sid accelerated.

The Pig skidded as something went under a tire. Animals flew from the hood and roof, while some gripped the mesh with all their strength. The van passed the truck that was slowing to a stop.

"Dogshit," breathed Darcy. "He doesn't have enough room to turn."

"What?" Lena's voice was shrill. "What do you mean doesn't have enough room?" She jumped into the rear and pressed her face against the window. Animals flowed to the truck like water to an enormous drain.

"Shit! Get 'em Toffee get 'em!" Caps's mouth ran at light speed as he slammed the truck into reverse. He set it into motion, unable to see what was behind him. Animals hung on the mirror, but he couldn't even see those, because of the squirrels on the mesh outside his window—the only thing between him and the teeth.

Gleaming steel shot past him, a bare centimetre from his eyes. He flinched back and felt the blade cut his hair on its next stab.

"Dammit, painter! Keep your head still."

Caps's spine became as rigid as an iron bar. The blade stabbed back and forth with the methodical speed of a sewing machine. It flashed past his eyes and whispered behind his head, speckling his face as the blade became encrusted with gore. Toffee's mesh was half off, and a squirrel was inside it, squatting in the newly-created pocket. It could find no purchase on the glass, but its rapid tapping nonetheless set a metronome that aided in driving Caps's mind near to the edge. He could hear himself talking but he had no idea what was coming out of his mouth. Toffee was leaning right into him, holding Caps's head with a fist in the hair, while his right arm did its thing. There was blood now, spattered across the wheel and the inside of the windshield. The hunter's breath was coming heavier, right into Caps's ear. Critters were coming up to the shredded net as fast as the hunter could drive them off. Toffee was working himself up into a froth, and his spittle joined the blood that already covered the artist's face.

There was a tap that followed each thrust. Caps realized the hunter was bringing the blade down against the window's broken edge each time he pulled back, scraping off whatever it was he'd just impaled. The window finally gave, and razor-sharp cubes of glass spilled into the artist's lap as the blade stopped, a large rat dangling right before his face. The rat stretched forward with its whole body, curving itself like a "C" from where the blade pierced it, trying to claw or bite Caps's face in its last dying moments. Toffee swung the blade down and cleared the rat off on the wheel. It fell into Caps's lap.

"Glaahhh!" He lurched forward as the rat jerked to its death. The blade, already slipping forward, bit into the flesh on the top of Caps's nose. At the same time, the squirrel Toffee had been aiming for, dodged under the blade's tip, and joined the rodent already in the artist's lap.

Time slowed to a standstill. The squirrel dug claws into the fabric of Caps's pant leg. Its mouth opened, and teeth oozed towards the vulnerable inner thigh. The hunter's blade plunged down, puncturing the squirrel just behind the head, going through and ending up in the cushion right by Caps's leg. The hunter flipped the blade up and went back to work, the impaled squirrel adding to its weight, making it more difficult to control.

Caps's perception narrowed to a single purpose, maneuvring the truck. The flashing steel, the growling at the window, the sheer bulk of animals trying to get in through the windshield, was only a peripheral thing. If he turned too soon, the trailer would get hung up on something, possible trapping them there. It was only the shifting movement of the truck that kept the animals from overwhelming himself and the hunter.

Now! his instincts shouted. He turned the wheel, knowing he'd come back far enough. The vehicle reversed without the awful bang that would announce failure. The worst part was yet to come, when he had to stop in order to go forward. He knew a big panic was coming, no, not a big panic, *the* big panic. But somehow, this wasn't it. Somehow he felt he'd get through this one.

"I have to stop. I have to stop the truck," he said, forcing a coherent sentence through his mouth that had a mind of its own.

"Down!" commanded the hunter, accenting the order by actually pushing on the back of Caps's head. "This is going to get messy."

How much messier can it get? Caps wondered, his hands slick and sticky on the blood-splattered wheel. Caps pulled right down as the barrel of a shotgun came up. The report was deafening. Blood and guts splattered over his left side as animals were blown from the window. He barely heard the second barrel go off. Something hard and grainy peppered his cheek as he shifted gears. Then he was up and accelerating, the speedometer's needle rising. The van, which was using a parking lot and a four-way intersection to do high-speed circles, broke off its pattern and zoomed in front of the truck.

Creatures fell from the running boards, and slid off the windshield, which was now cracked and spidering in a couple of places. Toffee scraped the squirrel off his blade and into the slipstream, then he picked up the rat and tossed it out the window as well. He was panting, and sweat glistened on his forehead. A tenacious squirrel, eyes peeled wide by airflow or terror, clung to the driver-side mirror's frame with all four legs. Its tail and fur were straight out. At last, its strength gave out and it tumbled backwards and out of sight. The hunter slumped back against his seat, and let his eyes close.

"We have to get something over these windows," said Caps.

"He'll know. Halbert knows that. Keep moving."

Caps wiped at his face with a strip torn from his shirt. Something had clawed the material open, he didn't know what, and he hadn't seen the hunter get it before it could do more damage. He tried to clean the inside of the windshield, but found he was just smearing gunk around. Toffee hadn't spoken since they'd freed themselves. Animals still pursued the vehicles, but they were fewer and farther between. The street they were on had gone commercial, cement buildings and shattered glass store fronts. There was less greenage, and therefore, less teeth. Some wasps had attempted a brief swarming of the truck, coming in from the front, but the semi's speed had smashed them against the windshield, or left them behind. A couple of them somehow made it in, clinging to the edge of the window. Caps crushed both of them, earning himself another wound as his hand swatted broken glass.

The van slowed, then came to a spot by the wide cement lot of a car dealership. A fleet of vehicles, prices no longer legible on weather-scourged placards, sat in much the same condition as those on the roads, save a lot less dents, and bit less fungus. The side door of the van opened and someone, Caps thought it might have been Noah under the net, jumped out and waved at him to keep going.

"Where?" he shouted as he slowed the truck.

"Straight, we'll catch up!" It was Noah. He had a pair of bolt cutters in his hands.

As soon as the rig passed, gunfire erupted from the door of the van, as someone from within, probably Darcy, covered Noah in whatever it was he was up to. In a short while, the van passed the rig, then turned into the parking lot of a gigantic market. Twenty-foot lettering spelled out "Superstore" on a long yellow wall. The parking lot, scattered with vehicles, and an accumulation of any other bit of junk the wind could drag across it, was an expanse of relatively unbroken tarmac. Caps brought the truck into the lot and stopped. The van opened, and Noah and Darcy popped out, each with a bit of rusted metal weave. Lena dropped down after with a tool kit.

Caps jumped down, and they embraced each other tightly, Lena forgoing her fear of affection in front of others. Toffee stayed in the truck while Noah and Caps fitted the metal to the windows.

"Where'd you get these?"

"Off some sort of box around a power metre. I'm glad I cut the squares large enough. This'll never keep bugs out."

"It doesn't have to. Undo that bolt we just put in." Caps went around to the front of the truck, and with a utility knife, cut the bug stopper from the front grill. "We'll put this under it. That'll stop everything." A gunshot rang out. "Let's hurry up."

Sid lowered his weapon. The coyote, a loner this time, lay on its side about twenty metres away. Its chest swelled and contracted as its life bled out.

"Aren't you worried about someone hearing us?" asked Darcy.

"I'm sure of it, but we'll be gone from here by the time they arrive. I think most of the city is left on its own. You notice some places there was almost no activity, but in others, it was like they'd never seen us before. It makes sense, what Toffee said about bow range. This was Canada. A heck of lot less guns lying around in these cities. Anyone setting up here would probably have to go with bows, or spears, even. A few handguns from the cops, some hunting rifles, but nothing like the firepower readily available in an American city. Lots of bows, though. They wouldn't even have to be homemade. Every sporting good place in Vancouver would have a few bows kicking around. Arrows and bowstrings are lot easier to manufacture than bullets and gunpowder."

"So, because the animals are attacking us, you think we're safe from people."

"That's about the size of it. Coyote at three o'clock. Want it?"

"You're weird, Sid. I love you, but you're weird." She shot the coyote.

Back on the road, Marine Drive curved up and to the north, leading away from Richmond, where the airport was. Caps had a small adhesive strip on his nose, holding the skin together. It had occurred to him that the hunter could have gone to work at a safer distance from his face, but it didn't matter. Toffee had saved his life. A few animals skittered from the overgrown ditches beside the road, but nothing like what they'd hit on Tenth. The thing was, where they were going, every building was likely to be surrounded by the thickness of trees that had blocked their earlier passage. They'd just have to worry about it when they got there.

A sign indicated the university turn off. The two lanes that led from Marine were laid amidst grassland, not trees, and although a few saplings had sprung up, the road was open. Human bones had been lifted into the air by vegetation growing up from beneath. It was more than a little discouraging. They came to a point where three cars blocked the road. The van stopped and pulled over to the side, waiting for the rig to do what the Pig couldn't. Caps, now much calmer than the critter-squashing fanatic he'd been, eased the truck up to the cars, and gently pushed them out of the way, then he accelerated, through and ahead. After the cars, a great crack had opened, running with the road, narrowing it to one lane. There was no room for the van to take point again, so Caps just kept going, figuring the Boss would honk or something when he was supposed to turn. Almost immediately they were plunged into trees again.

Animals surged from the flora, once again turning the road into an obstacle course of fur and bodies. Toffee's eyes were open, and he was adjusting the straps on his blade, making sure it was tightly secured. All at once, the road just ended. A massive tree had fallen across the road. The charred edge, evidence of a lightning strike, had reduced the girth of the tree, but even so, it still presented a five-foot wall of wood. To the left was the crevice, to the right, one of the university's buildings. Caps slammed on the brakes. The tires on both the trailer and the cab squealed as the semi skidded forward. It stopped a few feet before the tree. The van came to a similar sudden stop a few car lengths to the rear. Animals exploded over the roadblock and from the tree line to the left, beyond the crevice. Squirrels and raccoons leapt the gap, or down one side and up the other. Almost instantly the windshield was covered with claws and teeth, beady eyes that glossed over with rage at being unable to reach the humans through metal and glass.

"Come on girl, you can do it," said Sid, twisting the key.

The van had stalled when he'd slammed on the brakes in order to avoid rear ending the truck. A dog jumped and snarled at the driver's side window, while squirrels ran up and down the metal grid in front of the windshield, looking for an entrance. Sid turned the key again, to no better effect. The starter was trying, but the motor just wouldn't turn over.

"Don't flood it," said Darcy, eyes darting from the window to Sid's foot on the gas peddle.

"Come on, come on…"

Noah had left the .45 in its holster. The scratching from above was getting louder, and he needed both hands to hold his shotgun steady. Beside him, Lena was saying something under her breath, it might have been a prayer. The engine was still not turning over. He couldn't see out the back windows anymore, they were too fur covered. He heard the roars of at least two cougars from somewhere to the right of the vehicle. From the beyond the Pig's front end, a metal clanking increased in volume.

"What the..." said Sid, looking up. "No! He can't hear us...RICHARD! WE'RE STILL BEHIND YOU!" He pounded on the centre of the steering wheel, but the Pig's horn hadn't worked in years.

Animals were thrown from the windshield as the back end of the trailer smashed into the van's front. The Pig was pushed back and to the right as the trailer continued its motion. Lena dropped her gun and gripped tightly to the back of Sid's seat. Sid had quit with the engine and was pushing against the dashboard as if he could stop what was happening with his bare hands. The Pig's side was pushed up against the building, and finally the trailer stopped, pinning the van between metal and concrete. The impact had caused the side door of the van to buckle, and an opening, about two inches around, had opened near the bottom. As Noah stared with eyes round as saucers, squirrels and rats began to pour in.

35. UBC

Noah slammed the heel of his boot into the opening made by the buckled door. He caught the side of a rat as he did so. It squealed before squirming back and out of the hole. Three rodents—two rats and a squirrel—had made it inside and all of them were on his leg. He clubbed one of them with the butt of his gun, and Darcy was bare-handedly throttling the squirrel, but the unhindered rat bit down hard into the sensitive skin of Noah's inner thigh. He jerked his leg, then kicked it back down, re-covering the hole.

"Get it off of me! Get it off of me!"

Arms reached past his head as Lena bent forward and grabbed the rodent much in the same way Darcy had, closing her hands tightly around its throat and squeezing as hard and as fast as she could. The rat Noah had hit recovered with the devil's quickness. It sprang onto Lena's leg and bit, its head snapping back with confusion and pain almost instantly.

"Wrong leg," said Darcy, clubbing the creature off Lena's prosthetic.

"Get something to stuff this hole with! Now!" someone ordered. Noah would later recall with pride that it was his own voice issuing those commands.

The van's motor roared to life. Sid snatched up the radio handset.

"Richard! Come in!" he fiddled with the dial, then tried again. "Darcy, what frequency is that rig on?"

She didn't hear him, she was too busy in the back of the van. Blood was beginning to seep into Noah's pant leg, and if she didn't hurry, something was likely to chew right through his boot. Lena held her rat in the air, keening as she crushed its windpipe. Its struggling was nothing more than reflex action.

"Go forward," Toffee ordered.

"I can't see! If I'm hung up on–"

"Go forward dammit!"

"Richard, come in!" the Boss's voice crackled from the CB.

Caps snatched at the handset. He could see nothing through any window except writhing fur.

"Boss, we're stuck, I hit something!"

"You hit us! Go forward, we're pinned against this building."

The grate over Caps's window was beginning to buckle. He shifted into forward gear and accelerated. The truck lurched forward, chains jangling. He spoke into the mic again.

"Boss, are you clear?"

"Yes, we're backing up."

The whole cab shook from some heavy impact. Animals scattered from the windshield, making way for a much larger creature.

A grizzly bear was climbing up the grill onto the hood.

This is it, thought Caps, *this is the really big panic.*

It would be through the glass in one, two swipes at the most.

"Forward! FORWARD!" Toffee yelled.

The truck rocked forward, pinning the bear against the fallen tree. The bear's eyes bulged as it was crushed, its rib cage shattering, its chest squashed against its spine. Blood and innards flooded across the hood of the truck.

"That's enough," said Toffee, as the rig strained against the completely immovable obstacle.

Caps eased off the gas.

"Back up."

"I can't."

"BACK UP!"

"I can't, you idiot! On one side's the building, on the other is that doglicking trench. I can't see a thing."

As if commanded by the man's words, the windshield filled up again, a motley pattern of writhing fur and curved black claws. A wrenching noise announced a screw popping out of the grate over Toffee's window. The sound of climbing and scratching came through the rear of the cab, animals teaming on the headache rack. Another ripping sound, this time a screw from the driver-side grate.

"Shit! I hate driving this big bastard."

"Richard," Sid's voice announced, "Lena says there's a parking lot through to the right, we have to go through the bush."

Toffee's hand was first on the mic. "We can't see to back up."

"I'm working on it."

"Work fast."

"Lena, get a jerry can from the back, set the spout. Darcy, grab a shotgun." Sid had finally gotten the Pig started and jerked the vehicle backwards and forwards. He couldn't see much of anything, but the van's rocking was throwing a few animals at a time off the windshield's mesh, giving him brief glimpses of the semi. "I need to see where I'm going, then we put down a burn line. Noah, get ready."

"I can't clear the windshield, Sid." Darcy held the shotgun uselessly in her hands.

"Right, clear my window." He pulled a handle on the side of his chair and reclined as far back as he could go. Lena had to jerk her leg out of the way to avoid having it crushed.

Darcy smashed the inner window with a single jab of the gun barrel. Glass tinkled as it fell into the door well.

"Ready?"

Sid nodded. Darcy let go with both barrels. Blood splattered, fur flew. A huge hole was opened in the mesh, its curled edges blackened. Sid snapped upright into a cloud of smoke. Using the side mirror, he reversed as fast as he could. Seconds later he saw what he was looking for, a strip of pavement, barely three feet wide, that spanned the deep crevice. The problem was, it was on the wrong side of the road for what he needed. With a quick twist of the wheel, he reversed the van, so it was facing away from the rig.

"Darcy, clear your window."

Lena handed Darcy a loaded shotgun in exchange for the one she held. Darcy went to break her window, then simply rolled it down. She leaned her chair back as Sid had done, closed her eyes and fired.

"Clear that hole," Sid now used Darcy's mirror to guide him.

Lena snapped the shotgun closed on two fresh shells and offered it up.

"Noah, get ready," said Darcy, bringing the shotgun down by his foot.

Noah pulled his foot away and the shotgun's muzzle was pushed out through the hole. She fired off the first barrel, then the second an instant later. The van twisted and lurched.

"Pour it," said Sid, pushing the gas pedal down.

He'd used the small bridge to cross the gap with the wheels on the right side, now the van straddled it, and accelerated backwards. Noah shoved the gas nozzle out the hole and fumes assaulted his nose as fuel poured onto the road. They raced along, covering tarmac and animals with the flammable material. In no time they were next to the besieged semi. Enough animals had cleared the windshield that Sid could ride the gap safely.

"Keep pouring, load the double barrel," he said, setting the van forward again.

Squirrels and raccoons were avoiding the fuel, finding it thoroughly unpleasant. Sid drove to the bridge and crossed back over.

"Get ready to clear your windows," he said into the mic, then to Darcy, "Give me the gun."

He pushed the barrel through the hole and fired at the road. Nothing happened. He fired again. This time the fuel ignited, sputtering at first, then flames rose and raced up the road.

"Clear your windows!" he squeezed the handset as hard as he could, as if that would force the message through quicker.

Toffee blasted Caps's window first, then his own. The acrid smell of gunpowder filled the cab. Caps reversed, animals kept from his side by the flames, and from the hunter's side by...well, the hunter. Using the fire as a straight edge, he kept the trailer from drifting into the crevice.

"There," said Toffee. "They've punched through the bush."

"We're going to have to stop again. The flames are already giving up."

They passed the spot where scrub had been pushed aside by the van. It looked to Caps like a vertical rabbit hole. "Here we go." He pressed the brake and shifted into forward gear.

Toffee didn't waste any time. He fired a shotgun blast out of each window. Caps barely had enough time to get his head back, which he couldn't do near enough. Pushing on the gas, willing the truck to accelerate faster than it could, he followed the hole made by the Pig. Branches whipped at the naked window, the shotgun having torn the makeshift grate right off. One of them stung Caps's upper lip, and for a spine-tingling moment he thought some rodent had latched onto his face. The vehicle thundered over rough terrain, the cab victim to both the cab's and the trailer's gyrations, then they broke through onto blacktop, and with a last bounce from wheels fifteen through eighteen, were on something like open road. The van was ahead of them. The hood offered no purchase, and was soon clear of claws and teeth, but Caps could still hear them scrabbling up and down the headache rack.

"What's the best way? Lena? Give me my options!" Sid's voice was starting to break.

Lena looked up from the dead rat cradled in her hands. Outside the window, animals closed in from all sides. *Should have skipped school today,* said Caps's voice in her head. "There's a loading bay around back of the Walcott Building," she said. "That's where the fab lab is. There's a ramp down. Its not great, but it's defensible. Go left at the bus loop."

"Boss," said Noah, poking at his leg to see how bad the damage was. "How are we going to protect ourselves when we leave the Pig?"

"With our flamethrower."

"We brought a flamethrower? Why haven't we used it already?"

"Ever use one of those in a moving vehicle?" asked Darcy. She spied the rat Lena was holding onto. "We screw up doing that, we roast inside. Lena, give me that thing." She snatched the carcass from her friend and stuffed it through the hole in her mesh. She rolled up the window. "Sid, we have to cover that hole. Sorry about breaking the glass."

"Forget it. The window probably wouldn't roll down anyway. I don't think the door'll open. Richard hit us pretty good. Is that the bus loop?"

"Yes," said Lena, wiping her hands on her coveralls.

Sid relayed instructions over the radio, then took the road Lena had indicated. It was overgrown, but not enough to bar passage. They weren't going fast enough to keep squirrels from jumping on, but they were at sufficient speed to keep the creatures from staying on. Following Lena's directions they turned into the wide cement area to the rear of the building. Rotted wooden roadblocks and orange netting surrounded a hole beyond the turn-off. Near the end of the lot was a dung-brown trailer, its brake stand down and muck-encrusted.

"Richard," Sid said into the mic, "pass us and go down the ramp. It has to be past that trailer. If the loading doors aren't open, smash through them."

"Is there a bay down there? Like a motor pool?" came the crackling reply.

Sid checked with Lena, who shook her head.

"No. Just smash the doors and stop. Get ready to run." He dropped the handset. "Get geared up, weapons, ammo, food. We may find getting out is harder than getting in."

The rig sailed past them. It turned down the ramp, and with the sound of metal crunching, came to a stop, the trailer still visible, but the cab hidden. Sid used the lot to perform a wide circle, giving his team a few more seconds to prepare.

The blast-induced ringing in Noah's ears was gently nudged, then shoved aside by the pounding of his heart. He pushed things under his arms, Lena disappeared from view, then reappeared with a flame-thrower, the tank's straps cutting into one shoulder. Noah dropped half of what he carried, freeing an entire arm for his shotgun. He hoped he dropped the least important half. The building swung into view, sandstone brick drifting by in the rough oval hole blown through the mesh outside Darcy's window.

They were going to bail from the safety of the Pig. In that moment, Noah loved the ugly vehicle more than he'd ever loved a less mobile shelter. He didn't want to leave its warm embrace, compassion glowed from rust on the bolts, security beckoned from the stuffing pushing out of cracks in the upholstery.

Sid slammed on the brakes, screeching to a halt just before hitting the trailer.

"Everybody move!"

Darcy hit the ground running. Neither Sid's, nor the side door would open. It was a delay that might have cost them their lives had Noah not been quick enough with another shotgun blast. Then they were all out, and hauling ass down the ramp. Toffee and Caps were already inside the dark basement of the Walcott Building. Lena shoved the flamethrower into Sid's arms. He pointed it low and swept a crescent of fire, driving back creatures that were slipping past the truck.

"Go, go!" cried the Boss, illuminating the loading bay with another gout of flame. The bear was right where it died, a macabre hood ornament stamped to the metal.

Darcy clicked on a flashlight and led them to a door. It was locked. She shot the locking mechanism with her handgun, then kicked it open. Sid used two more squirts of fire. The Deep Six moved through the door and along a concrete hallway. After two more doors, which weren't locked and thankfully could be latched behind them, Darcy stopped at a hallway intersection with strong fire doors on all four sides.

"This should be far enough," she said, a little breathless.

"Check for rat holes," said Toffee.

The chief of security swung her light all around, at the same time offering a second flashlight to anyone who would take it. Noah grabbed it and helped her search. There were no gaps under the doors that he could see, nor were there heaters in this section of hallway, with easily pushed-aside inspection plates beneath them.

"Ssshhh, listen," said Sid.

The only sound was six people trying not to breath heavy.

"This won't last," said Toffee.

"No," replied Sid, equal certainty in his voice. "Okay Lena, which way?"

The pain in Noah's thigh made him want to limp, but it was better to walk through the pain. The muscle was bruised, but the rat never got the chance to start tearing. His mind hadn't yet pondered the less immediate ramifications of the bite, but it would, in its own due time. Lena didn't seem to know exactly where she was going, but she was covering it up well; choosing turns at random, but choosing them decisively. He was glad for the walk, he knew if he stopped moving, his stomach would knot up. At the same time as he was scared, he was exhilarated. He'd jumped from that vehicle without hesitation, and ran amongst the teeth, just the way Batman or the Duke would. They'd have been proud of him. So would his parents. He could picture himself telling them about it, breathless, after running all the way from school. From school? It was the anachronistic quality of the thought that jarred him. The only tools he had to visualize communication with his parents were those of a ten-year-old boy.

"Stop," said Toffee. "Girl, enough guessing. Where are we?"

"I was only down in this part of the building a few times." Her flashlight darted from door to dust-covered notice board, faculty meeting memos and lab schedules curling away from the staples that held them in place. "The lights were all on then, and…" her beam found a mummified skeleton in a lab coat. She didn't shriek. She'd done that the first two times. "There were living people to ask, 'Hey, where the hell am I?' "

Noah squatted by the corpse, braving the parchment-dry flesh to get a look at the name tag that depended from one pocket.

"Dr. T. Holland," he said, reading out loud.

"I know him," said Lena. "Well, I knew him." She hunkered down beside Noah. Nothing of the man she knew was present in the veil of flesh draped over the corpse's skull. "He was one of my profs. A good one. Those UBC profs, great researchers, but not a teacher among them. That was our reputation. It was true of some, but not Dr. Holland. There's no bloodstains on his clothes. Do you think he starved to death?"

A new dot of light appeared on the hallway floor.

"This guy didn't wait that long." Toffee's boot nudged a glass vial that lay near a skeletal hand.

"Where'd you get the flashlight?" asked Caps.

"I always carry one with me. Don't you?"

Lena picked up the open vial and scrutinized it, as if she could discern what had been in it. She sniffed it.

Yeah, that'll work, thought Toffee.

"Just because this vial is here doesn't mean it held poison." Lena waggled the vial at the hunter. "It could have just rolled here."

"Enough talk," said Sid. "Let's pick a room and give you time to get your bearings."

They fell back two sets of fire doors, then Sid picked a door. It, like all the other doors he'd tried, was locked. There was a number on the door, but no sign to indicate what lay behind it. Not wanting to waste a single bullet, he stepped back and kicked the door. It didn't budge. He shifted his balance to kick again, then stood easy.

"Toffee?" he waved an open hand at the door.

The hunter lashed out with his leg and the door burst open. The deadbolt hung from a cactus patch of splintered wood. Beyond the door was a cleaning station and an island of sinks and disposal receptacles that ran the length of the room. Past these were work stations, high desks with fire-retardant tops. A few microscopes were spread out among the stations. Bottles, vials, test tubes and other chemist's paraphernalia were also distributed. The implements of science stood and lay in a semi-organized mess, as if no one had bothered to clean up after frenzied, but precise work. There was a chalkboard on one wall, but it apparently hadn't been enough to sustain the amount of writing and drawing that had been going on. A pair of easels with giant pads of paper on them stood at each end of the room. Many pages had been flipped over the back of the easels, the sheets exposed were covered in chemist's jargon that none of the Deep Six understood.

"Lena, bring your light back to that second table," said Caps. "No, second from the door. That's a kerosene lamp." His foot hit something as he moved towards the lamp.

The object skittered across the floor, bounced off a stool leg, and ended up at Noah's feet. Caps paid no attention to it and picked up the lamp as Noah bent and retrieved the item. It was a blue plastic flashlight. He thumbed the switch, but it was long burnt out.

"Is there any fuel in it?" Darcy asked Caps.

"No." He picked a canister up from beside the station and shook it. Fluid sloshed around inside. "But I'll bet there's plenty in this."

All the flashlights went off once the lamp was filled and lit. It was of an hourglass configuration, the polished metal shade still reflective as ever. With a better overall picture of the lab, it was easy to piece together at least the beginning of a story. There were flashlights on all the workstations. There were also flashlights in the garbage pails, and on the floor. The torches were of all shapes and sizes, from a tiny penlight to a club-sized security guard's mag. The microscopes left on a high shelf had electric-powered light sources built into the base. Those on the workstations had adjustable mirrors underneath them. A Bunsen burner connected to the building's gas system had been pushed aside, it dangled from a table edge by the rubber hose that still attached it to a nozzle. In its place was a burner of a much older type, self-contained, much like the kerosene lamp.

"How long do you think they survived down here?" Noah asked nobody in particularly. He picked up a syringe. "Were they doing blood tests? Making a weapon, maybe?"

"Were they working on a cure?" asked Caps.

"Did they get out?" finished Lena.

"Let's teeth-proof this place before we do anything else." All flashlights came back on at the order. "Toffee, let's see what's through that door."

Circles of light probed corners and ceiling. Perimeter cupboards were thrown open, particularly those under sinks. There were always gaps around the pipes in those places. In this case, the holes had been plugged already, years ago.

Caps tried a couple of flashlights, then gave up. "I'll just guard the lamp, guys."

"You could pick it up and carry it," said Darcy.

"Oh. Yeah, I guess I could."

Toffee didn't have to hoof the lab's second door open. It was unlocked. Behind it lay a graveyard. There were seven bodies, draped with canvas sheets, like those used to pad elevator walls. The dead lay on long benches identical to those in the adjoining room. The surfaces not covered by human remains were taken up by those of animals, mummified in large plastic bags.

"Check this room, too," Sid called back to his subordinates. There was another door to the room, one that by its placement, led to the hall. "Seal off that door we came in, then stuff something under the one in here. There's bodies," he warned as an afterthought.

Toffee flipped up a couple of tarps, briefly examined what lay beneath, then let them drop. "Animal bit," he said, then flipped up a third. "That one, too. Lena," he called into the other room. "Can you at least remember if there was animal research down here?"

A beam of light rounded the doorpost and shone right into Toffee's eyes. He didn't flinch away.

"Not until you showed up," said the chief of communications, then very sweetly. "That was a different building." She ignored the bodies and moved towards the far door.

Toffee flipped another tarp.

"What are you expecting to find?" asked Sid.

"I want to see how many of the bodies were experimented on."

"What?" Sid moved to get a better view of the corpse. "You said they were animal-bit."

"They were. This guy got really mauled. But animals don't do this," he pointed at a section of the man's head. Despite the body's decay it was still possible to make a place above the ear where a patch of tissue, a few centimetres across, had been surgically removed. "The first two have bits of the skull gone."

"What was going on here? Brain research? Doesn't seem like they had the right equipment for that."

The rest of the team entered the morgue, searching for any hole not stuffed. Sid dropped the tarp and helped with the search. There was nothing in the room that added to their knowledge. It was simply a storage facility, and not a very good one. It must have smelled really bad to the people who had worked near it. When the proofing was all checked, the broken door held in place by two stools and packed all around by stuffing torn from a third, the crew became aware of their own states. Caps and Toffee were covered. Bits of innards glistened in the lamplight, patches of blood-matted fur stuck to their clothing. Noah had similar remains near the bottom of his pants. They all had something on them, except Lena.

"We need to wash up," said Darcy, "and tend to wounds."

"There might be some distilled water in one of these rooms," offered Lena.

"Did anyone grab a first aid kit?" asked Caps, noticing his injuries as if they'd just appeared.

There was a general shaking of heads.

"There's got to be plenty of them down here, what with all the labs," said Sid. "Although, there might not be much stuff in them."

Exhaustion seemed to take them all at the same time. Caps leaned back against a workstation and slid to the floor. Lena sat down next to him and collapsed into his shoulder, oblivious to the gore, dried and drying, that clung to every part of him.

"We can't stop now," said Sid, eyeing a stool regretfully. "If we're going to hole up here, and it looks like that's what's going to happen, we need supplies. Two groups. Caps, Lena, you're with me. Noah, Toffee, go with Darcy. I think we all know what we need."

"This is our hotel room?" asked Caps. "Isn't there a lounge or something down here? Something with a couch at least?"

"People worked in here for a long time after the lights went out. I don't see them lying around, that tells me this room is secure."

"Uh-huh," Caps wasn't buying it. "Where's the food? A chocolate bar wrapper, maybe? They didn't eat here. I don't see a pile of clothes bunched up in a pillow. They didn't sleep here either."

Sid's head drooped. He rubbed his brow for a few seconds. "We'll meet back here then. If there's a better place, I'm sure we'll find it. Look for keys on these bodies. I want these doors as intact as possible. Darcy, go right from here. We'll go left."

He picked up a marker from where it sat on the ledge of an easel. He uncapped it and tried to write. Its dry tip scratched pointlessly across the paper. He tried another one, same thing.

"You want us to mark arrows or something?" asked Toffee.

"That's the idea. No use getting lost again."

"I know exactly where we've been," the hunter shook his head derisively, then moved to unjam the door. "Darcy, step to it. I need some rest."

Caps held the lamp aloft, like an old coal miner, or Sherlock Holmes, peering through a London fog. He imagined that he looked cool, in a period sort of way. Except for all guck on him. He was certain one of the shotgun blasts had cooked the stuff to his skin. Dried bits of it flaked off as he scratched his cheek. They'd passed a few locked doors, and the Boss was adamant about finding keys. They'd found themselves in a hall of small offices, tiny things really, no bigger than large storage closets. Unlike the labs, there were names on these doors, plastic strips in cheap metal frames, easy to put in, easy to replace.

"Holy shit!" Caps stopped in place, the lantern gently swinging off its momentum.

The name on the door was Dr. M. Freeland.

"Do you think?" asked Caps.

"Can't be the same person," said Lena. "I never saw him on campus."

"Wasn't it a big campus?"

"Familiar faces stand out, no matter how vague. He never mentioned UBC. Ever."

"He did to me," said Sid, "when he told me about these panels he knew about. Never said he was a prof. Is it locked?"

Caps tried the handle. It was stiff, but it turned. The three of them stood outside the door, as if the rapist's ghost might be waiting behind it. Caps chuckled, then opened the door.

A mote of dust whorled in the lamplight. A small desk sat against the near wall, papers piled high, books lining one corner, held in place by a stapler that doubled as a bookend. A dented file cabinet, two drawers high, was wedged between the far wall and the chair. Three coat hooks had been spiked into the concrete. A lab coat hung from one them. There were three framed degrees hung from one wall, amid a circus of cartoons clipped from newspapers, or photocopied from books. They ranged in content from "Dilbert" to "Far Side."

"No way is this our guy," said Caps, reading a cartoon in which a pair of rhinos were doing something hideous to a tourist. "Y'know, I think Gary Larson may have been the greatest prophet of our generation. Dogshit! This is our Freeland."

"Is there a picture?" asked Sid.

"No, this bachelor degree. It's from the University of Regina. I have this pen of Freeland's from there. Going to make paint out of it one of these days."

"Then who's this guy?" Lena had her flashlight trained on a picture on the desk. It showed a thin, brown-haired man with a woman and a little girl. It was a studio shot, nicely lit, velvet background.

It was difficult for all three of them to move inside the office, but Caps and Sid maneuvered to look at the photo.

"Friends of his, maybe a brother," said Sid.

"Nope," Caps rebuffed. "Freeland said he was an only child, just like Jesus."

Another frame held three pictures, smaller, in ovals. The woman was in the centre, flanked by two pictures of the girl. A few metal figurines of British soldiers stood beside the frame, standing guard with painted muskets.

"This is just weird," said Caps, fingering a soldier. "I don't know what I expected, but cartoons and toys…"

"People changed," said Sid. "People changed a lot."

"Yeah, but this is…you'd think they're be one crucifix, or maybe a Bible quote. There's a stuffed rabbit over there, a cute one."

The described object was a gray-and-white plush toy, with big button eyes and a yellow bow tie. It was shoved into the space left between the filing cabinet and the wall closest to it. Stuffed in beside it was a tiny denim knapsack.

Lena wrenched a desk drawer open. It scraped along its guides. A pile of papers, small photos paper clipped to the top of each one, obscured what lay beneath. Lena dropped them on the desk. Under those was a textbook and a collection of pencils with broken tips. Caps fingered through the papers. They were applications for security passes. The usual vital statistics were there, department designation, personal histories, references.

"Hey," Caps lifted one of the papers by its edge. The photo was of a blue-eyed man, chubby, with thin blond hair. "This is Freeland…but…wow!" He held the application up to Lena. "Sweetheart, I'd like you to meet Edward Tremmel."

Lena took the page, studied it, then handed it to Sid.

Sid scanned the document, then flipped it up to read the sheet of paper clipped behind it. He blinked a few times, then leaned forward, supporting his weight on the desk. "He lied. He lied to all of us. He wasn't a doctor…he didn't even have a degree. He lied about who he was…he even lied on his application here."

Sid's cheeks sank in. He seemed to fold in on himself. It scared the hell out of Caps.

Caps took the application from the Boss's loose grip. He read the second page, it was written in a loose scrawl.

Dennis, I was a little late on checking references. According to U of C, he didn't graduate, he was asked to leave under "questionable circumstances." I'm not putting through his badge, and I want him off the team.

"Look, Boss," said Noah, "just because Freeland… Tremmel…lied about who he was, doesn't mean he lied about the panels."

Sid's recovery was almost instantaneous. "You're right. Why not be a doctor if nobody can prove otherwise?" He shoved papers around on the desk. Most of them had to do with photovoltaics, circuit diagrams, comparisons of masking materials, yield ratios…he uncovered a day-by-day calendar. It had a mock-helpful phrase at the top, "Don't put off till tomorrow what you can avoid all together." The date was June 10th. There were two notes on it. One was; "Meeting, 8:30," the other was; "Judy and Sam, 10:00."

On a hunch, Lena stooped and examined the backpack. The name "Samantha," was embroidered into the denim in pink lettering.

"They were here, his wife and daughter. They came to visit him." Lena was choked with grief for a perfect stranger.

Sid tore his eyes from Lena and resumed searching the desk. Caps took the backpack from her and for some reason known only to him, began to paw through it.

"This is it," said Sid, holding up a sheet of equations. At the bottom a large number was written in blue ink and circled in red. "Thirty-two percent. That was the number Freeland…well you know who I mean…always barked at me. Solar panels with a thirty-two percent yield. Unprecedented he said."

"I can do you one better," said Caps, holding out a fold-creased sheet of graph paper.

It was a map, drawn in blue crayon. It showed a few corridors, a crooked door or two, and a broken-line path from "Daddy's office," to "Daddy's lab." A crude, but recognizable doodle along the edge showed a smiling sun beaming down on a group of rectangles.

"We'll meet with the others, then follow this," said the Boss. "Thank you, Samantha Freeland."

On the way back, Lena allowed Caps to get ahead of them, so she could have a quiet word with Sid.

"I'm sorry about getting us lost. I was only here a few times."

"That's fine, Lena. You did well."

"I…I saved us, earlier, didn't I? Knowing where we could get through the bush."

"Yes, you did."

"Like, maps are good, but you needed someone who could remember things quickly, and stuff."

"Yes."

"So you did need me for this?"

"Of course I did. What made you think I didn't?"

"Oh, nothing. Thanks, Boss."

"You're welcome, although I don't know for what."

They met back at the lab. Darcy's group had not only found keys, they'd also found the sleeping area. Caps rushed out the truth about Edward Tremmel, speaking as if he alone had made the discovery. Although Sid was anxious to see his panels, as was Noah, the Boss decided to set up camp first, so to speak.

It was, or had been, a meeting room. Metal chairs were stacked in the hall outside in order to make room for mismatched cushions stripped from various places, laid out end to end. There were four of these "beds." There was another kerosene lamp and a few portable burners. Junk-food wrappers littered the floor, as well as other odds and ends: some coins, a watch, some pens, and a woman's corpse. Like the body of Dr. Holland, this one also had a small glass vial in close proximity. Toffee made a casual point of drawing it to Lena's attention. Noah and Darcy moved the body out into the hallway. It wasn't the first time moving dead for either of them. When they returned, Toffee was already on one of the beds, fast asleep.

Big plastic bottles from a water cooler lined one wall. Two of them were full, the seal standing the test of time. Using it sparingly, Lena went to work cleaning off her boyfriend. He stripped to the waist, then to his underwear. The way Lena calmly picked bits of fur off and dropped them in a pile both surprised and impressed Noah. They didn't talk much, not out of consideration to the sleeping hunter, but because they needed their energy just to keep going. Sid watched the proceedings from another of the beds. His eyes drooped occasionally.

Noah took one of the lanterns and moved outside to the hall, taking a chair down from the stack. Someone had to sit on guard duty. He rubbed his face with a damp rag, listening for the telltale scampering of animals in the ceiling, or along the hard floor of the hallway. Toffee had pointed out that dust levels indicated nothing had stirred in this basement in years. The fact that the man had just plunked down and gone to sleep, not even taking off the blade, gave Noah a feeling of security. Soon, his own lids began to close.

"Wake up, sun boy," said Darcy, standing over his chair.

"I wasn't...I was just resting my eyes. How's Caps?"

"Fine. Everything superficial. Your turn."

"For what?"

She tapped her palm with a first aid kit.

"I don't need that."

"That's my decision to make. Lose the coveralls."

Noah stood, too tired to enjoy Darcy's attention. He unzipped the front of his coveralls and clumsily stripped them off. Underneath he wore a frayed pair of shorts.

"I'm proud of you," said Darcy, holding the lamp over his legs once he'd sat down again.

"Huh?"

"The way you handled yourself in the Pig. I'd expected you to..."

"Faint?"

"No. Yes. I'm sorry." She tore open a tiny envelope, removing the antiseptic alcohol wipe from within.

"It's only dogs that make me...made me faint. I don't think it will happen anymore."

"Thanks to Caps?"

"Actually, I think it was thanks to Toffee."

She paused at this. "Well, whoever gets the credit, you did good."

She knelt by his side and cleaned dried blood off his leg. There wasn't that much of it.

"If you want to be proud of someone, it should be Len," said Noah, a little more conscious of her other hand resting above his knee. "I can't believe she didn't freak."

"She did, kind of. It was the rat, the one that bit you. She said getting her hands on it, being able to strike back, made her feel in control. I think she might still be holding onto it though, if I hadn't taken it away from her."

A long strand of Darcy's hair tickled the inside of his thigh as she bent close to examine the wound. His lethargy was banished, if not in his whole body, then certainly his loins. Warm breath blew on his skin, and he was suddenly embarrassed by the bulge that was forming in his shorts. Closing his eyes tightly, he pictured animals rushing at him. It almost did the trick.

"You were very lucky," she said, looking up at his face. "Oh, did I hurt you?" she asked, catching his expression.

"No! No, I'm just tired. How lucky am I?"

"No tearing, just punctures. Won't even scar. You can suit up again, if you want. I'm thinking we should hunt up some clean clothes."

"I'll put my coveralls back on for now. Are we crashing? What's watch rotation?"

Darcy gathered the kit together and stood, releasing a long sigh. "I'll go wake Sid up and ask him. I figure if Toffee sacked out, we're pretty safe." She studied Noah's face for a moment, then turned to re-enter the meeting room.

Noah hoped that if she'd caught him blushing, she'd just chock it up to excitement.

"Wait, Darcy…"

"Yes?"

"Do we have to rat-proof the room?" he asked, shrugging on his coveralls.

"Already done."

"That was fast, I must have conked out."

"Oh, we didn't do it. Some sort of insulation gunk was sprayed over steel wool. Real pro job."

Lena came into the hallway, Caps on her heels.

"Lena, we can check later."

"You don't have come with me, I'm not going to get lost again."

"Yeah, like I'd let you wander the halls alone."

Their voices faded as they turned a corner, then a fire door opened and closed, and the discussion vanished completely.

"I'm too tired to care," said Darcy, looking after her friends. "Yeah, our little sleep room here ain't the Pit, but it'll do for a night."

Noah wanted to tell her something. Instead, he asked her a question. "What if we were stuck down here for a while?"

"Don't worry, we won't be."

"I'm not worried. Hypothetically, if we were stuck down here, how long could we make it?"

Darcy cast her eyes at the meeting room. "We've got a few days worth of water. There'll be more water down here, Sid would figure out how to get us more anyway. Toffee and I could pop our heads out a window once in a while and shoot some food. If we leave out the sanity factor, we could survive down here for months."

Noah nodded, his expression sombre. "Thanks."

"How long can you stay awake?"

Noah mentally acknowledged the goose flesh that still covered his thighs. "I'll be up for a while." He stood and peered into the room as Darcy selected a cushion trail and lay down.

The Boss, though supine, was awake. His eyes met Noah's, then he rose and, after sparing a glance for his chief of security, stepped outside and gently closed the door.

"I heard your discussion with Darcy. I'm sorry to make you keep this secret."

"I understand. You hope it won't matter. I...I think it will."

Sid tugged at a chair, then simply pushed his back against the wall and slid down into a comfortable squat. "I think it will, too. Here," he handed Noah the sheet of paper he took from Freeland's—the real Freeland's—office. "This is what we're looking for, right?"

Noah scanned the equations and, to his eyes, poorly drawn diagram. As awake as his body had become, his mind was very tired. There were formulas he only half remembered, and a few notations that he didn't understand at all. It was like reading a language for which he'd only learned two thirds of the letters. As much as he wanted to put it away, in wasn't within his capacity to delay an answer to the Boss, so he worked at the scrawls, prying at them with his memory, undoing knots with his brain. Sid waited quietly, his eyes half closed.

After a few minutes of agonizing, Noah realized why he couldn't follow the equations. It was because what he had in front of him was only a fragment of the whole. "This is just part of it. Were there any more papers like this?"

"A mountain of them. Guess what you're doing tomorrow."

"I could get started now."

"Tomorrow. I saw how you struggled with that. Can you tell if it's sound?"

"Thirty-two percent yield from a cell? Bacon said it had never been done. Our best at the Pit were twenty-one. Freeland's...what's his real name?"

"Tremmel."

"Tremmel. Actually it really was Freeland's. Okay, Freeland's cell, the one Tremmel claimed was his, was twenty-five percent. Now that surprised me, because I always thought the ceiling was twenty-four. Australian guy did that. This is along the same lines, KOH-etched inverted pyramids, same passivation layer..."

"Noah, is it what we're looking for?"

"Can I go with a seventy-five percent yes?"

"That'll do for now. And the other?"

Noah scanned the ceiling, imagining what lay in wait above the ground. "I can do it…but Boss, there's so many teeth up there. Sooner or later…"

"Exactly. We'll worry about it later." He stood, pushing the top of Noah's leg to lever himself up. "You did your job, back in the Pig. Bacon would be proud."

"Would he? I got bit."

Sid ran a lazy finger down the scars that lined his cheek. "No, you didn't."

A door opened. Lena and Caps appeared from around the corner. He had his arm around her, but she shrugged out of it when she saw Noah and the Boss.

"Well?" asked Sid.

Lena held up two small glass vials. "These were by the bodies in halls, the ones we didn't check before. Dr. Kwon and Dr. Sulrami. Toffee was right. Some kind of suicide pact. I guess they went off to different places and…" She mimed tipping a vial to her lips.

Her eyes were downcast as she and Caps went into the sleeping quarters. Sid shut the door again.

"How do you feel now, knowing that the previous tenants here made that choice?"

"It's depressing, Boss. Really depressing."

"They didn't have guns, Noah. More importantly, they didn't have experience living in this world. Anyway, we'll find out tomorrow. Hang on, I'll get my gun. Pull off a chair for me, will you?"

Noah hefted a chair off the stack, then dumped it beside his, the metal legs clattering as they hit the floor. He understood the real reason for Sid delaying their visit to the fabrication lab. What he'd forgotten in his fatigue, was so did Toffee.

36. Done Deal

"So give me the run down, Mickey." Seth adjusted his sling as the mechanic stuffed tools into a belt slung over his shoulder.

"It's not a lemon. Some of the maintenance looks like it was done pretty recently. There's some improvisation here and there, but it's solid."

Seth's head gave a little shake, the mechanic's report not fitting in with his picture of the situation. "Did you check out the stuff in the trailer? The refrigeration unit and the cold tank?"

"Same thing. This is one hell of a deal you got, Seth. The defences on this truck are top notch. Look at this," he reached under the dented bumper of the rig and fiddled with a catch. The metal swung down on a hinge, revealing three strands of razor wire, strung between a pair of adjustable arms. Mickey turned a crank and the arms extended, spreading the wire out in an angled formation, like a staircase.

"This can be operated from the inside." He plucked the middle wire, eliciting a high-pitched tone. "This'll cut the ground stuff to shit, even when going slow. And this," he fiddled with a circular plate forced into the grill area. "Hmmm. I got this open earlier. I'll figure it out. There's a gun in here. Rifle, I think. Can't aim the sucker, 'cept by moving the cab. Still, you could shoot out some big critters, or maybe the back end of a car."

Seth stepped up to the running board and hauled on a window grill to hoist himself up. The interior wasn't too smelly, and the seats were in good condition. A drawn curtain hid the sleeping area. "This sounds like it's better than the two rigs we lost."

"It is, and it isn't," Mickey gave up on the gun portal. He ran a hand through thinning red hair, then dropped the belt from his shoulder and strapped it on in a single, smooth motion. "It's less fuel efficient. Even without driving it, I can tell you that. The underbody armour is overzealous if you ask me."

"Fisher's mentality," said Seth, swinging himself into the cab. "For them, the danger comes up from below. But from a structural point of view, this is a better truck?"

"Yes. Burle would've approved."

Seth swung back out and dropped to the ground. He still felt like he could have made a better deal. Burle was gone, but his knowledge remained, crammed haphazardly into the head of the store's janitor and stock boy—although it was odd calling a man in his late fifties a stock boy—Gerald Boone. The problem was getting him to talk. The man treated Seth like a usurper to the throne. Ten years in the Pit, nine of them under Burle, Boone truly felt the position should have fallen to him.

Seth's first deal as chief of stores was to buy the man's favour. He didn't want to waste time working out a relationship. The price tag was one bottle of scotch. Once Boone's mouth got going, it was as inescapable as an avalanche. Burle talked nonstop apparently, said some of the same things over and over again. With a little guidance, Boone's meandering tales bore fruit. The fishers had six trucks, a veritable fleet. True, they did a great deal more trading than the Pit, but then that was because they had to. Burle felt they had a fuel source in addition to what they got by trade, but they rigorously guarded its secret. Should Seth have traded SatCom equipment for access to the fishers' gas? No, that didn't seem right either. The travel involved in getting it would be prohibitive, unless the fishers were willing to deliver it by the truckload. The rig didn't look like one he'd send out to leave behind, but that made sense because the fishers didn't know about Gascan's embargo, or the Pit's war. Therefore, they didn't know the Pit needed a truck. So what else was there? He'd caught an expression on Dom's face when the truck was tabled as payment. It was fleeting, the man was good at keeping his features set, but Seth had recognized that brief drooping of lids as relief.

Bruno and Dom, freshly showered and carrying skinbags—care packages from Roshi—entered the pool. Both men wore the pained expression of the thoroughly hung over.

"Do you want me to explain the toys?" asked Bruno, eyeing the razor-wire cowcatcher.

"Tell Mickey," said Seth, "or better yet, tell Daniel. It's his rig now."

"I already did, I just like bragging about it."

The Pit's last expendable vehicle had been loaded with the SatCom components hours ago, as well as fuel and medicine. Dom was already inside, squirming in the passenger seat, testing its comfort value. Bruno was standing by the rig, giving it a last farewell.

"Your friend seems anxious to get on the road," said Seth. "I thought you'd want to stay a couple of days."

"I do. Dom's got a baby on the way. At least six weeks to go yet, but he's anxious."

"What type of security do you have for that?"

"Three rooms that absolutely nothing can get into. Not a pipe, not a vent. It's stuffy, but it's safe."

"How many kids do you have now?"

"Me? How do you know about my kids?"

"I meant your settlement, not you individually."

"Oh. Not enough. Never enough. I couldn't do it, live in this childless place."

Seth looked at the floor regretfully. It wasn't something he thought about often, because it brought him nothing but pain. He'd had both a wife and children, but that was before. His military service had allowed them little time together. Far too little time, in retrospect. His musings were shoved aside by a realization that popped out of his subconscious like a forgotten song lyric.

"You're the chief of transport, right?"

"Transport master, same thing."

"What's Dom?"

"He floats, sometimes he's with me, sometimes with the hunt master."

"Is he your heir apparent?"

"Hmmpph. Haven't heard that one for a while. He'd replace either me or Quinn. Quinn's the hunt master."

"Which one of you was up for bid?"

Bruno's eyebrows climbed for his hairline. "How do you mean?"

"It was Dom, wasn't it? You had no idea we'd want a rig. We might need another hunter though."

"Maybe, maybe not. Doesn't matter. Deal's done. I guess we'll be going now."

Seth wondered at a world where communication equipment held such high value. The fisher's captain would know Dominic could never bring a pregnant wife or child to the Pit, and yet he'd been willing to do that to the man anyway. And Dom, it appeared, would have gone through with it if he'd had to. This Captain of theirs inspired some loyalty. Would Seth leave his family on Sid's orders? He didn't think he would.

"I don't think I could have taken a man from his expecting wife," said Seth.

"Would've been your job, right? Do you have your next order ready?"

"Can't plan that far ahead right now. Give us a shout when you've set this up. We'll talk about it then."

Bruno gave the truck's grill an affectionate pat, then moved to join Dom in the car.

"Empty roads," said Seth.

The airlock doors groaned open, and the car moved beyond them. The big doors slammed shut again. Seth felt a wave of fatigue take him. He sat on the truck's running board and waited for it to pass. It would be just his luck for Patel to walk in at that moment, that I-told-you-so look stamped on his face. The chief of stores perceptions were so dimmed he didn't hear the approaching security officer until a hand fell on his shoulder.

"You'll have to leave," came the woman's voice from behind.

Seth raised his head, it was Patricia.

"Oh, excuse me, sir. Guess I didn't see the sling."

"It's still Seth, Patricia," he said, smiling weakly, "not sir. Why do I have to leave?"

"Well, you don't. Unless you want to. Mickey, are the keys in the hunters' van?"

"Yes. What's going on?"

"You have to leave, Mickey."

"Hey, I'm acting chief, this is my pool."

"Take a break, Mick," said Daniel striding over from the far door. "Go somewhere for about half an hour, please?"

Mickey grimaced at being ejected from his demesne, temporary as that position might be, and left the pool, the tools in his belt clicking with each step.

"Is that it?" called Purty's voice from the hall.

"We're locking Brennon McKay outside. You want to leave?"

"Locking…why?"

"He killed George Lethy. Crushed his windpipe. They've never liked each other, but things got worse, fast."

"Hey, Chief," Purty called again, "are we clear?"

"Seth?" Daniel raised an eyebrow.

"I'll stay." He had no desire to watch a man's final exit, but he felt too dizzy to walk, and was too proud to admit it. He'd seen this before, he'd even participated in lockouts in the past.

"We're clear," called Daniel.

Brennon was led in, Purtricil in front, Chiu-Keung behind. The man's eyes were red, as if from crying. A leather thong bound his hands behind him. Patricia opened the passenger door of the hunters' van, and Daniel, handgun held loose but ready, motioned for Brennon to get in. This was usually a breaking point, and Brennon didn't disappoint.

"I never meant to kill him. He attacked me, I was just defending myself."

"You could have moved away from the bars, Brennon. Get into the van."

Reason would be followed by indignation;

"You don't have the right to do this! That bitch isn't the boss. Halbert would never let you do this!"

Daniel simply motioned towards the van again.

The next step was pleading. Some people held themselves together, this guy looked like a gusher. Seth braced himself.

"Daniel, please! Please, you know me. You know I'd never do this on purpose. Daniel please! Daniel, pl–" the rest of the implorement was lost in a wracking sob.

At a look from Daniel, Purty and Chiu shoved Brennon up and into the van. Chiu got into the back, while Daniel moved around to take the wheel. For the second time that hour, the airlock doors slid open. When they closed, it seemed to Seth they did so with an air of finality not present when the fishers left.

"You ever think about the hypocrisy of it?" asked Purty, sitting down beside Seth.

"What hypocrisy would that be?"

"Lethy's dead. No family, not that many friends. You know what we're doing with him. Brennon's alive, so we're hauling him out there and leaving him to nature. Why don't we shoot him and just keep him here?"

"It comes down to who pulls the trigger," replied Seth. "No point in wasting ammo on a firing squad to, you know, spread the sin around. Plus, how much can Odega's critters eat?"

"Some people have a tooth pit inside the settlement. I heard D'Abo does."

"That's not for body disposal," said Seth, finally feeling capable of motion. "That's for gambling and entertainment. He says he only uses convicted criminals, but I'll bet the punishment doesn't always fit the crime."

"He tried to set up a deal with us a while back. Any time we wanted to lock someone outside, we could trade them to him instead. Apparently he gets a lot victims that way."

"As well as a ton of information. I pity that man."

Purtricil's eyes widened in surprise. "Pity him? Gascan? He's like a devil or something. You should hate him."

"He's got no soul, my friend," Seth stood, then sat down again, heavily. He hadn't recovered as much as he'd thought. "Purty, I'd like to be alone right now, if that's okay."

Sweat stood out in a fine sheen across the man's dark-skinned brow. Down, up, down again. Both hands pressed against the floor, an IV tube extending from one of them, he strained at his push-ups at the same time as he strained his ears for any sound of approach. The catheter that ran up beneath his gown and into his ureter was even more uncomfortable and unwieldy than the IV, but he knew that if he pulled it out, he'd never bring himself to put it back in. Down, up, two more, one more, done. He dropped heavily to the floor, his broad chest flattening against the cold tile. The man rolled over onto his back and raised one leg, flexing and extending it from the knee. He had to get his strength back and formulate a plan of escape. As long as his enemies, once trusted friends, thought him incapacitated, there'd be nobody guarding him directly; but maybe that, like their former benevolence, was a ruse. Maybe someone stood just out of sight beyond the exit door.

He was thirsty, as he often was. A plastic jug of water was always beside his bed, in case, he supposed, he awoke when no one was there to bring it to him, but he didn't drink from it. They checked the water level in that flask. They'd know then. The other source of liquid was at the far end of the room, and would mean wheeling over the IV stand, carrying the catheter bag. He'd be too far from the bed to make it back under the covers if someone appeared. He'd be caught red handed. Or yellow handed as the case may be. Still, he was quite thirsty, and no one had entered for some time now. He'd made the trip before, gone farther even, during his explorations. Undoing the clips that held the catheter bag to the bed frame, he gripped the IV stand and prepared to make the trip. He heard a door open. Hastily clipping the bag to the frame, he hurried himself under the covers as quietly as he could, and closed his eyes.

Dr. Patel washed his hands in his examination room's sink and mentally signed a death certificate.. George Lethy was a corpse before Patel had even reached the security office. It wasn't the crushed windpipe that had killed him, however. The man had a massive heart attack, most likely as a result of panic from not being able to breath. He'd need to do an autopsy to confirm that belief, but it wasn't necessary. Even if he had been able to save Lethy, the man's attacker would still have been locked outside. The decision had been hard on Sara, but she'd warned both men personally, one topside, then later the other, coming into the cells to make her intentions clear. She'd truly felt the words would be enough. They would have been enough coming from Sid.

The doctor sat at his desk and pulled open the top drawer. He removed a metal flask and unscrewed the top, but instead of drinking, he replaced the cap and put the flask away again. He couldn't afford to be less than a hundred percent if he was needed again, and his suspicion was that need could happen at any moment. Less than one week, and things were falling apart. The lower light levels, no personal electricity allotments, topside on lockdown…these all added to the vague discomfort, the uncertainty that was growing in the Pit's denizens. Rumors snowballed in the dark halls, old tensions surfaced. At least Roshi had some luxuries brewing in the kitchen. If the cook had any sense, he'd forego his plans to save the lobsters for a victory feast in Sid's honour, and cook them up as soon as possible.

Sara was going to make an announcement when dinner came, a carefully worded lie that would hopefully expel the need to name a traitor. She wasn't happy about it, but she saw the need. It was rare that Dr. Patel questioned Sid's decisions. Putting Sara in charge was one of those occasions, but not for any lack on Dr. White's part. She was a brilliant woman, caring and practical at the same time, but there was no authoritative presence about her. Daniel was doing his best, as were the other chiefs, to support her position when among others, but if weeks passed without the real Boss's return, things would change.

Dr. Patel stood and moved through the plastic curtain that separated him from the infirmary. One bed, Seth's, needed changing. His nurse, Katriona, was getting lax in her duties. He'd been easy on her of late, conscious of the gradual change in her behaviour. The world was getting to her. For about the millionth time, Patel cursed not having a capable therapist on staff. Even a clergyman would have been welcome, but those were very hard to find. Even harder, it seemed, than doctors.

Dr. Patel plucked at the sheets, comforted to note that there were no bloodstains on them. Not that he'd expected to see any. A few of Seth's black hairs clung to the pillow. The chief of store's hair was going. Slowly, but it was going. The man was thirty-eight, he'd had a good run of it in comparison to some people. Despite a decade away from having television and magazines scream "youth or bust" at people, some vanities were as entrenched as ever. Dr. Patel suddenly felt his fifty-seven years weigh heavily upon him. He'd need to train someone again, that always made him feel younger. Maybe an apprentice could be garnered from somewhere. There were rooms to fill, and two newly vacant bunks in the barracks.

Through the curtain, the flask called to him, luring him with a siren's song that promised temporary comfort. He resisted. What Dr. Patel wanted more than booze was someone to talk to. The fishers had been an enjoyable distraction, but they'd already left. He missed Burle terribly. Sara was too busy for a sit down, and Odega still lay in bed, no sign of regaining consciousness.

Dr. Patel leaned forward and placed his palm on Odega's forehead. It was clammy again, though it didn't feel feverish. One of the man's feet stuck out from beneath the sheets. Katriona must not have pulled the bedding taut after giving Ted his physio.

He needed his nurse back to her old self more than ever, both for himself, and for the Pit.

"Ted," said Patel, picking up the water flask beside the man's bed. It was as full as ever. "I really do wish you'd wake up. You're even more boring now than you were before." He tugged at the blanket, pulling a crease out. "We locked a man outside today. Brennon McKay. Murdered George Lethy, in the cells. Fancy that. Oh, sorry, Ted," he patted the man's belly through the blanket. "Probably don't need to hear that right now, do you? I've been thinking of training someone again. You might want to as well, save me the trouble of looking after your damnable animals the next time you go for a fortnight's nap."

Dr. Patel studied Odega's face, hoping for a flicker of lids, or if not that, then the indication of REM cycle, eyeballs jerking beneath lids, like hyperactive children under a pair of sheets.

"I've got a fresh batch of your favourite. There's a flask of it, right in my desk. Alright then, suit yourself. Thanks for letting me do all the talking, at least we're guaranteed intelligent conversation."

He checked the drip bag, Ted's pulse, and the catheter bag. One of the clips hadn't been properly fastened. He corrected the problem, and with a final tug at Odega's bedding, returned to his office to await the next disaster.

37. Rainbow's End

"Well this isn't good," Sid let the chain fall back against the door. It was heavy, and inconveniently placed. "Darcy, do you have a key for this lock?"

With a quick jingle of metal on metal, Darcy flipped through the ring. "Nope, no padlock key on here."

The chain was looped through the handles of a set of double doors between the Deep Six and Freeland's lab. It was held in place with a thick padlock of hardened steel.

Caps drew his sidearm and aimed it at the lock. The hunter stayed his hand.

"Better to save your ammo, painter."

"Oh, you gonna kick it open?"

The hunter didn't spare Caps a reply. He knelt, and put his ear to the door. "I don't hear anything," he said after a pause. He ran his fingers up the door, along the top, then down the sides. Then he swept them across the metal lip where one door overlapped the other. "Halbert, this door's been hit a few times. There topside access through these?"

"Yes," said Noah, surprising them all. "If we go straight instead of left, past these, one more set of fire doors, and there's stairs to an exit. Onto Agronomy Road."

"And you know this, how?" asked Darcy.

"I looked at that map," he swung his flashlight beam at a yellowed floor plan in a red wooden frame. "It's escape routes in event of a fire."

Lena slapped herself in the forehead.

The Boss moved to the map, meting out his own self recrimination, and tapped the glass with one finger. A sheen of dust fell ghostlike through the flashlight's glare.

"Toffee, is it safe?"

"For now. Don't know about after we open the door. Hunt for the key?"

"No. Is there a weak link?" a rustling of chain, a shake of the head. "Can we bash the lock?"

"If we had a sledgehammer."

"Can anyone pick it?" asked Caps.

Sid looked around, hopeful that someone might indicate in the affirmative. Nobody did. Not that it mattered. That lock hadn't been keyed in almost a decade. The tumblers were probably seized. Sid didn't want the sound of a gunshot to attract attention.

"There's bolt cutters in the van," said Noah.

Caps patted him on the shoulder. "You go get them then. The rest of us'll just stay down here."

"We could take the hinges out," he turned to see the hunter was doing just that.

The hinges were two eight-inch steel pins, screwed in from the top. Toffee had removed his blade and was using it as a torque wrench, the dull edge inserted into the slot at the hinge's top. After a few twists, Toffee extracted the first hinge pin. The second was harder to remove, but the hunter managed without putting the slightest bend in his prosthetic.

"Get ready," he said, grabbing the handle.

Guns came up. Sid was right behind the hunter. With the flame-thrower on his back, he reminded Noah of the fourth Ghostbuster. Though part of Sid's face looked more like the ghosts than the busters.

Toffee pulled the door loose. No daylight shone through the gap. The chain was now the hinge and the hunter swung the door until it leaned against its still-fastened counterpart. Sid threw light down the dark hallway. Past an intersecting corridor, his beam hit closed fire doors.

Toffee in the lead, they stepped through and into this new section of the Walcott Building's basement. Human bones littered the floor. Tooth marks showed where the last vestiges of meat had been scraped away. Clothing had been shredded, a leather wallet was torn to shreds. Petrified faeces were scattered amongst the remains, some in dull yellowish clumps, some in curled pies.

The hunter sniffed the air. "They must have been trapped in here with something, shut those doors," he indicated the far ones, "only to find those ones already chained." He scanned the faeces. "At least three different animals. A couple of dogs and a coon."

"You know your shit," said Caps.

"Okay, people died," said Darcy. "It's awful. Let's get these panels and go home. Sid, have you figured out how we're going to get back in the vehicles?"

"I'm working on it. I'm as eager as you to see our prize."

They passed the skeleton of a large dog on their way to the Freeland's lab. Part of it had been separated, dragged away from the body.

Noah shone his light through a window. The body of a raccoon, some of its desiccated hide still clinging to its bones, was curled up on a desk within the room. There were two large fish tanks, one standing, the other smashed on the floor.

That explains where they got their water, he thought. *Guess the coon was the last hold out.*

On the desk near the raccoon was what appeared to be a human jawbone. It was so small, it could only have been that of a child.

The doors to the lab, predictably, were locked. Darcy had what she felt was the key, but it wouldn't turn very far. At a nod from Sid, Toffee's boot smashed the double wooden doors open.

Noah wished he could do that, kick like the hunter. No bounce back, just one powerful thrust of the leg, throwing the doors aside like they were made of cardboard.

Every light available illumined the room. It was long, it was…empty.

"What the…" Sid took two strides into the room. He spun in all directions, whipping his flashlight about, scanning the ceiling when he ran out of floor and wall. There was a chalkboard, a desk piled with papers, and a workbench covered with same. No panels, or other equipment anywhere. "This can't be it. We must have the wrong room."

"No we don't," said Darcy. She held her lantern up to the chalkboard. Written on it, beneath a horde of mathematical gibberish, was;

"Short on the coffee fund: Freeland, Sulrami (again)."

Noah walked to the far end of the room, his beam picked out a large, discoloured rectangular area on the floor. "This is about the right size, Boss."

"Did someone get here first? Did someone beat us to it? No. Impossible. There'd be evidence."

Caps looked at the spot on the floor Noah had pointed out. If the rectangular area was where panels were stacked...well, there couldn't have been that many panels. If fact, the whole room couldn't have held the amount of panels the Boss had promised. Not if anyone had to actually work in there.

"Maybe the panels were relocated," said Darcy. "They could have been set up outside. Seems kind of dumb to keep the things down here. Those papers on the desk might tell us where to look," she began to rifle through the papers.

Toffee stood in the doorway, a big shit-eating grin on his face. "Don't bother, Halbert didn't expect to find any panels here."

"Yeah," said Caps, looking up from the mark on the floor, "where are they, Boss? They wouldn't be stored in here."

"No, he didn't expect–"

"That's enough, Ethan!"

Darcy froze at the desk, a sheaf of papers clutched between her fingers. Sid's sudden anger made her stomach knot. "Sid, what's going on?"

Everyone faced the Boss now, whose cheeks seemed to be growing darker. Sid turned from the hunter and glared at Noah.

The young man remembered his conversation with the hunter, just before he'd gone tooth crazy. He wanted to step backwards and melt into the wall.

"Tell 'em," said Toffee, "or I will. And don't blame the kid there. I didn't give him much of a choice."

"Sid..." Darcy breathed again.

Lena looked very unhappy, and Caps's eyes darted from Toffee to the Boss, like he was watching a tennis match.

"I didn't expect to find any panels here. Toffee's right. What I did expect was to find silicone wafers, gasses, certain chemicals, and a furnace. A very special furnace."

"Wait a minute," said Caps. "Why did you lie to us about that?"

"I didn't lie," said Sid. "I said we'd come out of here with all the panels we could use. I hoped they'd be here, ready to go. I just didn't expect it."

"So then we were going to what, make them?"

"That's right, we were going to make them."

Caps gestured around the empty room. "How?"

"That was my job," said Noah, quietly.

"You knew about this?" Caps was incensed. "Why didn't you say anything? How were you supposed to make solar panels without power?"

"That was also my job, getting power down here. Yours too. Between the two of us, we could do it."

It was Lena that caught on first. "Boss, how long were you planning to keep us here?"

"Here it comes," said Toffee, his grin, if anything, growing brighter.

"It doesn't matter," said Sid. "The panels aren't here, and neither is the equipment. Let's figure out how to get out of here."

"How long, Sid?" Darcy's voice quiet, so very quiet. "Weeks? Months? How long does it take a panel?"

Noah almost supplied an answer, but stopped himself. Why make matters worse?

"It wouldn't just be us," Sid defended himself. "At first it would be, but once we were situated, some of us could go home, send in replacements."

"And the guardians of the city?" asked Toffee. "You broke radio silence."

"I had to."

"Practically told them our names."

"Ethan..."

"Sure told them where we were–"

"Ethan, shut the hell up!"

The hunter stopped talking and sat down on the corner of the desk. He winked at Darcy, she looked away.

In the middle of the room, the Boss stood like a witch tied to the stake. All eyes burned into him now, except Noah's. The photovoltaic engineer stared fixedly at the floor, his cheeks burning from the shame of guilt by association.

"Why didn't you tell us?" asked Darcy.

Sid spread his hands wide. "Would any of you have come if I had?"

"At least you could have offered us the choice," said Caps, for perhaps the first time not even attempting to hide his displeasure at one of Sid's decisions.

"I...couldn't. I needed all of you on this. I picked the team carefully."

"Yeah, your blindest followers," said Lena bitterly, somehow excluding Toffee from her statement.

"Look, Lena, who are the most important people to you? Hmmm? Richard and Darcy. They're right here. Darcy, the same goes for you. The three closest people to you are right here. I didn't separate us. None of you are sitting at home wondering where your loved ones might be."

"No, we all get to die together," said Caps. "Or did you forget the thousands of teeth topside?"

"We got in, Richard. We'll get out."

"If the vehicles are even drivable. The animals'll be tearing the trucks apart. If not vital cables, then at the very least the upholstery. They'll be pissing in 'em and shitting in 'em. They'll be coming down for us, if they haven't started already."

Sid took a step forward and put his hand on Caps's shoulder. "That may very well be, but we'll still get out of here. I have the utmost faith in each and every one of you."

Caps looked at the Boss's hand like a rat had climbed to his shoulder. He pulled back out of the hand's reach. "But not enough faith to tell us the truth."

Sid looked at each of his subordinates in turn. They looked back, but something vital had been lost. Their unconditional trust in the man was tarnished, broken, possibly beyond repair. There were two exceptions. Toffee's allegiance to Sid was enigmatic at the best of times, and Noah had known the score since the onset of the expedition. In a way, it made him feel superior.

"I'll get us out of here," said Toffee. "You all follow me, and you'll be safe in your beds in less than two days. You can come too, Halbert."

"Like hell," said Darcy, pulling her gaze from the Boss and focusing on Toffee. "You think we'll just come to you like bitches to an alpha?"

"Fine, keep following your daddy. Maybe I'll live long enough to bury your remains."

Darcy jerked to a standing position. The chair she'd been in skidded back and fell over, clattering to the floor. The energy in the room changed that quickly. Gone was the accusation directed at Sid, now it was all about Darcy and the hunter.

Noah put it together in an instant. This was why the hunter had waited so long before springing the secret, though the complete absence of any photovoltaic equipment must have been as much a surprise to him as to Sid. Icing on the cake, really. But the hunter had made an error. Caps and Lena might actually have gone with him at that point, but not Darcy. Never Darcy.

Something above the desk caught Noah's eye. While the chief of the hunters and the chief of security stood locked in a contest of wills, he reached forward and snatched a sheet of paper from where it was stuck to the wall behind the desk. A small corner of it was left behind on the tape.

"Enough, both of you," said the Boss. "Darcy, pick up that chair. Toffee, back off."

"As if she's going to listen to you now," said the hunter, not taking his eyes away from the angry redhead. He could tell she was just looking for a reason to strike.

Noah read the sheet as quickly as he could. The materials had been transferred, but transferred where?

"Darcy…" Sid let the rest of his command hang. This was a critical moment in two ways; if the aggression kept building, Darcy and Toffee would come to blows, and that couldn't be good for anyone. Secondly, if Sid didn't re-establish his authority right away, he might not be able to again. It was for that reason that he chose Darcy to command. Of them all, she was the most likely to obey. And she did. With a gargle of rage, she stepped back and righted the chair. Lena, who stood rigid in the circle of Caps's arms, relaxed a little, and Toffee, watching the chair placed in its proper position, turned away with a look of disgust.

All of this passed Noah by as if he wasn't even there. He was too busy with the last two lines on the torn note.

"Dogshit!" he said. "Boss…"

"Good." Sid ignored him. "You've all stood by while I've misled others in the past, because you knew I was doing it for our greater good. The fact that it was you this time doesn't change my motivation for doing it."

"Boss," Noah persisted, "it's all here." He tapped the page. "Material transfer. The furnace, the wafers, all consigned to Green Day Industries. It was loaded into the back of a trailer on the night of June ninth. It was supposed to be picked up on the tenth. That trailer we saw coming in here, Boss, it's all packed up and ready to go."

Sid reached for the page but Toffee beat him to it, snatching the sheet out of Noah's hand. He scanned it quickly, a swirl of unidentifiable emotions passed across his face.

The Boss took the page gently from the hunter, read it through, then passed it to Caps.

"Richard, what would be involved in hooking up to that trailer and going?"

Caps read the sheet, not believing what had been said until he saw it with his own eyes. "Not a chance," he said. "That trailer will be in the same if not worse condition than the ones in the truck yards. We'd have to take the wheels off the trailer I fixed, and the air hoses, and even then…"

"I get you. Okay, I'm going to let you four talk about me behind my back for a minute. Toffee, come with me, please."

Sid moved back into the hallway. Toffee flicked his eyes at Noah, then squared his shoulders and followed the Boss.

Darcy moved as if she didn't know what to do with herself. First she sat down, then she stood, paced to one side of the room, then returned to the chair. Lena pushed herself away from her boyfriend and stared at wall.

"How long, Noah?" asked Caps.

"Well, that's kind of hard to answer."

Caps grabbed an equation-covered sheet at random from the desk and shoved it under Noah's nose. "Can you read this shit?"

"Yes."

"Don't try to protect the Boss. He dragged you out here like anything else bought and paid for. How long?"

"Weeks," he spoke as if the word had to be dragged from his mouth by a winch.

Caps's lower jaw protruded, as he turned to look in the direction the Boss had gone. "Why the hell do we follow that guy?"

"Because he's Sid," said Darcy, sudden weariness in her voice. "Because he's Sid."

From the darkened hallway came the faint sound of glass breaking. Darcy's head snapped up. "What the hell was that?" She moved to the door, gun at the ready. "Sid!" she whispered loudly. "Sid, was that you?"

The Boss and Toffee returned. Whatever had passed between the two of them didn't show in either of their faces. Sid held the map of escape routes.

"Noah, take all this," he swept his arm at the papers on the lab's desk, "and go to Freeland's office. Darcy, go with him. The rest of you with me. We're going to do something about those teeth. We'll need to unload that trailer and load ours. The quicker we're done, the quicker we're home."

"I've heard that before," said Caps. In spirit he'd already accepted the situation, but he had to get his verbal licks in.

They stood before the double doors, Toffee with his ear to the metal, Sid with the map in one hand and the flamethrower's nozzle in the other.

"Clear," said the hunter. Keys jangled as he worked the stiff lock.

It opened and subdued daylight filtered down stairs at the end of a short corridor. The evidence of animals was there in droppings and urine stains, but these were covered with a thin layer of dust. Cobwebs dangling from the ceiling wafted in the disturbed air.

"I don't think an external door's open," said Toffee, reading the quality of the light.

They moved ahead slowly. Toffee's footfalls were silent, as if the dust on the floor was all he needed to silence his movement. Sid was nearly silent, but their efforts were for naught. Lena had no agility whatsoever in her artificial ankle. She could walk, she could even run, but the hushed footsteps of the men before her was beyond her ability. But even her light offbeat padding was made moot by her boyfriend. Caps had not one iota of the quality known as grace. His every step echoed through the halls, as sure as the imprints of his boots were stamped in the dust.

They approached the bottom of the stairs warily. The hunter had been right. There was a door at the top of the steps, but it was shut. The light issued in from muck-encrusted windows that ran the height of the wall, all the way up to the building's top floor. Toffee motioned for the three of them to wait at the bottom. He ascended to the ground level floor prepared for nothing and everything at the same time. He got nothing. Empty, silent halls, bereft of life, animal or human.

"Clear," he said down the stairs. They moved to the second floor in similar fashion. Toffee first, then the rest.

Near the stairwell was a framed map of the second floor, its orange you-are-here dot about to become grossly inaccurate. Sid broke the glass and stripped the map from the wall. Beside the map's former home was a larger wooden case of the same colour. Empty pegs showed where a fire axe must have been.

Map in hand, Sid took the lead. Toffee forced a quieter gait from Caps with a brief, fierce look. The upper floors were students' facilities. The notices on bulletin boards mounted beside every classroom shouted fabulous deals on new cars, concerts that could not be missed, and tutelage available for everything from physics to a hundred different languages. Roommates were sought and computers offered for sale, as were textbooks and lab manuals two editions out of date.

The ceilings were quite high, and an almost wall-to-wall ventilation duct ran the length of the corridor. Beside and above it were more vents and pipes, steel ribbons that disappeared into the darkness. If the animals wanted in, there was no way to bar their passage. Scattered remains attested to that fact.

"This is good," said Sid, stopping at door 211.

The door, slightly ajar, creaked open at a push. Four rows of ten desks each faced a chalkboard and a podium. Across the room was a bank of windows, the shapes of other buildings vaguely outlined through the dirty glass. Toffee and Sid systematically tested the windows while Caps and Lena guarded the door. Old wooden frames, swelled and warped, refused to budge. Some of the latches had been painted right over, showing that they were stuck fast long before they were abandoned. In one sill a fingernail was embedded in the wood, so hard had its former owner pried at the window. A graphic snapshot of someone's last moments. That someone could be reassembled, at least partially, from the remains on the floor.

Sid winced as Toffee kicked the body aside. He'd caught himself once or twice standing on a bone. Even Lena seemed to regard the dead with no more care than she would a rusted pipe, or dust-covered bench. Acclimatization.

Toffee rubbed dust off the window with his sleeve. The outside of the glass was a nearly opaque film of bird droppings and dirt. After ten years of industrial extinction, the rain that fell on Vancouver was still filthy.

"Anybody pack some duct tape?" asked the hunter.

From the doorway, Caps patted his pockets, then snapped his fingers. "Damn, I knew I forgot something."

Toffee placed his hand against the glass, "There's critters out there. I can't tell how many. We'll have to break this quiet."

"We're in a school," said the Boss. "There has to be tape here somewhere."

"We never did find the third animal," said Noah, sorting sheets of paper under lantern light. He'd also selected a pair of binders, both green, that had more organized notes in them. In actual fact the panels weren't Freeland's baby. Dr. Kwon was the real brain behind the operation, Freeland's task had been to implement it.

"We never did find the third animal," repeated Noah. "We found the big dog and the coon, but not the third one."

Darcy hadn't said a word to him since they'd come to the tiny office. She just leaned in the doorway, watching the darkness.

Noah shook his head and returned to the pages. Dr. Sulrami assisted Freeland in this endeavour. There was no indication of Lena's professor, Dr. Holland, anywhere in the pages. The photovoltaic engineer scanned measurements of short-circuit currents, load resistance and cells per wafer. He understood what he was looking at, but he couldn't retain any of it. His mind, and eyes, kept drifting back to the woman in the doorway. He had work to do and he wanted to ignore her as she was ignoring him. His inability to do so was giving him a headache. Girl germs, girl germs, a child's voice chanted in his head. That was an interesting packet of forgotten thought patterns, to remember a time when he didn't like girls.

Girl germs, he thought back at the memory, *you didn't know the half of it, slugger.*

"Are you going to say something?" Since he couldn't avoid the problem, he decided to confront it.

"Don't you have work to do?" She didn't look at him as she spoke.

Paper crumpled as his hands bunched into fists. He forced them to relax. "Are you mad at me for something?"

Her head whipped up, then she bit back whatever it was she was going to say and resumed her vigil.

What would Caps do here? he asked himself. He'd crack a joke, something extreme.

"Say it, Darcy. Don't make me beat it out of you."

Her reaction was anything but humour. Her slouched posture against the jamb was instantly replaced by harsh rigidity. Her eyes burned.

"Darcy, I was joking!"

It was the tone of voice Noah had used, the intonation that had spurred her reaction. The look on his face, the same one she'd seen in the van, it locked into place and the connection she made appalled her. She took hold of herself, forgetting the vague discomfort she felt around Noah. There wasn't room for it now. Some major damage control had to be done, plus, she wasn't angry at him at all. She was angry because of him. She clicked off her flashlight, killing a beam growing dimmer at a depressing rate.

"Noah, that guy you came to the Pit with…"

"Bacon."

"Yes, Bacon. He was kind of like a father to you, wasn't he?"

"Don't ever let him hear you say that. Wouldn't take that on at all. If anyone asked him, he'd say I belonged to myself and no one else."

"But did you think of him as a father?"

"Uhm, I guess so. More like a father figure."

"I was sixteen when I lost my parents. I grew up real fast after that. I wouldn't…I can't believe I'm telling you this. Sid Halbert is…he's…people thought we were a couple anytime we moved to a new settlement. Some men thought he owned me. He even told some of them that he did, in order to protect me. Sometimes I did pretend to be his lover, or even his wife, depending on the situation. In all that time, he never laid a hand on me, and nobody else did either. He put me first in his decisions, and not once asked for anything in return. What else could he be but my father? And if you ask him in the right mood, he'll tell you that I'm his daughter."

Noah sat transfixed as if by an iron pole. The raw emotion in Darcy's voice overwhelmed him, the closeness she was offering, only moments after looking like she was going to smash his face open. He had no clue what direction she was headed in, he only wanted her to keep going.

"Noah, I'm angry at Sid, and I'm…I'm jealous of you. I'm jealous that Sid trusted you with something that he didn't trust me with. Some parts of me are still sixteen. I'm telling you this because I'm going to say something to you now, and not for the sake of picking on you. Do you understand?"

The wonderful flow of energy had taken a potentially unlikable turn, but he had to know what came next. He nodded.

"You're young, I am too in some ways, so I understand. You need a father figure to replace Bacon. Noah, Toffee ain't it. For your own sake, pick someone else."

It was as if a cold bucket of water had been poured over his head.

"What kind of dogshit is that?" he demanded.

She took in the measure of Noah's affront. "You don't even know you're doing it."

"Doing what?"

"That impression of Toffee. Your voice isn't as rough, but the tone, it's almost eerie. Better than Caps's. Caps just does Clint Eastwood and tries to pass it off as Toffee."

Noah was flabbergasted. Aping Toffee? Darcy pushed ahead before he could utter another denial.

"He's teaching you to fight, you credit him with helping you remember your past. Face it Noah, you think he's cool."

"I do not! He's an asshole, and a bully."

"And he's got a sword for an arm. That's got to appeal to a man who just found his inner child."

Speechless, then defeated, Noah turned his head away.

"Toffee is a capable hunter and a physically powerful man, but he has the heart of a raccoon. You saw what he tried to do back in Freeland's lab. Don't trust him, and certainly don't emulate him."

With a large square of packing tape over the window, Toffee broke the glass with his elbow. They peeled the tape away, careful not to let any shards fall. When the tape was all pulled back, they were greeted by more filthy glass.

"Double pane," said Toffee. "Figures."

He began flicking bits of glass away with his blade, clearing the inner pane completely. When that was done, he taped and broke the second layer. Pure sunlight burst through the ever-widening hole as Sid peeled the tape back. Toffee was the first to look. He pulled his head back and let the others have a go.

A few charred bodies lay on the ground where Sid had cleared their path with the flamethrower. The cab and front half of the trailer was hidden from view, but the back was visible, along with most of the Pig. A pair of kittens chased each other around one of the van's back tires. A large mother cat sat lazily by, occasionally hissing at a dog that came too close. The raccoons had retired, as had most of the rats, though a few scampered back and forth beyond notice of the cat. Some squirrels remained, but the rest of the creatures seemed to have vanished back into the trees surrounding the buildings. Down the wall from the van, the trailer sat like a rusted treasure chest. There was nothing printed on it to indicate its contents, but it had to be the one, it just had to be.

"We'll build a firewall," said Sid, looking around the room. "Let's hit some janitor's closets. Get everything flammable we can, maybe some stuff from downstairs. We'll need to find the fire axes, that'll make the job go quicker. Take a last look at the room as it is. We're about to renovate."

"That's infinity, right?" asked Darcy, pointing to a number eight that lay on its side beneath the notation f(x).

"Right, here it means as f of x..."

"That means function of x?"

"Yes. As f of x gets closer to zero, than x gets closer to infinity. I said that backwards, but you get the idea."

"No, actually I don't."

She'd taken an interest in the work partially to distract Noah from the heavy conversation they'd just had, but also as an excuse to stay within the false security of the lantern's illumination. Her flashlight had maybe minutes worth of juice left in it, and she didn't like having half her body exposed to darkness. If anything suddenly came through the door, she'd be ready for it. Noah leapt at the chance to explain things to her, but her simple question concerning a formula had led to a hunt through textbooks that lined the desk's edge, as Noah attempted to acquaint her with what he called the basics.

"It's very simple, actually. Okay, you know..."

"Stop. The last three times you said, 'okay, you know,' I didn't." She flipped the book closed, blowing a few sheets of paper off the desk.

"Well," Noah started, bending in the chair to retrieve the papers, "maybe when we get back to the Pit I can teach you under better circumstances."

She laughed, surprising herself as much as Noah. "I said this to my grade-ten math teacher, and I'll say it again. There is no way I am ever going to need this stuff." She scanned the disarray of research material on the desk, some handwritten, some neatly typed, all indecipherable. "You really get this stuff, don't you? You're not just putting on a big act."

"What? Too young to be smart?" his tone was only slightly defensive.

"Well, yes and no. Too young to be this educated. Not back then, but now. There's no schools outside the hearth, so to speak. Do all the panel jockeys trained at Underbel come out like you?" She tapped one of the framed degrees. "If this was old world, would you have one of these?"

"No and no. Bacon and Grearson taught me because I was willing to learn it. And I'd need to know a whole lot more about a whole lot more to get one of those degrees. Bacon knows everything. Look, I'm enjoying this conversation, and I really mean that, but I have to go through this stuff."

"Why? Let's find a sack or something and bag it all. You can sort it out at the Pit."

"That's...that's a great idea."

"There's some big plastic bags in the suicide squad's lab," said Caps, scaring the hell out of both of them.

"Very funny," said Darcy, recovering instantaneously.

"I didn't think so," said Noah, picking himself up off the floor.

"How the hell did you sneak up on me?"

"Elementary, my dear Darcy, I've been studying crater-nose. Plus," he looked down at his feet and waggled his bare toes, "I took my boots off. Let's go. Sid sent me to collect some stuff."

It was quick work. They obtained a few empty plastic bags from the graveyard, hardly paying any attention to the bodies under the tarps. Caps loaded a bag with bottles both full and empty, some with definitely flammable substances in them, some with possible. He carried the bag carefully, conscious of the glass tinking together with every step.

"They sure were diligent," said Noah, turning pages over on one of the easels. He couldn't tell how many experiments the researchers had done, all without the benefit of a proper animal research equipment. They sealed themselves in with what they had and went to work. "Too bad they gave up hope," he let go and the wad of paper slapped down against the easel.

"They didn't give up hope," said Darcy absently.

"What makes you say that?" asked Caps. "I think they were just working here to come up with the quickest poison they could make."

"They all had their name tags on, Caps. I don't think security was too stringent at the end, why would they have their ID on unless it was so people could identify them later? They may have given up hope for themselves, but not for mankind. Weird that we haven't found any suicide notes, or some sort of layman's explanation for whatever it was they were doing."

While Lena watched at the window, Sid and Toffee had hauled most of the desks out into the hallway where they could muffle the noise of destroying them. Caps returned with Noah and Darcy in tow, two bags of bottles, and one bag crammed with books and papers. Darcy then found where the axe had been relocated—it was near a staircase—and gave it to Sid. With swings of the axe and Caps and Noah enthusiastically hurling desks at the floor, they succeeded in changing scholastic furniture into a pile of kindling. This wood was piled up in the classroom, and saturated with flammable liquids.

"Whew, what a stench," said Caps, shaking the last few drops out of a jug of industrial-strength cleaner.

"Let's open the windows," said Sid.

"Those animals below are going to hear that," said Lena.

"I think they'll catch on anyway when we start throwing wood at them. Everybody load up, you know the plan."

Swinging the axe one-handed, Toffee smashed the windows, busting the next one before the glass from the previous one had hit the ground outside. Animals stared in confusion or interest at first, then with rage as they saw the human beings appearing at the broken glass. Smelly bits of wood arced from above as the Deep Six hurled their burdens to the ground below. The plan was to create as circular a barrier as possible around the two vehicles and the trailer. None of the projectiles were aerodynamic to begin with, so throwing with any accuracy seemed to be near impossible, except for Toffee, who was not only placing his missiles where he wanted them, but also hitting an animal on occasion.

Creatures charged the building. Some of them attempted to climb the walls, but only the squirrels could get real purchase on the sandstone, and Sid and his rifle easily dispatched them. Soon the wood was expended, and a rough crescent had been formed. It was nowhere near as tight as Sid had hoped for, but it would have to do. The animals at the base of the wall were in a frenzy now, cats and dogs shoulder to shoulder in their rage, their naturally enmity to each other forgotten.

"Toffee, Darcy, with me," said Sid, strapping on his flame-thrower. "The rest of you, give us ten minutes, then let fly. Come downstairs as soon as you've done that. Don't leave any doors open behind you."

Noah and Lena took over shooting squirrels as the three left. Caps kept a careful eye on his watch, as if time might somehow accelerate if he didn't. At nine minutes he handed a Molotov cocktail to each of his companions. At ten, they lit and threw.

None of their strikes were particularly accurate, but there were so many chemicals splattered around, it didn't much matter. Flames crawled between the detritus, jumped into the air, and spread out along the ground. There were a few breaks in the wall here and there, but none save the most courageous animals would dare them. The creatures outside the flaming barricade, the ones that had fallen back when the assault began, fell back even farther. Those inside pressed themselves against the wall, whimpering in fear, growling and hissing in anger. A staccato of gunfire added to the crackling flames, then Sid appeared, sweeping a tongue of fire across the creatures closest to the wall. From above it was impossible to tell how many creatures they'd killed in the loading bay before reaching the outside.

"Let's go," said Caps, tearing himself away from the window.

They didn't have to get the bolt cutters from the Pig, there was a pair in the loading bay. Up an internal ramp and through the doors, Sid crunched through the chain locking up the trailer, and with a bit of effort forced the doors open. No animals had breached it, although a few spiders had, judging by the cobwebs that depended from the ceiling. He looked at boxes, pulled tarps, and checked a manifest on a warped clipboard. Noah came into the trailer behind him, taking in the pressurized tanks, the metal cases.

"It's all here according to this," Sid wagged the clipboard. "All of it. Wafers, gas, and best of all…" he turned and shot the beam of his flashlight at the back end of the trailor. Whatever occupied that space lay beneath a tarp.

Noah grabbed the canvas and pulled. There was a lot of tarp, and it piled at his feet as he cleared it from its charge. Underneath was a bluish oval cylinder of metal, four feet long, two feet wide, and almost as high as the ceiling. There was a door in one end, small in relation to the rest of the object.

"I thought it would be bigger," said Sid.

"It will be. We have to brick it up on all sides. How are we going move it? It'll be way too heavy to lift. I didn't expect it to be assembled."

"Well, it was loaded on, it can be loaded off." The Boss stooped and pulled at the tarp. The furnace wasn't sitting on the floor of the trailer. Instead it rested upon two wooden pallets.

"This is incredible," said Noah, the moment taking him. "Once we get this going...Boss, we could make panels for everybody. We'll be heroes."

"Just worry about taking care of the Pit first. We have a limited number of those wafers you know." He exited the trailer.

In the loading bay, the rest of his crew industrially moved wood from the building to the outside. Caps and Lena dragged furniture from other rooms and smashed it, then Toffee and Darcy, sweating under their net-helmets, hauled the wood outside and added it to the barricade.

"Is it there?" called Darcy.

"Yes. All of it."

"Good, we need some extra hands." She tossed both halves of a coat rack over the hood of the truck, which still blocked the doors, then picked them up on the other side.

Sid hunted for a pallet jack. He found it pushed up against one wall, rust showing though flaked yellow paint. Next to it was something much better—a forklift.

"Richard, can you get this to work?"

Caps gave a chair's legs one final stomp, then trotted over to the forklift. He moved behind it, then came back out. "No can do, Boss. There might not even be anything wrong with it, but it's electric. No juice to charge the thing. Do you want me to try and start it?"

"No. Battery'll be dead. Noah, come out here and help us. I want this firewall thick."

38. Slave

The man was forty-two years old. What was left of his hair was a deep brown, almost the colour of mahogany. His shoulders were permanently hunched and his left arm was bent at an unnatural angle, just below the elbow; as if an extra joint was present, one that didn't move. His unruly beard was just a shade darker than his hair, and the untrimmed mustache irritated the tip of his nose and the top of his lips. A metal collar was fitted to his neck and held in place by a padlock the key to which had long since vanished. A chain dangled from the collar, the other end attached to a ring in the floor, near a drain through which ants had appeared once. Many of the tiny creatures had worked their way into his cell before help had come. He'd had to bellow, that time, and after the outburst had saved him, it had cost him. He wasn't allowed to speak, or make any verbal noise whatsoever. He didn't have the right. Speaking was for whole people. The man didn't even have his own name anymore, save what he was called when addressed; Slave.

Normally, he wouldn't have been chained to the ring, he would instead have been out, cleaning, hauling, accepting beatings; but he had to stay where he was now in case Luke wanted him. He hated Luke. He'd hated Archie, but he hated Luke more. At least Archie had been an intelligent lunatic, his successor was just a lunatic.

There was no door to his cell, at least not one in any wall. The access was through the ceiling, through a hatch that now swung open. A boy, no more than fifteen, appeared at the portal and gestured.

Slave unsnapped the hook that held his chain to his collar. That wasn't locked, not anymore. The consequences of having it unclipped without permission, those kept it fastened more securely than any combination of pins and tumblers. He couldn't have hidden his disobedience in any case. Three walls of the cell were concrete. The fourth was glass. Thick, well anchored glass that Slave had been unable to break when first imprisoned years ago. He'd been caught right away, and punished. He'd never tried again.

As Slave's chain hit the floor, a wooden ladder was lowered into his cell. He shambled awkwardly up the rungs, his movement hampered by the shape of his body and the short length of chain that hobbled him. His ankles had been punctured, and steel pins had been inserted. In addition, steel manacles were bound to his feet in much the same way as his collar. In time, Slave's flesh and joints had healed to accommodate the new shape of things. His legs had been limited to this short range of movement for so long, it was doubtful he could take longer strides even if the chain was removed.

His cell was all of concrete, lit by a torch that guttered away in a wall bracket. In the hallway outside, other torches lit the way. The styrofoam panels that made up the false ceiling had burned away over the torch holders. Years of heat and smoke had crumbled them, revealing coiled metal hoses and pipes that no longer carried anything.

The boy walked ahead of him, not looking back. Saying nothing, fearing nothing.

Slave trod the familiar path, past tarnished brass posts that had once supported opera rope, past glass walls, many of which would soon need cleaning again. He shuffled beneath a large plastic shark that dangled from twin chains in the ceiling. None of the building's occupants spared him a glance as he walked, these young ones, these savage ones.

The boy stopped before a door and knocked out of respect, rather than necessity. He was expected. He opened the door without being told and ushered Slave inside, then left. Slave waited in the alcove. Another door lay ahead of him, but he would wait for summons before going through. The room he was in was small, a brown desk held one corner, but any other original furnishing had been removed. What had once been a receptionist's office was now the anteroom of the master, the conduit between chosen and God.

"Enter," came a voice through the door.

Slave shuffled forward and turned the handle. He'd been this way many times before. Perhaps more times than anyone else who lived there, save the master himself. He shut the door behind him without being asked.

As spartan as the corridors outside were, the master's inner sanctum could have been considered opulent in comparison. The walls, none glass, were lined with pictures. Some photographs, some paintings, all seascapes. A few were devoid of life, save that of trees that lined a wave-beaten shore, but the rest were occupied, whales and fish, both above and below the waterline. The furnishings were old, but well maintained; a table with two chairs, a vanity against one wall and a pair of kerosene lamps instead of torches providing light.

The room's single occupant stood before a heavy drape which obscured the rest of the room. He was young, no more than twenty-one or twenty-two. A mop of curly blond hair was held in place by a leather headband. His beard was fair and thin, trimmed short, if not evenly.

He stood bare to the waist, his lower body fitted into a ragged pair of jeans. His eyes were bright with both frustration and malevolence.

Slave waited. He couldn't have spoken in any case, even if he'd wanted to.

"God is silent," said Luke, "and these don't help." He waved a hand at a pair of telephone books that sat on the table. "You lived here in the time before, didn't you?"

Slave nodded.

"Where is the Walcott Building?"

The name was familiar. Through the fog his mind had become a memory surfaced, a memory of better times.

"You do know it. Show me where."

He kept his head down. Luke had that same power Archie had, a piercing gaze that saw right through deception, or perhaps it was that Slave no longer had the capacity to deceive. Which would elicit the worst response, a false answer or no answer at all?

"If you don't tell me, I'll have another of your toes. You don't have many left."

A toe, the left ear—the only one he had—it didn't matter. What mattered another mutilation to the body when the spirit was already broken? Archie knew this. Slave moved to the only framed item not a seascape; a map of Vancouver and the Lower Mainland, circa 1997. He raised a slim, long-fingered hand—unharmed; they'd never injure his hands—and rested it on the University of British Columbia. He'd studied there, earned a bachelor degree and his wife. She'd died, and the children. Wasps.

"There?" Luke was aghast. "This place is forbidden. Why would She allow them to go there?"

Slave curled his hand into a claw and drew it across his throat.

"No. They're not dead. If She let them in, She'll protect them. But I've heard nothing since yesterday." From a drawer in the vanity he produced a thin, gray plastic case. "I want you to check it again." He held the case out, like a Catholic priest offering the host.

Slave reached out and took the case, its contents clicking together within. It was for this he was alive, for this that Archie had both saved him and damned him. He'd been allowed to speak then, when alone with the former master. The last words he'd ever spoken had been to the megalomaniacal potentate of this place. Archie had brought him in for two reasons; the first was to have someone of his own age to speak with, all the rest being scarcely more than children. It was for the second reason that Slave's tongue had been taken; nailed to a tabletop, then sawed off with a dull blade. Oh how he'd screamed, and been punished for the breach of silence, even considering the extenuating circumstances.

Luke drew the drape aside, and Slave shuffled through, opening the case to fulfill his purpose.

39. Tooth Crazy

"Ladies and gentlemen," said Sara, rising to her feet, "I have an announcement to make."

The mess hall fell silent. Not with the abrupt absence of noise like when Sid addressed the room, but with a gradual cessation, like people were stopping in their conversations only because others were. Although she may not have noticed the difference, Daniel did.

"Sid Halbert felt it was in the Pit's best interests to keep certain things from you. In light of recent events I feel it is better for you all to know. Security was searching for a traitor among us, and they did find one, of sorts. It was Burle's wish that if you blame anyone, you blame him."

Daniel almost choked on his mouthful of water. Dr. Patel would have done likewise had he been drinking at the time. This was not what they had discussed. Heads turned amongst the tables, a few words were murmured.

"You can make up your own mind once I tell you the facts," Sara continued. "None of the transport team were responsible, not October, not Ian, not any of them. Some goods that Burle got from the scavengers were bugged. It never occurred to him that they'd have that type of technology, and why should it? We located every item and destroyed them. It's over people, let it go. Thank you." She sat down.

Almost immediately conversation resumed, even louder.

"What the hell was that?" asked Dr. Patel, leaning closer to Sara.

"It just came to me. It's better than what they had, and now they won't be pointing the finger at anyone."

"No. They'll just be ripping open everything they own to find bugs."

"That's not all," said Daniel in Sara's other ear. "The scavengers wouldn't have bugs. They just wouldn't. And if they did, they'd trade 'em. If they were working for D'Abo, though…"

"But it's a lie, Daniel. Why is a hypothetical connection a problem?"

The acting chief of security jerked his thumb at the mess hall. "Because some of them are going to come up with that. Great, you've quashed the rumours that Ian was the traitor, at least for the people who believe you, but now people are going to be worried about mixing it up with D'Abo next."

"You should have discussed it with–" Dr. Patel started.

"Shut up, Harp. You too, Daniel. I can't have people at each others throats here. What we'd planned to say was unacceptable. I realized that as I was standing up. No, Harp. Don't say another word. I'm going to finish my meal." She forked up a piece of fish and held it before her mouth. "Daniel, maybe you should talk to Roshi, have him dish out the lobster early."

Dr. Patel leaned back in his chair and took a deep pull on his flask. It was one of his best batches, hardly any scathing of the throat whatsoever. Or maybe he'd finally succeeded in burning out his esophageal nerve endings. As far as he was concerned, he was off duty. Where most went to their rooms, Dr. Patel came to the infirmary. He'd been feeling edgy all day, and what the doctor recommended was some recreational drinking, and maybe a one-way discussion with Dr. Odega. He took another swig, this time noticing an aftertaste, not one of the usual ones that accompanied his creations. Curious, he drank again, this time focussing on the flavour. It was unpleasant and threatened to ruin an otherwise perfect batch. Was it part of the still? Flaking metal or a crumbling seal that was contaminating the cooker? The flask slipped through his fingers as if an unseen hand had yanked it. Dr. Patel bent forward to retrieve it, but the damn thing dipped away and the floor rushed up to meet him.

On the floor beside the chair, Dr. Patel struggled to rise. Everything he looked at seemed to rock slightly, and his limbs wouldn't quite obey his orders.

What's happening to me? His hands pushed on the floor, one of them slipped. *Is this a stroke? An aneurysm? An embolism?* There, his knees were under him, then his hands were on the edge of his desk and he was pulling himself up.

A huge shape rose above him. It quivered like everything else, but looked quite manlike.

Theodore Odega drove a meaty fist into Dr. Patel's nose, knocking the man to the floor. He straddled the doctor, placing his whole weight on the man's chest, then struck again. Blood spattered from Patel's lip. He hit him three more times, right, left, right again. The doctor's eyes rolled into the back of his head, and his lids closed.

Odega moved stealthily to the door and peeked into the hallway. As he suspected, there was no guard. They thought that little of him. He needed clothes, but reaching his room would be impossible. He padded down the hallway, mindful of interlopers in his lab. Cracking the door ever so slightly, he saw only darkness. He eased into the lab, listening for another's breath, a squeak of boot leather. With the door shut he flicked the switch. Only one of the three lights came to life. His lab was much as he'd left it, though Dr. Patel had neglected to tidy up completely after feeding. No doubt he'd been lax on cleaning up as well. Odega threw open the box beside his lab table. On top of a spare set of coveralls was a metal flask. He threw it disdainfully behind him, not even looking to see where it would land. It was slow poison, dulling his senses, blinding him to what had been going on right in front of his face. The man almost fell as he pulled on his clothing. His exertion on subduing the doctor was both taxing and unnecessary. The drug—flurazepam—a powerful hypnotic, would have done the job in a few more moments, but his wrath had demanded physical revenge against Patel. And Sara. Sweet Sara. Maybe she didn't know. Maybe she was as much a pawn in this as he was.

Odega opened the door to the zoo. The stench told him that his assessment of Dr. Patel's diligence was correct. The animals seemed to perk up a bit when he entered. At the far end, Ghandi worked at a bone.

"Ghandi, how are you girl?" asked Odega, moving slowly.

The dog rose to its feet and growled, not the warning growl of an animal protecting its food, but the fierce guttural—pregnant with violence—of a sworn enemy.

"I don't have time, girl. I can't leave you with these people either. I'm sorry."

Against the wall near Ghandi's cage leaned a sharp blade on a long pole. There were leather handgrips on the pole, making it a very sturdy weapon. He took this pole now, this killing stick, and held it before the cage. He hated the spear as it always meant failure—an animal too wild to control, or experimented on long past its usefulness. How much more bitter it was now, to use the spear in the face of his greatest success. The spear thrust forward, catching the caged animal beneath the jaw. He pushed hard and twisted, then pulled and stabbed again.

A bubbling hiss escaped the dog's mouth as it sank to the floor. The other animals tensed, but none made a sound. Such a death was commonplace in the zoo.

He wondered how much of the doctor's babbling was true, how much manufactured.

The killing done, Odega swept a final glance around his menagerie. There was no need to kill the other animals. He shut the door behind him and pondered footwear. His stomach twisted suddenly. The familiarity of the lab was adding to his despair rather than detracting from it. He'd been growing more suspicious of those he worked with, but thus far he'd succeeded in dismissing it, passing it off to long hours and maybe a bit too much drink. But still the doubts had persisted that Compton Pit wasn't for the future of humanity as its head of state declared, but that Compton Pit was for itself, or more specifically, for Sid. Once the man had what he needed he disposed of the excess. There was precedent. Like Gerard Fritz had just wandered off into the woods after completing Gershwin and the Mimis.

Odega must have known the truth long before he realized that he did. He thought he'd held off on telling Sid his new theories because none of them were more than supposition. He now knew he'd kept mum because revealing it would have been dangerous.

At Gershwin's side, in the heart of the Pit, he'd been struck down like an intruder. It was the only explanation. One moment he was revelling in success, Ghandi at his side, the next he was in the infirmary, with a throbbing headache and a tube up his privates. Ted didn't know who'd hit him, but he suspected Chiu-Keung. The others would have held him at gunpoint. Striking out was the Chinese man's style. And then to have to put up with Patel's constant drivel. That the physician had never suspected that the coma had been fake for almost five days only proved his incompetence and devotion to the bottle. It was a good thing not much surgery was required in the

Pit, or some poor fool was destined to wake up with a flask sewn into his stomach.

Odega rifled through his desk, pulling anything that might allude to his discovery. There wasn't much. It appeared his research hadn't even been touched, or perhaps the searchers had been very careful to replace everything where it was. Darcy was capable of that precision, as—Odega was sure—was Sid. He'd meant to stick hairs to his drawer, tiny filaments that would be broken unseen by trespassers, evidence of subterfuge. But he didn't have any hairs on his own head, and he didn't feel like yanking strands from anyone else's.

He shut the lights off and re-entered the hallway. He'd made an error. He should have hid Patel instead of leaving him there on the floor, but he didn't feel he had time now. Through the curtain and into the armoury, the chief of animal research armed himself with a revolver and a shotgun. He loaded up and pocketed bullets, constantly expecting security to come bursting through the other side. The subtle clicks of rounds being chambered were as loud as a parade drum. But no one came. Armed, but still barefoot, Odega peeked out into the central corridor. It was dim, what with the whole compound on low-light levels, but not empty. Two people stood by the notice board. Odega pulled his head back in. He heard a door open, then close. He took two deep breaths, his barrel chest swelling and contracting, then stepped out to find the corridor vacant.

He needed a vehicle, and he needed to get the airlock open. The best choice would be the hunters' van. It was always kept stocked, ready to go at a moment's notice. He approached the door to security and pushed himself up against the wall. The door was open a crack, and light spilled out into the corridor. Some rooms, apparently, still had full power.

The sliver of light on the floor expanded to a semi-circle as the door swung open. Purty stepped into the hallway, his eyes widening in shock as he saw Odega.

"Jeez, Doc. You scared me. It's good to see you up…" for the first time he noticed the shotgun. "Why are you…"

The stock of the rifle caught Purty under the chin. He stumbled back a step, and Odega quickly shifted his grip on the rifle so he could swing it like a bat, smashing the security officer in the side of the head. He looked both ways as he dragged the unconscious man into security. There was no one else there.

Odega dumped Purty to the floor, wiped blood and hair off the rifle's stock and onto the man's coveralls, then pushed the lever that opened the airlock. He'd have to hurry now, the big doors could be heard a long way from the motor pool.

Chiu-Kung stabbed a button on the console in the watchtower. "Purty," he said into the mic, "who's going out? I didn't...shit!"

The van, after clearing the ramp, smashed through the gate and accelerated.

Alarm bells rang through Compton Pit.

"One, two, three, push!" Sid, Caps and Toffee gave the pallet jack everything they had. The furnace made the last few pivotal inches up the loading ramp and into the back of the trailer. It was the final piece to be loaded.

Everyone was tired, sweaty and nauseous from the barricade. It was a dirty firewall, ignited by chemicals never meant for that purpose, and releasing countless substances better left in their manufactured state. The animals had retreated quite a distance from this toxic blaze. The Deep Six didn't have that luxury. Darcy, Noah and Lena toiled at feeding the beast, not even pausing to break things up anymore, just dragging items out and throwing on the fire whatever they felt would keep it going. Black smoke belched into the air, carrying with it threadlike cinders that drifted aimlessly, attaching themselves to any clothing or hair they came in contact with.

"We're done," said Caps, hauling the trailer doors shut with what felt like the last of his strength.

"No," said the Boss. "We have to seal our windows, and clean up a bit."

"I'll drive dirty. I could be covered in mud, I'd still put pedal to the metal."

"Not us. The vehicles."

The teeth had had a heyday. Upholstery was torn, the supplies in the back of the Pig were useless, and the excrement was everywhere. The Pig smelled like a dozen animals had laid claim to it. The bear draped over the truck's hood and grill had drawn a swarm of black flies, some of which remained even after the fire started. The smell coming off it was nearly as bad as that in the cab and sleeping area, where animals had also had their fun. Darcy and the hunter had cleared what few creatures had taken refuge from the initial blaze inside the vehicles. The mother cat had been one of them. Toffee stabbed her twice more after he thought she was dead. Cats were wily, and they could take a lot of abuse. Not like rats though; he'd seen rats keep going after they had a bullet right through them.

Despite the mess inside, luck was still with them. The cables, hoses and wires, the vulnerable circulatory systems of both van and truck, had been untouched.

Caps took Noah's place on fire duty. The chief of photovoltaics was happy to trade off until he discovered he was on shit detail.

Toffee considered peeling the bear off the truck, then decided he liked the idea of staring into its rotting face for the journey back to the Pit. He wondered who his chauffeur would be. Sid was also capable of driving the rig.

Wind screamed through the mesh as Senna pursued their stolen van on Travis Jones's stinking motorbike. The tires on the Hummer had been slashed, and the new rig was in no way a pursuit vehicle. She'd grabbed a jacket, but just her coveralls protected her legs, and they were freezing. Parts of the road that were inconvenient for the van were dire obstacles for her. It should have been Daniel, she thought. But Daniel had no experience on bikes. Goody for her. The acting chief of the hunters shifted her weight, drifting in order to bypass a rather large crack in the blacktop. There was a bit of road coming up that she'd practically have to walk the bike across, plus the van had one hell of a head start. She didn't even know what to do once she'd gotten to the van. What she did know was if she didn't catch it within half an hour, it would reach an intersection, then she'd have no clue which way to go.

From what chaotic threads of information she'd caught before Dr. White fired her out the airlock, it seemed that someone had taken out Purty and the doctor, then kidnapped Dr. Odega. That meant more traitors, but who were they working for?

The road turned nasty, uneven chunks of tarmac, like the highway was nothing more than a fallen house of cards. Senna slowed to a near stop. She wove between the curled lips of slab, conscious of how exposed she was at this moment. *I could be punching leather right now.*

The engine sounded loud enough to attract the attention of every animal for miles. At last she cleared the broken section—referred to affectionately by the Pit's regular drivers as the tumbledowns—and was able to accelerate.

She realized she wouldn't be punching. She'd be herding people into the mess hall where a headcount was surely being assembled. She throttled harder, a stopwatch ticking down in her head. The Pit couldn't afford to lose the van. The motor pool couldn't seem to win. It was emptying like the chip pile of an unlucky blackjack player. More importantly, the Pit couldn't afford to lose her. She barely slowed for the next bit of bad road, nothing like the tumbledowns, just a few cracks and potholes, but still her heart was pounding when the blacktop smoothed out. She opened the bike up, let it roar. Travis used to talk about the bike making him do it, singing to him to go faster, ride harder. Senna didn't hear anything, not a stanza, not a note. It was the van that impelled her, and the traitors within. Would it be someone she was close to? She didn't know what she'd do then.

"One man," crackled a voice through the speaker in the helmet. She whipped her head to the right, the direction from which the voice had come. Chastising herself, she flicked back to the road ahead and shouted into her mouthpiece.

"What?" There was no reply. She slowed and brought her left hand up, pushing a button on the helmet's chin. "What?"

"One man," repeated the voice. It sounded like Daniel.

"Screw protocol! Tell me what the hell that means!"

There was a long pause, then; "Purty's awake. He thinks it's just one man."

Just one man carrying a comatose Odega and overcoming security? The animal researcher was huge, dead lifting him would have been…one man…

"No passengers?" she said into her mic.

"Ten-four."

Her left hand gripped the handlebar and her right twisted as far as it could. It was Dr. Odega in the van. No kidnappers. Another betrayal. He was a traitor after all. Shangly's boys must have hit him as a red herring, and just done it too hard. Darcy was going to go ballistic when she got back. If she got back.

"What do I do?" she asked, thumbing the mic again. There was no reply. "Danny? Dan?" She must have exceeded the helmet's range. The Pit couldn't hear her, but if she was close to the van, Odega would have.

It appeared ahead of her for a moment, the green and brown camouflage pattern no use against the gray of the road, then it was gone, hidden by a downward incline. She realized that she had no idea of what to do once she reached the vehicle. Shoot out the tires? Was she to kill Odega or try to bring him back alive? *I'll pull up to the window and wave for him to pull over.* That thought elicited a bitter laugh.

She hit the downslope, and the distance between her and the prey rapidly decreased. Her complete lack of bike combat experience showed in the way she'd suited up. The throttle was controlled by her right hand, likewise her gun was holstered in that direction. With less than a hundred metres separating her from the van's bumper, she remembered the shotgun in the pouch on the left. She swung her hand back for the stock, missing the first two passes. Then her fingers closed on wood and she drew it forth and slid the barrel through a flap in the mesh, a knight readying her lance. Seventy-five metres. She'd take the tires, then subdue the turncoat if she could. Otherwise his rest would be even more severe than a coma. Fifty metres. The van began to weave back and forth. She wasn't even close to gun range yet and already Odega was taking evasive maneuvers. She couldn't key the mic without re-holstering the rifle, but maybe a warning shot would be sufficient command to stop. She aimed wide of the vehicle and stopped just short of pulling the trigger. If she did that, she'd only have one barrel left. Thirty metres. The road was getting rough again, but she couldn't slow. Twenty metres, almost there. The bike shuddered and hopped. Ten metres. She never knew what she hit. A pothole, the edge of raised slab, it didn't matter. The motorbike was thrown to the left. Her right hand tightened up, laying on the speed instead of easing off. Her left hand gripped uselessly at the shotgun. In an instant Senna was looking at the sky instead of the road as the bike passed its centre of gravity and smashed down. The protective bubble of mesh was now a fetter, keeping her pinned to the bike. Friction tore away the side mesh, shredded the material covering her left leg, and stripped skin from bone. She slid in a shower of blood and sparks until momentum ground itself out on uneven highway.

The van didn't stop, didn't even slow. Its reflection receded in the faceplate of her helmet, that thankfully, hadn't come off. Pain and shock numbed her mind, and coherent thought vanished, left behind in a desperate bid to hold onto tattered shreds of consciousness.

The rig had been backed out, and the van driven inside. There wasn't anything convenient left to burn. An exhausted Darcy and Lena had been sent to forage farther into the basement in order to retrieve barricade fuel.

Caps repeatedly spat on the ground as he drove screws through mesh on the Pig's door. No matter how much phlegm he coughed up, or how much water he swished in his mouth, he couldn't get rid of the burnt-plastic taste. This time the mesh had been stripped out of ventilation grates. They weren't fine enough to stop wasps, but they were strong enough to repel the teeth. Sid had gassed up both vehicles. Risky business considering the flames. There were no unfortunate incidents. The animals had retreated well back. They were smart enough to get as far away from the noxious fumes as possible. At the far end of the lot, a pack of dogs snarled and barked, as if the firewall could be intimidated into vanishing.

Noah was busy shoving padding back into shredded seats, and duct-taping it down. Some tears were too wide for a single strip of tape and the puffy material had somehow managed to pop out between double strands. All the physical lumps of excrement had been removed, but there was no getting rid of the smell. Their skinbags were trashed. Extra clothing torn, ammunition scattered everywhere, under seats, behind the wheel wells. Toffee's book was scattered everywhere. The hunter had cursed its loss and then used a handful of pages to wipe up a smear he identified as coon shit.

Sid had gone in search of fire extinguishers. He located two, only to discover they were empty, possibly used to repel animals. When they were ready to go, they'd have to climb into the vehicles and wait for the barricade to die of starvation.

"I feel like I've been drinking from the fuel tank," said Caps, pulling himself into the van and collapsing on the back seat, popping open a tear Noah had just taped. "Do you know how to drive the semi?"

Noah had a fleeting memory of Bacon asking him the same thing. "No."

"Dogshit. Toffee's riding shotgun. I figured since you two were getting so close and all..."

"Been talking to Darcy?"

"No. Why? She say the same thing? Forget about it. You're just toying with his affections right? Setting him up for a fall?" He dropped into a guttural European accent, half French, half German. "I read you like zee book!"

"Yeah, that's it." Noah retaped the seam, shoving Caps's leg out of the way in order to do so. "Darcy and Lena been gone a while, huh?"

"They're fine," said Caps. "I've got a Lena radar. If something was wrong with her, I'd know."

"You mean your spider sense would be tingling?"

"Noah, you've come a long way. Yup, spider sense. How 'bout this one, I'm registered as a level four telepath with the Psi Corp."

"Is that supposed to mean something? You're ripping up another seam, Caps. Could you slump in the front seat, I'm finished with that one."

"Yes, Mom." He moved to the indicated seat. "Noah, I forgive you."

"For what?"

"What do you mean 'for what?' For not telling me about the extended stay you and the Boss were planning."

"Oh, that. Uhm, I wasn't really feeling that bad about it. I was under orders, and I'll bet there's tons of stuff you don't tell me."

"Touché." Caps stretched his legs out, propping his feet on the dashboard. "I sure could use a hit right now. All those grow houses in this city…I'll bet we could find acres of the stuff just growing wild. Wouldn't be as good as what we get from H&H, but…"

"Dr. White lets you grow that stuff in hydroponics?"

"Noah, Sara asked me to help her with it. It's good for glaucoma, it's a natural appetite stimulant, alternative soporific, blah blah blah…If you have to pick a poison, it's better for you than Harpreet's liver killer. And don't think Sara doesn't sneak a puff here and there. She's got her own pipe, looks like Eggerson's work. He's a closet doper, too. Keeps his stash in the back of an Elvis puppet. There's a secret for you. Y'see, we should be using pot on the animals. Hit them with it constantly, bonfires and fans. They'd mellow out."

"I thought you said it was an appetite stimulant."

"There is that tiny flaw, but I'm working on it," his eyes widened suddenly, as if in alarm, then returned to normal.

"What was that?"

"Nothing. Lena just stubbed her toe, that's all."

"How did you…oh, that radar, huh? Very funny. You never told me why you two haven't gotten married."

"You're right, forgot all about it. Lena's got a lot of superstitions. I've knocked a few of them out of her but some of them are deep. Just give me time. Anyway, you've heard the saying, 'new wives make new widows?' " Noah nodded. "Lena believes that one completely. Thinks she might as well wear a black wedding dress if it comes to that. I've asked her. She always says no, if she even lets me get the question out."

Noah pulled a long strip of tape off the roll and fitted it to the edge of the seat. It was covered in gray. If it didn't hold now, it never would. "I'm sorry to hear that, Caps. It must bother you."

"More than you know. Forget about it. What do you think about Freeland/Tremmel?"

"Not much. I never met Freel…Tremmel. Just seen pictures, that's all. It's weird. One of the things I got from Burle…part of my inheritance…was a little soldier. Its team mates were on Freeland's desk. I stowed them in the Pig. Why not reunite them? But that means Tremmel stole one of them, or bought one just like it. What the hell for? Why not just pretend he was a higher-level scientist and keep his own name?"

"Who knows? Maybe he was worried he'd run into someone who'd remember his name. Kind of egotistical, that. But then look who we're talking about. Okay, you never met the guy, but trust me, thinking his real name would be etched in people's memories was right up his alley. My guess is that Tremmel really thought he was Freeland. There's all kinds of lunatics in the world. Do you remember David Letterman?" Noah shook his head. "He was a late-night talk show host. He had this lady stalker, used to break into his house and wait for him in bed. Did it over and over again. She totally believed that Letterman was in love with her, that they'd spent their lives together. Does the name Mark Chapman mean anything to you? No? Just take it from me, the world was, is, and always will be filled with wingnuts." Caps arched his back and flexed his shoulders, eliciting a few small pops from his spine. "We're almost home, pal. Man, I've got some great cartoon ideas. What do you think about–"

"Richard, get out here," the Boss's voice drifted through the open door.

"Dogshit. Just when I was getting relaxed. Coming! Sun boy, are you done in the cab?"

"I think Darcy's doing it."

"Darcy's off with Lena, remember? You've breathed too many fumes."

Caps answered the Boss's calling and Noah finished the back seat, then slumped down himself, stealing the brief luxury of closing his eyes.

"Noah, you too."

He pulled himself up and thumped heavily to the loading bay floor. The Boss waved for him to come over. Darcy and Lena had returned. He joined the semi circle around Sid.

"People, we're ready to go. I broke radio silence coming in here yesterday, and I spoke the name of our destination. If someone's on a scanner, and they know the layout of the city, they could be waiting for us outside the Endowment Lands."

"Could they be coming in for us?" asked Noah, looking around for the closest gun. His .45 was in the back of the van.

"I doubt it. The animals here don't display much knowledge of us. For most of them I think we're the first people they've seen. They don't fall back at gunshots. I think certain areas of the city are cleared on a regular basis. This certainly isn't one of them. Now so far we've seen absolutely nothing, but we've also seen nothing of past expeditions. We can estimate where they were when we lost contact, and all I see are Pre-Change wrecks. Those vehicles must have gone somewhere. Be alert. We have what we need, but don't get overconfident. Darcy, you're driving the Pig, I'm in the rig. Radio silence unless absolute emergency. Any questions?"

"We're not making anymore stops are we?" asked Lena.

"No. All the wish list stuff will have to wait until next time."

"I can't wait," said Caps.

Senna lay on her stomach, her left leg twisted and pinned beneath the motorbike. She didn't have the strength to extricate herself. The mic in her helmet was smashed, even if she wasn't out of range of the Pit. She could only hope that someone was on their way in the rig, or that the Hummer had gotten new tires in record time.

Her right hand wouldn't stop trembling and she'd missed the buck with her first two shots. It was a majestic specimen, fully ten points as old world trophy standards went. It was still a bit down the road, but it would be on her in seconds if it decided to charge. It did. Antlers lowered, cloven hoofs thundered across the highway. She fired. The bullet smashed through an antler, jerking the buck's head to one side. It faltered, then regained its balance and charged again. Senna rolled as best she could, excruciating pain shooting up her leg as she twisted it even farther. With tremendous force the antlers crashed into the bike, shoving it a couple of feet, tearing her flesh further. She jammed the gun into the buck's neck and pulled the trigger. The animal screamed and reared. She rolled again, but not enough. A hoof came down on her right shoulder, pulverizing the clavicle, popping the arm out of joint. The buck sidestepped then collapsed.

Blackness threatened to overtake her, but she breathed through the new pain, and with a clenched-teeth effort, repositioned herself.

Bone grated against bone as her left hand, the palm scraped nearly off, picked up the gun, and thumbed the hammer.

She knew she was dead. There was no way the rig would reach her in time. The wind carried the scent of her blood and scorched flesh to any questing nose. But she wasn't just going to lie there and be eaten. Brush rustled to her left. She turned her head and stared into the golden eyes of a wolf. Another wolf appeared behind it, then another.

"Come and get it," she said, shifting her aim. Five wolves had cleared the tree line. In the distance, an air horn sounded. If she could just hold them off for a few moments.

"I'm not ready, you hear me? I'm not ready."

There were stories told of moose and deer, run to ground, surrounded. They didn't give the wolves permission to eat them, and the pack would leave, its collective hunger unsated. But the relationship between animals and humans differed from the one the wolves had with their four-legged cousins. At some unseen command, they charged. Senna's brain sent the signal to her finger to pull the trigger, but it got lost somewhere along the way. The truck's air horn sounded again as powerful teeth sank into Senna's left arm somewhere past the wrist. A wolf jumped onto the cycle, leaning over the handlebars to savage the trapped leg. Gunfire sounded, but seemed to be coming from a great distance. A pair of jaws found her dislocated shoulder and went to work, biting and tearing. Pain and destruction assaulted her from every nerve ending. She screamed and thrashed, then fetid breath filled her nose and teeth clamped onto her throat.

Two of the wolves escaped the barrage of gunfire as Daniel and Chris dropped from the rig, guns blazing.

"Chief!" Chris shoved a carcass off her as he knelt by her side, "Chief, say something."

Senna's face was a mask of blood, her pale hair soaked through with crimson.

"We've got to get this off her," said the bald man, shoving at the bike.

Her eyes fluttered, reddish froth bubbled at her lips.

"NO!" Chris screamed, giving up on the bike, tugging at his acting superior.

Senna's eyes glossed over, the bubbling stopped. The hunter jostled her, said her name again and again.

"C'mon," said Daniel, tugging at the man's arm.

"We've got to take her back, the doc can fix her."

"Too late for that, Chris." Daniel picked up Senna's revolver and shoved it in his belt. "C'mon, or we'll wind up on the menu ourselves."

Chris choked back sobs as he was propelled to the rig. The surviving wolves were already nosing back out of the brush.

Sooner or later, a truck would push the bike off the road. Senna's body would be gone long before that.

40. Welcoming Committee

Sid put the truck into gear and let out a sigh. A few flames still guttered amid the jumble of the firewall. At the end of the hood, the bear's head stared accusingly.

"Now we see," said Toffee, "if your leprechauns have been paying attention. If they're waiting for us, it's on your head."

"Then you'll just have to kill them all before they take it."

The rig eased forward, then crushed charred wood to powder. The first wave of animals hit them as they left the lot. It was nowhere near the size of what they'd had coming in, but it would grow. Sid turned smoothly at the next corner, hardly losing any speed. The van was behind this time, acting as rear guard.

The farther from the Walcott Building they got, the more teeth sprang from the trees. But despite the rain of teeth, tension was eased by the fact that this was a voyage out, not a voyage in. They knew where they were going this time, and there would be no stops now until they reached Camper World.

The campus sped by, featureless two-story rectangles of brown siding, green army barracks left over from the university's original purpose, lopsided three-level constructions of plastic and glass, then the parking lots and finally the buildings passed into unbroken forest, and the Deep Six were on Marine Drive, leaving UBC and the Endowment Lands behind. Coyotes and rats, unable to keep up, turned instead to the buffet of tire-crushed animals that littered the road.

In the back of the van, Lena was saying a hundred thank yous to Buddha and Jesus Christ. Looming trees had been replaced with the high weeds of large paved areas surrounding warehouses and giant supermarkets. There were still trees on the far side of the road, but Marine Drive was quite wide, so teeth leaping from that particular foliage didn't stand a chance of making the vehicles. Clouds of flies lifted from well-chewed carcasses left over from the drive in.

"We did it," said Darcy, slapping the wheel. "We actually did it. Sun boy, how long before you've got the Pit back up to speed?"

"A few months, not much longer."

"Months!" Caps barked. "Back in the lab you said weeks."

"Months are just a collection of weeks. I didn't lie exactly."

"Great! You're as bad as the Boss." Caps slumped back into his seat and folded his arms over his chest. "Once we're back at the Pit…I don't know. I'm not happy with Sid at all."

"Get over it," said Darcy. "He hoped it wouldn't come to staying here, and it didn't. If Toffee hadn't tried to stir up trouble we never would've known. Besides, you're going to be too busy bragging to be worried about Sid."

"You've got a point there. Listen, I'll be distributing lists to each of you of the exaggerations I plan to make, so you can back me up under cross-examination. I'd hate to have a good story get shot down because one of you spills the truth. Man, I can't wait. We got boasting rights for at least a year, you know that? Conquerors of the dead zone, vanquishers of Vancouver! Yeah!"

"We're not out of the woods yet," said Darcy, eyeing the tree-thick zone they were entering. She watched road signs, trying to gauge where they were exactly. All she had to do was follow the rig, but she didn't want to get caught napping when their turn off came. She wasn't happy with driving, much preferring to have her hands wrapped around a rifle than a steering wheel.

"You're worse than I am," said Toffee, his eyes searching the trees. "They'd follow you right off a cliff, but you're still worse than me."

"And how do you figure that?"

"I know things, Halbert. I know lots of things I don't tell the others.

"Just waiting for the right moment are you? What do you think you know?"

"I know a certain experimental rat poison got into a few more animals than expected."

Sid kept a poker face but his hands tightened on the wheel.

"Lucky that batch of hunters decided to chow down in the field," continued Toffee. "Stew like that would've killed Roshi's reputation. And half the Pit."

"There was never any proof that–"

"Yeah, tox screens are so resource-intensive. You've got so many lies swept under the carpet it's starting to bulge, Halbert. One day I'm going to–"

"You're going to do nothing. I traded heavily for your life, Ethan. If not for me, Mount Baker would have strung you up for a bird feeder. You step out of line one more time, I'll leave you to the teeth, no matter what I paid for your clemency. Understood?" Sid took the hunter's silence as a yes. "Good."

"I've been locked outside before," said Toffee. "Didn't bother me much."

"You were younger then. How old are you now? Forty-eight? Forty-nine? Or has fifty come and gone for you?"

The hunter scanned his side mirror, assuring himself that the Pig was safely behind them. "I'll outlive you, Halbert, you can bet on that."

The two vehicles travelled with nothing more to slow them than a few patches of broken road and an intermittent pile-up of cars. In no time they'd reached Boundary Road, the border between Vancouver and Burnaby, and hopefully, an unobstructed path straight to the highway. It was wide, and although it would take them past Burnaby's Central Park, the Boss felt it the most expedient way to reach the highway.

"Central Park coming up," said Lena, counting down the streets from 57th Avenue. At 49th, they'd face a repeat of the Endowment Lands. As long as none of the larger trees had decided to lie down, they'd be fine.

Squirrels appeared once they reached 52nd. Not that the agile rodents hadn't been harassing them all the way, but not in numbers worth worrying about. By 49th and the edge of the park, the road was swarming with gray and black fur.

"Awe Jeez," said Caps, wrinkling his nose. "We should have put plastic over the mesh."

Darcy had run over a skunk, its musk covering the underside of the van. Its odour, one of the world's most pungent scents, would be with them until they had a chance to hose the vehicle off.

Noah kept his attention on the front and side windows. As the shotgun passenger it was his duty to protect the driver, and with Darcy holding that position, Noah's job was doubly important. The cougars had arrived, as well as dogs and smaller cats. Bodies thumped against the side of the van and shuddered under the tires. The carrion eaters were in for another feast, but hopefully one without human flesh.

A large bat smacked into the windshield. It grasped the mesh between its claws and spread its wings wide to help balance. Darcy barely managed to keep from flinching. Air and momentum now pressed the spread-eagled rodent against the mesh, trapping it. She had to tilt her head to the side to see around it.

Noah stared wide-eyed at the hideous, squealing creature. He knew what it was, but he'd never seen one this close before.

"I thought these things were nocturnal," he said, poking the windshield in front of him, as if that would somehow dislodge the creature.

"They are," said Caps. "We're like a late-night snack for it."

"It'll be dark soon enough," said Darcy. "I wonder how many of these things are in the city." She jogged the wheel, hoping the bat would be forced off by the motion. It wasn't.

As Noah studied its black-and-brown form, he noticed it had tiny handlike claws on its wingtips, it was using these as well as its feet to cling to the mesh. "I think it hurt itself when it hit us." A trickle of red oozed from the bat's mouth, then its wings curled up, and just as suddenly as it had appeared, it was gone.

"I vant to suck your blood," said Caps, doing a very cartoonish vampire accent, and crooking his fingers at Lena.

"Hey, Bela," said Darcy, "what's happening behind us? I've got another squirrel on my mirror."

"All clear, Chief. How long to the freeway?"

The trees vanished at a huge intersection. A weathered broadcasting tower stood on one corner.

"This is Kingsway," said Lena. "We're almost there."

The glut of animals thinned out once they put the park behind them. Once more it was just the occasional critter, not even a danger really.

Toffee let his eyes watch the road while his mind travelled to different places. He pondered the mistake he'd made in the underground lab, how he hadn't counted on Darcy's unswerving loyalty. It wasn't his brain that had made that mistake, it was his ego. She'd made it more than clear she wanted no connection to him whatsoever, but he continued to believe that was all a cover up. What disturbed him most about the failed coup d'etat wasn't the other's reactions, though. It was his own response to Darcy staring daggers at him.

Had he given her an excuse he was convinced she would have attacked, possibly with lethal intent.

That hurt.

Inside, past layers of cynicism, past dislike and low regard for fellow man, there was a part of the hunter that could still take things personally. Darcy had been a means to an end. Not that he hadn't taken pleasure of her body, it was certainly built for sin, but somewhere along the line, she'd slipped inside him, unknowingly, unobtrusively, and far deeper than he'd penetrated her.

A large dog protruded from the weeds, its paws splayed out of the road, its lifeless head draped over one leg.

"Halbert, something's wrong." As with many times in the past, the hunter couldn't immediately place what he'd seen.

"What?" Sid scanned the road and the ditches beside in all directions.

"I don't know, but we were through here on the way in and...Halbert, punch it!"

Sid's foot stomped down, he reached for the radio, "Talk to me, Ethan!"

The hunter had his gun up, he twisted in his seat trying to see more than the mirror and window would show him. "That dog we passed was a fresh kill. I didn't see any flies and I know we didn't run over anything on this stretch."

"That's it?" Sid relaxed a smidgen. "It could have lost a fight with another animal."

"Then the victor would be snacking. I..." There was a flurry of motion amongst the weeds, a glimpse of something gray. "Shit! Halbert there was a person back there!"

"Are you sure?"

"Unless dogs have learned to walk upright."

"Darcy, we've got company," the Boss said into the mic. "We're speeding up, be ready for anything."

"I don't see anything," came the chief of security's voice. "How many teeth? What kind?"

"Not teeth, people. Just..." something flew from the weeds and smashed on the hood, covering metal and windshield alike with an opaque, yellow fluid. Bits of glass sparkled in the fur around the bear's gaping mouth. Another missile of the same nature arced up, its launch timed to intercept the rig. It missed the hood, but shattered on the passenger side door. Toffee's face was splattered as the bottle's contents splashed through the protective mesh. His tongue darted out to sample the liquid.

"Whatever this shit is, it's flammable."

Then it was raining bottles. They struck the road beside the truck, smashed into the hood and the sides of the vehicles. Toffee had his gun up, but he didn't know where to shoot. He couldn't see anything within the high weeds that filled the ditches. The windshield was now awash with viscous fluid. Another couple of hits and it would be impossible to see the road ahead.

"Darcy, report!"

The radio crackled, "We're getting hit from all angles, I can barely see anything!"

"Go straight, don't slow down."

He twisted a knob and the truck's windshield wipers creaked to life, but the rubber on them had long since crumbled, and all the metal blades did was smear the yellow dye.

Toffee grabbed the mic from Sid and barked his own order into it. "Fire the weeds! Get that doglicking flamethrower going and torch the weeds!"

"Clear my window," said the Boss, pulling away from the mesh.

"This is getting to be a habit." The hunter hammered at the driver's side mesh with the barrel of his shotgun. The mesh bowed, but wouldn't separate. "It's on too tight, I can't knock it off."

With the unmistakable sound of metal on metal, the rig smashed into something, an abandoned car possibly. Toffee and Sid were thrown against their seatbelts. The wheel fought the Boss's hands, then the cab tilted to one side.

"We're going into the ditch!" shouted the hunter.

Sid hauled the wheel against the imbalance, and must have brought the rig back up onto level ground.

"Darcy, report!" this time it was Toffee barking into the mic, using the same command the Boss had given. There was no reply. "Darcy! C'mon, Red!"

There was another impact. Toffee lost both the mic and his shotgun. Whatever they'd hit this time was bigger than the first. The cab slued sideways, momentum from the trailer pushing it forward. Time lost its reference as they went into a blind skid. Sid slammed on the brakes and struggled with the wheel, trying to correct the vehicle's direction of travel by feel rather than sight. The windshield was completely covered.

The truck stopped and the two men undid their seatbelts even as they armed themselves.

"You said this stuff was flammable?" The Boss wiped his hand across a splatter on his shoulder.

Toffee didn't answer. He swung his door open and leapt to the road, crouching and rolling as soon as he hit the blacktop. Sid did the same on the other side. The truck was covered in yellow splotches. Across the road behind them was a pick-up truck, its front end twisted and bent. A hundred metres past that, the back end of the Pig poked out from the ditch, its front end buried in the scrub. All around, the high weeds shook as if stirred by an invisible wind.

Toffee let go two unaimed blasts into the weeds, then threw the shotgun aside and grabbed his .300 from the truck. Now, more than ever, he wished he'd brought a machine gun instead of his trusted hunting rifle. A cry came from the direction of the van. Toffee ran, chambering a round as he did so.

Darcy struggled with the horrible creature that attacked her. Gray arms flaking as caked-on mud fell from its limbs, small, beady eyes shining between swaths of cheesecloth wrapped around its head. It made no sound as it attempted to strangle the life out of her. Darcy tucked her chin in and grabbed her assailant's wrists. She pushed them against her, rather than away, bending the hands up, then forcing them down her chest. She grabbed two fingers and snapped them like twigs, then drove the heel of her hand into the cheesecloth where a nose should be. With a satisfying crunch her attacker fell back and out of the van, to be replaced almost immediately by another. It had all happened so quickly. She'd lost control of the van when a tire blew out, and they'd been set upon almost immediately upon crashing into the ditch. The second attacker was trying to stab her with a long-bladed knife. She jerked her body aside, cursing the seatbelt, and smashed this attacker in the face the same way she'd hit the first. She didn't have time to turn her head and she couldn't see what else was happening in the van, but she did know Noah had opened his door, or someone had opened it for him. Her palm-strike was off, she'd hit the enemy in the cheek maybe. More unnerving than the head wrapping was the silence. A few grunts of exertion had come from beneath the cheesecloth, but no words. She fought for control of the knife as her attacker's eyes twinkled. With two fingers rigid as steel, she drove her nails into those eyes until she felt soft tissue separate and wetness covered her fingers to the first set of knuckles. This time she was rewarded with a scream. The knife clattered to the uncarpeted floor of the van, and her foe staggered backwards. She slammed her door shut as she reached for her gun, scanning the interior of the van. Caps was in the backseat, head back, blood on his chest. Noah and Lena had vanished.

"Caps, are you okay? Lena! Noah! Where are you?"

A wave of heat came at her through the window, at the same time as a crackle of flames became a roar. Her left eye snapped shut as a trickle of blood stung the surface. She grabbed Caps and yanked him forward, then propelled him out the passenger door as a tongue of flame curled through her window. She heard gunfire, and another cloth-wrapped head appeared from the weeds. She dove from the van, barely missing Caps as she came up to crouch, her gun trained on where she'd seen the face, but it was gone. A shining blade on the end of a wooden shaft shot out from the weeds. It passed a hair's width from her head. She fired along the length of the spear. Flames raced around her, engulfing the weeds and the van alike. Black smoke was obscuring her vision. She dropped the shotgun and grabbed Caps, dragging him out of the weeds and onto the road. Toffee was there, shooting into the weeds where flames hadn't taken root. Sid was close behind, and although his face was full of alarm, he appeared unhurt.

"Caps, wake up!" She slapped him a couple of times, to no effect. An arrow struck the road beside her, its flaming tip crackling as it slid toward the van.

She spun. Another burning arrow streaked from the weeds on the far side of the road. Its trajectory would take it towards the truck, not her. Flames engulfed the van. Ignoring the possibility of an arrow in the back, she hooked Caps under the arms and dragged him away from the van. The bloodstain on his shirt spread and deepened as he bumped over the pavement. The smell of scorched rubber hit the air, flames licked and prodded the back of the Pig. There were three jerry cans and two full barrels of fuel in there.

"LENA! NOAH!" Darcy screamed into the burning ditch. They were nowhere on the road. One moment she'd been driving blind, the next a mud-covered ninja had been strangling her. How long could she have been out? A whistle of wind and an arrow streaked past her head. It nicked the side of the van and vanished into the fire. She winced as Caps's head bounced over a crack, then she was being pulled herself, hard.

"Get back!" growled Toffee in her ear. He gave a mighty yank and she lost her grip on Caps. She struggled, reaching for her friend. "I said back! God damn it!" He threw her away from the van, she almost lost her balance.

With a handful of shirt, Toffee hauled the artist up and draped him over one shoulder. Sid's hands were on Darcy, helping her move.

"Where are the others?" he demanded, as he hurried Darcy away from the Pig.

"I don't know! What the hell is going on?"

When the explosion came it was nowhere near as dramatic as Darcy had expected. One loud belch of displaced air, followed by two smaller ones. The glass blew out of the back windows and streams of fire shot for the sky like twin phoenixes bound for heaven. The air around the van grew thick until heat and flame obscured the Pig from view.

They'd come to rest against a small motorhome on flat tires. It was the type of camper built by dropping a miniature home on the back of a one-ton pickup. Flames spread out in either direction along the one side of the road, anyone in there would be dead.

Toffee dumped Caps on the road like a sack of potatoes, then moved to the rear of the camper and crouched, unslinging his rifle.

"They could have had us any time," said Toffee.

"They almost had me," said Darcy. She had her knife out and was cutting open Caps's shirt. There was a deep wound a few inches below his sternum. Blood swelled from the wound with each beat of his heart.

"Oh God! SID!" Darcy cut a swath off her coveralls. She bunched it up and shoved it against the wound.

"How bad?" asked the Boss, appearing at her side.

"Real bad. You didn't see the others? Sid, I conked out. I woke up with someone strangling me. They weren't there, just him. Caps, wake up!"

"They're bugging out," said Toffee.

Sid kept low as he moved beside the hunter. Through the shimmer of heat, four vehicles had taken to the road. They were black in colour, and seemed to be made up of triangular cages on wheels. They moved slowly at first, then high-pitched motors squeaked into life and the vehicles accelerated, back into Vancouver.

"Why are they leaving us alive?" asked Sid. "They didn't even manage to ignite the truck."

"Could be some left. Odd cars they had. Sounded like they were running on lawnmower engines."

"Sid, his eyes are open," called Darcy. He was disoriented, that much was clear. She wondered how she hadn't noticed the welt by his temple. "Caps, do you know where you are?"

The artist rolled his head back and forth, then tried to sit up. His mouth twisted in agony and the strength went out of his arms.

"Don't move. I've got you. Do you remember what happened?"

He gurgled, then coughed.

Darcy lifted the makeshift bandage and wiped blood away with her hand. She had to work fast. She needed...she needed...

"Caps, you're going to be okay. Stay calm, can you do that?"

His eyes gained focus and his body jerked with sudden tension. He tried to speak, but only wet coughs came out.

"Don't speak. You've got a bad wound, but you're going to be okay."

Sid settled into place beside them. "He's lost too much blood," he whispered into Darcy's ear.

"We can give him a transfusion. Him and Toffee are the same blood type. I remember from Harpreet's cards. We passed an ambulance on the way in, it's not far from here..."

"Halbert!" Toffee was up, his head tilted skyward.

Smoke was filling the air above the road. For the most part, it was a rich, billowing gray, but in the distance, it had taken on a darker quality, and a different texture. Wasps. Thousands of them.

The hunter took in the ditch with a sweep of his arm. "The fire is driving out the ground nests." He snapped his head around. "Nurse time is over, Red."

"The truck," yelled Sid, hauling at Darcy's sleeve.

Darcy pulled from his grasp, tucking her arms under Caps. "Wait, help me carry him!"

"We don't have time," he was already thirty feet away. "Leave him, that's an order!"

Darcy lifted the artist and, for a moment, stood like a groom carrying the bride across a threshold. Then the hunter's shoulder smashed into her and Caps fell to the road.

"NO!" she screamed as Toffee ensnared her wrist in an iron grip, pulling her shoulder nearly out of the socket as he ran.

The air filled with an angry droning. Sid reached the trailer and threw open the doors. Darcy ran after her arm, twisting her head to keep sight of the artist. Caps had rolled onto one side, he watched after his departing companions, mouth open, one arm raised. Sid's hand replaced Toffee's and Darcy was pulled into the back of the trailer. The swarm's forerunners had reached Caps, and black dots appeared on his body.

The hunter jumped up to the trailer and Sid slammed the doors. They were plunged into total darkness, not a bead of light shone through. The trailer had been solidly built, and seals that had stood up to weather, would now be put to a far more rigorous test.

"We need light," said Sid. Toffee's flashlight winked on. "Grab these tarps, stuff them around the door."

"Caps," said Darcy. "We just left him..."

"Not now," said the Boss, taking her roughly by the shoulders. "Get stuffing!"

They crammed canvas into the seams around the door. Just as they finished, Toffee's flashlight dimmed, then died. In darkness they listened to a thousand tiny taps as wasps struck the doors. The swarm's buzzing filled the trailer, vibrations echoing and amplifying. Without light they wouldn't know they were doomed until they felt it. It was maddening.

A warm body pressed itself to Darcy, pulling her into an embrace. After assuring herself that two arms entwined her, she returned the embrace, pushing her face into Sid's chest. It had all happened so suddenly. A drop of moisture touched her head, and she realized Sid was crying.

It sounded as if every inch of the trailer was covered with wasps. They'd chew away the seals, force their way past the tarps. It was only a matter of time.

41. Loose Lips

Donald Graff stared at the formidable gate through his binoculars. Built between convenient rocky outcroppings, it was all of brick and topped with barbed wire. The hillside he stood upon was barren. A slight breeze swirled motes of dust above ground that would never grow anything again. At the bottom of the hill, his car idled, running as it had been for almost two days now. It couldn't hold out much longer. He'd had to resort to the risky business of refuelling with the engine on.

"Don't move a muscle," said a man's voice. Heavy footsteps came from behind him and a gun was pressed into the back of his head. A hand reached over and took the binoculars. "Getting a good look?"

"I'm not a spy, I'm expected. My name is–"

"Shut up."

He was relieved of his sidearm, the rifle at his feet was kicked away.

"The car's clear," called another man.

Donald turned his head. The second man had the passenger door open and was leaning in to get at the ignition.

"Don't do that," called Graff, but it was too late, the engine died. "Wonderful. Now you'll have to tow me in."

"Why?" the gun pressed a little harder.

"Because the starter's shot. Why the hell do you think I left the car running? I knew the last time I turned it over it would be the last time I'd turn it over. Get that bedevilled gun off me."

"You're that cart maker guy, ain't you?" asked Morrey, sliding down after him.

"Cartographer, you imbecile."

"Why were you spying on us?"

"Everyone needs to know the lay of the land."

"Hey, Morrey, there's a bunch of books in here," said the second man.

"Get out of there," said Graff, forgetting the gun to his head and half trotting, half sliding down the hill. "Out, out!" he flapped his arm as if shooing flies away.

"It's okay, Armin, this is the guy we've been expecting."

Armin backed out of the car. He had dark hair and a thick beard, surrounding an olive-skinned face. Morrey was the larger of the two, with wide shoulders and watery blue eyes.

"Our car's back there," Morrey indicated a spot beyond the hill. "We'll send someone out for your ride later."

"I'm not leaving my things unattended," Graff said, shoving books back into skinbags. "You'll have to send out a tow truck. You do have a tow truck, don't you?" He settled himself in behind the steering wheel and shut the door. The two men stood watching him through the mesh-covered glass. Donald rolled the window down. "Go on. If it wasn't for you we'd be on our way already."

"Are all those books yours?" asked Armin, pointing to the back seat.

"No, they belong to the nun I've got in the trunk."

Armin made as if to move to the trunk.

"Forget it," said Morrey."He's being a smart ass. Let's get this dude his tow truck."

In a short while the gates opened and a tow truck approached. The driver said next to nothing as he hooked up Graff's car and winched the front wheels off the ground.

"You riding with me?" the driver asked through the window.

"I'm fine right here, thank you. Can we get this over with please?"

The driver mumbled something under his breath, and returned to his truck. Donald was towed through the gates and down a gently curving road. Past another gate, this one of steel mesh, but flanked on either side by machine-gun nests, the road ended its curve on a rocky plateau, and the settlement proper sprang into view. It consisted of a massive warehouse-type building, a field of solar panels that spilled over the plateau and down the eastern slope, and hundreds of metres of pipes, twisting and intertwining like a great worm. The warehouse doors opened and the truck drove inside. Wide-spaced skylights poorly lighted the dim interior. There were numerous vehicles inside; cars, small trucks, a pair of rigs, a large motorhome, and even a tank near the far wall—an American M1 from all appearances. Air compressors, tool chests and floods on moveable racks stood out amongst the vehicles. It was everything Graff had expected and more. If he couldn't get a new starter here, he wouldn't find one anywhere.

"This is your stop," said the driver, tapping Donald's window with a thick, hairy knuckle.

Three men approached, two of them carrying M16s, the third unarmed, his hands clasped before him.

"Mr. Graff, my name is Philip." He was Caucasion, but had a distinctive Asian cast about the eyes. His hair was jet-black, and cut short. "I've been instructed to tell you that you've arrived in time for dinner and the boss awaits your company."

"Good," said Donald. "It's nice to see at least one of his underlings has some manners. What about my things?"

"I am to assure you that nothing will be touched."

"Of course you are." Nonetheless, he locked all the doors. The front right-hand door didn't actually lock, though the button depressed. Still, there was no need to tell them that. "Well, gentlemen, take me to the fat man."

"I wouldn't call him that to his face, sir."

"Neither would I. Lead on."

Behind the tank, a set of stairs led underground. Whereas some settlements' tunnels were claustrophobic things, these corridors were high-ceilinged. They were lit by both fluorescents and fibreoptic cables that must have brought sunlight directly through the ground. The walls were painted a cheery, eggshell blue. But the doors were all steel, thick with strong locks.

"Interesting decor," Donald mused out loud. "It's like a nursery in a dungeon."

It was not the usual fanfare he expected to receive upon arriving announced. No wide-eyed, celebrity-starved commoners, no couples lingering in doorways whispering to each other, no one coming up with one of his books, or any old scrap of whatever, hoping for an autograph. In fact, the corridors were vacant with the exception of himself and his three escorts. No fans, which meant no witnesses. Not good.

"Does anyone else live here?" he asked.

"Quite a few people. The corridors were cleared to save you from tiresome admirers."

"Very thoughtful of you."

They descended another set of stairs. At the bottom of this was a security checkpoint. A tall, laconic black man waved them through to another checkpoint further down the hall. Past that, they arrived at a set of twin doors covered in burnished leather, but undoubtedly steel beneath. Philip pushed open the door.

"Mr. Donald Graff," he announced.

The cartographer stepped through the door and into Peter "Gascan" D'Abo's presence.

He was beyond fat. He was grotesque. A yellow silk muumuu could not conceal ponderous man-breasts that drooped to a bloated belly. A melted staircase of chins led up to puffy lips between heavy jowls. The nose was bulbous, the patch of graying hair comical atop a face so round it seemed even the man's skull was obese. D'Abo sat at the head of a lavishly set table. Green salad filled a large crystal bowl in the centre. Steam issued from beneath the lids of a pair of silver serving platters on a gas warmer. Some sort of fish was curled around olives and held in artistic place with tiny wooden skewers. The plates were fine china, the silverware polished, with intricately engraved ivory handles.

"Good evening, Mr. Graff. I was happy to receive your request for an audience. Do sit down."

There were only two place settings: D'Abo's and a second immediately to D'Abo's right.

Likes his enemies close, thought Donald. He seated himself, snapping out a folded linen napkin and placing it on his lap. "You weren't so forthcoming the last time I requested such."

"Yes," D'Abo paused. "It wasn't suitable for you to visit us at that time. Still, I regretted not being able to…ahh…entertain you. I was also unhappy about how I was portrayed in your sixth edition."

Donald's mouth watered as he eyed the repast. "Begging your pardon, but without actually meeting you, or seeing your establishment, I had to go on what others told me. I did state that it was not my own opinion."

"Still," D'Abo dropped one meaty arm on the table, effectively separating Graff from the food. "A bloated warthog, living like a parasite on the people around him? Not something I'd have expected from a scribe of your reputation."

"I merely published the common opinion of your reputation. I hope with this visit to set the record straight."

The arm withdrew. "Help yourself, that's what it's there for, Mr. Graff."

"Please, call me Donald." The cartographer lifted one of the silver lids. Slices of venison and dumplings floated in a rich gravy. Beneath the second lid were pea pods smothered in butter. Real butter by the smell of it. He loaded his plate, eschewing the salad in favour of the fish-wrapped olives.

"There are snails on the way, leave some room." D'Abo filled his own plate, taking anything left in both platters, then pulling the entire tray of olives to his left, claiming it for himself.

"What do you call this, by the way?" Graff asked around a mouthful of dumpling.

"Stew, I believe."

"No, not the food, this," he gestured around him. "I've heard Gastown, D'Abo's Pit, D'Aboville...what do you call it?"

"Home. Heh. You forgot Sodom & Gomorrah."

Graff paused in his eating. "Usually I'm flattered when someone remembers my work word for word. In this case I'm not sure I should be."

"We call it the Reservoir. The most insulting thing about your mention of me was how short it was. Barely half a page. Underbel received four full pages. They're hardly worth a sentence. Relax, Donald. I understand you had nothing concrete to work with."

"Thank you, Mr. D'Abo."

"Please, call me Peter."

The snails arrived, brought by a man in a chef's hat and apron stretched across a junior version of D'Abo's stomach. The cook apparently ate almost as well as his master. Once again, an obscene amount of butter had been used in the cooking process. If the snails were alive, they could have swum in it.

"If I'd had more warning of your arrival, I could have had a proper meal prepared."

"I won't hold it against you."

They ate in silence for a few minutes.

"The entire Reservoir will be open to you. I want a proper write-up this time, make sure to mention the many luxuries we have available to people of means. In particular..."

"I don't have that much time, I'm afraid. Oh, I'll look around a bit, but as far as an extended stay…needs must as the devil drives and all that."

"So we should get to business then," said D'Abo. "Here," he lifted a bottle from the floor to the table. "Johnny Walker Red."

"Excellent," Donald took the bottle. "One of the few advantages of our time is that any bottle of scotch one might come across is guaranteed to be at least ten years old." He was delighted to find the paper seal still intact. He cut the brittle ribbons with his thumbnail, and twisted off the cap. He poured a generous glass for both himself and his host.

"To mutually beneficial arrangements," said D'Abo, raising his glass.

Graff returned the toast, but waited until Gascan drank before he did himself.

"Now," D'Abo wiped his mouth off with the back of his hand, "you want a new starter for your car, and I assume you'd like it installed."

"Preferably. In exchange I offer you a more than fair write up in my next edition."

"And a retraction of your previous statements."

"My tires are getting a tad bald. Take care of that, and you have a retraction."

"Done." D'Abo held up his drink.

"Done." They drank, draining their glasses. "Well, that was easier than I had expected," Donald refilled both glasses.

"Oh we're not finished," said D'Abo. "To leave before fully enjoying my hospitality, and I believe that is your intention, requires an exit visa, so to speak."

Graff's drink stopped a few inches from his lips. "Peter, holding me prisoner can hardly inspire a positive account of the Reservoir."

"Oh but I've already got that, we drank to it. And I wouldn't dream of keeping you here indefinitely. I'd never see my review. A month should suffice."

"A month?" he barely resisted the impulse to slam his glass on the table. Instead, Graff took a gentle sip. "Impossible. I have schedule to keep."

"Why? Are these settlements going anywhere?"

"Well, actually, one of them is," he said cryptically. "What is the price of this visa?"

"Something I'm sure you have quite a bit of. Information. A little early warning of what's going in your next volume, something to give me an edge, as it were. Any notes you have currently would suffice. I'll have them copied."

"no one touches my notes. You'll have to settle for an oral account."

"Hmmm. It will have to be...tasty." Gascan tossed a snail in his mouth.

"Something you can use, a demand you can supply."

"Exactly."

"Do you trade solar panels?"

"Not usually. They're quite expensive," D'Abo hesitated, as if uninterested. "How large a demand?"

Graff paused. Something wiggled inside him, a worm of conscience telling him he was betraying some trust. But he couldn't be D'Abo's prisoner for a month. He'd never make it to Terpris in time, or else he'd have to cut the rest of his journey short, and that wouldn't provide him with enough for a whole book.

"A huge demand. Almost an entire array, I would imagine. Good buying power from what I know of the place."

"Go on."

"I assume you know of Compton Pit? I'm sure you've traded with them. I don't know what's happened there, but I checked it out from a distance. Their panels are in ruins. If it's their only source of power, they must be working in the dark."

D'Abo kept his face still, but couldn't resist licking his lips. "You inspected it from a distance? Why didn't you go in? Were you refused entry?"

"I was warned to steer clear, in a manner."

"Oh yes? Warned by who?"

"I believe it was Sid Halbert. The Boss."

"Mr. Graff, your visa is almost stamped. Tell me, did Halbert drive out to keep you from entering?"

"No. He..." *oh well, in for a penny, in for a pound,* "...I met him at a safe house outside Vancouver. He was on his way into the city."

"Alone?"

"No, there were some others with him," he hoped he could leave it at that.

"I'm sure you can do better than that, Donald."

"I don't just want my visa stamped, I want ink running down the page before I say anything else."

D'Abo slapped the table enthusiastically. "Done. Who else was with Halbert?"

"I believe his chief of security, Darcy McMillan–"

"McCullough."

"I thought I had that wrong. A big man with a fake arm, the right one…"

"Toffee. Interesting. Who else?"

"One Noah Thurlow, a panel jockey from Underbel. And two others; a self-proclaimed comic and a Chinese woman. Her name was Lena, if that helps. That's the lot."

D'Abo clapped his hands together. His poker face slipped away and mounds of flesh moved aside to accommodate his smile. "Donald, I am so glad you came to see me. Let me offer you a bonus for your help."

What Graff had taken to be a glass resting upside-down, turned out to be a crystal bell. D'Abo rang it, and a few seconds later a side door opened and five women, girls really, entered the room; four white, one Asian, all young.

"Take your pick," said Gascan. "You may have her for the evening. If you want more than one, that will cost extra."

Graff studied the women. He particularly liked the one in the middle, a short strawberry blond with a sprinkle of freckles across her nose. Her sad expression and barely contained fear was quite erotic and very enticing. He felt a stirring in his loins, but what good is man if he cannot resist temptations?

"My name is Donald Graff, the cartographer. Which one of you would like to warm my bed tonight?" None of them gave any indication of knowing who he was, or having any desire to accommodate his wishes. He turned to D'Abo. "Thank you for the gesture, but I make it a habit not to bed women who do not wish my company."

D'Abo tilted his head knowingly. "Shall I have a selection of boys brought in?"

"No. Absolutely not."

At a signal from D'Abo, the girls filed out. The blond, who'd picked up on the extra attention paid to her, looked relieved.

"I've enjoyed them all," said D'Abo. "You really don't know what you're missing."

"I have a fair idea. Just out of interest, was one of them your current companion? I'm just wondering at the value of the information I just gave you."

D'Abo dabbed his lips with his napkin and threw it on his plate. The door the chef had entered from opened and two servants immediately began clearing the table.

"I'm currently bedding none of them. I've taken to a more spirited, if less attractive woman. Looks aren't everything you know."

"I guess dinner is over," Graff snatched one more olive as the tray was carried past him.

"Yes. Philip will show you to your room, then give you an abbreviated tour."

Philip appeared as if by magic, pulling Donald's chair out. Graff followed his chaperone. The doors shut and D'Abo was alone in the room. The fat man took a swallow of scotch straight from the bottle. "Marco," he bellowed.

The chef appeared.

"Have my second dinner laid out, for two. I will be dining with my lady this time."

A spread surpassing the grandeur of the first was on the table as a tired-eyed woman was brought in by one of the Reservoir's goons. Her hair had been done, and she wore make-up, but it barely hid the bags under her eyes. She wore an off-the-shoulder dress of emerald green, specially—and quickly—made to compliment the reptilian scales tattooed on one arm.

"Menka, my dear," said D'Abo, bringing a bottle of wine to the table. "Your time with me here will soon be ending, but rather than being the dame of a crumbling prison, wouldn't you rather be queen of Compton Pit?"

42. Ethics

The droning faded. It was obvious from the sound that many of the wasps had left. Darcy had no idea how long they'd been in the trailer. There was hardly any room to move, what with the reefer packed with both Freeland's panel equipment, spare tires, tools and spare parts from the truck yards. Parts that Caps had selected. The only sounds were the wasps and three people breathing. It was impossible to tell how much time had passed. The buzzing faded some more, then vanished completely. What was left was an echo, almost like white noise, a residual throbbing as the eardrums adjusted to silence.

"They're gone," said Toffee.

"Is it night out?" Darcy asked. "Have we been here that long?"

"I don't think so," said Sid. "Is it getting warmer in here?"

"The fire! It must have reached us. The smoke would drive the stingers away."

It was getting decidedly warmer in the trailer, soon the heat would be unbearable.

"I'm opening the door, Halbert. Sting or bake, we're dead either way." There was the sound of canvas shoved aside, then the doors opened and smoke filled their lungs. They jumped down from the truck, not a wasp was in sight. The ditch where the fire started was burned out. The Pig was blackened metal and broken glass.

"Hmmph," snorted Toffee, "roast pig."

Smoke filled the air and all three of them stooped to get beneath it.

By the truck, the blaze was coming into its full glory. Sid eyed the yellow combustant that still adhered to the cab and the trailer.

"Come on," he grabbed a tarp. "We have to get the truck away from here." He pulled himself up the hood and rubbed the windshield till it was at least semi-clear.

Darcy scanned the road, bracing herself for the inevitable sight of her friend's swollen corpse, but it wasn't there.

"Sid, Caps is gone!"

He didn't hear her. The Boss was already in the cab of the truck, firing up the motor. Darcy ran, bent over, towards the camper. A smear of blood marked where she'd last seen the artist. Another smear of blood was on the door of the camper. She ripped the door open and jumped in. It was like an oven inside. Stretched out between the dining booth and what passed for the kitchen, Caps lay in a puddle of his own blood. Darcy lost herself. The heat vanished for her as she fell to her knees and tried to check Caps in a hundred different places at once. His face and chest were a mass of swollen red lumps, but the flesh between the mounds was so pale.

The camper rocked as Toffee came in. He grabbed Darcy and yanked her up, shoving her rudely into the booth. His fingers traced the side of Caps's neck.

"I don't believe it. He's still got a pulse."

With Toffee looking after Caps, Darcy began assembling details. Dead wasps on the floor of the camper, and on the counter top. Smears of blood on the door of the tiny oven. What Caps had done was incredible. Somehow, he'd gotten inside. Somehow, he'd had the presence of mind to stuff a strip of his shirt in his mouth. Even in his unconscious state, a hand pressed wadded cloth tightly to his wound.

A sheen of sweat stood out on Toffee's face. He squinted at her through the smoke that was filling the camper. "You're not going to leave here without him, are you?"

She shook her head.

Toffee backed out of the camper, then dragged Caps out by his feet.

With the artist draped over Toffee's shoulder, they ran for the truck. Sid had stopped it just outside the thickest of the smoke.

They piled into the cab, Toffee shoving Caps in before him. Sid threw the truck into gear and pulled away down the highway, outdistancing the spreading flames.

Darcy arranged Caps in the sleeping area. The wad of cloth was stuck to his chest. It was saturated, but possibly the bleeding had stopped. She'd pulled the stuffing out of his mouth, but could only hear his breathing by putting her ear right up to his face.

"There's the ambulance," called Sid through the curtain. "You've got five minutes."

Darcy leapt from the cab and ran to the back doors of the ambulance. They were locked. The front seats were empty. She was casting about for white-garbed corpses when Toffee shot the doors open with his rifle. He waited outside as Darcy rooted through the ambulance's contents for the equipment she thought she needed. She had bandages and a suture kit stuffed under one arm when she found the saline-filled IV bag.

"It won't work," said Toffee.

"What?"

"You want to take blood from me and stick it into the painter. How're you going to do that?"

"With this!" she shook the IV bag at him. A long tube hung from the bag, with a needle in the other end of it. "I'll squeeze out the fluid, and..."

"It won't work. You want to fill the bag up with my blood. That needle's bore is too small."

"How do you know?"

"I watched someone else try the same thing."

"Fine!" She threw her bundle to him. "Take that to Sid."

She rifled through boxes, grabbing more stuff; here a set of syringes, there some tubing. When one opened box revealed small glass vials marked antihistamine she took it and abandoned the ambulance.

The truck was already moving again as Darcy searched Caps's arm for a vein.

"His blood pressure's too low," said Toffee, examining the suture kit.

"Shut up!" She found what she hoped was a vein and shoved the needle in, then lifted the saline bag and fiddled with the valve that would allow fluid to flow down the tube. When the rate was at about a drop a second, she handed the bag to Toffee. "Here, make yourself useful."

She taped the needle in place with some non-allergic tape then plunged a syringe through the top of an antihistamine vial. She drew back the plunger, considered it, then drew it back some more.

"Do you have any idea what you're doing?" asked Toffee. He searched for someway to fasten the IV bag to the ceiling.

"If he goes into anaphylactic shock, he'll die."

"He's going to die anyway."

Darcy looked for a place on the IV setup she could stick the needle into. There was a valve that looked like it was designed for that purpose, but she didn't know how to work it. Fearful of getting an air bubble in the line, she picked a spot on Caps's other arm, and shot him up with the drug. A lurch of the truck nearly fouled the injection.

"Sid! Stop the truck."

After a few moments, the truck slowed, then halted.

"He's lost a couple pints at least," said Toffee. "There's a ton of sting juice running through him, plus the smoke inhalation. You're wasting your time, but have fun." The curtain swung closed as he slid out of the berth.

The IV tube still led upward, and Darcy followed it to the bag that was now pinned to the ceiling with three syringes.

She pawed through the rest of her medical booty until her eyes fell on a strip of sterilized wipes in individual packets. She should have used those before the injections, but hadn't thought of it. Still, infection was a rather minor consideration at the moment. She was hunting for butterfly bandages, but instead came up with a white packet marked Steri-Strip Skin Closures.

Sid's head and shoulders appeared through the curtain. "Can I help?"

Darcy began shaking all over. "I don't know, Sid. I may have killed him with that injection. I only have a vague idea. I don't know if I got veins…I don't know if…"

Sid took her by the shoulders. "It looks like you're doing fine. What's next?"

"We have to…help me with his wound." She handed him the packet of skin closures and took hold of the wad of cloth. "Pulling this off is going to open it up. I…"

"Pull it off."

She tried easing it at first, blood oozing out of the cloth as she squeezed it.

A wasp poked its head out from between two folds and crawled onto her wrist. She jerked back, yanking the makeshift bandage off. Immediately the ugly wound was running. Crimson rivulets ran down Caps's chest, slaloming around wasp-sting moguls. Darcy squashed the wasp with the heel of her hand. Her mind delivered a picture of the insect struggling beneath the cloth, trying to get inside Caps's wound. A wave of nausea overtook her and she hovered on the edge of vomiting.

Sid grabbed the edges of the gash and pinched it closed with his fingertips. Darcy tore open the Steri-Strip package and looked confusedly at the single sheet of shiny paper inside. On the back of it were five parallel lines of some thin, transparent material. She peeled one of the lines off and found it quite adhesive. The material separated into four pieces, each a little over an inch long. She used all four of them to hold the wound shut, cursing at herself for once again forgetting the alcohol wipes. When Sid removed his fingers, the wound stayed closed.

Darcy took up the suture kit. It contained thread and some curved needles. "It'll be just like sewing leather, right?" She tried to open the packet, but her hands were too unsteady.

Sid gently took the kit from her. "If we keep him still, those sticky strips should be enough. I'll take it from here. Get some rest."

"I'm fine."

"Just close your eyes for a moment."

She acquiesced. When her eyes opened again, Caps's face was clean, and he was wrapped in a blanket. The IV was still attached to the arm that protruded from the gray cocoon. Darcy lifted the blanket. A gauze bandage had been taped over his chest. The bandage was an orderly rectangle, but the tape was skewed every which way so that nothing was stuck directly over a sting. The redness in the stings themselves was fading, and although there was some swelling, it could have been a lot worse. She shuddered with relief. A part of her had screamed that she was making a big mistake with the antihistamine injection, that it was another anti-something altogether that was needed. Between his face and chest, she counted seventeen stings. There were a total of four more on his hands.

The bunk beneath her shook as the truck lurched to a stop.

"Darcy, wake up," came Sid's voice, accompanied by a knock on the curtain frame.

"I'm up. What's going on?"

She pulled herself from the sleeping area and settled into the space behind the seats. The Boss was drumming his fingers on the oversized wheel.

"Are you sure you saw nothing of Noah and Lena?"

"I'm positive, Sid."

"Close your eyes, think back. Caps was in the back seat. What else?"

"I was being attacked by the mud people."

"Makes sense," Toffee said. "Some mud blocks scent. They'd have to figure that out to survive here."

"What else?" prompted Sid. "Think, Darcy. Was there blood? Were their weapons there?"

Darcy concentrated. She'd been in such a frenzy it was difficult to picture the back of the Pig clearly. "I don't remember blood. Noah's shotgun was on the floor by his seat. Do you think they were taken? Why take them and not us?"

"I don't know," said Sid. "My gut tells me they were taken. If Caps was stabbed and left for dead, why weren't the others? How many of these mud people did you kill?"

"I don't know if I killed any of them, but I know one of them's blind." She brought her hand up and looked at the dried blood on the fingertips, and everywhere else.

"Sid, if Lena's alive…we can't let Caps die. What would we tell her when we got her back?"

"Who says we're going to?" snarled Toffee. "We've got the rig, we've got the panels. We're going back to the Pit, right Halbert?"

The Boss said nothing.

"Sid, you can't," Darcy was determined. "They are alive, they have to be. We can't just abandon them."

Sid gripped the wheel tighter. From a pragmatic point of view, he had what he needed. His rig, his equipment. He could get Bacon in on loan if not for good, embargo or no embargo. That would mean giving up panels to Underbel, though. Slowly, the Boss started the engine and turned the rig back towards the heart of the city.

Darcy let go the breath she was holding. "Hang on, Lena, we're coming."

"If we're going back," said Toffee, "we're going back for the sun boy, not for your friend. Are we going back, Halbert?"

The Boss was using an exit to give himself room to turn. "We're not going ahead, I'll tell you that much. They'll have other ambushes set up down the road. We'll need to find another way out of the city, or hole up somewhere until things cool off. I can't believe wasps saved our lives."

"I'll have to tell Conrad about this," Darcy said. "Wasps saved his life, too. Sid, we're not leaving are we?"

"I don't know."

"Sid!"

"Hush, Darcy. Let me think."

There was still a fair amount of smoke hanging in the air when they returned to the site of the crash. They drove along the ditch, staring into the blackened soil. There were two bodies, one on either side of the van, both blackened.

"Neither of 'em is Lena," said Sid, noting that both bodies had complete—if charred—legs. "We haven't a clue where they could have gone. This city is huge, and they know it. Even if Lena was still with us that wouldn't help. She knew the city then, they know the city now. We don't even know if they're alive. Maybe whoever these people are, they wanted a couple of bodies."

"You're the one who kept insisting that members of previous expeditions were still alive," said Darcy, indignant at his sudden change in tune.

"I never said they were alive, I simply pointed out that we didn't know. And we don't know now. Maybe they escaped the Pig and ran. They could be dead of wasp stings twenty feet into the bush and we'd never know it. Sorry, Darcy, but it's true. Now be quiet. I haven't made up my mind yet."

Sid chose the first exit beyond the flames. It turned out to be a poor choice initially, the road almost disappearing between the trees, but very few animals appeared. After a kilometre or so, the trees vanished and they were once again driving through an industrial area. There were more truck yards, not as many as on Douglas Road, but the ground, like before, was fairly desolate. There was more lichen, and more weeds, but as the city went, it wasn't that bad. Sid pulled in between two decrepit rigs close to the road. Nothing better than hiding in plain sight. "Let's get this crap off the van." There were only two net-helmets in the cab. "Darcy, stay inside."

Toffee and Sid used more tarps from the back of the trailer. They had no water other than a flask on Sid's belt. The rest had been in the Pig. Rubbing the yellow gunk off proved to be a repeated effort of smearing and re-smearing, taking a little bit more off each time. Only one animal attacked them, a mangy dog with patchy brown fur. Toffee threw a tarp over it as it pounced, then kicked it to death while it was trapped in the canvas net.

"We're going now, right?" said Toffee. "This is what you do, Halbert. You've got what you need. The Pit is waiting for their fearless leader to return." Sid didn't answer. "You have any idea where they might be? That's if they're still alive."

"Get back in the cab, have Darcy take care of your cheek. It's bleeding again."

Toffee pushed his hand up under his mesh. "No it ain't."

Sid's blow caught the hunter completely by surprise, not just that it came, but that it landed. He rocked on his feet, but didn't fall. They were behind the truck, out of view of Darcy if she'd been checking the mirrors.

The hunter touched his face again, this time the fingertips came away with blood on them.

"Don't, Ethan. You're right, I get what I need, and right now I need you in one piece, but don't push me."

The hunter took a couple of breaths to calm himself, then pointed his blade at Sid's heart. "It's coming, Halbert. Not now, but it's coming."

Always let the asshole get the last word, Sid thought, clamping his jaw shut, burying his anger. It had been one of his father's sayings. He motioned to the cab with a flick of his eyes. The blade dropped and the hunter moved off.

Sid turned his energy to cleaning the van, rubbing in circular motions. It was repetitive and somehow hypnotic, watching the paint spiral away to nothing. With the threat of violence in abeyance, at least temporarily, his anger/fear slackened into just anger, then sorrow. He'd thought they'd had it, gone to nature, shuffled off the mortal coil. The sheer number of wasps, the flimsiness of their defence. And though a few tears had escaped, wrung out by how suddenly everything had turned so bad, he'd spent those last moments being strong, for Darcy. And then they weren't the last moments.

The weight of all the emotions he'd been holding at bay fell on him like a hammer. Richard was near death, Noah and Lena were probably dead. The Pig was lost, but that was just a minor detail. Despite it all, he had what he'd come for. Just past the metal he was cleaning were the crown jewels. All he had to do was get them home. The equipment and materials were worth more to the Pit than Noah, more in fact than Sid himself, or the rest of the Deep Six. Deep four, now. But he hadn't wanted to lose any of them. In his heart of hearts, he didn't believe he would. Toffee always brought his whole team back, always. True the hunter's missions were nothing like this, but it was there nonetheless. It never occurred to the Boss that he was capable of anything less, but it should have. Settlement to settlement, refuge to refuge, Sid had always gotten what he'd needed. He'd improved things where he'd been, but always at a cost.

The Boss had left a trail of bodies behind him as he worked his way across the continent. All that was supposed to change once he'd assumed the helm of Compton Pit. A secure, well-supplied oasis beneath the ground. It was just the same, only the stakes were higher. He'd broken Fenwick Prison, but been merciful in the end. Not this time. Richard's life was going to be worth more than just a big metal box and a pile of silicone wafers. Sid wanted it all. Every book in every library, every can of soup, all the light switches and every inch of pipe that led to any sink. If these mud people were what stood between him and that, then so be it.

The very fact that Richard was still alive was nothing short of miraculous. That the ambulance had been within reach, that the equipment Darcy looted hadn't gone to rot...The antihistamine was years past the outdate inked on the bottles, and saline was saline, but still, nothing short of a miracle. If someone had been taking bets, though, Sid still would have put his money on the man never seeing the outside of the city. There was a limit to what a body could take, and Richard's chances would have been slim even if he was under Dr. Patel's care back at the Pit.

The Boss dropped to one knee and did something he hadn't done in a long time. He prayed. He thanked God for whatever aid had been rendered so far, and asked for a little more in what was to come.

"Here," said Sid, bringing the truck to a stop and letting it idle. They had only the cab now, the trailer hidden among several other trucks back where'd they taken the pit stop.

They were in a rundown area of the city, not that any part of Vancouver was up to code, but this section looked like it was marked for demolition long before the Change. The old brick façades were collapsed, three floors worth of a five-story fire escape had fallen off one building. There'd also been a recent fire, possibly from a lightning strike. The trees were blackened skeletons, and that meant a lot less teeth. He picked the spot for another reason; it had a landmark. For the most part the structures were slum apartments, but at the end of the block were golden arches that once proclaimed over five billion served.

"Here," Sid handed the CB handset to Darcy. "Assuming they think we were killed by the wasps, I don't want them recognizing my voice."

Darcy took a breath, then spoke into the mic. "Second team, this is Eagle, we're at the third checkpoint. Rendezvous at Dundas and Wall near the big M in three hours. Radio silence from here out."

She handed the handset back to Sid who returned it to its cradle. "Now we wait."

From the back, Darcy threw her arms around her adopted father and kissed his cheek. "Thank you, Sid. We'll find them, I know we will."

Two hours later, with the truck stashed between collapsing buildings a safe distance away, they raised their guns at the sound of motion. Instead of the tinny-sounding engines they'd heard out on the highway, a rhythmic clicking drifted up Dundas, as if made by metal on metal.

"They're coming in on bicycles?" Toffee speculated. "How the hell do they manage that?"

But it wasn't a two-wheeler coming up the road, it was a three-wheeler. One large wheel in front, two in back, mesh surrounding the drivers, they pedalled the trike up to the golden arches, then past it and behind the restaurant's building. Another trike arrived a minute later and joined its forerunner. From their vantage point behind one of the apartment buildings, Sid was able to make out a motor on the back of the second trike before it vanished.

"They've got motors on those things, but they can peddle them as well. Clever. Like giant mopeds."

People appeared from behind the restaurant. One of them made hand signals and the others began to spread out, finding hiding spots along the road. None of them spoke. They wore clothing both pre-Change and hand-made from animal hides. Each of them had cheesecloth wrapped around their heads, leaving only their eyes exposed. They all carried skinbags, some of them had bows slung over their shoulders and quivers hanging at their hips. Each of them was covered head-to-toe with gray mud. As city dwellers positioned themselves—Sid counted seven of them—another pair of trikes arrived, this time from the other direction.

"They're going to try the same tactic," said Toffee. "Blind us, then light us up."

"Not us," said Sid, a grim smile playing at his lips, "Eagle and the second team."

"There's too many of them," said Darcy. "They've got four or five in each of those trikes."

"We only need one."

The second pair of trikes unloaded, and the drivers pedalled off to find hiding spots for the vehicles, metal chains rotating gear wheels. The same mud-person who had directed the initial team—at least it looked like the same person, it was hard to tell—directed the second group, hands dancing in the air.

"Here we go," said Sid. One of the Vancouverites was approaching them, completely unaware of their presence. This one carried a skinbag, but no bow.

The cloth-wrapped figure turned into the alley, obviously seeing the same strategic value in it as Sid had, and was promptly locked in a choke hold by Toffee. The hunter had his arm around the person's throat, his biceps flexed as he cut off both oxygen and blood supply to the brain. The figure struggled, then spasmed and went limp. It took about nine seconds.

"Let's go," Sid ordered.

Toffee slung his victim over his shoulder, surprised at the lack of weight. They moved as quietly as they could, stepping on weed-free patches of concrete whenever able.

Darcy covered the rear, prepared to shoot at a moment's notice. Would the mud people hold their positions until the fictitious second team was supposed to arrive? If so, they had about forty-five minutes at the outside.

Darcy stood guard by the truck as Sid and Toffee took the prisoner inside the more sturdy of the flanking buildings. In the basement, in a rotted, mouldy apartment, windowless and illegal by old world laws, Toffee dumped the prisoner into a wood chair, and unwrapped the cheesecloth. The face beneath was as mud-caked as the rest. Toffee sliced the cheesecloth into two pieces and set about tying ankles to chair legs. Sid tied the captive's arms together behind the chair with the strap from his M16.

The hunter lifted the Vancouverite's head. Short hair was plastered to the top of it, its colour impossible to tell beneath the gray. "Halbert, it's a girl. And she's young." The mud conformed to the smooth quality of the girl's face.

"Wake her up."

Toffee slapped her gently a few times. The girl's eyes opened and her jaw dropped, but no sound came out. Her features twisted into a scowl and she struggled at her bonds.

"I'm Eagle," said Sid. "You were expecting me."

She looked from Sid to the hunter. Drying mud fell like dandruff as she writhed.

"You took two of my people. Where are they?" She continued to struggle. "If you free yourself we'll just tie you up again." The girl gave a mighty heave, tendons standing out on her neck as she pulled at her arms. She succeeded in nothing more than tipping the chair.

"Do you speak English?" Sid asked, righting the prisoner.

Toffee slapped her. "Answer the man."

She pressed her lips together and stared at them defiantly.

"What are you? Sixteen? Seventeen?" Still no reply. "We're under the ground. If you scream, no one will hear you."

The girl made no attempt to do so. Toffee grabbed her face and squeezed, forcing her mouth open. "Well, look at that. No tongue."

Sid was taken aback for a moment, then gained control of himself. "Do you understand English?"

She didn't nod, but her eyes flickered.

"Wait here," said Sid. He left, and returned a minute later with a street map of the city. He unfolded it and held it up to her. "Do you recognize this? It's a map of this city. Have you seen one of these? This is where we are now," he pointed. "Now I'm going to move my finger around the map. When I come to where you're holding our people, you nod. Understand?"

The prisoner stared through the map as if it wasn't even there.

"Maybe you can't read the map. I'll name off places as I come to them." He began a litany as his fingers moved past landmarks. The girl kept her face impassive, still staring at nothing.

Toffee scraped his blade along the edge of the chair. The girl jerked away. "She's not deaf."

Sid turned his back and let the map fall to his side. "No tongue. Great."

"They might all be like that," said Toffee. "Best way I've ever heard to teach 'em to keep quiet."

Sid looked at the girl again, taking in her youth. She would have been in grade eleven or twelve if the world hadn't shifted. She would be dating and preparing for college. Or maybe she would have been selling herself for heroin or mugging the elderly to support her habit. "I wish we'd grabbed a man."

"Should we go back out and get another? Give me the map, Halbert. Go outside and I'll get my hand dirty for you."

"Ethan…" a pained expression crossed his face, "Never mind. Here," he handed off the map and left to join Darcy.

When Toffee heard the sound of the basement door closing, he pulled a small table up to one side of the chair and sat down.

"I know you speak English, girl. Look at me," he let his blade rest on her lap. "Look at me."

She turned her head slowly. When her eyes were fixed on his, he resumed.

"You don't want to give up your home. I understand that. I don't care. But I'm a fair man. I want a secret from you, I'll give you one of mine. Even I have to spill them sometimes. The man who couldn't stomach this? He's Halbert. He wants his little engineer back. The woman, you saw her before I put you out, her name's Darcy. She wants to save her friends. Now I don't give a shit one way or another about the two people you kidnapped, but it's recently come clear to me that I'd do just about anything for Darcy. You don't know me, but if you did, you'd understand how much that pisses me off. She don't care too much for me, and that just makes it worse. Add to that the fact that Halbert blindsided me…first hit I've taken in a long time…well, I've got a lot of aggression to work out." He held the map up and lifted his blade, laying it flat against the girl's cheek. "Now it's your turn. Tell me a secret."

It was fifteen minutes by Darcy's watch that the hunter rejoined them. "They took our people. She figured they're still alive." He pressed the map flat against the side of the cab and stabbed a spot with his blade. "There." A drop of blood on the blade's tip soaked into the map. "Sorry, thought I cleaned all of that off."

"You're kidding," said Sid. "Are you sure you got the truth?"

"I'm sure."

"How…you're absolutely positive?"

"You want a second opinion? Let's get another one. I can go again."

"No. They must have…well, I guess we're going to find out, aren't we? How fast do you think those trikes can go?"

"Fully loaded? Thirty, forty maybe. They'll know shortcuts, though."

"We'll have to get a good head start." Sid pulled himself up to the cab.

Toffee caught Darcy's sleeve as she moved to follow. "Did he tell you it was a girl?" The chief of security jerked her arm out of Toffee's grasp, not answering one way or the other.

Sid fired up the engine. He imagined he could hear heads turning down by the restaurant. The rig rumbled out into the street and northeast, away from the corner of Dundas and Wall. With the trike motors running, the drivers wouldn't be able to hear the rig once Sid put enough distance between them. He turned south on Nanaimo Street and gave the truck some speed, smashing saplings and thundering over cracks. Without the trailer to hold it back, the cab was a much more powerful beast. From his high vantage point behind the wheel, Sid felt like he could drive through buildings if he had to. He threw caution to the wind and floored it. The animals they encountered were a non-issue, harmless teeth left in the distance, or smeared on blacktop.

"Sid, be careful," said Darcy from the back, casting a concerned glance at the sleeping area where their patient lay. Even the hunter looked a little uncomfortable as branches smacked into the windshield.

"I need an obvious trail and I need it fast." He checked the side mirror, then reached up and sounded the horn. "Come on you tongueless freaks. Come and get me!" He checked the side mirror, waiting as long as he could, then hauled on the wheel, taking the truck through the remains of a gas station, careful not to hit the larger growths or any of the structures, then headed up a different road, in the direction they'd come from. After a minute, he brought them to a stop, but kept the motor running. He eased them forward until they could see a patch of Nanaimo between the buildings. He realized the nose of the cab would then be visible, but it was a risk he needed to take. The trikes could be heard in the distance, motors gaining both pitch and volume as they came closer. They blurred past, three of them, then the fourth a second later.

Sid threw the truck into gear and drove.

"Nice," said Toffee. "Where are we going?"

"Back onto Dundas, then from there–"

"Halbert, are you serious about taking these people out, or just playing at it again?"

"I'm serious."

"Well you're driving a doglicking truck."

Sid had already weighed the odds of slipping in behind the trikes and running them down, but there were four of them, if the cab got so much as a flat tire, they were finished.

"Give me an ammo report."

"I've got eighteen rounds for my rifle, and some shotgun shells, if we find a shotgun." Toffee fished the shells out of his pocket and dropped them to the floor of the cab. "My sidearm's loaded, but I've got nothing to put in once it's empty."

Darcy patted pockets. "Sid, I'm loaded and I know I've got another…" her hand encountered something hard and cool in her right hip pocket. She ignored it, feeling for bullets. "Five more. How about you?"

"Whatever's in the clip for the M16, and a full load in my revolver. Don't shoot unless you have to. We need a lot more information before we can go in. There's something not right here."

"You mean more not right than the sand people from Star Wars chasing us around?" asked Darcy. She stopped, surprised. It was the type of thing Caps would have said. Except he would have called them Tuska…Tuskan something…She pulled from her pocket a stone pipe.

"Think how many have vanished into this city. None of them even got a warning off. We've been here for days. We've gotten away from them twice. If these are the people responsible for earlier disappearances, they've gotten rusty." He fiddled with the CB's dials. "I wish we had the radio from the Pig. We'd have at least a limited capability of scanning the airwaves. We only know that one of them was tongueless."

"I think they're all talkin' with their hands," said Toffee. "These ones anyway. According to that girl these folk ain't doing a lot of French kissing. It's some kind of religious thing, but I'm sketchy on the details."

"You got all that from a mute?" asked Darcy.

"Just got to know what questions to ask."

"That doesn't rule out Morse code, or a similar type of signal. Did you ask her if they had radios? Or just a scanner."

"Didn't get around to that."

"They'll have guards up," said Sid. "And patrols. I hate to say this, but we're going to have to do our recon on foot. This rig is too damn noisy."

43. objects of worship

All Noah could see through the glass was a faded wash of orange light, the source of which must have come from around the corner. He'd thrown himself against the floor-to-ceiling pane with all his weight, but that did nothing. He still wore his coveralls, but his boots had been taken, as had his sidearm, and anything in his pockets. The cell had no door, and the dim light didn't let him examine the ceiling, it disappeared into shadow a few inches above Noah's reach.

"Hello?" he called again. "Is there anybody out there?"

The metal bowl he assumed was for solid waste was bent in on one side. He'd tried to break the glass with it. There was a drain in the middle of the floor, and although the drain plate could have been a useful tool, Noah had been unable to remove it. He had managed to cut a few of his fingers in the attempt. He was thirsty, hungry and quite afraid. There was a tender lump on the right side of his head. It stung when he touched it, and there had been dried blood, now rubbed off, on the side of his head. He remembered nothing after bottles started hitting the Pig.

Noah checked his pockets again, hoping to find something both he and his captors had missed, but both parties had been quite thorough. He had called the names of the others, but that had produced the same result as everything else he'd called out. Nothing. In vain, he traced the walls again, walking slowly around the cell. It was four feet from wall to glass, and about six feet long, barely enough for him to lie down in. The hunter or Sid would both have to sleep at an angle if they were in similar cells, if they were even alive at all.

Maybe I'm dead, and this is hell. The light's colour suggested that it came from fire. As if to support his irrational thought, a hideous face appeared in the glass. One eye wider than the other, the nose bent and flattened, straggly hair and a patchy beard that grew out between a criss-cross of scars—it was certainly the face of a demon.

Noah lurched away from the glass, slamming his back against the rear wall. The face made no threatening moves, or any moves at all for that matter. It simply floated in the dim gloom outside.

"Who are you?" asked Noah in a hushed tone, unaware that no sound penetrated the glass. As his shock receded he realized he could make out a dim outline of the creature. It was hunched, one arm cocked at an odd angle, and the legs were bowed inwards. He looked, for all the world, like a troll; one of the so-ugly-they-were-charming statuettes his mother had collected. "Why have you brought me here? Where are my friends?"

The troll lifted a slender finger to its lips and gave the universal sign to be quiet. Despite the hideousness of its visage, there was a gentle quality in its eyes. Noah approached the glass and looked deeper into the creature's face. It was a man, not some mythical cave dweller. His deformities were not natural, but inflicted, constantly, and over a long period of time.

"Are you a prisoner, too?"

The man's eyes travelled down Noah, fixing on his chest, then he raised a hand and pressed it to the glass over Noah's heart.

The panel jockey looked down. "This?" he asked, pointing to the yellow stripe above his pocket. "This is my rank. I'm..." it suddenly occurred to him that he shouldn't say where he was from, or what he was capable of.

The troll gave the quiet sign again, then moved off, fading into the gloom.

"Wait!" Noah cried. "Come back! Tell me why I'm here!"

At the last moment Noah thought he saw something dangling between the man's feet. Then the hunched figure was gone.

"Where have you been?" demanded the boy, twisting Slave's ear and dragging him down the corridor. "The Master has had us looking all over for you." The ear was released.

Slave followed after the boy, Conner. In a few days the child would be old enough to chose his path, warrior or seeker. The boy had warrior written all over him, and Slave knew he would soon be cleaning Conner's blood off the tongue block. That was their privilege, to give up the distraction of speech for a purer spirit in service to God. No doubt the boy was proficient in handspeak, though he would never use it outside of lessons, not until his ascension at any rate. Only Luke and the warriors were allowed to communicate in that method. Slave understood the language as well, though was careful never to show it. He'd flicked something at Archie once. Though the previous Master would never touch Slave's hands, there had been nothing wrong with restructuring his arm.

The boy knocked, then opened the door. Slave entered, already bracing for the blow he was sure to receive. It didn't come. The wooden cudgel Luke used for that purpose was leaning safely against the wall; so, too, was the ceremonial staff that was likewise employed when closer at hand. The Master sat at his table, two large sheets of paper before him.

"Come, Slave. Look at these."

They were drawings, shredded near the top edges, but otherwise undamaged. One showed a young man on a rocky precipice, the sun between his hands. The other depicted three nudes of the same woman.

"These were brought to me from the car that crashed. There were more, but they'd been shredded, most likely by the cat that was in it. But God preserved these. They showed us who She wanted. I haven't harmed them yet. God hasn't told me what to do with them. She let them in to the city that we could bring them to Her. Slave, who are they?"

Slave studied each of the drawings, then cast his eyes at the floor and shook his head. Luke struck him open handed across the face.

"Don't lie to me. This one," he stabbed the drawing of Noah, "is wearing the same uniform you once had. Is he like you? Does he know what you know?"

Slave began to tremble inside. He didn't know the boy, but he did know the woman. There was nothing he could do to help, and he was ashamed.

"That's why you don't answer, this one is to be the new Slave. You have been with us too long. But what of the woman? Slave?"

He shuffled back and began the labourious process of removing his shirt. He had only a few, and he didn't want to get blood on this one. Soon the cudgel would be falling on his shoulders, or his legs. The Master liked to hit him in the legs.

Luke's eyes narrowed as he watched the man disrobe. "Do you think I'm going to beat you?" He stopped Slave from completely removing the shirt, then almost gently, pulled it back into place. Luke took him by the wrists. "I know more than you realize. The warriors give up speech to gain spiritual power, but they still have the hand speak. How much closer to God you are that you have nothing. I know She talks to you as well, tells you things that even I cannot hear. I give you permission, Slave, I give you privilege. Speak to me, make her will clear. None of us have ever been lost to outsiders before."

Do you know how insane you are? thought Slave. *I must be mad myself by now.*

A buzzing noise came from the table. Luke dropped Slave's wrists and hastily snatched a plastic egg timer, twisting the dial to silence it. "That's three. Three hours. How lucky you are to be here, to hear the last words of the intruders."

Luke threw the curtain aside, revealing a collection of interlinked communication devices. Soon a desperate cry would issue from it, heathens using their technology to announce their death, or cry for help. This time, thanks to a witless girl named Eagle, Luke had been able to pinpoint the exact time that that would happen. The minutes passed but nothing came from the speakers. The Master grew more and more agitated as the expected pleas failed to issue from the system.

Slave glanced at the cudgel. His relationship with it was intimate. He could almost feel its desire to strike emanating from across the room.

"It must be broken," announced Luke, sounding not entirely sure of himself. He moved to the chest and removed the box of implements: forceps, precision screwdrivers, a circuit tester. He slapped it into Slave's hands. "Check it, then check it again. If it's not working, I'll have your legs, I swear I will."

Slave didn't need to open anything to know the system was working. He'd given it a complete check-up only the day before. It was a marvel of engineering. It had three processing units and multi-band scanners that cycled from one end of the scale to the other, locking onto any transmission, then digitally recording it. Every transmission it had received since it had been turned on a year after the change could be played back at the touch of a few buttons. None but himself and the Master knew it was there. It was how Luke proved to his subjects that God spoke to him, how Archie had proven it before. The difference was Archie knew it was a pile of dogshit, a bunch of tricks no better than the wizard in his little cubical, berating Dorothy through a haze of holograms and smoke. But Luke believed the scanner was a divine instrument, built not by the hands of man, but by the will of a deity.

As Slave opened panels and ran diagnostics on a tiny screen located on the central unit, Luke turned his back, lest the sight of technology corrupt him. Though the scanner was the mouth of God, only a heathen could touch it.

Slave had thought many times of destroying the device, but he couldn't bring himself to do it. In what his world had become, the scanner was the only thing that reminded him of what he once was.

There was a new entry on the screen's menu selection, a recording he hadn't heard. He selected it and turned on the playback.

"Second team, this is Eagle. We're at the third checkpoint. Rendezvous at Dundas and Wall near the big M in three hours. Radio Silence from here out."

It was a husky alto voice that was as alien as it was achingly familiar. It filled him with a feeling of safety, and brought back a fleeting glimpse of who he used to be; Jonathan Crispin, chief of communications for Compton Pit.

"That was the last message," said Luke. "Three hours. That was three and a half hours ago. They couldn't have escaped unless She wanted. I don't understand. Enough! Slave, get out of here."

Jonathan was quick to comply. The Master yanked the curtain shut and followed him out to the hall, locking the door behind him with a small key. The boy, as ever, was waiting outside.

"I'm going to speak with our Lord," Luke said to the boy. "I'm not to be disturbed until the warriors return." He turned to Slave, speaking over his head rather than to his face as he did when they were alone. "Prepare the cleansing room. We'll need it tonight."

The Master walked off, his current herald right behind him. The uneasiness that was Jonathan's constant emotional state was pierced by something bittersweet and almost forgotten; hope. He perceived the illogic of the transmission even if Luke hadn't. Why would an exploratory team announce a rendezvous point so deep within hostile territory? It was a ruse, plain and simple. Never before had Luke proven himself to be so much less capable than the former Master. Whoever Eagle was, or whoever was pretending to be Eagle, had no idea how lucky she was.

Lena pushed her cheek to the cold, fourth wall of her cell. She was in complete darkness, and had only her sense of touch to go on. Her prison was tiny, she could cross its length in two strides, and its width in one. She couldn't reach the ceiling, though she'd jumped a couple of times. There was no door that she could find, although there was something in the floor, a drain it felt like, and an empty metal container that she'd stumbled over a couple of times before shoving it into one corner. She pulled her cheek away. The fourth wall, unlike the pitted concrete of the other three, felt very much like glass. She smacked the heel of her hand against it, testing its resiliency.

She'd called out a few times upon awakening in the dark place, at first afraid she'd been blinded. But examination proved that both her eyes were still there, and by pushing on closed lids, she could elicit bursts of colour. Her shouts had gained no response other than her own voice echoing off the inside of her prison. It was the quality of the echo that told her she was in a nearly soundproof oubliette. She didn't know how long she'd been there prior to regaining consciousness, and her short-term memory was a chaotic scattering of half-remembered sensations. A brief glimpse of Noah's door opening in the van, the feeling of movement, a bouncing, hard surface beneath her as she lay curled, her wrists bound behind her and hogtied to her ankles. She had nothing but her clothes, pants, blouse and socks. Lena's captors had taken everything, but had not been quite thorough enough in their search. She still had one weapon available to her.

Leaning against a wall for support, Lena stripped off her pants and unfastened her prosthetic, then she pulled her pants back on again, conscious of how much more vulnerable she felt without them. Balanced on one leg, she gauged her distance from the wall she was sure was glass, and swung. The leg struck with a thud, but tactile inspection showed no damage to either it or the wall. Taking a few breaths, she swung again, putting all her force into it. With a crunch, something gave, but it wasn't the glass. It was the bracket on top of the leg. Her fingers traced its new shape, knowing she couldn't put the leg back on. The wall, as before, was undamaged. "What do you want from me?" she asked the darkness.

At heart, she'd always been a pessimist. It was Caps's devil-may-care attitude that had kept her spirits buoyed in down times, and without him at her shoulder assuring her that he was alive, she could only assume that he and the others were dead. Lena slumped against the glass and slid to the floor. Thin tears drizzled down her cheeks. She held the leg to her chest like a child holding a teddy bear. There were no sounds other than those she made, and the vague, fish-like odour she'd detected upon awakening was gone now, her nose grown used to it. Unsure of her whereabouts, uncertain of her future, and effectively deprived of three of her senses, her desolation was absolute. Lena's limbs felt like they weighed a hundred pounds each. Her lids closed and misery carried her into unconsciousness.

In her sleep-like state, she didn't hear a door overhead slide open, nor did she see the orange light as a torch was placed, or lit, close to the opening. A rope ladder dropped into the cell.

Slave climbed haltingly down the ladder. Only exiting and entering his own cell in the same manner so many times allowed him to accomplish the task despite his body's disfiguration. He dropped to the floor and, with a furtive glance upwards, padded forward. His hands reached out to touch her face, stopping inches away. Slave had never seen a face so lovely as the one before him now. Even the dim memory of the wife he'd lost on New Wilderness Day paled in comparison. He touched her shoulder, then emboldened, gently pried Lena's fingers from the prosthetic. He had one hand almost off when her eyes snapped open.

She screamed, then swung with the leg, catching Slave upside the head. He staggered backwards, shaking. She screamed again and came at him, bludgeoning with a fury born of madness. The prosthetic became entangled in the rope ladder and Lena fell, jarring her hands against the floor. Slave rubbed the side of his face and looked up at the trap in the ceiling. He lunged for the ladder, intent to climb and be gone before he was discovered with the prisoner, but he was far too late.

The hall beyond the glass was suddenly visible as a lantern's hood was removed. Luke stood there, flanked by two of his seekers, their young heads shaved clean, red and blue paint across their cheeks.

Luke's smile never reached his eyes. He pointed at the trap door. Slave ascended. Lena was frozen in place, staring at the three people beyond her cell, and the creature disappearing through the ceiling. She spurred herself into motion as Slave's feet vanished from view. Lena grabbed at the rope ladder but it was whisked away, and the light from above winked out as the trapdoor was slammed shut. She could hear metal clicking against metal as a latch was thrown.

"Who are you?" she asked the figures beyond the glass. The central of the three, the one with hair, nodded to her, as if out of respect, then he turned and walked away, the two bald figures walking after, the light receding, then vanishing. She was again in darkness.

On her hands and knees she searched for her prosthetic, but it was gone, carried away in the ladder. Her fingers came across the bowl, and it was this that she hugged as she settled back against a wall and waited for light to appear once more.

After the seekers bound Slave to the table, they left at Luke's orders and closed the door behind them. It was an off-white room, lit via a skylight and two windows that looked out over barren earth. The table he was strapped to was both for torture and ceremony. It was upon this cruel bench that the seekers would be tied, to have the holy markings carved into their chests. At the base of the table was a wooden block, an altar of sorts, where warriors gave up their tongues.

"What did you hope to accomplish?" asked Luke, searching a box for the implement he desired. "Were you planning to fix her leg? Her mutilation wasn't apparent in the drawing. It surprised me. Do you know her?" He placed the box down, having found what he wanted. With a casual motion, Luke lowered secateurs to Slave's right foot and snipped off a toe. The man groaned, an animal sound, and went rigid against his bonds as warm blood oozed down his foot.

"That was for visiting the prisoner," said Luke, selecting another toe. "Did you also visit the other? Let's assume you did." Snip. "Now you have five toes left. You'll barely be able to walk if I cut off anymore. It was for this I had you prepare the room, Slave. Did you think it was for one of them? Maybe you don't need both eyes, hmmm?"

Slave's face contorted. He wanted to resist, more now than he had in years, but he couldn't lose an eye, he just couldn't. And he'd break eventually anyway. He always had in the past. Slave turned his head and mouthed one word, *please.*

"Good. You know them both?" Slave shook his head. "You know the girl?" A nod. "Do you know why God would want them?" A shake. "Don't lie to me now. She let them in to the city, kept them alive and delivered them into our hands. Do you know why She would want the girl?"

It didn't matter that Slave had no idea, except that it wasn't Her that wanted Lena, it was Luke. The Master needed something that would justify his beliefs, that the raiding party from Compton Pit had roamed the city on God's behest, rather than Luke's incompetence. Slave rifled through his memory like a man tearing pages from a book, desperate to find something he could give to save his eyes. It came to him, horrible as it was inevitable. Slowly, as if struggling against his own body, Slave nodded.

"Good. Tell me."

Luke unfastened Slave's wrists. The former chief of communication fluttered his fingers and hands as he wove the message. When he was done, Luke opened the door and bid a seeker to bandage Slave's foot.

Lena heard the latch disengage and pushed herself up, balanced on one leg, the metal pan clenched tight in both hands. If that creature came in again, she was going to bash its skull in and take the ladder. Instead of the hideous face that had greeted her last time, it was one of the bald, painted men she'd seen through the glass. He looked down through the rectangle of light, and lowered something on a rope. It was her prosthetic. He pointed to it and offered a hopeful smile.

He was too far up for Lena to hit, and she didn't trust her throwing abilities to accomplish much, so she placed the bowl on the ground and reached out to her leg. It had been repaired, crudely, but well enough that she could put it on. The face withdrew, but the trap remained open.

"Wait!" she cried. "Tell me where I am."

A strong wooden ladder was lowered, coming to rest firmly on the concrete floor. The face reappeared, it watched her expectantly.

"I have to put my leg on." She received a few blinks in reply. She looked at the glass, which gave back to her a faint reflection of herself. It wasn't pretty. Lena shucked her pants off and fastened the leg in place. It wasn't completely smooth and would chafe, but she'd be able to walk on it again. She drew her pants on and took a couple of tentative steps. She was surprised at how much relief she felt to have her prosthetic back. The painted man waited patiently, an unchanging look of bemusement on his face.

Lena placed her hands on the ladder and began to climb, cautiously, as if the man might start shaking it at any moment. But he didn't do anything to dislodge her, in fact he offered a hand to assist her as she neared the top. She refused it at first, but then accepted it when she realized how weak she was. Through the trapdoor, she emerged into a hallway lit by torches interspersed along the wall. In the better light, she realized the painted figure was no man, but still a boy. His youth showed through the red and blue. He wore a poor imitation of a toga, made by cutting a hole in a sheet and just draping it over its wearer.

"What are you?" she asked.

The boy, maybe seventeen by Lena's guessing, stepped back and gestured down the hallway. A few metres away stood a pair of differently attired people. They wore vests made from animal hides, and pants made of the same. Their faces weren't painted, but their scalps were bare. They appeared to be about the same age as the Hare Krishna wannabe.

"Where are my friends? Why have you brought me here?" She wanted to reach out and grab the boy by his throat, just like she'd done the rat, but a glance at the other two told her it wouldn't be a good idea. They were young, but they looked...vigilant.

The bald boy gestured again, this time adding a slight bow, and an expression that was almost apologetic.

Bewildered, Lena took a few steps in the indicated direction. The other two—she'd labelled them as guards—fell in beside her. They led her down the corridor, to a room where others, both painted and not, bustled in and out, bringing cushions, jugs, and other items. Allowing herself to be guided, Lena entered the room and, at another gesture, sat down on a dank-smelling love seat. The room was lit by a lantern, of a similar variety to the ones they used at UBC. The love seat was only one of the furnishings. There was also a mattress covered with blankets, a small table, a tub large enough for her to have a bath in, and a basket of fruit. Apples mostly, but she thought she saw the fat end of a pear among the red. Her mouth watered at the sight of them.

Her guide noticed her gaze and tripped over himself bringing the basket to her. The guards stood within the door, inconveniencing the constant tide of deliveries. She guessed the oldest among them would have been twenty. Some looked as young as sixteen.

"Do any of you speak?" Lena reached for the pear. At this point she had no fear of poison, there was no need for trickery. The pear was delicious, she practically inhaled it. When she was done she looked around for a place to throw the core. One of the delivery boys shot forward and snatched the core from her hand. He held it close to his chest, like it was a precious keepsake, then he bounded out the door.

"Somebody speak to me!" Lena stood and slapped the bowl out of her guide's hand. The guards kept their place, but the others stopped in their work and looked towards the boy who had brought her the ladder.

"They're not worthy," said a smooth voice from the doorway. It was the blond man that had stood outside her cell hours before. "Out, out." He waved everyone out of the room with the exception of Lena's guide. "This is Henry," he said, resting a hand on his subordinate's shoulder. "He was honoured to lead you here, as am I to receive you."

"Honoured. Honoured? You attacked us! You kidnapped me, put me in that hole."

"It was a test. One I almost failed. I apologize if you've been hurt in any way. I will leave you now. Come, Henry." The Master backed towards the door.

"Wait. Who are you? Where are my friends."

"Does She speak to you?" asked Luke, his face suddenly intent.

"Does she…who she? What the hell are you talking about?"

"Never mind, we'll speak of it later. I'll have water brought for you to bathe." He pulled the door shut behind him.

"NO!" Lena lurched for the door. She heard the sound of yet another latch being thrown. She hit the door a few times, then turned to survey her new cell, thinking she could use the lantern to start a fire, but that might not gain much more than the chance to asphyxiate before she burned to death. Whatever privileges her captors had decided to grant her, freedom wasn't one of them.

In a high-ceilinged room that may have once been a loading bay, Slave whimpered as he cored apples. His foot, now down to just two toes, throbbed. But pain, both real and phantom, was nothing in comparison to the ache in his heart. What he'd given up in the cleansing room, not only on Lena, but on the blond boy…all to keep from losing an eye. And what for? So he could continue to see clearly the hell in which he lived. But that wasn't entirely accurate. Hell would be much worse, though it was hard to imagine how. It was one of the last remnants of his Catholicism that still influenced him. To kill one's self meant eternal damnation, and if his life now was terrible beyond belief, he trembled at what hell might have in store. He often questioned God's cruelty—the real God, not the deity these young ones worshipped, a creation of fear and Archie's lies—that the real God would require so much suffering to be worthy of the gates of Heaven…still, faith didn't require explanations, and that was why it was so difficult to hold on to.

In the years before the Change, organized religion had less power than any time in history. Some people believed that was the cause, the Lord in Heaven had enough. Holding to his covenant never to flood the world again, The Almighty had chosen another tool with which to start over. Slave didn't believe that, though. If the animals were God's broom, the planet would have been swept clean in a few days, end of story. But he did believe in Jesus Christ, as amorphous as that was. In some ways, he envied the young ones their god. At least they could see their divine entity, even touch her on occasion.

The small paring knife was dull, and slicing the apples was difficult and time consuming. The calluses had formed on his thumb and knuckles over the years. The warriors harvested the apples by first blowing smoke through the trees to drive off the wasps. Once Slave was finished with them, seekers would make applesauce. He wondered if the children thought of that as they chose their path…not just what they would lose in articulation, but what they would have to eat.

Slave looked between the knife and the chain that transfixed his ankles. It was thick, but with enough time he could smash through it with a rock. He'd considered it many times before, but never followed through. Archie had told him if he ever broke the chain, then next one would have barbs.

Noah ascended the wooden ladder and into the hall above. He'd fixed in his mind how he was going to drive a fist through the face of whoever had lowered it, then jump the second person if there was one. He may have done well against one or two, but not four. They were on him as soon as his shoulders cleared the trap, blows upon his head and torso. One of them pulled at him so he wouldn't fall back to the cell below. Somehow Noah got his feet under him. A powerful kick found his chest. Noah fell to his knees, clutching his chest, surely a rib was broken. Blood and snot ran from his nose, and the welt he had before now pounded like thunder. A kick to his back knocked him flat. He felt sharp edges trace their way up his legs and back, then his coveralls were brutally yanked from his body, then his shorts in likewise manner. He tried to rise, but was kicked in the armpit, a quick, disabling blow. He rolled on his side as he fell, and looked up through blurry eyes into the faces of his attackers. They looked like children.

None of them spoke as they hoisted him up and dragged him down the hall. He tried to gain footing, to keep with them if nothing else, but he could barely catch his breath, never mind his balance.

Shortly after he was taken into a room that smelled like fear. He was bound to a table before which sat a wooden block, bloodstained and etched with a hundred cuts. Another person entered the room, this one taller, and a little older, late teens, maybe. He had no hair and his cheeks were painted red and blue.

"I told you to subdue him, not beat him half to death," he said. "You better not have broken anything." Henry checked each of Noah's bonds in turn. Satisfied, he dismissed the overzealous warriors, and probed Noah expertly for signs of damage. He clucked his tongue at Noah's sharp intake of breath when pressure was applied to the broken rib. "I'll take care of that for you."

Noah sucked his tongue, encouraging saliva to wet his mouth and throat. "Who…who are you?"

"Oh!" Henry started. He produced a small patch of hide and shoved it into Noah's mouth. "You don't have the right to speak," he said. "You're lucky you didn't say anything while the Master was around. You'll learn, though. You see, you're going to be our new slave. Now," he ran a finger down Noah's chest, "where should I start, the ankles or the tongue?"

44. Hail Caesar

Sara looked around the meeting room that was so familiar and yet so changed. For one thing, her view of the room was now from the Boss's chair at the head of the table. Whereas she used to have three people in her relaxed field of view, Dr. Patel, Odega, and lately, Noah, now she had the whole table to look at, and all of them focussed on her.

"I've been unable to access Dr. Odega's laptop," she said. "It's a password, and I don't know it."

Not only was the angle different, but the faces were as well. Even the faces that were familiar had changed. Dr. Patel's bandaged nose and blackened eyes marked the wake of his assault. Daniel, who usually sat in on meetings, was in Darcy's chair, and Purty beside him as second. The tracks of violence were on Purty's face as well. Mickey instead of Caps, Duff instead of Noah, and Chris...Cue Ball Chris of all people, the man whose animal impressions terrified newcomers, sat in as acting chief of the hunters. Mike would now be acting hunter second, but he wasn't present. Seth, face clear but arm still in a sling, talked quietly with Lyle Mercer, the dark-haired Nova Scotian who was acting chief of communications. Not that he had much of a job to do with the Pit on blackout.

"Lyle, do we have any decryption software in communications?"

Lyle held a finger up to Seth, as if for an inconsequential interruption in their conversation. "No, Dr. White. Not that can be applied right away. I suppose I could adapt something, but I'd have to brush up on my code."

"How long?"

"Uhm, a couple of weeks if I start today."

Two weeks, thought Sara, *might as well be two years.* "Thanks. I'll let you know. Daniel?"

"Nothing, not in the lab or in his room. I found no indication of outside contact. I also didn't find the journal you told me to look for."

"I think he transferred it to his laptop, I was hoping the paper copy was still around. If it was, I suppose he took it with him. Harpreet?"

The doctor was unsteady in his chair, the after affects of the flurazepam still with him. At least he knew what had been used. Chiu-Keung found the pill bottle under Odega's mattress in the infirmary. "I tried to necropsy Ghandi, but I just couldn't concentrate. I've got her in cold storage, I'll try again tonight."

"Understandable. No hurry, doctor, I doubt it will provide enlightenment. Opinions?"

"He went to D'Abo," said Chris.

"That doesn't add up," Seth spoke aloud for the first time, "D'Abo wanted Dr. Patel. Why have Odega rough him up, instead of kidnapping him?"

Sara nodded. Why indeed? "Lyle, did you contact Underbel?" She'd given the order to break silence just the one time, spending precious energy on the satellite system.

"Yes. They said they'd hold him for us if he showed up there, but the hunters' van was theirs by right of salvage. Sanderson did say they'd trade it back to us for a fair price."

"Trade it back to us!"

"Calm down, Boss," Seth said. "We'd do the same if our situations were reversed. If he doesn't go to D'Aboville, then he has to show up in Underbel."

"Underbel's a big place," Daniel cut in, "but how hard could it be to spot a six-foot-two, two-hundred-and-eighty-pound bald guy that can tame animals."

"I doubt," said Sara, "that he'll have a few dogs tagging along when he shows up. Still, even if they don't watch for him, they'll definitely be looking for the van. We'll deal with it as it comes. I suppose we should discuss the repercussions of him going over to the fat man."

"You seem to be discounting the other possibility," said Dr. Patel, voice thick from swollen lips. "The one, in fact, that you announced to the general population. He may be simply out of his mind. Temporarily disorientated as a result of his concussion. With any luck, he'll be knocking on the airlock door by tomorrow night."

"If he does," said Sara, "it might be worse, everything considered. If he comes home, I'll have to lock him outside."

"Oh come on," Dr. Patel slapped the table. "Extenuating circumstances. You know Ted. We know Ted. He would never..."

"And we thought we knew..." Sara cut herself short just before saying Burle's name. Mickey's ears perked up and Lyle was paying full attention for the first time since the meeting began. She spoke over her faux pas quickly, not wanting to be questioned on it. "Harpreet, I find it odd that you're his strongest proponent, considering you took the worst of his escape."

"I rather think that Senna got the worst of it."

There was a heavy pause in the discussion.

"The question is, what do we do now?" asked Seth.

"Get another hunter van," said Roshi. At least he was the same, in the right chair, grumpy as ever. He was serving the lobster that night, under protest. His victory feast for Sid had included three courses, with the lobster as the centerpiece. He'd searched places in his kitchen he hadn't seen in years, ferreting out every last dash of spice. It would have been a grand feast, the type he'd won blue ribbons for, the kind of meal that would have had him cooking in the White House if so many dishes' ingredients hadn't suddenly gotten mean. As it stood now, he'd been reduced to making a sort of chowder to spread it out. There simply weren't enough lobsters to go around. He'd kept his guest list for Sid's return down to twenty, including himself.

"We can still hunt with the Hummer," said Chris. "We'll just have to make more trips."

"Better teach more hunters! You got no leader now."

Chris growled in the back of his throat, like a wolf.

"Chris," snapped Dr. White, "that's enough. Roshi's right, to a degree. I want you hunting on a limited basis only. Day trips only."

"Do I get Senna's room?" asked Chris, ignoring the glowers that were shot at him across the table. "Hey, I'm acting chief of the hunters, doesn't look good for me to be a bunky. Even if Toffee does come back, I'll still be second. Look, I'm hurt to lose her. I cried out there, ask Danny. But fair's fair."

"Fine, you get her room, Chris. Someone would be promoted out of the barracks, it might as well be you. But don't get ahead of yourself. This is a battlefield promotion. If Seth were in any way capable, he'd be the acting chief."

"Okay, whatever."

"And no more growling at the table."

"I say we put the Pit on full alert," said Purty. "We have to prepare for Odega going to D'Abo. If the fat man finds out what state we're in, he'll come at us with everything."

Dr. White raised an eyebrow, surprised. That suggestion should have come from the acting chief of security, not his second. "Daniel?"

"I share my second's concern, but there is the morale of the Pit to consider."

"I agree. No need to panic the masses. We will tighten security, and plan for an attack, but putting the Pit on full alert would be unwise based on supposition."

Seth was in stores when Purty and Chiu-Keung entered and shut the door.

"Can I help you guys?" asked Seth, grinning at their serious expressions.

"You hear the people during dinner?" asked Purty.

"Yeah, they all liked the chowder. I did too. Think Roshi's got any of that left?"

"I'm not talking about the dinner."

"Well you should be. How hard would it be to pilfer the kitchen?"

"I got caught once," said Chiu. "You're on your own. Roshi scares me." Chiu caught Purty's dirty look. "What? It's Seth, I can't joke with the man?"

Purtricil put his hands on the desk and leaned towards Seth. "You heard them, the whispers, the jokes?"

"Purty, get out of my face," Seth smiled and shoved at the man's chest. "What are you, interrogating me? Yes, I heard them. Odega shot Senna, Odega and Senna were a team and Daniel killed Senna, but Ted got away. Odega and Senna were a team and both of them got away. The best one was we traded Odega, Senna and the van for a rig, and just don't want to tell nobody."

"That's not what I'm–"

"You're missing the point, Purty. One rig. All of that for one rig. Do you know how many rigs I could get for Odega alone?" For a moment, he actually considered what he'd ask for the researcher. He shook the thought off abruptly. Human trading did occur, but Noah Thurlow had been the first one at the Pit. And word had apparently gotten around, that fisher being offered up like that. It set a dangerous precedent.

Chiu was trying to stifle a laugh, but Purtricil was getting that look he got just before he hit someone. It wasn't often, but Seth had seen it before, and it was hard to forget.

"Calm down, Purty. I know what's going on, but why make a big deal about it? The Boss'll be back tomorrow. He told me one week, and he'd never blow a deadline. Dr. White will be fine."

"I don't really believe you're operating under the assumption that the Boss is still alive. I think you're deluding yourself, and you know it."

"So?" Seth shrugged his shoulders. "What do you want me to do about it?"

Purty exchanged a glance with Chiu, then turned back to Seth and leaned in again. "Look at what's happened. Last few days we've had two deaths, an escape and a lockout. Daniel can't even cut it as chief of security."

"What are you getting at?"

"Nobody'll back Daniel if he makes the play, but we will back you."

Seth noted that Chiu had gone to stand protectively by the door. "Back me for…No. No way. What did you two paranoids cook up?"

"It's not just us, we've spoken with a few people who feel the same way."

Seth stared at both of them, incredulous. "You nominated me Boss without even asking me first? You want me to lead a coup? How far does it go?"

"Think about it," said Chiu. "Dr. White's only Boss on Halbert's say so. It's still his authority that people are following, not hers. How long is that going to last? People taking orders from a ghost. The only question is do you take the lead now when things are just kind of bad, or do you wait until we get in a real mess?"

"The Boss will be back tomorrow, and if he's not, he'll be back the next day."

"How many next days are you going to let pass before you do something?" demanded Purty. "I'd do it but the Pit won't follow me, or Chiu. But they will follow you, Seth. Everyone loves you, man."

"You're forgetting I was passed over for chief of the hunters. Now you think I should be the Boss."

"Different situation," said Chiu. "Why have an angel when you can get the devil to do your killing?"

"I'm not an angel," said Seth, "and I resent the insinuation. Purty, how far does this go?"

"Are you in?"

"How far?"

They locked eyes, trying to stare an answer out of the other.

"This could go on forever," said Chiu.

"He's right," said Purty, easing off. "I like Dr. White, don't get me wrong, and it's not like I want to hurt her or anything, Christ, we need her. She won't give up the mantle willingly though, and there are some people who'll back her, Daniel and Dr. Patel I'm sure, but she's no Boss, Seth. We're hurting. Our lights are low, and people don't know what's really going on. Halbert took vital people with him on his suicide mission. It's like what Sara said, battlefield promotion. I'm looking around, and you're the only one standing. Three days, Seth. If D'Abo's guys drive hard, and we know they've got the resources to do it, they can be here in three days."

"The Boss. Will be back. Tomorrow."

"So you said. Three days. Think about it Seth, we'll talk again, tomorrow after breakfast."

The door closed behind the security officers, leaving Seth staring after them in utter disbelief. Of all the people who would try something like this, Purty was the last person he'd suspect. Devon from tanning maybe, one of the hunters, but not Purtricil. The chief of stores stood and looked around his domain. He took the visitor's chair and dragged it to the wall farthest from his desk. Pushing the boxes aside, he entered Burle's private reserve and moved something from it to a more reachable location. Satisfied, he locked his desk and left. There were some people he had to talk to.

"Sara, at least let me put a few people up here, and here," Daniel pointed to spots on a map indicating the road systems in and around the Pit. It had been drawn up in ink, then shaded with ochre.

"And what good will that do?" asked Sara. "If this force from D'Aboville comes, it'll be an army. We'll just be setting out people up for a fall."

"Then let's set up a blockade."

"What can we put up that D'Abo can't shove out of the way?"

"How 'bout mines?"

"Daniel, don't be ridiculous." The kettle whistled. It sat on a hotplate steam-heated by a pipe that ran through the wall of Sara's office. "Tea?"

"What are you making it out of this time?"

"Do you want some or not?"

"What the hell. Hit me."

She put some leaves in the bottom of a teapot and topped it off with boiling water. "We can't mine the roads. What happens if another surprise visitor shows up? I'd love to call Underbel and tell them that we accidentally blew up their convoy."

"What about remote-detonated mines? No pressure triggers."

Sara was taken aback. "Do we have those?"

"No. Seth could make some, though."

"Would that be risky?"

"I suppose. The mines we've got are old…claymores…going into 'em would involve a certain amount of…"

"Daniel, forget it. Ted went AWOL, that's all we know. It's not the first time it's happened. Gerard Fritz, Jason Worthy, they both gave up one day and went to nature. It's usually the people at the top that crack. The ones that care about people anyway."

"Fritz was testing a portable Mimi that didn't work. And besides, neither of them took vehicles, or attacked anybody on the way out."

"Gerard wasn't testing a portable Mimi," said Sara, pouring tea into a pair of mugs. She kept the spout high, enjoying the sound of liquid splashing as it hit the porcelain. "That was a cover story. As near as we can tell, he went out, stripped down, and ran beyond the sound net. Travis was in the watchtower at the time."

"Then the whole failed experiment thing…"

"Was a cover. The Pit had been animal free for only a few weeks at that point. A lot of people wondered if the animals knew to avoid them, then what were the Mimis doing to us? Sid felt it wouldn't be prudent to let the truth get out."

Daniel accepted his mug and pondered what he'd just been told. "I guess not."

"Fritz was an unstable man, you didn't know him. He was brilliant, as you can see by his work, and after his death, Ted had to compete with a ghost that announced itself every day that passed without an animal crossing the line. Only a handful of animals have gotten in since Gershwin's been running. Daniel, are you going to drink that?"

He blew across the surface, even though it had stopped steaming. He took a sip. "It's very…uh…" another sip. "Sara, this is terrible."

"Well, I like it. Drink, it'll relax you. Ted wanted to be the one to figure it out, Daniel. You should have seen him with Ghandi before she went normal. He loved that dog. More than he ever loved me, I'll tell you that much."

The acting chief of security glanced at the ceiling, uncomfortable with the intimate turn the conversation had taken. "If he loved the dog, why did he kill it?"

"I think he may have done it out of mercy."

"Mercy?"

"If Ghandi were still alive we'd have her strapped down with a dozen tubes coming out of her and electrodes strapped to her brain. Between the two of them, Harp and Ted could keep a critter alive under abhorrent conditions. All in the name of research. I'm sure Ted wanted to spare her that. Daniel, he wasn't a spy for Gascan or anybody else. He snapped, plain and simple. I blame myself for not seeing it coming. Concussion or no concussion, I think this would have happened."

Daniel put his mug down. "What if you're wrong?"

"How would we prepare if the fat man was on his way right now, and we knew it?"

"Mine the roads, man the machine guns, put the rocket launchers in the towers, post people at–"

"In other words, take a lot of people off their work detail to stand guard duty."

"Yes."

"No. This was a bad one, Danny, but we can't go jumping at shadows. Our production is down in all areas, everybody's uneasy. We didn't want to scare folk with Fritz's suicide back then, and I'm not going to panic people right now. Especially not now. Bottom line, if D'Abo really wanted to annex us, is there anything we could do besides hold him off for a while?"

"No," *not without Halbert we can't.* "You're right, Boss. We should pull the dish down, though."

"We don't have the juice to spare, and we wouldn't be able to hear Underbel if they contact us about Ted."

"Okay. Okay, but listen, if we are attacked, the first target will be the dish. D'Abo won't want us sending out an SOS."

"I appreciate the warning," she pulled a laptop out of her desk drawer and started punching buttons. "I'm going to have another go at the password. Sid could be back any minute now. Things will calm down once our beloved leader has come home, and you can get on with driving that fancy new rig of yours. Any choices for your transport team?"

"I put up a volunteer sheet on the main bulletin board, so far nobody's signed up."

"Hmmm. I guess we'll just have to draft folk, but that's for another day. Since you're not going to drink your tea, I can't see what's keeping you here. You've done your duty and made me consider all possibilities. Don't be too hard on Purty for going over your head like that. I'm sure he was just excited."

There were few smells fouler than those that came out of tanning. Animal hides in various stages of curing hung from hooks, some dangling loosely, some stretched taught within wire frames. Devon was busy smearing fat into the underside of an elk's hide with quick, easy motions.

"If you're here to campaign, Seth, don't bother. You've got my vote."

The chief of stores looked around at how many other people had heard the comment. Nobody seemed to notice, though. There were four other workers in the tannery, and Seth had come to draw Devon away to somewhere more private, not to solicit his support. "Dev," he said quietly, "shouldn't we go somewhere else?"

Devon stepped back from the hide and sucked his cheek. "Hey, anyone here got a problem with Seth being the Boss?"

"Not me," said a man bundling hides.

"I'm cool with it," said another.

The other two nodded, then went back to work.

Seth was shocked by how casual they were about it. It was as if he'd already been elected and just hadn't been told.

"C'mon," said Devon, putting his arm across Seth's shoulders, "let's go talk about details. Don't slack off anybody," he said loudly.

In a smaller room where tools were stored Devon stood before a wall of knives and hooks, his bare chest covered in the grease of his trade. "You shouldn't be so surprised. You wouldn't have started this if you didn't know, right?"

"I shouldn't have…" Seth stopped himself. "Devon, no offense, but how much did Purty tell you?"

"Oh don't worry, I'll keep my mouth shut. So will my boys back there. Maybe I should have kept it a secret, but me and the boys, we're tight. 'Sides, I wouldn't have told them if I didn't know what their answer would be."

Seth nodded, then forced a smile. "So with you five, that gives us..." He wondered how long he could hold the pause; fortunately it wasn't put to the test.

"Twenty-six. Unless you've brought some more people on board I don't know about."

"No, not since Purty talked to you. Is there anybody you think I should go after that I've missed?"

"Not really. As far as department heads are concerned, you've been pretty thorough. I guess you know who you could get and who you couldn't."

"Yes, I suppose." *Thanks, that told me absolutely nothing.* "Good to know you're behind me. I'll have Purtricil or Chiu keep you posted."

They exchanged a firm handshake, then Devon returned to his work.

Fabulous, thought Seth, as he left the tannery. *If I go to Sara with this, twenty-six people get locked outside for conspiracy to commit treason. Including all the tanners, and security second and third, at least.* He felt trapped in an untenable situation. If he refused to helm this revolution, who would be at the top if it succeeded...Purty? Not good enough. Seth agreed that for long term, Dr. White could not be the Boss, and odds were pretty good that Sid wasn't coming back. But what if he did return to find Seth sitting in the throne? And what of Sara? The Pit needed her badly. The more he thought about it, the more he realized that Sara hadn't been doing that bad a job, considering. She hadn't backed down from locking a man out, and she hadn't lost her head when Odega went ballistic. Sara wasn't the problem, it was the people's perception of her that was. *Why'd you have to take Caps, Boss? We could use a good PR guy right now.*

He caught Patricia in passing just outside of the mess hall. "Is Purtricil in the security office?"

"No, but Daniel is."

"I don't want Daniel," he said a little too quickly. "It's a non-security issue."

"Oh. I think Purty's in the motor pool. Chiu's with him."

The two security officers were speaking quietly with Mickey when Seth entered the pool. They all stopped at once and looked at him as he approached. He had no guarantee that the discussion was about the ensuing rebellion, but he had a gut feeling that it did. He normally went with his gut.

"We don't have to wait until breakfast. I'm in."

"In what?" asked Mickey. At first Seth thought he'd made a terrible error. "Is there a preemptive strike or something? Count me out. I'm not doing any strong-arm stuff."

The chief of stores tried to keep relief from flooding into his face. Obviously Purty and Chiu had sold the mechanic the same hogwash they'd given Devon; that the whole thing was Seth's idea.

"Don't worry, Mickey," said Purty, "we're not asking you to hold a gun. Seth, let's go to your office."

Once in stores, Seth sat down in his chair as Chiu shut the door and put his back against it. Purty moved for the second chair, found it absent, then spotted it on the far side of the room.

"I have two conditions," said Seth, locking eyes with Purty before he could move to get the chair. "I want to know everything, all the names, all the people, and how long you've been organizing this. If you don't tell me these things, you're out of the loop. I can't have lieutenants I don't trust."

"You can trust me. What's the second condition?"

"That we wait six days before we do anything."

"Six days?! Why that long? Seth, we can move tomorrow night if we have to."

"I want to give Sid the extra time," he held up his hand to stay any protest. "This is Sid Halbert we're talking about, and he's got Darcy and Toffee with him. If anyone could pull this off, it would be those three. The Pit will pick me over Dr. White, but I can't stand up against the real Boss, and I wouldn't want to. I don't particularly like the idea of being locked outside, do you?"

"But Gascan–"

"Forget him. It'll take Odega the better part of a week to get to D'Aboville. He doesn't have enough fuel to go straight there. His route's going to be pretty indirect if he wants to gas up and avoid attention. If, and only if, the fat man can mobilize right away, it'll then take him four days, four, not three, to get to us. Six days gives us plenty of time to be in the pilot's seat when he gets here."

"Do you think Dr. Odega would just split from here without some sort of plan? He probably has fuel stashed in places exactly for the purpose of going straight to Gascan's. That's where he was heading, Seth. Dammit. Maybe there's a tanker truck waiting for him, or a rendezvous. Two days. We wait two days."

"Yeah, right...someone's going to sit in a truck in the middle of nowhere, waiting indefinitely for Odega to come driving up in a stolen vehicle. There's no rendezvous. Maybe he could have stashed some fuel, but it couldn't have been that much. Burle accounted for every drop that came in and out of here. Five days."

"Bringing up Burle doesn't exactly strengthen your position, Seth. Three days."

"I'm starting to doubt your grasp of logic, Purty. Burle sold us out to Shangly, not Gascan. If Burle and Odega were working together, the fat man would have owned us long ago. Four days."

Purty nodded, "Done."

"And we do everything my way. You got the ball rolling on this, but if I'm going to be the Boss, then I'm your boss right now."

Purty spread his hands wide. "As it should be."

"Good. Grab that chair over there and take a load off. Chiu, in the top box of that pile back there, you'll find a bottle of Southern Comfort. No glasses, I'm afraid. We'll just have to pass the bottle."

"Seth," said Chiu-Keung, walking jauntily to the pile, "you are the man!"

"Okay, Purty, tell me everything."

Purtricil laid out the details. The bottle came, and Seth faked swallowing, then handed the bottle off. It was a crime, to have that fine liquor touch his lips, but not allow it to pass. He didn't want a drop of booze to dull his senses. He'd managed to buy four days. Seth had been prepared to fall back as far as two. Four days, ninety-six hours. At least it gave him room to breathe.

The chief of stores had no way of knowing that Peter D'Abo had been informed of the Pit's condition by another source, and as a result, a considerable force was already on the way.

In the trees beyond the Mimis' range, crows began to gather.

45. Visitations

Noah looked in abject terror at the lethal spike in the bald boy's hand. A length of chain rested across one leg, and two steel pins lay on the bench between his knees. The boy had been very clear about the process, the puncturing, the threading. The fact that his ankles had been swabbed with alcohol to prevent infection was even more insidious. He was going to be hobbled with no more concern than Dr. Patel and Dr. Odega would give lobotomising a cow.

"I won't lie to you, this is going to hurt." The boy took Noah's right foot in a firm grasp and raised the spike.

The door opened. A young man walked in, blond curly hair and a worn, if well-made cloak draped about his shoulders. "Henry, what are you doing?" he asked, his tone indicating that Henry was doing something he shouldn't.

"You...you said he was to be the new slave."

"Did I tell you to anoint him now?"

"No, I just assumed...forgive me, Master."

To Noah's astonishment, Henry—it was hard giving his tormentor such a mundane name—dropped out of sight, presumably prostrating himself on the floor. Every muscle in Noah's body, which had been as a taut as piano wires, let go at the same time. He crashed to the table, if it was possible to crash from a few inches away.

"Get up, Henry. You lead the seekers. It is your right to perform the ceremony, but not yet. I will let you know."

Henry rose, but kept his gaze on the floor. The Master tilted Henry's jaw with a finger till their eyes met.

"Leave us, seeker. I will speak with you later."

Henry didn't look back as he trotted out the door. The Master shut it, then yanked the chain from Noah's leg and dropped it to the floor. "I know what you do," he took Noah by the jaw. "You are a sun catcher. You can call the light into plates. We have these plates. Some of them no longer function. We have lost things. She has brought you here to serve us. But you will not be Slave. You cannot do what he does, so you will have a different name. Worm. You will be Worm."

The Master released his grip and allowed his hand to trail down Noah's chest. For a horrible moment, Noah though the man was going to cup his scrotum, but the hand pulled away. All Noah could do was choke on his gag as the Master opened the door and, with a gesture, summoned two of the speechless ones.

"This is Worm, but until he is anointed, he has no name. Unbind him, and take him to the cell I've had prepared."

The gag was pulled from Noah's mouth. His tongue was so dry it hurt. He tried to speak, but all that came out was an arid cough. The Master struck him across the face, fast and hard, very hard. Noah saw stars for a few seconds.

"Do not speak. Never speak. You will learn." He struck him again, as hard as the first time.

They dragged Noah to his new cell. This one at least had a door in the right place, but there was no pot, no drain. He was thrown to the cement floor, the door slammed shut, and Noah was plunged into darkness.

Slave hid in the doorway and watched Cyrus, the head warrior, flick his hands at Luke. The Master was furious, and given the circumstances, had every right to be. Not only had neither Eagle nor the "second team" showed up, but Caroline had disappeared without a trace. That brought the warriors' losses up to four now. Furthermore, and Slave had a little trouble making out what Cyrus was indicating, the boy moved his hands so quickly, they'd seen a rig, and were fairly sure it was the same one they'd considered destroyed. Slave pulled his head into the corridor as Luke strode past. He'd be summoned soon enough, but for now he had some time to himself.

I knew it was ruse, he thought, satisfied. But how many of them could there be? Just one rig? Not enough for an all out assault...barely enough for hit-and-run attacks. Luke was not the man that Archie was, but he'd catch on sooner or later, and he had both numbers and home-field advantage. Unless the rig was just a forerunner. Maybe an army was on its way, possibly it was already here. Slave shut the door on that line of thought as soon as it came. How many times had he fantasized about cavalry, only to be disappointed day after day?

"Nobody is coming to save you," said a voice in his head. It was Archie. "You belong to me, and as far as the children are concerned, you belong to Her."

Slave could remember his first days as if they'd only been weeks ago. Suffering in the dark from both the lack of food and water, excrement stinking up his cell...the abuse, both verbal and physical. Not as if that part of it had ever eased. Archie was in his fifties then, and already prone to spells of disorientation resulting from some sort of dementia—that is dementia over and above his normal level of insanity. He'd broken Jonathan quickly, but not by torturing him. Instead, he'd been forced to watch as Valerie, the only other survivor of the expedition, was cut to pieces bit by bit. His own disfigurement hadn't begun until he'd already agreed to maintain the radio scanner. Archie claimed to have built it, but Slave considered that a falsehood. The man demonstrated ignorance not becoming of a person who could have assembled such a complex system. No, it was more likely that someone else had been the scanner's creator, an adult that had been killed off once his purpose was fulfilled. There must have been adults, as the former Master could not have accomplished what he had with just the help of children. Gathering as many young ones as he had was not a task he could have accomplished by himself, either. But Archie never gave up where they'd come from, or how they'd ended up where they had. Slave had put together clues from Archie's more dated rambling towards the end. The man had been somehow involved in the school system, something to do with "special" children; kids prone to violence, or suffering from learning disorders. Perhaps he'd been a teacher, or a guidance counsellor, but whatever he had been, Luke's predecessor had used the Change to establish his own world, one in which he was king and God was tangible. And terrible.

Now there were more children, offspring from kids too young to appreciate their responsibility. Not that it mattered, babies weren't personal, they belonged to the tribe. Sex was forbidden below the age of sixteen, except, it seemed, in the Master's case. It was logical really; surrounded by children, sooner or later Archie would have to satisfy his needs. He'd dallied with both sexes, coming to find he preferred the boys. Luke had been his favourite, even as Conner was Luke's favourite now, but that would end as soon as Conner chose. Luke lost interest once his playmates lost their tongues. Despite the Master's—both of them—predilection towards pederasty, their victims, once older, displayed nothing more than the heterosexual tendencies of hormone-riddled teenagers without parental guidance. They rutted with girls every time they had the chance. Slave would come upon them in darkened corridors, in unused rooms, grunting in physical ecstasy even as they propagated their species. There was no marriage of any sort, no societal enforced bonding, although human nature had brought a few pairs together to the exclusion of all else. Yet for all the copulation going on, physical intimacy was another comfort denied Slave. Even were he not hideous to behold, and acts of kindness of any sort towards him forbidden, emasculation had been one of the first punishments Archie had inflicted. Perversely, Slave had also lost a toe as penalty for screaming when his manhood had been roughly hacked off.

It was a great loss to humanity everywhere that the former Master had been insane. He demonstrated an almost uncanny knowledge of animal behaviour. That he'd created a viable settlement where he had was nothing short of a miracle, and proof that higher powers supported him. However, the higher power that Luke, and the others gave themselves to, that was all of Archie's making. It wasn't the first time one of her kind had been viewed as deity. The Inuit had done so, perhaps still did, way up north where it was too cold for ants and wasps to live. But here, that she'd survived so long...sometimes even Slave wondered if there weren't at least minor supernatural forces at work.

Slave stooped and checked the bandage on his foot. The skin over the toes had been stitched as well. Henry was as good at healing as he was at causing the need for it. Soon the cycle of abuse would repeat itself on the unfortunate photovoltaic engineer, and even worse would be visited upon Lena. Dear, sweet Lena. He wondered if she was still in communications. She might even be chief by now.

Lena wiggled her hand in the tub, causing a light film of bubbles to form on the surface of the water. They'd brought it to her boiling hot, along with a skinbag of treasure. Soap, pre-Change stuff that, though a little misshapen, still bore the name "Ivory" stamped upon it. Shampoo, Vidal Sassoon, from a virgin bottle, conditioner of the same brand and scented bubble bath. Obviously the Master had sent someone to raid a supermarket or drugstore that hadn't been cleaned out in the first year. The same boy that had brought her the toiletries, handing the bag over like it contained a live raccoon, had also brought her a plank with which she could block the door. He'd even demonstrated, propping it under the handle. The plank was rotted and warped, and a solid hit would splinter it, but it would at least prevent casual entry. It amazed her that with the whole city at their disposal, there was very little evidence of them partaking of it.

There had been another bundle included in her care package. This one contained two dresses. Both faded, and a little large for her, but of a soft material. She ran her hand along the seam of one, almost laughing as she fingered the label that stated washing directions. They were the type of dresses Caps would have liked to see her in, would have loved to remove from her. Shutting out thoughts of her boyfriend, she undressed, leaving her clothes in a pile by the mattress. She unstrapped her prosthetic, then hopped the short distance that separated her from the tub. The water had cooled to a perfect temperature. She clambered in and allowed the scented water to envelop her. The tub was large enough that only her head and the top of her knee broke the water's surface. She kicked her legs and splashed with her hands, making more bubbles. She was a prisoner with future uncertain, might as well grab all the pleasure she could.

The bath had a truly relaxing effect. It had been years since she'd enjoyed this privilege; the single bathtub at the Pit was for Dr. Patel's patients only, people who were unable to stand whilst cleansing themselves. She closed her eyes and drifted awhile. Something scraped above her head. Lena opened her eyes and stared into those of a hideous creature. It was looking at her through a vent in the ceiling. The aperture was only large enough for the creature's face to show through. Her mouth opened and she nearly screamed, but was kept from it by vigorous shaking of the creature's head, and the desperate look in its eyes. Lena was acutely aware of her nudity. Bubble's obscured, but didn't completely hide her flesh. She thrashed in the tub, looking for the one thing she realized, belatedly, that hadn't been brought to her; towels. Lena squashed herself against the bottom of the tub, covering herself as best she could with her hands.

"What do you want?" she asked the head.

A hand joined the face within the rectangle in the ceiling. It was incongruous to the twisted features of its owner, slender, almost feminine. The creature, she noted it was a man, pointed at his eyes, then waggled a finger at her.

"You want me to look at something?"

The head shook, then another hand joined the first. He was miming something, and having a hard time of it, his movements restricted by his cramped quarters. Most likely it was an air vent he'd somehow crawled into. Lena watched his fingers, but didn't understand what he was doing. It was a twisting motion, like turning dials.

"There's something in here you want me to turn on?"

The expression on the man's face was clearly that of disappointment, recognizable even with his broken face.

"I've seen you before, haven't I?"

Like a light turning on, the man's face brightened. A wide smile stretched his mouth, showing black gaps between scattered teeth.

"You were in my cell, the first one. I hit you."

He nodded, but the smile vanished. Again his hands played at twisting air.

"I don't understand. You're…you're different from the rest of them, aren't you? You're not supposed to be here." A nod. "You can speak to me. I won't tell."

He opened his mouth and with two fingers, showed his tonguelessness.

"Oh. Did they do that to you?" Another nod. "The others who don't speak, do they have tongues?"

The head vanished.

"Wait!" she said loudly, then again quietly, wondering if perhaps someone might be listening at the door. There was a scraping sound again from above, as the man repositioned himself in the air vent. Lena wondered how she hadn't heard it when he'd crawled over her in the first place. She pulled herself up, then dropped back down again as the head reappeared.

The man forced a hand, then his whole arm through the vent opening, reached up and smeared two letters on the ceiling with a dust-covered finger; "CP."

"CP? Is that what you wrote? CP?"

His eyes brightened again, he nodded fervently.

"I don't know what that means." He pointed at her. "I'm CP? No, I'm Lena Wong. LW." The head shook and again the finger was pointing at her. An image came unbidden to her mind, college roommates frustrated during a drunken game of charades. "I'm going to be CP? I'm from CP? Compton Pit! That's it, isn't it? Compton Pit."

With a look of pleasure more deserving of a returned loved one than a right answer during a guessing game, the man stopped in his gestures, then slowly pointed to himself.

"You...you're from Compton Pit as well?" A nod, slow and full of regret.

Lena studied the face anew, looking past the flattened nose and the malformed jaw. There was something familiar about him, a quality to the eyes...

"Oh my God!" She felt as if her heart had stopped. "Jonathan...is that you?"

A series of emotions chased each other across his face. Relief, joy, sorrow, they all merged into one and tears splashed as they fell from the vent to the tub.

Forgetting her nudity, Lena stood, balancing awkwardly. She stretched up, her hand falling short of the ceiling, but he reached down and squeezed her fingertips. Tears flowed from his eyes as if he'd been saving them for years.

"Jonathan, what did they do to you?"

A low moan escaped from his throat, it was the cry of a wounded animal.

"Who else is here, Jonathan? Do you remember Caps? Is he here as well?"

There was a knock at the door. The hand vanished into the ceiling and the vent swung shut. She heard shuffling, then nothing. It was as if she'd imagined the whole thing. The knock came again.

"Hold on. I have to get dressed. You didn't bring me any towels."

She dried herself with a blanket as best she could, looked at the dresses, then pulled on her grimy pants and shirt. Lena had no interest in dressing up for her captors. She removed the plank and took a few steps back. "Okay, come in."

The door opened. Outside was a little girl, ten or eleven. In her arms was a stack of clean towels.

"Hhmph. You're a little late, but thank you."

The girl stepped into the room, placed the towels on the floor, then reached up and touched Lena's hand.

"What's your name, little one?"

The girl snatched her hand back, gripping it with the other as if her fingers had turned to gold. She ran out of the room. Before Lena could move to the door, it was pulled shut by one of the tongueless ones, and the latch was thrown.

Compton Pit's current chief of communications waited a few minutes, then replaced the plank and moved to stand under the vent. "Jonathan," she called in a loud whisper. "It's clear! Jonathan!"

There were no more sounds of motion from above, and the face didn't reappear. Lena flopped down on the love seat, her clothes clinging to the dampness of her skin. She pictured Jonathan Crispin's face, wondering what they'd done to him, wondering what they planned to do to her.

Noah closed his eyes and threw an arm across his face as the door opened and torchlight erupted in his cell. Rough hands grabbed him and threw him against the wall. His broken rib felt like a knife, cutting him from inside-out. The wind was knocked out of him as something struck him in the solar plexus, a fist, a foot, he couldn't tell.

"Look at me," said a man's voice.

Noah let his eyes open to a narrow slit. The door to his cell was closed, only the torchbearer stood within.

"I have questions. I give you privilege to speak."

The light didn't hurt as much, so Noah let his eyes come fully open. It was the blond man, the one who had felt him up earlier.

"How many of you came to the city?"

Noah pressed his lips together, and offered what he hoped was a defiant look. The torch loomed closer.

"I'll set your hair on fire. How many of you?"

Noah opened his mouth, intent on cursing the man, but his throat was too dry, and too raw.

The man nodded, then shouted at the closed door. "Bring us some water!" He turned back, eyes intent. "You will call me Master, while you are still able. You may speak only in my presence, and only when I give you permission."

The door opened and a boy entered with a plastic jug. He was bald and painted, but was shorter than Henry, and had darker skin. He left after giving the jug to the Master. Luke placed the torch on the floor and held the jug out to Noah, slapping his hands away as he reached for it.

"Drink from my hands, Worm. You will drink only what I bring you, eat only what I provide."

Thirsty beyond pride, Noah came forward and gulped from the jug. When he'd had a few mouthfuls, the jug was pulled away. Luke placed it on the floor.

"Now, answer my question, and maybe I'll give you some food."

"Go lick a dog." Noah was proud of his reply, it made him feel big, like Toffee or the Boss.

He didn't see the blow that took him on the side of the head, knocking him over. Thankfully, he fell on ribs unbroken.

"You have no idea how lucky you are that She wants you. Otherwise I would have your eyes for your impudence. Answer my question."

Forcing back tears, swallowing his fear, Noah pushed himself upright. "Or what? You'll beat me up and lock me in a room?"

"No. I'll torture your friend, the Chinese woman."

"Lena! She's here? What have you done to her?"

"Lena. That's her name? Funny, I never thought to ask. You stay here. Hmmm, she's short on legs, so I'll bring you one of her breasts."

"Don't touch her!" he lurched forward, grasping for Luke's robe.

Luke stepped back, shocked at this display of aggression. Surprise became anger, but for once he held it, resisted the urge to lash out. Noah struggled to his feet, clutching at his chest as he did so. As soon as he was standing, Luke kicked his legs out from under him.

"Is something broken?" asked the Master, genuine concern in his voice.

"My rib," Noah spat. "Henry said he was going to fix it, right after he punched holes in my ankles."

This time Luke could not restrain himself. He aimed a vicious kick at Noah's jaw. The young man saw it coming and rolled a little, not managing to avoid the blow, but at least abetting its force.

"Never speak a seeker's name, or anyone else's. You do not have the right!" The rage dissipated, and once more the Master spoke gently. "Will you answer my questions? If not, whatever happens to the woman is your fault."

He's nuts. Completely off his rocker. "You know how many of us there are. You kidnapped us." Noah checked his teeth with his tongue. None of them seemed loose, but there was a new cut inside his mouth, and warm, coppery blood trickled down his throat.

"I kidnapped no one. You were brought here by the grace of God. The others were inconsequential to Her. They are dead."

"I don't believe you."

"Six entered her domain. You, Lena, the black man, the sword swinger, the half-faced woman with red hair, and another man. She granted her protection until you were in our hands, for the others there was no use. They are dead."

Noah looked away.

"Who is Eagle? How many were in the second team? Answer me."

"I don't know who you're talking about. It was just us. The Deep Six," he laughed. He couldn't help it.

Luke straddled Noah and bent close to his face. "I will stick red-hot metal up inside her and split her apart."

"I'm telling you, I don't know any Eagle. It was just us."

Luke gripped him firmly by the throat, pushing his head back against the wall. He searched Noah's eyes, boring into them with his own. "I believe you. Tell me their names, the ones who were with you. I will ask the same of the woman. If your answers differ, she'll regret it."

Noah told him. What difference would it make if this lunatic knew their names?

Rather than loosening his grip, the Master tightened it, dropped his other hand dropped between Noah's legs and caressed him in a way that only Jenny and Cass had ever done. Noah struggled as best he could, but the fight had been knocked out of him, and the choke hold was quickly cutting off his oxygen.

"You will be hobbled, but I might let you keep your tongue. If you learn how to use it." Luke released both grips, grabbed the torch and jug, then knocked on the door with his elbow. The door opened and the Master left.

In the dark, Noah shivered, despair rushing in like a cattle stampede. Then he realized the Master had made a mistake. Why ask for names of people who were dead?

The tactile echo of a roaming hand shrivelled the skin around his balls. Noah rolled to his hands and knees, promptly vomiting up the precious water he'd just imbibed.

46. The Park

"I don't believe it," said Sid. "I'm looking at it, but I don't believe it."

They were on the fourteenth floor of a downtown high-rise, in the offices of what used to be Acadia Insurance. The stairs had been a good hike, but at last they'd found an office with a telescope in it, just like the Boss had said they would. It was through that instrument that he peered now, drawing it across a barren landscape, like a great wound in the earth.

"Looks like someone kicked Mother Nature's ass," said Toffee. Even without the telescope, the damage was amazing.

"But why?" Sid stepped back from the telescope and let Darcy have a turn. "Why go to all that trouble? There are so many better places to set up shop if you're determined to stay in the city."

"They must have wanted a challenge," said Darcy. The view was even more astounding when looking at it up close.

To the west, where Georgia Street had once left the city behind, was Stanley Park, a part of the city that Sid had wanted to avoid at all cost. The park consisted of thousands of acres of trees, woods that had been over-populated with animals even when people walked through them daily. There would be no teeth in Stanley Park now, though. Not when there weren't any trees, or grass, or anything. It looked as if a great war had been fought, like pictures of Ypres Darcy had seen in a WWI history text, earth pounded to nothing by weeks of artillery fire. Craters pocked ground that wasn't just barren, it was dead.

"Must have used dynamite," said Toffee, "and fire. They poisoned it too. City this size, bound to be a lot of herbicide around. They'd have to keep up with it."

The land upon which the park used to stand was surrounded on three sides by water. Its geographical contours formed the north shores of both English Bay and Coal Harbor. Near the easternmost tip of the peninsula was a cluster of totem poles that had somehow been preserved. The zoo, which had shut down a years before the Change, stood out as a concrete-gray blob amid the wasteland. It had few buildings, all small. There were two pool-like depressions, one that had been made for seals, the other a dry moat to separate onlookers from a single polar bear, so old and yellowed that most people joked it had been dead for weeks before anyone really noticed. There was only one large structure on the entire zoo grounds, the only thing that had kept stock when the rest of the enclosures had been emptied. It was designed to be an entity unto itself, a zoo within a zoo; the Vancouver Aquarium.

"What do you think?" Sid asked Darcy, guessing from the angle of the telescope that she was looking at their destination.

"I count five of those trikes outside. I see nothing moving. There's a radio antennae, and some solar panels on the roof, not enough to run much, though."

"There's enough to run a radio scanner. Could be that's all they want. Obviously we don't know what's inside, but I don't see any amenities outside. The people we've seen have only been armed with bows. I've never seen anything quite like those trikes they use, so they must have some mechanical capabilities…by all rights they should be using cars like everybody else."

"There's no cover, none whatsoever. In the truck, on foot, it doesn't matter. They'd spot us coming in the moment we hit the…park." Darcy stepped aside, giving Toffee his turn at the telescope. "So do we get back on the radio and lure them out again?"

"No," Sid rubbed his jaw. "I don't think they'd fall for that twice. Besides, they have Noah and Lena now, and I don't hold any misconceptions about either of their abilities to withstand torture. We have to assume these mud people know who we are by name. Noah couldn't tell them much, but Lena…she might even be able to anticipate our moves. We're going to have be very creative at this point."

Toffee swung the telescope away from the park to a sixteen-story apartment block a few blocks away. "Heh, this guy could see right into those bedrooms. I can make out the label on a beer can in there. Wonder how much time this telescope really spent pointed at the ocean." He tilted it down and swept his view slowly across Georgia Street. "You sure about going in on foot? We can take that road down by the bay."

"That's Beach Avenue," said Sid. "Doesn't matter. Wherever we came in, we'd be facing a hail of arrows. Probably more of that yellow napalm stuff. That's not taking into account what else they might have in store for us. The roads could be mined, for all we know."

"We need one of those trikes, Halbert. Wrap ourselves up, slap on some mud, and we can drive right up to their front door."

"I've been thinking about that. I haven't come up with a way to get one yet. No doubt there'll be people posted along the highway and the Port Mann Bridge. Any obvious exit from the city will be guarded, but knowing that and using it are two different things."

Darcy ran her finger along a mahogany desk, thick with dust. "Is there any way we could get a message to the Pit? There's satellite dishes on top of all of these buildings, and I bet we could get one of these computers to run if we gave it juice."

"And how are we going to do that?" asked Toffee.

"Pull the batteries from the truck. I doubt we'd drain them with a quick transmission."

"Different type of current," said Sid, shaking his head. "Noah would be able to do it, and Lena could probably figure out how to bounce a signal from somewhere, but not us, Darcy."

"Yeah, I know. Just wishing out loud." She'd drawn a tic-tac-toe board in the dust and had played a game against herself. It ended up being a draw. "We have to act fast. Who knows what's being done to them in there."

"What about some kind of distraction?" said the hunter. He'd left the telescope and was examining an enclosed elephant's tusk that had been carved to look like a Chinese fishing village. "I wonder if this is one of mine?"

"Not unless you were into manufacturing," said Sid. He pointed to an oval-shaped gold sticker on one corner of the glass case. It read; "Not real ivory."

The hunter sneered and smashed the case, lifting the tusk and rubbing a smooth part of it against his cheek. "This guy got the sticker from somewhere to keep eco-freaks from shitting on him. The tusk is real."

"You were one of those guys," said Darcy, folding her arms across her chest. "Did you at least kill them before you took the tusks?"

"Sympathy for elephants? Red, I didn't just take tusks, I took the whole animal. Didn't waste nothing. Anything that couldn't be made into a knickknack went to Hong Kong. Dealing with the Chinese was going to put me in a mansion by the time I was forty-five. But then I'd miss all this. So, what about another type of distraction if you don't want to use the radio?"

"Such as?"

"We could blow up this building."

"How?"

"That's your job, Halbert. You're the one who figures these things out."

"I think taking down a high-rise is a bit out of my league."

Darcy had pulled open the desk's middle drawer. She rifled through it, pushing aside paper clips, tiny memo pads, a letter opener…"Sid, we should loot the building while we're here? I mean, just think about how many computers we've seen so far. We could have one in every department instead of just the few laptops we've got kicking around."

"There'll be plenty of time for that later. Let's take the telescope and move to a lower floor. I don't want to leave Caps alone any longer than necessary. The seventh should do."

They relocated to the law offices of Prince, Heron, Katz & Blum. The decorations were even more lavish than those in the insurance office, leather furniture, gold and silver object d'arts, expensively-framed paintings and the like.

Caps lay on the floor by a hat rack, his IV bag—nearly empty—hanging next to a mouldy fedora. His breathing was shallow, but steady.

Darcy picked a thick book off a scrubbed-oak bookshelf, only to find that time and silverfish had their way with the binding. Pages fluttered about as the book fell apart in her hands.

"I'm hungry," said the hunter. "I'm going out to get us something to eat."

"Good idea," said Sid. "Darcy, go with him. I'll be here. Try not to take too long, you know how I worry," he offered her a smile.

Darcy kissed his cheek, then took off with the hunter.

Sid positioned the telescope before a window facing the park, and after cleaning the inside of the window and pulling up a chair, set to work studying the ground around the aquarium foot by foot. There was some activity now. A group had come from a door outside his line of sight. They were loading arrows and skinbags into two of the trikes. More people joined them, and the Boss's stomach tightened as they climbed in and started moving. He was concerned they might come across his teammates while they foraged, but realized the motors would be too loud for either Darcy or the hunter to miss. Sid watched the trikes, confused by the course they followed. Rather than taking the service road, they followed a serpentine path on and off the pavement. At one point they left the road all together, describing a wide circle before returning to the smoother blacktop. He watched them as far as he was able, losing sight of them at the fringe of the park.

"Get back," said Toffee, shoving Darcy into a doorway.

"What…" She heard the buzzing motors before she could finish her question. It irked her that the hunter had heard them first.

The trike went whizzing by, destination unknown. When the sound had receded, they stuck their heads back out and scanned the streets.

"They must have cleared more than the park," said the hunter. "I'll bet they routinely sweep the streets nearby, killing anything they come across. That bunch might actually be going out for food, rather than looking for us."

"Do you believe that?"

"Nope."

They crossed the road and ducked into another doorway.

"Toffee, did you kill that girl?"

"Of course. What am I, stupid?"

"No, I just thought you might have left her to starve to death, or be eaten by rats. That's your style."

"She would have bled to death before the teeth got to her."

"What did you do? You got our information pretty quickly."

"You don't want to know."

"Probably not, but tell me anyway. It's not like it could make me think less of you."

"Really? Here's a quick technique. Feed 'em a finger."

"What?"

"Cut off a fingertip and stick in their mouth, then cut off more fingertips until they swallow the first one. Ask anything you want after that. Nobody's got any will left in 'em once they've scarfed down one of their own digits."

"I was wrong. I do think less of you."

"We're moving again. Let's hit that apartment building," he indicated the one he'd seen through the telescope.

"Why that one?"

"Food, Red. I've got a craving for something I don't have to skin first. There's got to be something in a cupboard somewhere."

Darcy followed the hunter, but only because she'd been ordered to. Her hunger had completely vanished.

Sid stretched his back and arms before settling back down to the telescope. His teammates had been gone a little under an hour; longer than he was happy with, but not long enough for him to get scared. There was nothing happening in the park, and watching it had become...well, boring. A clanking noise came from the hallway, and Sid turned to find Toffee entering, a rucksack over his shoulder, and Darcy behind him with a gym bag.

"We hit pay dirt," said the hunter.

The city of Vancouver lay in earthquake country. A few tremors, rippling out from epicentres located in the state of Washington, occasionally rattled dishes and toppled picture frames, but that had been the worst of it. Despite this, earthquake preparedness had been almost a religion for some British Columbians, and warnings of the "Big One" were as common in the Lower Mainland as they were in LA, or San Francisco. It was in the apartment of one of these "prepared" people that Darcy and Toffee had found everything they needed: hermetically sealed first aid kits, two four-litre jugs of water, emergency blankets made of a thin foil-like material, and food. There were meal-replacement bars, chocolate and caramel, and even better army-surplus-type rations, in the form of boil-in-a-bag mulligan stew, stroganoff, chicken cacciatore and ravioli. Sid had expected to make a fire right in one of the offices, but they didn't have to resort to that. The seventh, as did most of the floors, sported a kitchenette, stocked with plates, cutlery and a pair of small pots. Along with food, the would-be quake survivor had a single-burner propane stove that folded down to the size of large book. There were also two small bottles of propane, both full.

"It's almost like being home again," said Darcy, spooning up a mouthful of stroganoff. Her hunger had returned as soon as the scent of cooked meat hit the air.

"I'll tell Roshi you said that," Sid joked, "I'm sure he'll be flattered that you think his cooking compares with," he picked up one of the foil packets and read the label, "Smith & Piedmont's survival food. I can remember when the earthquake was the biggest thing Vancouverites had to worry about. Richmond was a write-off if I remember the doggerel correctly."

"And the island," said Darcy, referring to Vancouver Island, sitting just off the western coast. "Although my Dad argued that it would be fine, what with its substrate being all bedrock."

Toffee bit a chunk out of a Power Bar, then spat it out.

"That stale?" asked Sid.

"Nope. Tastes just like they always did. I was hoping my memory was wrong. So, you come up with a plan yet?"

"I considered launching something from the roof somehow, but there'll be too many birds up there, especially since the gulls are nesting now. Taking a trike won't work either, even if we get one."

"Why not?" Toffee rinsed his mouth out with water and expectorated on the floor.

"I watched those two trikes, you must have heard them…"

"Saw them, actually."

"…yes, well they covered some bizarre path on their way out of the park. All twisty. I couldn't see what was guiding them, landmarks or just plain memory I don't know."

"You thinkin' mines?"

"Unlikely. Maybe covered pit traps. We'd need a trike and a driver." He looked out the window. "We'll be losing the light soon."

Faintly, trike motors buzzed from the street below. All three of them moved to the window. Toffee used the telescope as the vehicles came into view, following a reverse of the path they'd taken out. It was growing dark quickly.

The hunter straightened up. "Why are these things never mounted at a proper height? We probe the ground ahead of us. Only idiots fall into pit traps. They might even be designed not to spring under light weight. If it is mines, they'll be anti-vehicular. No problems there."

Orange lights appeared, one by one, as torches were lit around the outside of the building. As the first two vehicles pulled up, the other three started. Tiny yellow beams sprang to life once the vehicles were in motion. Toffee stooped to the eyepiece again.

"Halbert, those are bike lights, there's four on each of them. Y'know, the ones that get their power from motion."

"I had one of those," volunteered Darcy. "Made it harder to pedal. I think it was stolen about a week after I got it."

Sid took the telescope once more. A changing of the guard was going on with the two trikes not in motion. The previous occupants had gotten out and new teams were entering. Soon all five of the three-wheelers were drifting around in what looked like random directions.

"There must be something on the ground," said Darcy. "Look at that. How on Earth could anybody remember that many twists and turns."

"We won't know what it is, Darcy. It could be three pebbles together, or a stick broken in a specific place."

Toffee put his hand on Sid's shoulder and squeezed. "I'm telling you, Halbert, only idiots fall into pit traps."

"Can you make it through that?" Halbert waved his hand at the guards. "They may look like they're going all over the place, but I don't see too many gaps."

The hunter didn't answer. He dragged a chair to the window and sat down, intent on watching the trikes till he saw the hole in their search pattern.

47. Loophole

The door to Noah's cell opened and the two warriors were on him before his eyes could adjust to the light. They pinned his arms to the floor, but did little else. Pointed fingers pushed into his chest. He let out a sound as the broken rib was depressed. It was a quiet gasp, no more than a squeak. He was struck across the face.

"No speaking."

Noah opened his eyes and realized a third person had entered the room. He hadn't thought about the fact that the warriors were too busy holding his arms to poke and prod. Henry, at least Noah thought it was Henry, peeled shrink-wrap from a small, tan object. He flicked the wrapper to the floor distastefully. The object changed shape within his hands, going from roughly cubical to long and rectangular. Noah realized it was a tension bandage, one that had never been used.

"You're not worth this, you know," said Henry. "Lift him."

The warriors pulled Noah to his feet, still keeping his arms locked up, and away from his body. The one on the right was in his late teens, but the one on his left, if Noah hadn't been so weak, he was sure he could have crushed that one.

Henry wrinkled his nose as he wrapped Noah's torso. "Once you're anointed you'll get no special treatment. You'll really learn your place then. You fix our sun dishes, and you stay alive."

It was a much more severe version of the same thing Caps had said to him scant weeks before.

Henry secured the bandage with a pair of metal clips. "There, try to stay off your feet for a while." He laughed at his own joke, looking at the warriors for signs of their amusement. They just stared back blankly. "That was something doctors used to say in the old world. Don't you ever…forget it." Henry tilted Noah's head to one side and punched him in the temple. The chief of photovoltaic's head snapped to the side. "Drop him."

The warriors let go and Noah fell, one hand instinctively protecting his chest. As his vision cleared a fourth person entered the cell, this one was shorter and hairier than the others. He carried something.

"Have a few moments with your new friend," said Henry, drawing the warriors from the room. "Don't forget the light," he nodded at a torch propped in a wall bracket.

Noah looked up as the door closed. At first he was repulsed, then he recognized the troll that had stared at him through the glass.

"You were–"

The troll clamped his hand firmly on Noah's mouth and shook his ugly, shaggy head. He moved to the door and placed his ear up against it, gesturing at something through the door. It took nearly a minute for Noah to get it, his head still addled by the last blow, but finally he understood. The troll was telling him people were listening on the other side of the door. Somehow, the deformed man sensed his message had gotten across. Whatever he'd brought into the room was covered with an animal hide. The troll pushed it across the floor, and removed the covering. There was a jar of water and bowl of fruit. Two apples and a pear. All three were bruised, and a little mushy, but Noah didn't care. As he reached for the fruit, he saw the chain shackled between Slave's ankles. He realized he'd seen it earlier, but didn't understand until now. The reality of what was to become of him was terrible. He began to shake all over. Slowly, the troll knelt down, and put his arms around the young man. Then, lest he be caught bestowing kindness on the prisoner, he ended the embrace and shuffled to the door.

"Wait…"

Again the troll shook his head and gestured for silence with a finger to his lips. He knocked on the door.

"You talked. Twice," said Henry.

Noah brought his hands up, but not quickly enough. The kick took him the forehead.

"Take the tray away, Slave. He's obviously not hungry."

"You don't like the dresses?" asked Luke, disappointed. He stood alone in the room, but the warriors outside discouraged Lena from trying anything.

"I don't feel like dressing up. Is that what all this is?" she gestured at cushions and other luxuries she'd been brought. "You buttering me up to be your sex slave?"

The Master laughed like she'd said something quite funny indeed. Lena didn't get it.

"No. Tomorrow you will meet Her. I know She doesn't talk to you, but I do know why She wants you."

"Who is this woman? Is she the real leader here?"

"Woman?" his eyes darkened for a fraction of a second. "Tomorrow you will meet Her. You should be presentable. If these dresses are not suitable, I'll have others brought to you. Is there a colour you prefer?"

She was about to refuse to wear any dress he suggested, but felt she might be wrong to antagonize him. Her brief reunion with Crispin banished any illusions that these people might be kind to her.

"I like purple. With a high collar and a long skirt," she picked up the first two gowns. "These are…the right size." Why tell him they were too large? Baggy with lots of flesh covered was the way to go.

"Thank you. Do you have any special requests? I can't let you out of the room, but I could have something brought to you. We do have the whole city at our disposal."

"I'd like a dime, please."

"A dime?"

"Yes, it's a tiny coin about this size," she held her fingers a centimetre apart, "with a sailboat one side and…"

"Yes, I know what a dime is. I remember money." There, just for a moment, he sounded like a boy, instead of the pretentious aristocrat he pretended to be. "Why do you want a dime?"

"I had one for years, only coin I've ever kept. My lucky dime. I lost it somewhere and I'd like to have another one."

The Master narrowed his eyes suspiciously.

"Please?"

"Fine, I will have one brought to you."

Toffee crouched in the darkness. There was a good fifty metres between him and the place where the trikes passed the closest. Halbert would be furious with him for sneaking off, but who cares. And anyway, he'd left a note. The vehicles didn't alter from their individual courses. It was the type of thing that must have been practised constantly. Maybe they did it every night, watching for teeth. There wasn't much sound coming from the three-wheelers, just the occasional crunching of something, and the whisper of chain gliding across metal. From above he could tell they kept the grounds around the zoo pretty much covered, but they didn't maintain a constant speed, and once in a while, all five vehicles would be far enough away that he could make a break for one of the small concrete structures near the aquarium. Unfortunately, that opportunity wasn't as easy to see from ground level as it was from above, and he'd already missed it twice. His body was ready to sprint in an instant, and although he'd been holding the position for a while, he was neither tired, nor uncomfortable. A blob of light bobbed through the air as someone ran from the aquarium to intercept a trike. The vehicle slowed, then stopped, its lights winking out as it did so. The other four vehicles were still staggered enough in their circling that Toffee couldn't make it through, but if that one stayed still long enough…but it didn't. The torchbearer ran back towards the large building, while the lights on the trike lit up. But the vehicle wasn't rejoining its brethren, it was breaking off, heading out somewhere. With only four trikes to contend with, the hunter was going to have a much easier time of it.

Slave sat on the steps of the aquarium and watched the lights travel across the ground. He wondered at how different a place could look, and not change at all. He'd brought his children to the aquarium many times. Their favourite thing to see was the arapaima, a six-foot wedge-shaped fish with a mouth that looked like puckered lips. Three of them had shared a tank with a handful of what looked like giant catfish. A picture had stood on the mantle in his house, of himself and his wife, before a Haida Indian statue of a killer whale. The Vancouver Aquarium had looked one way then. The killer whale statue stood where it always had. It was even cleaned on a regular basis. Not surprising really, considering the part it played in Archie's religion. His eyes now saw the building, both inside and outside, not only with a familiarity born of years within, but through a haze of pain and hate. And now that had changed. He knew who was in the city now. Luke had given him names. It was Darcy's voice he'd recognized, though he still hadn't been able to put a face to the voice until Luke questioned him about Sid Halbert. That was the connection. Not only had Halbert managed to elude the warriors, but he'd taken care of four of them. It was small, but it was a start. Again the aquarium had taken on a different face. It looked like a place he would be leaving soon.

Conner came running back from delivering his message to Cyrus, and both of them went inside.

The Master stood in a long room, his cheek pressed up against a sheet of glass, beyond which lay complete darkness.

"I have displeased you, Mistress. I should have brought them to you sooner."

The glass ran the length of the room, broken into large windows by pillars. It was the lesser shrine, accessible only to the Master, and those he might give permission to accompany him. This time, he was alone. His need to commune was too personal to allow guests in Her presence. "Is it because she was treated roughly? I did not know."

He yearned for Her to speak with him, like She'd done with the former Master. Luke had grown up watching Archie have conversations with Her, although he never heard the words himself. He told the others that he did, of course. It wouldn't do for them to know their current high priest was not the conduit the former had been. Luke followed the rules to the letter. When to make offerings, what type of offerings to make…when to give a baby. Those were the best. New children brought such stress to the tribe, warriors going days without sleep, guarding the infant every second that they could. They also brought great joy. The females, truly women once producing a child, earned a closeness to Her when they freely gave of their own flesh and blood. For Luke, the sacrifice of a baby brought the expectancy of true contact, but it never came. The rapture of communion was denied him always. He did, however, put on a good show. He'd spread his arms, roll his eyes into the back of his head, and moan, just the way Archie had done. It never once occurred to him that his former master might also have been putting on an act.

Luke sank to his knees, his face still pressed to glass.

"Please. You have allowed the interlopers to escape us, protected them in the forbidden lands, enabled them to slay four of our number. What will make amends for my wrong? I am bringing her to you tomorrow, as the light begins to fade."

His head was knocked away as something heavy struck the glass from the other side.

"Is that too late? I could bring her to you at daybreak."

Again the glass was struck, but not quite so hard this time.

"It shall be done. Tomorrow as You bless us with your sun, the chosen one will be presented."

He gathered his cloak about him and ascended the stairs that lead to open air and the amphitheatre of the great shrine, but he would not trod upon those holy grounds until the morning. A double door opened to admit him to the building proper. Inside, Conner waited, his hands cupped together.

"I have it, Master," he said, holding up his hands. "Cyrus just got back. It didn't take him long."

"Well, it shouldn't have. Let me see it." He plucked the dime from the boys hand and looked at the coin from both sides. "Clean it, then take it to her. Conner, are you staying firm with your choice of the warrior's path?"

"Yes. I know it means I'll never speak again, but I don't mind. Do you think She'll come to me then, when I go to the block?"

"About that…I know I said you could take the cut at the same time as the offering is made, but that is not Her will. The sun catcher will be anointed then. You will have to wait until the next offering."

"Wait? But you promised this time! You said I could–"

Luke slapped him. "Never take that tone of voice with me again. Now, off with you. Take the dime to the chosen one."

Lena thanked the seeker who gave her the dime, waited until the door was shut, then placed the plank under the handle. She contemplated shoving the tub up against it, but it would be hard to pull it away quickly if someone came to the door. The coin was nice and shiny as she gave it an expert flip, and caught it in her other hand. It was so strange to be holding one of the coins again after so much time. Lena was superstitious, but she put no stock in lucky coins. She didn't really believe in lucky anything. Certainly the word incorporated into the name of her father's boat hadn't helped. She did however know that as innocuous as the tiny coin might seem, it made an excellent screwdriver. The vent opening above the tub was far too small for her to climb into, but if she unscrewed and removed the frame around it, there might just be enough space for her to get in.

Balancing precariously on the edge of the tub, she braced one hand against the ceiling and slotted the dime into one of the four screws that held the frame in place. She twisted, but the screw refused to budge. Pocketing the dime, she jumped down and tore the washing-instruction label from the seam of one of the dresses. She unscrewed the cap from where the oil was placed in her lantern, and dipped the label, allowing it to soak through. Stepping back up on the tub, she rubbed each screw with the label, hoping oil would seep in and lubricate them.

She dropped the label and tried the dime again. After a few finger-biting efforts, the first screw began to turn. None of them were easy to turn, but eventually she got all four of them out, putting them carefully in her pocket. With a glance at the door, she grabbed the frame and pulled. It didn't budge. Running her hand around the edges of it, she discovered it was caulked in place. Without proper leverage or a cutting tool, she had no hope of dislodging it. Cursing inwardly, she returned the screws to their rightful place, and threw the dime across the room. Nope, no such thing as lucky coins.

Noah became aware of the sound through the dim fog of semi-sleep. It was a furtive, thumping sound, and it was coming from above his head. Noah rolled onto his back and opened his eyes, as if he could see anything in the darkness. The sound came again. It wasn't footsteps of someone walking in a room above, it was more like something moving through the ceiling. An animal. From the sounds of it, maybe a coon. It was in the void space, or maybe in the ventilation system. Noah couldn't remember if there was a vent in his ceiling, he couldn't recall if he'd even looked up there the few times light had entered his world. To his dismay and terror, a rattling of metal told him there was a vent up there, and whatever was above him was trying to open it. If it got in, Noah was in no way capable of defending himself. To go through all he had, only to fall prey to teeth. Two words rang in his head; *this sucks*. A creak announced the vent opening, but instead of the dull thump of a raccoon landing on the floor, something solid dropped and clattered. With a creak and a snap, the vent closed again, and the shuffling sound moved off.

Noah crawled to where he thought the object might be. It took a long time to find it, but eventually his hand fell across cold metal. His hands recognized the object's shape a split second before his brain did. He turned his head towards the ceiling, offering silent thanks to whoever his benefactor had been.

Slave cleared the opening in the wall and shut the vent as quickly as he could. It had been hell for him, propelling himself through the duct with his wounded foot, but he had no choice. The Master had moved the schedule up from the evening to the morning. He couldn't wait for Sid to show. Now he had a delivery to make to Lena, but to get to her, he'd need to access a different set of ducts. As he moved to the hallway, he was almost bowled over by a pair of warriors racing by. One of them gestured to him to follow.

Why now? he asked himself. Warriors were always getting over-excited about the tiniest things.

He rounded the corner and into the foyer that led to the front doors. The Master was already there, Conner beside him, a sour expression on the boy's face.

The doors opened and a man limped in. He only had one full arm, the other ended just past the elbow. The broken shaft of an arrow protruded from his right hip. Two warriors preceded him, walking backwards, arrows trained on his heart. Three of them walked behind, faces tense, bowstrings taut. All of them looked scared, as if their prisoner might somehow overcome them, despite the five arrows aimed at him.

"You must be Toffee," said the Master, a smile of vindication curling his lips.

"Yeah. Who the fuck are you?"

One of the rear guard warriors dropped his bow and drew a cudgel from his belt, a fire-hardened knotted piece of wood. With a single, easy swing he struck Toffee across the back of the head. The hunter dropped to his knees, then crashed to the floor.

"I have acted upon God's will," said Luke, "and She has blessed us. How did you come upon this man?"

The warrior who had struck Toffee down, Cyrus, flicked his hands, describing how a flash of motion had drawn his attention, how he'd stopped the trike and feathered the man with his first shot.

"It is good. Have him taken to the cleansing room. Summon Henry. This man will tell us where his companions are. We will have them all before the ceremony. What a great day this is."

He raised his hands, indicating that the warriors should acknowledge his greatness. As a group, they bowed their heads. "Slave, has the sun catcher been fed?"

Slave hesitated, then shook his head.

"Well, feed him. No, not you. You stay with me. I want you with me until the ceremony. Conner, take food to the new one. I want him capable of walking to his anointment."

The boy chanced a sullen glance at the Master, then left to do his bidding. The warriors as a group lifted Toffee's limp body and dragged him down the corridor. Even unconscious, the hunter still made them uncomfortable.

When the door to his cell opened, Noah had his back pressed to the opposite wall. His mysterious benefactor had provided him with an opportunity and he didn't want to waste it. Though he didn't want to admit his need, he eyed the tray hungrily as it was brought in by the fair-haired boy he'd seen earlier. The boy looked at him with pure hatred as he placed the food upon the ground.

"I'd rather let you starve to death. You don't deserve the Master's blessing. It was my turn. My turn!"

"You can keep your master's blessing, I don't want any of it," Noah couldn't stop his tongue. "Doglicking pervert."

"You're not supposed to speak," the boy raised his hand as if to strike, then paused. "Pervert…I remember that word. What does it mean?" Noah kept silent. "Speak, I grant you privilege."

"It means someone who touches people in bad way."

The look on the boy's face was palpable. Noah felt odd, actually feeling pity for one of his captors. "He touches you, doesn't he, kid?"

"Shut up!" this time he did strike, a halfhearted slap that came more from obligation than from enmity. "This is your fault! It was supposed to be over."

This time, Noah wisely kept his mouth shut. He waited a few minutes after the door closed before moving to the tray. Knowing full well that guzzling the water or gulping the food down would lead to a stomachache didn't stop him from doing just that. It was the same tray he'd been brought earlier, the jar and the three pieces of bruised fruit, but in a way he was thankful for the mushy parts, as they were easier to consume. The act of biting and chewing caused no small amount of pain to his damaged face. Again, he was thankful no harm had befallen his teeth. While he dined, the metal object that had dropped from the ceiling was pressed tight to his skin, held in place by the tension bandage.

Noah had almost finished the second apple when the door opened again. A bundle of cloth flew through the portal and struck him in the shoulder.

"Put that on," said a voice, then the door closed.

Noah gulped what was left of the water, the cool liquid soothing his throat like the loving touch of an angel. He unwrapped the bundle and studied it with his hands as best he could. As near as he could tell, it was nothing more than a sheet with a hole in the middle. He shrugged into the cloth, surprised at how difficult it was to raise his arms above his head. If there was a specific front or back to the garment, he couldn't tell, but the feeling of cloth, any cloth, covering his legs and crotch was a comfort after spending so much time naked. The clothing would also help to conceal his prize. With the food eaten, Noah took his position against the far wall and waited. Blood rushed to his stomach to aid in the digestive process, and an almost irresistible fatigue came over him. He was determined not to sleep, but after a few minutes of staring at the darkness, his eyes betrayed him, the lids drooping, then falling shut.

"Wake him up," said the Master.

Henry covered both the hunter's mouth and nose. The man started in his sleep, his eyes opened and he tried to sit up. When he found he couldn't, being bound to the table and all, he ceased in his struggles and eyed the three people in the room with a disconcerting calmness.

"Where are the other three?" asked Luke. "The two men and the woman?"

"Other two," said Toffee. "The skinny guy must be dead by now."

Henry had taken two steps back from the table. Though the hunter was bound at the ankles, one wrist, and a strap across the chest, the seeker felt as though they'd brought a bear into their home. He'd never seen anyone quite so large as the hunter. In fact the man was too big to completely fit on the table, his feet dangled off the far end, and his head cleared the wood at the top.

"Tell me where they are, or you will be tortured."

"You can't torture me." Toffee looked at Slave. "You're an ugly son of a bitch, ain'tcha?" He returned his gaze to Luke. "You the boss here?"

He had an air about him, as though it were the Master strapped to the table instead of the other way around.

"Why can I not torture you?"

"Because I'll stop my heart, that's why. Think I'll just lie here and let you make me look like him?" he flicked his eyes at Slave.

"And how will you stop your heart?"

"With my mind, bonehead. Can't you?"

The Master looked at Henry. The seeker shrugged. "I've read about it being possible…"

Luke grasped the broken arrow shaft, still protruding from Toffee's hip. He wiggled it back and forth, eliciting a fresh trickle of blood, and most likely a great deal of pain. A slight narrowing of the hunter's eyes was his only reward for the effort.

"If you do not tell me where the other…two are, I will torture those I already have, the sun catcher and the woman. I will do it in front of your eyes."

"Go ahead, I don't care. Shit, I'll help you. What you should do is cut off one of their fingertips and–"

"Enough!" He struck, his fist smashing into Toffee's jaw. At least, that was the intent. The hunter rolled his head as the blow landed, allowing the fist to graze him, rather than making solid contact.

Slave eyed the door, wondering how to get away. He had to go, he had to get to Lena before the sunrise.

"I don't know what you kids think you are," said Toffee, "but I just came to get a look at you. I got caught, oh well. The other guy's name is Halbert, since you know who I am, I guess you knew that already."

The Master nodded, his own discomfort growing as the hunter failed to show any signs of fear.

"I don't owe that guy anything. I came in here to do a job, and I failed. My skin's more important than his, so we can keep wasting time, or we can deal."

"Deal? You are in no position to deal."

"Let me kill him," said Henry. "Let me kill him now."

"Silence!" Luke snapped at the seeker. "If it were Her will that he was dead, then he would be so."

Toffee sneered at the seeker, adding anger to the teenager's fear. "So you're not the boss, then. Okay, I'm done with you. Bring in your queen or whatever."

Quick as a cat, Luke snatched a pointed implement from a basket and plunged it through the hunter's arm, a few inches above the wrist. Toffee sucked air in through his teeth, but that was the extent of his reaction.

"You will not refer to Her in anyway," said Luke, his control fraying at the edges. The hunter's physical presence aside, his coolness given the circumstances was something the Master had never seen before, or even considered possible.

At the same time as Slave revelled in the man's demeanor, he too was discomforted, but for different reasons.

"So what," said the Master, "is your deal?" He left the spike where it was.

Toffee nodded, not even sparing a glance towards the slim piece of metal that pinioned his arm to the table. "There's a woman, not the one you have, the other one."

"The red-haired girl."

"Yeah. That's what I want. Halbert's the leader. With him taken care of, you've got no more worries. You get him, I get her, and we'll both be happy. I split. You can take us to the city limits and you'll never see either of us again."

"I see. And what if I decide to torture the red-haired woman? Darcy, isn't it?"

"You're not going to find her without me. I don't matter to Halbert. All he cares about is Noah."

"Noah? Is that the sun catcher's name?"

"Sun catcher? Haven't heard that one before. You didn't know his name? Heh. Not very good at this are you? How'd you manage to keep this city locked down for so long? No never mind, it wasn't you was it? You're too young." The Master reached for another spike. "Oh, give it up. I'll stop my heart, then you'll get nothing. Halbert and Darcy will hang around on the edges of this wasteland you've created and pick you off one at a time. They'll spend months doing it if they have to. You'll never find 'em till it's too late."

Luke's face stayed hard, but the spike hung loosely in his hands. "Henry, bring me the brazier."

The seeker, who had been unable to pull his gaze from the hunter, moved to the other side of the room and brought back a metal bowl on a wheeled cart. The bowl had glowing embers in it and a series of spikes similar to the one the Master now held.

"These are for something new," Luke explained to both Slave and Toffee. "I'm going to try skin writing. It is for the anointment of the sun catcher. Maybe I should practice on you."

"Fine," said Toffee. "I'm out of here." His eyes rolled into the back of his head and his body went rigid.

"Wait!" Luke screamed. The hunter's body had begun to jerk and spasm. "Don't die!" he grasped the hunter's head with both hands, but didn't know what to do. The only tools he had for forcing his will were fear and pain, but how did one use these to stop a man from killing himself? "Wait! I'll deal, I'll deal."

Toffee's body stopped thrashing. His eyes fluttered, then came into focus. "Almost passed the point of no return there. Okay, I know where they were when I left 'em. They could have moved by now, but I know where the rig is. You set up an ambush there. They have to return to it sooner or later."

"Tell me where," said the Master, visibly relieved.

Slave, by contrast, was growing more and more nervous. He looked at the brazier, knowing if Luke didn't practice on Toffee, he would find another canvass to work with.

"Not a chance. I don't trust you worth shit. I'll take your warriors there."

"You will not leave here until I have Halbert."

"Whatever. Bye." Again the hunter's eyes rolled up.

"No! You will take warriors to your vehicle, but you will be bound, and helpless."

"Wouldn't expect it any other way, kid. I'll tell you this though, the last time I saw Halbert and Darcy they were in the—"

Slave lurched forward, his hands wrapped around Toffee's throat before he knew what he was doing. He couldn't let this awful man lead the tribe to Sid. Luke grabbed Slave almost instantly, pulling him away and throwing him to the floor.

Toffee swallowed a couple of times. "Having some loyalty problems, are we?"

"What is that?" asked the Master, his focus on Slave now. Something white was showing from beneath the man's shirt.

Slave tried to move away as Luke reached for him, but he wasn't fast enough. Luke snatched the items—a few folded pieces of paper—from where they were tucked in Slave's waistband. He unfolded them, and another piece of paper fell out and fluttered to the floor. Luke bent and retrieved the additional item as Slave found his feet.

"Where did you get this?" asked the Master, holding up an edge-tattered, blue-and-yellow brochure, with the words "Vancouver Aquarium" on the front flap. "I thought all of these had been destroyed."

The brochure contained both a floor plan of the aquarium, as well as a local map, showing all the roads in and out of Stanley Park. Beside and beneath the maps were invitations to; "Stand face to face with a wolf eel," and "Dare the hunting grounds of a blacktip reef shark."

Henry moved to block the door as Luke unfolded the white paper. He scanned the text, his lips moving as he read. "Oh, dear. You've told her everything. Everything! What is this? Not a god...NOT A GOD? Blasphemer!" He cast the letter aside. The pages fluttered, one of them landing on Toffee's chest.

The Master's eyes were burning. An anger kindled by having another's will stronger than his own, now erupted into a voracious inferno. "Paper and ink are the province of the seekers! You do not have the right. And what you wrote...what you wrote...how were you going to get this to your precious Lena? God told me to keep you near. You will never be rescued, She has brought this heathen to lead us to Halbert!" During his tirade, he hadn't moved. Now he turned to Henry. "Bind the prisoner's wounds, remove the arrow. Prepare the table anew." His lips curled back into an expression of near-animal savagery. His next words to Slave came out in a snarl. "I will cut you 'till sunrise. The sun catcher's anointment will be heralded with your blood."

Toffee, almost forgotten on the table, finished reading and dropped his head back. Pain momentarily clouded his face.

Slave feinted towards the door and, as the Master moved to block him, whirled in the other direction, plunging his hands into the brazier. His mouth contorted in a silent scream as flesh sizzled and the sweet-sour aroma of burning flesh filled the air.

"NO!" Luke launched himself across the distance that separated them. He pushed Slave away from the brazier with both hands. Slave fell, coals scattered across the floor.

"What have you done?" the Master demanded, pulling Slave up by his wrists.

The deformed man surveyed the damage to his hands. Though he'd only had a few seconds, the destruction was complete. His palms were a ruin of charred and peeling skin, the fingers had been curved inwards, and there was nothing Henry would be able to do about it. With the destruction of his skillful extremities, Slave ceased to exist, his purpose could no longer be fulfilled. Though the pain was excruciating, Jonathan Crispin didn't cry out. He'd been taught nothing during his imprisonment if not how to accept pain. *Not by my own hand, I will not die by my own hand.* His jaw dropped, releasing powerful laughter that started at his belly and exploded from his mouth.

Luke's hands grasped Crispin by the throat, forcing him against the wall. He squeezed with all his might, seeking to crush not only the windpipe that was the source of that laughter, but the soul as well. He felt cartilage collapsing under his grip. His victim's eyes bulged at the assault, but still seemed to hold glee rather than pain. Saliva frothed on the Master's lips. Crispin's body began to thrash involuntarily, then it stopped. Forever.

The Master's hands fell to his side, the former chief of communications crumpled to the ground, a lifeless, misshapen pile of hair and rags.

"I like how you deal with traitors," said Toffee. "Better than wasting gas on locking them outside."

48. GasCan

Conrad gripped the wheel with his fat fingers and watched as Patricia worked away at a tough bit of jerky she'd dragged out from somewhere in the back of the Hummer. They worked their way back and forth on a stretch of road out of sight of the Pit. It was a duty that had quickly become known as "Boss Watch." It was likely that Sid would radio in on his approach, but possibly he wouldn't. Regardless, the patrol was pointlessly dull, with nothing much to look at besides what the headlights revealed, and not much to worry about except falling asleep.

"You ever think about hunting?" asked Connie.

"No. Why? You thinking of applying?"

"Why not? Not much future in security. There's three ahead of me for the big chair, but the way things are going, I could be chief of the hunters in a few weeks, get the double room, sit in on the special meals…"

"You mean be a special meal. You're not serious are you?"

"Nah, I'm just kidding around. I'm too set in my ways to jump now. So, you bet anything on Mike's pool?"

"The Deep Six pool? Yeah, I put a glass of milk on four."

"Which four?"

"The Boss, Toffee, Darcy and Caps."

"You know, if none of them come home at all, Mike keeps all that stuff. He stands to make a huge profit off of this."

"Why else would he do it? You?"

"I bet twice. Two each; The Boss and Darcy, Toffee and Darcy."

"Putting a lot of faith in the Chief, huh?"

"Kind of. Mostly I'm playing an angle."

"You know what's interesting? I don't think anybody's bet on all six."

Conrad had noticed the same thing when he'd seen the betting sheet. It was a little depressing, but then his money—so to speak—was riding on two and only two survivors.

"Connie, I think we're going to find out right now."

Twin beams of light broke the crest of the hill. They were about the right size and distance apart to be the Pig.

"Son of bitch! They're back!" His hand reached for the radio handset. Another pair of headlights appeared, these ones larger and higher. "And they got a rig!" His thumb pressed the button. "Base, I have good news…" another pair of truck-sized headlights popped into view, then a third and a fourth.

"Where did he get so many trucks?"

"Connie," Patricia grabbed his arm, "wouldn't the Boss be coming from the other direction?"

"Base! D'Abo!" Conrad screamed into the mic. He hauled on the wheel, g-force pressing him sideways in the seat as the Hummer did a U-turn. "D'Abo's coming! Full alert! D'Abo's coming!"

Patricia turned in her seat to watch behind them as Conrad pushed the Hummer to full speed. Two sets of smaller headlights, cars, had split from the truck convoy and were driving side by side.

"Shit, Connie, they've got some roadsters coming. Step on it!"

"I am stepping on it! Conrad to Base, Conrad to Base!"

"Chiu here."

"Dammit Chiu, where've you been? D'Abo's on his way!"

"What? Are you sure?"

"Oh, he's positive," said an oily voice. The fat man must have scanned their frequency. The radio went dead.

"Chiu! Did you hear that? Chiu! We're being jammed." He released the mic, letting it snap back on its coiled wire. "How many of them are there?"

"I can't tell. The trucks are coming single file. The cars are almost in gun range."

It was a sound quickly becoming familiar in Compton Pit, the alarm bells of full alert.

Sara was running full tilt to the battery bay. Daniel was at her side. They'd tried to bring the satellite dish down from both the tower and security, but nothing had happened. It sat there topside, tall and vulnerable. A target even a child could hit.

Duff hooked up with them, the front of his coveralls weren't completely done, and fat rolls jiggled with every step.

"Why won't the dish go down?" demanded Sara.

"No power to it. Thurlow cut that system before he left!"

They entered the workshop, Daniel stopping to find a light switch. Duff moved by memory, almost reaching the door to the battery bay before a single bank of fluorescents flickered to life.

"Daniel, go to communications," said Sara. "Lower the dish from there." The acting chief of security complied, Sara followed Duff into the power hub.

The temporary photovoltaic engineer—he hadn't even been granted acting chief status—pulled at a couple of cables, looking uncertain.

"Don't you know?" asked Sara, her heart racing, blood pressure threatening to blow a vessel.

Duff decisively shoved a dangling plug into an available socket. "There. That'll do it."

The door to the airlock gaped open, like the mouth of a mother Tilapia fish offering safety to her babies. The two cars had reached the top of Compton Pit's driveway, and weren't slowing down. In the southeastern tower, a pair of panic-stricken junior security officers loaded the heavy machine gun. The Hummer passed through the airlock, and the doors began their ponderously slow process of shutting. In the corridors of the Pit, people dragged themselves out of bed and threw on clothing. Others were already on their way to the armoury, and Chiu and Purty were on their way to Seth.

"I don't hear it," said Sara, referring to the telltale vibration of the dish being lowered.

"Maybe Daniel's waiting to hear from you," offered Duff.

Sara tore out of the battery bay and down the hall to communications. Her breath was coming heavier and the back of her throat was beginning to hurt. She hadn't done this much running in almost a decade. In communications, Daniel stood at the console, repeatedly stabbing a button, waiting for a light that would tell him his command was being followed.

"Shit!" She spun on her heel and raced back to the power hub.

"Are you sure it's him?" asked Seth, checking the clip of a handgun. There was no point in him bothering with a rifle.

"I've never heard his voice," said Chiu, "but it was exactly what I thought it would sound like."

"We've got to move now," said Purty. "Dr. White will just hand the Pit over to him."

Seth wrestled with the desire to argue the point, say that she'd do nothing of the sort, tell them to give her a chance, but he knew it wasn't the way to go.

"We don't have time right now. There's a couple of rookies in the tower right?"

"Yeah."

"Well get the hell up there! He won't just smash his way in. He'll have to deploy. We'll make our move when the time is right. Go!"

"I don't know!" said Duff, a thin sheen of sweat standing out on his forehead. "That should have been it."

"What the hell have you been doing these last few days? Sleeping?"

"Look, Thurlow rerouted a lot of power, more efficient. This isn't Freeland's configuration anymore, at least not the way I remember it."

"Well, figure it out, dammit!"

Heavy thudding announced Mike reaching the door. "The Hummer's in. Two cars have stopped outside the gate, but there's a string of trucks coming."

"Where're are Purty and Chiu?"

"I don't know. They must be in the tower."

"Duff!"

"I'm working on it."

The newly-drafted security officers stared in horror at the fleet of trucks approaching the pit. The vehicles stopped, just out of easy gun-range, and began to spread out, blocking the road and either side of the shoulder. There were five tractor-trailer rigs, a motorhome, an armoured personnel carrier, and the two cars. Two of the rigs towed flatbeds. On the back of one of them was a bulldozer. On the back of the other was a tank.

Chiu and Purty burst through the trapdoor.

"You're relieved," said Purtricil.

"Dogshit!" breathed Chiu, looking out at the tank. "Bring us a rocket launcher. Hurry. Oh man, Purty, the dish is still up!"

Daniel sounded like he was typing the way he rhythmically stabbed at the button. The tiny, green LED above failed to light.

Duff scrambled over the cables, tracing them with his eyes, the intense look from Dr. White making his job that much harder. She was right, he had been spending a lot of his time doing much of nothing in the workshop. Anything not vital to the Pit had been shut down already. What was there for him to do?

"That one!" He grasped a cable and yanked on it. He'd missed it at first because the plug had been hidden amongst other cables.

"You said that the last three times," said Sara.

Duff didn't reply as he unplugged one of his previous efforts and shoved the new one into place.

Topside, the large dish swivelled up, and the support tower began to rotate, even as it slowly eased into the ground.

The vibrations through the wall of the battery bay were like a deluge of cool water to Sara's overheated body. She left Duff behind, gasping with relief, and ran to communications. It was there she was needed most, now. The dim corridor sped by. Daniel was leaning on the desk with both hands. Lyle had appeared, finally. He looked up at Sara, indicating with a shake of his head that nothing had come through yet.

"Daniel, get up front. I want a rocket launcher in each tower, and two squads up topside. I'll take over here." She picked up the second set of headphones and slapped them on.

"We're being jammed," said Lyle. "Nothing coming in or out."

"That won't last long."

With Purty on the machine gun, Chiu shouldered the rocket launcher and took aim at the tank. There were only three rockets in total, two with him, and one in the northwest tower. Figures moved in the darkness by the panels as armed Comptonite's emerged from the hub and spread out. Down the road, people leapt from the backs of trucks, and the APC. The tank was unloaded, driven down an extended ramp. The vehicles shifted formation again, forming a protective circle around the motorhome. Chiu shifted his aim from the tank to the larger vehicle. It would be suicide to fire, for either of them to fire. There were probably a dozen heavy weapons pointed at the tower right now. Better weapons, with far more ammunition. It was a calculated standoff for now, and thanks to the Mimis there wasn't even the hope of teeth distracting D'Abo from his purpose. The sound net protected the enemy as well as the home team.

Sara listened carefully as Daniel described the situation to her through the Pit's intercom system, the alarm growing in his voice as he relayed information from the towers. It didn't occur to her to wonder what other people might be thinking at this moment, that they might blame her for not properly preparing. Though Odega was the most likely suspect, D'Abo would have had to mobilize before the animal researcher's escape, in order to be here now. How had he known? Was there truly another traitor in their midst?

"Hello, Compton Pit," said the same snakelike voice Conrad and Chiu had heard. "Who's going to talk to me?"

"This is Dr. White. Get off my driveway."

"Dr. White? I don't believe we've met. My name is Peter D'Abo. You might know me as Gascan. Why don't you put the Boss on?"

"He's busy right now, putting his cross-hairs on your forehead."

"Halbert must have a very long-range weapon indeed. Wherever did he get it? In Vancouver, perhaps?"

"Please hold," said Sara, pulling off the headset. "Lyle, patch this through to the tower. I'm not talking to this asshole blind. Don't talk to him, no matter what he says."

Again she was running, her slippered feet slapping the concrete floor as she turned into the main corridor. Seth met her as she reached the access door to the tower.

"What are you doing?" he asked, taking her arm.

"I can't talk if I don't know what's happening."

"He'll destroy the tower if you're up there in it."

"I'm not going to tell the bastard where I am, Seth. He knows. He knows about Vancouver."

"I'm coming with you."

"Fine."

Chiu's and Purty's eyes widened as Dr. White appeared through the trapdoor. A moment later, Seth followed. He shook his head slightly at them. *Now is not the time.*

Sara keyed on the speaker and mic. "Thank you for holding," she said.

"Very funny. Since I know Halbert isn't there, why don't you put the lovely and vivacious chief of security on?"

Sara bit her lip. Her hands worried at the hem of her cardigan. "Cut the crap, D'Abo. You're dealing with me. I'm the Boss. Turn around and go home. You're not welcome here."

"Have I made a single, aggressive move?" came the voice. She'd never seen D'Abo for herself, but she had seen some cartoon representations of him done by Caps. It was one of those images that came to mind, now. A titanic bulk squeezed into a little car. Somehow that helped take the edge off.

"You jammed our communications, I..." She almost said *see*, "... I've been told you have multiple guns and a tank pointed at us."

"I assume there are a number of guns pointed in my direction as well. I'm not here to hurt you, I'm here to help."

"We don't need any of your help."

"Come now, Sara. I can call you Sara, can't I?"

She glanced at Seth.

"We've got intel on him," said Seth. "Stands to reason he'd have the same on us."

"Are you still there?" asked D'Abo's voice, "or am I on hold again?"

"I'm here. Dr. White will do."

"What a shame. Dr. White, I know your panel array has been disabled, and all of your really important people are gone. I'm sure things can't be going too well for you. I offer my people and resources to aid in putting things back together, get you back on your feet again. Nobody needs to get hurt, here."

"Do you always do repair jobs with a tank?"

"It helps to keep misunderstandings from getting out of hand."

"I...I thank you for your concern, Peter. May I call you Peter?"

"I wouldn't have it any other way."

"We don't require your assistance. I'm sorry you came all this way for nothing. Why don't you just turn around and go home now."

"That would be a waste of a great deal of time and effort, Dr. White. I can see you're too proud for your own good. No matter. I'm glad you pulled your dish down, saves me the trouble of bringing in a new one."

"That sounded like a threat."

"Dr. White, open your airlock, throw down your guns. Compton Pit is clearly incapable of staying viable under its current situation. I'm stepping in, humanitarian reasons of course."

"No. You throw down your weapons, and get off our road. You have no clue how many guns are pointing at you at the moment."

"There are twenty people in the field, two people in the far tower, and three others besides yourself in the near tower."

She almost ducked in response, but managed to stymie the reaction.

"He must have some night goggles out there," whispered Seth, "or infrared. Shit, we don't even have stuff like that."

Sara's finger hovered over the intercom, torn between continuing or cutting the fat man off. D'Abo made the decision for her, speaking one more time before cutting off his own transmission.

"You will open the airlock and surrender the Pit to me. I know about your Screaming Mimis, and it's time your selfishness concerning that technology came to an end. You have until sunrise."

Dr. White punched the console. Unnoticed by her, Chiu and Purty looked askance at Seth. Again he shook his head. She flicked a switch that would allow her voice to be heard throughout Compton Pit. "People, this is the Boss. We are under siege. Please remain calm. This situation will be dealt with quickly and with a minimum of harm. All department heads, emergency meeting." She closed the channel and turned to Purtricil. "You two stay here. Do not, I repeat, do not fire first, no matter what happens. Am I understood?"

"Yes, ma'am."

She didn't realize the answer had come in response to a nod from Seth, just behind her shoulder.

A map of the Pit's surrounding area spread out on the table, Daniel explained the tactical situation as best he could.

"They're holding our only way in and out by vehicle. With the dish down, we can't ask for help from Underbel, not that it would do us much good if we could."

"Is Odega out there?" asked Chris.

"It doesn't matter whether he is or not!" snapped Dr. White, aware that the question was as much about her decisions as it was about Ted.

"If they charge us," said Daniel, "I estimate they can trash our topside defences in a few minutes. We have, three, count 'em, three rockets. D'Abo will open by launching dozens of them at the tower and the airlock doors. Eventually he'll breach both the airlock and the power hub. Now we can hold him inside, fight room to room if we have to, but as far as winning this..." he shook his head. "D'Abo won't risk his people on an all out assault. I'll bet one of those trucks is full of provisions. A second force may already be on its way. He can destroy what's left of the array, and wait us out."

"What about our back door?" asked Seth.

"I had the heavy machine gun from the northwest tower brought down to the caverns. It doesn't really do us much good up there anyway. The cave mouth is narrow enough that we can hold it indefinitely. If D'Abo knows it's there, and it's safe to assume that he does, then he also knows how defensible it is. Nope, this a siege, pure and simple."

"What about Sid?" asked Dr. Patel.

Sara raised an eyebrow to her acting second in command.

"If the Boss comes home now," said Daniel, "he'll be cut to pieces or used as a hostage."

"Do you have any good news?" asked Dr. White.

"None. We've always been capable of defending ourselves against a small attack, but nothing of this scale. Despite that, D'Abo would never try this if..." his voice faded off.

"I know, Daniel, if Sid were here. Well then, what would Sid do if he were here? What fabulous plan would the real Boss come up with?"

There was silence around the table. Nobody had an answer.

"So," Sara looked at each of them in turn, "you all think our only choice here is to surrender? Just hand Compton Pit and all it stands for over to that fat bastard? I can't accept that."

"You may have to if you want to save lives," said Patel.

"Daniel, could we send a team out through the caverns to flank him, or even come in from behind?"

"Maybe, but we're out of the Mimis' range then, they'd hear us shooting animals. Even if we could get through the scrub unmolested, I'm sure he has people watching for just such a move. Once again, we're either sending our people out to be killed or taken hostage. It's the numbers, Sara. Sid always said it would take an army to threaten us, and that's exactly what's out there."

"What have we got in the way of gas weapons?"

"A few smoke grenades, that's about it."

"What kind of smoke?"

"The kind that'll piss off wasps, but not much more."

Dr. White did something then that took them all by surprise. She spun her seat, putting its high back between herself and the senior staff. "You're all dismissed. Do your best to keep morale up."

The others looked back and forth between themselves.

"Dismissed? What are we going to do?" asked Chris. "We only have until sunrise."

"I'm well aware of that," came Sara's disembodied voice. "I was the one who talked with him. Go on, get out of here. The decision is mine to make."

"But…"

"This isn't a democracy. Get out, all of you."

They left, one by one. Both Dr. Patel and Daniel made an attempt to speak again, but they were ignored. In the hallway outside, Chris took Seth's arm and pulled him into a side corridor.

"What were you waiting for in there? I was ready to back you right away."

"Chris, everything's changed now. Our situation won't alter just because I'm the one calling the shots."

"Dogshit! She's going to surrender to him. Do you know what will happen to us?"

"Anyone useful who doesn't rebel too much will be moved to D'Aboville. Either that or he'll move in here, what with the Mimis and all. We'll be slaves, most likely—building things for him to trade off, any women he find's attractive enough will be made into whores. Harpreet will find himself making drugs that don't cure anything, and me…well I'll probably be killed outright, along with Daniel, and probably Purtricil."

"Sorry. Of course you thought about it. We can't surrender, Seth. We can't."

"And you'd rather die fighting, than live under the fat man's thumb, is that it? I don't think everyone here will agree with you."

"Die here, die out there, what difference does it make? When are you going to make your move, Boss?"

"Looks like it'll have to be before sunrise, won't it?"

"That's right."

"Have you been assigned a post?"

"I'm supposed to go back up topside."

"Go. I'll send for you when it's time."

49. Bjossa

With the sky beginning to lighten with the coming of the day, Toffee gritted his teeth against the pain and watched the ground blur beneath him. He was in the lead vehicle of three, giving directions to a silent, cloth-wrapped driver, as two warriors sat on either side, pedalling for all they were worth.

His arm was fine. The instrument used to puncture it had, thankfully, not hit anything vital. Also, it had been slim enough not to do that much soft-tissue damage. Toffee could still wiggle his fingers and make a fist, down by his side where the wrist was bound. His hip was a problem though. Henry, the painted one, had removed the arrowhead, but hadn't stitched the wound. He'd bandaged it tightly enough, but Toffee knew if he exerted himself in any way, he'd be in trouble. That had, no doubt, been the intent. His legs were tied at the ankles, about two feet of rope between them. They'd had problems figuring out how to bind his right arm securely enough, eventually resorting to wrapping strips of cloth all the way around the limb and his torso, making him look like a casualty from the American Civil War. They were still wary of him, no matter how much they tied him up. And they had a right to be. Toffee was pissed. Not only had he been seen going in, he'd been feathered, and the shock of that, more than the pain, had slowed his reactions to where he was actually captured. It was another sign that time, a much greater enemy than nature, was grinding him down.

"Turn here. Left." The driver complied.

Though the sky was growing ever brighter, the road between the high-rises was still in darkness. One thing that had not lessened with age, was his sense of direction. He was guiding them to where the semi was parked, in an alley behind a strip of restaurants.

"Just wait," demanded Seth, silencing the questions of his subordinates. "Chris isn't here yet, and I don't want to have to repeat myself."

There were six people there already, Purtricil and Chiu-Keung, Devon, Mickey, Lyle, and Patricia. With such a security-heavy core group, Seth noted it was always the military that attempted to seize control in a crisis. Somehow the former part of to serve and protect became swallowed up in the latter.

Chris arrived, a little breathless. "Took you long enough," he said.

"So what's the plan?" asked Purty.

Seth looked at the front door. "Come on, let's move back here in case someone comes in."

They preceded him into the rear room. Seth had an empty box waiting by the door.

"This is very simple, and I don't want to argue about it, is that clear?" They all nodded, or grunted affirmatives. "Dr. White is still in the meeting room. We're going to inform her of the change of power, then escort her to the cells. Purty, who's in the tower if you guys are down here?"

"Daniel and Conrad. It was his idea to relieve us. Lucky, huh?"

"Yes, it's a good break. Once Dr. White is locked up, you will be relieving him," he paused, giving them a chance to chuckle at the joke. "With Daniel locked up as well, we make a general announcement to the Pit and prepare to take casualties."

"What about Patel?" asked Chris. "We locking him up, too?"

"Did you hear that part about casualties? No, the doctor will forget his politics once the wounded start rolling in. We need to hit that motorhome out there with a rocket. It's where D'Abo will be, and if we take him out, this whole thing might go away. The problem is, whoever takes the shot will be pulverized by return fire almost instantly. Any volunteers?"

"I'll do it," said Purtricil.

Seth reached out and squeezed the man's shoulder. "Thank you. I wish it could be me."

"Pit needs you, buddy."

"What if Gascan's moved?" asked Chris. "He'll be expecting us to try and get him."

"Or what if he's not here at all?" suggested Lyle. "He could be back home, sending his voice through a series of relay vehicles, or even a satellite uplink."

"It's a chance we'll have to take." Seth stooped and picked up the box. "The motorhome is the only vehicle with antennae arrays on it. If nothing else we'll at least cut off their communications. Later I'll be sending a team out the back way, to try and reach Underbel anyway they can. Now," he held out the box. "I want to see every bullet from every gun in this box."

"What?" Chris held his rifle protectively to his chest. "Like hell I'm doing this unarmed."

There was a jumble of agreements.

Seth jiggled the box. "So you refuse my first order. This is going well. Not unarmed, Chris, you'll have your weapons, but for psychological effect. This is really tense right now, and I don't want Sara, or anyone getting shot by accident. We need her, remember? Pretty soon we're only going to have H&H to rely on for both power and food. In the box people, now."

One by one they emptied their clips and chambers into the box. After checking the breach of each weapon, Seth jiggled the box again. "Now what's in your pockets. Sorry, I don't trust y'all not to reload. Tense times and all."

More shells thumped into the box. Seth put it down and shoved it out the door with his foot. "Okay, good. Back there is something else we can use," he jerked his chin at the rear of the room.

As soon as everyone's head was turned, Seth stepped out of the room and slammed the door. His heart pounded as he fitted the key and threw the deadbolt. It was a solid door, built with the intention of being a strong room for guests' valuables, back when Compton Pit was preparing to be Compton Hotel.

Seth's subordinates yelled at him through the door. It didn't even give as heavy shoulders hit it from the other side.

"Sorry, guys," Seth called out. "I'll be back to let you out at sunrise."

Ignoring the harsh language coming from his makeshift prison, Seth pressed his hand to his face and prayed that he was doing the right thing. He couldn't violate his own code of honour. He'd pledged allegiance to Sid Halbert, and if Sid told him to follow Sara, then that was what he was going to do. From the desk in his office he took a bottle of scotch, thinking about how quickly he was emptying Burle's cache. If Dr. White decided to surrender, if this was indeed his last hour of freedom, he intended to spend it in the company of friends, or at least a friend. Sara would appreciate the gesture.

As he entered the main corridor, Dr. White came storming past him. "Seth, good, come with me."

Surprised, he turned to follow her.

"Is that scotch? We'll drink it later."

"Where are we going?"

She was headed towards the motor pool, was she going outside to surrender in person? She turned before the pool's door and entered security. One of the newly-appointed officers was at the desk. Seth didn't even know his name, but thought he was one of Roshi's kitchen helpers.

"Communications, patch an open channel to security," Dr. White said into the mic.

"Yes, ma'am," came a woman's voice.

"Who is this? Where's Lyle?"

"This is Katherine. Lyle had to go."

"Go? Go where? Never mind. Do I have my channel?"

"Just a second."

The speaker crackled. "Dr. White to Peter."

"Well, the jury is back," came the reply, voice heavy with self-satisfaction. "And early, too. Have you made your decision?"

"Yes. I'm pulling all my people inside, I'm abandoning the towers. Please don't shoot any of them." She switched back to internal communications. "Katherine, cut that channel and shutdown all outgoing and incoming traffic. Shut the whole thing down."

"Yes, ma'am. Dr. White, what's happening?"

"You'll find out soon enough." She switched channels again, connecting to the towers. "All personnel come down from the towers. I repeat, come down from the towers. Sound the all-inside alarm." Without waiting for a reply, she selected all speakers. "Bob Dufferin, report to the battery bay immediately."

Seth handed the bottle to the security officer. "Hold on to this, will you? Don't even think about opening it."

The man took the bottle, somehow able to be surprised at its label in the face of everything else that was going on around them.

"Sara, what have you figured out?"

"We need an army to fight an army, right?"

"Well, yeah."

"We've got one."

Then she was running, and Seth was pushing hard to keep up with her.

Lena was led from her cell and along a corridor with a slight upward incline. The four warriors hadn't touched her, but it was clear from the way they carried themselves she shouldn't stray from the path. She looked for Jonathan, but he was nowhere to be seen. The Master walked ahead, a long, intricately carved staff held in one hand. His cloak had been replaced with a much finer one, black, with gold stitch work along the hem. Lena was wearing a dress of the type she'd described, blue not purple. Apparently whoever had been sent for it was colour blind.

"So I'm finally getting to meet this woman you keep talking about."

"Not only will you meet Her," said Luke, "you will hear Her name."

They passed through a door, and almost immediately the walls seemed familiar. Lena looked at the ceiling where chains dangled. She felt she should know what had hung from them. As they moved farther down the hall, she could make out faint chanting, but couldn't hear exactly what was being said. They stopped at a set of double doors. Though all glass, they had been painted black.

"Are you ready?" asked the Master. "She awaits you now."

Lena shrugged. What else was she going to do? At least now she'd get some answers. "Lead on."

The doors opened and Lena knew exactly where she was. She was led into the open air of what Luke had referred to as the Greater Shrine, but it was simply the amphitheatre of the Vancouver Aquarium. Below, across the curving stone seats like a giant staircase, people, warriors, seekers, and others that showed no affiliation to either caste, prostrated themselves, genuflecting and chanting in sequence, those that had tongues, anyway.

"Bee-yoh-sah, Bee-yoh-sah."

It was the same three syllables, over and over again.

Past the stairs was a massive pool of water, dark beneath the warming sky. Lena gaped at the worshippers, realizing what it was that they were chanting. Bjossa. It was the name of the last killer whale owned by the aquarium. A female, the death of her mate,

Finna, had spurred a series of free-the-whale protests that had coincided with a number of similarly themed films from Disney.

She'd been brought here to meet a ghost. The whale habitat was huge, but nothing could have survived in it for ten years without proper care, especially not a mammal that would kill anyone trying to do the job.

They brought her around the pool to the place where a trainer had once used hand signals to command the creature, getting her to swim around and leap to the delight of children of all ages. The chanting grew in pitch as Luke ascended the platform.

They're going to drown me! The thought came with complete certainty. These lunatics worshipped the ghost of a killer whale. That was how Lena was going to meet their god.

At an unseen signal, the warriors seized her, two for her arms, the other two stooping to hold her legs.

The Master raised his staff over the water, then swung his arm so it pointed skywards.

Lena's entire world, any grasp of hope or even reality, was shattered as a massive killer whale, very much alive, burst from the pool, its tail almost clearing the surface before it crashed back down again in a deluge of water.

Noah awoke to blinding light and arms locked around his. He was out of his cell and being dragged down the corridor before he'd fully gotten his bearings. He didn't say anything as they stopped before a wooden door. One of them knocked. The fair-haired boy opened the door and Noah was brought into the chamber of horrors.

The table had been cleaned, the hooks and knives polished. A brazier sat upon a metal cart, slim bits of metal sticking out of burning embers.

Henry stood by the tongue block, a cleaver in his hand.

"Put him down," said the seeker.

The warriors kicked at the back of Noah's legs, forcing him to his knees. One of them pushed the panel jockey's head forward.

"I'm glad the Master changed his mind about your anointment. Slaves never learn, not really. Okay, one of you fish his tongue out."

"Here," said Toffee, "it's in here. Turn right."

The trike turned, the two behind it followed. Again Toffee wondered what method they'd used to clear the animals from the area of the city surrounding the park. Constant, methodical hunting?

Mass use of poison? Whatever they'd done, they'd been relentless about it.

The rig sat where Toffee had last seen it, pressed up against a wall of cream coloured stone.

"There it is. Now all you have to do is set up and wait."

The vehicles disgorged their passengers. The hunter was pulled to his feet, and made to stand against the lead trike. In all, ten warriors approached the truck. An eleventh stayed back at the trikes, a sharp knife held to Toffee's throat.

"Don't be scared," Toffee called to them, "it's not going to bite you," he looked down at the kid guarding him, "but I will." He jerked his head down and fastened his teeth on the mud-covered wrist holding the knife. There are few muscles in a body stronger than those of the jaw, and the hunter bit down as hard as he could. At the same time he dropped, allowing his weight to pull the warrior off balance and to the ground. Bone gave between his teeth and he snapped his head to the side, like a tiger ripping out a gazelle's throat. Tissue and cartilage came away in his mouth and he spit the gruesome morsel to the ground. He plunged forward, pressing his face into the warrior's neck, pinning him down with his weight. Like a lover his lips probed the neck, then the hunter bit down, going for the jugular.

The other warriors, momentarily stunned by the savagery that was taking place in their midst, fell like tenpins as machine gun fire erupted from a doorway across the alley. It was a short burst, followed up by rapid single shots as Darcy stepped into view and took care of those Sid hadn't.

Toffee rose to his knees, his victim gurgling and dying on the ground before him. Warm blood ran down the hunter's jaw and neck, and he could tell from the look on Darcy's face he looked to her a monster. He was angered that it pained him. He covered it up with bravado, smiling through the crimson mask. "This Trojan-horse shit gets easier every time I do it."

"Are you insane!" cried Sid, storming towards the kneeling man.

"It was your plan, Halbert. I left a note."

"It was *a* plan, Ethan, *a* plan. When you didn't come back…"

"Glad I have more faith in me than you do."

"I had enough faith to wait for you. Did you let yourself get captured?"

"Yeah, that's what happened. There's two trikes still there, doing guard duty. The rest of the kids will be busy elsewhere. They mark the pit traps with two small animal skulls on a stick. Steer clear of those and we're through."

"I want to go back up to the telescope, scout the place again."

"We don't have time for that, Halbert! When the sun comes up, sun boy's never gonna ask another question, and Lena's going to be whale food."

"Shut down the Mimis," said Sara.

"What?" Duff looked from her to Seth.

"Did I stutter? Shut down the Mimis. We're below, D'Abo's above. Shut down the Mimis."

"I can't. Not from in here. Thurlow hardwired 'em, and protected them somehow. We'd have to do it from above."

Sara clenched her fists in frustration. "Cut the cables then, I don't care."

"I don't...I don't know which ones to cut. Should I cut them all?"

"I thought you looked after this between chiefs. You complained that Thurlow was copping an attitude with you, treating you like you didn't know anything."

Duff looked at his feet, his shoulders slumped and he appeared for all the world like a small boy being chastised by his mother. "Freeland never changed much of anything. All the system specs were the same as they were before he took over. Thurlow...I could tell the kid was just so smart. I'm at least twenty years older than him and...I was jealous."

"So when Noah was telling you things, you weren't really listening?"

"That's about it. I didn't know how much he'd changed the system until after he was gone. He showed me where to find stuff on the laptop, but I didn't pay much attention there either."

"Great," she wrapped her arms around herself, hugging tightly. "Shut down Gershwin."

"What?" this time it was Seth's turn to freak out. "You can't be serious."

"I'm deadly serious. If we can't kill power to the Mimis, cut power to Gershwin. You can do that, can't you, Duff?"

Duff considered, "Yes. That cable's unchanged...but it's bolted into place, I'd have to..."

"Cut it! Just cut the damn cable. Now!"

"Sara," Seth interposed himself between the Boss and the engineer, "if we do that, we might not get Gershwin back on line again."

"Look, Seth, Gershwin is just another computer. There's no access to it because Fritz wanted it that way, but he had to be prepared for power outages. If Gershwin is turned back on again, it should reinitialize, bring all its programming back online again. What's in the trees?"

"Animals."

"What else? Remember Toffee's warnings about travelling beyond the Mimis? Remember Conrad?"

"Bald-faced hornets. More nests than we've ever seen before."

"Give the man a prize. Duff, cut the cable."

The whale floated on her side, one eye fixed hungrily on the food. She knew it was food, because it struggled. It struggled a lot. And it screamed, much louder than other food had screamed before. It was the best food, but she'd learned the hard way that she could only eat it when the stick was there. A different face held it than before, but it was the same stick, and the same motions.

Bjossa was an old whale, and she'd spent over thirty of her years in this tiny world. The food had changed, but the rules were the same. Behave, and be rewarded. The reward was more vital now, the reward was survival. She'd eaten the walkers before, without the stick being there; walkers that stood by the edge, or collected water in tiny vessels. The food was rich, but the punishment severe. No food, of any type, for a long time. It was during this period she'd eaten her companion, a sleek dolphin she'd lived in harmony with for years. But she'd been hungry, and it was the way of things. After a while the birds learned not to land on the surface of the habitat, what birds there were.

"Bjossa," said the stick-holder, "we bask in your glory, we live in your protection."

She didn't understand the sounds, but the stick moved, a twisting motion. Bjossa dropped from the surface of the water and sped for the bottom, past rock work transplanted from a nearby island. She banked, pointing herself at the end of water, and drove her tail, ready to fly.

It was all the whale knew. She had no concept that her universe was a four-million-litre habitat connected to the ocean with underground pipes with intakes that worked by the power of the tide, constantly supplying fresh sea water without need of electricity. She didn't have the tools to envision an infinite sea a short swim away.

"Bjossa," the Master intoned, "show us that You are pleased."

The water ended and she was airborne. One eye on the stick, the other on the food, she twisted her body and smashed into the water.

Noah struggled as best he could, but so many hands held him down, and he was still so weak. He'd tried to bite the hand that reached into his mouth, but his jaw was clamped open. It was the boy, pulling his tongue, pushing it down against the rough, foul-tasting wood. Noah tried desperately to reach what he had hidden, not caring if they saw it. But it was inaccessible, strapped to his back.

"Almost sunrise," said Henry. "Blessed be the name of Bjossa, blessed be She."

"Blessed be She," echoed Conner.

Henry raised the cleaver.

"Wait," said the boy. "Do me first. Do me at sunrise, then him. The Master'll never know the difference."

"But She will," said Henry. "The Master is sorry that you have to wait, that's why you're being allowed to participate in the anointing. She will bless you for your service to Her, and be mindful of your sacrifice."

"No!" he released his grip and stepped back. Noah pulled his tongue back into his mouth so far he thought he might choke on it. "I'm not waiting for the next offering! It'll be months before Juanita's baby. He promised me!" The boy was on the verge of tears.

"Conner! Fulfill your duty or I'll have you beaten."

"Do you know what he does to me?" he demanded of the seeker, then, to the warriors, "Do you? He can't touch me anymore once I'm a warrior. Everyone knows that. Please, seeker, please! I'll do anything. Anything."

Henry's eyes drooped, but not in sympathy. "Get his tongue, now."

The boy, deep in misery, reached out to do the seeker's bidding. Noah fixed his eyes on Conner's and rocked a little, grunting like he was being sodomized.

"NO!" Conner launched himself at Henry, grappling for the cleaver, possibly to cut his tongue out himself. Escape from his own version of hell was too close to be denied.

The seeker held the cleaver above his head, out of Conner's reach. With his other hand he pushed at the boy, who was quickly overcoming him. With a grunt of rage, Henry shoved at the boy's chest, smashing him into the far wall. A hook, that hung point outward, punctured Conner's back, coming out his chest below the sternum.

Henry dropped the cleaver and ran to the boy. Lifting and pulling at the same time.

"You two, get over here! Help me with him. Do you know what will happen to me if I kill the Master's favourite…" he looked at the warriors who still held Noah's arms. "Forget him! He's useless. Help me. It his Her will that this boy lives."

The warriors relinquished their hold, Noah ceased in his struggles and went limp.

Go on, he urged them, *I'm completely helpless.*

All three teenagers lifted the boy, Henry guiding the hook from the wall. Henry muttered things like "careful, careful," and "you're going to be fine," just like a real doctor would. They laid the boy on the table, blood was running everywhere.

Completely forgotten, Noah stood. The sleep he had fought against unsuccessfully had done him good. His head throbbed, but his vision was clear, and the earlier nausea had gone away. He reached an arm behind him, twisting painfully to get up beneath the sheet and his bandages. The object's tip slipped between his fingers, and he pulled. It caught inside the bandage, and for a terrible second, refused to budge, then it was moving again, sliding against his skin.

Henry was in the process of working the hook out through Conner's back. The warriors held the screaming boy down while staring at the procedure with morbid fascination.

With one more tug, the nickel-plated .45 was in Noah's hands. He'd already chambered a round before hiding it away. Though he'd never used this one, he had fired one like it a few times. He raised the barrel, one hand braced on the other, preparing for the kick that would skew his aim upwards. He sighted on the back of the closest warrior, and paused. Suddenly, none of them seemed to be a threat, with their attention elsewhere, on the other side of the gun. He'd never killed a human before, and these people, savage as they were, were just children.

"You stupid little idiot," barked Henry, his veneer of care falling away. "Stop squirming! I'm trying to save your worthless hide." There was a tearing sound. "No!"

The hook was out, but with a substantial amount of tissue on it.

Noah pulled the trigger. It was as if the direction of gravity had momentarily shifted, and the warrior simply fell up into the air and against the wall. They turned and looked at him, even Conner. Noah shot the second warrior, he too, did the gravity dance. He aimed the gun at Henry.

"Please, No!" Henry pushed himself off the table and to the floor, curling himself up into a ball. "Don't kill me. Please don't kill me!"

On the table, Conner died.

"Do I have the right to speak?" asked Noah. "Huh? Can I?"

"Yes! Yes of course!"

"Isn't it, 'I grant you privilege?' "

"I grant it! I grant it!"

"Where are my friends?"

"There's just one, Lena."

"Don't lie to me!" he stabbed at the air with the gun.

"I'm not lying. We just have you and her."

"Then where is she?"

"With Bjossa. She is with Bjossa."

"Take me."

Darcy pulled hard on the tiny wheel, sending the trike into a skid. Under any other circumstances she might have enjoyed bouncing over the dead earth in a jouncy ATV, but now every time she saw a pair of skulls, she had to alter course, or blow up, or fall in, or something. Toffee was in the lead, somehow driving despite his injuries. Sid was in the rear. The earth lit up as the top crescent of the sun broke the horizon.

Please, she begged, *let sunrise mean the whole sunrise, not just the tip.*

"Bjossa, You have commanded," the stick came to rest parallel with the water. "This one escaped You, but bore your mark. Now she is returned to You."

The chanting of the worshippers had reached a fevered pitch. It echoed off the amphitheatre's walls, drowning out the Master's voice. He spread his arms wide and the warriors threw Lena into the water.

50. Sunrise

The sun was one-third up when Peter "Gascan" D'Abo stepped from his motorhome and stood free beneath the sky. He wore no helmet or netting, no protection of any kind. He noted, with no small surprise, that many of his people had removed their own uncomfortable headgear. Though Philip had argued strongly against it, D'abo had to come. This was too tasty not to take the first bite in person. Compton Pit, crippled and brainless, animal-free and waiting to be plucked like a ripe peach. Halbert was dead. Lost on some fool's attempt to get something from the city. Probably trucks. Well, there were going to be plenty of trucks at Compton Pit now.

"Menka," he spoke into the RV, "come out here."

Her head appeared at the door. She eyed the not-too-distant trees and pulled back a little. "I'll stay in here, thanks."

"Don't be silly. Look at all my men, they're enjoying this. You should, too."

"There could be a sniper out there."

"No, I don't think there could. I have men everywhere in the woods. A sunrise, Menka, come and watch it. When was the last time you watched the sunrise?"

"I've seen it. I know how it ends."

"Be that way. Your loss. Stay by the radio, we'll call in when the sun is full."

The fat man lifted his arms, as if to encompass the Pit's topside in a possessive hug. His men cheered him on, the attention befitting of a despot. He was rather surprised when gunfire erupted from the trees.

Distant screams accompanied the shots. His men spun to return fire, but there was none to return. It wasn't an attack from the tree line, it seemed to be a war going on from within it, but on all sides.

"Morrey," yelled D'Abo, "what's going on?" He wasn't concerned with getting shot. He stood within a fortress of steel, trucks on all sides.

"I don't know," came the guard's reply as he appeared, rolling out from beneath a trailer. He tapped the headphones.

As conscripts faced the trees and awaited orders, nobody heard the puffs of a mortar from amid the panels, nor did they see tiny projectiles arcing towards the forest.

"Peter," called Menka, "White's on the radio! She wants to know what you're shooting at?"

"It's a trick! Morrey, destroy the towers, get a team to their power hub and destroy that too. No wait! Disconnect it if you can."

A wind seemed to have kicked up. He could hear it, but not feel it. That's how secure he was, even the wind couldn't get to him. D'Abo turned towards the motorhome, to see Menka staring out of it, eyes bulging in stark-naked terror. She slammed and locked the door.

"Menka, what…"

Screams came from everywhere. Gunshots erupted as everyone on the perimeter opened fire at once. The wind grew more ferocious, sounding like the prelude to a hurricane. The infant daylight dimmed, as if the sun had changed its mind and decided to sleep in. D'Abo's head turned and his eyes climbed skyward, where a writhing cloud of darkness was massing above the trees. It was a swarm of a thousand nests, countless hornet drones, normally fulfilling their function as they always had, but all it took was one. One hornet to scent a human, one tiny part to release the pheromone and summon the whole. But D'Abo knew there was more to it than that. They'd come too quickly, they'd been stirred up, somehow. And the breakthrough devices that were supposed to keep the stingers at bay, weren't.

He threw himself against the motorhome, pounding the door with his hand.

"Menka! Open this door. Open it now!"

"Forget it, you fat bastard! You brought us out here."

"You said they couldn't turn those things off."

"I didn't think they could. Bye, Peter."

A gunshot sounded from within, then the motorhome's engine started.

"Where do you think you're going to go?" the fat man screamed. "You're boxed in!"

But that wouldn't be true in a moment. Motors rumbled to life all around him. As the swarm thickened, vehicles were moving. Men jumped on the sides of trucks, pulled at doors held shut tight from within. Gunfire sounded as men tried to ward off hornets with bullets. D'Abo's conscripts were fleeing in all directions. Some of them were running towards the Pit.

Morrey had disappeared. D'Abo jogged to the cab of the motorhome, maybe she hadn't locked those doors. He was not accustomed to any fast motion, and even the short trot was difficult for him. As he reached the passenger door of the cab, the motorhome moved backwards, heading for an opening created when the APC drove forward. The cab disappeared from his reach, he could see Menka laughing at him from behind the steering wheel. Philip was dead, slumped against the very door D'Abo had hoped to open.

Menka's escape was cut short as one of the flatbed trucks, going for the same opening she was, slammed into the motorhome, skewing it sideways. The sky darkened, the cacophony of screams lessened only because there were less voices to add to it. Another impact thundered behind D'Abo as vehicle collided with vehicle. Beyond the swarm something else was taking flight. A gathering of black shapes larger, and almost as numerous as the hornets. What little of the sky that wasn't blotted out by the swarm, was hidden by the crows. Another truck pulled away and behind it lay the tank, somehow missed in the chaos. Its hatch lay open, like a call to safety. D'Abo ran as fast as he could, his ponderous belly slapping the tops of his legs. He reached the tank and clambered up its treads, sweat making his hands slick. He shoved his legs into the hatch and pushed. Less than a third of the way in, he got stuck. His ass and thighs, a mass of legendary proportions, formed a perfect airtight seal with the lip of the hatch. D'Abo grabbed the side of the tank and pulled as hard as he could, but it was physically impossible to force his bulk through the hatch. He pushed, but he wasn't getting out, either. The wind was a hurricane now, and Gascan felt the movement of air across his skin. There was nothing to see but the dark blizzard, and then even that was gone as hornets found his mouth and eyes.

"This isn't the way," said Noah, his gun pressed to the back of Henry's head.

"It is! It is!"

"The chanting's coming from up there."

"This is the way."

There was no one else to bar their passage as they moved through the corridors. They passed glass-walled cells and Noah wondered if one of them might have been his.

"Where's the troll? The beaten man?"

"Slave? He's dead. The Master killed him."

Henry threw open another door, the torch in his hand guttering as he did so. Noah still thought the seeker was misleading him, but if that really was the case, the panel jockey was prepared to kill him, and anyone else that appeared.

"Where is everybody?"

"With Bjossa. All with Bjossa."

Another set of doors and Noah was in a long room, even longer, it seemed, than the mess hall in Compton Pit. Dim bluish light filtered into the room through enormous floor-to-ceiling windows. Beyond the first few was an underwater world of white curves. It looked like something from the arctic. Past those, the colour and texture changed. The new environment was made of dark rock, and appeared larger than the arctic one.

"What is this place?"

Henry stopped and pressed himself against a window. It was long enough for ten men to stand before it, shoulder to shoulder.

"What are you doing? Where's Lena?"

"There, she's up there. Bjossa, save me."

Noah looked through the window, the habitat beyond made brighter as sunlight hit it from above. A pair of legs kicked near the translucent ceiling, one of the legs detached below the knee and sank. There was another shape in the water, this one impossibly huge.

"Oh. My. God."

"Yes," whispered Henry. "My God."

It was impulse, an action born of instinct rather than thought. Noah raised the gun, pointed it at the whale and emptied it into the glass.

The glass had been constructed to withstand the constant pressure of a small lake worth of water, and to absorb the impact of an angry whale if it had to, but the engineers who constructed the habitat never took into account the effect of forty-five caliber slugs smashing into it from close range. Chunks like divots had been blasted out of the glass. It spiderwebbed, cracks racing along the massive pane. Instinct took Noah again, propelling him towards a set of stairs near a huge mural of killer whales basking in the water off a tree-lined shore.

With a mighty roar, the window shattered and water hammered the seeker to the floor. Noah was halfway up the stairs when the wave crashed into him, knocking him down and sucking him under..

Bjossa turned from the food, something new was happening. The water pulled around her and a great sound had entered her world. She hesitated, torn between the thrashing legs, one of which had fallen apart—that was also new—and investigated what was happening. Was her world getting bigger? No. The end of water was coming closer to her, rather than her growing closer to it. A current caught her then, pulling her with a force stronger than she could resist.

From the trainer's platform, Luke stared dumbfounded as the waters receded and a whirlpool began to form near the far edge, near the worshippers. Bjossa, who had been heading toward her prize, her bulk swelling beneath the surface, suddenly vanished.

Lena had been floating above the amphitheatre, free as a bird. She looked down upon the blond man with his upraised stick, down upon the kneeling teenagers and near-adults that cried for her body's death. She looked down upon herself, thrashing amidst the arms of strangers. This was a place she'd been before, though she didn't clearly remember when. She watched as her other self was tossed into the water, and she wondered how long before she would be moving on. It was peaceful, where she was, on a different plane from the violence before her. She was separate, free from harm, a witness and nothing else. She noted idly that her body had begun to turn in circles as it struggled to stay afloat.

Her tranquility fractured as the scene became more chaotic. The water was moving, whirling, pulling. Elsewhere called, a simple act to go, but her other self called as well, wanting her to return. It was a difficult choice, she wanted both.

"You must live, Lena." It was not quite a voice, not really a string of words, more of an emotion, a sensation.

The choice was made.

Lena gained control of herself, coughing out what felt like a lung full of brackish water. It was real, she was in a pool with a killer whale, and now the water fought against her. A great sucking noise assaulted her ears and she fought the current. Old rules, tenants of the sea, ingrained by her father, saved her. Rather than struggle against the water's pull, she swam perpendicular to it. The walls around the pool were irregular, carved of dark stone. On one of these, she found purchase, clinging to it as the sucking noise became even louder. The force against her lessened as the water sank, pulling at her to the waist, then just the legs, then just her foot. The rock was slippery, and she slid as the water left her, but her foot found purchase, and between that and her arms, she was able to stay put as the pool vanished beneath her.

Noah shoved at the door that topped the stairs. It was locked, bolted from the other side, and water kept rising. If he couldn't get the door open, he'd drown inside a building. The irony of it was not lost on him. He'd lost his gun when the wave hit him, but it wouldn't have done him much good, he was sure the clip was empty. There was no sign of the seeker, but that was just as well, Noah had no desire to face him again under the circumstance. For what seemed an eternity he watched the dark liquid engulfing the stairs, cutting his land off with an unceasing flow.

Luke screamed at Lena, then at his warriors to dislodge her from the rock. This was all her fault. Somehow she was cursed, her presence had caused this. One of the windows in the lesser shrine must have broken, it was the only explanation. The drawings weren't an expression of desire, they were a warning not to let her survive. How could he have misunderstood Her to such an extent? But all was not lost. There was still enough depth to the enclosure for Her to survive. Water would continue to pour in from the sea. The lesser shrine would now become part of her home. Perhaps that was what was intended. The warriors were leaning over the edge, trying to push at the woman, but she was just out of reach.

"I'll do it myself," he said, jumping down from the platform. His staff was long enough. He'd beat Lena's head until she dropped to Bjossa's reach.

"Hey, Master," a rough voice called, like stone grating against stone. He looked up and Toffee's bullet took him square in the forehead. His last vision, his final glimpse, was the sun clearing the horizon as his God once cleared the water.

"Get away from her," Darcy screamed at the warrior, her trigger finger squeezing to enforce the command. The hammer clicked on an empty, or dud chamber. But it didn't matter. The warriors were up, and away from the edge.

"All of you stay down," said Toffee, turning his rifle on the worshippers. He shot one of them just to make his point.

Darcy dropped her pistol and ran. She bounced down the steps and swung her arm at the warriors. "Get away, away!"

One of them didn't move fast enough. Darcy grabbed him under the jaw and threw him out of her way. He slipped on the edge and slid down the rock form, splashing into the water below. She dropped to the edge, and stuck her hand out to Lena. "Grab hold of me, honey, c'mon you can reach."

"Ohmygod, Darcy! Where did you come from? I can't reach!" Her half leg made gripping the substrate very difficult. Adrenaline was fading, leaving behind numb and feeble limbs. "I'm slipping. Lower something down to me."

In the water below, the warrior, now treading water, barked like a walrus, then vanished. A patch of white moved through a blooming red cloud.

"Dogshit," said Darcy. "Sid! Get me something to pull her up with!"

"What was that?" asked Lena, afraid to look down. Her foot gave. She slid, screaming. Her hand caught in a seam, a space where the rock form had separated. Her downward motion wedged the hand in place, tearing her skin as it halted her descent.

"Darcy," Sid shoved his M16 into Darcy's hands and dropped to the edge of the pool. "Cover these guys." He lowered the Master's staff. "Lena, grab on."

Lena looked up the length of her arm, to where the end of the staff was. She could take it, if she could just lift her other hand. She tried. She couldn't.

Darcy raised the weapon, aiming at a swell of water. "This thing should have died years ago."

"Darcy, no!" Sid kicked at her leg. "If Toffee is right, that whale is their god. They're cowed right now." And they were, all of them on their hands and knees, heads bowed. "It looks like they've had submissiveness beaten into them. But if you shoot their god, they'll go nuts. Lena, grab on. Come on, girl, you can do it."

Bjossa rose, sunlight gleaming off her white patches. She gazed at her new world. She'd eaten the food. It didn't look like what she'd expected. There were new caves to explore, and that was exciting, but she was confused, and the whirlpool had scared her. The end of water now met a high wall, not a short one. Parts of her world once free to her were now inaccessible. The one she had been expecting was still there, on the wall. Was it still food? Yes. The stick was there, and it was pointing. The face behind the stick had changed again, both in shape and in colour, but the stick pointed at the food. It a was new motion, one unfamiliar to her. The food was out of reach, but Bjossa could reach her if she leaped. That's what the new motion must mean. Jump for the food. The whale swam for the far end of the habitat, preparing for her flight.

"Lena, grab the stick dammit!"

"You'd better hurry, girl," called Toffee. "God's on her way."

Darcy, who'd been watching her friend dangle from the trapped extremity, lifted her eyes for water. It was an image that called back to childhood horror films. The whale's massive dorsal fin, far bigger than that shark's, cleaving the surface as the orca torpedoed towards them.

"Lena," Darcy dropped to the edge, adding her grip to Sid's on the staff, "grab the staff, honey. Lena, grab the staff!"

The dorsal fin plunged as the Bjossa began her arc. It was a different type of jump, what with less depth to work with.

"Lena!" cried Darcy, "if you don't grab this staff *right now,* you're going to die!"

The woman reached, really reached within herself. It felt like pushing through molasses. Her leg kicked, her arm came up, and grabbed the end of the staff.

"Hold on," said Sid, pulling slowly. If he jerked, she'd lose her grip. Her hand came towards him with agonizing slowness. Closer, but not yet within reach.

Bjossa cleared the water.

Sid's hand clamped on Lena's wrist and he pulled. The whale's titanic jaws slammed shut just below Lena's amputated knee. If she'd had a leg there, both she and Sid would have been pulled down. Between Darcy and Sid, they hauled her up and onto safe ground. Darcy hugged her tightly, trying to give her own body warmth to her shivering friend.

"Lena," said Sid, "where's Noah?"

It was freezing in the compartment made up of walls, a floor of water, and an unopenable door. He crouched at the bottom of the portal, numb through and through. If he passed out, he'd slide into the water, sure to drown. His dizziness had returned, along with the nausea, and all the other lovely things getting hit in the head imparted. Forcing his eyes to open, he resumed pounding on the door.

"Hello? Anybody out there? I'm speaking. Somebody want to come and punish me?"

"Isn't he with you?" Lena asked pulling away from Darcy and looking around. "Where's Rick?"

"He's outside," said Sid, quickly. "He's fine." He'd hate himself a long time for that one. "This is the Vancouver Aquarium. Do you know it?"

"I know what it is. Sort of. I came here a few times."

"Lena, the only way this could have happened is if someone blew it out from below. Do you know how to get there?"

"Yes, I think so."

"Show me." He handed Darcy the staff and scooped Lena up in his arms.

Darcy stared daggers at Sid for what he was doing, even though she understood it.

Sid carried her through a set of doors. Toffee kept a watchful eye on the supplicants, his half arm looking naked without its blade. He wouldn't be leaving until he found it. Darcy looked at the cowering teenagers nearby, then at the horde of them on the giant steps.

Keeping an eye, and her gun on the group, she moved to stand next to the hunter. "What the hell are we going to do with them?"

"I think Halbert'll wimp out. Maybe even load 'em up in a trailer and take them home with us."

"I doubt that. What if they stop being so…amenable?"

"Who cares. I just wish I had more bullets."

Tears welled up in Darcy's eyes. She'd be the one to tell Lena. She'd asked for the responsibility, but that was before Sid had lied to her. Now it wasn't just going to be crushing, it was going to be…there wasn't a word for it.

"You bastards!" she shouted at the tribe. "We didn't come here to hurt any of you! We were leaving! Was that your master down there? Well I'm your master now! There's your god, go to her. Go to your god!" She shook the staff at them, rage filling her cheeks with blood.

Darcy dropped the staff and gripped her rifle with both hands as worshipper rose en mass. But none of them came at her, or Toffee. One by one, they dropped to the edge of the habitat, and jumped into the water. The ones that could chant, did.

"Bee-yoh-sah, Bee-yoh-sah."

Darcy rushed to the edge, stupified by what she'd just witnessed.

"I think we should keep that staff," said Toffee.

Darcy ran back to the staff and snatched it up. It was a part of whatever madness these children existed in. She held it over the habitat and threw it down amongst the worshippers.

Bjossa watched the stick twirl as it fell into the people-clogged water. What does that mean? God knew what she wanted it to mean. All food.

"Let's get the hell out of here," said Darcy as the screams hit the air.

"Here," said Lena, touching a door at the bottom of a short flight of steps. "Do you think he would be down here?"

"Someone must have done something, I can't think of who else would, but him." Sid put his hands to the door. It was freezing. He checked the seals around the door. They were airtight, but he couldn't tell if they would stop water or not. "Lena, head back to the top of the stairs. These doors might be holding back a lot of water." He struck the door. "Hello? Is there anybody in there?"

"It could have been Jonathan."

"Jonathan?"

"Crispin. He's here. They'd done horrible things to him."

"Oh. Was one of his arms bent funny?"

"Yes. Have you seen him?"

"No, but Toffee has." He struck the door again. "I'm going to open this. Get ready." A dull thump came from the other side of the door. Sid unlocked the bolt and pulled. Noah fell through and collapsed at his feet.

"Noah!" Sid wrapped his arms around the young man and lifted him.

"Hi, Boss," Noah sounded as if his voice was coming from a million miles away. "My rib's broken. I'm going to sleep now." He closed his eyes, and went limp.

As Sid hugged the chief of photovoltaics to his chest, Lena worked her way down the steps, and ran her fingers through Noah's wet hair. "You did it, Boss. We made it."

Sid was unable to look at her. He swallowed hard and stared at the water that lapped at the steps through the open door. "Lena, there's something I have to tell you."

51. The Wake

Dear Lena,

It's been a long time since I've written to anyone, so if this gets hard to read, forgive me.

I do not know how long I've been a prisoner here, there's not much to mark the passing of time, except the seasons, and those don't change much. It does rain more in the winter, and we had snow for a few days once. Seeing your face, touching your hand, these were the only good things that have happened to me since I left Compton Pit.

You and the panel jockey (they call him a sun catcher here) are the only two prisoners. No matter what they tell you, Sid and the others are still alive, and Luke isn't happy about it. Luke is the blonde-haired monster who controls these children, the one who wants you to call him master. Luke's not the one who started this. He must have been eleven or twelve when the real master, Archie Humboldt, brought him and the other children to the aquarium. That's where we are if you haven't figured it out. Archie's been dead for a while now, don't know how long for sure.

I'm a slave here, that's what they call me, too. Archie made me look the way I do, and cut my tongue out so I couldn't tell anyone about the radio scanner. That's why they keep me alive, to maintain a radio scanner, though only Luke knows that. The scanner can lock onto a radio frequency and jam it, though Archie never told Luke about that capability, and I've kept it a secret also. That's how communication with the outside was always cut off so quickly. We had satellite equipment, but our dishes were the first target when we were hit. The others are all dead. I'm the only survivor.

I told him about how you lost your leg. I'm sorry, but I was afraid. They have a god, but it's not really a god. It's Bjossa, the aquarium's whale. The habitat is self-sustaining, and Archie taught them how to keep the water clean and stuff. The whale understands enough not to attack these people while they're going about their jobs. Their religion is pretty basic; Luke tells them what Bjossa wants, he just makes it up, but the others think he hears the whale's voice in his head. They feed their babies to it. It's all part of Archie's plan. Warriors can fight and hunt, but can't talk or read. The seekers, they're the bald ones painted like hockey fans, can read and talk, but aren't allowed to touch weapons. Information is completely compartmentalized, keeps rebellion or new ideas from getting around. Some technology is allowed, the solar panels, the motors on the trikes they drive, but only because she (Bjossa) "wills it." Everything else is completely forbidden. No one gets to keep a baby, because Archie didn't want his subjects caring for anything but the whale. They call me slave, but Luke's the real prisoner. He completely believes every bit of dogshit Archie spewed out, and so do the other kids.

They intend to smash your friend up, make him look like me, but keep him alive to fix the solar panels that power the scanner. They're going to feed you to the whale. Be brave. Sid is on his way. Luke keeps a museum of stuff they've taken from outsiders. There was only one gun, and I'm going to sneak it to the panel jockey. We're going to get out of here.

Seeing you has given me courage I didn't think I had anymore, made me remember so many things. After I give you this letter, I won't be able to come by again, but I'm out here, and I'll be ready when Sid shows.

You have no idea how lucky you are that Archie's not still running the show. Luke let most of the watch posts go untended, and didn't maintain the traps in and around the city. Archie was a genius, to accomplish what he did with so little…

Noah folded the letter and let it drop to his side. There were two more pages, but reading while the truck moved was making him feel ill. He sat in the space behind the seats. Lena was in the sleeping area with the curtain drawn. She hadn't said anything since they'd left the aquarium. Darcy had slipped under the curtain an hour ago to be with her friend.

"If this Archie guy was so smart, why didn't he put together a real settlement, instead of this cult?"

"There's all kinds of crazy," said Sid. He was driving as fast as was safe, wanting nothing more than to get home. "This one sounds like megalomania, with some sadism thrown into the mix. It doesn't matter. Not anymore."

Noah propped himself up to get a better view of the hunter, who was riding shotgun.

"And they all jumped into the water? Just like that?"

"Uh-huh," grunted Toffee. "Red waved the stick, said jump, and down they went. Y'know Halbert, I've killed a few folk, but that girl is a mass murderer now. Kinda makes a man proud, don't it?"

Noah knocked a few times on the wood panelling beside one edge of the curtain.

Darcy popped her head out. "What?"

"How're they doing?"

The chief of security gave him a sad shake of her head, then disappeared behind the curtain. Fresh tears welled up in his eyes, but he blinked them away. His face felt like it was ten feet wide, all lumps and bruises. With the short beard he'd grown—none of them had shaved since they'd left the Pit—the few glimpses of himself he'd caught in reflective surfaces showed him he was on his way to looking like Jonathan Crispin. Darcy had told him he'd gotten off lucky, that once he healed up, a couple of small scars on the lips was all he had to worry about. A small part of Noah actually enjoyed the thought, thinking it would make him look manlier.

"Why do we do it, Boss?" Noah asked. "These kids, the scavengers…I remember this group that raided Underbel for a while a few years back…with all the animals, why do we still kill each other?"

"Yeah, Halbert," sneered the hunter, "why can't we all just get along?"

They rode in silence for a while as Sid pondered how to answer a question he'd asked himself a thousand times. "Some people think that since the Change we've become more like the animals. Predatory and territorial, but we've always been quicker to kill than to question. Every time we made progress we'd take huge steps back. I'm not going to preach here, Noah. I don't have the answers. I've done things…and I'll do more things…that I'll regret, because it serves a purpose, but it always means making someone else's needs irrelevant in the face of my own."

Halbert, you're breaking my heart, Toffee thought sarcastically. "It's survival of the fittest, kid. We're not the only species that preys on their own, we're just the best at it. Tell you one thing about the world, it's never boring. Our race needed this kick in the ass. And if the animals hadn't turned…shit, we'd have blown ourselves to pieces by now."

"You really believe that?" asked Sid. "What about that mansion you were going to buy?"

"It was gonna have a bomb shelter. All those countries Russia used to be? Nuclear weapons, but no food. You do the math."

Noah had to lie down again. He'd been through a lot, both physically and emotionally. He thought about pulling himself into the sleeping area to see Caps, but there'd be time for that later. Right now he needed everything he had just to keep himself online. He knew things now, things he'd never desired to have revealed to him. Things like what it felt like to kill someone, end their existence with a finger motion. What it felt like to scare a person so badly he cried and wet himself as he hurried to do Noah's bidding. The power it bestowed gave him a better understanding of Toffee. The pain it brought gave him a better understanding of Sid. And it wasn't just power, he'd seen the farthest extreme of both ends of the stick. The Master's hand on him, it was a memory that would torment him for a long time. His own inability to defend himself, how much farther it could have gone...Conner.

"The bumps are making me sick again, Boss. Do we have anymore...uh..."

"Gravol? Sure. Ethan, hand him the bag, will you?"

They'd made a couple of stops for supplies. One of them had been a drugstore with a fortune locked away inside.

The hunter scooped a gym bag up by the handles with his blade. He flipped it into the back area. They hadn't left the aquarium right away. Toffee had located his possessions and his deadly prosthetic, as well as Lena's watch and few other items. He'd also found what remained of Caps's sketchbook. He destroyed that. The letter he'd kept for a laugh. All that stuff about courage, and freedom at last. Lena hadn't even read it yet.

On the other side of the curtain, on a mattress that had been pressed into a happier service mere nights ago, Darcy sat with her knees against her chest, and watched Caps's condition worsen. It was all she could do, just be there close by. Lena had stopped crying hours ago. Not that her grief had ended, the body could only produce so many tears at one go. Now she just lay on her side, holding Caps's half hand tightly in both her full ones.

The silence had become unbearable for Darcy. She hadn't wasted breath on platitudes, nor was she going to resort to it now, but she had to say something.

"Sid's really sorry for what he said earlier." *Why the hell did I say that? Might as well say 'we lied to you, nananana!'*

Lena rolled and her head came up, slowly, like it was tremendously heavy. "I understand why he did it."

"So you don't hate him?'

"I haven't got the energy. Maybe tomorrow. Joke. That's what Rick would do...joke...I'd never have forgiven myself if I'd lost it before I could help find Noah."

They were silent again. Darcy wanted to reach out and touch her friend, but resisted, as she'd done twenty times already. There were times for physical comfort, and times where any contact, any attempt at warmth, was rejected. Her own grief for Travis was still present, though in ever-diminishing quantities, but the first few nights...so much loss, so much darkness...a loving hand felt like an intrusion. Lena was like that now, wrapped up in a barbed-wire coat of if only and never again.

Passing away in bed, surrounded by loved ones, that never happened. No one ever got to say goodbye.

"If Rick doesn't make it...I'll wish Noah hadn't saved me." Lena's voice was flat, delivering a fact and nothing more.

"No you won't. Look, I know how you feel–"

"Did you want to die when Travis did? Did you want to run out to nature, or shoot yourself?"

"No. I wanted to...I guess turn off for a while, but not forever. I still had Sid. I still had you and—"

"Darcy, do you remember...no, you weren't at the Pit yet. Rick had made his intentions clear to me, but I thought he was weird. Cute, but weird. You can remember when we didn't have the Mimis, but we'd gotten a lot better by the time you showed up. We found all the places animals could get in because...because animals kept getting in. There were mice here and there. People would wake up with one of them hanging onto some body part or another. Two people a night would sit in the mess hall, in darkness, as bait. Sara and Harpreet had come up with this odourless glue. You'd sit in a circle of this gunk and listen to them skitter across the floor, then squeal as they tore themselves apart trying to get at you. One night my turn came. He pretended it was a coincidence, but Rick had pulled strings to switch to my shift. The whole time we were in there, he reeled off cartoon mouse dialogue. Nailed their voices. Stuff like, 'Hey, Minnie, I'm stuck to this floor like I'm stuck on you!' and 'I'd kiss you Mickey, but my jaw just came off.' I laughed so much that night. I thought I'd literally torn something in my stomach. All the animals are just...just muppets to him." Her eyes closed and a wash of fresh pain rippled beneath her skin. "That was the night I fell in love with him. He gave me back something I'd lost. But now I realize it was just a loaner. He's my smile. Rick is my smile." The trembling came, and along with it a sparse offering of tears.

Caps made a noise, half cough, half sigh. His eyelids twitched slightly, but didn't open.

"We owe you," said Purty, pouring himself another finger of scotch. The substance was being gulped down all over the Pit, but it didn't matter. There'd been a case of it in D'Abo's motorhome, only one bottle broken in the crash. Good packing.

"I'll drink to that," Seth raised his glass and knocked it back. He plopped the glass back on his desk. "Bartender, another."

"It's all over. Chiu and I talked to everyone involved and we're just going to forget it ever happened. Dr. White pulled through for us. The Pit thinks she's up there with the Boss. Well, most of them do."

"Yeah, I heard the new one. Sid left a book of contingency plans and Dr. White's just claiming the idea was hers. It never stops. And listen, I won't forget about this."

Purty's eyes grew serious. "What do you mean? Are you going to turn us in?"

"Hell, no. But you said it yourself, you owe me, all of you. And I'll collect, you bet I will." He held his glass out. Eventually, Purty tapped it with his.

"We've got company," said Sid, slowing the truck. There was a car up ahead, an unfamiliar one. It was sideways across the road. A net-helmeted figure in fatigues and a flak jacket stood on the far side, a bazooka on his shoulder. "Toffee, get ready. Damn, we're almost within radio range of the Pit."

"He's calling to us," said the hunter.

The truck stopped. Cautiously, Sid rolled down the window. If the bazooka was really loaded, he didn't have much of a choice.

"Step out of the vehicle and identify yourself," called the figure.

Darcy scrambled to the front of the cab and leaned over Sid's lap. "Daniel? Is that you?"

"Chief?"

Darcy threw open the door and crushed Sid in some sensitive places as she crawled over him. "What the hell are you doing out of uniform?" she yelled as soon as her feet hit the ground.

"Chief!" the bazooka dropped and Daniel was running. The car started up and followed. Sid stepped down, as the acting chief of security swept the real McCoy up in a bear hug.

"Where did you get that car?" Darcy asked. "Where did we get a bazooka?"

"We got a lot of things," he pulled off his net-helmet and kissed Darcy's forehead. "Sorry, breach of conduct, but…"

"It's okay."

He pulled his headgear back on.

Patricia got out of the car. This close to the mesh that covered the windshield, she could make out Toffee in the cab, Noah beside him. Lena appeared from the gloom behind the seats. "How many of you, Boss?"

"All of us," said Sid, tossing a net-helmet to Darcy. "Where'd you get the car, Daniel?"

"Let me show you. Is this for me?" he gestured to the truck.

"Yes."

He shook his head and smiled. "Do you want me to call in?"

"No. Let's surprise them."

"Boss, they're not going to be the only ones."

And they weren't. There were two rigs parked within the fence, an APC and a tank. A tank for Pete's sake. A crew was busy clearing human remains off the road. A sizable pile had already accrued off to one side.

Daniel stopped at the gate, and rather than simply use his radio, stepped out of the car and yelled up at the tower, "Delivery from Vancouver!"

There was a flurry of motion in the tower, Sid couldn't quite make out who was up there, but everyone working had stopped in their motion and were walking or running towards the truck.

Sid dropped to the road and feigned humility as he basked in admiration.

Darcy popped her head through the curtain. "You ready for this?"

"No," said Lena, not wanting to leave her man. "I can't. Tell them…just tell them we're sleeping."

"Wait, quiet," the Boss silenced the questions and declarations that were coming in on top of each other. "Will someone please tell me where all these vehicles came from?"

The airlock doors opened. Sara walked up the ramp as the gate slid away.

"Welcome home. You missed a hell of party." She hugged Sid, pushing her head hard against his chest.

"Sara, what's going on?"

She told him, brief details, overriding his questions. People were spilling out of the airlock like worker ants defending their colony.

"Come on," said Sara. "Let's get you inside. You can leave the truck out here."

It was a party. Dr. Patel fussed over all of them, and was particularly reluctant to leave Caps alone in the infirmary, but in the end relented and joined the festivities. Responsibilities were forgotten as the Comptonites gathered in the mess hall. Roshi was exhausting himself, running out of the kitchen to slap backs and shake hands, then running back in again to torment subordinates who weren't working fast enough. That the grand speech master had reneged on his promised encore was a pall over the gathering, but a light one. All six had returned. It was a miracle. Even Toffee was treated with warmth and admiration, albeit cautiously. As tales were urged from Noah's lips, he found himself exaggerating details where no exaggeration was needed. The animals at UBC tripled in number, especially the bear population. Caps gained heroic status, crushing teeth barehanded like a barbarian from a childhood comic book. Daniel handed the chief of security's mantle over to Darcy with a newly-acquired Ruger automatic and a skinbag of manure. Dr. White officially did the same, leading a cheer of; "The queen is dead, long live the king."

"You did good, Sara," said the Boss, taking her by the shoulder.

"Don't say that. You'll want me to do it again. H&H is in a mess. I blame you for that."

Everyone in their own way was given back the torch they left behind. Duff gave Noah a light bulb. Chris whimpered like a beaten dog, rolled at Toffee's feet and exposed his throat. But Lyle stood with a microphone dangling from his hand, nobody to give it to—Lena had slipped away after the first few congratulatory minutes—and Mickey sat by himself, contemplating his brush with chiefdom, and the still possible loss of a friend.

There were passes thrown at Noah that night, though he refused them all. None were thrown at Darcy, but many men thought about it. Miranda slipped away, as smoothly as Lena had, to prepare her own welcome home for the Boss, after first confirming he'd appreciate it. She knew it would be the last time. There were no misconceptions.

The party dwindled, as all parties do. The noise lessened and the crowd thinned until just the last few diehards remained, picking up empty bottles, scrounging for the last of the booze. Claiming I-knew-its and repeating stories as if they'd been the ones to take the trip.

The transition was amazing, from darkness to light, from one end of the spectrum to the other. Vancouver lay open to them like a giant oyster bed, its pearls perfect and waiting to be taken. Sid had announced his plan to block the roads, allowing them exclusive access for as long as they could get away with it. Sooner or later someone would figure out where Compton Pit's sudden wealth was coming from. A joint plan would also be enacted with Underbel to execute a take-over of D'Aboville. The Reservoir was now only a skeleton crew of leaderless thugs, and a horde of discontented slave labourers and conscripts. Between the fat man's supply, and the reservoirs in Vancouver, especially the huge one on Burnaby Mountain, fuel would become much cheaper. Trade and exploration in the area would enjoy a surge like it hadn't seen since the first regular deliveries began between the settlements.

Amongst the others who had their fill and called it a night, Noah Thurlow walked the length of the residential corridor just to see it again, then returned to his room, number 26.

Bare feet slapped the floor, leaving small puddles behind. Darcy was walking towards him, her hair wet and clinging to the sides of her face and neck. Her robe was bunched from the towel wrapped around her beneath it.

"Normally I dry my feet," she said, looking at her wet footprints, "but I wanted to feel the water between my toes."

Noah offered her a slight smile, the only type he could manage without pain. He flicked his eyes at Caps's door.

"He made it home, sun boy. Harpreet won't let him die now. Aren't you going to shower?"

"My time slot's not until tomorrow."

Darcy laughed. "I don't think that really matters, do you?" She cupped his chin and rubbed her fingers in his short beard. "You should shave, too. Sid already has." He winced as she squeezed a tender spot. "Oops," she pulled her hand away. "Sorry."

"Do you...do you want to come in?"

"Okay."

They entered number 26. Someone had cleaned the room in Noah's absence. Fresh sheets were tight across the cot with precise, hospital corners. The floor had been mopped, and even the small vent shone like it was new steel.

"I didn't ask anyone to clean my room."

"Do you want to file a complaint? My privacy was violated, too. Violated quite nicely. It's good to come home."

Above the desk was Noah's house-warming gift; the poster of the cement trucks paving the ocean.

"Kind of prophetic, huh?" asked Noah, fingering a corner that had come loose from its putty. "Is Lena going to be okay if..."

"I don't know. I hope so."

"Is there anything I can do for her?"

"Just wait. Have faith in our doctor."

"Is there anything I can do for you?"

There was a long pause. Noah didn't mean anything by it, but realized the implications were there the moment the words left his mouth. They held each other's gaze, her with glistening skin and flushed cheeks, him with swollen face and bloodshot eyes. Beauty and the beast, the classic couple.

"I'm going to bed, Noah. Sleep well. I'll see you at breakfast." She hesitated, then kissed him, a dry and sisterly brush of lips on cheek. She turned to leave.

"Darcy, wait." A fresh set of coveralls lay crisp and folded at the foot of the bed. Noah picked them up and ran his finger across the bold yellow stripe that marked his rank.

"What?"

"I was thinking about those scientists at UBC. The suicide squad."

"What about them?"

"Do you think they killed themselves because they didn't find anything...or because they did?"

Brian S. Matthews

Brian S. Matthews is capable of sleeping anywhere and can stare directly at the sun for long periods of time. His hobbies include classical music, judging others and trying to convince the bank that it's really their fault when one of his cheques goes NSF.

Brian is currently living in Vancouver, with two cats he doesn't particularly trust.

City on the Currents by Brians S. Matthews
Book II of the New Wilderness Trilogy
Coming December 2005
Aydy Press

The author can be contacted by emailing
newwilderness@shaw.ca

Acknowledgments

I would like to extend my thanks to the following people:

My father, for sitting at my bedside when I was a child and reading to me the works of Jack London, Conan Doyle, Rudyard Kipling, and many others at a time when most children my age were being read Dr. Seuss, or sadly, nothing at all.

My mother, for refusing to read my work until I was published, giving me even more determination to break into print.

Dwight Hill for demanding more pages as soon as I could type them.

Ron Gavin for midnight visits to the Douglas Road truck yards.

Jim Mason for fastidious nitpicking.

Wendy Porter for even more fastiduous nitpicking.

Chaim Katz for eyes keener than mine.

Bill Richards for the wonderfully creepy cover art.

Jerry Morales for his encouragement and some very useful last-minute advice.

Brian Bethune for providing a key that opened many doors.

Dr. John Q. Pinkney for unlimited access to the treasure trove of knowledge which is his brain.

Shannon Mobley, without whom this book might still be only a dog-earred manuscript cluttering a desk drawer.

Paula Turner for tireless proofreading and miles of footwork.

Tom Bulmer for his time.

Ron Herron for his faith.

And finally, my sister Fiona for her unending support, and her ability to find the silver lining without ever bothering to see the cloud.

65492534R00355

Made in the USA
Lexington, KY
14 July 2017